A TEXT BOOK OF

# THERMODYNAMICS

**FOR**

**SEMESTER - I**

## SECOND YEAR DEGREE COURSE IN MECHANICAL, MECHANICAL SANDWICH & AUTOMOBILE ENGINEERING

**Strictly According to New Revised Credit System Syllabus of Savitribai Phule Pune University**

(w.e.f June 2016)

**Dr. S. N. SAPALI**
B.E., M.E. (Mech.) Ph.D. (IIT Kharagpur)
Professor & Head, Mech. Engg. Deptt.
College of Engineering (COEP),
Pune.

**Dr. S. V. DINGARE**
B.E., M.E., Ph.D (Mech.)
Professor, Mech. Engg. Deptt.
MIT College of Engineering,
Kothrud Pune.

**Dr. S. S. KORE**
B.E., M.E., Ph.D (Mech.)
Associate Professor & Head
Mech. Engg. Deptt.
Sinhgad Academy of Engineering,
Kondhwa (Bk), Pune.

**Dr. S. S. GHORPADE**
B.E., M.E. (Mech.)
Assistant Professor,
Mech. Engg. Deptt.
Sinhgad Academy of Engineering,
Kondhwa (Bk), Pune.

N3532

**THERMODYNAMICS (SE MECHANICAL)**     **ISBN 978-93-86084-06-4**

Second Edition   :   June 2017

©   :   **Authors**





**Published By :**        Polyplate

**NIRALI PRAKASHAN**

Abhyudaya Pragati, 1312, Shivaji Nagar,
Off J.M. Road, Pune – 411005
Tel - (020) 25512336/37/39, Fax - (020) 25511379
Email : niralipune@pragationline.com


☞ **DISTRIBUTION CENTRES**

**PUNE**

| | | |
|---|---|---|
| **Nirali Prakashan** | : | 119, Budhwar Peth, Jogeshwari Mandir Lane, Pune 411002, Maharashtra |
| | | Tel : (020) 2445 2044, 66022708, Fax : (020) 2445 1538 |
| | | Email : bookorder@pragationline.com, niralilocal@pragationline.com |
| **Nirali Prakashan** | : | S. No. 28/27, Dhyari, Near Pari Company, Pune 411041 |
| | | Tel : (020) 24690204 Fax : (020) 24690316 |
| | | Email : dhyari@pragationline.com, bookorder@pragationline.com |

**MUMBAI**

| | | |
|---|---|---|
| **Nirali Prakashan** | : | 385, S.V.P. Road, Rasdhara Co-op. Hsg. Society Ltd., |
| | | Girgaum, Mumbai 400004, Maharashtra |
| | | Tel : (022) 2385 6339 / 2386 9976, Fax : (022) 2386 9976 |
| | | Email : niralimumbai@pragationline.com |

☞ **DISTRIBUTION BRANCHES**

**JALGAON**

| | | |
|---|---|---|
| **Nirali Prakashan** | : | 34, V. V. Golani Market, Navi Peth, Jalgaon 425001, |
| | | Maharashtra, Tel : (0257) 222 0395, Mob : 94234 91860 |

**KOLHAPUR**

| | | |
|---|---|---|
| **Nirali Prakashan** | : | New Mahadvar Road, Kedar Plaza, $1^{st}$ Floor Opp. IDBI Bank |
| | | Kolhapur 416 012, Maharashtra. Mob : 9850046155 |

**NAGPUR**

| | | |
|---|---|---|
| **Pratibha Book Distributors:** | | Above Maratha Mandir, Shop No. 3, First Floor, |
| | | Rani Jhanshi Square, Sitabuldi, Nagpur 440012, Maharashtra |
| | | Tel : (0712) 254 7129 |

**DELHI**

| | | |
|---|---|---|
| **Nirali Prakashan** | : | 4593/21, Basement, Aggarwal Lane 15, Ansari Road, Daryaganj |
| | | Near Times of India Building, New Delhi  110002 |
| | | Mob :  08505972553 |

**BENGALURU**

| | | |
|---|---|---|
| **Pragati Book House** | : | House No. 1, Sanjeevappa Lane, Avenue Road Cross, |
| | | Opp. Rice Church, Bengaluru – 560002. |
| | | Tel : (080) 64513344, 64513355,Mob : 9880582331, 9845021552 |
| | | Email:bharatsavla@yahoo.com |

**CHENNAI**

| | | |
|---|---|---|
| **Pragati Books** | : | 9/1, Montieth Road, Behind Taas Mahal, Egmore, |
| | | Chennai 600008 Tamil Nadu, Tel : (044) 6518 3535, |
| | | Mob : 94440 01782 / 98450 21552 / 98805 82331, |
| | | Email : bharatsavla@yahoo.com |


**niralipune@pragationline.com | www.pragationline.com**

Also find us on  www.facebook.com/niralibooks

# PREFACE TO THE SECOND EDITION

We are glad and excited to announce that the First Edition of this book received an overwhelming response from the engineering student community, compelling us to release its **Second Edition** within a very short period of time.

This thoroughly revised **Second Edition** has been updated with additional matter, many solved problems, including solutions to Numerous Exercises and University Question Papers (December 2013 to May 2017) for practice.

Special care has been taken to maintain high degree of accuracy in the theory and numericals throughout the book.

We take this opportunity to express our sincere thanks to Dineshbhai Furia of Nirali Prakashan, a reputed pioneer in the publication field. Our special thanks to Jignesh Furia for their effective cooperation and great care in bringing out this revised edition. We also appreciate the efforts of M. P. Munde and the entire staff of Engineering Books Deptt. of Nirali Prakashan namely Mrs. Deepali Lachake (Co-ordinator) for bringing this book to the students in a timely manner.

We sincerely hope that this "**Second Edition**" will also be warmly received by all concerned as in the past.

Valuable suggestions from our esteemed readers to improve the book are most welcome and highly appreciated.


**Pune**                                                                                          **Authors**

# PREFACE

It gives us great pleasure in publishing this text book on **"Thermodynamics"** for the Students of Second Year Degree Course in Mechanical and Automobile Engineering. This book is strictly written According to New Revised Credit System Syllabus of Savitribai Phule Pune University (2015 Pattern).

As per the policy of the University, Engineering Syllabi is revised every five years. Last revision was in the year 2012. New revision is coming little earlier, as university has introduced **Online** system of examination from year 2012.

As per the New Credit System, the **In Sem (Online - 50 Marks) Examinations** (Combined Phase-I and Phase-II) will be conducted based on first, second, third and fourth units. The **Online** examinations will have objective types of questions with multiple choices. **End Semester Examination (Theory Paper 50 Marks)** will be based on all the six units and that will be conducted in traditional way and the theory course will have 4 credits.

Authors have tried to introduce the subject to the average students, with a large number of solved examples. The subject matter has been developed in a logical and coherent manner with neat illustrations along with a fairly large number of solved examples and exercises. Answers to many unsolved numerical problems are also given.

**The Main Objectives of this Text are :**

- To cover the basic principles of thermodynamics.
- To develop a very good understanding of the subject matter.
- To give practice to solve the numerical examples in thermodynamics.
- To give practice to solve the multiple choice questions in the subject.

**We have given Free Separate book of Multiple Choice Questions (MCQ's) which will be very useful to the students, especially for Online Examinations.**

We take this opportunity to express our sincere thanks to Shri. Dineshbhai Furia, Shri. Jignesh Furia, Mrs. Nirali Verma and Shri. M. P. Munde and entire team of Nirali Prakashan namely Mrs. Deepali Lachake (Co-ordinator), who really have taken keen interest and untiring efforts in publishing this text.

Finally, we express our gratitude to our family members for their continuous support and encouragement, thanks to all.

We have no doubt that like our earlier texts, student's community will respond favourably to this new venture.

The advice and suggestions of our esteemed readers to improve the text are most welcomed, and will be highly appreciated.


**23 June 2016**  
**Pune**

Authors

# SYLLABUS

**Unit I : Laws of Thermodynamics** **[6 Hrs]**

Introduction of thermodynamics, Review of basic definitions, Zeroth law of thermodynamics, Macro and Microscopic Approach, State Postulate, State, Process and Thermodynamic Cycles, First law of thermodynamics, Joules experiment, Applications of first law to flow and non flow processes and cycles. Steady flow energy equation and its application to different devices. Equivalence of Clausius and Kelvin Planck Statement, PMM I and II, Concept of Reversibility and Irreversibility.

**Unit II : Entropy** **[4 Hrs]**

Entropy as a property, Clausius inequality, Principle of increase of Entropy, Change of entropy for an ideal gas and pure substance.

**Ideal Gas** **[6 Hrs]**

**Ideal Gas definition Gas Laws:** Boyle's law, Charle's law, Avagadro's Law, Equation of State, Ideal Gas constant and Universal Gas constant, Ideal gas processes- on P-V and T-S diagrams Constant Pressure, Constant Volume, Isothermal, Adiabatic, Polytropic, Throttling Processes, Calculations of heat transfer, work done, internal energy. Change in entropy, enthalpy.

**Unit III : Thermodynamic Cycles** **[6 Hrs]**

**Gas Power Cycles:** Air Standard Cycle, Efficiency and Mean Effective Pressure, Carnot Cycle, Otto Cycle, Diesel cycle, Dual cycle, Comparison of cycles, Brayton cycle,

**Gas Refrigeration Cycle:** Reversed Carnot, Bell Coleman Cycle.

**Availability** **[4 Hrs]**

Available and unavailable energy, concept of availability, availability of heat source at constant temperature and variable temperature, Availability of non flow and steady flow systems, Helmholtz and Gibbs function, irreversibility and second law efficiency.

**Unit IV : Properties of Pure Substances** **[5 Hrs]**

Formation of steam, Phase changes, Properties of steam, Use of Steam Tables, Study of P-v, T-s and Mollier diagram for steam, Dryness fraction and its determination, Study of steam calorimeters (Barrel, Separating, Throttling and combined)

Non-flow and Steady flow vapour processes, Change of properties, Work and heat transfer.

**Thermodynamic Vapour Cycle** **[5 Hrs]**

**Vapour Power Cycles:** Carnot cycle, Rankine cycle, Comparison of Carnot cycle and Rankine cycle, Efficiency of Rankine cycle, Relative efficiency, Effect of superheat, boiler and condenser pressure on performance of Rankine cycle, **Vapour Refrigeration Cycles:** Reversed Carnot Vapor Cycle, Vapor Compression Cycle and representation of cycle on P-h and T-s diagram, Refrigerating effect, Compressor power and COP estimation **(Numerical treatment using R134a only and enthalpy Cp, Cv data should be provided in tabulated form).**

**Unit V : Steam Generators** **[6 Hrs]**

Introduction to fuels, Theoretical amount of Oxygen / Air required for combustion. Stoichiometric Air: Fuel ratio, Excess air, lean and rich mixtures, Stoichiometric A: F ratio for petrol **(No Numerical Treatment on fuels and combustion, only basic definitions and terminologies to be covered).**

Classification, Constructional details of low pressure boilers, Features of high pressure (power) boilers, Introduction to IBR, Boiler performance calculations-Equivalent evaporation, Boiler efficiency Energy balance, Boiler draught (natural draught numerical only).

**Unit VI : Psychrometry** **[6 Hrs]**

Psychrometry and Psychrometric Properties, Basic Terminologies, Psychrometric Relations, Psychrometric Chart, Psychrometric Processes, Thermodynamics of Human Body, Comfort Conditions **(Numerical treatment using Psychrometric chart only).**

# CONTENTS

## Unit III : Thermodynamic Cycles and Availability

## Chapter 4 : Thermodynamic Cycles     4.1-4.46

## Chapter 7 : Vapour Power Cycle — 7.1-7.60



## Unit V : Steam Generators

## Chapter 8 : Steam Generators — 8.1-8.66

## Unit VI : Psychrometry

# Chapter 1

# LAWS OF THERMODYNAMICS

## 1.1 INTRODUCTION

Thermodynamics is a science that deals with matter, energy and interactions between matter and energy.

The subject of thermodynamics is based essentially on three main concepts, these are

- **Energy**, is an idea central to the development of all branches of science and engineering. A fundamental postulate of thermodynamics is that matter has energy (which can be in several forms) and energy is conserved.

- **Thermodynamic Equilibrium**; a state which every isolated system with no internal constraints eventually attains.

- **Entropy**; which determines whether a specified type of the change can occur or not.

## 1.2 SCOPE OF THERMODYNAMICS

Every engineering activity involves an interaction between energy and matter, thus it is hard to imagine an area which does not relate to thermodynamics in some respect. Therefore, a good understanding of thermodynamic principles has been an essential part of engineering education.

One does not need to go very far to see some application areas of thermodynamics. These areas are where one lives. Many household utensiles and appliances are designed, by using thermodynamic principles. For example, electric heaters, LPG stove, heating and air conditioning systems, the refrigerator, pressure cooker, water heater, shower, electric iron. On large scale, thermodynamics plays a major part in the design and analysis of automotive engines, rockets, jet engines, and conventional power plants (thermal power plants) and also nuclear power plants. At this stage, it is essential to mention that human body is an interesting application area of thermodynamics.

Under thermodynamics, we study the working and performance of (i) Conventional or nuclear power plant, (ii) Compression Ignition (C.I.) and Spark Ignition (S.I.) engines, (iii) Gas turbines, (iv) Steam turbines, (v) Refrigerators, (vi) Air conditioners, (vii) Air compressors, (viii) Refrigerant compressors, (ix) Pumps, etc.

# 1.3 BASIC DEFINITIONS

## 1.3.1 Working Substance

In heat engine, a fluid is used to receive heat, expand and produce work output. In refrigerators and heat pumps, a fluid is used to receive heat at a low temperature and reject at higher temperature. Such a fluid with essential properties is known as a working substance.

A working substance absorbs heat and rejects heat. Working substance does work or work is done on it. It is compressed or expanded, heated or cooled so that the desired energy transfer is achieved.

Examples of working substances are: air in an air compressor, water in hydraulic turbines, air and fuel mixture in gas turbines and I. C. engines, steam in a steam power plant, carbon dioxide or water in nuclear power plant.

**Pure Substance**

This has a homogeneous and invariable chemical composition, even if the substance changes its phase from solid to liquid or liquid to vapour.

Water is a pure substance; the chemical composition (formula) of $H_2O$ will not change, even if it undergoes phase change from ice to water and water to vapour.

## 1.3.2 System

Thermodynamic system or simply a system, is defined as a quantity of matter or a region in space chosen for study. The region outside the system is called as *surroundings*. The real or imaginary surface that separates the system from its surroundings is called the *boundary*. These are illustrated in **Fig. 1.1**.

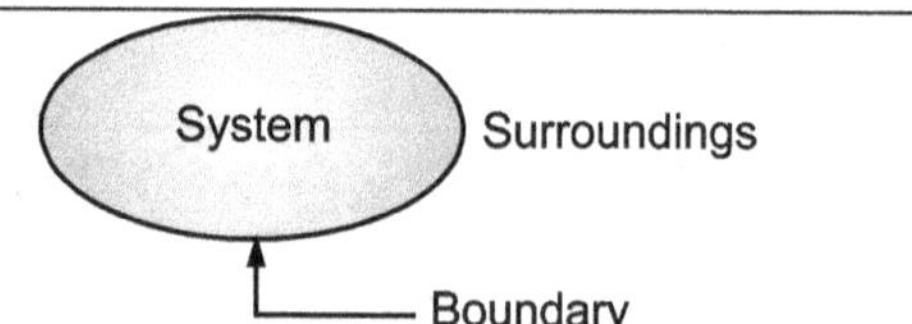


**Fig. 1.1: System, surroundings and boundary**

The boundary of a system can be fixed or movable.

**Classification of Systems:**

(i)   System may be classified as closed, open and isolated.

**(a) Closed System (Non-flow system):**

It consists of fixed amount of mass and no mass can cross its boundary. That is, no mass can enter or leave a closed system as shown in **Fig. 1.2**. But energy, in the form of heat or work can cross the boundary and the volume of a closed system does not have to be fixed.

It consists of fixed mass while volume changes. Boundaries of such system are real and moving.

For example, pressure cooker, stirling cryogenerator.

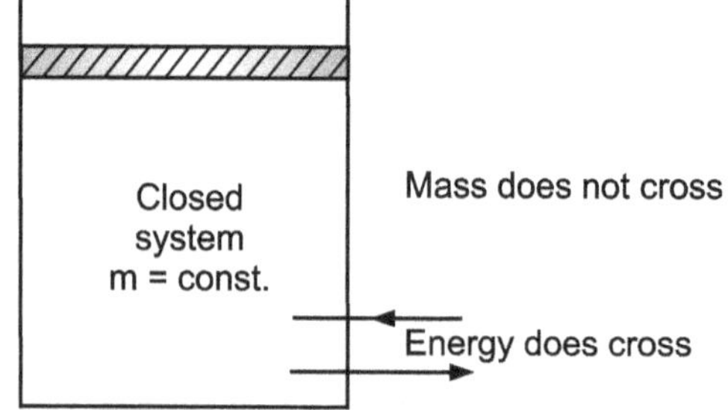


**Fig. 1.2: Mass cannitot cross the boundaries of a closed system but energy can**

## (b) Open System or Control Volume (Flow system):

The system which can exchange both mass as well as energy with the surroundings is called as open or flow system. It consists of fixed volume while mass enters and leaves the system. Boundaries of such system are fixed and may be imaginary.

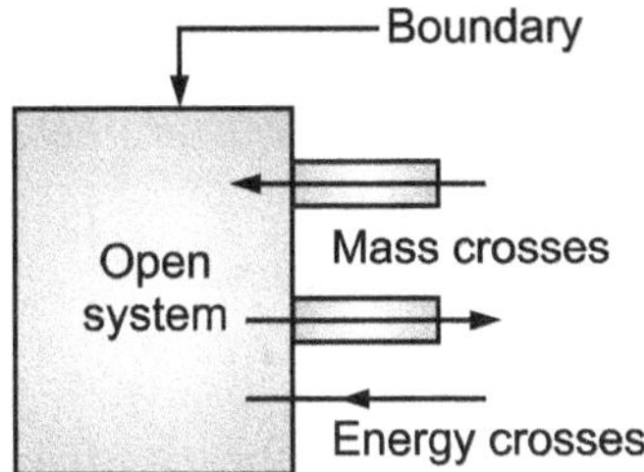


**Fig. 1.3: Both mass and energy can cross the boundaries of a system**

As an example of open system, consider the water heater as shown in Fig. 1.4.

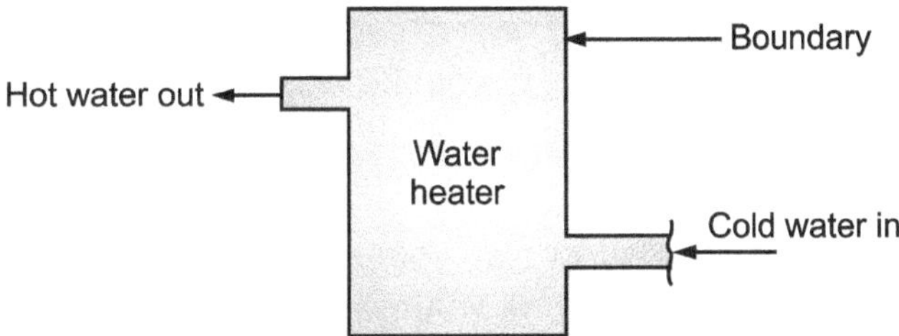


**Fig. 1.4: An open system with one inlet and one exit**

For example, air compressor, turbines, nozzles, etc.

## (c) Isolated System:

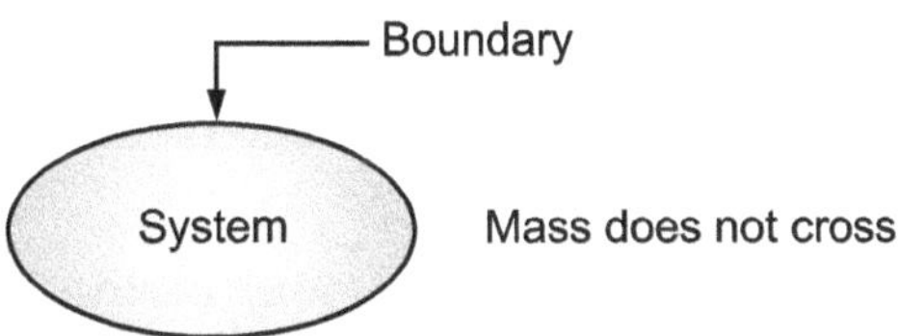


**Fig. 1.5: Isolated system**

This is one in which there is no interaction between the system and the surroundings. No transfer of mass and energy across the boundary.

For example, thermos flask, cryogenic gas container.

**(ii)** System can also be classified as homogeneous and heterogeneous.

## (a) Homogeneous system:

In this working substance is present a single phase. e.g. air, water, crude oil.

## (b) Heterogeneous system:

In this working substance is present in more than one phases. e.g. fog, mixture water and ice.

**Control Volume and Control Surface:**

If the volume of system under study remains constant and has a fixed position, then this volume is called as a control volume. The control volume is bounded by a control surface.

Fig. 1.6 shows a control volume bounded by a control surface. Both mass and energy entering and leaving the system are shown in the figure. Control volume is same as open system. The volume may change in open system, but it remains constant in control volume.

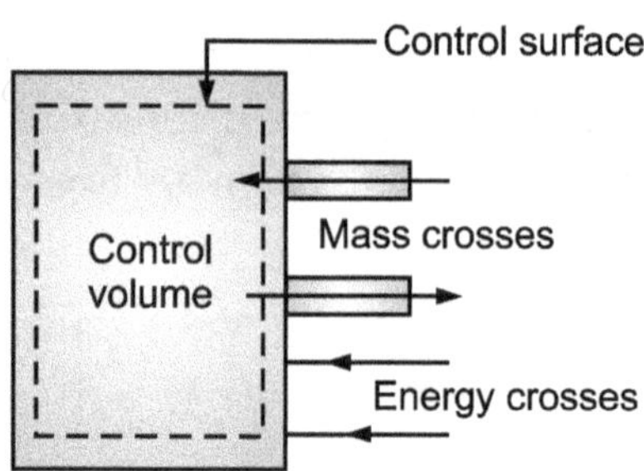


**Fig. 1.6: Control volume**

## 1.3.3 Properties

Any measurable characteristic of a system is called a property. Some familiar examples are pressure P, temperature T, volume V, and mass m. Other properties are viscosity, thermal conductivity, modulus of elasticity, electric resistivity and even velocity and elevation.

Not all properties are independent, however, some are defined in terms of other ones. For example, density is defined as mass per unit volume.

$$\rho = \frac{m}{V} \ (kg/m^3) \qquad \qquad ...(1.1)$$

Properties are considered to be either intensive or extensive.

**Intensive and Extensive Properties:**

Intensive properties are those which are independent of the mass (size) of a system. For example, temperature, pressure and density.

Extensive properties vary directly with mass (or size) of the system. For example, mass, volume, and total energy.

An easy way to determine whether a property is intensive or extensive is to divide the system into two equal parts as shown in Fig. 1.7.

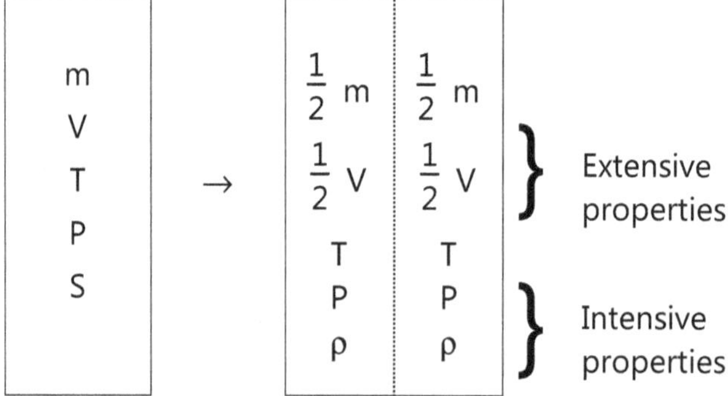


**Fig. 1.7: Extensive and intensive properties**

Each part will have the same value of intensive properties as the original system, but extensive properties are half the original.

## 1.3.4 State

It is the condition of a system. This condition or state of a system is described by the thermodynamic properties, such as pressure, temperature and volume.

The state of a pure substance can be defined by any two independent properties.

Thermodynamics deals with equilibrium states. The word equilibrium implies a state of balance. In an equilibrium state, there are no unbalanced potentials (or driving forces) within the system. A system which is in equilibrium, experiences no spontaneous changes.

## 1.3.5 Processes

Any change that a system undergoes from one equilibrium state to another is called a **process** and the series of states through which a system passes during a process is called the path of the process. (Fig. 1.8). To describe a process completely, one should specify the initial and final states of the process, as well as the path it follows and the interactions with the surroundings. The system changes its state from one state to another, by energy transfer across the boundaries.

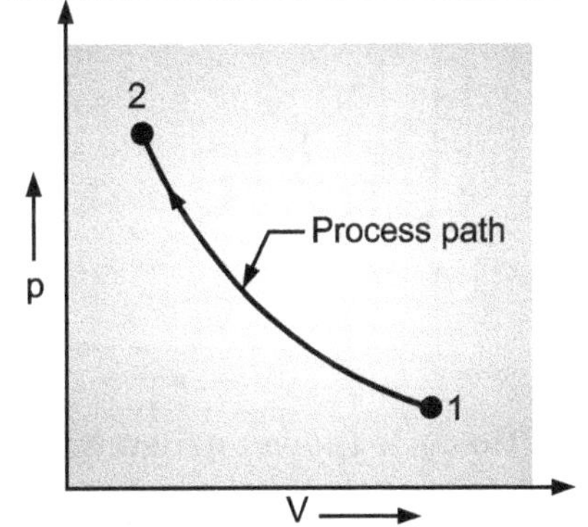


**Fig. 1.8: Process between states 1 and 2**

The values of the properties at the beginning and at the end of a process are different.

If the value of one of the properties is kept constant, the process is known by the property which is kept constant.

The various processes are as listed below:

(a) **Constant pressure or Isobaric process:** The pressure is maintained constant during the process.

(b) **Constant volume or Isochoric process:** The volume is kept constant during the process.

(c) **Constant temperature or Isothermal process:** Temperature is kept constant during the process.

(d) **Constant entropy or Isentropic process:** The entropy remains constant during the process. This is also known as reversible adiabatic process.

## 1.3.6 Cycle or Cyclic Process

A **thermodynamic cycle** or simply cycle is defined as a series of state changes such that the final state is identical with the initial state. It can also be defined as if the number of processes in sequence bring the system back to its initial state, then the system is said to execute a cycle or cyclic process.

The cyclic process plays an important role in the study of thermodynamics. Because, a net effect of a cyclic process may be conversion of heat into work or maintaining a system at lower temperature than surroundings (refrigerator) by means of work input.

Cyclic processes are classified as closed cycles or open cycles. In **closed cyclic** process, the same working substance is used again and again and only heat and work transfer take place between system and surroundings. The steam power plant and refrigeration system work on a closed cycle. In an **open cycle**, the working fluid once used during the cyclic process is thrown out and new mass of working fluid is taken in during the next cyclic process. Internal combustion engines and gas turbines work on an open cycle.

Different ideal closed cyclic processes are shown in Fig. 1.9.

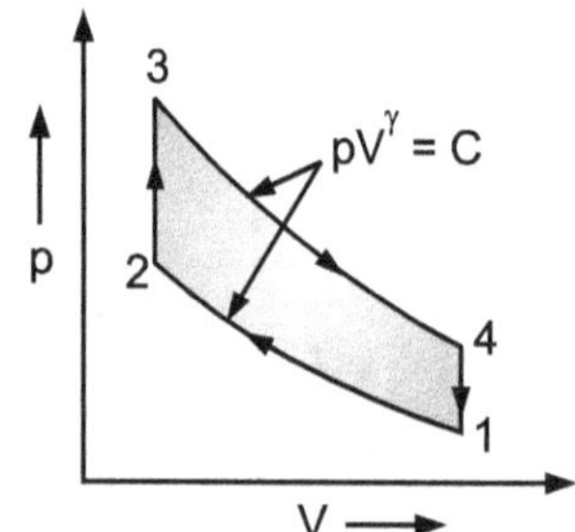


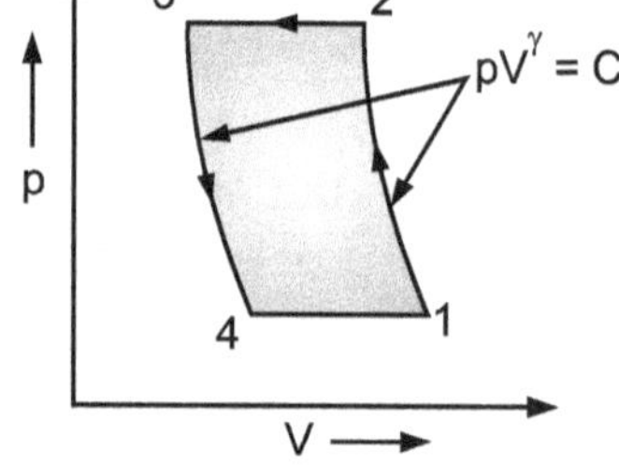


**(a) Otto cycle (power generation)**　　　　**(b) Reversed Joule cycle (Refrigeration)**

**Fig. 1.9: Otto and Joule cycles**

The cyclic process shown in Fig. 1.9 (a) is used for power generation and Fig. 1.9 (b) shows a refrigeration cycle.

## 1.3.7 Reversible and Irreversible Process

When a process proceeds in such a manner that the system remains infinitesimally close to an equilibrium state at all times, it is called a quasi - static or quasi - equilibrium process.

Quasi means **'almost'. Infinite slowness** (dead slow) is the characteristic feature of a quasi - static process.

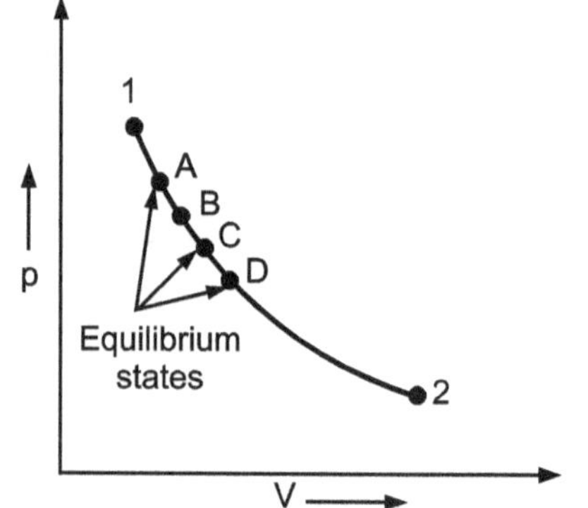


**Fig. 1.10: Quasi-static process**

Consider a process wherein the involved energy transfers are extremely small, i.e. infinitesimal in magnitude (Refer **Fig. 1.10**). Starting from state 1, a new equilibrium state 'A' very close to state 1 will be reached due to a very small energy exchange. If any process consists of such a large number of equilibrium states, say A, B, C, D ......... as in the figure, it may be represented by a continuous curve joining states 1 to 2. Such a process should occur extremely slowly, through a succession of equilibrium states. It is therefore, called a **quasi-static process**.

All the states in quasi-static process are equilibrium states. If the process is carried out in the reverse direction, it should reach the same equilibrium states at the same time by evolving the same amount of energy exchange. Therefore, *quasi-static* process is a *reversible process*.

A process which is not a quasi-static process, is known as an **irreversible process**. For an irreversible process, only end states are in equilibrium state. The other states are non-equilibrium states. The values of properties at intermediate non-equilibrium states are not known. Therefore, irreversible process cannot be shown on thermodynamic plane. (P - V plane, P - T plane etc.). Therefore, it is shown as a dotted curve on thermodynamic plane. (See **Fig. 1.11**)

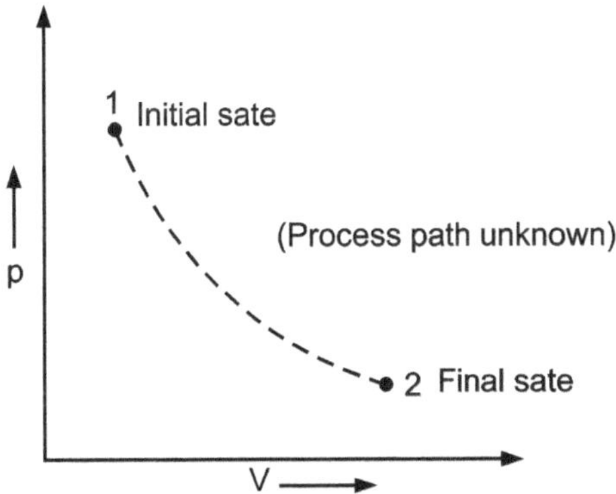


**Fig. 1.11: Irreversible process**

## 1.3.8 Point Function

Any point on x - y plane can be defined by x and y co-ordinates. Similarly, thermodynamic planes (such as P - V, P - T and T - s) can be formed by any two variables. On such planes, any two properties are sufficient to define a state.

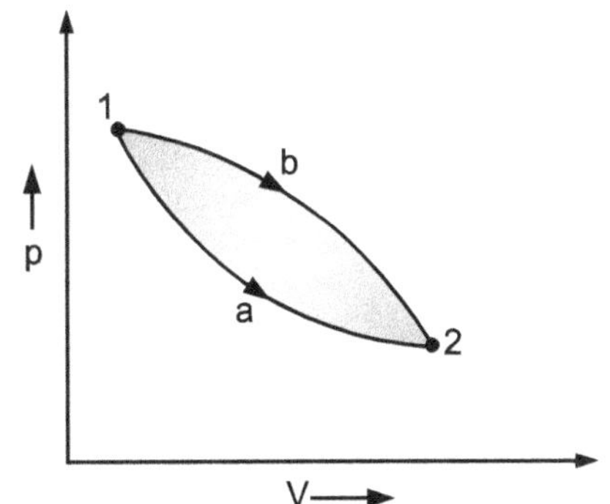


**Fig. 1.12: Point function**

Consider a P - V plane as shown in **Fig. 1.12** and any point 1 defined by the pressure $P_1$ and volume $V_1$. Also, let $P_2$ and $V_2$ define a state point 2 on P - V diagram. The state point 2 is reached from state point 1 by two ways: (i) through 1 - a - 2 and (ii) through 1 - b - 2. It is clear that the values of $P_2$ and $V_2$ are same at the end of two processes. Therefore, the change in the values of pressure P and volume V are not dependent on the path followed but only dependent on end state.

Two properties define a state. Therefore, all the properties are state or point functions. The characteristics such as pressure, temperature, volume, internal energy and entropy are state functions and are properties of a system. The property which is not a state or point function, then it is not a property. Examples are heat, work, etc.

Let $\phi$ is any property and $d\phi$ is its differential. As property is a point function, we can write $\int_{1}^{2} d\phi = \phi_2 - \phi_1$. This change depends only on end states. Therefore, $d\phi$ is an **exact differential**.

A characteristic of a system which has an exact differential is a property of the system and otherwise it is a non-property.

Therefore, we can have the following points: (i) A property is defined by a point on any thermodynamic plane. (ii) The change in thermodynamic property depends on only end states and not on the path. (iii) The properties are exact differentials.

## 1.3.9 Path Function

Heat and work are path functions.

The amount of heat transferred when a system changes from a state 1 to state 2 depends on the intermediate states through which the system passes i.e. its path. Therefore, dQ is an inexact differential.

$$\int_{1}^{2} dQ = Q_{1-2} \text{ i.e. } \int_{1}^{2} dQ \neq Q_2 - Q_1$$

Heat is represented by an area under the curve on Temperature-entropy (or T – s) diagram. T - s diagrams for three-processes are illustrated in Fig. 1.13.

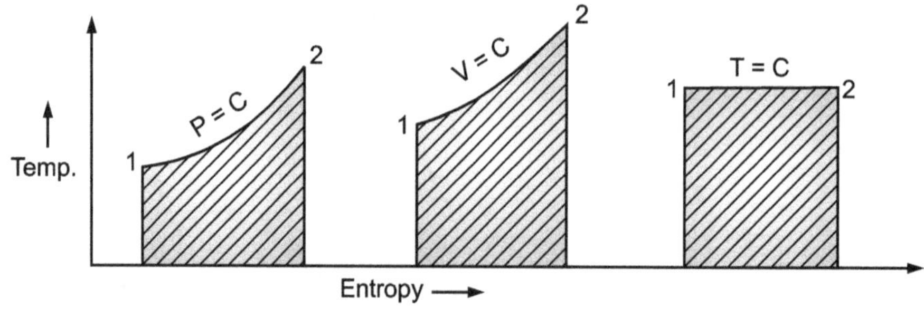


Fig. 1.13: Heat transfer depends on path. $Q_{1-2}$ is different for different paths

Work is represented by an area under the pressure - volume (or P - V) diagram. Therefore, work cannot be represented by a point on P - V plot.

The P - V diagrams for three processes are illustrated in Fig. 1.14.

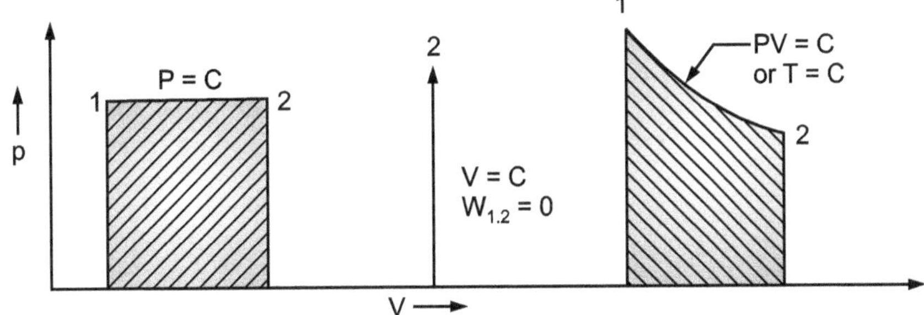

**Fig. 1.14: Work depends on path. Its value is different for different paths**

$$\int_{1}^{2} dW \neq W_2 - W_1 \text{ or } \int_{1}^{2} dW = W_{1-2}$$

A little consideration shows that, the quantities heat and work are different for different processes. Hence heat and work are path functions. Their differentials are **inexact** differentials.

## 1.3.10 Heat

Heat is defined as the form of energy that is transferred across a boundary by virtue of temperature difference.

Heat is an interaction which may occur between two systems, when they are brought into communication.

The concept of heat is related with the temperature difference between the two systems or between the system and surroundings.

Heat is not stored in the system, it is the **energy in transit**. It is not a property of the system, and it is a path function. It is represented by an inexact differential $\int \delta Q = Q_{1-2}$.

**Comments:**

- Heat is not that which inevitably causes temperature rise. For example, boiling of water at 100°C to convert into steam.
- Heat is not that which is always present when temperature rise occurs. For example, (a) A compression of gas in an adiabatically insulated cylinder, (b) Conversion of water into vapour at 100°C.

**According to Rutherford**

- Heat is not a conserved fluid which can be transferred from one body to another. Heat exists in transition phase only.
- Heat should not be confused with temperature.

**Sign Convention for Heat:**

The heat supplied to a system is considered as positive while the heat rejected by the system is considered as negative.

## 1.3.11 Work

In mechanics, work is defined as the product of force and distance, while the direction of application of force on the body is in the direction of motion.

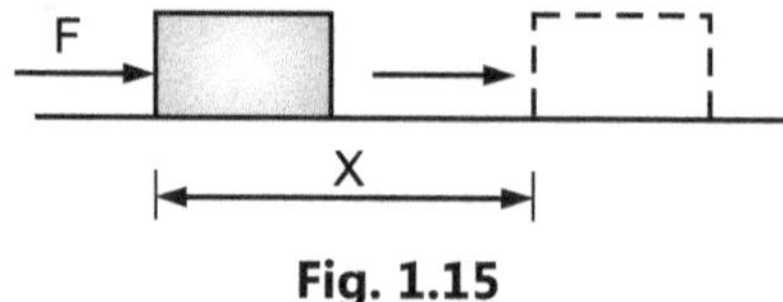

**Fig. 1.15**

$W = F \cdot X$ (Nm), where F = force, N; X = distance in metres.

Work is one of the basic modes of energy transfer. In thermodynamics, work transfer occurs between the system and surroundings. ***Work is said to be done by a system, if the sole effect external to the system can be reduced to the raising of a weight.***

Thus in thermodynamics,

- Work is either done on a system or it is done by the system.

- The weight may not be raised actually, but the net effect of work can be converted to raise the weight.

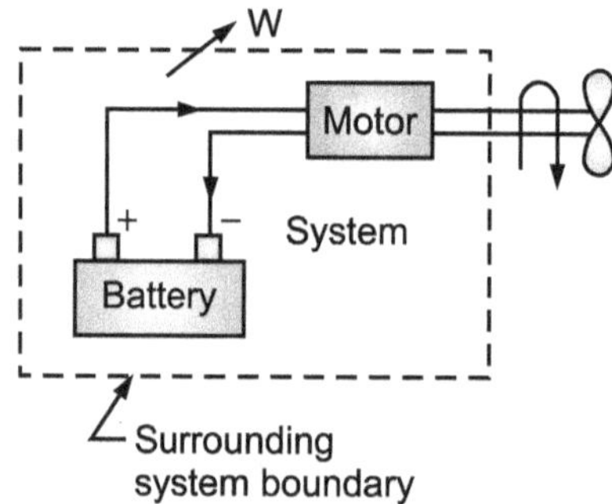


**Fig. 1.16: Battery - motor system driving a fan**

Let us consider an example of a battery driving a motor (Fig. 1.16). The motor is driving a fan. If we limit the system boundary for battery and motor as shown, then work is done by the system (battery and motor) on the surroundings (fan). It means work crosses the boundary.

Now, replace a fan with a pulley and weight as shown in Fig. 1.17.

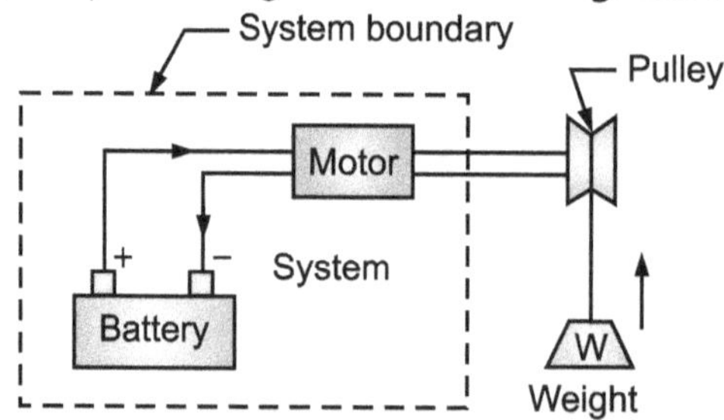


**Fig. 1.17: Work transfer from a system**

The weight may be raised with the pulley and motor. It means total effect external to the system is to raise the load.

If work is done by a system, then it is considered as positive and when work is done on a system, it is taken as negative (Fig. 1.18).

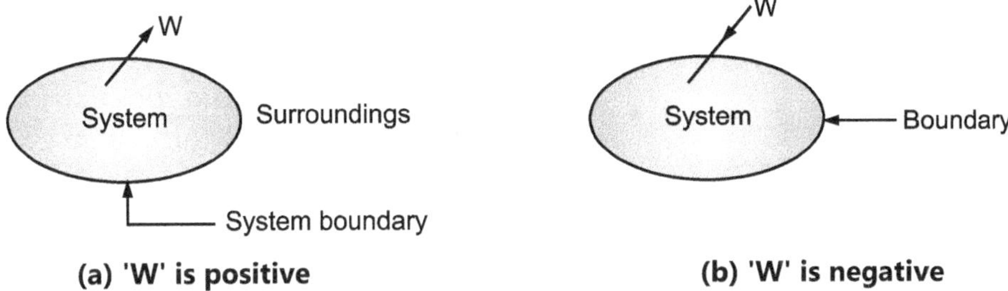


**(a) 'W' is positive**                              **(b) 'W' is negative**

**Fig. 1.18: Sign conventions for work**

**Comments:**

- Work is energy in transit. It appears only when it crosses the boundary.

- It is a path function and not a property of the system.

- The work is an inexact differential i.e. $\int dW \neq W_2 - W_1$.

## 1.3.12 Similarities Between Heat and Work

- Both are boundary phenomena and in both cases energy should cross the system boundary.

- Both are transient phenomena and exist whenever a system executes a process.

- Both are path functions and therefore form the inexact differentials. Hence they are not thermodynamic properties.

## 1.3.13 Difference between Heat and Work

- If a system is in a stable equilibrium state, then work interaction between the system and the surroundings cannot take place whereas there is no such restriction for the heat interaction. This is clear from the example of a gas contained in a rigid container at high pressure and temperature. The rigidness of the container provides an upper limit to the volume of the system. In this case, no work interaction will occur. But due to temperature difference between the system and surroundings, heat interaction occurs.

- For heat interaction between the system and the surroundings, the temperature potential difference should exist between them, but no temperature difference is required for work interaction.

## 1.3.14 Different Forms of Work

| | |
|---|---|
| (a)   PdV work or displacement work. | (b)   Shaft work |
| (c)   Flow work | (d)   Paddle wheel work or stirring work |

(e)  Electrical work                          (f)  Work done in stretching a wire

(g)  Magnetization work                       (h)  Surface tension work

(i)  Free expansion work

## (a) PdV Work or displacement work:

Consider a cylinder and piston arrangement as shown in Fig. 1.19.

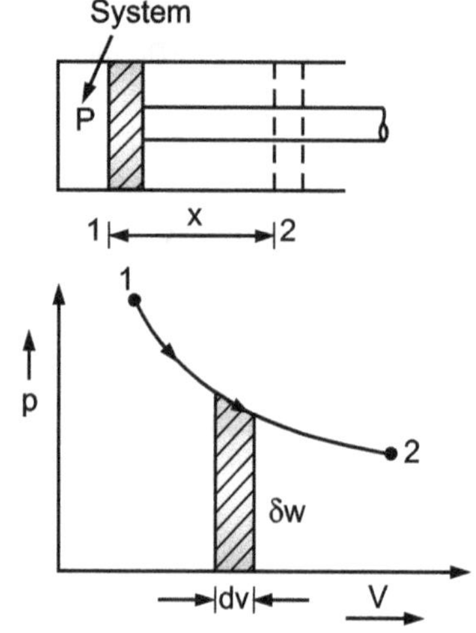


**Fig. 1.19: P-v diagram**

As the piston moves from position 1 to position 2, work is done by the system on the piston i.e. work is obtained from the system.

The work done by the system to move the piston through a small distance δx is say δW.

$\therefore$        δW  = Force × distance moved

$\therefore$        δW  = Pressure × area of piston × δx

         = P (A · δx) = PdV

Total work done for the expansion of system from state point 1 to state point 2 is

$$W = \int_1^2 PdV \qquad \text{... (1.2)}$$

         = Area under the curve.

Thus we can say PdV work is a path function. The above equation (1.2) is valid only when:

- The piston has very slow movement so that change in pressure is uniform throughout, i.e. it must be a quasi-static process.

- It should be frictionless process.

- System is closed.

- The boundary of the system moves so that work can be transferred.

The above equation (1.2) can be solved if the exact relation between P and V is known and the process must be **non-flow process**.

## (b) Shaft work:

A rotating shaft can raise a weight, if a pulley is fixed to its end. (See **Fig. 1.20**).

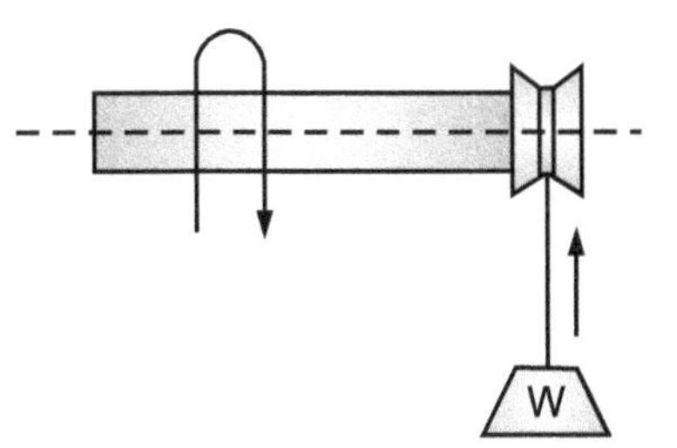

The work done is given by

$$\delta W = T \, \delta \theta$$

where,    $T$ = torque, in N-m

$\delta\theta$ = angle of rotation.

If the shaft rotate at N-rpm, then rate of work (Power) is

$$= \frac{2\,\pi\,NT}{60} \text{ N-m/s or watt}$$

**Fig. 1.20: Shaft work**

## (c) Flow work (Flow energy):

It is the energy associated with the flowing fluid. The flow work represents the amount of work that must be done to push a unit mass into or out of the system boundary.

Mathematically, work done per unit mass = p dv, Joule                                    ... (1.3)

where p is the pressure, N/m², normal to the boundary, and v = specific volume of fluid, m³/kg which crosses the boundary. It is explained in detail in further text.

## (d) Paddle wheel work or stirring work:

Consider a fluid (system) in a container alongwith a paddle wheel mounted at the end of a shaft and pulley and weight arrangement as shown in Fig. 1.21.

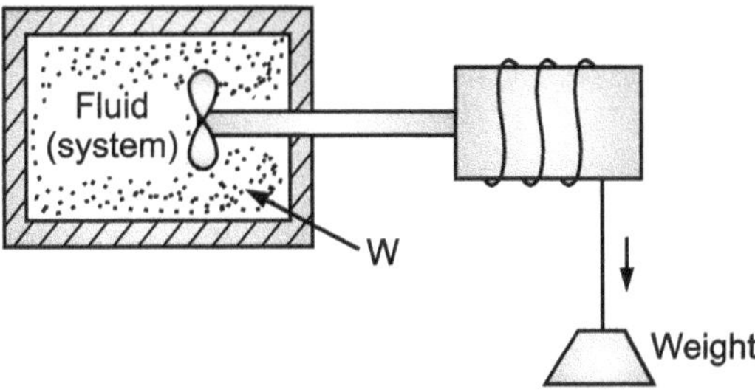


**Fig. 1.21: Paddle wheel work**

As the weight is lowered, the paddle wheel rotates, doing the work on the system. Due to this, temperature of the fluid increases and hence internal energy of the fluid increases.

Boundary of the system does not move, hence there is no change in the volume.

$$\therefore \qquad \int p\,dv = 0 \text{ but } \delta W \neq 0$$

## (e) Electrical work:

Consider a resistor as a system as shown in Fig. 1.22. As the current passes through the resistor, heat is generated. If the resistor is replaced by a motor, motor can drive a pulley and pulley can raise a weight.

The rate of work transfer $= I \cdot V$        ... (1.4)

where I = current in amperes, V = potential difference in volts.

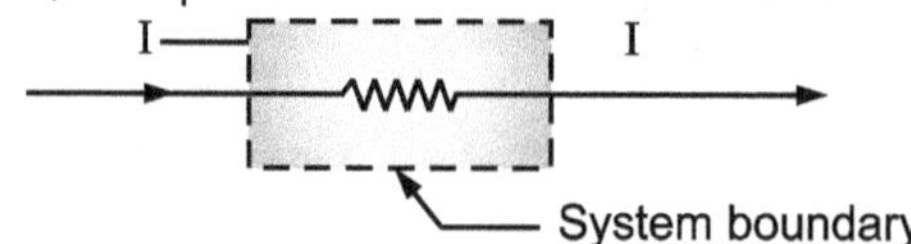


**Fig. 1.22: Electrical work**

### (f)  Work done in stretching a wire:

If L is the length of wire which is subjected to a tension 'T', it will change its length to L + dL, the small quantity of work done is

$$dW = -T \cdot dL$$

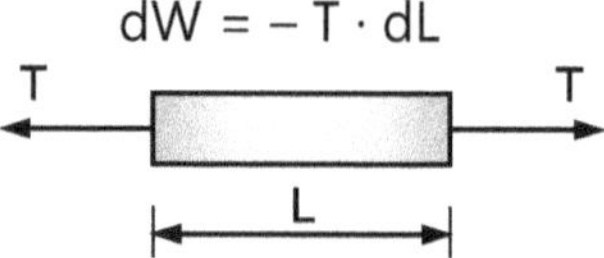


**Fig. 1.23: Work doe in stretching a wire**

Negative sign is due to the work done on the wire (system).

For a finite change of length from $L_i$ to $L_f$

$$W_{i-f} = \int_{L_i}^{L_f} -T \cdot dL \qquad ... (1.5)$$

### (g) Magnetization work:

The work done per unit volume on a magnetic material through which the magnetic and magnetization fields are uniform is

$$dW = -H \cdot dI$$

$$W_{1-2} = -\int_{I_1}^{I_2} H \cdot dI \qquad ... (1.6)$$

where H is field strength and I is the component of magnetization field in the direction of field. Negative sign is on account of work done on the system.

### (h) Surface tension work:

The work done on the homogeneous liquid film in changing its surface area by an infinitesimal amount dA is

$$dW = \sigma\, dA \ \text{Or} \ W_{1-2} = \int_{A_1}^{A_2} \sigma \cdot dA \qquad ... (1.7)$$

where $\sigma$ is the surface tension in N/m.

### (i) Free expansion work:

The expansion of gas against vacuum is called as free or unstrained expansion. The gas expands in a rigid vacuum container, hence no work is done and hence dW = 0 although pdv ≠ 0.

### Total Work done by a System:

Different forms of work transfer may occur simultaneously during a process. But the net or total work done by the system would be equal to the algebraic sum of these as given below:

$$W_{total} = W_{displacement} + W_{flow} + W_{electrical} + \ldots \qquad \ldots (1.8)$$

## 1.4  THERMODYNAMIC PROPERTIES OF THEIR UNITS

In this book the International System of Units or System International d' Units (SI) is used. The units are divided into base units and derived units. The following table will give information about their names and symbols.

**Base Units :**

| Quantity | Unit Name | Unit Symbol |
|---|---|---|
| Mass | Kilogram | kg |
| Length | Meter | m |
| Time | Second | s |
| Temperature | Kelvin | K |
| Amount of Matter | Mole | mol. |

**Derived Units (I) :**

| Quantity | Unit Name | Unit Symbol |
|---|---|---|
| Area | Square meter | $m^2$ |
| Volume | Cubic meter | $m^3$ |
| Velocity | Meter per second | m/s |
| Acceleration | Meter per second | $m/s^2$ |
| Density | Kilogram per cubic meter | $kg/m^3$ |
| Specific Volume | Cubic meter per kilogram | $m^3/kg$ |

**Derived Units (II) :**

| Quantity | Name | Symbol | Expression in terms of other units | Expression in terms of base units |
|---|---|---|---|---|
| Force | Newton | N | – | $kg \cdot m/s^2$ |
| Pressure | Pascal | Pa | $N/m^2$ | $kg/ms^2$ |
| energy, work, heat | Joule | J | N.m | $kg \cdot m^2/s^2$ |
| Power | Watt | W | J/s | $kg \cdot m^2/s^2$ |

## 1.4.1 Common multiples of SI Units

The most common multiples and submultiples used in SI units can be summarised as follows:

| Multiplication factor | Prefix | Symbol |
|---|---|---|
| $10^6$ | Mega | M |
| $10^3$ | Kilo | k |
| $10^{-3}$ | Milli | m |
| $10^{-6}$ | Micro | μ |
| $10^{-9}$ | Nano | n |
| $10^{-12}$ | Pico | p |

## 1.4.2 A Note on Additional Units

1. **Volume:** The unit of volume is cubic meter ($m^3$). The unit litre is also commonly used and 1 litre equals $10^{-3}$ $m^3$. The basic unit of $m^3$ however should be used in technical work.

2. **Mass:** The basic unit of mass is kilogram (kg). For large masses 1 tonne or 1 Megagram ($10^3$ kg) is used. For small masses 1 milligram ($10^{-6}$ kg) is used.

   The term weight should not be used in place of mass. Weight is force while mass is quantity of matter.

3. **Force:** The unit of force is Newton (N) and it is defined as the force which will accelerate one kg of mass with an acceleration of one meter per second.

   Newton's $2^{nd}$ law gives us the relation

   $F \propto m \times a$ where F is force, m is mass, and a is acceleration.

   or $\qquad\qquad\qquad F = \dfrac{ma}{g_c}$ where $g_c$ is constant of proportionality $\qquad$ ... (1.9)

As one Newton produces acceleration of $1 m/s^2$ in 1 kg of mass we have

$$1 \text{ Newton} = \frac{1}{g_c} \times 1 \text{ kg} \times 1 \text{ m/s}^2$$

$$\therefore \qquad g_c = 1$$

when $g_c = 1$ the system is said to be coherent or consistent and the product of units of mass and acceleration becomes the unit of force.

If the mass is allowed to fall freely under the action of standard gravitational force it is accelerated at the rate of $9.806 \text{ m/s}^2$ ($9.81 \text{ m/s}^2$) and we have

$$\text{Force} \; = \; 1 \, kg \times 9.81 \; m/s^2 = 9.81 \; N \qquad \qquad \text{... (1.10)}$$

It follows that the weight of 1 kg mass equals 9.81 Newtons

**4.   Density:** Density $\rho$ is defined as mass (not weight) per unit volume. Its units are kilogram per cubic metre ($kg/m^3$). Density of water is 1000 $kg/m^3$ or 1 tonne/$m^3$. The reciprocal of density is called specific volume and is defined as volume occupied by unit

Most common unit of pressure is 1 bar which is equal to $10^5$ $P_a$. mass of a substance. Its units are cubic metre per kilogram ($m^3/kg$)

$$v \; = \; m^3/kg \text{ and } v = \frac{1}{\rho} \qquad \qquad \text{... (1.11)}$$

**5.   Specific weight:** It is defined as the force of gravity on unit volume (not unit mass). It is denoted by $\gamma$ and its units are Newton per cubic meter ($N/m^3$).

$$\gamma \; = \; \frac{\text{force of gravity}}{\text{volume}} \; = \frac{m \cdot g \cdot}{g_c \, V} \; = \frac{\rho g}{g_c} \qquad \qquad \text{... (1.12)}$$

Where g is local acceleration due to gravity. At earth's surface $g = g_c$ and $\gamma = \rho$.

Also
$$\frac{\gamma}{g} \; = \; \frac{\rho}{g_c}$$

**6.   Pressure:** It is defined as force per unit area. Its units are Newton per square meter ($N/m^2$). This unit is also called as *Pascal* ($P_a$).

$$\therefore \qquad P_a \; = \; \frac{N}{m^2} \text{ or } 1 \text{ Pascal} = \frac{1 \text{ Newton}}{1 \text{ meter}^2} \qquad \qquad \text{... (1.13)}$$

Pascal is a small unit and kilo pascal (1 $kN/m^2$) and Megapascal (1 $MN/m^2 = 10^6 \, N/m^2$) may be used.

Also $\qquad \qquad$ 1 $MN/m^2 \; = \; 1 \, N/mm^2$

$\therefore \qquad \qquad$ 1 bar $\; = \; 10^5 \, N/m^2 = 10^5 \, P_a = 100 \, kP_a$

The pressure exerted by the atmosphere is known as atmospheric pressure and is denoted by 1 atm. In various units the values of 1 atmospheric pressure are given below :

$$1 \text{ atm} \; = \; 760 \text{ mm. of Hg} = 10.33 \text{ meter of } H_2O = 101325 \, N/m^2$$

$$= \; 1.01325 \text{ bar} = 1.033 \text{ kgf/cm}^2$$

Another useful unit of pressure is,

$$1 \text{ tor} \; = \; 1 \text{ mm of Hg} = 133.32 \, N/m^2 = 133.32 \text{ Pa}$$

## 1.4.3 Absolute and Gauge Pressure

- **Pressure measurement is done by**
- **Barometer:** This measures atmosphere pressure
- **Bourdon pressure gauge:** This measures pressure in any closed container or pipe etc.
- **Manometer:** This also measures pressure in a container or pipe as Bourdon gauge.

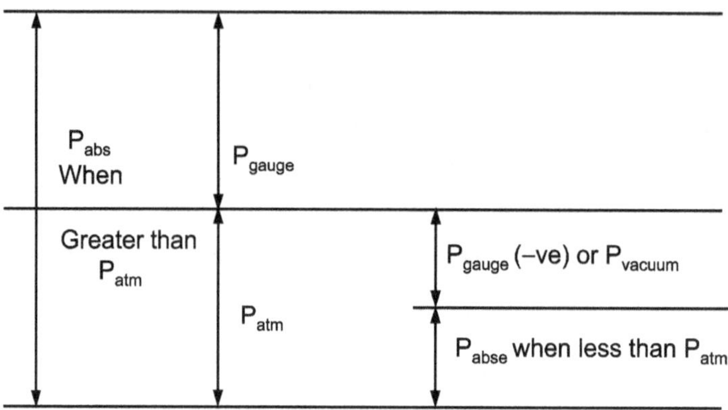


**Fig. 1.24: Relation between absolute and gauge pressure**

The pressure of atmosphere acts both on the container and the gauge which measures pressure inside the container. The gauge thus measures pressure on and above atmospheric pressure. If we wish to find the real pressure or absolute pressure we have to add the atmospheric pressure to the gauge pressure. This can be written as

$$\text{Absolute Pressure} = \text{Atmospheric Pressure} \pm \text{Gauge Pressure}$$

or
$$P_{abs} = P_{atm} \pm P_{gauge}$$

The negative sign is used when the absolute pressure is less than the atmospheric pressure. Fig. 1.24 gives an idea of this relation.

## (b)  Fluid Pressure

Consider a vessel filled up with fluid of density $\rho$. The fluid pressure at any point which is at distance Z from the surface is given by

$$P = \rho g Z = \frac{kg}{m^3} \cdot \frac{m}{sec^2} \cdot m$$

$$= kg \left(\frac{m}{sec^2}\right) \frac{1}{m^2}$$

$$= \frac{\text{Mass} \times \text{Acceleration}}{m^2}$$

$$= \frac{\text{Force}}{m^2} = \frac{N}{m^2} \text{ or Pa}$$

**Fig. 1.25: Fluid Pressure**

If the fluid is mercury with a density of 13596 kg/m$^3$ the pressure exerted by 760 mm of Hg which is atmospheric pressure is given as

$$P = 13596 \times 9.806 \times 0.76 = 1.01325 \times 10^5 \text{ N/m}^2 = 1.01325 \text{ bar}$$

and height of mercury corresponding to a pressure of 1 bar is given by,

$$h \text{ of mercury} = \frac{760}{1.01325} \approx 750 \text{ mm of mercury}$$

The pressure corresponding to 1 mm of mercury which is called 1 Tor is given by,

$$1 \text{ Tor} = 13596 \times 9.806 \times \frac{1}{1000} = 133.32 \text{ Pascals}$$

# 1.5 THERMODYNAMIC EQUILIBRIUM

- Thermodynamics deals with equilibrium states.

- Equilibrium means state of balance.

- Therefore, in an equilibrium state, there is no unbalanced potential (or driving force) within the system or between system and surroundings).

- A system which is in thermodynamic equilibrium, does not undergo any spontaneous change.

When a system is isolated from its surroundings, it reaches a state of thermodynamic equilibrium. The system is said to be in **thermodynamic equilibrium** state if it is in mechanical, chemical and thermal equilibrium.

**Mechanical Equilibrium:** In the absence of any unbalanced force within the system itself and also between the system and surroundings, the system is said to be in **mechanical equilibrium**.

**Chemical Equilibrium:** If there is no spontaneous chemical reaction or transfer of matter from one part of the system to another, such as diffusion, then the system is said to be in **chemical equilibrium**.

**Thermal Equilibrium:** When a system existing in chemical and mechanical equilibrium is separated from its surrounding by a diathermic wall (**diathermic wall** means which allows heat to flow) and if there is no spontaneous change in any property of the system, the system is said to be in a state of **thermal equilibrium**. Such a system exists with equality of temperature.

## 1.5.1 Zeroth Law of Thermodynamics

When a body is brought into contact with another body which is at a different temperature, heat is transferred from the body at higher temperature to the body at lower temperature until both bodies attain the same temperature (Fig. 1.26). At that instant (point), the heat transfer stops, and the two bodies are said to have reached **thermal equilibrium**. *The equality of temperature is the only* requirement for thermal equilibrium.

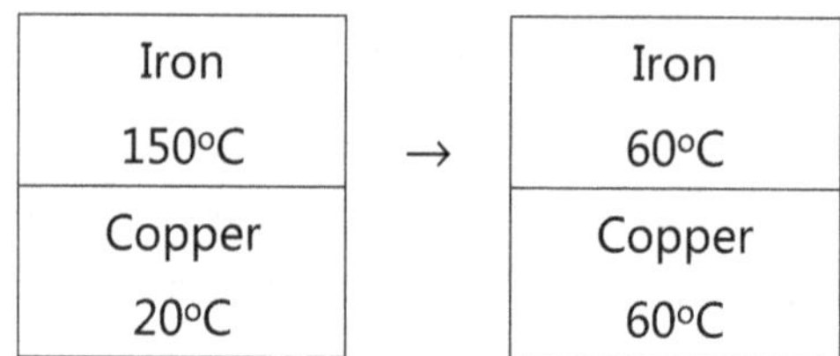


**Fig. 1.26: Two bodies reaching thermal equilibrium after being brought into contact**

The two bodies are said to be in thermal equilibrium if they attain same (equal) temperature.

**Zeroth Law of Thermodynamics:**

When a body 'A' is in thermal equilibrium with a body 'B' and also body 'A' is in thermal equilibrium with body 'C' separately, then bodies B and C will be in thermal equilibrium with each other. (Fig. 1.27).

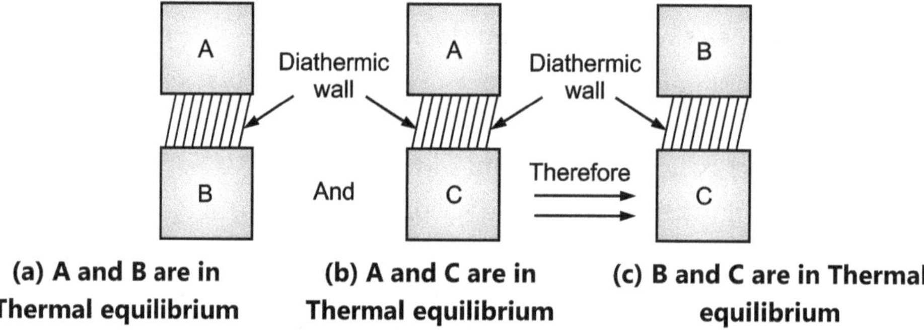


**(a) A and B are in          (b) A and C are in          (c) B and C are in Thermal**
**Thermal equilibrium        Thermal equilibrium              equilibrium**

**Fig. 1.27: Zeroth law of thermodynamics**

Diathermic wall is one which allows heat transfer in both directions, but impermeable to electrical, magnetic and other types of work interactions and isolated from the surroundings. In general, energy exchange occurs as heat between them.

Zeroth law of thermodynamics is the base for temperature measurement.

# 1.6 MACROSCOPIC AND MICROSCOPIC VIEWS

There are two points of view from which the behaviour of matter can be studied: the macroscopic and microscopic.

**Macroscopic View**

In this analysis, the system or equipment is considered as a whole. It considers the whole effect of matter without taking into account the events occurring at the molecular level. The branch which takes this view is termed as classical thermodynamics.

Macroscopic thermodynamics is only concerned with the effects of the action of many molecules and these effects can be perceived by human senses. For example, Macroscopic quantity, pressure is the average rate of change of momentum due to all the molecular collisions occurring per unit area. The effect of pressure can be felt. Similarly, temperature of a gas is due to average value of translational kinetic energies of millions of individual molecules. This can also be sensed.

**Microscopic View**

From the microscopic point of view, matter is composed of myriads of molecules. If it is a gas, each molecule at a given instant has a certain position, velocity and energy and for each molecule, these change vary frequently as a result of collisions. The behaviour of the gas molecule is described by summing up the behaviour of each molecule. Such a study is made in microscopic or statistical thermodynamics.

To find the behaviour of a system, statistical methods are used.

The properties like velocity, momentum, kinetic energy which describe the molecule cannot be easily measured with required accuracy. They cannot be felt by our senses.

The analysis of behaviour of a system is same by both the methods and the results are also compatible.

Only macroscopic study i.e. classical approach to thermodynamics is adopted in this book.

# 1.7  FIRST LAW OF THERMODYNAMICS

Heat and work, the forms of energy which are discussed in the earlier articles, are related by the first law of thermodynamics. This is a law of conservation of energy which states that 'energy can neither be created nor be destroyed'. This law cannot be proved mathematically, but no exception has been observed.

## 1.7.1 First Law of Thermodynamics and Joule's Experiment

Before defining the first law of thermodynamics, it is better to discuss some experimental results on which it is based. Such an experiment was carried out by a scientist J. P. Joule, during the period 1840-1849. In one of the experiment, he used the apparatus similar to that shown in **Fig. 1.28**.

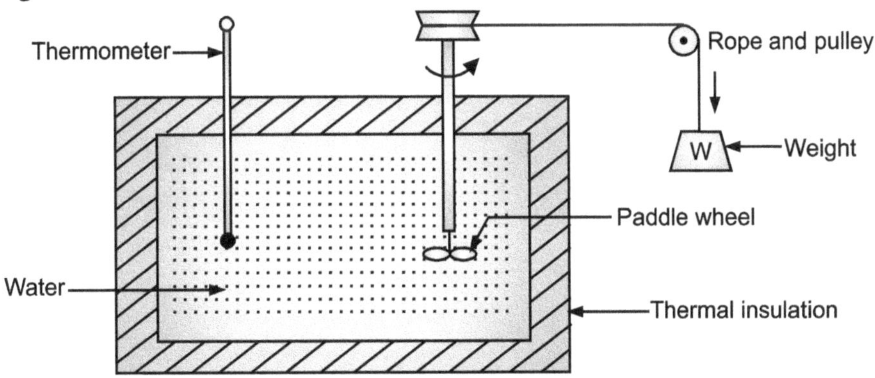


**Fig. 1.28: Joule's Experiment**

It consists of a closed container insulated from outside, filled with certain amount of water, having thermometer and a paddle wheel.

The temperature of water is measured before and after the work is done on it through a paddle wheel, which rotates due to the weight moving down. The rise in the temperature of water is always proportional to the work done on it due to the potential energy lost by the weight.

Let $W_{1-2}$ is the work done on the water (system), $t_1$ = initial temperature of water, $t_2$ = temperature of water after the work is done ($t_2 > t_1$). This process is as shown in Fig. 1.29.

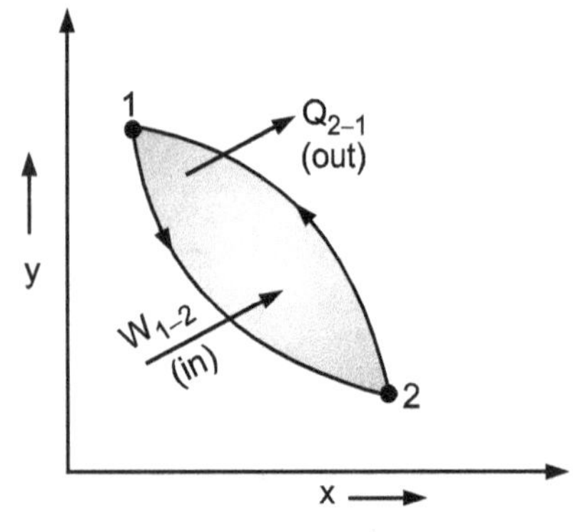


**Fig. 1.29: Cycle**

Now, assume the insulation is removed, therefore heat transfer takes place from the system to the surroundings. Therefore, its temperature reaches to the original temperature $t_1$. The amount of heat $Q_{2-1}$ is transferred to the surroundings. Thus, a system completes a cycle, with definite amount of work $W_{1-2}$ input to the system and followed by $Q_{2-1}$, amount of heat dissipated from the system.

Joule had conducted this experiment number of times for different weights moving through different distances. Each time he measured the temperature rise of the system.

He found that $Q_{1-2}$ is proportional to $W_{1-2}$. ($Q_{1-2} \propto W_{1-2}$). This constant of proportionality is known as **'Joule's equivalent or the mechanical equivalent of heat'**.

In SI units, work is measured in N-m and heat in joules (J) and the relation is
1 N-m = 1 joule and hence Joule's constant is unity.

If the cycle shown in Fig. 1.29 involves many more heat and work transfers, the same conclusion will be found. Expressed mathematically,

$$(\Sigma W)_{cycle} = J (\Sigma Q)_{cycle} \qquad \qquad ... (1.14)$$

It can be written as $\oint \delta W = J \oint \delta Q$

As $\qquad J = 1, \quad \oint \delta W = \oint \delta Q \qquad \qquad ...(1.15)$

where the symbol $\oint$ denotes the cyclic integral for the closed path. This is the first law applied to a closed system undergoing a cyclic process.

**Other Statements of First Law of Thermodynamics:**

**(i)   Principle of Energy Conservation:**

According to this concept, energy can neither be created nor be destroyed. This implies that the sum of the energies of a system at the microscopic and macroscopic levels is fixed, unless there is an interaction with the surroundings, involving an energy exchange.

This can be simply stated as

**"The total energy of an isolated system, measured with respect to any given frame of reference remains constant."** Mathematically, for an isolated system,

$$E \text{ (total)} = U + K.E. + P.E. + \text{Chemical energy} + \ldots\ldots$$

$$= \text{Constant}$$

## 1.7.2   First Law Applied to a Closed System Undergoing a Change of State

The expression $(\sum W)_{cycle} = (\sum Q)_{cycle}$ applies only to a system undergoing a cyclic process. But in practice, a system may undergo a *non-cyclic* process which produces a change of state in the system.

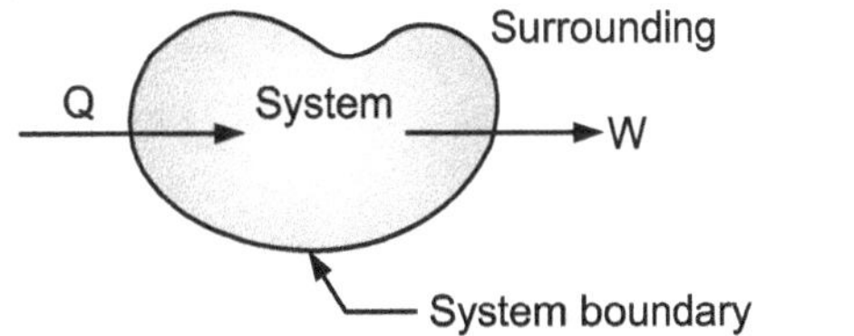


**Fig. 1.30: A system interacting with the surroundings which involves work and heat transfer**

Let us consider a system interacting with surroundings which involves work and heat transfer (Fig. 1.30)

If Q is the amount of heat transferred to the system and W is the work obtained from it, then $Q - W$ is the energy stored in the system. This stored energy in the system is not a heat or work but referred as internal energy or simply energy of the system.

$\Delta E = Q - W$, where $\Delta E$ is the increase in internal energy of the system.

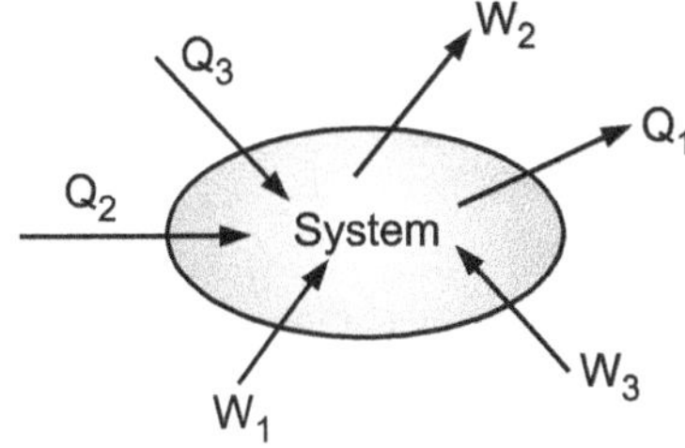


**Fig. 1.31: System interacting with the surroundings involving more energy transfers**

If more energy transfers are involved in the process, as shown in Fig. 1.31, the first law gives

$$(Q2 + Q3 - Q1) = \cdot E + (W2 + W1 - W3)$$

Energy is conserved in this operation also.

## 1.7.3 Internal Energy

Let a system undergoes a cyclic process as shown in Fig. 1.32. Consider this system changes its state from state 1 to state 2 following the path A. Apply first law to this process.

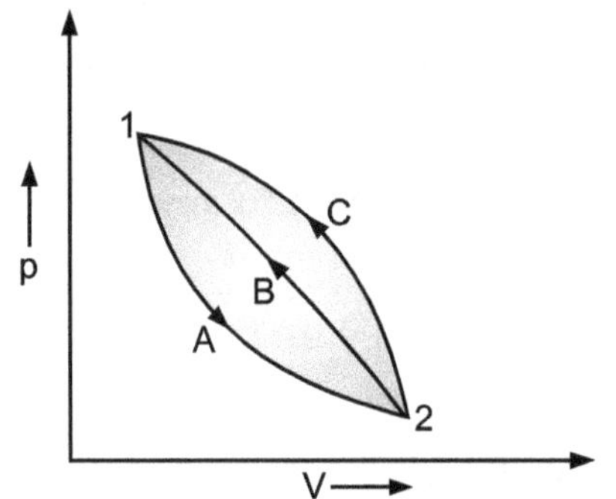

**Fig. 1.32: Energy - a property of a system**

$$Q_A = \Delta E_A + W_A \qquad \ldots (1.16)$$

The system returns from state 2 to state 1 along the path B.

$$\therefore \quad Q_B = \Delta E_B + W_B \qquad \ldots (1.17)$$

These two processes form a cycle, for which,

$$(\Sigma W)_{cycle} = (\Sigma Q)_{cycle}$$

$$\therefore \quad W_A + W_B = Q_A + Q_B$$

$$\therefore \quad Q_A - W_A = W_B - Q_B \qquad .. (1.18)$$

From equations (1.16), (1.17) and (1.18), it results,

$$\Delta E_A = - \Delta E_B \qquad \ldots (1.19)$$

Similarly, if we consider the cycle as $1 - A - 2 - C - 1$, then,

$$\Delta E_A = - \Delta E_C \qquad \ldots (1.20)$$

Comparison of the equations (1.18) and (1.19) will lead to,

$$\Delta E_B = \Delta E_C \qquad \ldots (1.21)$$

Hence, the change in energy between the states 1 and 2 is same for the paths B and C. It means the internal energy is independent of the path of the process. It is fixed for a particular state of the system. Therefore, one can conclude that internal energy is a point function and property of the system.

We have, $\qquad \delta Q - \delta W = dE$

The total energy change, $\delta E = \delta U + \delta KE + \delta PE$

where, $\qquad\qquad \delta KE \rightarrow$ change in K.E.

$\qquad\qquad\qquad \delta PE \rightarrow$ change in P.E.

$\qquad\qquad\qquad \delta U \rightarrow$ change in internal energy

If there is no change in K.E. and P.E., then

$$\delta PE = \delta KE = 0,$$

hence, $\qquad \delta Q - \delta W = \delta U \qquad \ldots (1.22)$

As $(\delta Q - \delta W)$ is independent of path and depends only on end states, the internal energy $U = \int (\delta Q - \delta W)$ is also independent of path and therefore, a property of the system.

# 1.8  STEADY FLOW PROCESS

A steady flow process is said to exist when the working substance flows in and out of the control volume and the properties of the working substance at any section of flow do not vary with time. A steady flow process must satisfy the following conditions:

- The rates of work and heat transferred across the control surface do not change with time.
- The mass flow rates at entrance and exit sections of the control volume are equal and do not change with time. Naturally, the mass within the control volume does not change with time and there is no change in energy within the system.
- The state of the working substance at any section within the control volume or at entrance or exit sections does not change with respect to time.

## 1.8.1 Mass Balance

By the conservation of mass, for steady flow, the mass flow rate entering the control volume must be equal to the mass flow rate leaving the control volume. (Volume flow rate at entry and exit of control volume may be different). See **Fig. 1.33**.

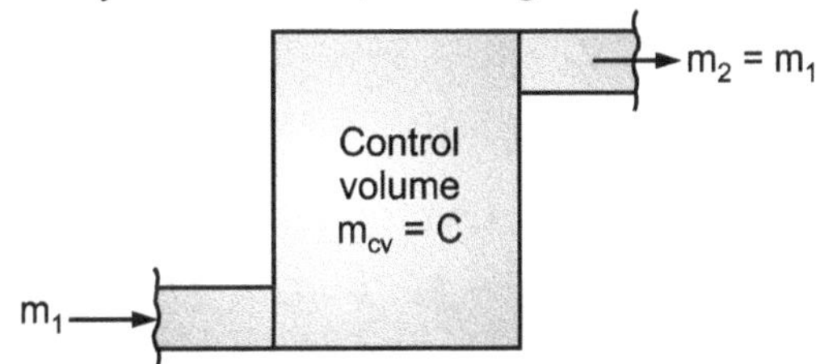


**Fig. 1.33: During a steady flow process, the amount of mass entering the control volume equals the amount of mass leaving**

## 1.8.2 Flow Work

Unlike closed systems, control volumes involve mass flow across their boundaries, and some work is required to push the mass into or out of the control volume. This work is known as the flow work or flow energy and is necessary for maintaining a continuous flow through a control volume (open system).

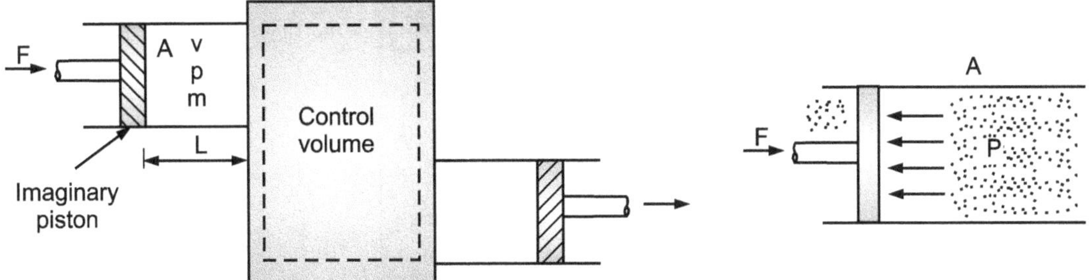


**Fig. 1.34: Schematic for flow work**      **Fig. 1.35: The force applied on a fluid by a piston is equal to the force applied on the piston by a fluid**

To obtain a relation for flow work, consider a volume 'V' of the fluid element shown in Fig. 1.34. The fluid immediately upstream will force this fluid element to enter the control volume, thus it can be regarded as an imaginary piston. The fluid element can be chosen to be sufficiently small.

If the fluid pressure is P and cross-sectional area of the fluid element is A, (Fig. 1.35), the force applied on the fluid element by the imaginary piston is $F = P \cdot A$.

To push the entire fluid element into the control volume, this force must act through a distance L. Thus the work done in pushing the fluid element across the boundary (i.e. the flow work) is

$$W_{flow} = F \cdot L = P \cdot A \cdot L = PV, \text{ kJ} \qquad \qquad \text{... (1.23)}$$

The flow work per unit mass is obtained by dividing both sides of this equation by the mass of the fluid element.

$$W_{flow} = PV_s \text{ (kJ/kg)} \qquad \qquad \text{... (1.24)}$$

where $V_s$ = Specific volume of fluid, $m^3/kg$

The total energy of the flowing fluid is

$$= PV_s + (U + KE + PE)$$

But,    $U + PV_s$ = enthalpy h

∴    Total energy of flowing fluid per unit mass

$$= h + KE + PE \qquad \qquad \text{... (1.25)}$$

$$= h + \frac{V^2}{2} + gZ \qquad \qquad \text{... (1.26)}$$

## 1.9  FIRST LAW APPLIED TO A STEADY FLOW PROCESS

A steady flow system is shown in Fig. 1.36, where one stream of fluid enters the control volume at section 1 – 1 and other stream of the fluid leaves the control volume at section 2 – 2. The properties at any location within the control volume are steady with time.

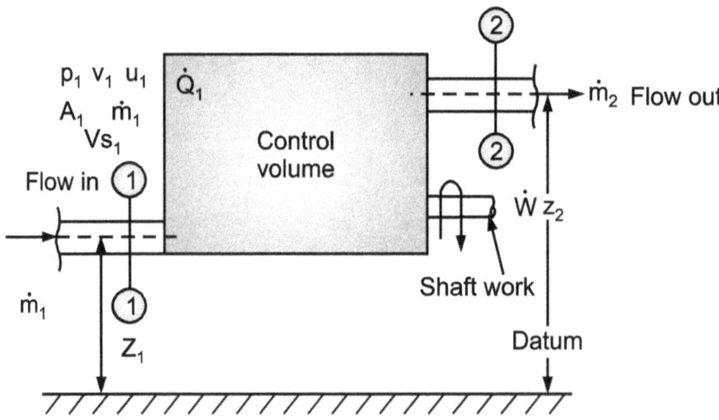


**Fig. 1.36: Steady flow process**

The following quantities are expressed with reference to Fig. 1.36.

$A_1, A_2$　– cross section of stream, $m^2$

$m_1, m_2$　– mass flow rate, kg/s

$P_1, P_2$　– absolute pressure, $N/m^2$

$V_{s1}, V_{s2}$　– specific volume, $m^3/kg$

$u_1, u_2$　– specific internal energy, J/kg

$v_1, v_2$– velocity of fluid, m/s

$z_1, z_2$– elevation above an arbitrary datum, m

$Q$　– net rate of heat flow into control volume, J/s

$W$　– net rate of work transfer through control volume, J/s

Subscripts 1 and 2 refer to the inlet and outlet sections.

The sum of energy quantities entering into the system

$$= \quad Q + m_1 \left( u_1 + \frac{v_1^2}{2} + gz_1 + PV_{s1} \right) \qquad \dots (1.27)$$

$$= \quad Q + m_1 \left( h_1 + \frac{v_1^2}{2} + gz_1 \right) \qquad \dots (1.28)$$

The sum of energy quantities leaving the control volume

$$= \quad W + m_2 \left( h_2 + \frac{v_2^2}{2} + gz_2 \right) \qquad \dots (1.29)$$

The change in energy $\Delta E$ of the control volume (system) is zero for **steady state conditions**.

Apply first law, i.e. the total energy entering the control volume is equal to the total energy leaving the control volume plus $\Delta E$.

For steady flow, $m_1 = m_2 = m$ and $\Delta E = 0$.

$$\therefore \quad Q + m \left( h_1 + \frac{v_1^2}{2} + gz_1 \right) = W + m \left( h_2 + \frac{v_2^2}{2} + gz_2 \right) \text{ J/s}$$

$$\therefore \quad Q - W = m \left( h_2 + \frac{v_2^2}{2} + gz_2 \right) - m \left( h_1 + \frac{v_1^2}{2} + gz_1 \right) \text{ J/s} \qquad \dots(1.30)$$

In words,

$$\begin{pmatrix} \text{Total energy} \\ \text{crossing boundary} \\ \text{as heat-work} \\ \text{per unit time} \end{pmatrix} = \begin{pmatrix} \text{Total energy} \\ \text{transported out} \\ \text{of CV with mass} \\ \text{per unit time} \end{pmatrix} - \begin{pmatrix} \text{Total energy} \\ \text{transported into} \\ \text{CV with mass} \\ \text{per unit time} \end{pmatrix} \qquad \dots (1.31)$$

It can be expressed as

$$Q - W = m\left[(h_2 - h_1) + \left(\frac{v_2^2 - v_1^2}{2000}\right) + \frac{g\,(z_2 - z_1)}{1000}\right] \text{ kW} \qquad \ldots (1.32)$$

$$Q - W = m\,(\Delta h + \Delta KE + \Delta PE) \text{ kW} \qquad \ldots (1.33)$$

Dividing these equations by m, we obtain the "steady flow energy equation (SFEE)" on a unit mass basis as

$$q = Q/m, \qquad w = W/m \text{ kJ/kg}$$

$$q - w = h_2 - h_1 + \frac{v_2^2 - v_1^2}{2000} + g\,\frac{(z_2 - z_1)}{1000} \text{ kJ/kg} \qquad \ldots (1.34)$$

## 1.9.1 Application to Different Devices

### (a) Nozzle and Diffuser:

A nozzle is a device used to accelerate the fluid flow while the diffuser is a device used to convert the kinetic energy of a flowing fluid into pressure head.

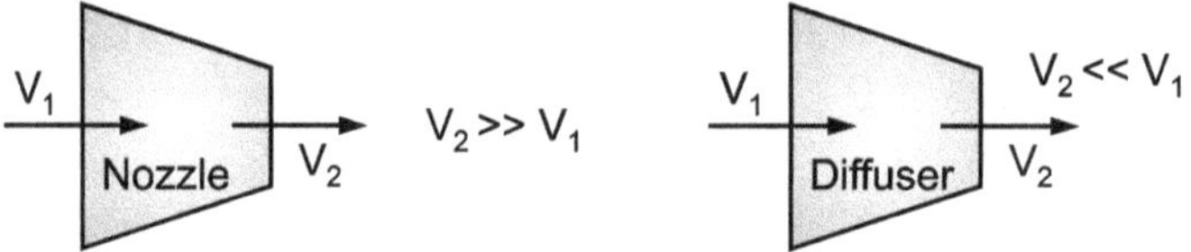


**Fig. 1.37: Nozzle and Diffuser**

$Q = 0$, The rate of heat transfer between the fluid and surroundings is very small and neglected.

$W = 0$, As there is no shaft work available from these or even work is not supplied.

$\Delta PE \approx 0$, The fluid usually experiences no change of elevation.

The SFEE equation (1.34) reduces to

$$0 = h_2 - h_1 + \frac{v_2^2 - v_1^2}{2000}$$

Usually $v_1$ is very small ($v_1 <<< v_2$) for nozzle,

$$\therefore \quad v_2 = \sqrt{2000\,(h_1 - h_2)} \text{ m/s} \qquad \ldots (1.35)$$

Here $(h_1 - h_2)$ is in J/kg.

### (b) Turbine and Compressor:

Turbines are prime-movers which generate power, whereas compressors and pumps require power input.

As the turbine is insulated, no heat exchange takes place, therefore, $Q = 0$. The flow velocities are often small in steam turbines, and K.E. term can be neglected. Also for steam turbines, $\Delta PE = 0$.

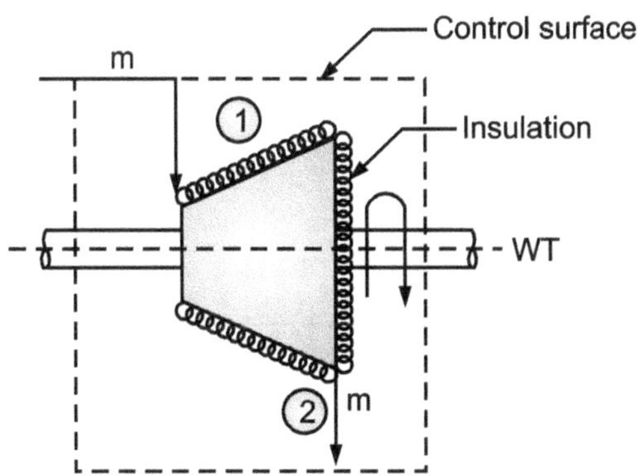


**Fig. 1.38: Flow through a turbine**

$\therefore$    SFEE then becomes $h_1 = h_2 + W$

or                    $W = h_1 - h_2$ kJ/kg

$$= m (h_1 - h_2) \text{ kW} \qquad \qquad \text{... (1.36)}$$

where m = mass flow rate in kg/s.

Similarly, for an adiabatic pump or compressor, the SFEE is,

$$W = (h_2 - h_1) \cdot m \text{ kW} \qquad \qquad \text{... (1.37)}$$

where '$h_1$' and '$h_2$' are in kJ/kg.

## (c) Throttling Valves:

Throttling valves are a kind of flow restricting devices that cause a significant pressure drop in the fluid. Some familiar examples are ordinary adjustable valves, capillary tubes and porous plugs. Unlike turbines, they produce a pressure drop without involving any work. The pressure drop in the fluid is often accompanied by a large drop in temperature and for that reason throttling devices are commonly used in refrigeration and air conditioning applications.

Throttling devices are very small in size, therefore flow through them is adiabatic (Q = 0). No work is involved, hence W = 0. Change in potential energy, $\Delta PE \approx 0$, Increase in KE of the fluid is insignificant, $\Delta KE = 0$.

$\therefore$                    $Q - W = \Delta h + \Delta KE + \Delta PE$

$$0 = \Delta h + 0 + 0$$

$\therefore$                    $0 = \Delta h$

i.e.                    $h_1 = h_2$ kJ/kg $\qquad \qquad$ ... (1.38)

i.e. enthalpy values at the inlet and exit of a throttling valve are same.

## (d) Heat Exchanger:

Heat exchanger is a device, where two moving fluid streams exchange heat without mixing.

The simplest form of a heat exchanger is a double tube (also called tube and shell) heat exchanger shown in Fig. 1.39.

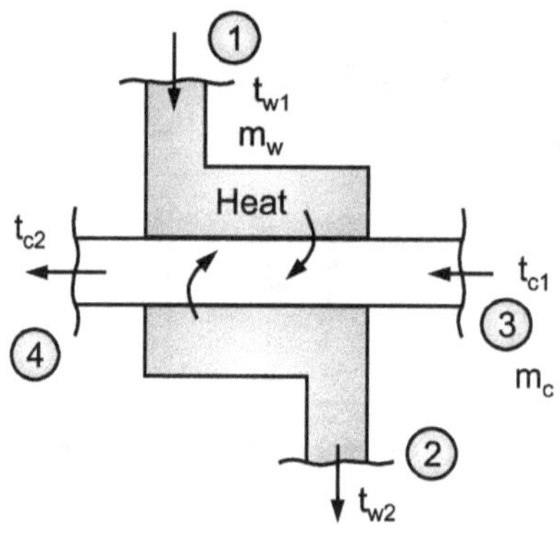


**Fig. 1.39**

$$W = 0, \Delta PE = 0, \Delta KE = 0$$

$$m_w h_1 + m_c h_3 = m_w h_2 + m_c h_4$$

$$\therefore \quad m_w (h_1 - h_2) = m_c (h_4 - h_3) \qquad \qquad \dots (1.39)$$

c = cold fluid, w = water (hot fluid)

## 1.9.2  Work Done in a Reversible Steady Flow Process

Refer Fig. 1.40.

We know that SFEE is

$$Q + \left( h_1 + \frac{v_1^2}{2000} + \frac{gz_1}{1000} \right) = W + \left( h_2 + \frac{v_2^2}{2000} + \frac{gz_2}{1000} \right)$$

$$\therefore \qquad Q - W = \Delta h + \Delta PE + \Delta KE \text{ kJ/kg}$$

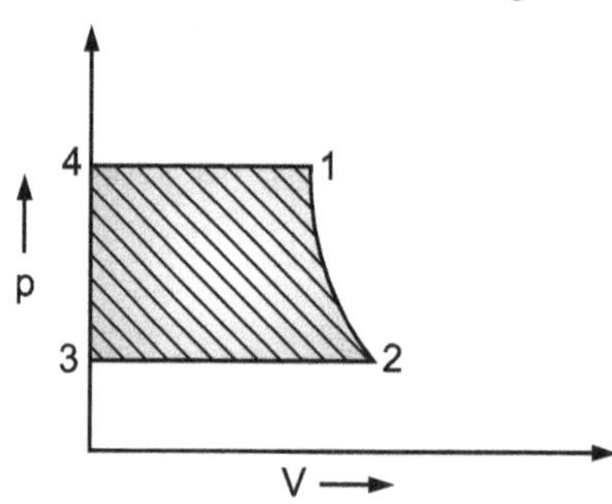


**Fig. 1.40: Meaning of – ∫ VdP**

In the differential form,

$$\delta q = \delta W + dh + dPE + dKE \qquad \qquad \dots (i)$$

From first law, $\qquad \delta q = \delta W + dU$

and $\delta W = P \, dV$ for a reversible work

$$\delta q \;=\; PdV + dU \qquad\qquad \text{... (ii)}$$

Enthalpy,
$$h \;=\; U + PV$$

$$dh \;=\; dU + PdV + VdP \qquad\qquad \text{... (iii)}$$

Substituting values of $\delta q$ and dh from equations (II) and (III) in equation (I),

$$PdV + dU = \delta W + dU + PdV + VdP + dPE + dKE$$

$$\therefore \qquad - \int VdP \;=\; \int \delta W + \Delta PE + \Delta KE \qquad\qquad \text{... (1.40)}$$

which is to say that, in a reversible steady flow process, $- \int VdP$ equals the shaft work 'W' plus changes in KE and PE.

(a) If $\Delta PE$ is negligible,

$$- \int V\, dP \;=\; W + \Delta KE$$

(b)  If $\Delta KE$ is negligible,

$$- \int V\, dP \;=\; W + \Delta PE$$

(c)  If $\Delta KE$ and $\Delta PE$ both are negligible, then

$$- \int V\, dP \;=\; W_{shaft} \qquad\qquad \text{... (1.41)}$$

i.e. in a reversible steady flow process, $- \int V\, dP$ equals shaft work 'W' when changes in kinetic energy and potential energy are neglected.

# 1.10 SIGNIFICANCE OF $\int_{1}^{2}$ PDV IN CASE OF STEADY FLOW PROCESS

Refer **Fig. 1.41**.

The SFEE is

$$Q + \left( h_1 + \frac{v_1^2}{2} + gz_1 \right) = W + \left( h_2 + \frac{v_2^2}{2} + gz_2 \right)$$

$$\therefore \qquad Q + \left( U_1 + P_1V_1 + \frac{v_1^2}{2000} + \frac{gz_1}{1000} \right) = W + \left( U_2 + P_2V_2 + \frac{v_2^2}{2000} + \frac{gz_2}{1000} \right) \; kJ/kg$$

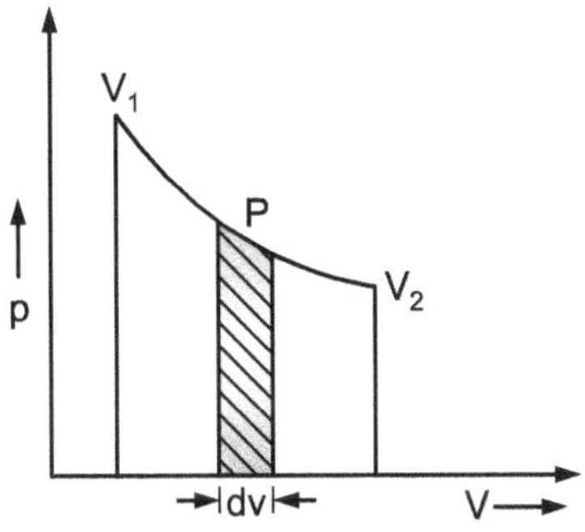

**Fig. 1.41**

$$Q \;=\; \Delta U + \Delta (PV) + \Delta KE + \Delta PE + W$$

In differential form,    $\delta Q = dU + d(PV) + d(KE) + d(PE) + \delta W$

For any reversible process,

$$\delta Q = dU + PdV$$

$$\therefore \quad dU + PdV = dU + d(PV) + d(KE) + d(PE) + \delta W$$

$$\therefore \quad PdV = d(PV) + d(KE) + d(PE) + \delta W$$

Integrating

$$\therefore \quad \int_1^2 PdV = \Delta PV + \Delta KE + \Delta PE + W \qquad \ldots (1.42)$$

$\int_1^2 PdV$ for a steady flow process is sum of change in flow work plus change in kinetic energy, plus change in potential energy and shaft work.

**Note:** For **non-flow** reversible process, $\int_1^2 P\,dV$ is the area under the curve and it represents shaft work when the pressure changes from $P_1$ to $P_2$ and volume from $V_1$ to $V_2$.

$$\int_1^2 P\,dv = W_{1-2} \qquad \ldots (1.43)$$

## 1.11 PERPETUAL MOTION MACHINE OF FIRST KIND, PMM - I

First law states that energy can neither be created nor be destroyed but only gets transformed from one form to another.

A device which violates the first law of thermodynamics is called as perpetual motion machine of first kind.

A device which continuously produces work without consuming any energy, is known as perpetual motion machine of first kind. This is illustrated in **Fig. 1.42**. PMM - I is against first law, hence PMM - I is impossible.

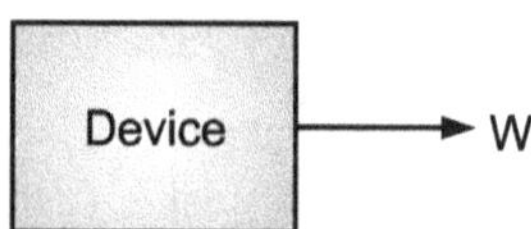


**Fig. 1.42: PMM - I**

The converse of PMM - I is, there can be no machine which would continuously consume work without some other form of energy appearing simultaneously (Fig. 1.43).

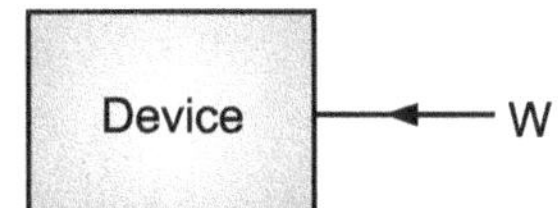


**Fig. 1.43: Converse of PMM - I**

This is also not possible.

## 1.12 LIMITATIONS OF FIRST LAW OF THERMODYNAMICS

- First law of thermodynamics tells that energy can be transformed from one form to another, but it does not tell how much energy can be transformed from one form to another. It means it is not quantitative law.

- Energy of an isolated system remains constant, as stated by first law. But it does not give information regarding whether a system which undergoes a process or not.

- Let us consider the following examples. Let a room is heated by an electric resistor (**Fig. 1.44**).

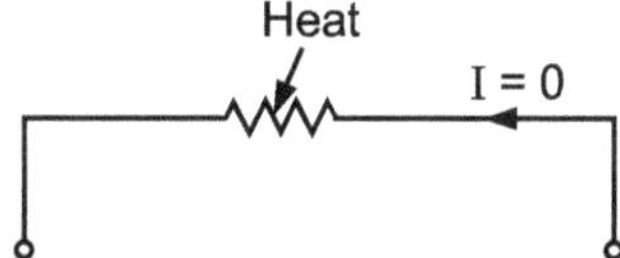


**Fig. 1.44: Transferring heat to the wire will not generate electricity**

Again the first law dictates that the amount of electrical energy supplied to the resistance wire be equal to the amount of energy transformed to the room air as heat. Now, attempt to reverse this process. If the same amount of heat supplied to the resistance wire will not generate electric energy, still it will not violate first law.

Again consider a paddle - wheel mechanism that is operated by the fall of mass. (**Fig. 1.45**).

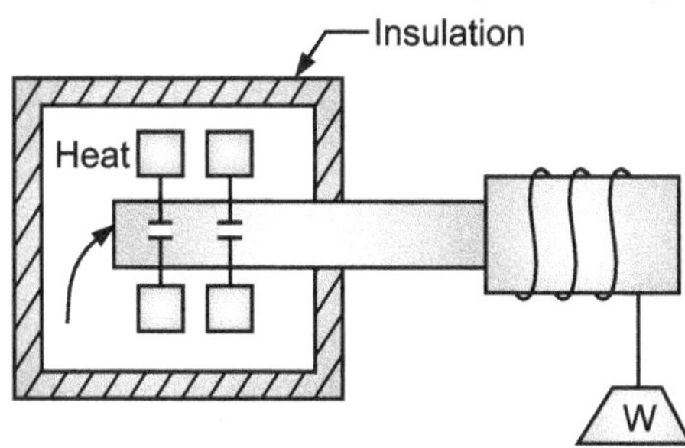


**Fig. 1.45: Transferring heat to paddle wheel does not cause it to rotate**

As the weight falls, paddle wheel rotates, stirring the fluid. Therefore, fluid gets heated. Now, attempt to reverse the process. That is transferring heat from the fluid to the paddle wheel, does not make the paddle wheel to rotate in reverse direction raising the weight from lower level to higher level. Still it will not violate the first law.

It is clear from above, that processes proceed naturally in a **certain** direction and not in the reverse direction. The first law places no restriction on the direction of a process; but satisfying the first law does not ensure that process will actually occur.

These limitations of first law make necessary to study second law of thermodynamics.

## 1.13 THE SECOND LAW OF THERMODYNAMICS

### 1.13.1 Thermal Energy Reservoirs

A hypothetical body with a large thermal capacity (mass × specific heat) that can supply or absorb finite amount of heat energy without undergoing a change in temperature is termed as **thermal energy reservoir**. In practice, large bodies of water such as oceans, lakes and rivers as well as the atmospheric air are considered as thermal reservoirs.

A reservoir that supplies energy in the form of heat is called a **source** and one that absorbs energy in the form of heat is called a **sink**.

### 1.13.2 Heat Engine or Carnot Engine

Work can easily be converted into other forms of energy, but converting other forms of energy into work is not that easy. A device used to convert heat energy to work is known as **heat engine**.

Heat engines differ considerably from one another, but all are characterised by the following (**Fig. 1.46**).

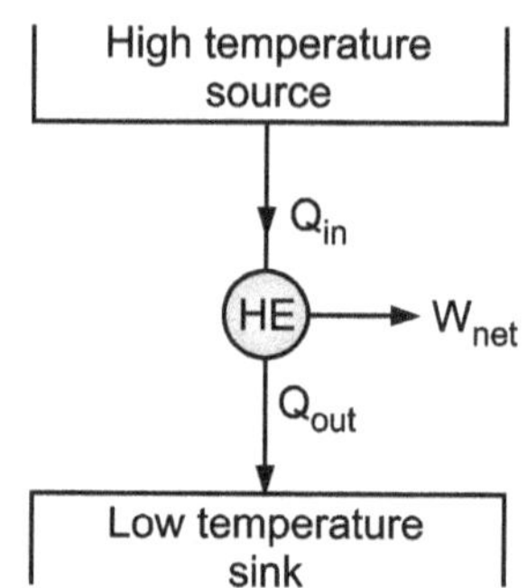


**Fig. 1.46: Part of the heat received by a heat engine is converted to work while the rest is rejected)**

- They receive heat from a high temperature source (solar energy, oil furnace, nuclear reactor, etc.)
- They convert part of this heat to work (usually in the form of a rotating shaft).
- They reject the remaining waste heat to a low temperature sink (the atmosphere, rivers, oceans etc.)
- They operate on a cycle.

Heat engines and other cyclic devices usually involve a fluid to and from which heat is transferred while undergoing a cycle. This fluid is called a working substance.

A steam power plant is best example of heat engine, which operates on thermodynamic cycle.

The work developing devices such as Internal combustion type (gas turbines and car engines) are also heat engines but they operate on mechanical cycle.

Let, $Q_{in}$ = amount of heat supplied to heat engine, kJ

$Q_{out}$ = amount of heat rejected to heat engine, kJ

The net work output, $W_{net} = Q_{in} - Q_{out}$ kJ

**Thermal Efficiency:**

$Q_{out}$ is never zero. Therefore, $W_{net}$ of heat engine is always less than $Q_{in}$.

$$\therefore \quad \text{Thermal efficiency} = \frac{\text{net work output}}{\text{total heat input}}$$

$$\eta_{th} = \frac{W_{net}}{Q_{in}} = \frac{Q_{in} - Q_{out}}{Q_{in}}$$

$$= 1 - \frac{Q_{out}}{Q_{in}} \qquad \qquad \text{... (1.44)}$$

## 1.13.3 Refrigerator

A device which transfers heat from a low temperature body (medium) to a high temperature one is called as a **refrigerator**.

A refrigerator is a cyclic device which uses refrigerant as a working fluid. The most frequently used refrigeration is a vapour - compression refrigeration cycle.

A refrigerator is shown schematically in **Fig. 1.47**. Here $Q_L$ is the amount of heat removed from the refrigerated space at temperature $T_L$, $Q_H$ is the amount of heat rejected to the warm environment at temperature $T_H$ and $W_{net}$ is the net work input to the refrigerator.

The efficiency of a refrigerator is expressed in terms of the ***coefficient of performance*** (COP), denoted by $COP_R$.

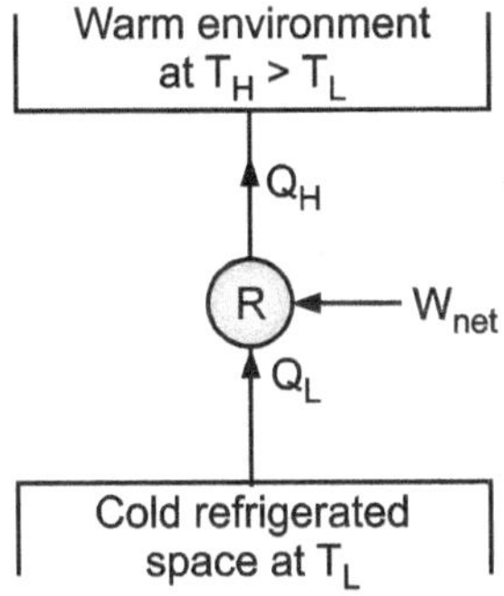


**Fig. 1.47: Schematic of refrigerator**

**Coefficient of Performance:**

The objective of a refrigerator is to remove heat ($Q_L$) from the refrigerated space. To accomplish this, it requires $W_{net}$ work as input. Therefore, COP of a refrigerator is

$$COP_R = \frac{\text{desired effect}}{\text{required input}} = \frac{Q_L}{W_{net}} \qquad \qquad \text{... (1.45)}$$

but, $\qquad W_{net} = Q_H - Q_L$

$$\therefore \qquad COP_R = \frac{Q_L}{Q_H - Q_L} = \frac{1}{(Q_H/Q_L) - 1} \qquad \qquad \text{... (1.46)}$$

COP may be greater than unity also.

## 1.13.4 Heat Pump (HP)

Another device that transfers heat from a low temperature space to a high temperature one is the heat pump. (**Fig. 1.48**). The objective of a heat pump is to maintain a heated space at high temperature.

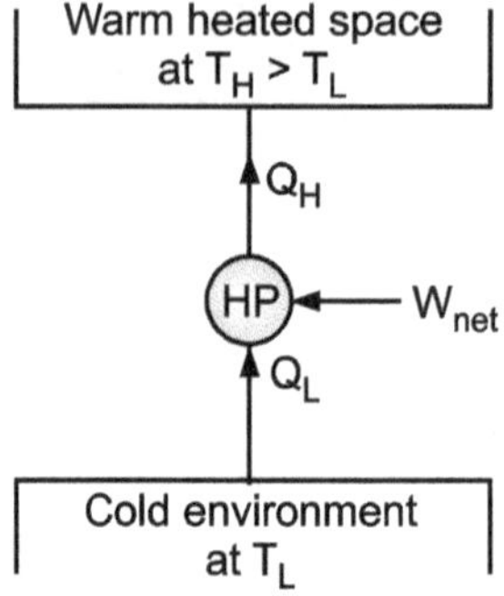


**Fig. 1.48: Schematic of heat pump**

The measure of performance of a heat pump is also expressed in terms of the coefficient of performance ($COP_{HP}$), defined as

$$COP_{HP} = \frac{\text{desired output}}{\text{required input}} = \frac{Q_H}{W_{net}} \qquad \text{... (1.47)}$$

$$= \frac{Q_H}{Q_H - Q_L} = \frac{1}{1 - \dfrac{Q_L}{Q_H}} \qquad \text{... (1.48)}$$

A comparison of equations (1.44) and (1.46) reveals that

$$COP_{HP} = COP_R + 1$$

## 1.13.5 The Second Law of Thermodynamics

In the last section, it is discussed that heat engine must reject some heat to a low temperature reservoir to complete the cycle, i.e. no heat engine can convert all the heat it receives to useful work. This limitation on the thermal efficiency of heat engine forms the basis for the *Kelvin-Planck statement.*

### (a) Kelvin - Planck - Statement:

"It is impossible to construct a device that operates on a cycle and produces no effect other than withdrawal energy as heat from a single reservoir and converting all of it into work".

Simply, it can also be stated as "It is impossible for any device that operates on a cycle to receive heat from a single reservoir and produce an equivalent amount of work."

It can also be stated as "No engine can have thermal efficiency of 100 percent" (**Fig. 1.49**).

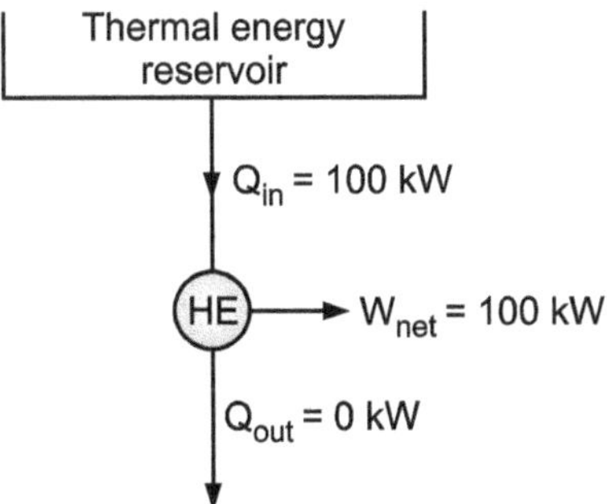


**Fig. 1.49: A heat engine that violates Kelvin-Planck statement of second law (PMM - II)**

**(b) Clausius - Statement (Second Law of Thermodynamics)**

"It is impossible to construct a device that operates in a cycle and produces no effect other than the transfer of heat from a low temperature body to a higher temperature body without external aid".

It simply states that a refrigerator will not operate unless its compressor is driven by an external power (electric motor). It means a device requires external energy to transfer heat from a low temperature body to a higher temperature body.

A device that violates Clausius statement is shown in **Fig. 1.50**.

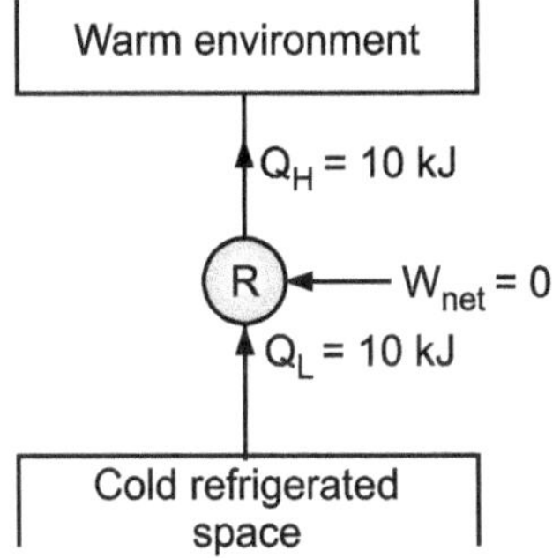


**Fig. 1.50: A refrigerator that violates the Clausius statement of the second law (PMM - II)**

## 1.13.6 Perpetual Motion Machine of Second Kind, PMM-II

A device that violates the second low of thermodynamics is called a perpetual motion machine of the second kind (PMM-II) is practically impossible.

Fig. 1.49 and 1.50 represent PMM II. Refer Fig. 1.49. This engine converts heat completely into work i.e. it is 100% efficient. This is violation or Kelvin-planck statement.

Refer Fig. 1.50. This device transfers heat from low temperature body to high temperature body without any external aid.  Hence such a device violates classics statement. Such a device violates claesics statement. Such type of heat transfer is possible in practice only with help of external aid. Hence the cyclic devices shown in Fig. 1.49 and 1.50 are not possible in practice.

## 1.13.7 Equivalence of Kelvin-Planck and Clausius Statements

- Kelvin-Planck statement tells that any heat engine will not convert the thermal energy of heat source completely into useful work. It means that a heat engine does not have 100 percent efficiency.

- Clausius statement tells that it will not be possible to transfer heat from a body at lower temperature to a body at higher temperature without external aid (energy input).

- From above paragraphs, one feels that the two statements are totally different and have no way interlinked. But conceptually the two statements of second law of thermodynamics are equivalent in all respect and can be proved here.

- The proof is not in the form of mathematical steps but violation of one statement implies the violation of the second and vice-versa.

(a)   Consider a cyclic heat pump 'P' shown in Fig. 1.51 which transfers heat from a low temperature reservoir ($T_2$) to a high temperature reservoir ($T_1$) with no other effect i.e. with no expenditure of work, violating Clausius statement.

Let us assume a heat engine 'E' working between the same thermal reservoirs producing net work ($W_{net}$) in a thermodynamic cycle. Assume that the rate of working of the heat engine is such that it draws an amount of heat $Q_1$ from the reservoir equal to that discharged by the heat pump (P). It means there is no need of high temperature reservoir and the heat $Q_1$ discharged by the heat pump (P) is directly fed to the heat engine. So one concludes that heat pump 'P' and the heat engine 'E' working together constitute a heat engine operating in cycles and producing net work while exchanging heat only with one body at a single fixed temperature. This violates the Kelvin-Planck statement.

(b)   Let us consider a perpetual motion machine of second kind (PMM-II) 'E' which produces net work in a cycle by exchanging heat with only one thermal energy reservoir (at $T_1$) and thus violates the Kelvin-Planck statement (See Fig. 1.52).

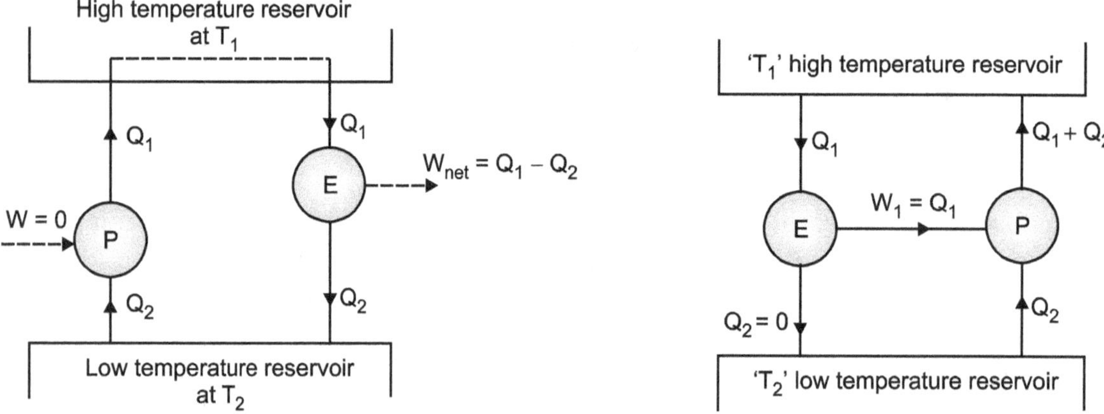


**Fig. 1.51: Violation of Clausius statement**         **Fig. 1.52: Violation of Kelvin-Planck statement**

Now, consider a cyclic heat pump (P) extracting heat $Q_2$ from a low temperature reservoir at $T_2$ and discharging heat to the high temperature reservoir at $T_1$ with the expenditure of work 'W' equal to that of the PMM-II delivers to a complete cycle. So E and P together constitute a heat pump working in cycles and producing the sole effect of transferring heat from a body at low temperature to a body at high temperature, thus violating the Clausius statement.

# 1.14  CONCEPT OF REVERSIBILITY AND IRREVERSIBLITY

- A reversible process is carried out infinitely slowly with an infinitesimal gradient, so that every state passed through by the system is an equilibrium state.

- Any natural process carried out with a finite gradient is an irreversible process. A reversible process consists of a succession of equilibrium states. So it is an idealized hypothetical process. It is said to be an asymptote to reality. All spontaneous processes are irreversible.

- Time has an important effect on reversibility. If the time allowed for a process to occur is infinitely large, even though the gradient is finite, the process becomes reversible. However, if this time allowed is reduced to a finite value, the finite gradient makes the process irreversible.

## 1.14.1 Causes of Irreversibility

The irreversibility of a process may be due to either lack of equilibrium during the process or involvement of dissipative effects.

### (a)  Irreversibility Due to Lack of Equilibrium

When there is no thermodynamic equilibrium (mechanical, thermal or chemical) between the system and its surroundings, or between two systems, or two parts of the same system, causes a continuous change which is irreversible. The following are few specific examples in this regard:

**(i)  Heat Transfer through a Finite Temperature Difference:** To transfer a finite amount of heat through an infinitesimal temperature difference would require an infinite amount of time, or infinite area. All actual heat transfer processes are through a finite temperature difference and are, therefore, irreversible, and greater the temperature difference, the greater is the irreversibility.

We can demonstrate by the second law that heat transfer through a finite temperature difference is irreversible.

- Let us assume that a source at $T_A$ and a sink at $T_B$ ($T_A > T_B$) are available, and let $Q_{A-B}$ be the amount of heat flowing from A and B (See Fig. 1.53).

- Let us assume engine operating between A and B, taking heat $Q_1$ from A and discharging heat $Q_2$ to B.

- Let the heat transfer process be reversed, and $Q_{B-A}$ be the heat flowing from B to A (See Fig. 1.54) and let the rate of working of the engine be such that

$$Q_2 = Q_{B-A}$$

Then the sink B may be eliminated. The net result is that E produces net work W in a cycle by exchanging heat only with A, thus violating the Kelvin-Plank statement. So the heat transfer process $Q_{A-B}$ is irreversible, and $Q_{B-A}$ is not possible.

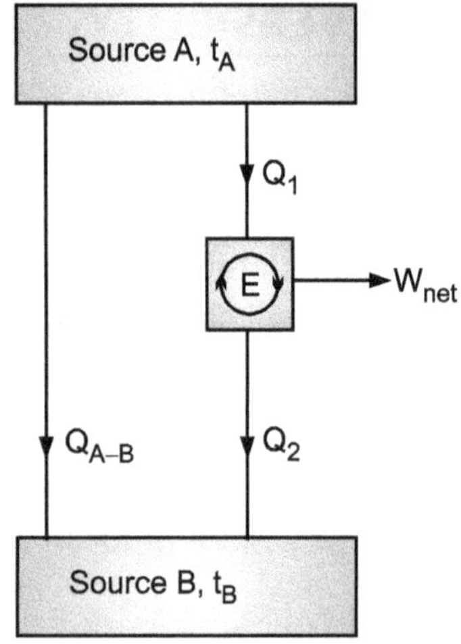


**Fig. 1.53: Heat transfer through a finite temperature difference**



**Fig. 1.54: Heat transfer through a finite temperature difference is irreversible**

**(ii) Lack of pressure: Equilibrium within the Interior of the System or between the System and the Surroundings:** When there exists a difference in pressures between the system and the surroundings, or within the system itself, then both the system and its surroundings, will undergo a change of state. For example, let any system is at a pressure $p_1$ greater than the surrounding. In this case, a process occurs wherein the system pressure reduces to surrounding pressure resulting into the mechanical equilibrium. The reverse of this process is not possible spontaneously without producing any other effect.

**(iii) Free Expansion:** Let us consider an insulated container (See Fig. 1.55) which is divided into two compartments A and B by a thin diaphragm.

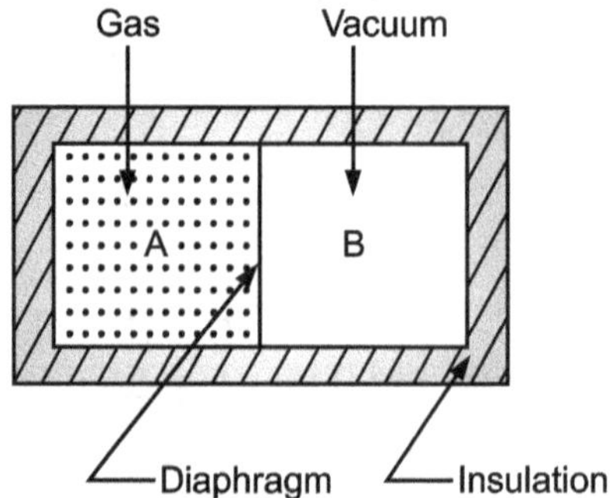


**Fig. 1.55: Free expansion**

Compartment A contains a mass of gas, while compartment B is completely evacuated. If a hole is made in the diaphragm, the gas in A will expand into B until the pressures in A and B compartments become equal. This is known as free or unrestrained expansion. We can demonstrate by the second law, that the process of free expansion is irreversible.

- To prove this, assume that free expansion is reversible, and that the gas in B returns into compartment A with an increase in pressure, and compartment B becomes evacuated as before (See Fig. 1.56).

- There is no other effect. Let us install an engine (a machine, not a cyclic heat engine) between A and B, and permit the gas to expand through the engine from A to B.

- The engine develops a work output W at the expense of the internal energy of the gas. The internal energy of the gas (system) in B can be resorted to its initial value by heat transfer Q (=W) from a source.

- Now, by the use of the reverse free expansion, the system can be resorted to the initial state of high pressure in A and vacuum in B.

- The net result is a cycle, in which we observe that net work output W is accomplished by exchanging heat with a single reservoir.

- This violates the Kelvin-Planck statement. Hence, free expansion is irreversible. The same argument will hold if the compartment B is not in vacuum but at a pressure lower than that in compartment A (case b).

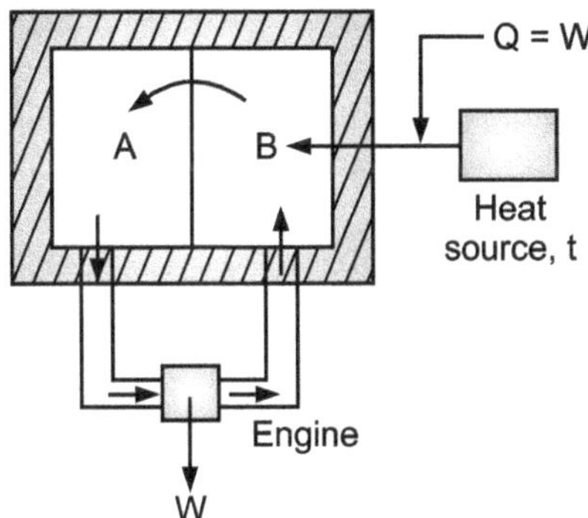


**Fig. 1.56: Second law demonstrates that free expansion is irreversible**

## (b)  Reversibility due to Dissipative Effects

The transformation of work into molecular internal energy either of the system or of the reservoir takes place through the agency of such phenomena as friction, viscosity, inelasticity, electrical resistance, and magnetic hysteresis. These effects are known as dissipative effects, and work is said to be dissipated. The irreversibility of a process may be due to the dissipative effects in which work is done without producing an equivalent increase in the kinetic or potential energy of any system.

**(i)  Friction:** Friction is always present when two moving surfaces are in contact. Friction may be reduced by suitable lubrication, but it can never be completely eliminated. If this were possible, a movable device could be kept in continual motion without violating either of the two laws of thermodynamics. The continual motion of a movable device in the complete absence of friction is known as perpetual motion of the third kind.

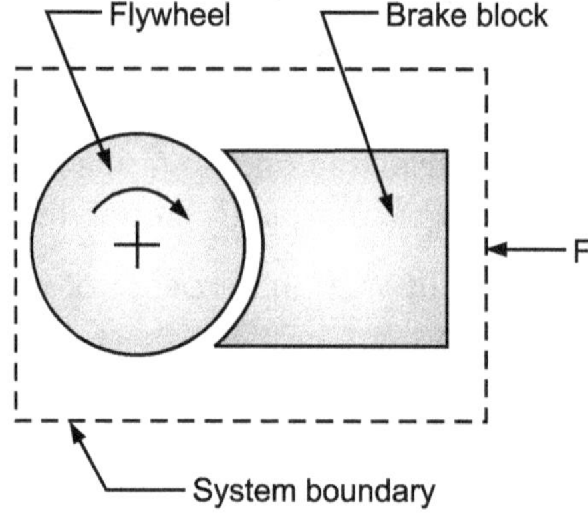


**Fig. 1.57**

- That friction makes a process irreversible can be demonstrated by the second law. Let us consider a system consisting of a flywheel and a brake block (See Fig. 1.57).

- The flywheel was rotating with a certain rpm, and it was brought to rest by applying the friction brake.

- The distance moved by the brake block is very small, so work transfer is very nearly equal to zero.

- If the braking process occurs very rapidly, there is little heat transfer. Using suffix 2 after braking and suffix 1 before braking, and applying the first law, we have

$$Q_{1-2} = E_2 - E_1 + W_{1-2}$$
$$0 = E_2 - E_1 + 0$$
$$\therefore \quad E_2 = E_1 \qquad \qquad \qquad \dots (1.49)$$

The energy of the system (isolated) remains constant. Since the energy may exist in the forms of kinetic, potential, and molecular internal energy, we have,

$$U_2 + \frac{mV_2^2}{2} + mZ_{2g} = U_1 + \frac{mV_1^2}{2} + mZ_{1g}$$

Since the wheel is brought to rest, $V_2 = 0$, and there is no change in P.E.

$$U_1 = U_1 + \frac{mV_1^2}{2} \qquad \qquad \qquad \dots (1.50)$$

Therefore, the molecular internal energy of the system (i.e., of the brake and the wheel) increases by absorption if the K.E. of the wheel. The reverse process, i.e., the conversion of this increase in molecular internal energy into K.E. within the system to cause the wheel to rotate is not possible to prove it by the second law, let us assume that it is possible, and imagine the following cycle with three processes:

**Process A:** Let initially the wheel and the brake are at high temperature as a result of the absorption of the K.E. of the wheel, and the flywheel is at rest. Let the flywheel now start rotating at a particular rpm at the expense of the internal energy of the wheel and brake, the temperature of which will then decrease.

**Process B:** Let the flywheel be brought to rest by using its K.E. in raising weights, with no change in temperature.

**Process C:** Now, let heat be supplied from a source to the flywheel and the weights, with no change in temperature.

Therefore, the processes A, B, and C together constitute a cycle producing work by exchanging heat with a single reservoir. This violates the Kelvin-Planck statement, and it will become a PMM2. So the braking process, i.e., the transformation of K.E. into molecular internal energy, is irreversible.

### (ii)  Paddle-Wheel Work Transfer:

- Consider an insulated tank with a fluid (system) in it. Work may be transferred into a system by means of a paddle wheel (See Fig. 1.58) which is also known as stirring work. Here work transferred is dissipated adiabatically into an increase in the molecular internal energy of the system.

- To prove the irreversibility of the process, let us assume that the same amount of work is delivered by the system at the expense of its molecular internal energy, and the temperature of the system goes down (See Fig. 1.59).

- The system is brought back to its initial state by heat transfer from a source. These two processes together constitute a cycle in which there is work output and the system exchanges heat with a single reservoir.

- It becomes a PMM2, and hence the dissipation of stirring work to internal energy is irreversible.

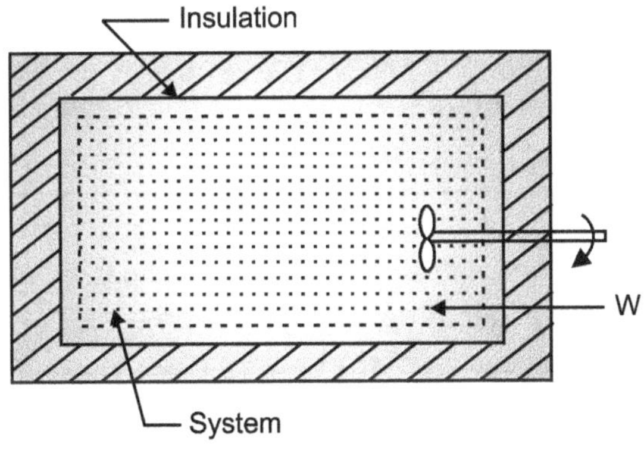


**Fig. 1.58: Adiabatic work transfer**

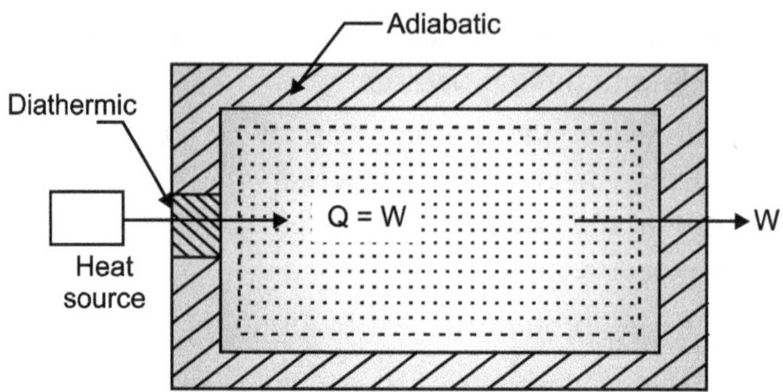


**Fig. 1.59: Irreversibility due to dissipation of stirring work into internal energy**

**(iii) Transfer of Electricity through a Resistor:** The flow of electric current through a wire represents work transfer, because the current can drive a motor which can raise a weight. Taking the wire/ the resistor as the system (See Fig. 1.60) and the first law as,

$$Q_{1-2} = U_2 - U_1 + W_{1-2}$$

Here both $W_{1-2}$ and $Q_{1-2}$ are negative.

$$W_{1-2} = U_2 - U_1 + Q_{1-2} \qquad \ldots (1.51)$$

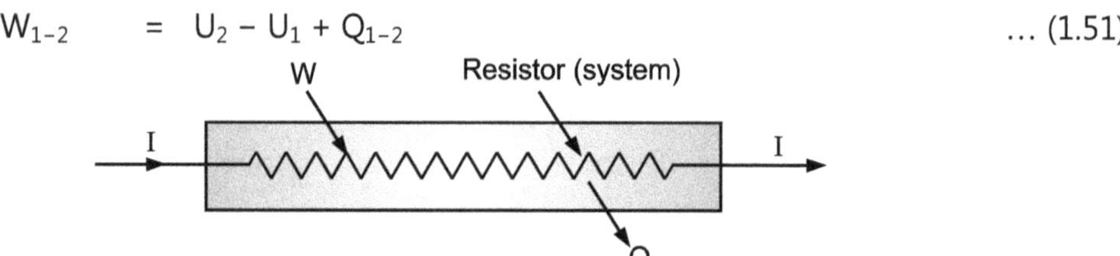


**Fig. 1.60: Irreversibility due to dissipation of electrical work into internal energy**

A part of the work transfer is stored as an increase in the internal energy of the wire (to give an increase in its temperature), and the remainder leaves the system as heat. At steady state, the internal energy and hence the temperature of the resistor become constant with respect to time and

$$W_{1-2} = Q_{1-2} \qquad \ldots (1.52)$$

The reverse process, i.e. the conversion of heat $Q_{1-2}$ into electrical work $W_{1-2}$ of the same magnitude is not possible. Let us assume that this is possible. Then heat $Q_{1-2}$ will be absorbed and equal work $W_{1-2}$ will be delivered. But this will become a PMM2. So the dissipation of electrical work into internal energy or heat is irreversible.

## 1.14.2 Conditions for Reversibility

- A natural process is irreversible because the conditions for mechanical, thermal and chemical equilibrium are not satisfied, and the dissipative effects, in which work is transformed into an increase in internal energy, are present.

- For a process to be reversible, it must not possess these features. If a process is performed quasistatically, the system passes through states of thermodynamic equilibrium, which may be traversed as well in one direction or in the opposite direction.

- *If there are no dissipative effects, all the work done by the system during the performance of a process in one direction can be returned to the system during the reverse process.*

- A process will be reversible when it is performed in such a way that the system is at all times infinitesimally near a state of thermodynamic equilibrium and in the absence of dissipative effect of any form. Reversible processes are, therefore, purely ideal, limiting cases of actual processes.

## 1.14.3 Types of Irreversibility

A process becomes irreversible if it occurs due to a finite potential gradient like the gradient in temperature or pressure, or if there is dissipative effect like friction, in which work is transformed into internal energy increase of the system. Two types of irreversibility can be distinguished:

(a)   Internal irreversibility

(b)   External irreversibility

The internal irreversibility is caused by the internal dissipative effects like friction, turbulence, electrical resistance, magnetic hysteresis, etc. within the system. The external irreversibility refers to the irreversibility occurring at the system boundary like heat interaction with the surroundings due to finite temperature gradient.

Sometimes, it is useful to make other distinctions. If the irreversibility of a process is due to the dissipation of work into the increase in internal energy of a system, or due to a finite pressure gradient, it is called mechanical irreversibility. If the process occurs in account of a finite temperature gradient, it is thermal irreversibility, and if it is due to a finite concentration gradient or a chemical reaction, it is called chemical irreversibility.

A heat engine cycle in which there is a temperature difference (i) between the source and the working fluid during heat supply, and (ii) between the working fluid and the sink during heat rejection, exhibits external thermal irreversibility. If the real source and sink are not considered and hypothetical reversible processes for heat supply and heat rejection are assumed, the cycle can be reversible. With the inclusion of the actual source and sink, however, the cycle becomes externally irreversible.

## 1.15  CARNOT CYCLE (REVERSIBLE CYCLE)

It is also called as **reversible cycle** because all the processes are reversible one. It works between two different temperature reservoirs. It consists of two reversible adiabatic and two reversible isothermal processes.

Carnot engine working between two thermal reservoirs is shown in Fig. 1.61.

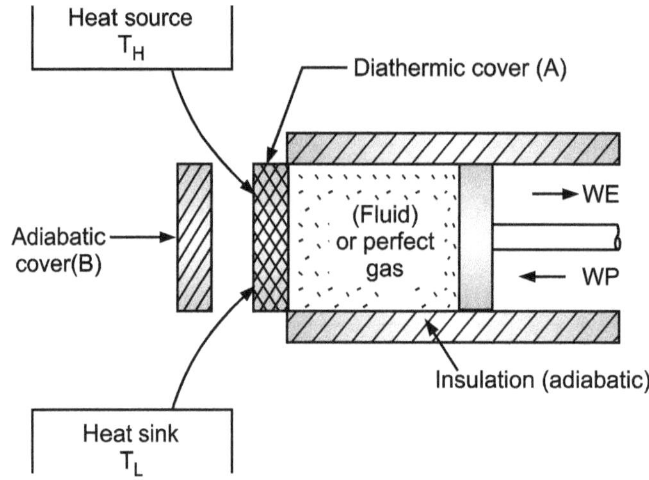



**Fig. 1.61: Carnot heat engine**

Carnot cycle is represented on p-V plane [Fig. 1.62 (a)] and on T-s plane [Fig. 1.62 (b)].

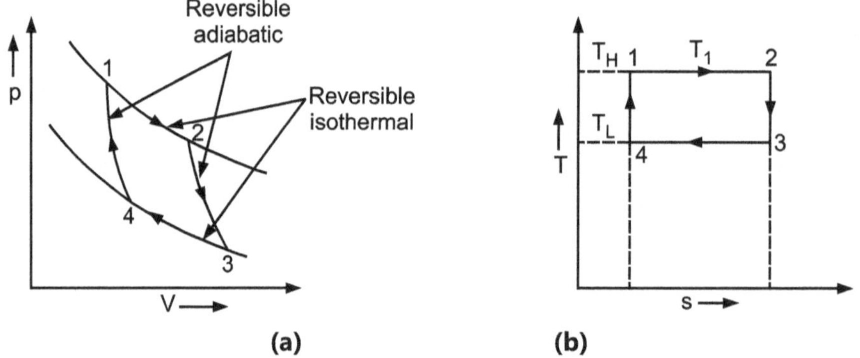



**Fig. 1.62: p-V and T-s diagrams**

## Process 1 - 2 : Reversible Isothermal Expansion process:

The hot body at temperature $T_H$ is brought in contact with working fluid (diathermic cover A is in contact with cylinder head), so that heat is transferred isothermally.

∴      According to the first law of thermodynamics,

$$Q_{1-2} = \Delta U + W_{1-2} \qquad\qquad (\because \Delta U = 0)$$

∴

$$Q_{1-2} = W_{1-2} = m \cdot R \cdot T_H \ln\left(\frac{V_2}{V_1}\right)$$

$$= T_1 (s_2 - s_1) \text{ kJ} \qquad\qquad \dots (1.53)$$

## Process 2 - 3: Reversible Adiabatic (Isentropic) Expansion process :

In this process, diathermic cover 'A' is assumed to be replaced by the adiabatic cover 'B'. No heat transfer occurs. Work $W_E$ is obtained from the system; at the cost of internal energy.

Therefore, temperature decreases from $T_H$ to $T_L$ ($T_2$ to $T_3$).

$$\therefore \qquad Q_{2-3} \;=\; 0$$

## Process 3 - 4: Reversible Isothermal Compression process :

Again adiabatic cover 'B' is replaced by cover 'A'. It is assumed that the fluid is brought into contact with low temperature sink ($T_L$). The heat is rejected isothermally from the fluid to sink.

$$Q_{3-4} \;=\; W_{3-4} = -\, mRT_L \cdot \ln\left(\frac{V_4}{V_3}\right)$$

$$=\; mRT_L \ln\left(\frac{V_3}{V_4}\right)$$

$$=\; T_3\,(s_3 - s_4)\ \text{kJ} \qquad\qquad \ldots (1.54)$$

## Process 4 – 1: Reversible Adiabatic (Isentropic) Compression process :

This compression process is continued till the fluid reaches initial state at point 1. The work is done on the fluid in this process and therefore internal energy increases. So temperature increases from $T_L$ to $T_H$.

$$\text{Thermal efficiency} = \frac{\text{Heat supplied} - \text{Heat rejected}}{\text{Heat supplied}}$$

$$= \frac{mRT_H \ln\left(\dfrac{V_2}{V_1}\right) - mRT_L \ln\left(\dfrac{V_3}{V_4}\right)}{mRT_H \ln\left(\dfrac{V_2}{V_1}\right)}$$

$$\frac{V_3}{V_2} = \frac{V_4}{V_1} \quad \text{or} \quad \frac{V_2}{V_1} = \frac{V_3}{V_4}$$

$$\eta_{th} \;=\; \frac{T_H - T_L}{T_H} \ \text{or}\ \frac{T_1 - T_3}{T_1} \qquad\qquad \ldots (1.55)$$

$$=\; 1 - \frac{T_L}{T_H}$$

If $T_L$ is constant (i.e. the temperature of heat sink such as atmosphere, lake water etc.) and source temperature $T_H$ increases, the thermal efficiency of the cycle increases.

The relative work outputs of various piston engine cycles are given by mean effective pressure (mep or $p_m$). The **mean effective pressure** is defined as the constant pressure producing the same net work output while causing the piston to move through the same swept volume as in the actual cycle (See Fig. 1.63).

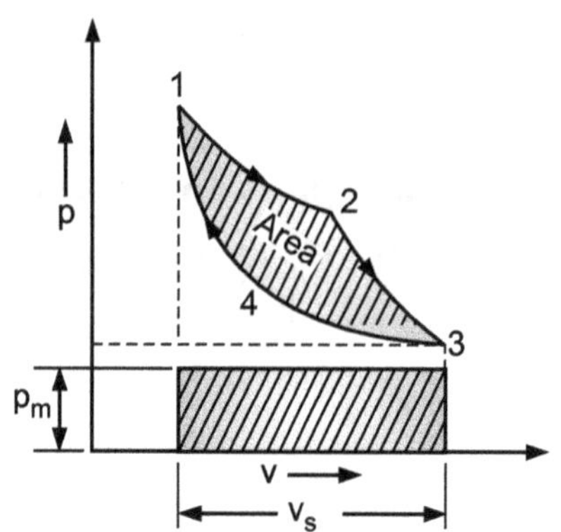


**Fig. 1.63: Mean effective pressure**

Let $p_m$ = Mean effective pressure, N/m$^2$

$V_s$ = Swept volume, m$^3$

W = Net work output per cycle, N-m

Then, $p_m = \dfrac{\text{Work done per cycle}}{\text{Stroke volume}}$

$$= \frac{W}{V_s} = \frac{\displaystyle\int pdV}{V_s} \qquad \ldots (1.56)$$

$\therefore \qquad p_m = \dfrac{\text{Area of indicator diagram}}{\text{Stroke volume}}$

## SOLVED PROBLEMS

**Problem 1.1:** A gas at pressure of 1500 kPa is expanded in a cylinder - piston arrangement. The piston has a diameter of 10 cm. The expansion curve is a straight line. At the end of expansion, the pressure of the gas is 120 kPa. Find the work done by the gas on the piston if stroke length is 0.25 m.

**Solution:**

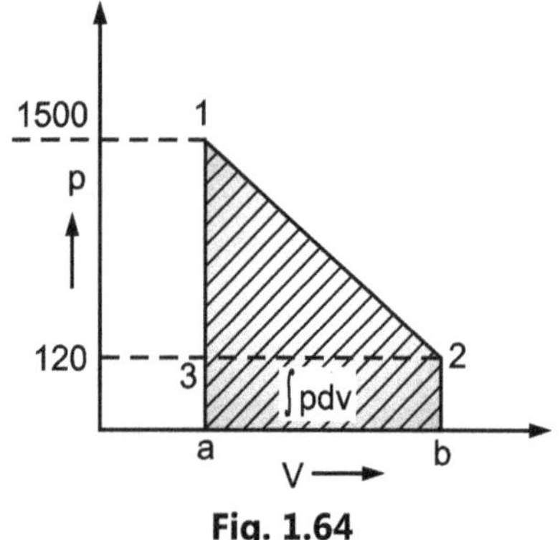


**Fig. 1.64**

$$W = \int_{1}^{2} P \, dV$$

$$= \text{Area under the curve}$$

$$\therefore \qquad V_b - V_a \; = \; \frac{\pi}{4} d^2 \cdot L = \frac{\pi}{4}(0.1)^2 \times 0.25 = 1.96 \times 10^{-3} \text{ m}^3$$

$$\therefore \qquad W \; = \; \text{Area } 1 - 2 - 3 + \text{Area } a - b - 2 - 3$$

$$= \; \frac{1}{2} \times (1500 - 120) \times V_s + 120 \times V_s$$

$$= \; \left[\frac{1}{2}(1500 - 120) + 120\right] \times 1.96 \times 10^{-3}$$

$$W \; = \; 1.355 \text{ kN-m} \qquad\qquad\qquad \text{... Ans.}$$

**Problem 1.2:** In a cylinder - piston arrangement, the pressure is inversely proportional to the square of volume. The initial pressure in the cylinder is 20 bar and initial volume is 0.1 m$^3$. The volume is increased so that final pressure reduces to 2 bar. Find the work done in kJ.

**Solution: Given:**

$$P_1 \; = \; 20 \times 10^5 \text{ N/m}^2 \text{ or Pa}$$

$$P_2 \; = \; 2 \times 10^5 \text{ N/m}^2 \text{ or Pa}$$

$$P \; \propto \; \frac{1}{V^2} \qquad \text{and } V_1 = 0.1 \text{ m}^3$$

$$\text{Work done} \; = \; \int_1^2 P \, dV$$

$$P \; = \; \frac{C}{V^2} \therefore \text{Work done} = \int_1^2 \frac{C}{V^2} \cdot dV$$

$$\text{Work done} \; = \; C \int_1^2 \frac{dV}{V^2} = C \left[\frac{V_2^{-1} - V_1^{-1}}{-1}\right] = C \left[\frac{1}{V_1} - \frac{1}{V_2}\right]$$

$$C = PV^2 = P_1 V_1^2 \; = \; 20 \times 10^5 \times (0.1)^2 = 20{,}000$$

$$\therefore \qquad W \; = \; 20{,}000 \left[\frac{1}{V_1} - \frac{1}{V_2}\right]$$

$$P_2 V_2^2 \; = \; C$$

$$\therefore \qquad V_2 \; = \; \sqrt{\frac{C}{P_2}} = \sqrt{\frac{20000}{2 \times 10^5}} = 0.31 \text{ m}^3$$

$$\therefore \qquad W \; = \; 20{,}000 \left[\frac{1}{0.1} - \frac{1}{0.31}\right] = 135.4 \times 10^3 \text{ N-m}$$

$$W \; = \; 135.4 \text{ kJ} \qquad\qquad\qquad \text{... Ans.}$$

**Problem 1.3:** The volume of a sample of a gas is 0.04 m³ and at a pressure of 10 bar. If the final volume of gas is 0.1 m³ after the following processes were carried out, evaluate the work done in each process.

   (i)  Constant pressure process

   (ii)  PV = constant

**Solution:** The work done in each case is calculated by the formula $\int P\,dV$.

### (i) Constant pressure process:

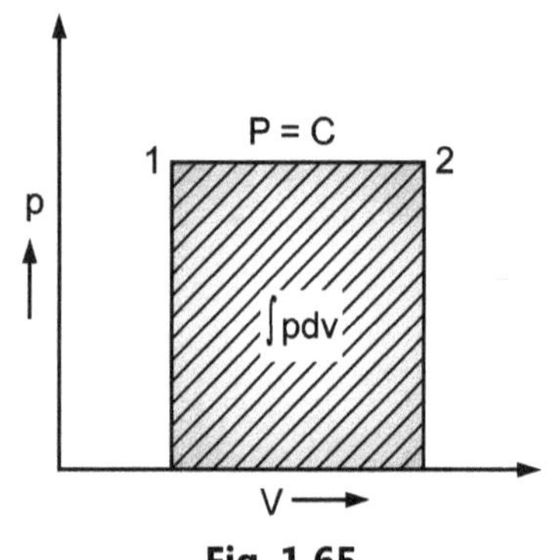


**Fig. 1.65**

$$P_1 = 10 \times 10^5 \text{ N/m}^2, \; P_2 = P_1$$

$$V_1 = 0.04 \text{ m}^3, \; V_2 = 0.1 \text{ m}^3$$

$$W = \int_1^2 P\,dV = P\,(V_2 - V_1)$$

$$= 10 \times 10^5 \, [0.1 - 0.04]$$

$$= 60{,}000 \text{ J} = 60 \text{ kJ} \qquad \textbf{... Ans.}$$

### (ii) PV = Constant for isothermal process:

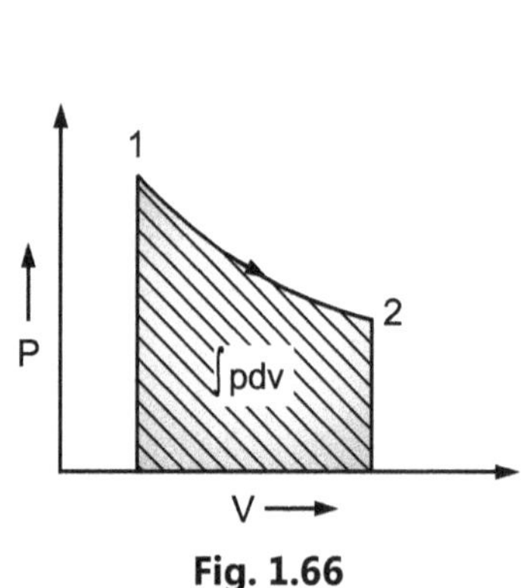


**Fig. 1.66**

$$W = \int_1^2 P\,dV = \int_1^2 \frac{C}{V} \cdot dV$$

$$= C \int_1^2 \frac{dV}{V}$$

$$= C\,[\ln_e V_2 - \ln_e V_1]$$

$$= C \ln \frac{V_2}{V_1}$$

but $C = PV = P_1 V_1$

$$\therefore \quad W = P_1 V_1 \ln V_2/V_1$$

$$= 10 \times 10^5 \times 0.04 \ln 0.1/0.04$$

$$W = 36651.6 \text{ joule} = \textbf{36.651 kJ} \qquad \textbf{... Ans.}$$

**Problem 1.4:** A system of gas in a cylinder-piston arrangement expands according to $\left(P + \dfrac{a}{V^2}\right)(V - b) = mRT$, where a, b and R are constants. Obtain the expression for the work done by the system on the piston for the expansion process.

**Solution:** The work done is

$$W = \int_{1}^{2} P \, dV$$

Given relation is, $\left(P + \dfrac{a}{V^2}\right)(V - b) = mRT$

$$\therefore \qquad P = \frac{mRT}{V - b} - \frac{a}{V^2}$$

$$\therefore \qquad W = \int_{1}^{2} \left(\frac{mRT}{V - b} - \frac{a}{V^2}\right) dV$$

$$= mRT \ln\left(\frac{V_2 - b}{V_1 - b}\right) + \frac{a}{V_2} - \frac{a}{V_1} \qquad \textbf{... Ans.}$$

---

**Problem 1.5:** A refrigerator is loaded with food and the door of the refrigerator is closed. During a certain period, the machine required 1 kWh energy and internal energy of the system drops by 6000 kJ. Find the net heat transferred to or from the system.

**Solution:**

$$1 \text{ kWh} = 3600 \text{ kJ}$$
$$Q = \Delta U + W$$

Internal energy drops,

i.e. $\qquad \Delta U = -6000 \text{ kJ}$

$$W = -3600 \text{ kJ}$$

$$\therefore \qquad Q = -6000 + (-3600)$$

$$= -9600 \text{ kJ (Heat rejected)} \qquad \textbf{... Ans.}$$

---

**Problem 1.6:** A cylinder contains 5 kg of working fluid. During the period the piston moves out; the temperature of the system falls from 95°C to 40°C and net heat rejected through the cylinder walls is 20 kJ.

The specific internal energy and temperature are related to each other by

$$U = \left(30 + \frac{t}{1.25}\right) \text{ kJ/kg}$$

where t is the temperature in °C. Calculate the work transferred.

**Solution:** Initial internal energy $= mU_1$

Final internal energy $= mU_2$

Change in internal energy,

$$\Delta U = U_2 - U_1$$

$$\Delta U = m(U_2 - U_1)$$

---

$$= m\left[\left(30 + \frac{t_2}{1.25}\right) - \left(30 + \frac{t_1}{1.25}\right)\right]$$

$$= 5\left[\frac{40 - 95}{1.25}\right] = -220 \text{ kJ}$$

$$Q = -20, \text{ because heat is rejected}$$

$\therefore$
$$Q = \Delta U + W$$

$$-20 = -220 + W$$

$\therefore$
$$W = 200 \text{ kJ} \qquad\qquad \textbf{... Ans.}$$

**Problem 1.7:** A system undergoes a frictionless non-flow process according to the law

$$P = \frac{4.5}{V} + 2$$

where P is in bar and V in m³/kg. During the process, volume changes from 0.12 m³/kg to 0.04 m³/kg and temperature increases by 133°C. The internal energy of the fluid varies as $dU = C_v \cdot dT$, where $C_v = 0.71$ kJ/kg °C. Find out the heat transfer and its direction for fluid of mass 10 kg.

**Solution:** Given,

$$P = \frac{4.5}{V} + 2, \ V_1 = 0.12 \text{ m}^3/\text{kg}, \ V_2 = 0.04 \text{ m}^3/\text{kg}, \ (\Delta T)_{increase} = 133°C$$

$$C_v = 0.71 \text{ kJ/kg °C}, \ m = 10 \text{ kg}$$

$$dU = C_v \, dT$$

Work done in a frictionless non-flow reversible process

$$= \int_1^2 P \, dV = 10^5 \int_1^2 \left(\frac{4.5}{V} + 2\right) dV \text{ joule/kg}$$

$$= 10^5 \left[4.5 \ln_e V_2/V_1 + 2 (V_2 - V_1)\right]_{0.12}^{0.04}$$

$$= 10^5 \left[4.5 \ln_e \frac{0.04}{0.12} + 2 (0.04 - 0.12)\right] \text{ joule/kg}$$

$$= -510375 \text{ joule/kg} = -510.375 \text{ kJ/kg}$$

$$\Delta U = \int C_v dT = C_v \cdot \Delta T = 0.71 \times 133 = 94.43 \text{ kJ/kg}$$

$$q = \Delta U + W = 94.43 - 510.375 = -415.94 \text{ kJ/kg}$$

$$Q = m \cdot q = 10 \times (-415.94) \text{ kJ} = \textbf{-- 4159.4 kJ} \qquad\qquad \textbf{... Ans.}$$

**Problem 1.8:** A closed system undergoes a thermodynamic cycle. There are four processes AB, BC, CD and DA in the cycle. The heat transfer and work transfer in kW for each process are given below:

| Process | Heat transfer, kW | Work, kW |
|---------|-------------------|----------|
| AB | Nil | – 366.67 |
| BC | 300 | Nil |
| CD | – 66.67 | + 500 |
| DA | – 33.33 | + 66.667 |

Show that the data is consistent with the first law of thermodynamics and determine:

(a)  Net rate of work output in kW

(b)  Efficiency of the cycle.

(c)  Change in internal energy of each process.

**Solution:** For cyclic process,

$$\oint \delta Q = \oint \delta W$$

For the cycle,      $\oint \delta Q = 0 + 300 - 66.67 - 33.33 = 200$ kW

$$\oint W = -366.67 + 0 + 500 + 66.67 = 200 \text{ kW}$$

$\therefore$      $\oint \delta Q = \oint \delta W$, the data is consistent with first law of thermodynamics

(a)   Net rate of work/sec. = 200 kW                                      ... **Ans.**

(b)   Efficiency of cycle $= \dfrac{\text{Net work output}}{\text{Heat supplied}} = \dfrac{200}{300} = 66.67$ %      ... **Ans.**

(c)   According to first law,

$$\delta Q = \delta U + \delta W$$

$$\delta U = \delta Q - \delta W$$

Hence for all processes, change in internal energy can be calculated.

| Process | $\delta Q$ | $\delta W$ | $\delta U = \delta Q - \delta W$ | |
|---------|------|--------|---------------------------------|---|
| AB | Nil | – 366.67 | = | $0 - (- 366.67) = 366.67$ |
| BC | 300 | Nil | = | $300 - 0 = 300$ kW |
| CD | – 66.67 | + 500 | = | $- 66.67 - 500 = - 566.67$ kW |
| DA | – 33.33 | + 66.67 | = | $- 33.33 - 66.67 = - 100$ kW |

... **Ans.**

**Problem 1.9:** Steady flow process is applied to nozzle. Steam enters a horizontal steam nozzle at a pressure of 10 bar. The pressure of steam at the exit of the nozzle is 1 bar. The internal energy of the steam decreases by 250 kJ/kg and the specific volume increases from 0.2 m³/kg to 1.7 m³/kg as the steam flows through the nozzle. Find the exit velocity of steam if its inlet velocity is 900 m/min. Heat transferred from the nozzle is negligible.

**Solution:** Steady flow energy equation

$$Q + \left( u_1 + P_1 V_{S1} + \frac{v_1^2}{2} + gz_1 \right) = W + \left( u_2 + P_2 V_{S2} + \frac{v_2^2}{2} + gz_2 \right)$$

$$gz_1 = gz_2 \text{ horizontal}$$

No work is transferred $\therefore$ W = 0. Also, Q = 0.

$$u_1 + P_1 V_{S1} + \frac{v_1^2}{2} = u_2 + P_2 V_{S2} + \frac{v_2^2}{2}$$

$$\frac{v_2^2}{2} = (u_1 - u_2) + (P_1 V_{S1} - P_2 V_{S2}) + \frac{v_1^2}{2}$$

$$= 250 \times 10^3 + 10^5 (10 \times 0.2 - 1 \times 1.7) + \frac{15^2}{2}$$

$$= 250{,}000 + 30{,}000 + 112.5$$

$$\frac{v_2^2}{2} = 280112.5$$

$\therefore$ $\quad v_2 = 748.5$ m/s $\qquad$ ... **Ans.**

**Problem 1.10:** A nozzle is used for increasing the velocity of a steam. The enthalpy and velocity of the steam entering the nozzle are 2750 kJ/kg and 50 m/s respectively. The enthalpy at the exit of nozzle is 2600 kJ/kg. The heat losses from this horizontal nozzle are negligible.

(i)  Find the velocity at exit from the nozzle.

(ii)  If the inlet area is 0.1 m² and specific volume at inlet is 0.18 m³/kg, find the mass flow rate.

(iii)  If the specific volume at the outlet is 0.498 m³/kg, find the area at the exit of the nozzle.

**Solution: Given :** $h_1 = 2750$ kJ/kg, $v_1 = 50$ m/s, $h_2 = 2600$ kJ/kg

(i)   Steady flow energy equation is

$$Q + \left(h_1 + \frac{v_1^2}{2} + gz_1\right) = W + \left(h_2 + \frac{v_2^2}{2} + gz_2\right)$$

$Q = 0$, $W = 0$, $\Delta PE = 0$

$$\therefore \qquad h_1 + \frac{v_1^2}{2} = h_2 + \frac{v_2^2}{2}$$

$$\therefore \qquad 2750 + \frac{50^2}{2000} = 2600 + \frac{v_2^2}{2000}$$

$$\therefore \qquad v_2 = 550 \text{ m/s}$$

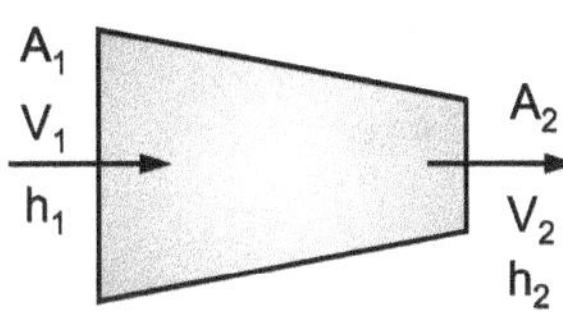


**Fig. 1.67**

(ii)  For nozzle,

$$\text{Mass flow rate (at inlet)} = \frac{\text{(Inlet area)} \cdot \text{(Inlet velocity)}}{\text{Specific volume at inlet}}$$

$$= \frac{(0.1) \times 50}{0.18} = 27.7 \text{ kg/s} \qquad \text{... Ans.}$$

(iii) For nozzle, Mass flow rate at inlet = Mass flow rate at outlet

$$27.7 = \frac{A_2 \times V_2}{\text{Specific volume at exit}}$$

$$27.7 = \frac{A_2 \times 550}{0.498}$$

$$\therefore \qquad A_2 = 0.025 \text{ m}^2 \qquad \text{... Ans.}$$

**Problem 1.11:** Air at 100 kPa and 280 K is compressed steadily to 600 kPa and 400 K. The mass flow rate of the air is 0.02 kg/s and a heat loss of 16 kJ/kg occurs during the process. Assuming the changes in kinetic and potential energies are negligible, determine the necessary power input to the compressor.

Assume enthalpy of air at inlet and exit as 280.13 kJ/kg and 400.98 kJ/kg respectively.

**Solution:** Steady flow energy equation is

$$q + \left(h_1 + \frac{v_1^2}{2} + gz_1\right) = w + \left(h_2 + \frac{v_2^2}{2} + gz_2\right)$$

$$q - w = \Delta h + \Delta PE + \Delta KE$$

$$\therefore \qquad q - w = \Delta h + 0 + 0$$

$$\therefore \qquad q - w = h_2 - h_1$$

$$\therefore \qquad -16 - w = (400.98 - 280.13)$$

$$w = -136.85 \text{ kJ/kg}$$

This is the work done on the air per unit mass. The power input to the compressor is determined by multiplying this value by the mass flow rate.

$$W = m \cdot w \ = \ (-136.85) \times (0.02) = -2.74 \text{ kW} \qquad \textbf{Ans.}$$

**Problem 1.12:** A water turbine receives water through a nozzle at the rate of 36000 kg/min. The head of water from the centre of the turbine is 300 m and discharge 5 m below the centre line of turbine. The velocity of water at outlet is 8 m/s. Neglecting the initial velocity of water, find the power output of the turbine.

**Solution: Given:** $m_w = \dfrac{3600}{60}$ kg/s = 600 kg/s, $v_1 = 0$, $v_2 = 8$ m/s

SFEE is,

$$Q + \left( h_1 + \frac{v_1^2}{2} + gz_1 \right) = W + \left( h_2 + \frac{v_2^2}{2} + gz_2 \right)$$

$$h_1 = h_2 = 0, \ Q = 0, \ v_1 = 0, \ z_2 = 0$$

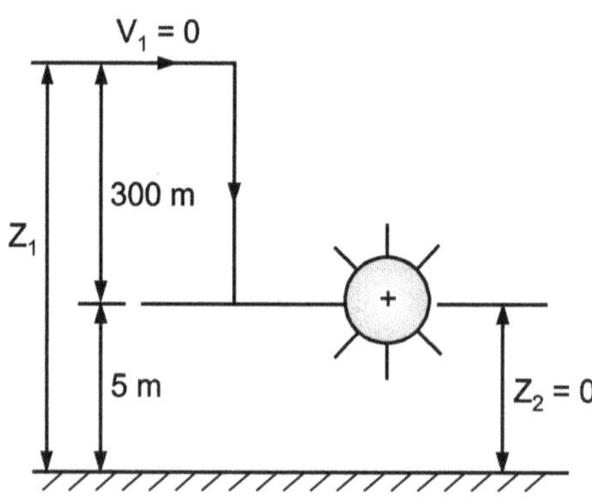


**Fig. 1.68**

$$\therefore \qquad W \ = \ gz_1 - \frac{v_2^2}{2} \ \text{J/kg}$$

$$W \ = \ 9.81 \times (305) - \frac{8^2}{2} \ = \ 2960 \text{ J/kg}$$

$$\text{Power output} \ = \ 2960 \times m_w = \frac{2960 \cdot 600}{1000} \ = \ 1776 \text{ kW} \qquad \text{... Ans.}$$

**Problem 1.13:** In a steady flow machine, 405 kW of work is done by the machine. The flow of fluid is 3 kg/s. The specific volume of the fluid, pressure and velocity at inlet are 0.37 m³/kg,  6 bar and 16 m/s respectively. The inlet is 32 m above the floor and discharge pipe is at the level of floor. The discharge conditions are 0.62 m²/kg, 1 bar and 270 m/s respectively. The total heat loss between the inlet and discharge is 9 kJ/kg of the fluid. Find the change in specific internal energy.

**Solution:** Refer Fig. 1.56.

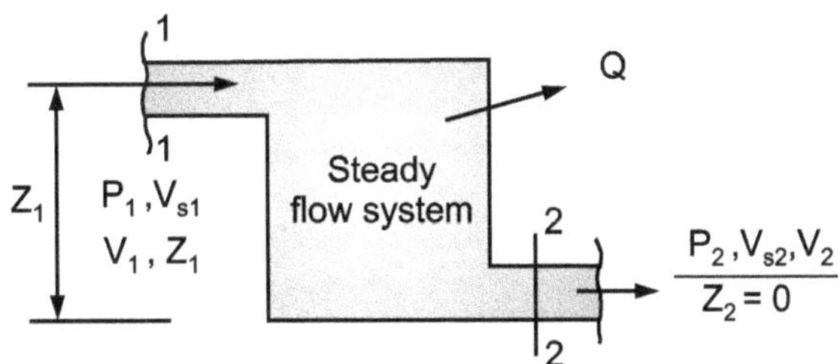

**Fig. 1.69**

**Given:** W = 405/3 = 135 kJ/kg

$$m \quad = 3 \text{ kg/s} \qquad\qquad z_1 \quad = 32 \text{ m}$$
$$V_{s1} = 0.37 \text{ m}^3/\text{kg} \qquad V_{s2} = 0.62 \text{ m}^3/\text{kg}$$
$$P_1 \quad = 6 \text{ bar} \qquad\qquad P_2 \quad = 1 \text{ bar}$$
$$v_1 \quad = 16 \text{ m/s} \qquad\qquad v_2 \quad = 270 \text{ m/s}, z_2 = 0$$
$$Q \quad = 9 \text{ kJ/kg} \qquad u_2 - u_1 \quad = ?$$

Using SFEE

$$Q + \left( u_1 + P_1 V_{s1} + \frac{v_1^2}{2} + gz_1 \right) = W + \left( u_2 + P_2 V_{s2} + \frac{v_2^2}{2} + gz_2 \right)$$

$$- 9 + \left( u_1 + 6 \times 10^5 \times 0.37 + \frac{16^2}{2} + 9.81 \times 32 \right)$$

$$= 135 + \left( u_2 + 1 \times 10^5 \times 0.62 + \frac{270^2}{2} + 9.81 \times 0 \right)$$

$$\therefore \qquad\qquad u_2 - u_1 = - 20 \text{ kJ/kg}$$

$$\therefore \qquad\qquad \text{Total } \Delta U = - 20 \times m = - 20 \times 3 = - 60 \text{ kJ/s} = - 60 \text{ kW} \qquad \textbf{... Ans.}$$

**Problem 1.14:** Air flows steadily at the rate of 0.5 kg/s, through an air compressor entering at 7 m/s velocity, 100 kPa and 0.95 m³/kg and leaving at 5 m/s, 700 kPa and 0.19 m³/kg respectively. The internal energy of the air leaving is 90 kJ/kg greater than that of air entering. Cooling water in the compressor jacket absorbs heat from the air at the rate of 58 kW.

   (a)  Compute the rate of shaft work input to the compressor in kW.

   (b)  Find the ratio of inlet and outlet pipe diameter.

**Solution:**

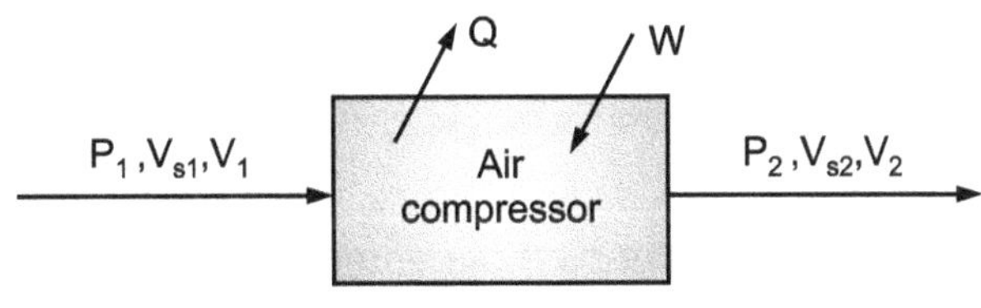

**Fig. 1.70**

**Given:** m = 0.5 kg/s

$$v_1 = 7 \text{ m/s} \qquad\qquad v_2 = 5 \text{ m/s}$$

$$V_{S1} = 0.95 \text{ m}^3/\text{kg} \qquad\qquad V_{S2} = 0.19 \text{ m}^3/\text{kg}$$

$$P_1 = 100 \times 10^3 \text{ N/m}^2 \qquad\qquad P_2 = 700 \times 10^3 \text{ N/m}^2$$

$$u_2 - u_1 = 90 \text{ kJ/kg} \qquad\qquad Q = -5.8 \text{ kW}$$

$$Q = \frac{-58}{m} = \frac{-58}{0.5} = -116 \text{ kJ/kg}$$

$$Q + \left( u_1 + P_1 V_{S1} + \frac{v_1^2}{2} + gz_1 \right) = W + \left( u_2 + P_2 V_{S2} + \frac{v_2^2}{2} + gz_2 \right)$$

(a) 
$$W = \left[ (u_1 - u_2) + P_1 V_{S1} - P_2 V_{S2} + \frac{v_1^2}{2} - \frac{v_2^2}{2} \right] + Q$$

$$= \left[ -90 \times 10^3 + 100 \times 10^3 \times 0.95 - 700 \times 10^3 \times 0.19 + \frac{7^2}{2} - \frac{5^2}{2} \right] - 116 \text{ J/kg}$$

$$= [-90 + 95 - 133 + 0.012 - 116] \text{ kJ/kg}$$

$$= -223.98 \text{ kJ/kg}$$

Mass flow rate is m = 0.5 kg/s

Net work done/s = W × m = − 223.98 × 0.5 = − 112 kW                        ... **Ans.**

(b) $m \times V_{S1} = A_1 v_1$ ∴ $\qquad A_1 = \dfrac{m \cdot V_{S1}}{v_1} = \dfrac{0.5 \times 0.95}{7} = 0.0678 \text{ m}^2$

$$A_2 = \frac{m \cdot V_{S2}}{v_2} = \frac{0.5 \times 0.19}{5} = 0.019 \text{ m}^2$$

$$\frac{A_1}{A_2} = \frac{\frac{\pi}{4} \cdot d_1^2}{\frac{\pi}{4} \cdot d_2^2}$$

$$= \frac{0.0678}{0.019} = 3.568$$

∴ $\qquad \dfrac{d_1^2}{d_2^2} = 3.568$

∴ $\qquad \dfrac{d_1}{d_2} = \dfrac{\text{inlet pipe diameter}}{\text{outlet pipe diameter}} = 1.889$                        ... **Ans.**

**Problem 1.15 :** The following data is given for an air compressor :

(i)    Rate of air flow 5 kg/s

|                      | Inlet         | Outlet      |
|----------------------|---------------|-------------|
| Pressure             | 80 kPa        | 600 kPa     |
| Sp. volume           | 0.65 m³/kg    | 0.12        |
| Sp. internal energy  | 40 kJ/kg      | 140 kJ/kg   |
| Velocity             | 6 m/s         | 4 m/s       |

Heat rejected to cooling water is 50 kW.

Find (i) Power required to drive the compressor in kW.

(ii)    Ratio of inlet pipe diameter to outlet pipe diameter.

**Solution:** $\Delta PE = 0$, $Q = \dfrac{50}{5} = 10$ kJ/kg

The SFEE is

$$Q + \left( u_1 + P_1 V_{s1} + \frac{v_1^2}{2} + gz_1 \right) = W + \left( u_2 + P_2 V_{s2} + \frac{v_2^2}{2} + gz_2 \right) \text{ J/kg}$$

$$Q + \left( u_1 + P_1 V_{s1} + \frac{v_1^2}{2} \right) = W + \left( u_2 + P_2 V_{s2} + \frac{v_2^2}{2} \right)$$

$$10 + \left( 40 + 80 \times 0.65 + \frac{6^2}{2} \times 10^{-3} \right)$$

$$= W + \left( 140 + 600 \times 0.12 + \frac{4^2}{2} \times 10^{-3} \right) \text{ kJ/kg}$$

$\therefore \qquad\qquad\qquad W = -129.99$ kJ/kg $\qquad\qquad\qquad$ **... Ans.**

For determining the ratio of diameters, use continuity equation.

$$\dot{m} = \frac{A_1 v_1}{V_{s1}} = \frac{A_2 v_2}{V_{s2}}$$

$$\therefore \qquad \frac{A_1}{A_2} = \frac{V_{s1}}{V_{s2}} \times \frac{v_2}{v_1} = \frac{0.65}{0.12} \times \frac{4}{6} = 3.611$$

$$\therefore \qquad \frac{d_1}{d_2} = \sqrt{\frac{A_1}{A_2}} = \sqrt{3.611} = 1.9 \qquad\qquad \text{... Ans.}$$

**Problem 1.16:** Air flows in a compressor at a rate of 0.7 kg/sec. The air enters at 5 m/sec velocity, 100 kPa pressure, 0.85 m³/kg, volume leaving at 3 m/sec, 700 kPa and 0.17 m³/kg. The internal energy of the air leaving is 80 kJ/kg greater than that of air entering. Cooling water in the compressor jacket absorb heat from air at the rate of 60 kW.

(a)  Determine the rate of shaft work input to the air in kW.

(b)  Find the ratio of inlet pipe diameter to outlet pipe diameter.

**Solution:**

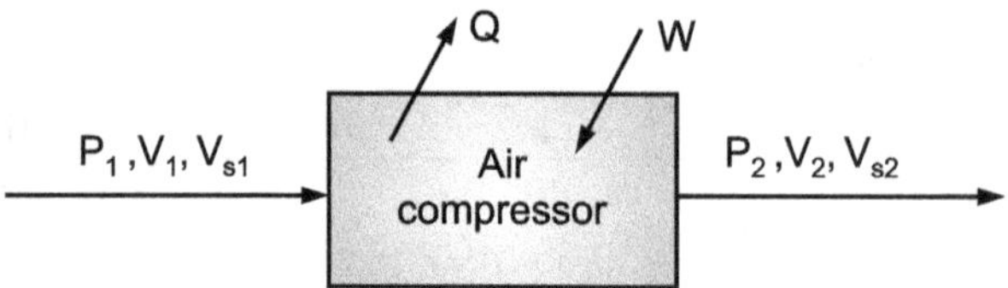


**Fig. 1.71: Block diagram of a compressor**

**Given:**

$$m = 0.7 \text{ kg/sec.}$$

$$v_1 = 5 \text{ m/sec, } v_2 = 3 \text{ m/sec}$$

$$v_{s_1} = 0.85 \text{ m}^3/\text{kg, } v_{s_2} = 0.17 \text{ m}^3/\text{kg}$$

$$P_1 = 100 \times 10^3 \text{ N/m}^2, P_2 = 700 \times 10^3 \text{ N/m}^2$$

$$u_2 - u_1 = 80 \text{ kJ/kg, } Q = \frac{-60}{0.7} = -85.7 \text{ kJ/kg}$$

**(a) Shaft work:** Steady flow energy equation:

$$Q + \left( u_1 + P_1 v_{s_1} + \frac{v_1^2}{2} + gz_1 \right) = W + \left( u_2 + P_2 v_{s_2} + \frac{v_2^2}{2} + gz_2 \right)$$

$$\therefore \quad W = \left[ (u_1 - u_2) + P_1 v_{s_1} - P_2 v_{s_2} + \frac{v_1^2}{2} - \frac{v_2^2}{2} \right] + Q$$

$$= \left[ -80 \times 10^3 + 100 \times 10^3 \times 0.85 - 700 \times 10^3 \times 0.17 + \frac{5^2}{2} - \frac{3^2}{2} \right] - 85.7$$

$$= -80 + 85 - 119 - 0.008 - 85.7$$

$$= -199.7 \text{ kJ/kg}$$

Mass flow rate of air $= 0.7$ kg/sec.

Net work $= m \times W = 0.7 \times (-199.7) = -139.8$ kW  **... Ans.**

**(b) Ratio of inlet to outlet pipe diameter**

$$= mv_{s_1} = A_1 v_1$$

$$\therefore \quad A_1 = \frac{m \cdot v_{s_1}}{v_1} = \frac{0.7 \times 0.85}{5} = 0.119 \text{ m}^2$$

Similarly, $$A_2 = \frac{m \cdot v_{s_2}}{v_2} = \frac{0.7 \times 0.17}{3} = 0.0396$$

$$\therefore \quad \frac{A_1}{A_2} = \frac{\frac{\pi}{4} \cdot d_1^2}{\frac{\pi}{4} \cdot d_2^2} = \frac{0.119}{0.0396} = 3$$

$$\therefore \quad \frac{d_1}{d_2} = \frac{\text{Inlet pipe diameter}}{\text{Outlet pipe diameter}} = 1.732 \quad \textbf{... Ans.}$$

**Problem 1.17:** 1 kg of fluid contained in a cylinder receives 150 kJ of work by paddle wheel together with 50 kJ in the form of heat. At the same time, the piston in the cylinder moves in such a way that pressure remains constant at 200 kN/m$^2$ and fluid expands from 2m$^3$ to 5 m$^3$. Estimate the change in internal energy and change in enthalpy.

**Solution:**

$$P = \text{constant} = 200 \text{ kN/m}^2$$

$$v_1 = 2 \text{ m}^3, v_2 = 5 \text{ m}^3$$

$$W = 150 \text{ kJ done on the gas.}$$

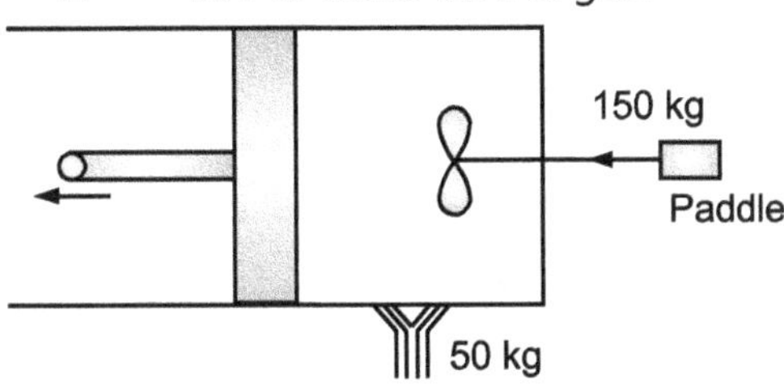


**Fig. 1.72**

$$Q = \Delta U + W$$

Change in internal energy,

$$\Delta U = Q - W = 50 - 150 = -100 \text{ kJ} \qquad \textbf{... Ans.}$$

Change in enthalpy, $\Delta H = \Delta U + d(Pv)$

$$= \Delta U + P \cdot dv$$

$\therefore \qquad P\,dv = P(v_2 - v_1)$

$$= 200 \times 10^3 (5 - 2) = 600 \times 10^3 \text{ Nm} = 600 \text{ kJ}$$

$\therefore \qquad \Delta H = \Delta U + P\,dv$

$$= -100 + 600 = +500 \text{ kJ} \qquad \textbf{... Ans.}$$

Positive sign indicates that the enthalpy increases.

**Problem 1.18:** In a particular non-flow system, a certain amount of working substance undergoes a frictionless process according to the law

$$P = \left(\frac{5}{v} + 3\right)$$

where P is in bar and v is in m$^3$. During the process, volume changes from $v_1 = 0.12$ m$^3$ to $v_2 = 0.04$ m$^3$. The system rejects 93 kJ of heat during the process. Determine the change in internal energy and the change in enthalpy.

**Solution: Given:** Initial volume, $v_1 = 0.12$ m$^3$

Final volume, $v_2 = 0.04$ m$^3$.

It is a compression process.

$$\text{Work done,} \quad W = \int_1^2 P\,dv = \int_1^2 \left(\frac{5}{v} + 3\right) dv \cdot 10^5$$

$$= [5 \log v + 3v]_1^2 \times 10^5$$

$$= \left[5 \log \frac{v_2}{v_1} + 3\,(v_2 - v_1)\right] \times 10^5$$

$$= -5.73 \times 10^5 \text{ joule}$$

$$= -573 \text{ kJ, work is done on the gas.}$$

Now, $\qquad Q = \Delta U + W$

where $\qquad \Delta U$ = change in internal energy

$$= Q - W$$

$$= -93 \text{ kJ} - (-573)\text{ kJ} = 480 \text{ kJ} \qquad \textbf{... Ans.}$$

$$\Delta H = dU + d\,(Pv) = dU + P\,dv$$

$$= 480 - 573 = -93 \text{ kJ} \qquad \textbf{... Ans.}$$

**Problem 1.19:** Air at 100 kPa and 280 K is compressed steadily to 600 kPa and 400 K. The mass flow rate of air is 0.02 kg/s and heat loss 16 kJ/kg occurs during the process. Assuming changes in kinetic and potential energies to be negligible, determine the necessary power input to the compressor. Assume enthalpy of air at inlet and exit at 280.13 kJ/kg and 400.98 kJ/kg respectively.

**Solution: Given:**

$$P_1 = 100 \text{ kPa} \qquad \dot{m}_{air} = 0.02 \text{ kg/s}$$
$$T_1 = 280 \text{ K} \qquad Q = -16 \text{ kJ/kg}$$
$$P_2 = 600 \text{ kPa} \qquad h_1 = 280.13 \text{ kJ/kg}$$
$$T_2 = 400 \text{ K} \qquad h_2 = 400.98 \text{ kJ/kg}$$

The steady flow energy equation is

$$q + \left(h_1 + \frac{v_1^2}{2} + gz_1\right) = w + \left(h_2 + \frac{v_2^2}{2} + gz_2\right)$$

Change in K.E. and P.E. are negligible.

$\therefore \qquad q - w = \Delta h$

$$w = q - \Delta h$$

$$= -16 - (400.98 - 280.13)$$

$$= -136.85 \text{ kJ/kg}$$

Power input, $W = m \cdot w$

$$= 0.02 \frac{kg}{s} \times (-136.85)\frac{kJ}{kg} = -2.737 \text{ kW} \qquad \textbf{... Ans.}$$

**Problem 1.20:** A cylinder fitted with frictionless piston containing gas at a pressure $200 \times 10^3$ N/m$^2$ executes the cycle by undergoing the following processes :

(i)   1200 N-m of stirring work is done on gas by paddle wheel and cylinder is well insulated. As a result, volume increases by 0.0028 m$^3$.

(ii)  With the insulation removed and paddle wheel stationary, heat transfer from the gas restores the gas to its initial state. Evaluate :

(a)  net work done by gas during process (i)

(b)  net work done and heat transfer by gas in process (i)

(c)  increase in energy of gas in processes (i) and (ii)

(d)  the increase in energy of gas for combined processes (i) and (ii).

**Solution:** (a) Work done by the gas on the piston

$$= P \cdot dv \; = \; 200 \times 10^3 \, \text{N/m}^2 \times (0.0028 \, \text{m}^3) = 560 \, \text{N-m}$$

The work supplied to the gas by paddle = 1200 N-m.

$\therefore$  The difference between 1200 N-m and 560 N-m is stored in the gas in the form of internal energy.

$\therefore$  Increase in internal energy = 1200 – 560 = 640 N-m.                    ... **Ans.**

(b)  Net work done in process (i) = 560 N-m.

Since the cylinder is well insulated, the rate of heat transfer is zero.          ... **Ans.**

(c)  In process (i), internal energy increases by 640 N-m. In process (ii), the insulation is removed, it means heat transfer from gas to the surroundings takes place. It means internal energy decreases by 640 N-m, so that the gas returns to the original state.          ... **Ans.**

(d)  The gas undergoes a cyclic process because it expands from initial state due to addition of work by paddle wheel. The gas returns to the initial state as the internal energy decreases by the same amount. Therefore, the net change in internal energy in the combined processes (i) and (ii) is zero.

---

**Problem 1.21:** A gas turbine receives gases at 7.2 bar and 850°C and velocity of 160 m/s. The gases come out of turbine at 1.15 bar and 450°C and a velocity of 250 m/s. Find out the work output from the gas turbine in kW/kg. The process may be assumed as adiabatic.

Take $C_p$ = 1.04 kJ/kg-°C for gas.

**Solution:**  The general energy equation on the basis of 1 kg flow can be written as

$$\left( \frac{V_1^2}{2} + gZ_1 + h_1 \right) \pm Q \pm W \; = \; \left[ \frac{V_2^2}{2} + gZ_2 + h_2 \right]$$

For the gas turbine,      $Z_1 \; = \; Z_2, \; Q = 0$

(as the flow is adiabatic (given)

Gas turbine is work developing system.

$$\therefore \quad \left(\frac{V_1^2}{2} + h_1\right) - W = \left(\frac{V_2^2}{2} + h_2\right)$$

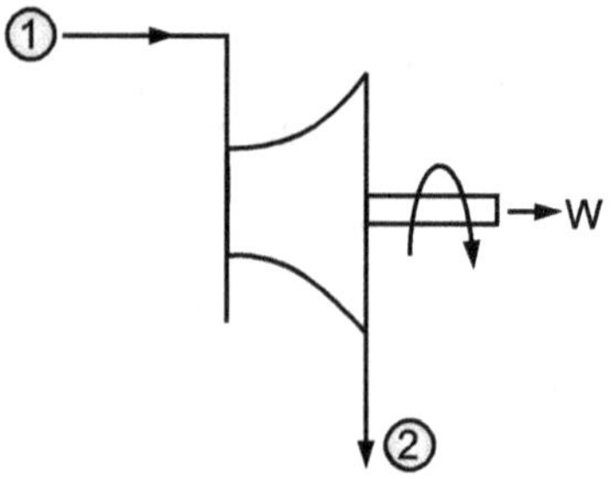

**Fig. 1.73**

$$\therefore \quad W = \frac{V_1^2 - V_2^2}{2} + (h_1 - h_2) = \frac{V_1^2 - V_2^2}{2} + C_p\,(T_1 - T_2)$$

$$= \left[\frac{(160)^2 - (250)^2}{2}\right] + 1.04 \times 10^3 \times (850 - 450)\ \text{joules}$$

$$= (-18450 + 416 \times 10^3)\ \text{joules} = -18.45 + 416 = 397.55\ \text{kJ/kg}$$

... **Ans.**

---

**Problem 1.22 :** The internal energy of a system is given by,

$$U = (100 + 50\,T + 0.04\,T^2)\ \text{joules}$$

and heat transfer Q is given by

$$Q = (4000 + 16\,T)\ \text{joules, where T is in K.}$$

If the temperature of the system changes from 300 K to 500 K, find the work transfer and its direction.

**Solution:**

$$U = 100 + 50\,T + 0.04\,T^2$$

$$\therefore \quad \frac{dU}{dT} = 50 + 0.08\,T$$

$$\therefore \quad dU = (50 + 0.08\,T)\,dT$$

$$Q = 4000 + 16\,T$$

$$\therefore \quad \frac{dQ}{dT} = 1.6$$

$$\therefore \quad dQ = 16\,dT$$

As per first law of thermodynamics,

$$dQ = dW + dU$$

---

$$\therefore \quad dW = dQ - dU = (16\ dT) - (50 + 0.08\ T)\ dT$$

$$= (16 - 50 - 0.08\ T)\ dT = -(34 + 0.08\ T)\ dT$$

$$\therefore \quad W = -\int_{T_1}^{T_2} (34 + 0.08\ T)\ dT$$

$$= \int_{T_2}^{T_1} (34 + 0.08\ T)\ dT$$

$$= 34\ (T_1 - T_2) + 0.08 \left( \frac{T_1^2 - T_2^2}{2} \right)$$

$$= 34\ (300 - 500) + 0.04\ [(300)^2 - (500)^2]$$

$$= -6800 - 6400 = -13200\ J = -13.2\ kJ \qquad \textbf{... Ans.}$$

The negative sign indicates that the work is done on the system.

**Problem 1.23:** A steam turbine receives steam at 15 bar and velocity of 300 m/s. The internal energy at inlet is 2000 kJ/kg and specific volume is 0.15 m³/kg. The steam leaves the turbine at 130 kPa with a velocity of 200 m/s, internal energy of 1500 kJ/kg and specific volume of 1.2 m³/kg. If inlet condition is 3 m above the discharge, find out the power output of the turbine if the steam flow rate is 300 kJ/min. Heat lost to the surrounding is 50 kJ/kg.

**Solution:** The generalised flow energy equation on the basis of 1 kg mass is given by,

$$\left( \frac{V_1^2}{2} + Z_1 g + p_1 v_{s1} + u_1 \right) \pm Q \pm W = \left( \frac{V_2^2}{2} + Z_2 g + p_2 v_{s2} + u_2 \right)$$

As it is work developing system, it can be written as

$$\left( \frac{V_1^2}{2} + Z_1 g + p_1 v_{s1} + u_1 \right) - Q - W = \left( \frac{V_2^2}{2} + Z_2 g + p_2 v_{s2} + u_2 \right)$$

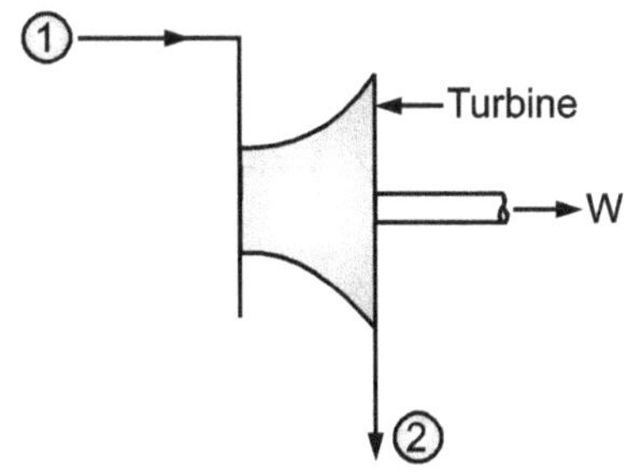


**Fig. 1.74**

$$\therefore \quad W = \frac{V_1^2 - V_2^2}{2} + g\ (Z_1 - Z_2) + (p_1 v_{s1} - p_2 v_{s2}) + (u_1 - u_2) - Q$$

$$= \frac{(300)^2 - (200)^2}{2} + 9.81 \times (3) + 10^5 \times (15 \times 0.15 - 1.3 \times 1.2)$$

$$+ 10^3 \times (2000 - 1500) - 50 \times 10^3$$

$$= 2.5 \times 10^4 + 29.43 + 10^5 \times (2.25 - 1.56) + 10^3 \times 500 - 50 \times 10^3$$

$$= 10^3 \times [25 + 0.0294 + 69 + 500 - 50] \text{ joules} = 544.03 \text{ kJ/kg} \qquad \textbf{... Ans.}$$

As steam flow (m) = 300 kg/min = 5 kg/sec

$\therefore$　　P　=　m·W = 5 × 544.03 = 2720 kW $\qquad$ **... Ans.**

**Problem 1.24:** A closed system executes a process in which it develops 8000 kJ of work by receiving 1500 kJ of heat. What is the change in internal energy? The system then is brought to original state with the rejection of 800 J of heat. What is the work done during the second process?

**Solution:** The first process is represented by 1-a-2 and second process is represented by 2-b-1 on p-v diagram as shown in Fig. 1.62.

Consider the process 1-a-2.

$$Q_{1a2} = + 1500 \text{ kJ}, \ W = 1000 \text{ kJ}$$

$\therefore \qquad Q_{1a2} = W_{1a2} + U_2 - U_1$

$\therefore \qquad \Delta U = U_2 - U_1$

$$= Q_{1a2} - W_{1a2}$$

$$= 1500 - 1000 = 500 \text{ kJ}$$

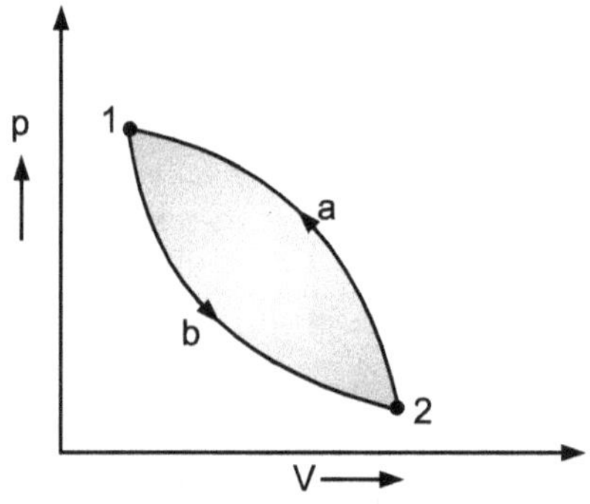

**Fig. 1.75**

For closed cycle,

$$\oint dQ = \oint dW$$

$\therefore \qquad Q_{1a2} + Q_{2b1} = W_{1a2} + W_{2b1}$

$\therefore \qquad 1500 - 800 = 1000 + W_{2b1}$

$\therefore \qquad W_{2b1} = -300 \text{ kJ} \qquad$ **... Ans.**

The negative sign indicates that the work is done on the system.

**Problem 1.25:** A turbine operates under steady flow conditions with the following inlet and outlet conditions of the working fluid.

| Property | Inlet | Outlet |
|---|---|---|
| Pressure (kPa) | 1177 | 19.6 |
| Specific volume (m³/kg) | 0.218 | 7.79 |
| Velocity (m/s) | 35 | 100 |
| Internal energy (kJ/kg) | 2792.7 | 2456.5 |
| Elevation (m) | 3 | 0.0 |

Heat lost to the surrounding is 25 kJ/min. If the rate of steam flow through the turbine is 240 kg/min, what is the power output of the turbine?

**Solution:** The general flow energy equation considering mass flow rate m kg/sec can be written as

$$m\left[\frac{V_1^2}{2} + Z_1g + u_1 + p_1v_{s1}\right] - Q - W = m\left[\frac{V_2^2}{2} + Z_2g + u_2 + p_2v_{s2}\right]$$

where m is mass flow in kg/sec and Q and W are also on second basis.

where Q is heat rejected in J/sec $= \dfrac{25 \times 1000}{60} = 416.6$ J/s

and W is the work developed in J/sec = watts

and m is mass of working fluid passing through the turbine $= \dfrac{240}{60} = 4$ kg/sec

$$\therefore \quad W = m\left[\frac{V_1^2 - V_2^2}{2} + g\,(Z_1 - Z_2) + (u_1 - u_2) + (p_1v_{s1} - p_2v_{s2})\right] - Q$$

Substituting the given values in proper units,

$$W = 4\left[\frac{(35)^2 - (100)^2}{2} + 9.81\,(3 - 0) + 10^3\,(2792.7 - 2456.5) + (0.1177 \times 0.218 - 19.6 \times 7.79) \times 10^3\right] - 416.6$$

$$\therefore \quad W = 4 \times [-4387.5 + 29.43 + 10^3 \times 336.2 + 10^3 \times 103.9] - 416.6$$

$$= 4 \times 10^3\,[-4.38 + 0.029 + 336.2 + 103.9] - 416.6$$

$$= 4 \times 10^3\,[435.8] - 416.6$$

$$= 1742.6 \text{ kWz} \qquad \text{... } \textbf{Ans.}$$

**Problem 1.26:** A Carnot engine which rejects heat to a cooling pond at 27°C has an efficiency of 30 percent. If the cooling pond receives 837.2 kJ/min, what is the power developed by the cycle? Find the temperature of the source.

**Solution:** $\qquad\qquad\qquad\qquad T_L = 27 + 273 = 300$ K

$$\eta_{th} \; = 30\,\%, \; Q_L \; = 837.2 \text{ kJ/min} = 139.5 \text{ kW}$$

$$\eta_{carnot} \; = \frac{T_H - T_L}{T_H}$$

$$0.3 \; = \frac{T_H - (300)}{T_H}$$

$$\therefore \qquad T_H \; = \textbf{428.5 K}$$

For reversible engine,

$$\frac{Q_L}{Q_H} \; = \frac{T_L}{T_H}$$

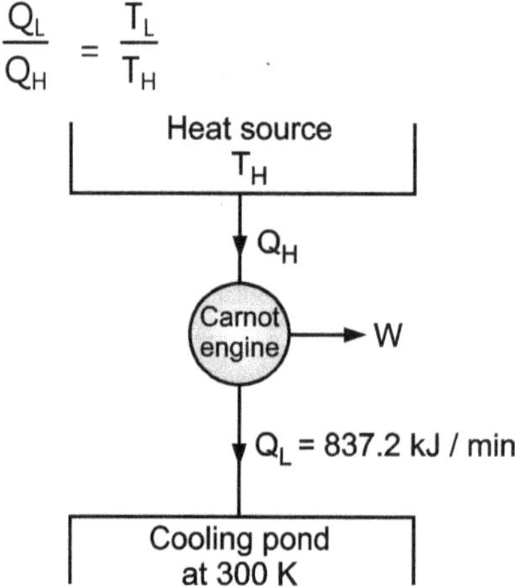


**Fig. 1.76: Heat engine**

$$Q_H \; = \frac{Q_L}{T_L} \cdot T_H$$

$$= \frac{837.2 \times 428.5}{300} = \textbf{1196 kJ/min.}$$

$$\text{Power developed, } W \; = Q_H - Q_L$$

$$= 1196 - 837.2 = 358.6 \text{ kJ/min} = \textbf{5.97 kW}$$

**Problem 1.27:** The working substance in a Carnot engine is 0.05 kg of air. The maximum cycle temperature is 900 K and maximum pressure is 8.5 MPa. The heat added per cycle is 5 kJ. Determine the maximum cylinder volume if the minimum temperature during the cycle is 300 K.

**Solution: Given :** m = 0.05 kg, $T_H$ = 900 K

Maximum pressure = $p_1$ = $8.5 \times 10^6$ N/m$^2$

The maximum temperature and pressure corresponds to a point 1 on p-V diagram (See Fig. 1.32) and maximum volume at state 3.

We apply gas equation to find the volume $V_1$.

$$p_1V_1 = mRT_1 \qquad \therefore \ V_1 = \frac{mRT_1}{p_1} = \frac{0.05 \times 0.287 \times 900}{8.5 \times 10^3} = 1.52 \times 10^{-3} \text{ m}^3$$

Heat supplied, $Q = p_1V_1 \ln V_2/V_1$

$$5 \times 10^3 = 8.5 \times 10^6 \times 1.52 \times 10^{-3} \ln \frac{V_2}{V_1}$$

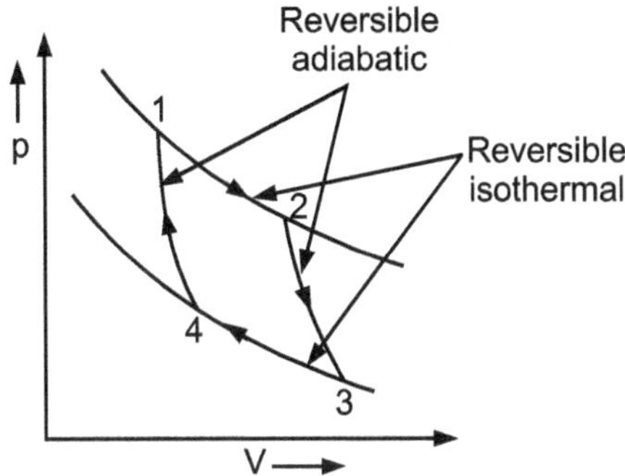


**Fig. 1.77: Carnot cycle**

$$\therefore \qquad \log \frac{V_2}{V_1} = 0.387 \qquad \therefore \ \frac{V_2}{V_1} = 1.4727$$

$$\therefore \qquad V_2 = 1.52 \times 10^{-3} \times 1.4727 = 2.23 \times 10^{-3} \text{ m}^3$$

$$\text{But} \qquad \frac{V_3}{V_2} = \left(\frac{T_2}{T_3}\right)^{1/\gamma - 1}$$

$$\therefore \qquad V_3 = V_2 \left(\frac{T_2}{T_3}\right)^{1/\gamma - 1} = 2.23 \times 10^{-3} \left(\frac{900}{300}\right)^{1/1.4 - 1}$$

$$= 0.0347 \text{ m}^3$$

$\therefore$   Maximum cylinder volume = **0.0347 m³**

# EXERCISE

1. What is thermodynamics?

2. How thermodynamics is studied?

3. Explain the difference between microscopic and macroscopic studies.

4. What is meant by pure substance?

5. Explain with suitable sketches, following thermodynamic systems : closed, open, isolated and adiabatic.

6. What do you understand by control volume and control surface?

7. What is thermodynamic property? Explain intensive and extensive properties.

8.   What is meant by state, process and a cycle?

9.   What is thermodynamic equilibrium?

10.  What is a quasi-static process? Is it a reversible process?

11.  Distinguish between reversible and irreversible processes.

12.  What is point function and path function?

13.  Discuss : 'Property is an exact differential'. Discuss property and non-property.

14.  What is heat and work? What are the similarities in heat and work? Also differentiate heat and work.

15.  What is displacement work?

16.  What are the different forms of work?

17.  What do you understand by equation of temperature?

18.  Explain zeroth law of thermodynamics.

19.  What is energy? What are the forms of energy?

20.  What do you understand by internal energy?

21.  What is the outcome of Joule's experiment?

22.  Give different statements of first law of thermodynamics.

23.  Prove that energy is a property of the system.

24.  What is meant by steady flow process?

25.  Explain the meaning of flow work.

26.  Apply first law of thermodynamics to steady flow process.

27.  Explain few examples of steady flow process with the assumptions.

28.  What are the limitations of first law of thermodynamics?

29.  What is the meaning of $- \int V\, dP$ in a steady flow process?

30.  What is meant by perpetual motion machine of first kind?

31.  What do you understand by thermal reservoirs?

32.  What is heat engine? Explain its working with block diagram. What is its thermal efficiency?

33.  Define second law of thermodynamics.

     Explain: (i) Kelvin - Planck statement, (ii) Clausius statement

     Give suitable examples.

34.  What is meant by perpetual motion machine of second kind?

35.  What is refrigerator and heat pump? What is meant by COP?

36. A cycle comprises of three processes. The energy transfers in each process are tabulated below:

| Process | Q (kJ) | W (kJ) | $\Delta U$ (kJ) |
|---------|--------|--------|--------|
| 1 – 2 | + 50 | + 30 | – |
| 2 – 3 | – | – 40 | + 30 |
| 3 – 1 | – | – | – |

If the cycle rejects 30 kJ of heat and if 10 such cycles are completed per minute, complete the table and find the power. State whether it is a power producing or power absorbing system.

$$\textbf{(Ans. } \Delta U_{1-2} = +20 \text{ kJ}, Q_{2-3} = -10 \text{ kJ},$$

$$\Delta U_{3-1} = -50 \text{ kJ}, Q_{3-1} = -70 \text{ kJ}, W_{3-1} = -20 \text{ kJ}$$

$$\text{Net power} = -5 \text{ kW, Power absorbing system)}$$

37. The power output of an adiabatic steam turbine is 5 MW and the inlet and exit conditions of steam are as under.

|       | Pressure | Temp. | Velocity | Elevation |
|-------|----------|-------|----------|-----------|
| Inlet | 2 MPa | 400° C | 50 m/s | 10 m |
| Exit | 15 kPa | 0.9 dry | 180 m/s | 6 m |

Determine the work done / kg of steam and the mass flow rate in kg/s.

$$\textbf{(Ans. } W_S = 871.91 \text{ kJ/kg}, \dot{m} = 5.734 \text{ kg/s)}$$

38. During a certain reversible process, volume changes from 0.5 m$^3$ to 1.5 m$^3$. The law of the process is P = (10 – 3 V), where 'P' is in bar and 'V' in m$^3$. The internal energy of the air decreases by 150 kJ.

Find:

(i)   $\int$ PdV, Q and $\Delta h$ and work transfer if it is a reversible non-flow process.

(ii)  $\int$ PdV, $-\int$ vdp, Q, $\Delta h$ and work transfer if it is steady flow process with $\Delta P = 0$ and $\Delta K = 0$ kJ.

39. Prove the statement that "It is not possible to attain absolute zero K temperature."

40. Two heat pumps are connected in series between two heat reservoirs  at $T_1$ and $T_3$. Heat pump 'A' transfers heat from a reservoir at '$T_3$' and rejects heat to a intermediate reservoir at '$T_2$' while the other heat pump 'B' transfers heat from reservoir at $T_2$ to the reservoir at '$T_1$'. If $T_1 > T_2 > T_3$, show that (i) intermediate temperature '$T_2$' is arithmetic mean of '$T_1$' and '$T_3$' when work input to both heat pumps is same,  (ii)  intermediate temperature '$T_2$' is a geometric mean of '$T_1$' and '$T_3$' if both the heat pumps have same C.O.P.

41. An inventor claims to have developed a refrigerating machine which operates between –20°C and +30°C and consumes 1 kW power. The machine gives a refrigerating affect of 21.6 MJ/h. Verify the validity of his claim.

42. A domestic food freezer maintains a temperature of – 15°C. The outdoor ambient is at 30°C. If the heat load on the freezer is 1.75 kW, what is the minimum power necessary to pump out this heat? If the actual C.O.P. of the freezer is half that of the ideal C.O.P., what is the actual power required?

$\quad\quad$ (**Ans.** Minimum power required = 0.305 kW, Actual power required = 0.61 kW)

43. A reversible heat pump is driven by a reversible heat engine. The heat rejected by the heat pump and by the heat engine is used to warm up a building. If the thermal efficiency of the heat engine is 27 % and the C.O.P. of the heat pump is 4, find the ratio of heat supplied to building to the heat supplied to the heat engine.

$\quad\quad$ (**Ans.** Ratio = 2.08)

44. Prove that for a Carnot cycle,

$$\left.\frac{d\eta}{dT_2}\right|_{T_1=c} = \frac{-1}{T_1} \text{ and } \left.\frac{d\eta}{dT_1}\right|_{T_2=c} = \frac{T_2}{T_1^2}$$

and state which is a more effective way to increase the thermal efficiency of a Carnot cycle.

45. A reversible heat engine used for a satellite operates between a hot reservoir at $T_1$ and a radiating panel at $T_2$. The heat radiated from the panel is proportional to its area and $T_4^2$. For a given work output and a fixed temperature $T_1$, show that the area of the panel will be minimum when $\dfrac{T_1}{T_2} = \dfrac{4}{3}$.

46. A centrifugal pump operates under steady flow conditions. It delivers 0.3 m³ of water per minute at 20° C. The suction pressure is 80 kPa, and the delivery pressure is 3 bar. Diameters of suction and delivery pipes are 15 cm and 10 cm respectively. The pump axis is 5 m above the sump level and is 15 m below the level in the overhead tank. Neglecting change of internal energy, calculate the power required to operate the pump. Given: g = 9.81 m/s², $e_w$ = 1000 kg/m³.$\quad$ (**Ans.** $w_s$ = – 2.1623 kW)

# UNIVERSITY QUESTION PAPERS

## DEC. 2013

1. Define any three and give suitable example wherever necessary:                **[6]**

   (i)   Enthalpy

   (ii)  Intensive and extensive properties

   (iii) Quasi–static Process.

   (iv)  Zeroth law of thermodynamics

   (v)   Heat Sink and Heat Source

2. During a Thermodynamic cycle of processes (A–B–C–D–A), the heat transferred during each process are: 120 kJ, –16 kJ, –48kJ and 12 kJ respectively. Estimate net work transferred during the Thermodynamic cycle, direction of work transfer, Change in Internal energy and Total energy during the cycle using the first law for Thermodynamic cycle.                **[6]**

## MAY 2014

1. State and explain Steady Flow Energy Equation and write the equation when applied to following devices (any Six),                **[6]**

   (a)  Throttling device.    (b)  Boiler.

   (c)  Condenser.           (d)  Nozzles

   (e)  Diffusers.            (f)  Turbines

   (g)  Compressor

2. A cylinder containing air undergoes a thermodynamic cycle through following two processes.

   **Process 1:** During compression 82 kJ of work is done on the system (air) by piston and 45 kJ heat is rejected.

   **Process 2:** During expansion 100 kJ of work is done by the system (air). Using the first law of thermodynamics for cycle estimate

   (a)  The heat transfer during process 2 and

   (b)  Direction of this heat transfer.                **[6]**

## DEC. 2014

1. State limitations of first law of thermodynamics. Explain how Clausius and Kelvin Planck statements overcome these limitations using the heat engine, heat pump and refrigerator concept. Define thermal efficiency of heat engine and COP for refrigerator and heat pump.                **[6]**

2. A reversible heat engine working as a refrigerator absorbs heat from low temperature reservoir of 650 kg, when work input is 250 kJ: **[6]**

   (i) Find its COP and heat transferred to the surrounding.

   (ii) If the same device works as a heat engine, find out its thermal efficiency.

   (iii) If the same device works as a heat pump, estimate the COP.

### MAY 2015

1. State Kelvin–Planck and Clausius statement of the second law of thermodynamics and prove that the violation of Kelvin–Planck statement results into violation of Clausius statement. **[6]**

### NOV. 2015

1. Explain the following concepts of thermodynamics : **[6]**

   (i) Thermodynamics cycle

   (ii) Flow work

   (iii) P-dV work.

2. What are the Kelvin–Planck and Clausius statements of second law of thermodynamic ? Also establish their equivalence. **[6]**

### MAY 2016

1. Discuss the concept of point function and path function. Explain with examples and suitable diagram. **[6]**

◈ ◈ ◈

# Chapter 2

# ENTROPY

## 2.1 INTRODUCTION

Entropy is a useful property and serves as a valuable tool in the second law analysis of engineering devices. Entropy is not a common word as energy is. But with continued use, our understanding of entropy will deepen and we will grow in understanding entropy. In the following paragraphs, it has been tried out to introduce the entropy to the reader.

Entropy can be defined as a measure of molecular disorder or molecular randomness. Let us discuss the entropy of a fluid which could exist in three different phases. A common fluid water exists in vapour, liquid and solid phase depending upon the temperature at a fixed pressure. In vapour state, the molecular distance is more as compared with liquid and solid state. It means the molecules in vapour phase have more freedom to move in any direction, it means the molecules arranged in most disorderly manner. Hence, the entropy of a system (fluid) in vapour state is more as compared with its liquid state. Similarly, the water molecules are more systematically/orderly organised in the solid state than liquid. Therefore, the entropy of liquid water is always more compared to that it in solid state. This discussion is equally applicable to all the systems which could be in different phases. This is as shown in Fig. 2.1.

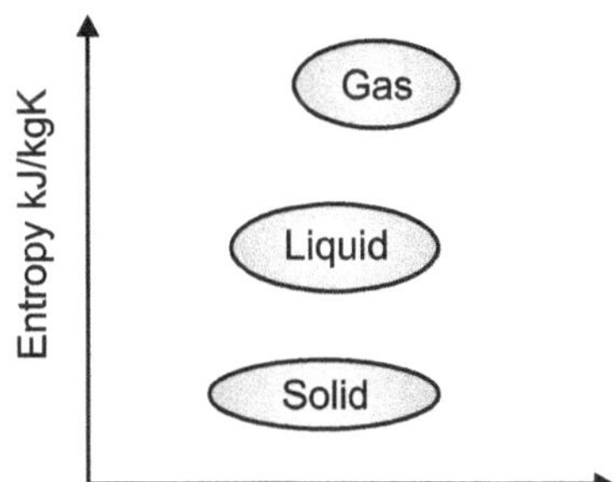


**Fig. 2.1: The entropy (molecular disorder) of a substance increases as it changes its phase to liquid or gas**

Molecules in the gas phase possess a considerable amount of kinetic energy. However, no matter how large their kinetic energy are, the gas molecules will not rotate a paddle wheel inserted into the container and produce work. This is so because the gas molecules and the energy they carry with them are disorganised. Probably the number of molecules which try to rotate the paddle wheel in one direction is equally opposed by the remaining gas molecules, resulting in no rotation of the paddle wheel. Hence, one cannot extract useful work directly from disorganised energy (See Fig. 2.2).

**Fig. 2.2: The disorganised energy does not create useful effect**

**(equal and opposite forces applied to a load will not move it)**

Now, consider a rotating shaft as shown in Fig. 2.3. Here all the molecules of shaft are organised and rotate in one direction. Hence, one can extract useful work from the organised molecules as exist in the form of solid shaft. The rotation of the shaft can be utilised to raise or lower the load. Being an organised form of energy, work is free of disorder or randomness and thus free of entropy. There is no transfer of entropy associated with energy transfer as work.

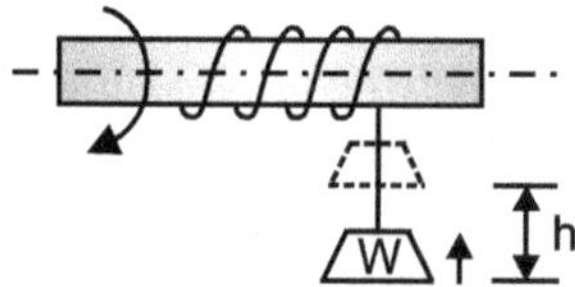


**Fig. 2.3: Weight can be raised or lowered by a rotating shaft which does not create any disorder (entropy)**

Let us consider one more example in which heat is transferred from a hot body to a cold body as shown in Fig. 2.4.

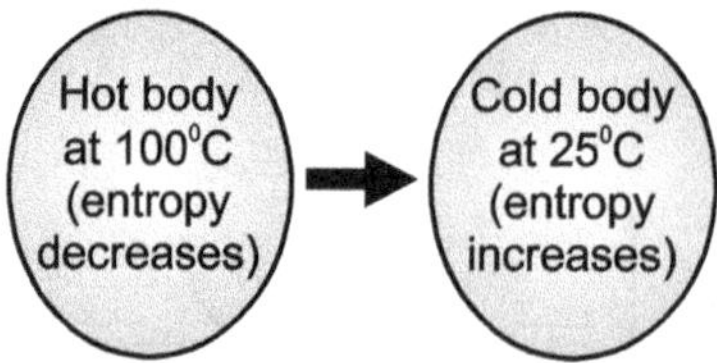


**Fig. 2.4: During a heat transfer process, the net disorder (entropy) increases**

Heat, a disorganized energy, and disorganization (entropy) will result with heat. As a result, the entropy of the hot body will decrease while the entropy and disorder of the cold body increase. As per second law, the increase in entropy of cold body be greater than the decrease in entropy of the hot body, and thus the net entropy of the combined system (cold body and hot body) increases. It means the combined system is at a state of greater disorder at the end state.

"Steel has got a great strength and looses all when red hot". You may be surprised at this stage to read the sentence. Let us apply entropy concept to our life style. When a person is angry it means the body organs are in the most disordered state. Therefore, when an angry person will perform badly or he does unwanted/not useful task, which may lead to any type of distruction. Therefore, every person should try to keep entropy of his body to a minimum level to do the constructive job.

## 2.2 CLAUSIUS INEQUALITY                                    [Dec. 10]

An important inequality that has major consequences in thermodynamics is the Clausius inequality, which is expressed as,

$$\oint \frac{\delta Q}{T} \leq 0 \qquad \qquad \text{... (2.1)}$$

The cyclic integral of $\frac{\delta Q}{\delta T}$ is always less than or equal to zero. This inequality is valid for all

cycles, reversible or irreversible. The $\oint$ is used to indicate that integration is to be carried out over the entire cycle.

The validity of the Clausius inequality can be illustrated with the help of two heat engines, one reversible and the other irreversible both operating between the same temperature limits of $T_H$ and $T_L$.

Here $T_H$ represents the temperature of high-temperature reservoir while $T_L$ is that of low-temperature reservoir as shown in Fig. 2.5.

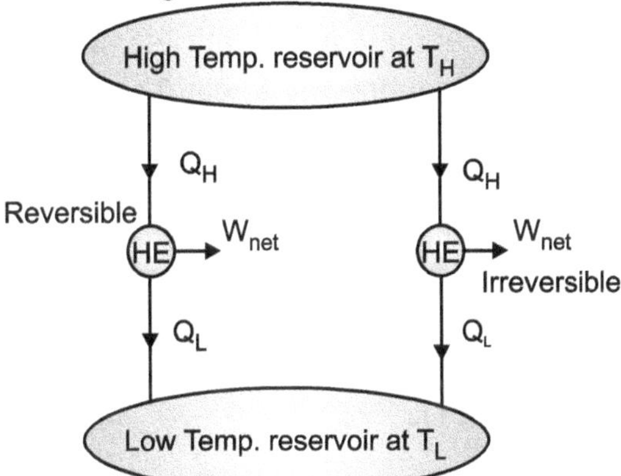


**Fig. 2.5: A reversible and irreversible heat engine operating between the same temperature limits (same reservoir)**

Here $Q_H$ and $Q_L$ are the rate of heat transfer taking place at constant temperatures $T_H$ and $T_L$ respectively.

(A) For reversible heat engine, the cyclic integral of $\frac{\delta Q}{T}$ becomes,

$$\oint \left(\frac{\delta Q}{T}\right)_{rev} = \int \frac{\delta Q_H}{T_H} - \int \frac{\delta Q_L}{T_L}$$

$$= \frac{1}{T_H} \int \delta Q_H - \frac{1}{T_L} \int \delta Q_L$$

$$= \frac{Q_H}{T_H} - \frac{Q_L}{T_L} = 0$$

Since, $\dfrac{Q_H}{T_H} = \dfrac{Q_L}{T_L}$ for reversible cycle, thus, for a reversible heat engine cycle,

$$\oint \left( \frac{\delta Q}{T} \right)_{rev} = 0 \qquad\qquad \text{... (2.2)}$$

Equation (2.2) is developed for totally reversible heat engine, but is equally valid for heat engines that are only internally reversible. In such a situation, $T_H$ and $T_L$ can be considered as the temperature of the working fluid at locations heat is received and rejected respectively. Therefore, equation (2.2) can be written as,

$$\oint \left( \frac{\delta Q}{T} \right)_{int\ rev} = 0 \qquad\qquad \text{... (2.3)}$$

(B) Now, consider the irreversible heat engine operating between the same thermal reservoirs (temperature limits) as the reversible one and receive the same amount of heat $Q_H$ during a cyclic operation. But as per the Carnot principle, the irreversible heat engine will deliver less net work and which rejects more waste heat. Therefore,

$$Q_{L,\ irrev} > Q_L$$

$$Q_{L,\ irrev} = Q_L + Q_{diff}$$

where, $Q_{diff}$ is a positive quantity.

Carrying out the cyclic integral of $\dfrac{\delta Q}{T}$ for this irreversible heat engines results,

$$\oint \left( \frac{\delta Q}{T} \right)_{irrev} = \frac{Q_H}{T_H} - \frac{Q_{L,\ irrev}}{T_L}$$

$$= \frac{Q_H}{T_H} - \frac{Q_L}{T_L} - \frac{Q_{diff}}{T_L}$$

$$= - \frac{Q_{diff}}{T_L} < 0$$

$\therefore$   For an irreversible heat engine cycle,

$$\oint \left( \frac{\delta Q}{T} \right)_{irrev} < 0 \qquad\qquad \text{... (2.4)}$$

The Clausius inequality is obtained by combining the equations (2.3) and (2.4) as,

$$\oint \frac{\delta Q}{T} \leq 0 \qquad\qquad \text{... (2.5)}$$

The equation (2.5) is valid for totally or just internally reversible cycles. Equality sign is for reversible engine while inequality sign is for irreversible engine.

## 2.3 ENTROPY AS A PROPERTY                                          [Dec. 10]

The Clausius inequality discussed in Section 2.1 forms the definition of new property called entropy.

Consider a cycle that consists of two internally reversible processes, A and B, as shown in Fig. 2.6. Applying equation (2.3) to this internally reversible cycle, we obtain

$$\oint \left(\frac{\delta Q}{T}\right)_{int\ rev} = \int_1^2 \left(\frac{\delta Q}{T}\right)_A + \int_2^1 \left(\frac{\delta Q}{T}\right)_B = 0$$

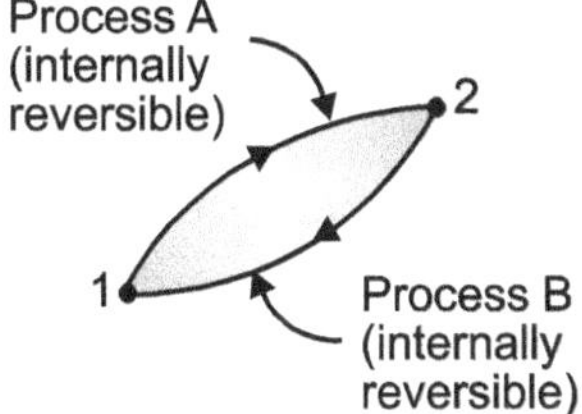


**Fig. 2.6: Reversible cyclic processes between two end states**

Reversing the limits of the last integral and changing its sign,

$$\int_1^2 \left(\frac{\delta Q}{T}\right)_A - \int_1^2 \left(\frac{\delta Q}{T}\right)_B = 0$$

$$\int_1^2 \left(\frac{\delta Q}{T}\right)_A = \int_1^2 \left(\frac{\delta Q}{T}\right)_B$$

Since A and B are any two internally reversible process paths between states 1 and 2, the value of this integral depends on the end states only and not on the path followed. Therefore, it must represent the change of a property. This property is called **entropy.** It is designated by s and is defined as,

$$ds = \left(\frac{\delta Q}{T}\right)_{int\ rev} \quad (kJ/K) \qquad \ldots (2.6\ a)$$

Entropy is an extensive property of a system and sometimes is referred to as total entropy. Entropy per unit mass, designated s, is an intensive property and has the unit kJ/(kg·K). The term entropy is generally used to refer to both total entropy and entropy per unit mass.

The entropy change of a system during a process can be determined by integrating equation (2.6 a) between the initial and the final states:

$$\Delta s = s_2 - s_1 = \int_1^2 \left(\frac{\delta Q}{T}\right)_{int\ rev} \quad (kJ/K) \qquad \ldots (2.6\ b)$$

## 2.4 PRINCIPLE OF INCREASE OF ENTROPY                              [Dec. 10]

Consider a cycle that consists of two processes, one internally reversible and the other irreversible as shown in Fig. 2.7.

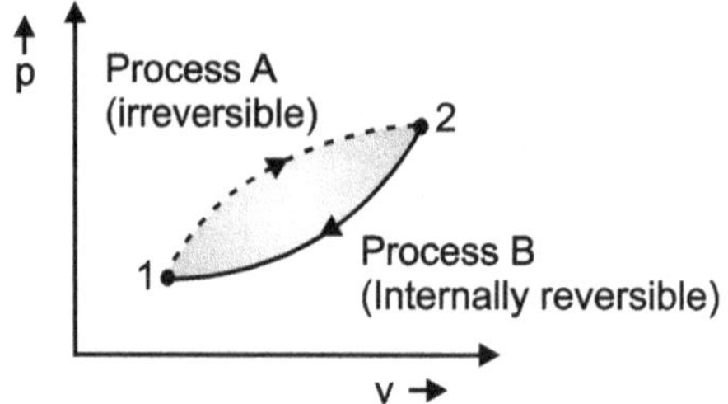


**Fig. 2.7: A cycle composed of a reversible and an irreversible process**

Clausius inequality tells that the cyclic integral of $\dfrac{\delta Q}{T}$ for the irreversible cycle is less than zero, i.e.

$$\oint \left(\frac{\delta Q}{T}\right)_{irrev} < 0$$

or $$\int_{1,\,A}^{2} \left(\frac{\delta Q}{T}\right)_{irrev} + \int_{2,\,B}^{1} \left(\frac{\delta Q}{T}\right)_{int,\,rev} < 0$$

The second term in the above equation represents entropy change $s_1 - s_2$. Thus,

$$\int_{1,\,A}^{2} \left(\frac{\delta Q}{T}\right)_{irrev} + (s_1 - s_2) < 0$$

This can be rearranged as,

$$\Delta s = (s_2 - s_1) > \int_{1,\,A}^{2} \left(\frac{\delta Q}{T}\right)_{irrev} \qquad \ldots (2.7)$$

From equation (2.7) one can say *"the entropy change of a closed system during an irreversible process is greater than the integral of $\dfrac{\delta Q}{T}$ evaluated for that process"*.

In general, the relation between the change of entropy of a closed system and the integral of $\dfrac{\delta Q}{T}$ can be expressed as,

$$\Delta s \geq \int_{1}^{2} \frac{\delta Q}{T} \qquad \ldots (2.8)$$

or in the differential form,

$$ds \geq \frac{\delta Q}{T} \qquad \qquad \text{... (2.9)}$$

Here the equality sign holds for a totally or just internally reversible process and the inequality for an irreversible process. $\delta Q$ represents a differential amount of actual heat transfer between the system and surroundings and 'T' is the absolute temperature at the boundary.

Let us now consider an isolated system. It is known that in an isolated system, matter, work and heat cannot cross the boundary of the system. Hence, according to the first law of thermodynamics, the internal energy of the system remains constant.

For isolated system, $\delta Q = 0$, from equation (2.9), we get,

$$(ds)_{isolated} \geq 0 \qquad \qquad \text{... (2.10)}$$

Equation (2.10) tells that the entropy of an isolated system either increases or remains constant. This is a corollary of second law of thermodynamics. It explains the principle of increase in entropy.

## 2.5 CHANGE IN ENTROPY OF THE UNIVERSE

The entropy of an isolated system either increases or remains constant i.e.

$$(ds)_{isolated} \geq 0$$

Let us consider a system at temperature T and a surrounding at temperature $T_o$ within a single boundary as shown in Fig. 2.8, where it forms an isolated system.

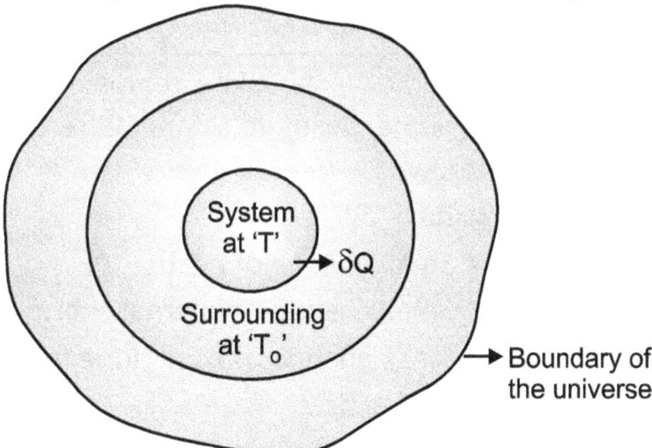


**Fig. 2.8: A combination of a system and surrounding to form an universe**

The combination of the system and the surroundings within a single boundary is sometimes called the universe. Let us apply principle of increase of entropy to the universe.

$$(ds)_{universe} \geq 0$$

$$\therefore \qquad (ds)_{universe} = (ds)_{system} + (ds)_{surroundings}$$

Let $\delta Q$ be the quantity of heat transferred from the system at temperature 'T' to the surrounding at temperature '$T_o$'.

$$(ds)_{system} \geq -\frac{\delta Q}{T}$$

(−ve sign indicates that heat is rejected from system.)

Similarly, since an amount of heat $\delta Q$ is received by the surroundings, for a reversible process,

$$(ds)_{surroundings} = \frac{\delta Q}{T_o}$$

Hence, the total change in entropy for the combined system

$$(ds)_{system} + (ds)_{surroundings} \geq -\frac{\delta Q}{T} + \frac{\delta Q}{T_o}$$

$$(ds)_{universe} \geq dQ\left(-\frac{1}{T} + \frac{1}{T_o}\right)$$

The same result can also be obtained for the open system. Therefore, for both closed and open system, one can write

$$(ds)_{universe} \geq 0 \qquad \qquad \text{... (2.11)}$$

Equation (2.11) states that the process involving heat interaction between the system and surroundings takes place only if the net entropy of the combined system increases or in the limit remains constant. Since all the real processes are irreversible, the entropy increases continuously.

## 2.6 ENTROPY CHANGES FOR A CLOSED SYSTEM

### 2.6.1 Change of Entropy of a Gas

Let 1 kg of gas at a pressure $p_1$, volume $V_1$, absolute temperature $T_1$ and entropy $s_1$, be heated such that its final pressure, volume, absolute temperature and entropy are $p_2$, $V_2$, $T_2$ and $s_2$ respectively. According to first law,

$$dQ = du + dW$$

where,

$$dQ = \text{Small change of heat}$$

$$du = \text{Small change of internal energy and}$$

$$dW = \text{Small change of work done } (pdV)$$

Now

$$dQ = c_v dT + pdV$$

Dividing both sides by T, we get

$$\frac{dQ}{T} = \frac{c_v dT}{T} + \frac{pdV}{T}$$

But

$$\frac{dQ}{T} = ds$$

and as

$$pV = RT$$

$$\therefore \qquad \frac{p}{T} = \frac{R}{V}$$

Hence,
$$ds = \frac{c_v dT}{T} + R\frac{dV}{V}$$

Integrating both sides,

$$\int_{s_1}^{s_2} ds = c_v \int_{T_1}^{T_2} \frac{dT}{T} + R \int_{V_1}^{V_2} \frac{dV}{V}$$

or
$$(s_2 - s_1) = c_v \log_e \frac{T_2}{T_1} + R \log_e \frac{V_2}{V_1} \qquad \dots (2.12)$$

This expression can also be obtained in the following way:

According to the gas equation, we have

$$\frac{p_1 V_1}{T_1} = \frac{p_2 V_2}{T_2}$$

or
$$\frac{T_2}{T_1} = \frac{p_2}{p_1} \times \frac{V_2}{V_1}$$

Substituting the value of $\frac{T_2}{T_1}$ in equation (2.12) we get,

$$s_2 - s_1 = c_v \log_e \frac{p_2}{p_1} \times \frac{V_2}{V_1} + R \log_e \frac{V_2}{V_1}$$

$$= c_v \log_e \frac{p_2}{p_1} + c_v \log_e \frac{V_2}{V_1} + R \log_e \frac{V_2}{V_1}$$

$$= c_v \log_e \frac{p_2}{p_1} + (c_v + R) \log_e \frac{V_2}{V_1}$$

$$= c_v \log_e \frac{p_2}{p_1} + c_p \log_e \frac{V_2}{V_1}$$

$$\therefore \qquad s_2 - s_1 = c_v \log_e \frac{p_2}{p_1} + c_p \log_e \frac{V_2}{V_1} \qquad \dots (2.13)$$

Again, from gas equation,

$$\frac{p_1 V_1}{T_1} = \frac{p_2 V_2}{T_2}$$

or
$$\frac{V_2}{V_1} = \frac{p_1}{p_2} \times \frac{T_2}{T_1}$$

Putting the value of $\frac{V_2}{V_1}$ in equation (2.12), we get,

$$(s_2 - s_1) = c_v \log_e \frac{T_2}{T_1} + R \log_e \frac{p_1}{p_2} \times \frac{T_2}{T_1}$$

$$= c_v \log_e \frac{T_2}{T_1} + R \log_e \frac{p_1}{p_2} + R \log_e \frac{T_2}{T_1}$$

$$= (c_v + R) \log_e \frac{T_2}{T_1} - R \log_e \frac{p_2}{p_1}$$

$$= c_p \log_e \frac{T_2}{T_1} - R \log_e \frac{p_2}{p_1}$$

$$\therefore \qquad s_2 - s_1 = c_p \log_e \frac{T_2}{T_1} - R \log_e \frac{p_2}{p_1} \qquad \ldots (2.14)$$

## (a) Heating a Gas at Constant Volume

Refer Fig. 2.9. Let 1 kg of gas be heated at constant volume and let the change in entropy and absolute temperature be from $s_1$ to $s_2$ and $T_1$ to $T_2$ respectively.

Then
$$Q = c_v (T_2 - T_1)$$

Differentiating to find small increment of heat dQ corresponding to small rise in temperature dT,

$$dQ = c_v \, dT$$

Dividing both sides by T, we get

$$\frac{dQ}{T} = c_v \cdot \frac{dT}{T}$$

or
$$ds = c_v \cdot \frac{dT}{T}$$

Integrating both sides, we get

$$\int_{s_1}^{s_2} ds = c_v \int_{T_1}^{T_2} \frac{dT}{T}$$

or
$$s_2 - s_1 = c_v \log_e \frac{T_2}{T_1} \qquad \ldots (2.15)$$

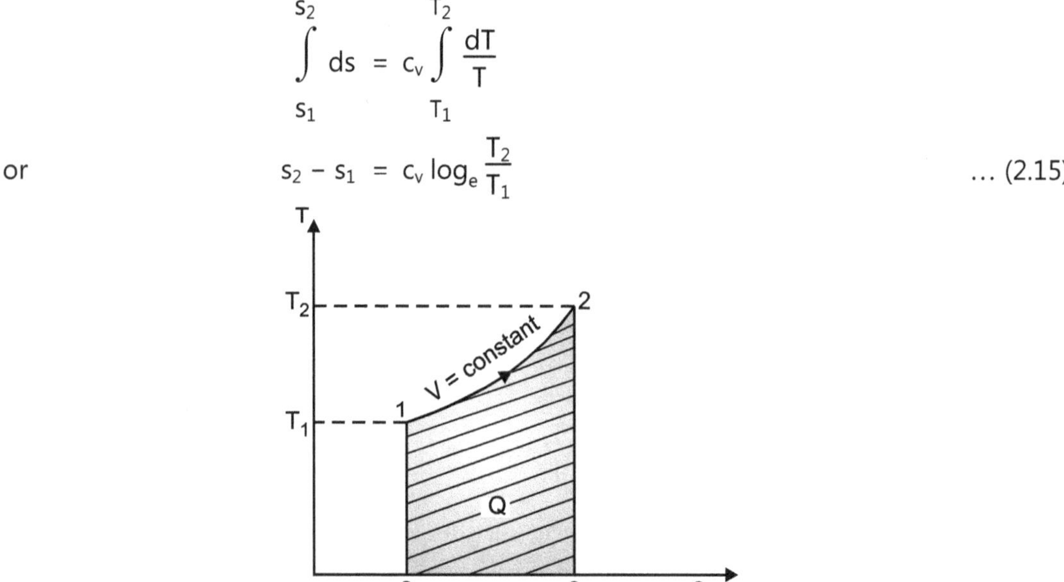


**Fig. 2.9: Constant volume process on T-s diagram**

## (b) Heating a Gas at Constant Pressure

Refer Fig. 2.10. Let 1 kg of gas be heated at constant pressure, so that its absolute temperature changes from $T_1$ to $T_2$ and entropy $s_1$ to $s_2$.

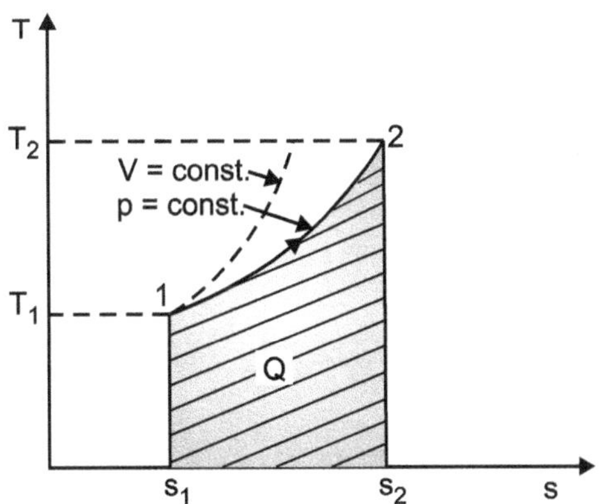

**Fig. 2.10: T-s diagram: Constant pressure process**

Then,                                   $Q = c_p (T_2 - T_1)$

Differentiating to find small increase in heat, dQ of this gas when the temperature rise is dT.

$$dQ = c_p \cdot dT$$

Dividing both sides by T, we get

$$dQ = dT$$

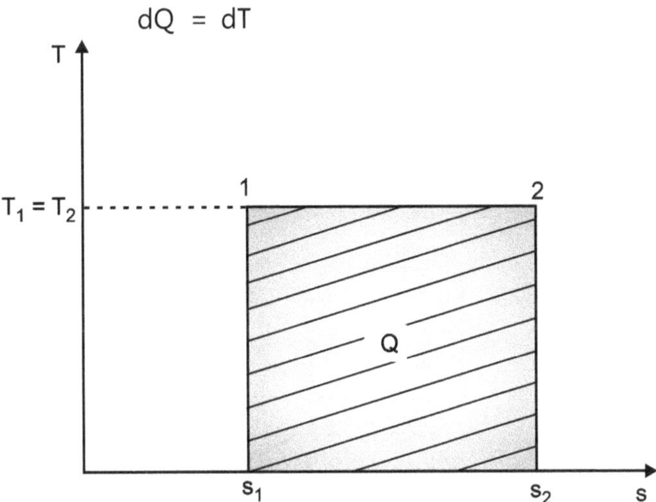

**Fig. 2.11: T-s diagram: Isothermal process**

$$\therefore \qquad T(s_2 - s_1) = RT_1 \log_e \frac{V_2}{V_1}$$

$$s_2 - s_1 = R \log_e \frac{V_2}{V_1} \qquad [\because T_1 = T_2 = T] \ \ldots (2.16)$$

## (c) Adiabatic Process (Reversible)

During an adiabatic process as heat is neither supplied nor rejected,

$$dQ = 0$$

$$\frac{dQ}{dT} = 0$$

$$ds = 0 \qquad\qquad\qquad \ldots (2.17)$$

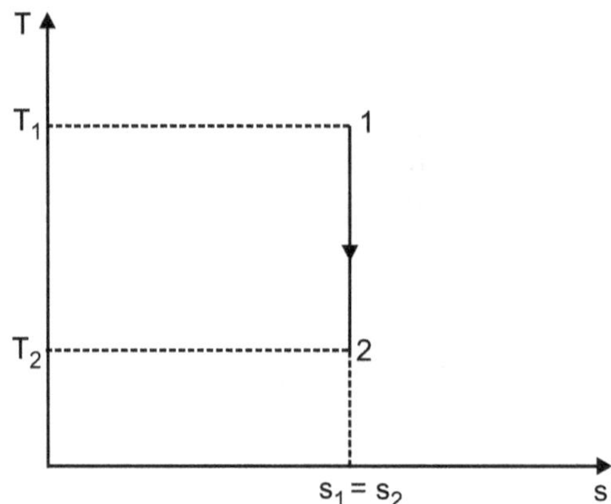

**Fig. 2.12: T-s diagram: Adiabatic process**

This shows that there is no change in entropy and hence it is known as isentropic process.

Fig. 2.12 represents an adiabatic process. It is a vertical line (1-2) and therefore area under this line is nil; hence heat supplied or rejected and entropy change is zero.

**(d) Polytropic Process**

Refer Fig. 2.13.

The expression for 'entropy change' in polytropic process ($pV^n$ = constant) can be obtained from equation (2.12).

i.e.
$$s_2 - s_1 = c_v \log_e \frac{T_2}{T_1} + R \log_e \frac{V_2}{V_1}$$

**Fig. 2.13: T-s diagram: Polytropic process**

Also
$$p_1 V_1^n = p_2 V_2^n$$

or
$$\frac{p_1}{p_2} = \left(\frac{V_2}{V_1}\right)^n \qquad \ldots \text{(i)}$$

Again, as
$$\frac{p_1 V_1}{T_1} = \frac{p_2 V_2}{T_2}$$

or
$$\frac{p_1}{p_2} = \frac{V_2}{V_1} \times \frac{T_1}{T_2} \qquad \ldots \text{(ii)}$$

From equations (i) and (ii), we get

$$\left(\frac{V_2}{V_1}\right)^n = \frac{V_2}{V_1} \times \frac{T_1}{T_2}$$

or

$$\left(\frac{V_2}{V_1}\right)^{n-1} = \frac{T_1}{T_2}$$

or

$$\frac{V_2}{V_1} = \left(\frac{T_1}{T_2}\right)^{\frac{1}{n-1}}$$

$$= c_v \log_e \frac{T_2}{T_1} - R\left(\frac{1}{n-1}\right) \log_e \frac{T_2}{T_1}$$

$$= c_v \log_e \frac{T_2}{T_1} - (c_p - c_v) \times \left(\frac{1}{n-1}\right) \log_e \frac{T_2}{T_1} \qquad [\because R = c_p - c_v]$$

$$= c_v \log_e \frac{T_2}{T_1} - (\gamma \cdot c_v - c_v) \times \left(\frac{1}{n-1}\right) \log_e \frac{T_2}{T_1} \qquad [\because c_p = \gamma \cdot c_v]$$

$$= c_v \left[1 - \left(\frac{\gamma - 1}{n - 1}\right)\right] \log_e \frac{T_2}{T_1} = c_v \left[\frac{(n-1) - (\gamma - 1)}{(n-1)}\right] \log_e \frac{T_2}{T_1}$$

$$= c_v \left(\frac{n - 1 - \gamma + 1}{n - 1}\right) \log_e \frac{T_2}{T_1}$$

$$= c_v \left(\frac{n - \gamma}{n - 1}\right) \log_e \frac{T_2}{T_1} \text{ per kg of gas}$$

$$\therefore \quad s_2 - s_1 = c_v \left(\frac{n - \gamma}{n - 1}\right) \log_e \frac{T_2}{T_1} \text{ per kg of gas} \qquad \ldots (2.18)$$

## (e) Approximation for Heat Absorbed

The curve AB shown in Fig. 2.14 is obtained by heating 1 kg of gas from initial state A to final state B. Let temperature during heating increase from $T_1$ to $T_2$. Then heat absorbed by the gas will be given by the area (shown shaded) under curve AB.

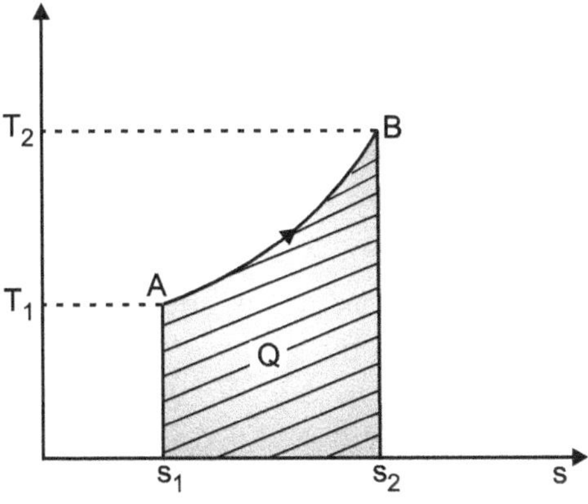


**Fig. 2.14**

As the curve on T-s diagram which represents the heating of the gas, usually has very slight curvature, it can be assumed a straight line for a small temperature range. Then,

$$\text{Heat absorbed} = \text{Area under the curve AB}$$

$$= (s_2 - s_1)\left(\frac{T_1 + T_2}{2}\right) \qquad \dots (2.19)$$

In other words, heat absorbed approximately equals the product of change of entropy and means absolute temperature.

Table 2.1: Summary of Formulae

| Sr. No. | Process | Change of Entropy (per kg) |
|---|---|---|
| 1. | General case | (i) $\quad c_v \log_e \frac{T_2}{T_1} + R \log_e \frac{V_2}{V_1}$ (in terms of T and V) <br><br> (ii) $\quad c_v \log_e \frac{p_2}{p_1} + c_v \log_e \frac{V_2}{V_1}$ (in terms of p and V) <br><br> (iii) $\quad c_p \log_e \frac{T_2}{T_1} - R \log_e \frac{p_2}{p_1}$ (in terms of T and p) |
| 2. | Constant volume | $c_v \log_e \frac{T_2}{T_1}$ |
| 3. | Constant pressure | $c_p \log_e \frac{T_2}{T_1}$ |
| 4. | Isothermal | $R \log_e \frac{V_2}{V_1}$ |
| 5. | Adiabatic | Zero |
| 6. | Polytropic | $c_v \left(\frac{n - \gamma}{n - 1}\right) \log_e \frac{T_2}{T_1}$ |

## 2.6.2 Entropy Changes for an Open System

In an open system, as compared with closed system, there is additional change of entropy due to the mass crossing the boundaries of the system. *The net change of entropy of a system due to mass transport is equal to the difference between the product of the mass and its specific entropy at the inlet and at the outlet of the system.* Therefore, the total change of entropy of the system during a small interval is given by,

$$ds \geq \frac{dQ}{T_0} + \Sigma s_i \cdot dm_i - \Sigma s_o \cdot dm_o$$

where,

$$T_0 = \text{Temperature of the surroundings, in K}$$

$$s_i = \text{Specific entropy at the inlet, J/kg·K}$$

$$s_o = \text{Specific entropy at the outlet, J/kg·K}$$

$$dm_i \ = \ \text{Mass entering the system, kg/sec}$$

$$dm_o \ = \ \text{Mass leaving the system, kg/sec}$$

(Subscripts i and o refer to inlet and outlet conditions.)

The above equation in general form can be written as,

$$ds \ \geq \ \frac{dQ}{T_0} + \Sigma s \cdot dm \qquad \qquad \ldots (2.20)$$

In equation (2.20), entropy flow into the system is considered positive and entropy outflow is considered negative. The equality sign is applicable to reversible process in which the heat interactions and mass transport to and from the system is accomplished reversibly. The inequality sign is applicable to irreversible processes.

If equation (2.20) is divided by dt, then it becomes a rate equation and is written as,

$$\frac{ds}{dt} \ \geq \ \frac{1}{T_0} \cdot \frac{dQ}{dt} + \Sigma s \cdot \frac{dm}{dt} \qquad \qquad \ldots (2.21)$$

In a steady-state, steady flow process, the rate of change of entropy of the system $\left(\dfrac{ds}{dt}\right)$ becomes zero.

$$\therefore \qquad \qquad 0 \ \geq \ \frac{1}{T_0}\frac{dQ}{dt} + \Sigma s \cdot \frac{dm}{dt}$$

$$\text{or} \qquad \qquad \frac{1}{T_0} \dot{Q} + \Sigma s \cdot \dot{m} \leq 0 \qquad \qquad \ldots (2.22)$$

$$\text{where} \qquad \qquad \dot{Q} \ = \ \frac{dQ}{dt} \qquad \text{and}$$

$$\dot{m} \ = \ \frac{dm}{dt}$$

For adiabatic steady flow process,

$$\dot{Q} \ = \ 0$$

$$\Sigma s \cdot \dot{m} \ \leq \ 0 \qquad \qquad \ldots (2.23)$$

If the process is reversible and adiabatic, then,

$$\Sigma s \cdot \dot{m} \ = \ 0 \qquad \qquad \ldots (2.24)$$

## 2.7 THE Tds RELATIONS

Earlier in this chapter, it is shown that the quantity $\left(\dfrac{\delta Q}{T}\right)_{int \ rev}$ corresponds to a differential change in property, called as entropy. The entropy change for various processes like constant volume process, constant pressure process, isothermal process etc. was evaluated and shown in the preceding sections. When the temperature varies during a process, we have a relation between $\delta Q$ and T to perform this integration.

Finding such relations is the task done in this section.

The differential form of the conservation of energy equation for a closed stationary system having a simple compressible fluid for internally reversible process can be written as,

$$\delta Q = \delta w + \delta u$$

But

$$\delta Q = Tds$$

$$\delta w = pdV$$

Thus

$$Tds - pdv = du$$

$$Tds = du + pdV \qquad \dots (2.25)$$

or

$$Tds = du + pdV \qquad \text{for unit mass} \dots (2.26)$$

This equation is known as first Tds or Gibb's equation.

The second Tds equation is obtained by eliminating du from equation (2.26) by using the definition of enthalpy ($h = u + pv$).

$$h = u + pV \rightarrow dh = du + pdV + Vdp$$

But

$$du + pdV = Tds$$

$\therefore$

$$Tds = dh - Vdp \qquad \dots (2.27)$$

Equations (2.26 and 2.27) are extremely valuables as they relate entropy changes of a system to the changes in other properties.

## 2.8 ENTROPY CHANGE OF A PURE SUBSTANCE

The Tds relations developed in the previous section are not limited to a particular substance in a particular phase. These are valid for all pure substances at any phase or combination of phases. The use of these equations, however, depends on the availability of the property relations between T and du or dh and the p-V-T behaviour of the substance. The Tds relations for pure substance, in general are very complicated. Therefore, instead of using such complicated equations to find entropy, these are tabulated in exactly the same manner as other properties u, V and h. In steam tables, the entropy of a saturated liquid $s_f$ at 0.01°C is assigned the value of zero. For refrigerant $R_{22}$, the zero value is assigned to saturated liquid at −40°C. The entropy values become −ve at temperature below the reference value.

The entropy values of any pure substance are obtained just as any other property. It can be directly obtained in the compressed liquid and superheated regions. In the saturated mixture region, it is determined from,

$$s = s_f + x\, s_{fg} \qquad \dots (2.28)$$

where, 'x' is the dryness fraction or quality of vapour and $s_f$ and $s_{fg}$ are listed in the property tables.

## 2.9  THE ENTROPY CHANGE OF SOLIDS AND LIQUIDS

The Tds equation is,

$$Tds = du + pdV \qquad \dots (2.29)$$

$$\text{or} \qquad ds = \frac{du}{T} + \frac{pdV}{T}$$

The solids and liquids are idealized as incompressible substances since their volumes remain essentially constant during a process.

Thus, change in volume, dV = 0 for solids and liquids.

Equation (2.29) reduces to

$$ds = \frac{du}{T} = c\,\frac{dT}{T} \qquad \dots (2.30)$$

As $c_p = c_v = c$ for incompressible substances and $du = c\,dT$, the entropy change for a process is determined by integration.

$$s_2 - s_1 = \int_1^2 c(T)\,\frac{dT}{T} \ \text{kJ/kg·K} \qquad \dots (2.31)$$

The specific heat 'c' of liquids and solids depend on temperature. We need a relation for 'c' as a function of temperature to perform the integration. In many cases 'c' may be taken as average value.

$$\therefore \qquad s_2 - s_1 = c_{av} \cdot \ln\left(\frac{T_2}{T_1}\right) \ \text{kJ/kg·K} \qquad \dots (2.32)$$

## SOLVED PROBLEMS

**Problem 2.1:** A heat engine operates between two thermal reservoirs which are at 900 K and 300 K. The heat engine receives 500 kJ heat from the source and rejects 300 kJ to heat sink at 300 K. Determine if this heat engine violates the second law of thermodynamics on the basis of (a) Clausius inequality and (b) the Carnot principle.

**Solution:** Refer Fig. 2.15.

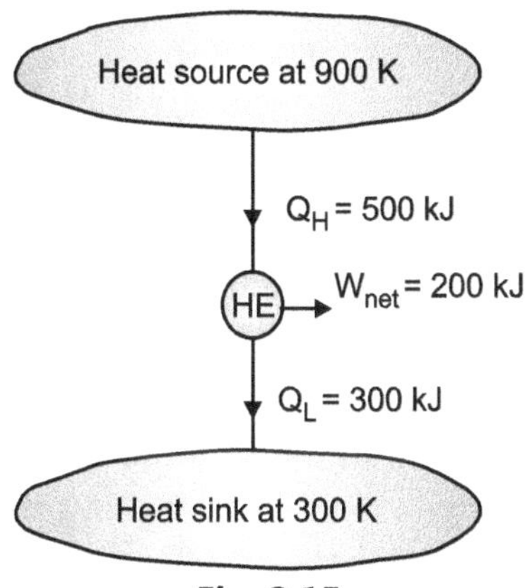


**Fig. 2.15**

(a)  The cyclic integral of $\dfrac{\delta Q}{T}$ for the heat-engine cycle under consideration is,

$$\oint \frac{\delta Q}{T} = \frac{Q_H}{T_H} - \frac{Q_L}{T_L} = \frac{500 \text{ kJ}}{900 \text{ K}} - \frac{300 \text{ kJ}}{300 \text{ K}}$$

$$= -0.444 \text{ kJ/kg}$$

The value is negative, this satisfies the Clausius inequality and the second law of thermodynamics.

(b)  To check Carnot principle,

$$\eta_{th} = 1 - \frac{Q_L}{Q_H} = 1 - \frac{300}{500} = 0.4$$

$$\eta_{th \text{ rev}} = 1 - \frac{T_L}{T_H} = 1 - \frac{300}{900} = 0.66$$

The efficiency of reversible engine (0.66) is higher than the efficiency of actual heat engine (0.4) i.e. $\eta_{th} < \eta_{th \text{ rev}}$. The cycle that violates the Clausius inequality will also violate the Carnot principle.

**Problem 2.2:** In a heat exchanger, water flows through a tube which is surrounded by air. Water at 80°C and 1 bar pressure rejects 600 kJ heat to the air at 300 K. Assume the heat exchanger is insulated (water rejects heat to air only). Air flows through shell-side of the heat exchanger. Determine (a) the entropy change of the water, (b) the entropy change of air during the process and (c) whether this process is reversible, irreversible or impossible.

**Solution:** (a) The temperature of flowing water is 80°C. Therefore, the entropy change of water during internally reversible, isothermal process (since temperature of water at 80°C will not change) can be found.

$$\Delta s_{water} = \frac{Q_{water}}{T_{water}} = \frac{-600 \text{ kJ}}{(80 + 273) \text{ K}} = -1.69 \text{ kJ/K}$$

$Q_{water}$ is negative, since heat is rejected.

(b)  The entropy change of air

$$Q_{air} = +600 \text{ kJ as it receives.}$$

$$\Delta s_{air} = \frac{Q_{air}}{T_{air}} = \frac{600 \text{ kJ}}{300 \text{ K}} = 2.0 \text{ kJ/K}$$

(c)  The total change of entropy for this process

$$\Delta s_{Total} = \Delta s_{water} + \Delta s_{air}$$

$$= -1.69 + 2.0 = 0.31 \text{ kJ/K}$$

The total energy change of the whole process is positive. Hence, it is an irreversible process.

**Problem 2.3:** A 100 kg iron casting at 600 K is put into a well having a large quantity of water at 285 K. Eventually, the iron casting attains thermal equilibrium with well water. The specific heat of cast iron is 0.5 kJ/kg·K. Determine (a) Entropy change of the cast iron block, (b) Entropy change of well water, (c) Total entropy change for this process.

**Solution:** (a) Cast iron block is treated as incompressible substance.

$$\Delta s_{iron} = m\,(s_2 - s_1) = m \cdot c_{av} \log\left(\frac{T_2}{T_1}\right)$$

$$= 100 \text{ kg} \times 0.5 \text{ kJ/kg·K } \ln\left(\frac{285}{600}\right)$$

$$= \mathbf{-37.2 \text{ kJ/K}}$$

(b) The well water acts as a thermal reservoir which does not experience increase in temperature.

$$Q_{iron} = m \cdot c_{av} \cdot (T_2 - T_1)$$

$$= 100 \times 0.5 \times (285 - 600)$$

$$= -15750 \text{ kJ}$$

$$Q_{well} = -Q_{iron} = +15750 \text{ kJ}$$

$$\Delta s_{well} = \frac{Q_{well}}{T_{well}} = \frac{15750 \text{ kJ}}{285 \text{ K}} = \mathbf{55.2 \text{ kJ/K}}$$

(c) The total entropy change for the process is,

$$\Delta s_{total} = \Delta s_{iron} + \Delta s_{well}$$

$$= -37.2 + 55.0 = \mathbf{18 \text{ kJ/K}}$$

The total entropy change is positive, hence the process is irreversible.

**Problem 2.4:** An iron cube at a temperature of 400°C is dropped into an insulated bath containing 10 kg water at 25°C. The water finally reaches a temperature of 50°C at steady state. Given that the specific heat of water is equal to 4186 J/kg·K. Find the entropy changes for the iron cube and the water. Is the process reversible? If so why?

**Solution: Given:** Temperature of iron cube $\qquad = 400°C = 673 \text{ K}$

Temperature of water $\qquad\qquad\qquad\qquad = 25°C = 298 \text{ K}$

Mass of water $\qquad\qquad\qquad\qquad\qquad = 10 \text{ kg}$

Temperature of water and cube after equilibrium $\quad = 50°C = 323 \text{ K}$

Specific heat of water, $c_{pw} \qquad\qquad\qquad = 4186 \text{ J/kg·K}$

**Entropy changes for the iron cube and the water:**

Now, Heat lost by iron cube = Heat gained by water

$$m_i\, c_{pi}\,(673 - 323) = m_w\, c_{pw}\,(323 - 298)$$

$$= 10 \times 4186\,(323 - 298)$$

$$\therefore \qquad m_i\, c_{pi} = \frac{10 \times 4186\,(323 - 298)}{(623 - 323)} = 2990$$

where, $\qquad\qquad\qquad m_i$ = Mass of iron, kg, and

$$c_{pi} = \text{Specific heat of iron, J/kg·K}$$

The iron cube rejects heat $= Q_{iron}$

$$\text{The entropy of iron } = m_i c_{pi} \ln\left(\frac{T_2}{T_1}\right)$$

(a) Entropy of iron at 673 K $= m_i\, c_{pi} \ln\left(\frac{T_2}{T_1}\right)$

$$= 2990 \ln\left(\frac{323}{673}\right)$$

$$= -2195 \text{ J/K}$$

Water receives heat ($Q_w$ is positive).

(b) $\quad$ Entropy of water at 298 K $= m_w \cdot c_{pw} \ln\left(\frac{T_2}{T_1}\right)$

$$= 10 \times 4186 \ln\left(\frac{298}{273}\right) = 10 \times 4186 \ln\left(\frac{323}{298}\right)$$

$$= 3372 \text{ J/K}$$

(c) The total entropy change for the process is,

$$\Delta s_{total} = \Delta s_{iron} + \Delta s_{water}$$

$$= -2195 + 3372$$

$$= 1177 \text{ J/K}$$

$$\text{Net change in entropy } = 3372.24 - 2195$$

$$\text{Net change in entropy} = 3372.24 - 2195 = \mathbf{1177.24 \text{ J/K}}$$

Since $\Delta s > 0$, hence, the process is **irreversible.**

---

**Problem 2.5:** An ideal gas is heated from temperature $T_1$ to $T_2$ by keeping its volume constant. The gas is expanded back to its initial temperature according to the law $pv^n$ = constant. If the entropy changes in the two processes are equal, find the value of n in terms of the adiabatic index $\gamma$.

**Solution:** Change in entropy during constant volume process

$$= m\, c_v \ln\left(\frac{T_2}{T_1}\right) \qquad\qquad \text{... (i)}$$

Change in entropy during polytropic process ($pv^n$ = constant)

$$= m\, c_v \left(\frac{\gamma - n}{n - 1}\right) \ln\left(\frac{T_2}{T_1}\right) \qquad\qquad \text{... (ii)}$$

For the same entropy, equating (i) and (ii), we have

$$\frac{\gamma - n}{n - 1} = 1$$

or $\qquad\qquad (\gamma - n) = (n - 1) \text{ or } 2n = \gamma + 1$

$\therefore \qquad\qquad n = \dfrac{\gamma + 1}{2}$

---

**Problem 2.6:** 1 kg of air has a volume of 56 litres and a temperature of 190°C. The air then receives heat at constant pressure until its temperature becomes 500°C. From this state the air rejects heat at constant volume until its pressure is reduced to 700 kN/m$^2$. Determine the change of entropy during each process stating whether it is on increase or decrease.

Take $c_p$ = 1.006 kJ/kg·K and $c_v$ = 0.717 kJ/kg·K

### Solution: Given:

Mass of air = m = 1 kg.

Initial volume of air = $V_1$ = 56 litres

Initial temperature of air = $T_1$ = 190 + 273 = 463 K

Final temperature of air = $T_2$ = 500 + 273 = 773 K

Final pressure of air = $p_3$ = 700 kN/m$^2$

Calculate: (i) Change of entropy during each process.

The given process is drawn in Fig. 2.16.

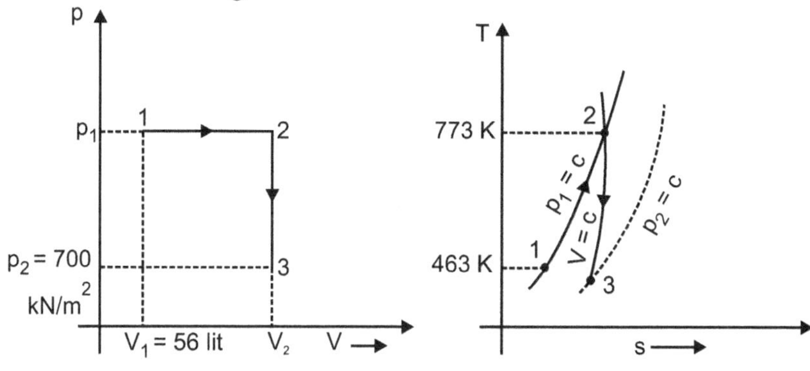

**Fig. 2.16**

### For process 1-2 (Constant Pressure Process):

$$p_1 = p_2$$

By general gas equation,

$$\frac{p_1 V_1}{T_1} = \frac{p_2 V_2}{T_2}$$

$$\therefore \quad \frac{V_1}{T_1} = \frac{V_2}{V_1}$$

$$V_2 = \frac{V_1}{T_1} \times T_2 = \frac{56 \times 10^{-3}}{463} \times 773$$

$$\therefore \quad V_2 = 0.09353 \text{ m}^3$$

Using the equation of change of entropy,

$$s_2 - s_1 = mc_v \cdot \log_e \frac{T_2}{T_1} + mR \log \frac{V_2}{V_1}$$

$$= 1 \times 0.717 \log \frac{773}{463} + 1 \, (1.006 - 0.717) \log \frac{0.09353}{0.056}$$

$$= 0.3675 + 0.48268$$

$$= \textbf{0.85 kJ/kg·K (Increase)}$$

**Process 2-3 (Constant Volume): $V_2 = V_3$**

From general gas equation,

$$p_2 V_2 = mRT_2$$

$$\therefore \qquad p_2 = \frac{mRT_2}{V_2}$$

$$= \frac{1 \times 0.289 \times 773}{0.09353}$$

$$= \textbf{2388.51 kN/m}^2$$

and

$$\frac{p_2 V_2}{T_2} = \frac{p_3 V_3}{T_3}$$

$$\frac{p_2}{T_2} = \frac{p_3}{T_3} \qquad\qquad (\because V_2 = V_3)$$

$$\therefore \qquad T_3 = \frac{p_3 T_2}{p_2} = \frac{700 \times 773}{2388.51}$$

$$T_3 = 226.54 \text{ K}$$

Using the equation of change of entropy,

$$s_3 - s_2 = mc_p \cdot \log_e \frac{T_3}{T_2} - mR \cdot \log_e \frac{p_3}{p_2}$$

$$= 1 \times 1.006 \log \frac{226.54}{773} - 1 \times 0.289 \log \frac{700}{2388.51}$$

$$= -1.23472 - (-0.3547)$$

$$= \textbf{-0.88002 kJ/kg·K (Decrease)}$$

**Problem 2.7:** A mass 'm' kg of a gas at temperature $T_1$ K is isobarically and adiabatically mixed with an equal mass of same gas at temperature $T_2$ K ($T_1 > T_2$). Show that the change in entropy of the universe during the process is given by:

$$(\Delta s)_{uni} = 2m \cdot c_p \ln \left[ \frac{T_1 + T_2}{2\sqrt{T_1 \cdot T_2}} \right]$$

**Solution:** Consider 'm' kg of gas at temperature $T_1$ in the compartment (A) and same mass i.e. 'm' kg of gas at temperature $T_2$ in another compartment (B). The gas from (A) and (B) is allowed to mix together as shown in Fig. 2.17.

The gases in compartment (A) and compartment (B) are allowed to mix together as shown in Fig. 2.17.

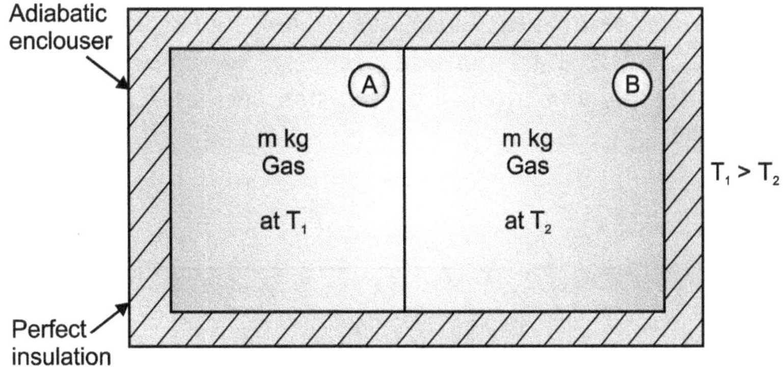


**Fig. 2.17**

Let the temperature of gas after mixing be $T_3$.

Heat given out by gas at $T_1$ = Heat lost by gas at $T_2$

$$\therefore \quad mc_p (T_1 - T_3) = mc_p (T_3 - T_2)$$

$$\therefore \quad T_3 = \frac{T_1 + T_2}{2} \qquad \qquad \dots (1)$$

(a) The change of entropy of gas in compartment (A) at constant pressure,

$$(\Delta s)_A = \int_{T_1}^{T_3} \frac{dQ}{T} = \int_{T_1}^{T_3} \frac{m \cdot c_p}{T} \, dT = mc_p \cdot \log_e \frac{T_3}{T_1} \qquad \dots (2)$$

(b) The change of entropy of gas in compartment (B),

$$(\Delta s)_B = \int_{T_2}^{T_3} \frac{m \cdot c_p}{T} \, dT = mc_p \cdot \log_e \frac{T_3}{T_2} \qquad \dots (3)$$

(c) The change of entropy of surroundings $(\Delta s)_{surr} = 0$ because it is an adiabatic process.

$$\therefore \quad (\Delta s)_{universe} = (\Delta s)_A + (\Delta s)_B + (\Delta s)_{surr}$$

$$= m \cdot c_p \cdot \log_e \frac{T_3}{T_1} + m \cdot c_p \cdot \log_e \frac{T_3}{T_2} + 0 \qquad \dots (4)$$

Substituting value of $T_3$ from equation (1) in equation (4), we get,

$$(\Delta s)_{universe} = mc_p \left[ \log_e \frac{T_1 + T_2}{2T_1} + \log_e \frac{T_1 + T_2}{2T_2} \right]$$

$$\therefore \quad (\Delta s)_{universe} = mc_p \left[ \log_e \left( \frac{T_1 + T_2}{2T_1} \right) + \log_e \left( \frac{T_1 + T_2}{2T_2} \right) \right]$$

$$= mc_p \cdot \log_e \left[ \frac{(T_1 + T_2)^2}{(2\sqrt{T_1 T_2})^2} \right] = mc_p \log_e \left[ \frac{T_1 + T_2}{2\sqrt{T_1 T_2}} \right]^2$$

$$(\Delta s)_{universe} = 2 \cdot m \cdot c_p \log_e \left[ \frac{T_1 + T_2}{2\sqrt{T_1 T_2}} \right] \qquad \dots (5)$$

Hence proved.

**Problem 2.8:** The two compartments of insulated air box contain air at 200 kPa, 300 K, 1 kg mass and at 150 kPa, 300 K, 1 kg mass respectively. By removing the partition of the compartment, prove that the entropy of isolated system increases. Also find out the change in entropy.

**Solution:**

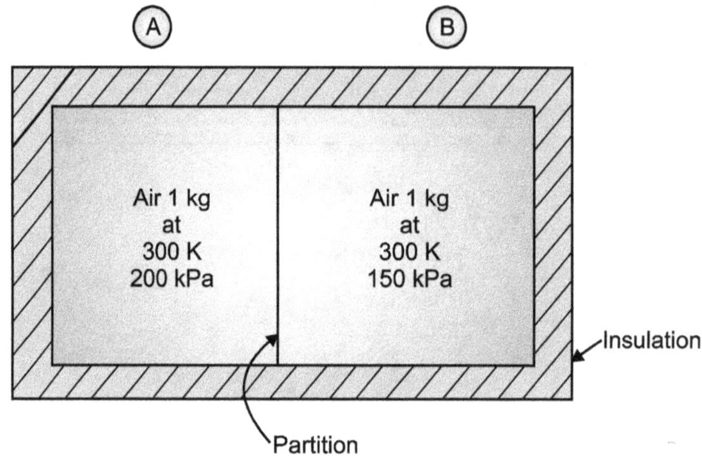


**Fig. 2.18**

**Required:**

(i)   Proof of entropy of isolated system increases.

(ii)  Change in entropy = $\Delta s$ =?

Consider the volume of compartment (A) is $V_A$.

Apply ideal gas equation to the compartment 'A'

$$p_A V_A = m_A \, RT$$

$$\therefore \qquad V_A = \frac{m_A \, RT}{p_A} = \frac{1 \times 287 \times 300}{200 \times 10^3} = 0.4305 \text{ m}^3$$

Similarly, for compartment B,

$$V_B = \frac{1 \times 287 \times 300}{150 \times 10^3} = 0.574 \text{ m}^3$$

The temperature in both compartments is same,

$$T_A = T_B = 300 \text{ K}$$

As the process is adiabatic mixing, the temperature reached after mixing is also 300 K.

$$\text{The total mass of mixture} = m_A + m_B = 1 + 1 = 2 \text{ kg}$$

$$\text{The total volume, } V = V_A + V_B$$

$$= 0.4305 + 0.574$$

$$= 1.0045 \text{ m}^3$$

Now, using the characteristic gas equation,

$$pV = mRT$$

$$p = \frac{mRT}{V}$$

$$= \frac{2 \times 287 \times 300}{1.0045}$$

$$p = 171.43 \text{ kPa}$$

The partial pressure of air after mixing is given by,

$$p_{air(A)} = p \times \frac{n_{air}}{n} = p \times \frac{m_A}{M_A} \times \frac{M}{m}$$

$$= \left(171.43 \times \frac{1}{28.97}\right) \times \frac{28.97}{2}$$

$$= 85.715 \text{ kPa}$$

and $\qquad p_{air(B)} = 85.715 \text{ kPa}$

Then, entropy change per kg is given by,

$$\Delta s = \left[\int_{T_1}^{T_2} c_p \frac{dT}{T} - \frac{\overline{R}}{M} \log (p_2/p_1)\right]$$

$$(\Delta s)_{air(A)} = 0 - \frac{8314.4}{28.97} \log \left(\frac{85.715}{200}\right)$$

$$= 243.17 \text{ J/kg}$$

and $\qquad (\Delta s)_{air(B)} = 0 - \frac{8314.4}{28.97} \ln \left(\frac{85.715}{150}\right)$

$$= 160.61 \text{ J/kg}$$

$$= 0.161 \text{ kJ/kg}$$

Total change in entropy of the mixture

$$(\Delta s)_{mix} = (\Delta s)_{air(A)} + (\Delta s)_{air(B)}$$

$$= 0.24317 + 0.161$$

$$= \textbf{0.404 kJ/kg}$$

The change in entropy of the mixture is 0.404 kJ/kg, which is a positive value. Hence, entropy of the total system always increases.

---

**Problem 2.9:** 1 kg of nitrogen at a temperature of 155°C occupies a volume of 0.3 m$^3$. The gas undergoes constant pressure expansion to a volume of 0.4 m$^3$. The gas is then expanded isothermally to a volume of 0.5 m$^3$. Determine change of entropy for each process and total change of entropy. Represent the process on p-V and T-s diagrams. Take:

$$c_v = 0.743 \ \frac{kJ}{kg \cdot K}$$

and

$$R = 0.297 \ \frac{kJ}{kg \cdot K}$$

**Solution: Given data:** $m = 1$ kg, $T_1 = 155°C = 428$ K, $V_1 = 0.3$ m$^3$, $V_2 = 0.4$ m$^3$, $V_3 = 0.5$ m$^3$.

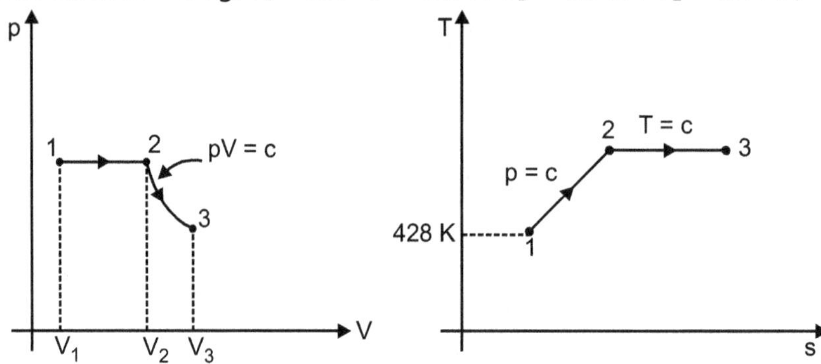


**Fig. 2.19: p-V and T-s diagrams**

**At state point 1:**

$$p_1 V_1 = mRT_1$$

$$\therefore \quad p_1 = \frac{mRT_1}{V_1} = \frac{1 \times 297 \times 428}{0.3}$$

$$\therefore \quad p_1 = 4.2372 \ \text{bar}$$

From general gas equation,

$$\frac{p_1 V_1}{T_1} = \frac{p_2 V_2}{T_2}$$

$$\therefore \quad T_2 = T_1 \cdot \frac{V_2}{V_1} \qquad\qquad (\because \ p_1 = p_2)$$

$$= 428 \times \frac{0.4}{0.3}$$

$$= 570.67 \ \text{K}$$

Change in entropy for 1-2 process,

$$s_2 - s_1 = mR \log_e \frac{V_2}{V_1} + mc_v \log_e \frac{T_2}{T_1}$$

$$= 1 \times 0.297 \log_e \frac{0.4}{0.3} + 1 \times 0.743 \times \log_e \frac{570.67}{428}$$

$$= 0.08544 + 0.213752$$

$$= \mathbf{0.2992 \ kJ/kg}$$

**For process 2-3,**

$$T_2 = T_3 = 570.67 \ \text{K}$$

Change in entropy for 2-3 process,

$$s_3 - s_2 = mR \log_e \frac{V_3}{V_2} + mc_v \log_e \frac{T_3}{T_2}$$

$$= 1 \times 0.297 \log_e \frac{0.5}{0.4} + 1 \times 0.743 \times \log_e \frac{570.67}{570.67}$$

$$= \textbf{0.06627 kJ/kg}$$

Overall change in entropy,

$$s_3 - s_1 = (s_2 - s_1) + (s_3 - s_2)$$

$$= 0.2992 + 0.06627$$

$$= 0.36547 \text{ kJ/kg}$$

$$\therefore \quad \text{Total change of entropy} = \textbf{0.36547 kJ/kg}$$

**Problem 2.10:** 1 kg of ice at −6°C is exposed to atmosphere which is at 30°C. The ice melts and comes into thermal equilibrium. Determine entropy increase of the universe. Take $c_p$ of ice = 2009 kJ/kg·K and latent heat of fusion of ice = 333.3 kJ/kg.

**Solution:** Refer Fig. 2.20.

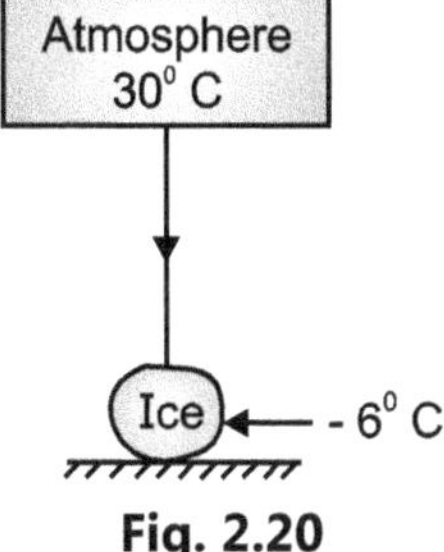


**Fig. 2.20**

$$\text{Mass of ice} = m_1 = 1 \text{ kg}$$

$$\text{Temperature of ice} = -6 + 273 = 267 \text{ K}$$

$$\text{Temperature of atmosphere} = 30 + 273 = 303 \text{ K}$$

Heat absorbed by ice from the atmosphere

= Heat absorbed in solid state + Latent heat + Heat absorbed in liquid phase

$$= m_i \times c_{pi} \times \Delta t + L_i + m_w c_{pw} \Delta t$$

$$= 1 \times 2.09 \times [0 - (-6)] + 333.33 + 1 \times 4.187 \times (30 - 0)$$

$$= 12.54 + 333.33 + 125.61$$

$$= \textbf{471.27 kJ}$$

Entropy change of the atmosphere

$$(\Delta s)_{atm} = -\frac{Q}{T} = -\frac{471.27}{303}$$

$$= \textbf{−1.5553 kJ/K}$$

(a)　Entropy change of system (ice) as it gets heated from −6°C to 0°C,

(b)　　　　$$(\Delta s_I)_{system} = \int_{267}^{273} m_i c_{pi} \frac{dT}{T} = 1 \times 2.09 \times \log_e\left(\frac{273}{267}\right) = 0.04645 \text{ kJ/K}$$

(c)　Entropy change of system as ice melts at 0°C to become water at 0°C,

$$(\Delta s_{II})_{system} = \frac{333.33}{273} = 1.2209 \text{ kJ/K}$$

(d)　Entropy change of water as it gets heated from 0°C to 30°C,

$$(\Delta s_{III})_{system} = \int_{273}^{303} m_w c_{pw} \frac{dT}{T} = 1 \times 4.187 \times \log_e\left(\frac{303}{273}\right) = 0.4365 \text{ kJ/K}$$

Total entropy change of ice as it melts into water,

$$(\Delta s)_{total} = \Delta s_I + \Delta s_{II} + \Delta s_{III}$$
$$= 0.04645 + 1.2209 + 0.4365 = 1.70385 \text{ kJ/K}$$

The temperature-entropy diagram for the system as ice at −6°C converts to water at 30°C is shown in Fig. 2.21.

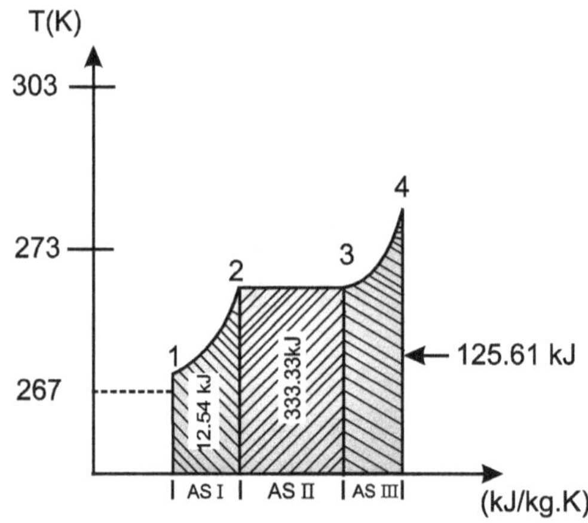


**Fig. 2.21**

∴　Entropy increase of the universe,

$$(\Delta s)_{universe} = (\Delta s)_{system} + (\Delta s)_{atm}$$
$$= 1.70385 + (-1.5553)$$
$$= \mathbf{0.14855 \text{ kJ/K}}$$

---

**Problem 2.11:** One kg of water at 300 K is first heated to 400 K by bringing it in contact with an intermediate heat reservoir at 400 K and then to 500 K as before. What will be the entropy change of the universe in this case?

**Solution: Heating of water:**

Heat transfer in each reservoir (i.e. for I and II, it is same at $\Delta T = 100$ K)

$$Q = m_w \cdot c_{pw} \cdot \Delta T = 1 \times 4.1868 \times 100 = 418.7 \text{ kJ}$$

---

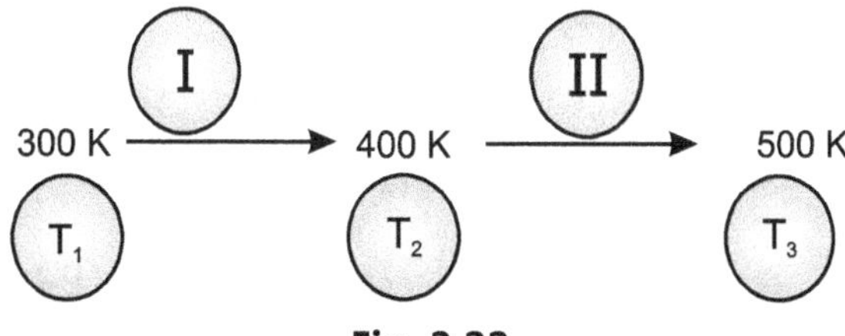



**Fig. 2.22**

Entropy change of water, heat reservoir and universe,

$$(\Delta s)_{water} = m_w \cdot c_{pw} \cdot \left[ \log_e \frac{T_2}{T_1} + \log_e \frac{T_3}{T_2} \right]$$

$$= 1 \times 4.1868 \left[ \log_e \frac{400}{300} + \log_e \frac{500}{400} \right]$$

$$= 2.1387 \text{ kJ/K}$$

$$(\Delta s)_{reservoir\ I} = \frac{-418.7}{400} = -1.04675 \text{ kJ/K}$$

$$(\Delta s)_{reservoir\ II} = \frac{-418.7}{500} = -0.8374 \text{ kJ/K}$$

Negative sign indicates that both reservoirs loss heat.

Then,

$$(\Delta s)_{universe} = (\Delta s)_{water} + (\Delta s)_{reservoir\text{-}I} + (\Delta s)_{reservoir\text{-}II}$$

$$= 2.1387 - 1.04675 - 0.8374$$

$$= \textbf{0.25455 kJ/K}$$

**Problem 2.12:** At constant pressure 138 kPa, 5 kg of oxygen is cooled from 500 K to 300 K. The temperature of the surrounding is 277 K. Find the available part of heat removed and entropy increase of universe.

**Solution: Given data:** m = 5 kg, $p_1$ = 138 kPa, $T_1$ = 500 K, $T_0$ = 277 K, $p_0$ = 1 bar = 100 kPa.

Initial availability of $O_2$,

$$A_1 = (u_1 - u_0) + p_0 (V_1 - V_0) - T_0 (s_1 - s_0)$$

$$s_1 - s_0 = c_p \cdot \log_e \frac{T_1}{T_0} - R \log_e \frac{p_1}{p_0}$$

$$= 0.9169 \log_e \frac{500}{277} - 0.287 \log_e \frac{138}{100}$$

$$= 0.54151 - 0.09243$$

$$= 0.4491 \text{ kJ/kg·K}$$

$\therefore$

$$A_1 = mc_v (T_1 - T_0) + mR\, p_0 \left[ \frac{T_1}{p_1} - \frac{T_0}{p_0} \right] - mT_0 [0.4491]$$

$$= 5 \times 0.653 (500 - 277) + 5 \times 0.287 \times 100 \left[ \frac{500}{138} - \frac{277}{100} \right]$$

$$- 5 \times 277 \times 0.4491$$

$$= 728.095 + 122.4325 - 622.00$$

$$= \mathbf{228.524 \ kJ}$$

Final availability at $T_2$ = 300 K, $T_0$ = 277 K, $p_2 = p_1$ = 138 kPa, $p_0$ = 100 kPa

$$A_2 = mc_v (T_2 - T_0) + mR \ p_0 \left[\frac{T_2}{p_2} - \frac{T_0}{p_1}\right] - mT_0 (s_2 - s_0)$$

$$s_2 - s_0 = c_p \cdot \log_e (T_2/T_0) - R \log_e (p_2/p_0)$$

$$= 0.9169 \log_e \left(\frac{300}{277}\right) - 0.287 \log_e \left(\frac{138}{100}\right)$$

$$= -0.0193 \ kJ/kg \cdot K$$

$$A_2 = 5 \times 0.653 (300 - 277) + 5 \times 0.287 \times 100 \left[\frac{300}{138} - \frac{277}{100}\right]$$
$$- 5 \times 277 (-0.0193)$$

$$\therefore \qquad A_2 = 75.095 + (-85.54) + 26.7305 = 16.287 \ kJ$$

Available part of heat removed = 16.287 − 228.524

$$= \mathbf{-212.237 \ kJ}$$

**Problem 2.13:** 0.04 m$^3$ of nitrogen contained in a cylinder behind a piston is initially at 1.05 bar and 15°C. The gas is compressed isothermally and reversibly until the pressure is 4.8 bar. Calculate: (i) Change of entropy, (ii) Heat flow, (iii) Work done.

Sketch the process on a p-V diagram and T-s diagram. Assume nitrogen to act as a perfect gas. Molecular weight of nitrogen = 28.

**Solution: Given data:**

$$V_1 = 0.04 \ m^3$$
$$p_1 = 1.05 \ bar = 1.05 \times 10^5 \ N/m^2$$
$$T_1 = 15°C = 15 + 273 = 288 \ K$$
$$p_2 = 4.8 \ bar = 4.8 \times 10^5 \ N/m^2$$
$$T_2 = T_1 = 288 \ K$$

The process is shown on p-v and T-s diagrams as below.

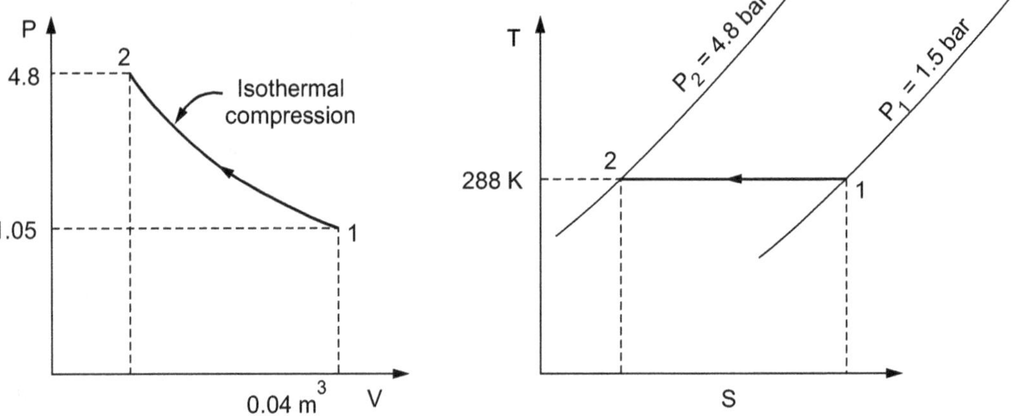


**Fig. 2.23**

Characteristic gas constant,

$$R = \frac{\text{Universal gas constant, } R_0}{\text{Molecular weight, M}} = \frac{8314}{28}$$

$$= 297 \text{ N-m/kg·K}$$

Now, we have $p_1 V_1 = mRT_1$

$$\therefore \quad m = \frac{p_1 V_1}{RT_1} = \frac{1.05 \times 10^5 \times 0.04}{297 \times 288}$$

$$= \mathbf{0.0491 \ kg}$$

**The change of entropy:**

$$s_2 - s_1 = mR \ln \frac{p_1}{p_2}$$

$$= 0.0491 \times \frac{297}{1000} \times \ln \left( \frac{1.05}{4.8} \right)$$

$$= \mathbf{-0.02216 \ kJ/K}$$

**Problem 2.14:** 1 kg of air is allowed to expand reversibly in a cylinder behind a piston in such a way that the temperature remains constant at 260°C while the volume is doubled. The piston is then moved in, and heat is rejected by the air reversibly at constant pressure until the volume is the same as it was initially. Calculate the net heat flow and the overall change of entropy. Sketch the processes on a T-s diagram.

**Solution: Given data:**

$$m = 1 \text{ kg}$$

$$T_1 = T_2 = 260 = 260 + 273$$

$$260 = 533 \text{ K}$$

$$V_1 = V_3$$

$$V_2 = 2V_1$$

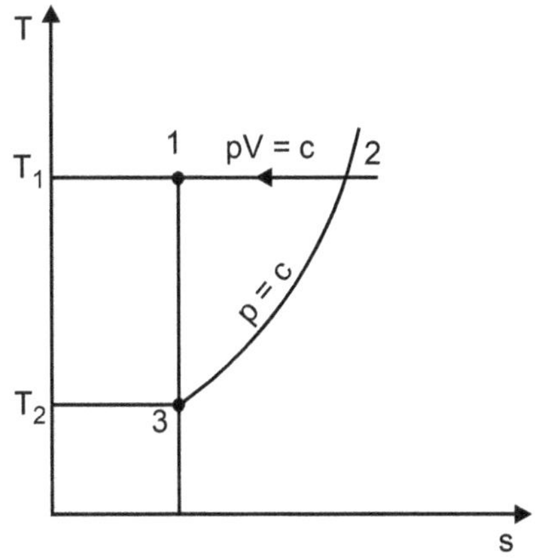

**Fig. 2.24**

**For process 1-2:**  $\qquad pV = c$

$$\text{Heat transfer, } Q = mc\,(T_2 - T_1)$$

$$Q_{12} = 0 \text{ kJ}$$

$$\text{Change in entropy} = \Delta s_{1-2}$$

$$= mR \ln\left(\frac{V_2}{V_1}\right)$$

For air, $c_p = 1.005$ kJ/kg·K, $c_v = 0.718$ kJ/kg $+ R = $ kJ/kg·K

$$\Delta s_{1-2} = 1 \times 0.287 \times \ln\left(\frac{2V_1}{V_1}\right)$$

$$= 0.1989 \text{ kJ/K}$$

**For process 2-3:**  $\qquad p = c$

$$\frac{V_2}{T_2} = \frac{V_3}{T_3}$$

Now,  $\qquad\qquad V_2 = 2V_1 \text{ and } V_3 = V_1$

$$\frac{2V_1}{T_2} = \frac{V_1}{3}$$

$\therefore \qquad\qquad T_3 = \dfrac{T_2}{2} = \dfrac{533}{2}$

$$= 266.5 \text{ K}$$

$\therefore \qquad$ Heat transfer, $Q_{2-3} = m \cdot c_p\,(T_3 - T_2)$

$$= 1 \times 1.005 \times (266.5 - 533)$$

$$= -267.83 \text{ kJ}$$

$$\Delta s_{2-3} = m \cdot c_v \cdot \ln\left(\frac{T_3}{T_2}\right)$$

$$= 1 \times 0.718 \times \ln\left(\frac{266.5}{533}\right)$$

$$\Delta s_{2-3} = -0.4976 \text{ kJ/K}$$

$\therefore \qquad$ Overall heat transfer $= Q_{1-2} + Q_{2-3}$

$$\Delta Q = \mathbf{-267.83 \text{ kJ} \text{ (Heat is rejected)}}$$

and overall entropy change $= \Delta s_{1-2} + \Delta s_{2-3}$

$$= 0.1989 - 0.4976$$

$$\Delta s = \mathbf{-0.2987 \text{ kJ/K} \text{ (Entropy decreases)}}$$

## EXERCISE

1. Suppose you have to explain entropy production to a child, how will you explain it?
2. Think a process of a closed system for which the entropy of both the system and its surroundings increase.
3. Is it possible for the entropy of both a closed system and its surroundings to decrease during a process?
4. Discuss the transfer of entropy into or out of a closed system.
5. How will you calculate the entropy production in a nuclear reactor?
6. How will you calculate the entropy production during a storm?
7. All state of an adiabatic and internally reversible process of a closed system have the same entropy, but is a process between two states having same entropy necessarily adiabatic and internally reversible?
8. Define Clausius inequality and prove it.
9. Define entropy and show that it is a property of the system.
10. Give a physical explanation of entropy.
11. Why is the Carnot cycle on T-s plot a rectangle?
12. What do you understand by entropy principle?
13. Show that the entropy of an isolated system increases in all real process and is conserved in reversible process.
14. Why is the entropy increase of an isolated system a measure of the extent of irreversibility of the process undergone by the system?
15. State the summary given by Rudolf Clausius about first and second laws of thermodynamics.
16. Show that the transfer of heat through a finite temperature difference is irreversible.
17. Show that the adiabatic mixing of two fluids is irreversible.
18. What causes an increase in entropy?
19. Why is the second law called a directional law of nature?
20. Derive the expression for entropy generation (production) in a closed system.
21. Derive the expression for entropy generation in a open system (control volume).
22. What do you mean by absolute value of entropy?

## UNIVERSITY QUESTION PAPERS

### DEC. 2013

1. A reversible heat engine operates between three isothermal heat reservoirs. The engine receives 4000 kW heat from reservoir A at 1000 K produces work output of 1600 kW. Heat source reservoir B and Heat sink reservoir C are at 300 K and 400 K respectively. Calculate the heat transfer with the reservoir B and C using Clausius inequality theorem. Also estimate the thermal efficiency of the heat engine.          **[6]**

2. State and explain Clausius inequality. Explain law of increase of entropy principle and change in entropy for reversible, irreversible and impossible process.                    **[6]**

## MAY 2014

1. 30 kg of copper block, Cp = 0.386 kJ/kg K at 95°C is dropped in 30 litres of water at 24°C. Assume perfect heat transfer, and no heat lost to the surrounding. Find the final equilibrium temperature reached for water and copper block and entropy generation.                    **[6]**

2. Derive the general equation for change in entropy for any thermodynamic process. Further apply the same for Constant Volume process.                    **[6]**

## DEC. 2014

1. 1 kg of ice at –5 deg. C is exposed to atmosphere at 20 deg. C. The ice melts and attains thermal equilibrium with surrounding. Determine :                    **[6]**
   (i)   Change in entropy of the universe
   (ii)  Total heat transfer during the process.
   $C_{p\,ice}$ = 2.093 kJ/kg K, Latent heat of fusion = 333.3 kJ/kg.
   $C_{p\,water}$ = 4.187 kJ/kg K.

2. Derive expression for the following quantities for an ideal gas undergoing a constant pressure process :                    **[6]**
   (i)   Heat transfer            (ii)  Non–flow work transfer
   (iii) Steady flow work transfer   (iv)  Change in entropy
   (v)   Change in internal energy and change in enthalpy during the process.

## MAY 2015

1. In a certain heat exchanger, 50 kg of water is heated per minute from 50°C to 110°C by hot gases which enter the heat exchanger at 250°C. If the flow rate of gases is 100 kg/min, estimate the net change of entropy. Assume no loss of heat to surroundings. $C_p$ (water) = 4.186 kJ/kg–K, $C_p$ (gas) = 1 kJ/kg–K.                    **[6]**

## NOV. 2015

1. Find the change in entropy of universe when 1 kg of ice at –5°C is exposed to atmosphere which is at 30°C, ice melts and comes in thermal equilibrium with atmosphere. Consider specific heat of ice 2.1 kJ/kgK, latent heat of fusion of ice 330 kJ/kg.                    **[6]**

2. Air is initially at 1 bar and 27°C is compressed reversibly and adiabatically in a reciprocating engine to final pressure of 25 bar. Find work done, change in enthalpy and change in entropy per kg of air. Assume $C_p$ and $C_v$ of air 1.005 kJ/kgK and 0.717 kJ/kgK respectively.                    **[6]**

# Chapter 3

# IDEAL GAS

## 3.1 INTRODUCTION

The principles of thermodynamics are associated with gases and vapours. It is desirable to study the behaviour of such substances in different phases (solid, liquid and gaseous). For practical purpose, the gases are heated, cooled, expanded and compressed. Therefore, already eminent scientists have conducted some experiments and investigated the behaviour of such gases and formulated in the form of laws.

The gas which obeys all the gas laws at all ranges of pressure and temperature is known as **ideal gas**. Practically, ideal gas does not exist, but it is hypothetical one.

No real gases are ideal gases, but they behave as ideal gases at low pressure and at high temperature conditions. Examples of real gases are air, oxygen, hydrogen, nitrogen, helium, etc.

The behaviour of ideal gas is governed by **Boyle's law, Charle's law, Avogadro's law and characteristic equation of state**.

Let us discuss these laws as outlined below.

## 3.2 BOYLE'S LAW

It states that if the temperature of gas is held constant, the volume of the gas varies inversely with the absolute pressure of the gas.

It is invented by Robert Boyle (1627 – 1691) during an experiment conducted on air.

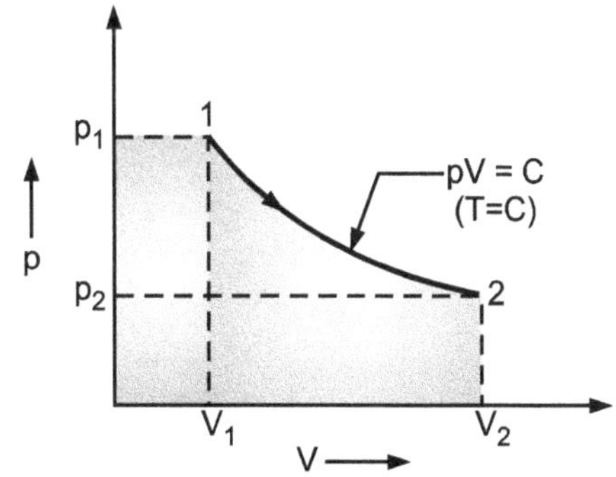


**Fig. 3.1: Boyle's law**

According to this law, $p \propto \dfrac{1}{V}$ for constant temperature

$$\therefore \qquad pV = c \qquad\qquad \text{... (3.1)}$$

where,

$p$ = absolute pressure, $N/m^2$

$V$ = volume of gas, $m^3$

This (pV = c) represents a rectangular hyperbola on p-V diagram. The isothermal process is also known as **hyperbolic process**.

Consider a certain mass of gas which undergoes an equilibrium state 1 to equilibrium state 2 at constant temperature as shown in Fig. 3.1.

For this process, Boyle's law can be written as,

$$p_1 V_1 = p_2 V_2 = \text{constant}$$

## 3.3 CHARLE'S LAW

This law can be stated in two ways:

(1) When a given quantity of gas changes from one equilibrium state to another at constant pressure, the volume of gas varies directly with its absolute temperature.

Mathematically, $V \propto T$ ... (3.2)

$$\frac{V}{T} = \frac{V_1}{T_1} = \frac{V_2}{T_2} = \text{constant}$$

where $V_1$, $T_1$ and $V_2$, $T_2$ are the volume and temperature at state 1 and state 2 respectively.

(2) When a given quantity of gas changes from one equilibrium state to another, at constant volume, the pressure of gas varies directly with its absolute temperature.

Mathematically, $p \propto T$ ... (3.3)

i.e. $$\frac{p}{T} = \frac{p_1}{T_1} = \frac{p_2}{T_2} = \text{constant}$$

where $p_1$, $T_1$ refer to state 1 and $p_2$, $T_2$ refer to state 2.

The Charle's law can be represented on T-V and T-p diagram as shown below in Fig. 3.2.

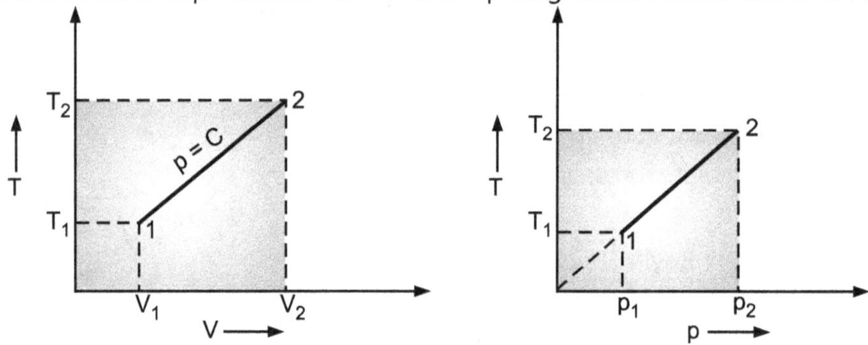


**Fig. 3.2: Charle's law**

## 3.4 AVOGADRO'S LAW

It states that equal volumes of all gases at standard temperature and pressure conditions contain the same number of molecules.

If two ideal gases are contained in two separate vessels of equal volume at the same temperature and pressure, they will contain the same number of molecules. Let n indicate the number of molecules.

The total mass of the gas is proportional to its molecular weight and number of molecules present.

i.e. $\qquad m \propto M \cdot n \qquad$ ... (3.4)

where, $\qquad m$ = mass of gas

$\qquad M$ = molecular weight

$\qquad n$ = number of molecules

Molecular weight is expressed in terms of unit mass and is called as mole.

The equation (3.4) can also be written as

$$\frac{m_1}{m_2} = \frac{M_1}{M_2}$$

$$\frac{\rho_1}{\rho_2} = \frac{M_1}{M_2} \qquad \left(\begin{array}{l} m = \rho V \text{ and } v \text{ is same} \\ \text{for both gases} \end{array}\right)$$

or $$\frac{v_2}{v_1} = \frac{M_1}{M_2}$$

where, $v_1$ and $v_2$ are specific volumes of two gases.

So we have, $M_1 v_1 = M_2 v_2 = $ constant.

It means that the product of molecular weight and specific volume for all gases is constant at the same temperature and pressure conditions.

The product of a mole and specific volume of a gas at same temperature and pressure is constant. This is known as molal volume and is denoted by $\bar{V}$.

$$\bar{V} = M \cdot v \ m^3/kg \text{ - mole} \qquad \text{... (3.5)}$$

$$\text{Molal volume} = \text{Mole} \times \text{Specific volume}$$

At a pressure of 760 mm of Hg and temperature of $0^\circ$C (these are known as NTP conditions), one kg mole of all gases occupy a volume of 20.4 $m^3$.

## 3.5 CHARACTERISTIC GAS EQUATION

The relation between pressure, volume and temperature of an ideal gas is known as characteristic gas equation or equation of state.

Boyle's law gives relation between p and V at constant temperature. Charle's law gives the relation between p and T when V is constant or relation between V and T when p is constant.

In this section, we shall obtain the relation between p, V and T as an equation of state for an ideal gas.

Consider a constant mass of gas whose original state is $p_1$, $V_1$ and $T_1$ and let this gas change its state to $p_2$, $V_2$ and $T_2$ as shown in Fig. 3.3.

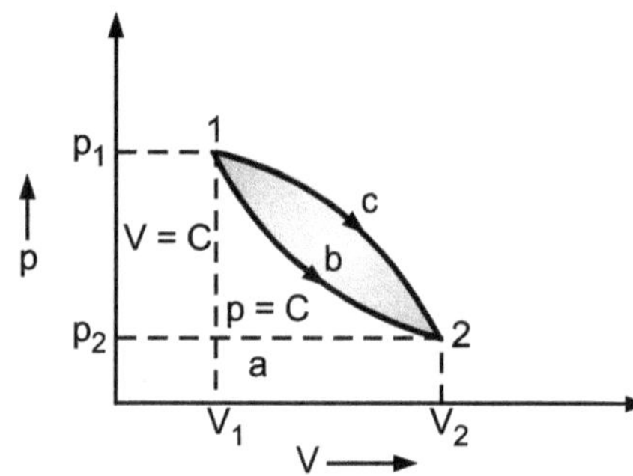


**Fig. 3.3: Ideal gas undergoing a cyclic process**

A little consideration will show that there are number of possible paths (1 – a – 2, 1 – b – 2 and 1 – c – 2), connecting states 1 and 2 on p-V plane.

Let us apply Charle's law for a constant volume process (1 to a).

$$\frac{p_1}{p_a} = \frac{T_1}{T_a}$$

$$\therefore \quad T_a = \frac{p_a}{p_1} \cdot T_1 = \frac{p_2}{p_1} \cdot T_1 \qquad \qquad \text{... (3.6)}$$

Also, applying Charle's law for constant pressure process (process a to 2)

$$\frac{V_a}{V_2} = \frac{T_a}{T_2}$$

$$\therefore \quad T_a = \frac{V_1}{V_2} \cdot T_2 \qquad \qquad \text{... (3.7)}$$

Equating equations (3.6) and (3.7), we get,

$$\frac{p_2}{p_1} \cdot T_1 = \frac{V_1}{V_2} \cdot T_2$$

$$\therefore \quad \frac{p_1 V_1}{T_1} = \frac{p_2 V_2}{T_2}$$

$$\text{or} \qquad \frac{pV}{T} = \text{Constant} \qquad \qquad \text{... (3.8)}$$

where,  p = pressure, $N/m^2$; V = volume, $m^3$; T = temperature, kelvin

$\therefore$  If V is taken as specific volume as v, then

$$\frac{pv}{T} = \text{Constant} = R \qquad \qquad \text{... (3.9)}$$

Multiply by mass 'm' on both sides to the above equation

$$\frac{p\,(mv)}{T} = m\,R$$

but $\qquad\qquad\qquad\qquad$ V = m v

$$\therefore \qquad pV = m\,RT \qquad \qquad \dots (3.10)$$

This equation (3.10) is known as a perfect gas equation or characteristic gas equation or an equation of state for an ideal gas.

'R' is known as specific gas constant or characteristic gas constant. For air, the value of R is 287 J/kg·K (0.287 kJ/kg·K). The value of 'R' varies for different gases.

## 3.6 UNIVERSAL GAS CONSTANT ($\bar{R}$)

We know that, $p\,(mv) = m\,RT$        $\dots (3.11)$

If m = unity,        $p \cdot v = RT$

    where, v = specific volume, kg/m³

Multiplying both sides of above equation by molecular weight of gas M,

$$p \cdot v\,M = M\,RT$$

But           $Mv = \bar{V}$, where $\bar{V}$ is molal volume.

$$\therefore \qquad p\bar{V} = MRT \text{ J/kg-mole} \qquad \dots (3.12)$$

$MR = \bar{R}$ is known as universal gas constant.

$$\therefore \qquad \frac{p\bar{V}}{T} = \bar{R} \qquad \qquad \dots (3.13)$$

It is discussed earlier that, at NTP conditions, 1 kg mole of any gas occupies a volume of 22.4 m³. Therefore, p = 1.01325 bar (760 mm of Hg)

T = 273 K, $\bar{V}$ = 22.4 m³/kg mole

$$\therefore \qquad \bar{R} = \frac{1.01325 \times 10^5 \times 22.4}{273}$$

$$= 8313.8 \text{ J/kg mole - K}$$

$$\bar{R} = 8.314 \text{ kJ/kg mole - K} \qquad \dots (3.14)$$

The value of characteristic gas constant R can be obtained for any gas by dividing $\bar{R}$ by the molecular weight of that gas.

    $\therefore$ Example: R for oxygen.

Molecular weight of $O_2$ = 32 kg/kg mole

$$\therefore \qquad R = \frac{8313.8}{32} = 259.8 \text{ J/kg K}$$

## 3.7 ENTHALPY (H)

Enthalpy is defined by the relation

$$h = u + p \cdot V \qquad \qquad \text{... (3.15)}$$

where,  $h$ = enthalpy, kJ/kg, $u$ = internal energy, kJ/kg

and  $pV$ = flow work, kJ/kg, $p$ is in kN/m$^2$ and $V$ in m$^3$.

For unit mass,

$$h = u + pv \qquad \qquad \text{... (3.16)}$$

where, $h$ = enthalpy, kJ/kg; $u$ = internal energy, kJ/kg; $p$ = pressure, kN/m$^2$; and $v$ = specific volume, in m$^3$/kg.

As $u$, $p$ and $v$ are point function and properties of the system, then combination of these, is enthalpy, which is also a point function and property of the system.

## 3.8 ENTHALPY IS A FUNCTION OF TEMPERATURE ONLY

Enthalpy of a gas is  $h = u + pv$  for unit mass

The internal energy, $\Delta u = c_v \cdot \Delta T$ where $c_v$ is the specific heat at constant volume, kJ/kg·K and $\Delta T$ is the change in temperature.

From characteristic gas equation for unit mass,

$$pv = RT$$

Hence

$$\Delta h = c_v \cdot \Delta T + R\Delta T \qquad \qquad \text{... (3.17)}$$

In this equation, $c_v$ and $R$ are constants, 'h' will be dependent only on temperature. Therefore enthalpy is a function of temperature only.

## 3.9 INTERNAL ENERGY (U)

The internal energy is a point function and property of the system.

It is proved experimentally that internal energy is a function of temperature only and is independent of pressure and volume. This is valid for an ideal gas.

Mathematically,

$$\therefore \qquad u = f(T) \qquad \qquad \text{... (3.18)}$$

$$\Delta u = m \cdot c_v \cdot \Delta T \text{ kJ} \qquad \qquad \text{... (3.19)}$$

where, $m$ = mass, kg; $c_v$ = specific heat at constant volume, kJ/kg·K; $\Delta T$ = temperature rise.

## 3.10 SPECIFIC HEAT (C)

**Specific heat (c)** is defined as the amount of heat required to raise the temperature of unit mass of a substance through one degree.

The total quantity of heat absorbed by a system having mass 'm' and whose temperature rise is $\Delta T$ is given by,

$$Q = m \cdot c \cdot \Delta T \text{ kJ} \qquad \qquad \text{... (3.20)}$$

where, $Q$ = heat, in kJ; $m$ = mass, kg; $c$ = specific heat, kJ/kg·K;

$\Delta T$ = temperature rise, °C.

There are two types of specific heats.

(i)  Specific heat at constant volume ($c_v$) and

(ii)  Specific heat at constant pressure ($c_p$)

## 3.10.1 Specific Heat at Constant Volume ($c_V$)

The amount of heat required to raise the temperature of a unit mass of a substance through one degree under constant volume is known as specific heat at constant volume.

From first law of thermodynamics, we have

$$\delta Q = du + \delta w$$

$$= du + p\,dV$$

But for constant volume,   $dV = 0$,

$\therefore$                    $p\,dV = 0$

$\therefore$  $(\delta Q)_v = du$. For unit mass, $(\delta q)_v = du$          ... (3.21)

But, heat supplied under constant volume process is,

$$(\delta Q)_v = m \cdot c_v \cdot dT \qquad \text{... (3.22)}$$

and for unit mass,    $(\delta q)_v = c_v \cdot dT$          ... (3.23)

From equations (3.21) and (3.23), we can write,

$$du = c_v \cdot dT$$

$\therefore$                    $c_v = \left(\dfrac{du}{dT}\right)_v$          ... (3.24)

Now, $c_v$ is the rate of change of internal energy with respect to temperature when volume is kept constant.

## 3.10.2 Specific Heat at Constant Pressure ($c_p$)

It is defined as the amount of heat required to raise the temperature of a unit mass of a substance through one degree of temperature change at constant pressure.

Refer Fig. 3.4 during heating at constant pressure, the piston moves upwards to keep the pressure of the system (gas) constant. As the piston moves from position 1 to position 2, the work is obtained from the system (equal to $p \times dV$).

Here it is assumed that there is no friction between the piston and cylinder walls.

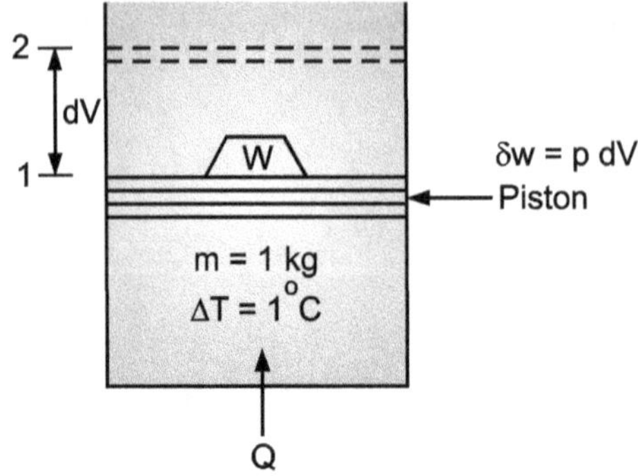


**Fig. 3.4: Specific heat at constant pressure**

From first law of thermodynamics,

$$\delta q = du + \delta w \qquad \text{for unit mass}$$

$$\therefore \qquad \delta q = du + p\,dV$$

$$\text{or} \qquad dq = du + d\,(pV) \quad \text{as } p = \text{constant}$$

$$(dq)_p = d\,(u + pV)$$

$$(dq)_p = dh \quad \text{as } u + pV = h \qquad \qquad \dots (3.25)$$

It means heat supplied at constant pressure is equal to the change in enthalpy.

But heat supplied at constant pressure process is given by,

$$(dq)_p = c_p \cdot dT \text{ for } m = 1 \qquad \qquad \dots (3.26)$$

From equations (3.25) and (3.26), we can write,

$$dh = c_p\,dT \text{ or } c_p = \left(\frac{dh}{dT}\right)_p \qquad \qquad \dots (3.27)$$

This indicates that $c_p$ is the rate of change of enthalpy with respect to temperature when pressure is kept constant.

**Comments on $c_p$ and $c_v$:**

$$(\delta Q)_v = du = m \cdot c_v \cdot dT$$

$$\text{and} \qquad (\delta Q)_p = dh = m \cdot c_p \cdot dT$$

- These two equations are valid for all reversible or irreversible processes.
- They do not depend upon the path of the process.
- The values of specific heats $c_p$ and $c_v$ increase with increase in temperature. But for calculation purpose, average values of $c_p$ and $c_v$ are taken. The average values of these for air are $c_p = 1.005$ kJ/kg·K and $c_v = 0.718$ kJ/kg·K.

- The heat supplied under constant volume is used to increase the internal energy of the system. But heat supplied under constant pressure is used to *increase internal energy plus to do the external work*. Therefore, heat supplied under constant pressure is always greater than that of heat supplied at constant volume. Therefore, $c_p$ is greater than $c_v$.

Mathematically,

$$c_p = \frac{dh}{dT} \quad \text{and} \quad c_v = \frac{du}{dT}$$

As,      $dh > du$,                $c_p = c_v$

## 3.11 RELATION BETWEEN $C_P$ AND $C_V$

The ratio of specific heat at constant pressure and specific heat at constant volume is known as adiabatic index or index for adiabatic process. This ratio is denoted by $\gamma$.

$$\therefore \qquad \gamma = \frac{c_p}{c_v} \quad \text{or} \quad c_p = \gamma \cdot c_v \qquad\qquad \text{... (3.28)}$$

$c_p$ is always greater than $c_v$, therefore, $\gamma$ is greater than one.

### 3.11.1 To Obtain Relation Between $c_p$, $c_v$ and R

Let us consider expression for enthalpy.

$$h = u + pV \quad \text{for unit mass}$$

but
$$pv = RT \quad \text{for unit mass}$$

$\therefore$
$$h = u + RT$$

In differential form,
$$dh = du + R\,dT$$

but
$$dh = c_p \cdot dT \quad \text{and} \quad du = c_v \cdot dT$$

$\therefore$
$$c_p \cdot dT = c_v \cdot dT + R\,dT$$

Dividing this equation by dT

$$c_p = c_v + R$$

$\therefore$
$$c_p - c_v = R \text{ kJ/kg·K} \qquad\qquad \text{... (3.29)}$$

where,   R = characteristic gas constant.

### 3.11.2 Relation Between $c_p$, R and $\gamma$

We know that,        $c_p - c_v = R$

Dividing this equation by $c_v$,

$$\therefore \qquad \frac{c_p}{c_v} - 1 = \frac{R}{c_v}$$

but
$$\frac{c_p}{c_v} = \gamma$$

$$\therefore \qquad \gamma - 1 \;=\; \frac{R}{c_v}$$

$$\text{or} \qquad c_v \;=\; \frac{R}{\gamma - 1} \qquad \qquad \text{... (3.30)}$$

$$\text{also} \qquad c_p \;=\; \gamma \cdot c_v$$

$$\therefore \qquad c_p \;=\; \frac{R \cdot \gamma}{(\gamma - 1)} \qquad \qquad \text{... (3.31)}$$

# 3.12 IDEAL GAS PROCESSES (NON-FLOW PROCESSES)

A system (an ideal gas) may undergo various processes, with one of the variables, such as pressure, volume, temperature, entropy, etc. changing and other remaining constant. Such processes are analysed in the following section.

Only non-flow processes are explained here. Non-flow process is a process in which mass of the system does not cross the boundary. The same mass undergoes all cyclic processes.

The non-flow processes are:

- Constant volume or Isochoric process (V = c)
- Constant pressure or Isobaric process (p = c).
- Constant temperature process (isothermal)
- Isentropic or reversible adiabatic process
- Polytropic process.

For all these processes, relations for work done, internal energy and heat transfer are obtained by applying first law of thermodynamics.

## 3.12.1 Isochoric or Constant Volume Process (V = C)

In this process, volume of the system remains constant throughout the process. This can be represented on p-V diagram [**Fig. 3.5 (a)**].

Heating of air in a rigid closed container is an example [**Fig. 3.5 (b)**].

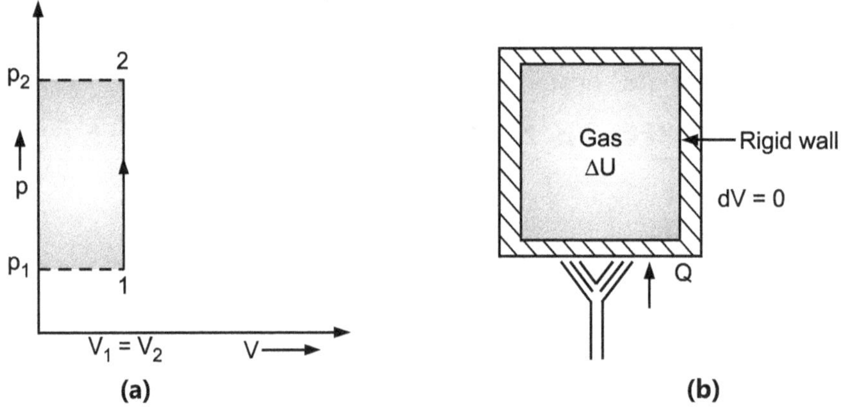


**Fig. 3.5: Constant volume process**

## (a) Work done:

Applying first law of thermodynamics,

$$\delta q = du + \delta w$$
$$\delta q = du + p\,dV$$

$\therefore$      Since $dV = 0$, $\delta w = 0$

Work done during the process, $w = 0$.

## (b) Heat supplied:

As $\delta w = 0$,      $\delta Q = du = m \cdot c_v \cdot dT$

$\therefore$      $Q = u_2 - u_1$

$$Q = m \cdot c_v (T_2 - T_1) \text{ kJ} \qquad \ldots (3.32)$$

The addition of heat increases the internal energy of the system.

The equation (3.32) equally holds good for reversible as well as irreversible process.

## SOLVED PROBLEMS

**Problem 3.1:** A closed vessel contains 2 kg of $CO_2$ at 20° C and pressure of 0.7 bar. Heat is supplied to the vessel till the gas acquires a pressure of 1.4 bar. Calculate:

(i)      Final temperature

(ii)      Work done on or by a gas

(iii)      Change in internal energy.

Assume $c_v$ for $CO_2$, $c_v = 0.653$ kJ/kg·K

**Solution: Given:** A closed container means volume is constant ($v = C$)

$p_1 = 0.7 \times 10^5$ N/m$^2$, $T_1 = (20 + 273) = 293$ K

$p_2 = 1.4 \times 10^5$ N/m$^2$, $m = 2$ kg

(i)   As $V = C$,      $\dfrac{p_1}{p_2} = \dfrac{T_1}{T_2}$

$\therefore$      $T_2 = \dfrac{p_2}{p_1} \times T_1 = \dfrac{1.4}{0.7} \times (293) = 586$ K

(ii)   $dV = 0$,      $\therefore$   $W = \displaystyle\int_1^2 p\,dV = 0$

     i.e. work done is zero.

(iii)      $q = u_2 - u_1$

         $= m \cdot c_v \cdot (T_2 - T_1)$

         $= 2 \times 0.653 \times (586 - 293) = 382.6$ kJ

Change in internal energy = **382.6 kJ (increases)**

## 3.12.2 Constant Pressure (p = C) Process

Pressure of the system remains constant throughout the process.

Heating of a gas in a frictionless cylinder - piston arrangement is an example [See Fig. 3.6 (a)].

The process is represented on p-V diagram [Fig. 3.6 (b)].

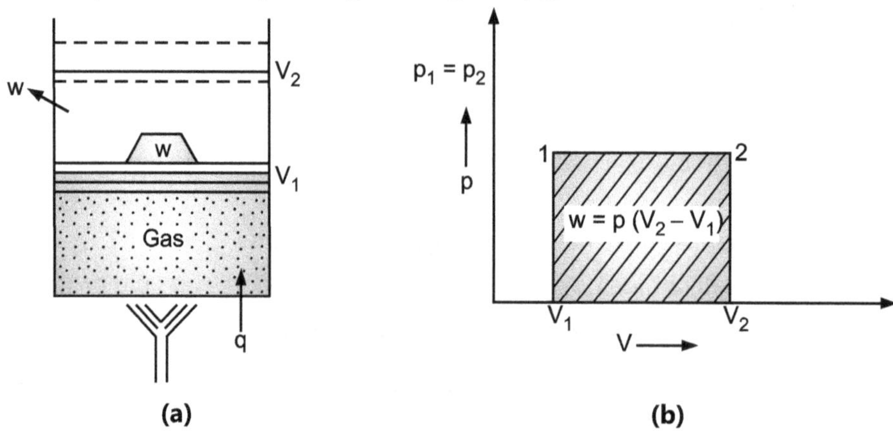


**Fig. 3.6: Constant pressure process**

**(a) Work done:**
$$w_{1-2} = \int_1^2 p \, dV = p \int_1^2 dV$$

$$= p (V_2 - V_1) = p_2 V_2 - p_1 V_1 \qquad \ldots (3.33)$$

$$= \text{Area under the curve}$$

As $p_2 V_2 = mRT_2$,     $p_1 V_1 = mRT_1$

$\therefore \qquad w_{1-2} = m \cdot R (T_2 - T_1) \qquad \ldots (3.34)$

**(b) Heat supplied:**

$$\delta q = du + dw$$
$$= du + p \, dV$$
$$= d (u + pV), \qquad\qquad p = \text{constant}$$
$$dq = dh$$
$$\text{Heat supplied} = \text{Change in enthalpy}$$

**(c) Internal energy:**

$$\Delta u = u_2 - u_1$$
$$\therefore \qquad \delta q - \delta w = du$$

**Problem 3.2: (Constant pressure process):** A 3 kilogram nitrogen at a temperature of 150° C occupies a volume of 0.55 m³. The gas undergoes a fully restricted constant pressure expansion without friction to a final volume of 0.8 m³. Evaluate the final pressure, final temperature, work done and heat transfer. Assume $c_p$ = 0.743 J/kg·K and R = 0.297 kJ/kg·K.

**Solution: Given:** $m = 3$ kg,

$T = 150 + 273 = 423$ K,    $V_1 = 0.55$ m$^3$

$R = 0.297$ kJ/kg·K,     $c_p = 0.743$ J/kg·K

(i)   Use characteristic gas equation

$$pV = m\,RT$$

i.e. $\quad\quad\quad\quad\quad\quad p_1 V_1 = m\,RT_1$

$$\therefore \quad\quad\quad p_1 = \frac{m\,RT_1}{V_1}$$

$$= \frac{3 \times 297 \times 423}{0.55} = 6.85260 \text{ N/m}^2 = \textbf{6.85 bar}$$

It is a constant pressure process, therefore, $p_1 = p_2$

$$\therefore \quad\quad\quad p_2 = 6.85 \text{ bar}$$

(ii) $\quad\quad\quad \dfrac{p_1 V_1}{T_1} = \dfrac{p_2 V_2}{T_2}$ where, $p_2 = p_1$

$$\therefore \quad\quad\quad \frac{V_1}{T_1} = \frac{V_2}{T_2}$$

$$\therefore \quad\quad\quad T_2 = \frac{V_2}{V_1} \cdot T_1 = \frac{0.8}{0.55} \times 423$$

$$\therefore \quad\quad\quad T_2 = \textbf{615 K}$$

(iii) Work done, $\quad\quad w_{1-2} = \int_1^2 p\,dV = p\,(V_2 - V_1)$

$$= 6.85 \times 10^5 \,(0.8 - 0.55)$$

$$= \textbf{1.7125 kJ}$$

(iv) $\quad\quad\quad dQ = dH = m \cdot c_p \cdot dT$

$$Q = \Delta H = 3 \times 0.743\,(615 - 423) = 427.96 \text{ kJ}$$

$Q = 427.96$ kJ (Supplied), $\Delta H = \textbf{427.96 kJ (increases)}$

## 3.12.3 Constant Temperature (Isothermal) Process (pv = C)

It is also known as hyperbolic process. The temperature of the gas remains constant throughout the process. This is represented on p-V diagram [Fig. 3.7 (a)]. Heating a gas in a cylinder - piston arrangement such that temperature should remain constant. This is possible only when all the heat supplied is utilized to perform the work. [Fig. 3.7 (b)].

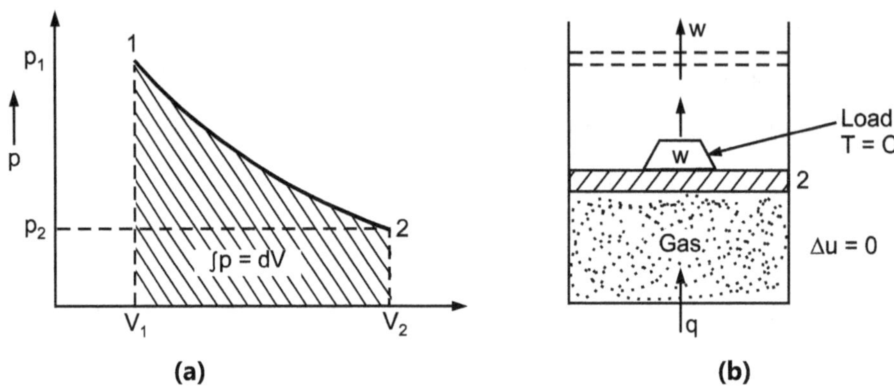


**Fig. 3.7: Isothermal process**

**(a) Work done:** Apply first law of thermodynamics,

$$\delta q \;=\; du + \delta w$$

$$w_{1-2} \;=\; \int_{1}^{2} p\,dV \quad \text{as } pV = C \;\therefore\; p = \frac{C}{V}$$

$$=\; \int_{1}^{2} \frac{C}{V}\cdot dV$$

$$=\; C\cdot \ln V_2/V_1 = p_1 V_1 \ln \frac{V_2}{V_1}$$

$$=\; p_1 V_1 \ln \frac{p_1}{p_2} \qquad\qquad \text{... (3.35)}$$

$$=\; m\,RT_1 \ln \frac{p_1}{p_2} \qquad\qquad \text{... (3.36)}$$

**(b) Internal energy:** $\qquad du \;=\; m\cdot c_v\,dT \quad \text{where } dT = 0$

$\therefore \qquad\qquad\qquad\qquad du \;=\; 0$

**(c) Heat supplied:** $\qquad \delta q \;=\; \delta w$

$$q_{1-2} \;=\; w_{1-2} = p_1 V_1 \ln \frac{V_2}{V_1} \qquad\qquad \text{... (3.37)}$$

$$q_{1-2} \;=\; p_1 V_1 \ln \frac{p_1}{p_2} \qquad\qquad \text{... (3.38)}$$

**Problem 3.3:** 2 kg of air is compressed isothermally from pressure of 103.5 kPa and temperature 30°C to a pressure of 600 kPa. Find q, w and Δu for the process. R = 0.287 kJ/kg·K.

**Solution:**

(1)
$$w_{1-2} = \int_1^2 p\, dV \quad pv = V$$

$$\therefore \quad p = \frac{C}{V}$$

$\therefore$
$$w_{1-2} = p_1 V_1 \ln \frac{p_1}{p_2}$$

$$= m\, RT_1 \ln p_1/p_2$$

$$= 2 \times 0.287 \ln \frac{103.5}{600} = -\,305.64 \text{ kJ (done on the air)}$$

(2)
$$\Delta u = u_2 - u_1 = m\, c_v \cdot dT \quad \text{where} \quad dT = 0$$

$\therefore$
$$\Delta u = 0$$

(3)
$$q = w = -\,305.64 \text{ kJ (rejected)}$$

## 3.12.4 Polytropic Process

This is a general process without any restriction, and it is represented by the law $pV^n = C$, where 'n' is called as polytropic index. Different curves are drawn on p-V plane for different values of 'n'.

By giving different values to 'n', we can get different relations representing different processes. This is shown in Fig. 3.8 and the data is collected in Table 3.1.

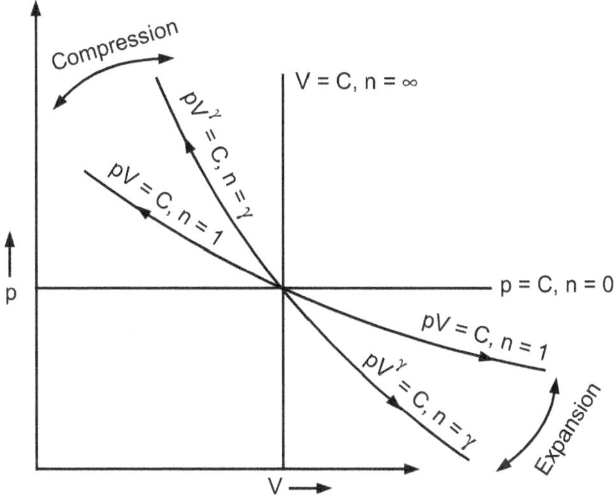


**Fig. 3.8: General process**

## Table 3.1: Various non-flow processes

| Value of n | $pV^n = C$ becomes | Law of process | Name of process |
|:---:|:---:|:---:|:---|
| $n = 0$ | $pV^0 = C$ | $p = C$ | Constant pressure process |
| $n = 1$ | $pV^1 = C$ | $pV = C$ | Constant temperature process |
| $n = \gamma$ | $pV^\gamma = C$ | $pV^\gamma = C$ | Constant entropy or reversible adiabatic process |
| $n = \infty$ | $pV^\infty = C$ | $V = C$ | Constant volume process |

**(a) Work done:**

$$w_{1-2} = \int_1^2 p \, dV = \int_1^2 \frac{C}{V^n} \cdot dV \qquad \text{as } pV^n = C$$

$$= \int_1^2 C \cdot V^{-n} \, dV = \frac{C}{1-n} \left(V^{1-n}\right)_1^2$$

$$= \frac{C}{1-n} \left[ V_2^{1-n} - V_1^{1-n} \right] \qquad \text{where } C = p_2 V_2^n = p_1 V_1^n$$

$$\therefore \qquad w_{1-2} = \frac{1}{1-n} \left[ p_2 V_2 - p_1 V_1 \right] \qquad \qquad \dots (3.39)$$

$$= \frac{p_1 V_1 - p_2 V_2}{n-1} \qquad \qquad \dots (3.40)$$

$$w_{1-2} = \frac{m R (T_1 - T_2)}{n-1} \qquad \qquad \dots (3.41)$$

**(b) Internal energy:**

$$du = m \cdot c_v \cdot dT$$

$$\therefore \qquad \Delta u = c_v (T_2 - T_1) \text{ kJ/kg for } m = 1 \qquad \qquad \dots (3.42)$$

**(c) Heat supplied:** By first law of thermodynamics for unit mass,

$$\delta q = du + \delta w \ \text{ or } \ \delta q = du + p \, dV$$

$$\therefore \qquad q_{1-2} = c_v (T_2 - T_1) + \frac{R}{1-n} (T_2 - T_1) \qquad \text{for unit mass}$$

$$= (T_2 - T_1) \left( c_v + \frac{R}{1-n} \right)$$

$$= (T_2 - T_1) (c_v - n\, c_v + c_p - c_v) \qquad \text{as } R = c_p - c_v$$

$$= \frac{(T_2 - T_1)(c_p - n\, c_v)}{1-n}$$

$$q_{1-2} = \frac{(T_2 - T_1) \cdot c_v}{1 - n} \left( \frac{c_p}{c_v} - n \right)$$

$$q_{1-2} = (T_2 - T_1) \frac{c_v \cdot (\gamma - n)}{1 - n} \qquad \because c_v = \frac{R}{\gamma - 1}$$

$$= \frac{R}{\gamma - 1} \left( \frac{\gamma - n}{1 - n} \right) (T_2 - T_1) \qquad \ldots (3.43)$$

$$= \left( \frac{\gamma - n}{\gamma - 1} \right) \frac{R}{1 - n} (T_2 - T_1)$$

$$= \frac{\gamma - n}{\gamma - 1} \times \text{work done} \qquad \ldots (3.44)$$

$$\text{Work done} = \frac{mR (T_2 - T_1)}{1 - n} \ , m = 1$$

$$w_{1-2} = \frac{R (T_2 - T_1)}{1 - n} \qquad \ldots (3.45)$$

**Problem 3.4:** 2 kg of air at 150° C and 3 bar pressure expands according to law $pv^{1.2} = C$ to a final pressure of 1 bar. Calculate work done, heat supplied and internal energy. Assume R = 0.287 kJ/kg K and $\gamma = 1.41$.

**Solution:** m = 2, $p_1 = 3 \times 10^5$ N/m², $p_2 = 1 \times 10^5$ N/m², $T_1 = (150 + 273) = 423$ K

**(1) For non-flow polytropic process,**

$$w_{1-2} = \frac{m R (T_1 - T_2)}{n - 1}$$

First find the value of $T_2 =$?

We know that, $\qquad \dfrac{p_1 V_1}{T_1} = \dfrac{p_2 V_2}{T_2}$

$$\therefore \qquad T_2 = \frac{p_2}{p_1} \cdot \frac{V_2}{V_1} \cdot T_1 \qquad \ldots (1)$$

but $\qquad p_1 V_1^n = p_2 V_2^n$

$$\therefore \qquad \frac{p_1}{p_2} = \left( \frac{V_2}{V_1} \right)^n \text{ or } \left( \frac{p_1}{p_2} \right)^{1/n} = \frac{V_2}{V_1} \qquad \ldots (2)$$

Put in equation (1)

$$\therefore \qquad T_2 = \frac{p_2}{p_1} \cdot \left( \frac{p_1}{p_2} \right)^{1/n} \cdot T_1$$

$$T_2 = \left(\frac{p_2}{p_1}\right) \cdot \left(\frac{p_2}{p_1}\right)^{1/n} \cdot T_1$$

$$T_2 = \left(\frac{p_2}{p_1}\right)^{\frac{n-1}{n}} \cdot T_1$$

$$\therefore \quad T_2 = \left(\frac{1}{3}\right)^{\frac{0.2}{1.2}} (423) = 351.9 \text{ K}$$

$$\therefore \quad w_{1-2} = \frac{2 \times 0.287\,(423 - 351.9)}{1.2 - 1}$$

$$= 203.9 \text{ kJ (work done by system)}$$

**(2) Heat supplied:**

$$q_{1-2} = \left(\frac{\gamma - n}{\gamma - 1}\right) \times \text{Work done}$$

$$= \frac{(1.41 - 1.2)}{(1.41 - 1)} \times 203.9 = 104.4 \text{ kJ}$$

**(3) Change in internal energy:**

$$\Delta u = m\, c_v \cdot (T_2 - T_1)$$

$$= m \cdot \frac{R}{\gamma - 1} (T_2 - T_1) \qquad \because c_v = \frac{R}{\gamma - 1}$$

$$= 2 \times \frac{0.287}{1.41 - 1} \times (351.9 - 423) = -99.54 \text{ kJ (decreases)}$$

Or by first law of thermodynamics,

$$\Delta u = q - w$$

$$= 104.4 - 203.9 = \mathbf{-\,99.5 \text{ kJ (decreases)}}$$

## 3.12.5 Analysis of Polytropic Process

In the previous section, we have derived an equation for heat transfer $q_{1-2}$ as

$$q_{1-2} = \left(\frac{\gamma - n}{1 - \gamma}\right) \times \text{Work done in non-flow polytropic process.}$$

Whether a system receives heat or it rejects heat during a compression and expansion process for different values of 'n' is discussed below.

### (a) Compression process:

In compression process, work is done on the system (i.e. work is negative).

(i)   If $n > \gamma$, then $\left(\frac{\gamma - n}{1 - \gamma}\right)$ is negative. Also work is negative.

Then $q_{1-2}$ is positive. It means system receives heat during compression process.

(ii)  If $n < \gamma$ then $\left(\frac{\gamma - n}{1 - \gamma}\right)$ is positive.

But work is negative (work is done on the system).

Therefore, $q_{1-2}$ becomes negative. It means heat is rejected during the process.

**(b) Expansion process:**

In expansion process, work is obtained from the system. Therefore, work is positive.

(i) If $n > \gamma$, then $\left(\dfrac{\gamma - n}{1 - \gamma}\right)$ is negative.

Therefore, $q_{1-2}$ is negative. It means heat is rejected during the process.

(ii) For $n < \gamma$, $\left(\dfrac{\gamma - n}{\gamma - 1}\right)$ is positive and the net effect of $q$ is positive. It means that heat is received by the system.

**(c) For $n = \gamma$**

$q_{1-2} = 0$. Heat transfer is zero during the process, means it is an adiabatic process.

If $n = 1$, then $\left(\dfrac{\gamma - n}{\gamma - 1}\right) = 1$.

Therefore, $\qquad q = $ Work done

It means whatever may be the heat supplied it is utilized to perform the work.

From the above analysis, it is possible to control the value of 'n', by controlling the quantity of heat to or from the system in compression or expansion process.

## 3.12.6 Polytropic Specific Heat ($c_n$)

For polytropic process for unit mass of a gas, we have derived the equation for heat transfer,

$q_{1-2} = \left(\dfrac{\gamma - n}{\gamma - 1}\right) \times$ Work done in a non-flow polytropic process.

The above equation can also be written as,

$$q_{1-2} = \frac{\gamma - n}{\gamma - 1} \times \frac{R}{1 - n} (T_2 - T_1)$$

$$\text{but} \qquad c_v = \frac{R}{\gamma - 1}$$

$$\therefore \qquad q_{1-2} = \left(\frac{\gamma - n}{1 - \gamma}\right) c_v \cdot (T_2 - T_1) \qquad \qquad \dots (3.46)$$

$$= c_n \cdot (T_2 - T_1) \qquad \qquad \dots (3.47)$$

The constant $c_n$ is called as polytropic specific heat given by

$$c_n = \left(\frac{\gamma - n}{1 - n}\right) \cdot c_v \text{ kJ/kg·K} \qquad \qquad \dots (3.48)$$

If the value of $(1 - n)$ is negative, meaning of $c_n$ is also negative. The value of polytropic specific heat is negative. This indicates that temperature of the system decreases even though heat is being supplied and the temperature of the system increases even when heat is being rejected by the system.

## 3.12.7 Characteristic Gas Equation and Polytropic Process

The characteristic gas equation for an ideal gas

$$\frac{pV}{T} = \text{Constant} \qquad \qquad \text{... (3.49)}$$

and the law of polytropic process is

$$pV^n = c \qquad \qquad \text{... (3.50)}$$

These two equations (3.49) and (3.50) become an important tool to find the properties at salient points of a thermodynamic cycle.

Let us consider few co-ordinates which are obtained.

By polytropic process,

$$p_1 V_1^n = p_2 V_2^n \qquad \qquad \text{... (3.51)}$$

By characteristic gas equation,

$$\frac{p_1 V_1}{T_1} = \frac{p_2 V_2}{T_2} \qquad \qquad \text{... (3.52)}$$

$$\frac{T_1}{T_2} = \frac{p_1}{p_2} \cdot \frac{V_2}{V_1} \qquad \qquad \text{... (3.53)}$$

But from equation (3.51),

$$\left(\frac{p_1}{p_2}\right) = \left(\frac{V_2}{V_1}\right)^n$$

$$\therefore \quad \frac{T_1}{T_2} = \left(\frac{V_2}{V_1}\right)^n \cdot \frac{V_1}{V_2} = \left(\frac{V_2}{V_1}\right)^n \left(\frac{V_2}{V_1}\right)^{-1}$$

$$\therefore \quad \boxed{\frac{T_1}{T_2} = \left(\frac{V_2}{V_1}\right)^{n-1}} \qquad \qquad \text{... (3.54)}$$

Adopting above procedure of simplification, following co-relations can be obtained.

$$\frac{T_1}{T_2} = \left(\frac{p_1}{p_2}\right)^{\frac{n-1}{n}} \qquad \qquad \text{... (3.55)}$$

Equations (3.54) and (3.55) can be written as,

$$\frac{T_1}{T_2} = \left(\frac{p_1}{p_2}\right)^{\frac{n-1}{n}} = \left(\frac{V_2}{V_1}\right)^{n-1} \qquad \qquad \text{... (3.56)}$$

Similarly, following relations can be obtained.

$$\frac{p_1}{p_2} = \left(\frac{V_2}{V_1}\right)^n = \left(\frac{T_1}{T_2}\right)^{\frac{n}{n-1}} \qquad \qquad \text{... (3.57)}$$

$$\text{and} \quad \left(\frac{V_2}{V_1}\right) = \left(\frac{p_2}{p_1}\right)^{1/n} = \left(\frac{T_1}{T_2}\right)^{\frac{1}{n-1}} \qquad \qquad \text{... (3.58)}$$

## 3.12.8 To Obtain Polytropic Index 'n'

The polytropic process is, $pV^n = c$.

$$\therefore \qquad p_1V_1^n = p_2V_2^n$$

Taking log on both sides,

$$\log p_1 + n \log V_1 = \log p_2 + n \log V_2$$

$$\therefore \qquad \log \frac{p_1}{p_2} = n \log \frac{V_2}{V_1}$$

$$\therefore \qquad n = \frac{\log\left(\dfrac{p_2}{p_1}\right)}{\log\left(\dfrac{V_2}{V_1}\right)} \qquad\qquad \dots (3.59)$$

## 3.12.9 Adiabatic Process

A process during which there is no transfer of heat is called as **adiabatic process**.

Following are the examples of an adiabatic process:

- Consider a well insulated (adiabatic) room heated by an electric heater as a system (Fig. 3.9).

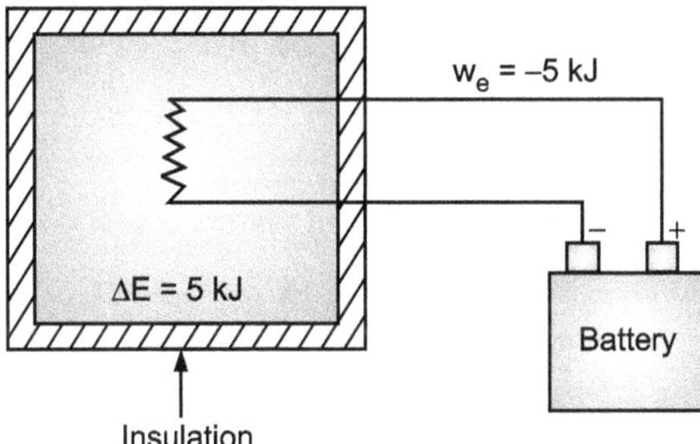


**Fig. 3.9: The work done (electrical) on an adiabatic**

**System is equal to the Increase in the energy of the system**

- A well insulated (adiabatic) container having a fluid in it and supplied with a paddle wheel work (stirring work) (See Fig. 3.10).

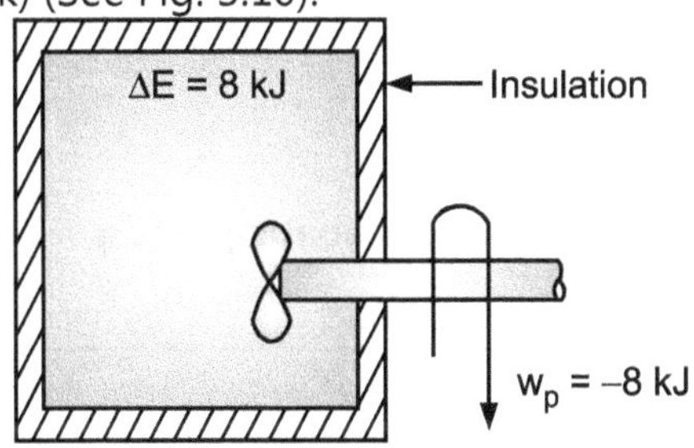


**Fig. 3.10: The work done on an adiabatic system**

**is equal to the Increase in the energy of the system**

- The temperature of air increases when it is compressed as shown in Fig. 3.11. This is because energy is added to the air in the form of boundary work. In the absence of any heat transfer (Q = 0), the entire boundary work will be stored in the air as part of the total energy.

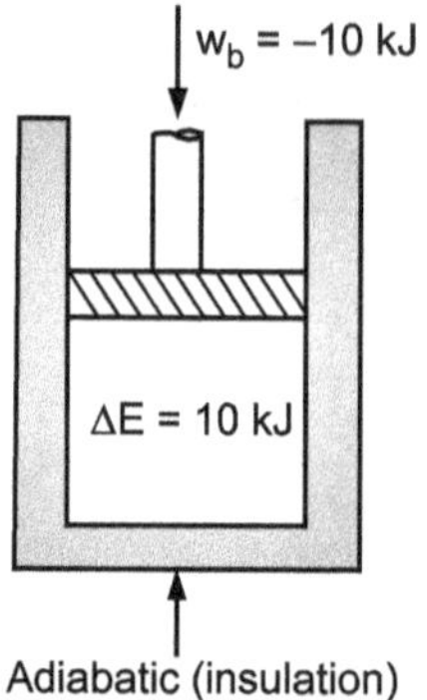


**Fig. 3.11: The work (boundary) done on an adiabatic system = increase in the energy of the system**

When adiabatic process is reversible, it is known as reversible adiabatic or isentropic process (i.e. constant entropy process).

This reversible adiabatic process is represented by $pV^\gamma = C$, where $\gamma$ is known as adiabatic index and is equal to $\dfrac{c_p}{c_v}$.

The adiabatic process for the change of state of a system (ideal gas) is as shown in Fig. 3.12.

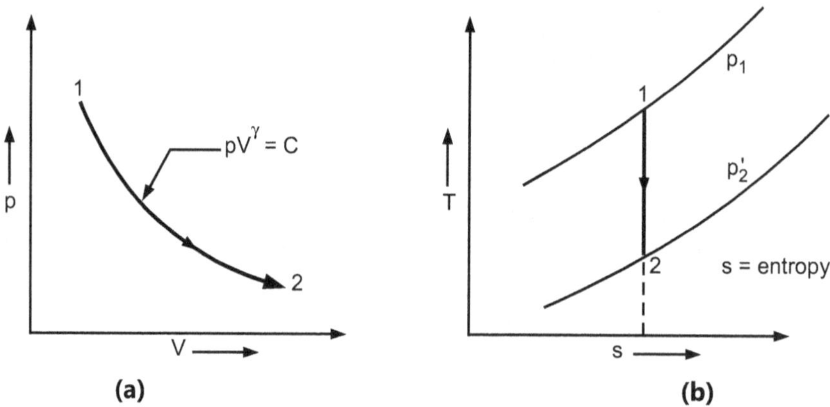


**Fig. 3.12: Adiabatic process**

## 3.12.10 The Law of Adiabatic Process

For non-flow system, for unit mass, first law of thermodynamics in the differential form is

$$\delta q = du + p\, dV \text{ for } m = 1 \qquad \text{... (3.60)}$$

$$\text{and } dq = dh - V\, dp \text{ for } m = 1 \qquad \text{... (3.61)}$$

For adiabatic process,  $dq = 0$

Also  $du = c_v \cdot dT$  and $dh = c_p \cdot dT$  for m = 1.

Putting these values in equations (3.60) and (3.61) above,

$$c_v \cdot dT = -p \, dV \qquad \qquad \ldots (3.62)$$

and $$c_p \cdot dT = V \, dp \qquad \qquad \ldots (3.63)$$

Dividing equation (3.63) by equation (3.62),

$$\frac{c_p}{c_v} = -\frac{V}{p}\frac{dp}{dV} \quad \left( \because \frac{c_p}{c_v} = \gamma \right)$$

$$\therefore \qquad \gamma \cdot \frac{dV}{V} = -\frac{dp}{p} \qquad \qquad \ldots (3.64)$$

Integrating the equation (3.64) between the states 1 and 2,

$$\gamma \cdot \log\left(\frac{V_2}{V_1}\right) = -\log(p_2/p_1)$$

$$\log\left(\frac{V_2}{V_1}\right)^{\gamma} = \log\left(\frac{p_1}{p_2}\right) \qquad \text{Removing log from both sides}$$

$$\therefore \qquad \left(\frac{V_2}{V_1}\right)^{\gamma} = \frac{p_1}{p_2}$$

$$\therefore \qquad p_1 V_1^{\gamma} = p_2 V_2^{\gamma} = pV^{\gamma} = C \qquad \qquad \ldots (3.65)$$

If $$\gamma \times m = V$$

then $$pV^{\gamma} = C \qquad \qquad \ldots (3.66)$$

This is known as the law of adiabatic process.

**(a) Work Done:**

The work done for the reversible adiabatic process is represented by the area under the curve 1 – 2 (Fig. 3.13).

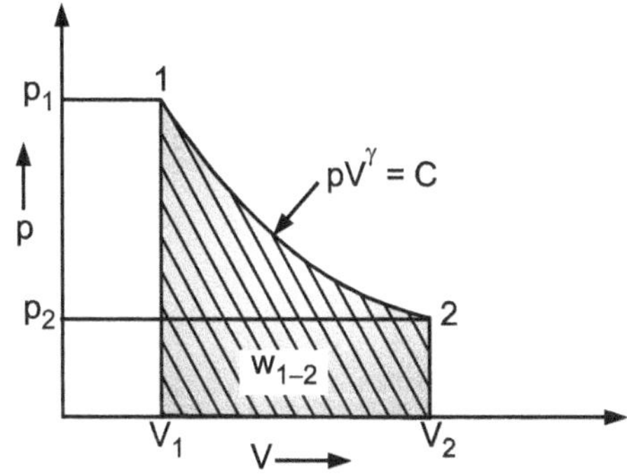


**Fig. 3.13: Work done under the curve 1-2**

For polytropic process,

$$w_{1-2} = \frac{p_2 V_2 - p_1 V_1}{1 - n}$$

Replace n by $\gamma$ for adiabatic process.

$$\therefore \qquad w_{1-2} = \frac{p_2 V_2 - p_1 V_1}{1 - \gamma} \qquad \qquad \dots (3.67)$$

$$\text{or} \qquad w_{1-2} = \frac{p_1 V_1 - p_2 V_2}{\gamma - 1} \qquad \qquad \dots (3.68)$$

**(b) Internal Energy:**

The first law of thermodynamics is

$$\delta q = du + \delta w$$

For adiabatic process, $\qquad \delta q = 0$

$$\therefore \qquad \delta w = -\,du$$

$$\therefore \qquad w_{1-2} = \int_1^2 \delta w = -\int_1^2 du = -\,m \cdot c_v\,(T_2 - T_1)$$

$$\therefore \qquad w_{1-2} = -\frac{m\,R}{\gamma - 1}\,(T_2 - T_1) \qquad \left(\text{as } c_v = \frac{R}{\gamma - 1}\right)$$

$$p_2 V_2 = mRT_2 \text{ and } p_1 V_1 = mRT_1$$

$$= -\frac{(p_2 V_2) - (p_1 V_1)}{\gamma - 1} = \frac{p_2 V_2 - p_1 V_1}{1 - \gamma} \qquad \dots (3.69)$$

It indicates that, work done on the system is utilised to increase the energy of system. On the other hand, if work is obtained from the system, energy of the system decreases.

## 3.12.11 To Prove $\gamma = \dfrac{c_p}{c_v}$

In last section, we have derived that

$$w_{1-2} = \frac{p_1 V_1 - p_2 V_2}{\gamma - 1} = \frac{m\,R\,(T_1 - T_2)}{\gamma - 1}$$

For adiabatic process, $\qquad q = 0.$

$\therefore$ First law becomes, $\quad w = -\,\Delta u$

$$\frac{m\,R\,(T_1 - T_2)}{\gamma - 1} = -\,m \cdot c_v\,(T_2 - T_1)$$

$$\frac{m\,R\,(T_1 - T_2)}{\gamma - 1} = m\,c_v\,(T_1 - T_2)$$

$$\frac{R}{\gamma - 1} = c_v \qquad \qquad \dots (3.70)$$

But, $\qquad \qquad R = c_p - c_v$

$$\therefore \qquad \frac{c_p - c_v}{\gamma - 1} = c_v$$

$$\frac{c_p}{c_v} - 1 = \gamma - 1$$

$$\therefore \qquad \frac{c_p}{c_v} = \gamma \qquad \qquad \dots (3.71)$$

For adiabatic process, the heat transfer (dQ = 0), the index $\gamma$ of the process is equal to the ratio of the specific heat at constant pressure to the specific heat at constant volume.

## 3.13 THROTTLING PROCESS

When a fluid flows through a constricted passage like a partially opened valve or an orifice or a porous plug then there is an appreciable pressure drop and the flow is said to be throttled.

Fig. 3.13 shows the process of throttling by a partially opened valve on a fluid flowing in an insulated pipe.

As it is insulated, therefore,

$$\frac{dq}{dm} = 0$$

$$\text{and} \qquad \frac{dw}{dm} = 0$$

$\therefore$　The change in potential energy is very small and neglected. Thus, the SFEE reduces to,

$$h_1 + \frac{V_1^2}{2} = h_2 + \frac{V_2^2}{2}$$

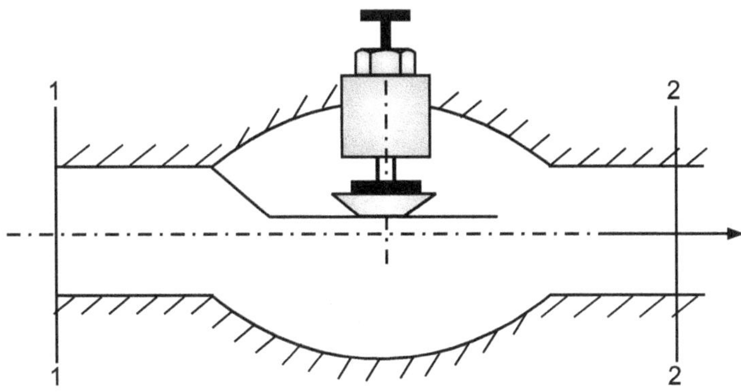

**Fig. 3.13 : Flow through a valve**

The velocity through a pipe flow (through a valve opening) is very small. Then, if one neglects K.E. term, then,

$$h_1 = h_2$$

i.e. the enthalpy of fluid before throttling is equal to the enthalpy of fluid after throttling.

It means energy content of the fluid before and after throttling remain constant. This is as per the first law of thermodynamics. Though there is a process irreversibly involved, but it cannot be quantified by the first law.

**Problem 3.5:** A certain gas expands adiabatically from a pressure of 800 kPa and volume 0.015 m³ to a pressure of 140 kPa. Determine work done and change in internal energy. Take $c_p$ = 1.046 kJ/kg·K and $c_v$ = 0.752 kJ/kg·K

**Solution: Given:** $p_1$ = 800 kPa, $v_1$ = 0.015 m³, $p_2$ = 140 kPa.

$$\gamma = \frac{c_p}{c_v} = \frac{1.046}{0.752} = 1.39$$

The adiabatic process $p_1 V_1^{\gamma} = p_2 V_2^{\gamma}$ is represented on p-v and T-s diagram as shown in Fig. 3.14.

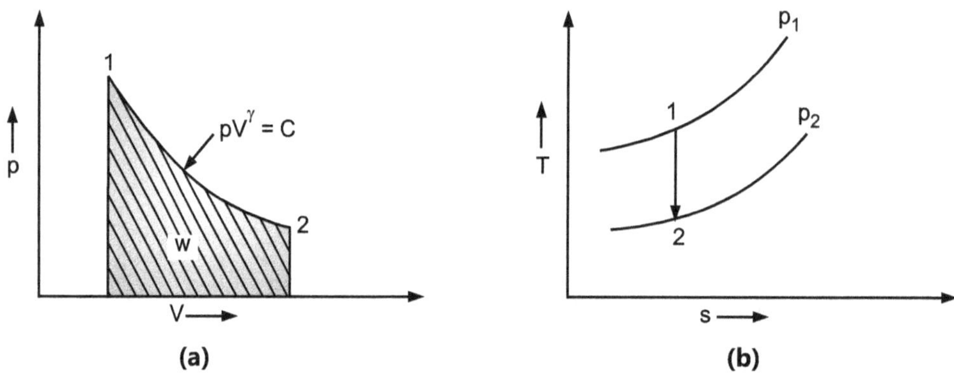


**Fig. 3.14: p-v and T-s diagrams**

Now, $$p_1 V_1^{\gamma} = p_2 V_2^{\gamma}$$

$$\therefore \quad V_2 = \left(\frac{p_1}{p_2}\right)^{1/\gamma} \cdot V_1 = \left(\frac{800}{140}\right)^{1/1.39} \times 0.015 = 0.0525 \text{ m}^3$$

$$\text{Work done} = w_{1-2} = \int_1^2 p \, dV = \frac{p_1 V_1 - p_2 V_2}{\gamma - 1}$$

$$= \frac{800 \times 0.015 - 140 \times 0.0525}{1.39 - 1}$$

$$= \textbf{11.92 kJ (work done by system)}$$

For adiabatic process, $q = 0$.

$$\therefore \quad \Delta u = -w = \textbf{- 11.92 kJ (decreases)}$$

**Problem 3.6 (Comparison of isothermal, polytropic and adiabatic):** 1 kg of air is compressed in a non-flow process from a pressure of 1 bar and 27°C to a pressure of 6 bar according to (a) adiabatically, (b) isothermally, (c) polytropically with n = 1.25.

Find work done, heat transferred, in each case. Also represent these on p-V and T-s diagrams. Take $c_p$ = 1.033 kJ/kg·K and $\gamma$ = 1.4.

**Solution: Given:** m = 1, $p_1$ = 1 bar, $p_2$ = 6 bar and $T_1$ = 27 + 273 = 300 K.

**(a) Adiabatic process ($pv^\gamma$ = C):**

(i) Work done,
$$w_{1-2} = \int_1^2 p\,dV = \frac{p_1 V_1 - p_2 V_2}{\gamma - 1}$$

$v_2$ is unknown.

$$\therefore \qquad p_1 V_1^\gamma = p_2 V_2^\gamma$$

$$\therefore \qquad V_2 = \left(\frac{p_1}{p_2}\right)^{1/\gamma} \cdot V_1$$

$\therefore$ To calculate $V_1$, consider characteristic gas equation.

$$pV = mRT$$
$$p_1 V_1 = mRT_1$$

$$\therefore \qquad V_1 = \frac{mRT_1}{p_1}$$

$$= \frac{1 \times 0.287 \times 10^3 \times 300}{1 \times 10^5} = 0.861 \text{ m}^3$$

$$\therefore \qquad V_2 = \left(\frac{p_1}{p_2}\right)^{1/\gamma} \cdot V_1 = \left(\frac{1}{6}\right)^{1/1.4} \times 0.861 = 0.239 \text{ m}^3$$

$$w_{1-2} = \frac{p_1 V_1 - p_2 V_2}{\gamma - 1}$$

$$= \frac{1 \times 10^5 \times 0.861 - 6 \times 10^5 \times 0.239}{1.4 - 1}$$

$$j = -1.4325 \times 10^5 \text{ joule} = -143.25 \text{ kJ}$$

Negative sign indicates that work is done on the system.

(ii)   Heat transfer, q = 0 for adiabatic process.

(iii)  Internal energy: By first law

$$q = \Delta u + w_{1-2}$$
$$\Delta u = -w_{1-2}$$
$$= -(-143.25) = \textbf{143.25 kJ}$$

Due to adiabatic compression, internal energy of the system increases.

**(b) Isothermal process (pv = C):**

(i)  Work done,
$$w_{1-2} = \int_1^2 p \, dV$$

$$= \int_1^2 \frac{C}{v} \cdot dV$$

$$= m RT_1 \log \frac{V_2}{V_1} = p_1 V_1 \log \frac{V_2}{V_1}$$

$$= 1 \times 10^5 \times 0.861 \log \left(\frac{0.239}{0.861}\right) = -110348 \text{ joule}$$

$$= -110.348 \text{ kJ (work done on the system)}$$

(ii) Internal energy:
$$\Delta u = m \, c_v \cdot \Delta T, \text{ where } \Delta T = 0$$

$$\therefore \quad \Delta u = 0$$

(iii) Heat transfer, q

According to first law of thermodynamics,

$$q = \Delta u + w_{1-2}$$

$$= 0 - 110.348 = \textbf{-110.348 kJ (rejected)}$$

**(c) Polytropic compression: $pV^n = C$, where n = 1.25**

(i)  Work done,
$$w_{1-2} = \int_1^2 p \, dV$$

$$= \frac{p_1 V_1 - p_2 V_2}{\gamma - 1}$$

$$= \frac{1 \times 10^5 \times 0.861 - 6 \times 10^5 \times 0.239}{1.25 - 1}$$

$$= -229200 \text{ joule} = -229.2 \text{ kJ (work done on the system)}$$

(ii) Heat transfer :
$$q_{1-2} = \left(\frac{\gamma - n}{\gamma - 1}\right) \times \text{Work done}$$

$$= \frac{1.4 - 1.25}{1.4 - 1} \times (-229.2) = -85.9 \text{ kJ (rejected)}$$

(iii) Internal energy: $\Delta u$

By first law,
$$q = \Delta u + w_{1-2}$$

$$\Delta u = q - w_{1-2}$$

$$= -85.9 - (-229.2) = \textbf{143.2 kJ (increases)}$$

---

**Problem 3.7:** A certain quantity of air has a volume of 0.028 m³ at a pressure of 1.25 bar and 25°C. It is compressed to a volume of 0.0042 m³ according to the law $pv^{1.3}$ = constant. Find the final temperature and work done during compression. Also determine the reduction in pressure at a constant volume required to bring the air back to its original temperature.

**Solution:** The processes are represented on p-V diagram shown below.

**Given:** $V_2 = 0.0042$ m³, $p_1 = 1.25$ bar, $V_1 = 0.028$ m³, and $T_1 = 25° + 273 = 298$ K

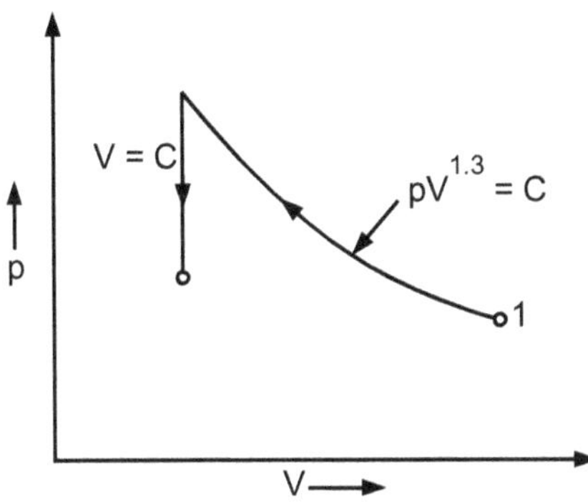


**Fig. 3.15: p-v diagram**

$$\frac{p_1 V_1}{T_1} = \frac{p_2 V_2}{T_2}$$

$$\therefore \qquad \frac{T_2}{T_1} = \frac{p_2 V_2}{p_1 V_1} \qquad\qquad \dots \text{(I)}$$

but $\qquad p_1 V_1^n = p_2 V_2^n \qquad\qquad \dots \text{(II)}$

Solving equations (I) and (II),

$$\frac{T_2}{T_1} = \left(\frac{V_1}{V_2}\right)^{n-1}$$

$$T_2 = T_1 \left(\frac{V_1}{V_2}\right)^{n-1}$$

$$= 298 \left(\frac{0.028}{0.0042}\right)^{0.3} = 526 \text{ K}$$

$$\frac{p_2}{p_1} = \left(\frac{T_2}{T_1}\right)^{\frac{n}{n-1}}$$

$$p_2 = 1.25 \times \left(\frac{526}{298}\right)^{\frac{1.3}{0.3}}$$

$$p_2 = 14.663 \text{ bar}$$

Work done during process 1 – 2 is

$$w_{1-2} = \frac{p_1 V_1 - p_2 V_2}{n - 1}$$

$$= \frac{(1.25 \times 10^5 \times 0.028 - 14.663 \times 10^5 \times 0.0042)}{1.3 - 1}$$

$$= -8861.5 \text{ joule}$$

$$= -8.8615 \text{ kJ}$$

**Process 2 – 3: Constant volume:**

$$\frac{p_2}{T_2} = \frac{p_3}{T_3}, \quad T_3 = 298 \text{ K}$$

$$p_3 = \frac{T_3}{T_2} \cdot p_2$$

$$= \frac{298}{526} \times 14.663 = \textbf{8.3 bar}$$

Pressure reduces from 14.6 bar to 8.3 bar.

**Problem 3.8:** 0.45 kg of gas is expanded adiabatically until the pressure is halved and the temperature of gas falls from 220°C to 130°C. During the expansion, there is a work transfer of 27 kJ. Determine (i) the adiabatic index of the gas, (ii) the characteristic gas constant.

**Solution: Given:** $m = 0.45$ kg, $p_2 = \dfrac{p_1}{2}$, $T_1 = 220 + 273 = 493$ K, $T_2 = 403$ K, $w_{1-2} = 27$ kJ.

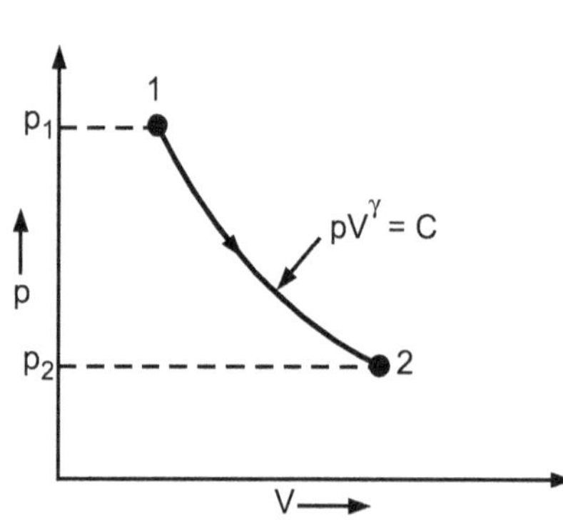


**Fig. 3.16: Adiabatic process**

$$\frac{p_1 V_1}{T_1} = \frac{p_2 V_2}{T_2}$$

$$\therefore \quad \frac{T_2}{T_1} = \frac{p_2 V_2}{p_1 V_1}$$

$$p_1 V_1^\gamma = p_2 V_2^\gamma$$

$$\left(\frac{V_2}{V_1}\right)^\gamma = \frac{p_1}{p_2}$$

$$\therefore \quad \frac{V_2}{V_1} = \left(\frac{p_1}{p_2}\right)^{1/\gamma}$$

$$\therefore \quad \frac{T_2}{T_1} = \frac{p_2}{p_1} \left(\frac{p_1}{p_2}\right)^{1/\gamma}$$

$$= \left(\frac{p_2}{p_1}\right)^{\frac{\gamma - 1}{\gamma}}$$

$$\therefore \qquad \frac{403}{493} = \left(\frac{1}{2}\right)^{\frac{\gamma-1}{\gamma}} \qquad\qquad \because p_1 = 2p_2$$

$$\log(0.817) = \frac{\gamma-1}{\gamma}\log 0.5$$

$$-0.2015 = -\frac{0.693\,\gamma + 0.693}{\gamma}$$

$$0.693 = -0.2015\,\gamma + 0.693\,\gamma$$

$$\therefore \qquad \gamma = \frac{0.693}{0.4915} = 1.4095$$

$$w_{1-2} = m \cdot c_v\,(T_1 - T_2)$$

$$27 = 0.45 \times c_v \times (493 - 403)$$

$$c_v = 0.6666 \ \text{kJ/kg·K}$$

$$c_v = \frac{R}{\gamma - 1} \qquad\qquad \therefore\ R = c_v\,(\gamma - 1)$$

$$\therefore \qquad R = 0.6666 \times (1.4095 - 1)$$

$$= \mathbf{0.273\ kJ/kg·K}$$

**Problem 3.9:** In a certain thermodynamic process of an ideal gas, the volume changes from 0.2 m³ to 0.5 m³, while the pressure changes according to the law $p = 1500\left(\dfrac{V}{100} + 1\right)$, where p is in N/m², V is in m³. Find the work done by the gas in kJ.

**Solution:** It is an non-flow expansion process.

$$\therefore \qquad w_{1-2} = \int_1^2 p\,dV$$

$$= 1500 \int_1^2 \left(\frac{V}{100} + 1\right) dV$$

$$= 1500 \left[\frac{V^2}{200} + V\right]_1^2$$

$$= 1500 \left[\frac{V_2^2}{200} + V_2 - \frac{V_1^2}{200} - V_1\right]$$

$$= 1500 \left[\left(\frac{V_2^2 - V_1^2}{200}\right) + (V_2 - V_1)\right]$$

$$= 1500 \left( \frac{0.5^2 - 0.2^2}{200} + 0.5 - 0.2 \right)$$

$$= 451.5 \text{ joules} = \textbf{0.451 kJ}$$

**Problem 3.10:** 1 kg of a certain gas undergoes a thermodynamic constant pressure process whereby the volume changes from 1 m³ to 1.8 m³ while the temperature changes from 50ºC to 450ºC. The specific heat at constant pressure is given by,

$$c_p = \left( 2.5 + \frac{40}{T + 20} \right) \text{ kJ/kg·K, where T is in ºC. Find out}$$

(i) heat supplied, (ii) change in internal energy, (iii) work done, (iv) change in enthalpy. Take $\gamma = 1.4$

**Solution: Given:** $V_1 = 1$ m³, $V_2 = 1.8$ m³, $T_1 = 50$ºC, $T_2 = 450$ºC

**(i)  Heat supplied in constant pressure:**

$$q = \int m\, c_p \cdot dT = \int_{T_1}^{T_2} \left( 2.5 + \frac{40}{T + 20} \right) dT, \; m = 1$$

$$= \int_{50}^{450} 2.5 \, dT + \int_{50}^{450} \frac{40}{T + 20} \, dT = [2.5 \, T]_{50}^{450} + [40 \log (T + 20)]_{50}^{450}$$

$$= 2.5 \, (450 - 50) + 40 \log \left( \frac{470}{70} \right) = \textbf{1076.2 kJ}$$

**(ii)  Change in internal energy:**

$$u_2 - u_1 = \int_{T_1}^{T_2} m\, c_v \, dT \qquad \text{where } m = 1, \; c_p = \gamma \cdot c_v$$

$$= \frac{1}{\gamma} \int_{T_1}^{T_2} c_p \cdot dT = \frac{1}{\gamma} \int_{50}^{450} \left( 2.5 + \frac{40}{T + 20} \right) dT$$

$$\therefore \qquad \Delta u = \textbf{768.69 kJ (increases)}$$

**(iii) Work done ($w_{1-2}$):**

By first law of thermodynamics,

$$q = \Delta u + w_{1-2}$$

$$w_{1-2} = q - \Delta u$$

$$= 1076.2 - 768.69 = \textbf{307.45 kJ/kg (work done by system)}$$

**(iv)** Change in enthalpy $= \begin{bmatrix} \text{heat supplied under} \\ \text{constant pressure process} \end{bmatrix}$

$$= \textbf{1076.2 kJ (increases)}$$

**Problem 3.11:** 0.5 kg of air is compressed adiabatically from 160 kPa, 60°C to  0.8 MPa and is then expanded at constant pressure to the original volume. Sketch the processes on p-V diagram and find out the heat transfer and work transfer from the whole path. Take $c_p$ = 1.005 kJ/kg·K and $c_v$ = 0.710 kJ/kg·K.

**Solution: (a) p-V and T-s diagrams**

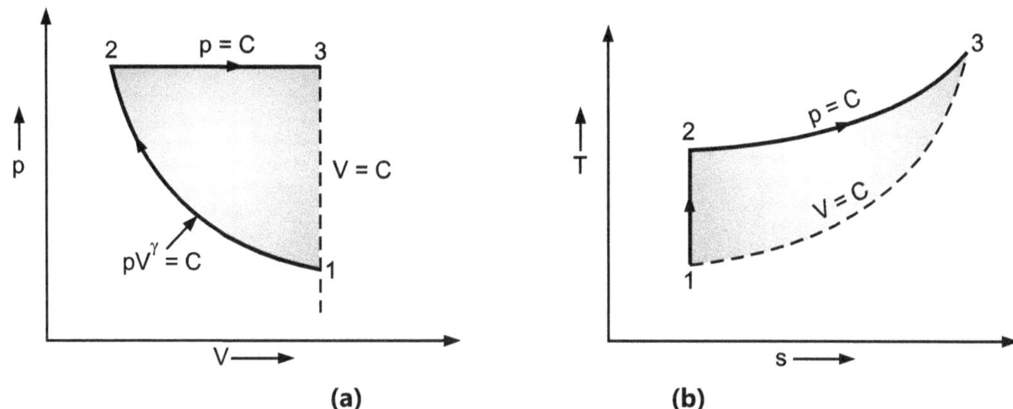


**Fig. 3.17**

**Given:** m = 0.5 kg, $p_1$ = 160 kPa, $T_1$ = (60 + 273) = 333 K, $p_2$ = 800 kPa

**(i) Process 1 – 2:**
$$\frac{T_2}{T_1} = \left(\frac{p_2}{p_1}\right)^{\frac{\gamma-1}{\gamma}}$$

$\therefore$
$$T_2 = T_1\left(\frac{p_2}{p_1}\right)^{\frac{\gamma-1}{\gamma}}$$

$\therefore$
$$T_2 = 333\left(\frac{800}{160}\right)^{\frac{1.4-1}{1.4}}$$

$$= 527.4 \text{ K}$$

R = $c_p - c_v$ = 1.005 – 0.710 = 0.295 kJ/kg·K

Work done in non-flow adiabatic compression process, $w_{1-2}$,

$$w_{1-2} = \left(\frac{p_1V_1 - p_2V_2}{\gamma-1}\right) = mR\left(\frac{T_1 - T_2}{\gamma-1}\right)$$

$$= \frac{0.5 \times 0.295 \times (333 - 527.4)}{1.4 - 1} = -71.68 \text{ kJ}$$

Heat transfer during reversible adiabatic compression process is zero.

**(ii) Process 2 – 3: Constant pressure expansion:**

$$w_{1-2} = p_2\,(V_3 - V_2) = mR\,(T_3 - T_2) \qquad \text{from } p = C$$

$$\frac{V_3}{V_2} = \frac{V_1}{V_2} \qquad \ldots (1)$$

$$\frac{T_3}{T_2} = \frac{V_3}{V_2} \qquad \ldots (2)$$

but
$$\left(\frac{V_1}{V_2}\right) = \left(\frac{P_2}{P_1}\right)^{\frac{1}{\gamma}} = \left(\frac{800}{160}\right)^{\frac{1}{1.4}} = 3.156$$

From equation (2),   $T_3 = T_2 \cdot \dfrac{V_3}{V_2} = 527.4 \times 3.156 = 1664.9$ K

$\therefore$
$$w_{2-3} = mR\,(T_3 - T_2)$$

$$= 0.5 \times 0.295\,(1664.9 - 527.4) = +167.78 \text{ kJ}$$

Work is done by the air.

$\therefore$   Work done for the whole path

$$= (-71.68 + 167.7)$$

$$= +96.1 \text{ kJ}$$

Positive sign indicates that work is done by air.

**(b) Heat transfer during constant pressure process (2 – 3)**

$$q_{2-3} = m \cdot c_p\,(T_3 - T_2)$$

$$= 0.5 \times 1.005\,(1664.9 - 527.4)$$

$$= 571.32 \text{ kJ}$$

Heat transfer for complete path

$$= q_{1-2} + q_{2-3} = 0 + 571.32$$

$$= \mathbf{571.32 \text{ kJ}}$$

**Problem 3.12:** In a vessel, 10 kg of oxygen is heated in a reversible, non-flow, constant volume process so that the pressure of $O_2$ is increased two times that of initial value. The initial temperature is 25°C. Calculate:

(i)  The final temperature

(ii) The change in internal energy

(iii) Change in enthalpy

(iv) Heat transfer.

Take R = 0.259 kJ/kg·K, and $c_v$ = 0.652 kJ/kg·K for oxygen.

**Solution:** This is a constant volume process.

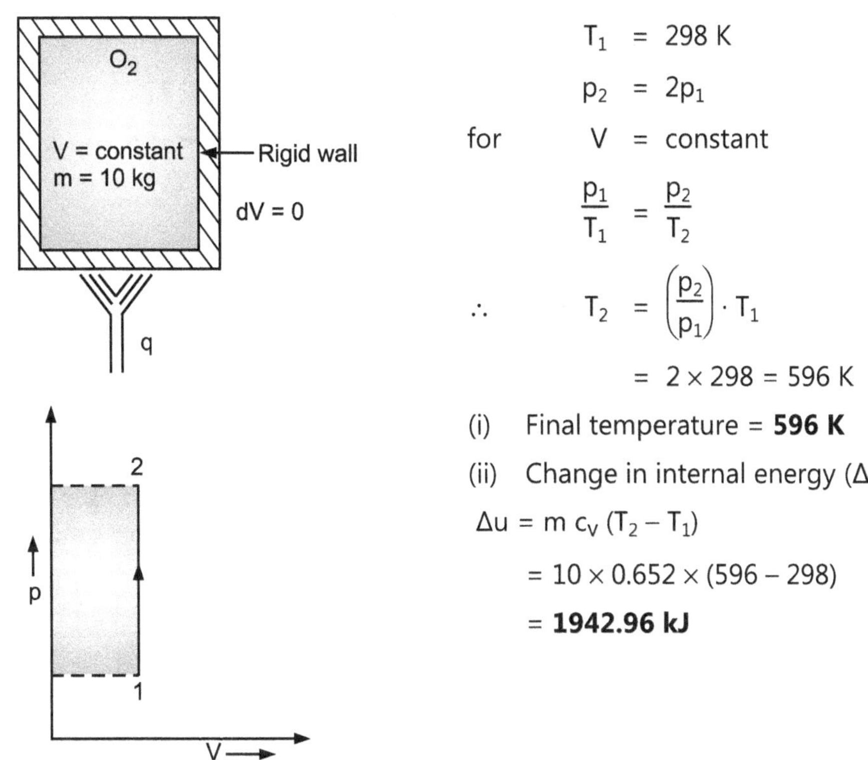



$$T_1 = 298 \text{ K}$$

$$p_2 = 2p_1$$

for $\quad V = \text{constant}$

$$\frac{p_1}{T_1} = \frac{p_2}{T_2}$$

$$\therefore \quad T_2 = \left(\frac{p_2}{p_1}\right) \cdot T_1$$

$$= 2 \times 298 = 596 \text{ K}$$

(i)  Final temperature = **596 K**

(ii)  Change in internal energy ($\Delta u$)

$$\Delta u = m\, c_v\, (T_2 - T_1)$$

$$= 10 \times 0.652 \times (596 - 298)$$

$$= \textbf{1942.96 kJ}$$

**Fig. 3.18: Constant Volume Process**

(iii) Change in enthalpy, $\quad \Delta h = du + d\,(pV)$

$$\Delta h = 1942.96 + V\,(p_2 - p_1) = 1942.96 + mR\,(T_2 - T_1)$$

$$= 1942.96 + 10 \times 0.259\,(298)$$

$$\Delta h = \textbf{2714.78 kJ (increases)}$$

(iv) Heat transfer, $q_{1-2}$

By first law, $\quad q_{1-2} = \Delta u + \int p\, dV$ where $dV = 0$ $\qquad \therefore p\, dV = 0$

$$\therefore \quad q_{1-2} = \Delta u = \textbf{1942.96 kJ (supplied)}$$

**Problem 3.13:** 10 kg of a gas at 40° C occupies 3 m³. Determine the gas pressure in bar. An additional mass of the gas is then very slowly added to raise the tank pressure to 10 bar. Assuming that the gas temperature remains constant, how much extra mass must have been added? Take R = 0.297 kJ/kg·K.

**Solution: Given:** Mass of gas, $m_1$ = 10 kg; Volume of gas, $V_1$ = 3 m³

Temperature of gas, $\quad T_1 = 40°C$

Pressure of gas after addition, $p_2$ = 10 bar.

Temperature of gas remains constant during addition of mass, $R = 0.297$ kJ/kg·K.

$$p_1 V_1 = m_1 R T_1$$

$$\therefore \quad p_1 = \frac{m_1 R T_1}{V_1} = \frac{10 \times 0.297 \times (40 + 273)}{3} = 309.8 \text{ kN/m}^2$$

$$= \mathbf{2.098 \ bar}$$

Mass of gas is added to the tank at constant temperature.

$$\therefore \quad p_2 V_2 = m_2 R T$$

$$\therefore \quad m_2 = \frac{p_2 V_2}{RT} = \frac{10 \times 10^5 \times 3}{0.297 \times 10^3 \times 313} = 32.3 \text{ kg}$$

$$\therefore \quad \text{Mass of gas added} = m_2 - m_1 = 32.3 - 10 = \mathbf{22.3 \ kg}$$

**Problem 3.14:** A fluid passes through a thermodynamic cycle comprising of four processes. The energy transfers in each process are given in the following table. If the sum of all the heat transfers in the cycle is –17000 kJ, complete the following table showing method for each item.

| Process | Q (kJ/min) | W (kJ/min) | ΔE (kJ/min) |
|---------|-----------|-----------|------------|
| 1 – 2 | 0 | 2170 | – |
| 2 – 3 | + 21000 | 0 | – |
| 3 – 4 | – 2100 | – | – 36600 |
| 4 – 1 | – | – | – |

**Solution:** Process 1-2:

$$Q_{12} = \Delta E_{12} + W_{12}$$

$$\Delta E_{12} = Q_{12} - W_{12}$$

$$= 0 - 2170 = - 2170 \text{ kJ/min}$$

Process 2-3:

$$Q_{23} = \Delta E_{23} + W_{23}$$

$$\Delta E_{23} = Q_{23} - W_{23}$$

$$= 21000 - 0 = + 21000 \text{ kJ/min}$$

Process 3-4:

$$Q_{34} = \Delta E_{34} + W_{34}$$

$$W_{34} = Q_{34} - \Delta E_{34}$$

$$= - 2100 - (- 36600) = + 34500 \text{ kJ/min}$$

As stated in the problem, $\quad Q = Q_{12} + Q_{23} + Q_{34} + Q_{41} = - 17000 \text{ kJ/min}$

$$\therefore \quad Q_{41} = - 17000 - 0 - 21000 - (- 2100)$$

$$= - 35900 \text{ kJ/min}$$

For a cyclic process,     $\Sigma\,\Delta E\ =\ 0$

$-\,2170 + 21000 - 36600 + \Delta E_{41} = 0$   $\therefore$   $\Delta E_{41} = +\,17770$ kJ/min

The table becomes:

| Process | Q (kJ/min) | W(kJ/min) | $\Delta E$ (kJ/min) |
|---------|------------|-----------|---------------------|
| 1 – 2   | 0          | 2170      | – 2170              |
| 2 – 3   | 21000      | 0         | + 21000             |
| 3 – 4   | – 2100     | 34500     | – 36600             |
| 4 – 1   | – 35900    | – 53670   | 17770               |

Since,           $\Sigma\,Q_{cycle}\ =\ \Sigma\,W_{cycle}$

$$=\ -\,17000\ \text{kJ/min} = \textbf{–\,283.3 kW}$$

**Problem 3.15:** The compression ratio in an Otto cycle is 8. The pressure and temperature at the beginning of compression process is 1 bar and 300 K respectively. The heat supplied to the air per cycle is 900 kJ/kg.

Determine: (i) Air standard efficiency, (ii) MEP.

**Solution: Given:** Compression ratio, r = 8, $p_1$ = 1 bar, $T_1$ = 300 K.

Q = Heat supplied per cycle = 900 kJ/kg

$$\text{Air standard efficiency}\ =\ 1 - \frac{1}{r^{\gamma-1}}$$

$$\text{For air, } \gamma = 1.4\ =\ 1 - \frac{1}{8^{(1.4-1)}} = 0.5647$$

The Otto cycle on p-v diagram can be seen from Fig. 3.25.

Temperature at the end of compression process,

$$T_2\ =\ T_1 \cdot r^{\gamma-1} = 300\,(8)^{1.4-1} = 689.2\ \text{K}$$

$$\frac{p_2}{p_1}\ =\ \left(\frac{v_1}{v_2}\right)^{\gamma} = (r)^{\gamma}$$

$\therefore\qquad p_2\ =\ p_1 \cdot (r)^{\gamma} = 18.37$ bar

$$Q = \text{Heat added}\ =\ c_v \cdot (T_3 - T_2)$$

$$900\ =\ 0.72\,(T_3 - 689.2)$$

$\therefore\qquad T_3\ =\ 1939.2$ K

For constant volume heat addition process,

$$\frac{p_2 v_2}{T_2}\ =\ \frac{p_3 v_3}{T_3}\quad \therefore\ \frac{p_2}{T_2} = \frac{p_3}{T_3}$$

$$\therefore\qquad p_3\ =\ \frac{T_3}{T_2} \cdot p_2 = \frac{1939.2}{689.2} \times 18.37 = 51.68\ \text{bar}$$

$$\alpha \;=\; \frac{p_3}{p_2} = \frac{p_4}{p_1} = \frac{51.68}{18.37} = \mathbf{2.81}$$

$$\therefore \qquad MEP \;=\; \frac{p_1 \cdot r \cdot (\alpha - 1)\,(r^{\gamma-1} - 1)}{(\gamma - 1)\,(r - 1)}$$

$$=\; \frac{1 \times 8\,(2.81 - 1)\,(8^{1.4-1} - 1)}{(1.4 - 1)\,(8 - 1)} = \mathbf{6.7\ bar}$$

**Problem 3.16:** A closed system undergoes a thermodynamic cycle. There are four processes AB, BC, CD and DA in the cycle. The heat transfer and work transfer in kJ/min for each process is as below:

| Process | Heat transfer kJ/min | Work transfer kJ/min |
|---|---|---|
| AB | Nil | −22000 |
| BC | 18000 | Nil |
| CD | −4000 | +30,000 |
| DA | −2000 | +4000 |

Show that the data is consistent with first law of thermodynamics and determine:

(a)  Net rate of work output in kW.

(b)  Efficiency of the cycle.

(c)  Change in internal energy for each process.

**Solution:** Process A-B:

$$Q_{A\text{-}B} \;=\; \Delta E_{A\text{-}B} + W_{A\text{-}B}$$
$$\Delta E_{A\text{-}B} \;=\; Q_{A\text{-}B} - W_{A\text{-}B}$$
$$=\; 0 + 22000 \text{ kJ/min}$$

Process B-C:

$$Q_{B\text{-}C} \;=\; \Delta E_{B\text{-}C} + W_{B\text{-}C}$$
$$\Delta E_{B\text{-}C} \;=\; Q_{B\text{-}C} - W_{B\text{-}C}$$
$$=\; 18{,}000 - 0 = 18000 \text{ kJ/min}$$

Process C-D:

$$Q_{C\text{-}D} \;=\; \Delta E_{C\text{-}D} + W_{C\text{-}D}$$
$$\Delta E_{C\text{-}D} \;=\; Q_{C\text{-}D} - W_{C\text{-}D}$$
$$=\; -4000 - 30{,}000 = -34{,}000 \text{ kJ/min}$$

Process D-A:

$$Q_{D\text{-}A} \;=\; \Delta E_{D\text{-}A} + W_{D\text{-}A}$$
$$\Delta E_{DA} \;=\; Q_{D\text{-}A} - W_{D\text{-}A}$$
$$=\; -2000 - 4000 = -6000 \text{ kJ/min}$$

(a) $\qquad$ Net work output $\;=\; -22000 + 0 + 30{,}000 + 4000$

$$= +12000 \text{ kJ/min} \qquad \qquad \dots (1)$$

$$\text{Net heat supplied} \quad = \quad 0 + 18000 - 4000 - 6000$$

$$= 12000 \text{ kJ/min} \qquad \qquad \dots (2)$$

(c) $\quad$ Net change in internal energy $\quad = 22000 + 18000 - 34000 - 6000 = 0$

From equations (1) and (2) above, one can write

$$\oint Q = \oint W$$

It satisfies the first law of thermodynamics. We cannot say this cycle has a 100 percent efficiency because this otherwise would be in disagreement with second law of thermodynamics.

---

**Problem 3.17:** A cylinder contains 0.24 m³ of air at 1 bar and 90°C. It is compressed to 0.06 m³ and its final pressure is 6 bar. Find the index of compression, increase in internal energy and heat transfer. Take R = 0.287 kJ/kg·K and $c_v$ = 0.72 kJ/kg·K for the air.

**Solution:** The index of compression is given by,

$$n = \frac{\log_e\left(\dfrac{p_1}{p_2}\right)}{\log_e\left(\dfrac{V_2}{V_1}\right)} = \frac{\log_e\left(\dfrac{1}{6}\right)}{\log_e\left(\dfrac{0.06}{0.24}\right)} = 1.293$$

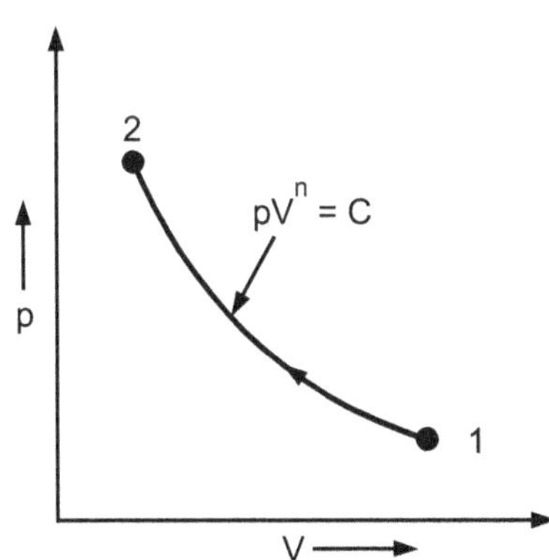


**Fig. 3.19**

$$c_p = c_v + R = 0.712 + 0.287 = \textbf{0.999 kJ/kg·K}$$

$$\gamma = \frac{c_p}{c_v} = \frac{0.999}{0.72} = \textbf{1.403}$$

Using characteristic gas equation,

$$p_1 V_1 = m R T_1$$

---

$$\therefore \quad m = \frac{p_1 V_1}{R T_1} = \frac{1 \times 10^5 \times 0.24}{287 \times 363} = \mathbf{0.230\ kg}$$

Again using gas equation for conditions 1 and 2,

$$\frac{p_1 V_1}{T_1} = \frac{p_2 V_2}{T_2}$$

$$\therefore \quad T_2 = T_1 \cdot \frac{p_2 V_2}{p_1 V_1} = 363 \times \frac{6 \times 10^5 \times 0.06}{1 \times 10^5 \times 0.24} = \mathbf{544.5\ K}$$

The work done during compression is given by,

$$w = \frac{p_1 V_1 - p_2 V_2}{n - 1} = \frac{10^5 \times (1 \times 0.24 - 6 \times 0.06)}{1.293 - 1}$$

$$= -40995 = \mathbf{-40.955\ kJ}$$

The negative sign indicates that the work is done on the system.

As per the first law of thermodynamics,

$$q = w + \Delta u = w + m c_v (T_2 - T_1)$$

$$= -40.95 + 0.23 \times 0.712 \times (544.5 - 363)$$

$$= -11.22\ kW$$

The negative sign indicates that the heat is rejected by the system.

**Problem 3.18:** The specific heat at constant pressure of one kg fluid undergoing non-flow constant pressure process is given by

$$c_p = \left( 3 + \frac{40}{T + 20} \right) kJ/kg\text{-}^{\circ}C$$

where T is in °C. The pressure during the process is maintained at 2 bar and volume changes from 1 m³ to 1.8 m³ and temperature changes from 50°C to 450°C. Determine the heat added, work done, change in internal energy and change in enthalpy.

**Solution:** The work done is given by

$$w_{12} = \frac{p (V_2 - V_1)}{1000}\ kJ$$

$$= \frac{2 \times 10^5 \times (1.8 - 1)}{1000}$$

$$= \mathbf{160\ kJ}$$

$$\text{Heat supplied,} \quad q_{12} = \int_{T_1}^{T_2} c_p\ dT$$

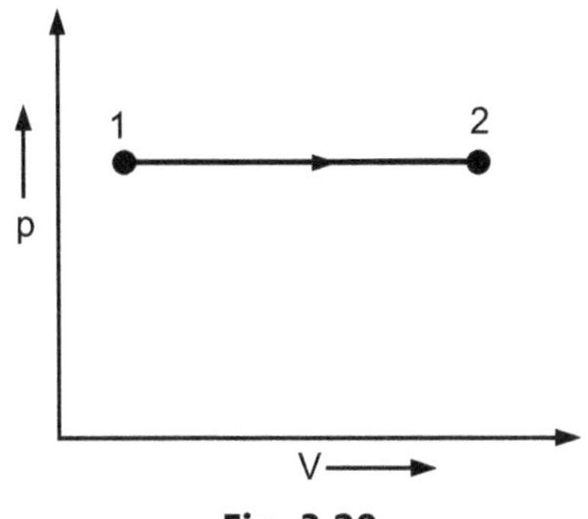

**Fig. 3.20**

$$= \int\limits_{T_1}^{T_2} \left(3.0 + \frac{40}{T + 20}\right) dT$$

$$= \Big[3.0\,T + 40\,\log_e (T + 20)\Big]_{50}^{450}$$

$$= 3.0 \times (450 - 50) + 40\,\log_e \left(\frac{450 + 20}{50 + 20}\right)$$

$$= 1200 + 40 \times 1.9 = \mathbf{1960\ kJ}$$

According to first law for the given process,

$$q = w_{12} + \Delta u$$

$\therefore$ $\qquad \Delta u = q - w_{12} = 1960 - 160 = \mathbf{1800\ kJ}$ (change in internal energy)

$\Delta h$ (change in enthalpy) = Heat supplied = **1800 kJ.**

**Problem 3.19:** 2 kg of air at 25°C is heated at constant pressure until the volume is doubled and then it is heated at constant volume until the pressure is doubled. Draw the processes on p-V diagram. For the total path of the process, find the work transfer, heat transfer and change in entropy. Assume the processes to be non-flow.

Take $c_v$ = 0.712 kJ/kg·K and $c_p$ = 1.00 kJ/kg·K for air.

**Solution:** R = $c_p - c_v$ = 0.288 kJ/kg·K

(a) $\qquad w = w_{12} + w_{23}$

$$= p_1 (V_2 - V_1) + 0{\cdot}0 \text{ as } dV = 0$$

$$= p_1 (2V_1 - V_1) \text{ as } V_2 = 2V_1 \text{ (given)}$$

$$= p_1 V_1 \times 1$$

$$= mRT_1$$

$$= 2 \times 0.712 \times (25 + 273)$$

$$= \mathbf{424.3\ kJ/kg}$$

(b) $\quad q \; = \; q_{12} + q_{23}$

$\qquad = \; mc_v \, (T_2 - T_1) + mc_v \, (T_3 - T_2)$

$\qquad = \; c_v \, [(p_2 V_2 - p_1 V_1) + (p_3 V_3 - p_2 V_2)]$

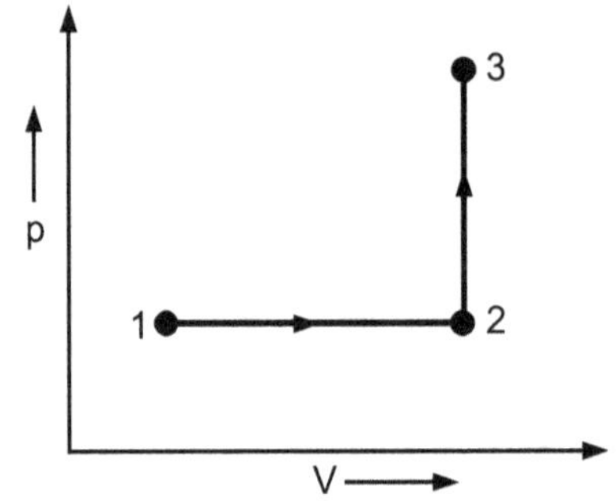

**Fig. 3.21**

$\qquad = \; c_v \, [p_1 \, (V_2 - V_1) + V_2 \, (p_3 - p_2)]$ as $p_2 = p_1$ and $V_3 = V_2$ (given)

$\qquad = \; c_v \, [p_1 \, (2V_1 - V_1) + V_2 \, (2p_2 - p_2)]$ as $V_2 = 2V_1$ and $p_3 = 2p_2$ (given)

$\qquad = \; c_v \, [p_1 V_1 + p_2 V_2]$

$\qquad = \; c_v \, [p_1 V_1 + p_1 \times 2V_1]$ as $p_2 = p_1$ and $V_2 = 2V_1$

$\qquad = \; c_v \times 3 p_1 V_1 = 3 c_v \times mRT_1$

$\qquad = \; 3 \times 0.712 \times 424.3 = \textbf{1272.9 kJ}$

(c) $\qquad ds \; = \; ds_1 + ds_2$

$$= \; c_v \, \log_e \left(\frac{T_2}{T_1}\right) + c_p \, \log_e \left(\frac{T_3}{T_2}\right)$$

$$= \; c_v \, \log_e \left(\frac{p_2 V_2 / mR}{p_1 V_1 / mR}\right) + c_p \, \log_e \left(\frac{p_3 V_3 / mR}{p_2 V_2 / mR}\right)$$

$$= \; c_v \, \log_e \left(\frac{p_2 V_2}{p_1 V_1}\right) + c_p \, \log_e \left(\frac{p_3 V_3}{p_2 V_2}\right)$$

$$= \; c_v \, \log_e \left(\frac{V_2}{V_1}\right) + c_p \, \log_e \left(\frac{p_3}{p_2}\right) \text{ as } p_2 = p_1 \text{ and } V_3 = V_2$$

$$= \; c_v \, \log_e (2) + c_p \, \log_e (2) \text{ as } V_2 = 2V_1 \text{ and } p_3 = 2p_2$$

$$= \; (c_v + c_p) \, \log_e (2) = (0.712 + 1.0) \times 0.693 = \textbf{1.186 kJ/kg·K}$$

**Problem 3.20:** 1 kg of air has a volume of 56 litres and a temperature of 190°C. The air then receives heat at constant pressure until its temperature becomes 500°C. From this state the air rejects heat at constant volume until its pressure is reduced to 700 kN/m². Determine the change of entropy during each process stating whether it is on increase or decrease.

Take $c_p = 1.006$ kJ/kg·K and $c_v = 0.717$ kJ/kg·K.

**Solution: Given:**

Mass of air = m = 1 kg

Initial volume of air = $V_1$ = 56 litres

Initial temperature of air = $T_1$ = 190 + 273 = 463 K

Final temperature of air = $T_2$ = 500 + 273 = 773 K

Final pressure of air = $p_3$ = 700 kN/m$^2$

Calculate: (i) Change of entropy during each process.

The given process is drawn in Fig. 3.22.

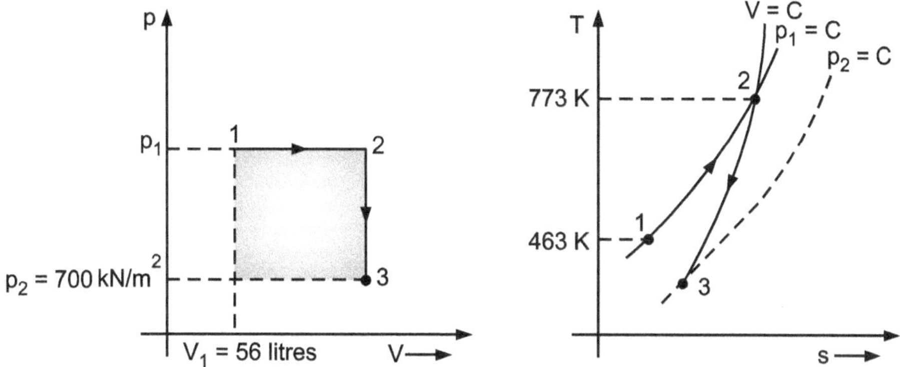



**Fig. 3.22: p-V and T-s diagrams**

**For process 1-2** (constant pressure process):

$$p_1 = p_2$$

By general gas equation,

$$\frac{p_1 V_1}{T_1} = \frac{p_2 V_2}{T_2}$$

$\therefore \qquad \dfrac{V_1}{T_1} = \dfrac{V_2}{T_2}$

$$V_2 = \frac{V_1}{T_1} \times T_2 = \frac{56 \times 10^{-3}}{463} \times 773$$

$\therefore \qquad V_2 = 0.09353 \ \text{m}^3$

Using the equation of change of entropy,

$$s_2 - s_1 = m\, c_v \cdot \log_e \frac{T_2}{T_1} + mR \log \frac{V_2}{V_1}$$

$$= 1 \times 0.711 \log \frac{773}{463} + 1(1.006 - 0.717) \log \frac{0.09353}{0.056}$$

$$= 0.3675 + 0.48268$$

$$= \textbf{0.85 kJ/kg·K (Increase)}$$

**Process 2-3** (Constant volume):

$$V_2 = V_3$$

From general gas equation

$$p_2V_2 = mRT_2$$

$$\therefore \qquad p_2 = \frac{mRT_2}{V_2} = \frac{1 \times 0.289 \times 773}{0.09353}$$

$$= \textbf{2388.51 kN/m}^2$$

and

$$\frac{p_2V_2}{T_2} = \frac{p_3V_3}{T_3}$$

$$\frac{p_2}{T_2} = \frac{p_3}{T_3} \text{ (as } V_2 = V_3)$$

$$\therefore \qquad T_3 = \frac{p_3T_2}{p_2} = \frac{700 \times 773}{2388.51}$$

$$T_3 = 22654 \text{ K}$$

Using the equation of change of entropy,

$$s_3 - s_2 = mc_p \cdot \log_e \frac{T_3}{T_2} - mR \cdot \log_e \frac{p_3}{p_2}$$

$$= 1 \times 1.006 \log \frac{226.54}{773} - 1 \times 0.289 \log \frac{700}{2388.51}$$

$$= -1.23472 - (-0.3547)$$

$$= \textbf{-0.88002 kJ/kg·K (Decrease)}$$

**Problem 3.21:** A closed system of 2 kg of air initially at pressure 5 bar and temperature 227°C, expands reversibly to pressure 2 bar following the law $pV^{1.25}$ = constant. Assuming air as an ideal gas, determine the work done and heat transferred.

**Solution: Given:**

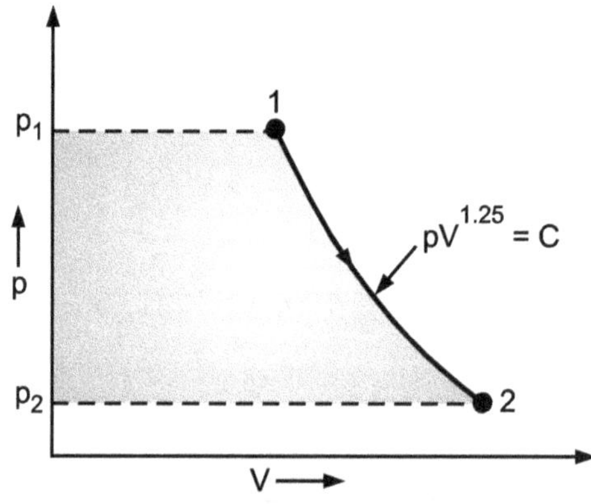


**Fig. 3.23: p-V diagram**

Mass = m = 2 kg, $p_1$ = 5 bar, $T_2$ = 227°C = 500 K, $p_2$ = 2 bar and $pV^{1.25}$ = constant.
Determine: (i) Work done, (ii) Heat transferred.

For the process, $\quad pV^{1.25} = C$

$$p_1 V_1^{1.25} = p_2 V_2^{1.25}$$

$$\therefore \quad \frac{T_2}{T_1} = \left(\frac{p_2}{p_1}\right)^{\frac{1.25 - 1}{1.25}}$$

$$\therefore \quad T_2 = T_1 \left[\frac{p_2}{p_1}\right]^{\frac{0.25}{1.25}}$$

$$= (2274273) \left[\frac{2}{5}\right]^{\frac{0.25}{1.25}}$$

$$= (500) \times (0.4)^{0.2}$$

$$T_2 = \mathbf{416.28\ K}$$

and at point 1, $\quad p_1 V_1 = mRT_1$

$$\therefore \quad V_1 = \frac{mRT_1}{p_1} = \frac{2 \times 287 \times 500}{5 \times 10^5} = \mathbf{0.574\ m^3}$$

and $\qquad p_1 V_1^{1.25} = p_2 V_2^{1.25}$

$$\therefore \quad V_2 = V_1 \,(p_1/p_2)^{1/1.25}$$

$$= 0.574 \left(\frac{5}{2}\right)^{1/1.25}$$

$$= 0.574 \times (2.5)^{0.8}$$

$$V_2 = 1.195\ m^3$$

**(i) Work done (w):**

$$w = \frac{p_1 V_1 - p_2 V_2}{n - 1}$$

$$= \frac{mR\,(T_1 - T_2)}{n - 1}$$

$$= \frac{2 \times 0.287 \times (500 - 416.28)}{1.25 - 1}$$

$$w = \mathbf{192.22\ kJ}$$

**(ii) Heat transferred (q):**

$$q = m \cdot c_p \left(\frac{n - \gamma}{n - 1}\right)(T_2 - T_1)$$

$$= 2 \times 0.743 \times \left(\frac{1.25 - 1.4}{1.25 - 1}\right)(416.28 - 500)$$

$$q = \mathbf{74.64\ kJ}$$

**Problem 3.22:** 1 kg of nitrogen at a temperature of 155°C occupies a volume of 0.3 m$^3$. The gas undergoes constant pressure expansion to a volume of 0.4 m$^3$. The gas is then expanded isothermally to a volume of 0.5 m$^3$. Determine change of entropy for which process and total change of entropy. Represent the process on p-V and T-s diagrams. Take:

$$c_v = 0.743 \text{ kJ/kg·K}$$

$$R = 0.297 \text{ kJ/kg·K}$$

**Solution: Given Data:** m = 1 kg, $T_1$ = 155°C = 428 K, $V_1$ = 0.3 m$^3$, $V_2$ = 0.4 m$^3$, $V_3$ = 0.5 m$^3$.

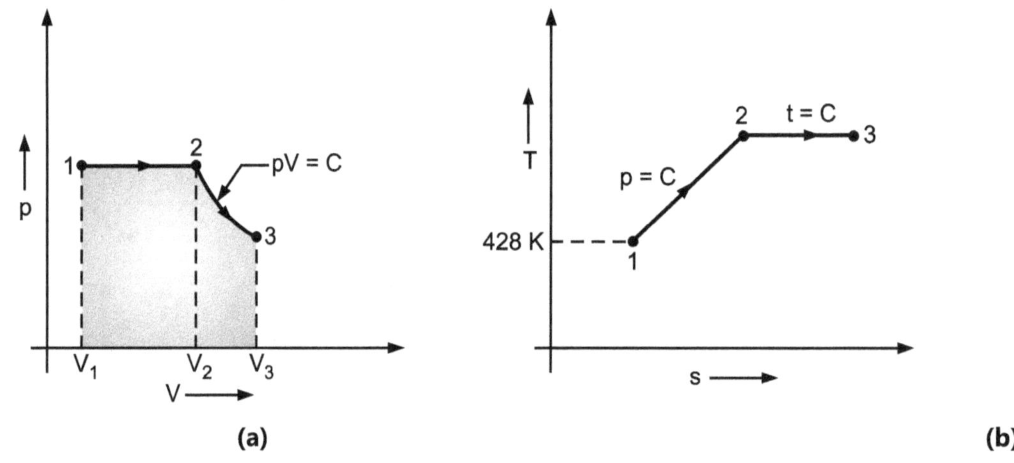


**Fig. 3.24: p-V and T-s diagrams**

**At state point 1:**

$$p_1 V_1 = mRT_1$$

$$\therefore \quad p_1 = \frac{mRT_1}{V_1} = \frac{1 \times 297 \times 428}{0.3}$$

$$\therefore \quad p_1 = 4.2372 \text{ bar}$$

From characteristic gas equation,

$$\frac{p_1 V_1}{T_1} = \frac{p_2 V_2}{T_2}$$

$$\therefore \quad T_2 = T_1 \cdot \frac{V_2}{V_1} \qquad\qquad (\because p_1 = p_2)$$

$$= 428 \times \frac{0.4}{0.3}$$

$$= 570.67 \text{ K}$$

Change in entropy for 1-2 process,

$$s_2 - s_1 = mR \log_e \frac{V_2}{V_1} + mc_v \log_e \frac{T_2}{T_1}$$

$$= 1 \times 0.297 \log_e \frac{0.4}{0.3} + 1 \times 0.743 \times \log_e \frac{570.67}{428}$$

$$= 0.08544 + 0.213752$$

$$= 0.2992 \text{ kJ/kg·K}$$

**For process 2-3,**

$$T_2 = T_3 = 570.67 \text{ K}$$

Change in entropy for 2-3 process,

$$s_3 - s_2 = mR \log_e \frac{V_3}{V_2} + mc_v \log_e \frac{T_3}{T_2}$$

$$= 1 \times 0.297 \log_e \frac{0.5}{0.4} + 1 \times 0.743 \times \log_e \frac{570.67}{570.67}$$

$$= 0.06627 \text{ kJ/kg·K}$$

Overall change in entropy,

$$s_3 - s_1 = (s_2 - s_1) + (s_3 - s_2)$$

$$= 0.2992 + 0.06627$$

$$= \mathbf{0.36547 \text{ kJ/kg·K}}$$

$\therefore$　Total change of entropy = 0.36547 kJ/kg·K.

---

**Problem 3.23:** 1 m$^3$ of an ideal gas expands polytropically from a pressure of 10 bar and 300°C to 1 bar. Find work done; heat; change of I.E., change of enthalpy assuming index of expansion, n = 1.3.

Take R = 0.287 kJ/kg·K, c$_p$ = 1.005 kJ/kg·K, $\gamma$ = 1.4

**Solution: Given data:** V$_1$ = 1 m$^3$, p$_1$ = 10 bar, T$_1$ = 300°C = 573 K, p$_2$ = 1 bar, n = 1.3.

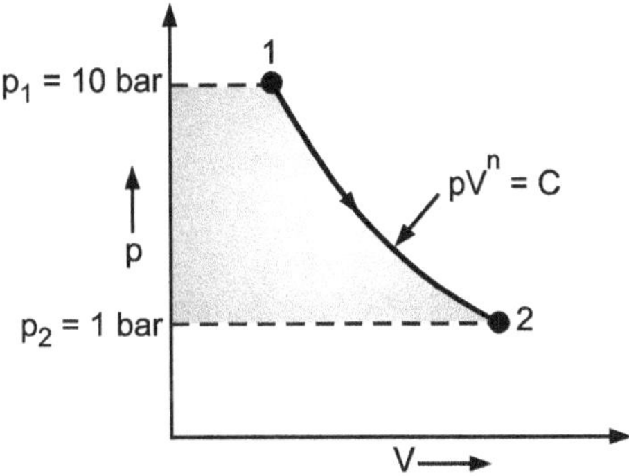


**Fig. 3.25: p-V diagram**

$$p_1 V_1 = m R T_1$$

and

$$p_1 V_1^n = p_2 V_2^n$$

$$V_2 = \left(\frac{p_1}{p_2}\right)^{\frac{1}{n}} \times V_1$$

$$= \left(\frac{10}{1}\right)^{\frac{1}{1.3}} \times 1$$

$$= 5.8780 \ m^3$$

And

$$\frac{T_2}{T_1} = \left(\frac{p_1}{p_2}\right)^{\frac{n-1}{n}}$$

$$\therefore \qquad T_2 = T_1 \left(\frac{p_2}{p_1}\right)^{\frac{n-1}{n}}$$

$$= 573 \left(\frac{1}{10}\right)^{\frac{1.3-1}{1.3}}$$

$$= 336.81 \ K$$

$$\text{Work done} = w = \frac{mR \cdot (T_1 - T_2)}{n - 1}$$

$$= \frac{1 \times 0.287 \times (573 - 336.81)}{1.3 - 1}$$

$$= 225.955 \ kJ/kg$$

$$\text{Heat transferred, } q = \left(\frac{\gamma - n}{\gamma - 1}\right) \times \text{Work done}$$

$$= \left(\frac{1.4 - 1.3}{1.4 - 1}\right) \times 225.955$$

$$= 56.488 \ kJ/kg$$

$$\text{Change in I.E.} = \Delta u = m c_v (T_2 - T_1)$$

$$= 1 \times 0.718 \times (336.81 - 573)$$

$$u_2 - u_1 = -169.58 \ kJ/kg$$

Change in enthalpy $(\Delta h)$,

$$\Delta h = m c_p \cdot (T_2 - T_1) = 1 \times 1.005 \times (336.81 - 573)$$

$$= -237.37 \ kJ/kg$$

**Problem 3.24:** A gas has a density of 1.875 kg/m$^3$ at a pressure of 1 bar and with a temperature of 15°C. A mass of 0.9 kg of the gas requires a heat transfer of 175 kJ to raise the temperature from 15°C to 250°C, while pressure of the gas remains constant.

Determine:

   (i)   Characteristic gas constant of the gas

   (ii)  $c_p$ of the gas

   (iii)  $c_v$ of the gas

   (iv)  Change of internal energy

   (v)  Work transfer.

**Solution:**

**(i) For a gas,**

$$pV = mRT$$

$$R = \frac{pV}{mT} = \frac{100 \times 1}{1.875 \times 288} = \mathbf{0.185 \ kJ/kg \cdot K}$$

**(ii) For constant pressure heating,**

$$\text{Heat transfer} = mc_p \cdot (T_2 - T_1)$$

$$\therefore \qquad 175 = 0.9 \times c_p \,(250 - 15)$$

$$\therefore \qquad \mathbf{c_p = 0.828 \ kJ/kg \cdot K}$$

**(iii)** Now,

$$c_p - c_v = R$$

$$\therefore \qquad c_v = c_p - R = 0.828 - 0.185$$

$$\mathbf{c_v = 0.643 \ kJ/kg \cdot K}$$

**(iv)** Change of internal energy is,

$$mc_v \,(T_2 - T_1) = 0.9 \times 0.643 \times (250 - 15)$$

$$= 0.9 \times 0.643 \times 235$$

$$\Delta u = 136 \ kJ$$

**(v)**

$$q = \Delta u + w$$

$$\therefore \qquad w = q - \Delta u$$

$$= 175 - 136$$

$$= \mathbf{39 \ kJ}$$

**Problem 3.25:** 1 kg of certain working substance undergoes a reversible constant pressure process at 1.2 bar during which its volume changes from 1 m$^3$ to 1.8 m$^3$ and temperature changes from 50°C to 370°C. The specific heat for the substance at constant pressure is given by,

$$c_p = \left[1.1 + \frac{40}{T + 30}\right] kJ/kg \cdot °C$$

where, T is in °C. Find heat supplied, work done, change in internal energy and change in enthalpy.

**Solution: Given Data:**

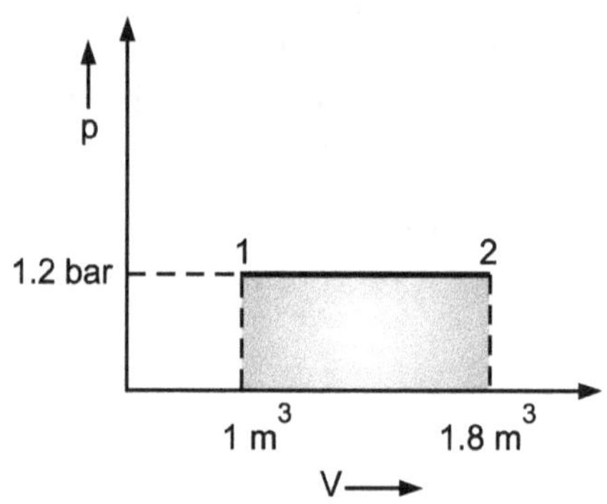



**Fig. 3.26: Constant pressure process**

$T_1 = 50°C$ and $T_2 = 370°C$

For constant pressure process,

$$\delta q = dh$$

$\therefore$

$$\delta q = dh = \int_{T_1}^{T_2} mc_p \cdot dT$$

$$= \int_{T_1}^{T_2} 1 \times \left[ 1.1 + \frac{40}{T + 30} \right] \cdot dT$$

$$= [1.1]_{T_1 = 50}^{T_2 = 370} + 40 \, \{log_e (T + 30)\}_{T_1 = 50}^{T_2 = 370}$$

Heat supplied = 416.38 kJ = Change in enthalpy

Also,  Work done = $p (V_2 - V_1) = 120 (1.8 - 1) = 96$ kJ

According to first law of thermodynamics,

$$q - w = \Delta u = \text{Change in internal energy}$$

$\therefore$  Change in internal energy = $\Delta u = 416.38 - 96$

$$= 320.38 \text{ kJ}$$

---

**Problem 3.26:** Helium gas is expanded polytropically from 4 bar, 300°C to 1 bar such that final volume is 2.5 times the volume at inlet. Velocity of the gas at exit is 50 m/sec.

Find out:

(i)  Index of expansion

(ii)  Work done/kg

(iii)  Mass flow rate to produce 1 MW

(iv)  Heat transfer

(v)  Exit area of turbine if $c_p = 5.193$ kJ/kg·K

**Solution: Given:**

$$p_1 \ = \ 4 \text{ bar} = 400 \text{ kPa}$$

$$p_2 \ = \ 1 \text{ bar} = 100 \text{ kPa}$$

$$T_1 \ = \ 300°C = 573 \text{ K}$$

$$V_2 \ = \ 2.5 \ V_1$$

$$c_2 \ = \ 50 \text{ m/s}$$

**(i)  For polytropic process:**

$$p_1 V_1^n \ = \ p_2 V_2^n$$

Taking log on both sides,

$$\log_e p_1 + n \log_e V_1 \ = \ \log_e p_2 + n \log_e V_2$$

$$\therefore \qquad n \ = \ \frac{\log_e (p_2/p_1)}{\log_e (V_1/V_2)} = \frac{\log_e (1/4)}{\log_e (1/2.5)}$$

$$\mathbf{n \ = \ 1.51}$$

**(ii)  Work done:**

$$\text{W.D.} = w \ = \ \frac{n}{n-1} p_1 V_1 \left[ 1 - (p_2/p_1)^{\frac{n-1}{n}} \right]$$

$$\frac{\text{W.D}}{\text{kg}} = w \ = \ \frac{n}{n-1} RT_1 \left[ 1 - (p_2/p_1)^{\frac{n-1}{n}} \right]$$

$$= \ \frac{1.51}{1.51-1} \times 0.287 \times 573 \left[ 1 - \left(\frac{100}{400}\right)^{\frac{1.51-1}{1.51}} \right]$$

$$w \ = \ \mathbf{182 \text{ kJ/kg}}$$

**(iii) Mass flow rate to produce 1 MW power:**

$$= \ \frac{1000}{182} = \mathbf{5.493 \text{ kg/sec}}$$

**(iv) Heat transferred:**

$$q \ = \ c_v \left(\frac{\gamma - n}{1 - n}\right) (T_2 - T_1)$$

$$\frac{T_2}{T_1} \ = \ (p_2/p_1)^{\frac{n-1}{n}} = \left(\frac{100}{400}\right)^{\frac{1.51-1}{1.51}} = 0.626$$

$$\therefore \qquad T_2 \ = \ 0.626 \times 300 = 358.765 \text{ K}$$

Also, $\qquad c_v \ = \ c_p - R = 5.193 - 0.287 = 4.906 \text{ kJ/kg·K}$

$$q \;=\; 4.906 \times \left[\frac{1.4 - 1.51}{1 - 1.51}\right][358.765 - 573]$$

$$q \;=\; \mathbf{-226.694 \ kW}$$

Negative sign indicates that heat is rejected.

**(v) Outlet area of turbine:**

$$p_2 V_2 \;=\; mRT_2$$

Let m = 1.

$$\therefore \qquad V_2 \;=\; \frac{RT_2}{p_2} = \frac{0.287 \times 358.765}{100}$$

$$V_2 \;=\; 1.03 \ \text{m}^3/\text{kg}$$

$$\therefore \qquad \text{Density} = \rho_2 = \frac{1}{V_2} \;=\; \frac{1}{1.03} = 0.971 \ \text{kg/m}^3$$

$$\text{The mass flow rate} \;=\; \text{Area} \times \text{Velocity} \times \text{Density}$$

$$5.493 \;=\; A \times 50 \times 0.971$$

$$\therefore \qquad A \;=\; \mathbf{0.113 \ m^2}$$

**Problem 3.27:** 0.04 m$^3$ of nitrogen contained in a cylinder behind a piston is initially at 1.05 bar and 15°C. The gas is compressed isothermally and reversibly until the pressure is 4.8 bar. Calculate:

(i) Change of entropy, (ii) Heat flow, (iii) Work done.

Sketch the process on a p-v and T-s diagram. Assume nitrogen to act as a perfect gas. Molecular weight of nitrogen = 28.

**Solution: Given Data:**

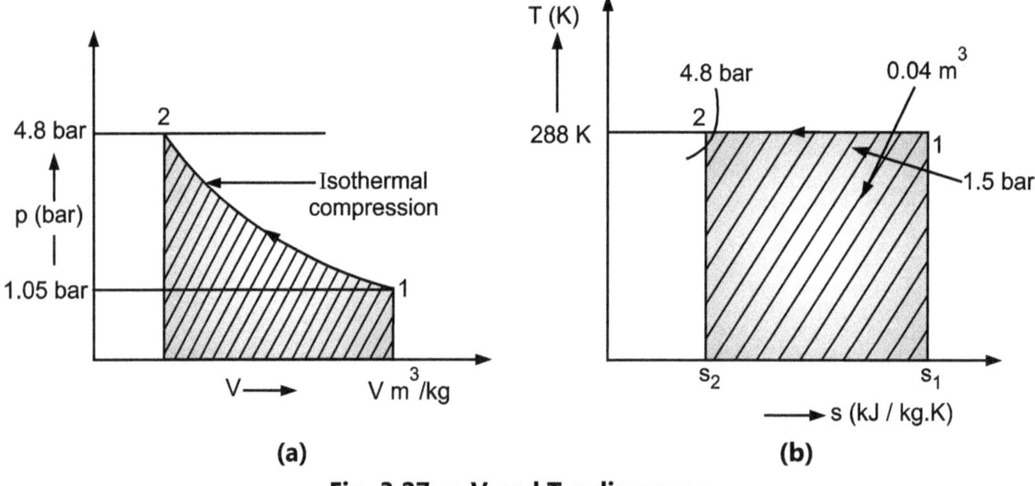


**Fig. 3.27: p-V and T-s diagrams**

$$V_1 = 0.04 \text{ m}^3$$
$$p_1 = 1.05 \text{ bar} = 1.05 \times 10^5 \text{ N/m}^2$$
$$T_1 = 15°C = 15 + 273 = 288 \text{ K}$$
$$p_2 = 4.8 \text{ bar} = 4.8 \times 10^5 \text{ N/m}^2$$
$$T_2 = T_1 = 288 \text{ K}$$

The process is shown on p-V and T-s diagrams as below.

Characteristic gas constant

$$R = \frac{\text{Universal gas constant}}{\text{Molecular weight}} = \frac{R_o}{M} = \frac{8.314}{28} = 297 \text{ N-m/kg·K}$$

Now, we have $\quad p_1 V_1 = mRT_1$

$$\therefore \quad m = \frac{p_1 V_1}{RT_1} = \frac{1.05 \times 10^5 \times 0.04}{297 \times 288} = 0.0491 \text{ kg}$$

**(i) The change of entropy:**

$$s_2 - s_1 = mR \ln \frac{p_1}{p_2}$$

$$= 0.0491 \times \frac{297}{1000} \times \ln \left( \frac{1.05}{4.8} \right)$$

$$= -0.02216 \text{ kJ/K}$$

$\therefore \quad$ Decrease in entropy, $s_1 - s_2 = $ **0.02216 kJ/K**

**(ii)** 			**Heat rejected** $=$ Shaded area on T-s diagram

$$= T (s_1 - s_2)$$

$$= 288 \times 0.02216 = \textbf{6.382 kJ}$$

**(iii) For an isothermal process,**

$$w = q = 6.382 \text{ kJ}$$

$\therefore \quad$ Work done on air $= $ **6.382 kJ**

**Problem 3.28:** 1 kg of air is allowed to expand reversibly in a cylinder behind a piston in such a way that the temperature remains constant at 260°C while the volume is doubled. The piston is then moved in, and heat is rejected by the air reversibly at constant pressure until the volume is the same as it was initially. Calculate the net heat flow and the overall change of entropy. Sketch the processes on a T-s diagram.

**Solution: Given Data:**

$$m = 1 \text{ kg}$$
$$T_1 = T_2 = 260$$

$$= 260 + 273$$

$$260 = 533 \text{ K}$$

$$V_1 = V_3$$

$$V_2 = 2V_1$$

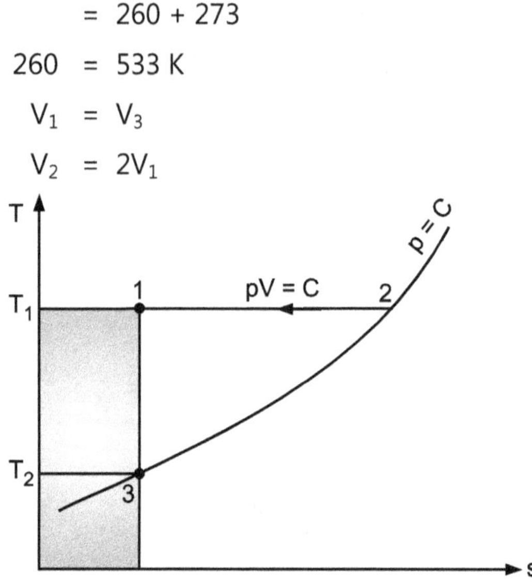


**Fig. 3.28: T-s diagram**

**For process 1-2:** pV = C

$$\text{Heat transfer, } q = mC\,(T_2 - T_1)$$

$$\mathbf{q_{12} = 0 \text{ kJ}}$$

$$\text{Change in entropy, } \Delta s_{1-2} = mR \ln\left(\frac{V_2}{V_1}\right)$$

For air,  $\quad c_p = 1.005 \text{ kJ/kg·K}, \ c_v = 0.718 \text{ kJ/kg} + R = \text{kJ/kg·K}$

$$\therefore \quad \Delta s_{1-2} = 1 \times 0.287 \times \ln\left(\frac{2V_1}{V_1}\right) = 0.1989 \text{ kJ/K}$$

**For process 2-3:** p = C

$$\frac{V_2}{T_2} = \frac{V_3}{T_3}$$

Now,  $\quad V_2 = 2V_1$

and  $\quad V_3 = V_1$

$$\frac{2V_1}{T_2} = \frac{V_1}{3}$$

$$\therefore \quad T_3 = \frac{T_2}{2} = \frac{533}{2} = 266.5 \text{ K}$$

$$\therefore \quad \text{Heat transfer, } q_{2-3} = m \cdot c_p\,(T_3 - T_2) = 1 \times 1.005 \times (266.5 - 533)$$

$$= -267.83 \text{ kJ}$$

$$\Delta s_{2-3} \;=\; m \cdot c_v \cdot \ln\left(\frac{T_3}{T_2}\right) \;=\; 1 \times 0.718 \times \ln\left(\frac{266.5}{533}\right)$$

$$\Delta s_{2-3} \;=\; -0.4976 \text{ kJ/K}$$

$\therefore$    Overall heat transfer $\;=\; q_{1-2} + q_{2-3}$

$$\Delta q \;=\; \textbf{-267.83 kJ} \text{ (Heat is rejected)}$$

and overall entropy change $\;=\; \Delta s_{1-2} + \Delta s_{2-3}$

$$= 0.1989 - 0.4976$$

$$\Delta s \;=\; \textbf{-0.2987 kJ/K} \text{ (Entropy decreases)}$$

**Problem 3.29:** Air expands in a cylinder in a reversible adiabatic process from 13.73 bar to 1.96 bar. If the final temperature is to be 27°C, what would be the initial temperature? Also calculate the change in specific enthalpy, heat and work transfer per kg of air.

**Solution: Given Data:**

$$p_1 \;=\; 13.73 \text{ bar}$$
$$p_2 \;=\; 1.96 \text{ bar}$$
$$T_2 = 27°C \;=\; 27 + 273 = 300 \text{ K}$$
$$T_1 \;=\; ?$$
$$\Delta h, \Delta q \text{ and } \Delta w \;=\; ?$$
$$pV^\gamma \;=\; C$$

For reversible and adiabatic process,

$$\frac{T_2}{T_1} \;=\; \left(\frac{p_2}{p_1}\right)^{\frac{\gamma-1}{\gamma}}$$

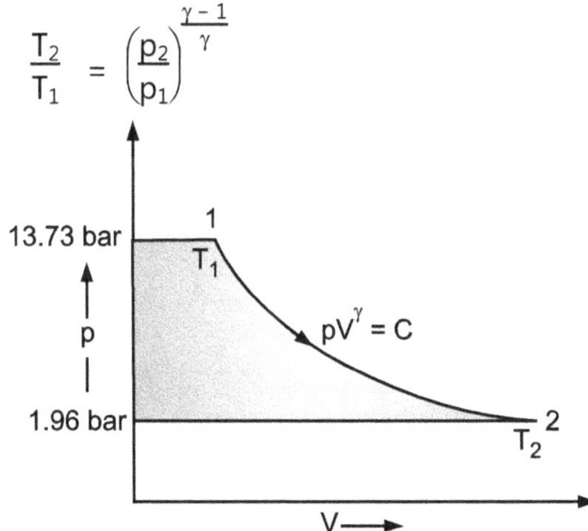


**Fig. 3.29: p-V diagram**

For air, $\gamma = 1.4$, $c_p = 1.005$ kJ/kg·K and $c_v = 0.718$ kJ/kg·K

$R = c_p - c_v = 0.287$ kJ/kg·K

$$\therefore \qquad \frac{T_2}{T_1} \;=\; \left(\frac{1.96}{13.73}\right)^{\frac{1.4-1}{1.4}}$$

$$= \textbf{0.5734}$$

$$\therefore \qquad T_1 = \frac{T_2}{0.5734} = \frac{300}{0.5734} = 523.2 \text{ K or } \mathbf{250.2°C}$$

Change of specific enthalpy,

$$\Delta h = c_p (T_2 - T_1) = 1.005 \times (300 - 523.2)$$
$$= \mathbf{-224.316 \text{ kJ/kg}}$$

$$\text{Heat transfer, } \Delta q = c_v (T_2 - T_1)$$
$$= 0$$

$$\text{Work transfer} = \frac{R (T_2 - T_1)}{1 - \gamma} = \frac{0.287 \times (300 - 523.2)}{1 - 1.4}$$
$$= \mathbf{160.146 \text{ kJ/kg}}$$

**Problem 3.30:** A cylinder contains 0.12 m$^3$ of air at 1 bar and 90°C. It is compressed to 0.3 m$^3$, the final pressure being 6 bar. Find the index of compression, increase in internal energy and heat transfer. R = 0.287 kJ/kg·K, $c_v$ = 0.717 kJ/kg·K.

**Solution: Given Data:**

$$p_1 = 1 \text{ bar}$$
$$V_1 = 0.12 \text{ m}^3$$
$$T_1 = 90°C = 90 + 273 = 363 \text{ K}$$
$$V_2 = 0.3 \text{ m}^3$$
$$p_2 = 6 \text{ bar}$$
$$R = 0.287 \text{ kJ/kg·K}$$
$$c_v = 0.717 \text{ kJ/kg·K}$$

Now, Index of compression,

$$n = \frac{\ln (p_2/p_1)}{\ln (V_2/V_1)} = \frac{\ln (6/1)}{\ln (0.3/0.12)}$$
$$n = \mathbf{1.955}$$

For polytropic process,

$$\frac{T_2}{T_1} = \left(\frac{V_1}{V_2}\right)^{1-n} = \left(\frac{p_2}{p_1}\right)^{\frac{n-1}{n}}$$

$$\frac{T_2}{363} = \left(\frac{6}{1}\right)^{\frac{1.955-1}{1.955}}$$

$$\therefore \qquad T_2 = 871 \text{ K}$$

$$\text{Now, mass of air,} \qquad m = \frac{p_1 V_1}{R T_1} = \frac{1 \times 10^5 \times 0.12}{0.287 \times 10^3 \times 363}$$
$$= \mathbf{0.1152 \text{ kg}}$$

$\therefore$    Change in internal energy,

$$\Delta u = mc_v (T_2 - T_1) = 0.1152 \times 0.717 \times (871 - 363)$$

$$= \textbf{41.96 kJ}$$

$$q = \Delta u + w$$

Now,    $$w = \frac{p_1 V_1 + p_2 V_2}{n - 1} = \frac{mR (T_1 - T_2)}{n - 1} = \frac{0.1152 \times 0.287 \times (363 - 871)}{(1.955 - 1)}$$

$$= \textbf{-17.59 kJ}$$

$\therefore$    $$q = 41.96 - 17.59 = 24.37 \text{ kJ}$$

## EXERCISE

1.  Define ideal gas (perfect gas). Derive characteristic equation of a perfect gas.

2.  Define specific gas constant. What are its units?

3.  Define universal gas constant and give its units. What is the use of it?

4.  Define enthalpy. Is it a function of temperature? Give reasons.

5.  Define $c_p$ and $c_v$. Obtain the relation between them.

6.  Why $c_p$ is always greater than $c_v$?

7.  Obtain the relation between $c_p$, $c_v$ and R.

8.  Represent the following processes on p-v and T-s diagrams
    (a) Isochoric process        (b)   Isobaric process
    (c) Isothermal process       (d)   Reversible adiabatic process.

9.  Define polytropic process. Explain how all the remaining processes can be obtained from polytropic process for different values of n.

10. Derive an expression for work done and heat supplied for polytropic process for non-flow systems.

11. Define polytropic specific heat. What is the importance of its negative sign?

12. Explain the meaning of adiabatic process with suitable examples.

13. For reversible adiabatic process, prove that $pv^\gamma = C$.

14. What are the assumptions made in the analysis of air standard cycles?

## PROBLEMS FOR PRACTICE

1.  50 litres of air at 1.013 bar and 100°C is compressed to 28 bar. Volume of air at the end of polytropic compression is found to be 4 litres. Air is now heated at constant volume till pressure rises to 56 bar. Assuming $c_p$ = 1.00 kJ/kg-K and $c_v$ = 0.71 kJ/kg·K, determine (i) polytropic index of compression, (ii) mass of air, (iii) final temperature.

$$(\textbf{Ans.} \ n = 1.31, \ m = 21.35 \text{ kg}, \ T = 1632.2 \text{ K})$$

2.  2.5 kg of oxygen at a pressure of 1 bar and temperature 27°C is compressed isentropically to a pressure of 15 bar. The gas is then cooled at constant volume till it reaches its original pressure. Calculate (i) heat transferred, (ii) work done.

**(Ans.** Q = 1000.6 kJ, W = − 570.4 kJ)

3.  10 kg of air at 40 bar and 500°C is heated at constant pressure to a temperature of 1250°C. It is then expanded to six times its volume at the end of heat addition. The expansion follows the law $pv^{1.3}$ = constant. Calculate (a) change in internal energy, (b) change of enthalpy, (c) work done, (d) heat transfer in each process and for the overall process. Take $c_p$ = 1.0045 kJ/kg·K, $c_v$ = 0.7175 kJ/kg·K.

4.  A quantity of gas occupies a volume of 0.28 $m^3$ at 1.03 bar and 21°C. The gas is compressed isothermally to a pressure of 5.15 bar and is then expanded adiabatically to its initial volume of 0.28 $m^3$. Determine (i) heat transferred in kJ, (ii) change in internal energy during expansion in kJ, (iii) mass of gas in kJ.

Assume $\gamma$ = 1.4 and $c_p$ = 0.921 kJ/kg·K.

## UNIVERSITY QUESTION PAPERS

### DEC. 2013

1.  Determine the total enthalpy and total Internal energy for the following cases:     **[6]**
    (i)   3kg of steam at 11 bar and 60% dry.
    (ii)  5kg of steam at 10 bar and 250°C.

2.  Explain heating of ice from −10°C to Super heated steam at 150°C and 1 atmospheric pressure on T–h Diagram (Show sensible heating and latent heating regions clearly).**[6]**

### DEC. 2014

1. Steam initially at 1.5 MPa, 300 deg. C expands isentropically in a steam turbine to 40 deg. C. Determine the ideal work output of the steam per kg of steam.     **[6]**

### MAY 2015

1.  Derive expression for the following quantities for an ideal gas  undergoing a constant temperature process:     **[6]**
    (i)   Non-Flow System-Work done, Change in internal energy, Heat transfer
    (ii)  Flow System—Work done, Heat transfer, Entropy change.

### MAY 2016

1.  Steam at a 6.87 bar, 205T, enters in an insulated nozzle with a velocity of 50 m/s. It leaves at a pressure of 1.37 bar and a velocity of 500 m/s. Determine the final enthalpy of steam.     **[6]**

2.  Draw the P-v diagram of various thermodynamic processes for ideal gas; clearly indicating polytrophic index or slope of each process.     **[6]**

# Chapter 4

# THERMODYNAMIC CYCLES

## 4.1 INTRODUCTION

Analysis of engine cycle is an important tool to design and study the internal combustion engines. A thermodynamic cycle consists of a series of processes through which the working fluid progresses (passes). In other words, a thermodynamic cycle implies a closed system with no exchange of matter with surroundings. Truly speaking internal combustion engine element operate on a thermodynamic cycle as it consists of an open system wherein a new fluid continuously enters the engine at one set of conditions and leaves at another condition. This is shown in Fig. 4.1

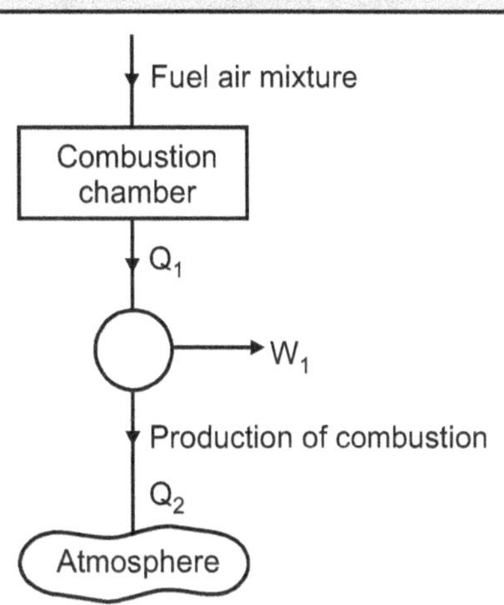


**Fig. 4.1: Internal combustion engine:**

**A block diagram**

An accurate analysis of an internal combustion engine is very difficult due to the complex chemical reactions that take place when fuel burns. Not only it involves friction between piston and cylinder walls, but also heat transfer between the gases and cylinder walls. Hence, it is an usual practice to analyse the cycle making some simplifying assumptions.

The two commonly employed approximation of an actual engine in order of their increasing accuracy are:

- Ideal or air standard cycle analysis.

- Fuel-air cycles analysis.

These two cycles are theoretical cycles.

Numerical result obtained by the above theoretical analysis are different from actual results due to above approximations. The results so obtained are not only for academic interests but have a great practical importance. The analysis of the theoretical cycle indicates the upper limit of the performance of an engine.

## 4.2 IDEAL OR AIR STANDARD CYCLE

Air standard cycles are defined as cycles using a perfect gas (ideal gas) as the working substance. Air is almost invariably used as the working fluid in internal combustion engines (I.C. engines). Air is assumed to behave as a perfect gas.

The **following assumptions are made in the analysis of standard cycles**:

- The working substance is a *perfect* gas, i.e. it follows the characteristic gas equation, $pv = mRT$.
- The working substance (fluid) is a fixed mass of air contained in a closed system.
- The physical constants of the working medium (substance) such as $c_p = 1.005$ kJ/kg·K, $c_v = 0.718$ kJ/kg·K and $\gamma = 1.4$ are taken in the calculations, for air.
- The specific heat of working substance is assumed constant.
- The working medium does not undergo chemical changes.
- Heat is supplied and rejected in a reversible manner and if necessary, can be supplied and rejected instantaneously. (In actual engine, energy is supplied by combustion of fuel and rejected by exhaust gases).
- The compression and expansion processes are reversible adiabatic (isentropic).
- The operation of the engine is frictionless.
- Kinetic and potential energies are neglected.

The work output, peak pressure, peak temperature and *thermal efficiency* based on ideal cycle are higher than those of actual engine.

Thermal efficiency is the ratio of work output to the heat supplied to the engine.

Mathematically, $$\eta_{th} = \frac{\text{Work output}}{\text{Heat supplied}}$$

Thermal efficiency is referred as **Air standard efficiency** for the cycle which uses air as the working substance.

## 4.3 OTTO CYCLE                                    [Dec. 10, 12, May 12]

It is also known as constant volume cycle. It consists of two constant volume processes and two reversible adiabatic processes.

This Otto cycle is the theoretical cycle for the spark - ignition engine.

The cycle is represented on p-v and T-s planes [Fig. 4.2 (a) and (b)].

In the air cycle analysis, the induction and exhaust processes, represented by lines $0 - 1$ and $1 - 0$ respectively are neglected. The work done during both the processes is equal and opposite and hence cancel each other.

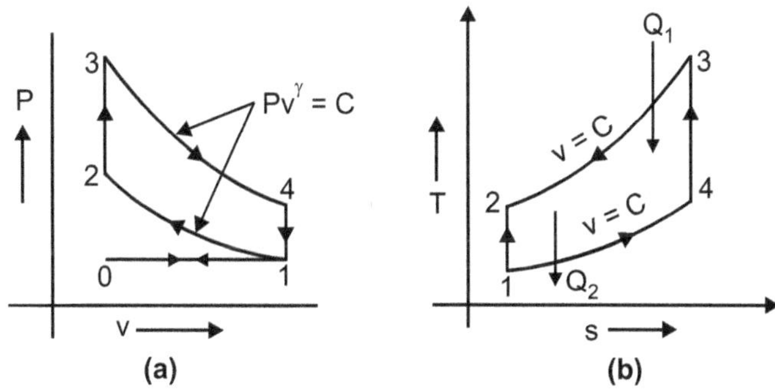


**Fig. 4.2: Otto Cycle on P-v and T-s diagram**

## Process 1-2:

Reversible adiabatic compression of the air. The piston moves from Bottom Dead Centre (BDC) position to the Top Dead Centre (TDC) position. No heat transfer takes place during the process.

## Process 2-3:

Heat is added at constant volume so that the state of air changes from point 2 to 3.

For unit mass of air, heat supplied,

$$Q = c_V (T_3 - T_2) \qquad \ldots \text{(i)}$$

## Process 3-4:

Isentropic (reversible adiabatic) expansion of the air takes place. During this process, piston moves from TDC position to BDC position. No heat transfer occurs during the process.

## Process 4-1:

The heat is rejected at constant volume. It is assumed that the heat rejection occurs instantaneously.

For unit mass of air, heat rejected,

$$Q_2 = c_V (T_4 - T_1) \qquad \ldots \text{(ii)}$$

$$\therefore \quad \text{Work done} = \text{Heat added} - \text{Heat rejected}$$

$$= c_V (T_3 - T_2) - c_V (T_4 - T_1)$$

$$\text{Thermal efficiency} = \frac{\text{Work done}}{\text{Heat supplied}}$$

$$= \frac{c_V (T_3 - T_2) - c_V (T_4 - T_1)}{c_V (T_3 - T_2)}$$

$$= 1 - \frac{(T_4 - T_1)}{(T_3 - T_2)} \qquad \ldots \text{(iii)}$$

$$\text{Now, compression ratio} = \frac{v_1}{v_2} = r_c$$

$$\text{Expansion ratio} = \frac{v_4}{v_3} = r_e$$

Here, $r_c = r_e = r$

For ideal gas,    $pv = RT$ and $pv^\gamma = C$

$$\frac{p_1 v_1}{T_1} = \frac{p_2 v_2}{T_2} \qquad\qquad p_1 v_1^\gamma = p_2 v_2^\gamma$$

$$\frac{T_2}{T_1} = \frac{p_2 v_2}{p_1 v_1} \qquad\qquad \frac{p_2}{p_1} = \left(\frac{v_1}{v_2}\right)^\gamma$$

$$= \left(\frac{v_1}{v_2}\right)^\gamma \cdot \frac{v_2}{v_1}$$

$$\therefore \quad \frac{T_2}{T_1} = \left(\frac{v_1}{v_2}\right)^{\gamma-1}$$

$$= \left(\frac{v_4}{v_3}\right)^{\gamma-1} = \frac{T_3}{T_4} = r^{\gamma-1}$$

$$\therefore \quad T_3 = T_4 \cdot r^{\gamma-1} \text{ and } T_2 = T_1 \cdot r^{\gamma-1}$$

Put these values of $T_3$ and $T_2$ in equation (iv).

$$\therefore \quad \text{Thermal efficiency} = 1 - \frac{(T_4 - T_1)}{(T_4 - T_1)\, r^{\gamma-1}}$$

$$\eta_{thermal} = 1 - \frac{1}{r^{\gamma-1}} \qquad\qquad \dots \text{(iv)}$$

## Mean Effective Pressure (mep) of Otto Cycle:

See Fig. 4.3.

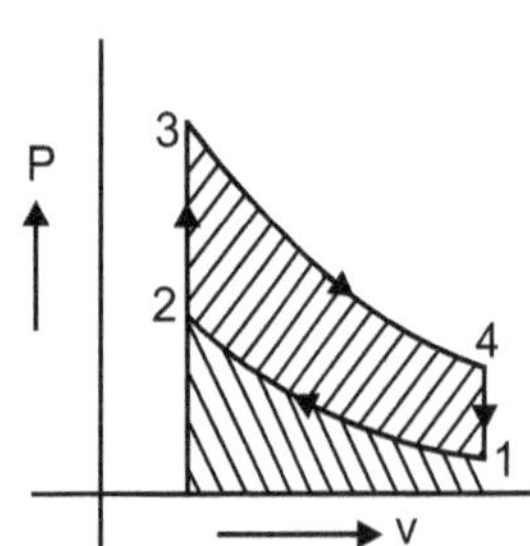


**Fig. 4.3: Otto cycle on P-v plot**

Let clearance volume,

$$v_2 = v_3 = 1$$

and

$$v_1 = v_4 = r$$

Also

$$\frac{p_3}{p_2} = \frac{p_4}{p_1} = \alpha$$

$$\frac{p_2}{p_1} = \frac{p_3}{p_4} = r^\gamma$$

Work done = Area of the P-v diagram

$$= \frac{P_3 v_3 - P_4 v_4}{\gamma - 1} - \frac{P_2 v_2 - P_1 v_1}{\gamma - 1}$$

$$= \frac{1}{\gamma - 1}\left[ P_4 v_4 \left(\frac{P_3}{P_4} \cdot \frac{v_3}{v_4} - 1\right) - P_1 v_1 \left(\frac{P_2 v_2}{P_1 v_1} - 1\right) \right]$$

$$v_4 = r, \text{ because } v_4 = v_1 = r$$

$$= \frac{1}{\gamma - 1}\left[P_4 \cdot r\left(\frac{P_3}{P_4 \cdot r} - 1\right) - P_1 \, r\left(\frac{P_2}{P_1 \, r} - 1\right)\right]$$

$$\frac{P_3}{P_4} = r^\gamma \text{ and } \frac{P_2}{P_1} = r^\gamma$$

$$= \frac{r}{\gamma - 1}\left[P_4\,(r^{\gamma - 1} - 1) - P_1\,(r^{\gamma - 1} - 1)\right]$$

$$= \frac{r}{\gamma - 1}(r^{\gamma - 1} - 1) \cdot (P_4 - P_1), \quad \frac{P_4}{P_1} = \alpha$$

$$= \frac{r}{\gamma - 1} \cdot P_1\,(\alpha - 1)\,(r^{\gamma - 1} - 1)$$

Length of the diagram = r − 1

$$\therefore \qquad \text{mep} \;=\; \frac{\text{Area of the P-v diagram}}{\text{Length of diagram}}$$

$$= \frac{P_1 \cdot r\,(\alpha - 1)\,(r^{\gamma - 1} - 1)}{(\gamma - 1)\,(r - 1)} \qquad\qquad \dots \text{(v)}$$

## SOLVED PROBLEMS

**Problem 4.1 (Air Standard Efficiency of Otto Cycle):** The bore and stroke of an engine working on the Otto cycle are 17 cm and 30 cm respectively. The clearance volume is 0.002025 m³. Calculate the air standard efficiency.

**Solution:** d = $17 \times 10^{-2}$ m, L = 0.3 m, $v_c$ = 0.002025 m³.

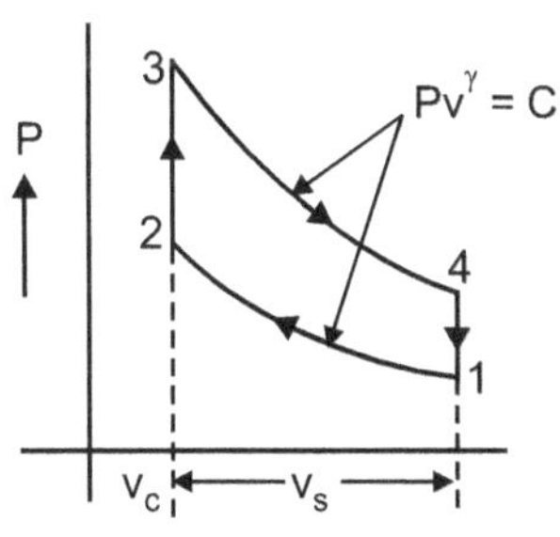


**Fig. 4.4**

$$\text{Swept volume} \;=\; \left(\frac{\pi}{4}\right) d^2 \cdot L = \left(\frac{\pi}{4}\right)(0.17)^2 \times 0.3$$

$$v_s \;=\; 6.8094 \times 10^{-3} \text{ m}^3$$

$$\text{Clearance volume} \;=\; v_c = 0.002025 \text{ m}^3$$

$$\text{Total cylinder volume} \;=\; v_1 = v_c + v_s$$

$$= 8.8344 \times 10^{-3} \text{ m}^3$$

$$\text{Compression ratio} \;=\; r = \frac{v_1}{v_c} = 4.36$$

$$\text{Air standard efficiency} \;=\; 1 - \frac{1}{r^{\gamma-1}} = 1 - \frac{1}{(4.36)^{1.4-1}}$$

$$= 0.445 \text{ or } 44.5\,\% \qquad\qquad \textbf{... Ans.}$$

**Problem 4.2 (Otto Cycle: P, v, T at Salient Points):** In an ideal Otto cycle, the compression ratio is 6. The initial pressure and temperature of the air are 1 bar and 373 K. The maximum pressure in the cycle is 35 bar. For 1 kg of air flow, calculate the values of pressure, temperature at the four salient points of the cycle. What is the ratio of heat supplied to the heat rejected?

Assume, for air, $R = 0.287$ kJ/kg·K, $\gamma = 1.4$.

**Solution: Given:** $r = 6$, $P_1 = 1$ bar, $T_1 = 373$ K, $P_3 = 35$ bar

**(i)  Point 1:**

To calculate $v_1$

$$P_1 v_1 = mRT_1, \; m = 1$$

$$\therefore \qquad v_1 \;=\; \frac{287 \times 373}{1 \times 10^5} = 1.0705 \text{ m}^3$$

$$P_1 = 1 \text{ bar}, \; v_1 = 1.0705 \text{ m}^3, \; T_1 = 373 \text{ K}$$

**(ii) Point 2:**
$$P_1 v_1^{\gamma} \;=\; P_2 v_2^{\gamma}$$

$$p_2 \;=\; p_1 \left(\frac{v_1}{v_2}\right)^{\gamma} = 1 \times (6)^{1.4} = \textbf{12.28 bar}$$

$$v_2 \;=\; \frac{v_1}{6} = \frac{1.0705}{6} = \textbf{0.1784 m}^3$$

$$\frac{P_1 v_1}{T_1} \;=\; \frac{P_2 v_2}{T_2} \;\therefore\; T_2 = \frac{P_2 v_2}{P_1 v_1} \cdot T_1$$

$$\therefore \qquad T_2 \;=\; \frac{12.28 \times 0.1784}{1 \times 1.0705} \times 373 = \textbf{763.4 K}$$

$$p_2 = 12.28 \text{ bar}, \; v_2 = 0.1784 \text{ m}^3, \; T_2 = 763.4 \text{ K}$$

**(iii) Point 3:**
$$v_3 \;=\; v_2 = 0.1784 \text{ m}^3$$

$$\frac{P_3}{T_3} \;=\; \frac{P_2}{T_2}$$

$$T_3 \;=\; \frac{P_3}{P_2} \cdot T_2 = \frac{35}{12.28} \times 763.4 = \textbf{2175.8 K}$$

$$\therefore \quad P_3 = 35 \text{ bar}, \; v_3 = 0.1784 \text{ m}^3, \; T_3 = 2175.8 \text{ K}$$

**(iv) Point 4:**
$$P_3 v_3^{\gamma} \;=\; P_4 V_4^{\gamma}$$

$$\therefore \qquad P_4 = P_3 \left(\frac{v_3}{v_4}\right)^{\gamma} = 35 \left(\frac{1}{6}\right)^{1.4} = \textbf{2.85 bar}$$

$$v_4 = v_1 = 1.0705 \text{ m}^3$$

$$\frac{P_4}{T_4} = \frac{P_1}{T_1} \quad \therefore \ T_4 = \frac{P_4}{P_1} \cdot T_1 = \mathbf{1062.5 \ K}$$

$\therefore \quad P_4 = 2.85$ bar, $v_4 = 1.0705 \text{ m}^3$, $T_4 = 1062.5$ K

$$\text{Heat supplied} = C_V (T_3 - T_2)$$

$$= \frac{R}{\gamma - 1} (T_3 - T_2) \text{ where, } C_V = \frac{R}{\gamma - 1} = \mathbf{0.7175}$$

$$= \frac{0.287}{1.4 - 1} (2175.8 - 763.4) = \mathbf{1013.4 \ kJ/kg}$$

$$\text{Heat rejected} = C_V (T_4 - T_1)$$

$$= 0.7175 (1062.5 - 373) = \mathbf{494.72 \ kJ/kg}$$

$$\frac{\text{Heat supplied}}{\text{Heat rejected}} = \frac{1013.4}{494.7} = \mathbf{2.05} \qquad \text{... Ans.}$$

**Problem 4.3:** In an ideal Otto cycle, if $T_3$ and $T_1$ represent the maximum and minimum temperatures respectively, show that for the maximum work to be done in the cycle,

$$T_2 = \sqrt{T_1 T_3}$$

where, $T_2$ is the temperature after the compression.

**Solution:**

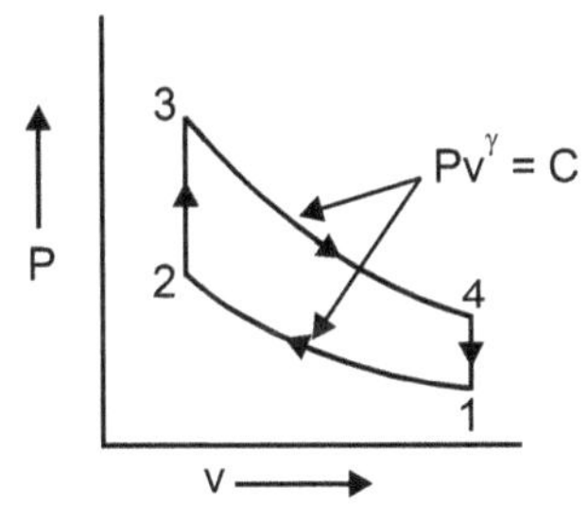


**Fig. 4.5**

Heat added during the process 2-3 is

$$Q_1 = C_V (T_3 - T_2) \text{ for unit mass} \qquad \text{... (I)}$$

Heat rejected during the process 4 – 1 is

$$Q_2 = C_V (T_4 - T_1) \text{ for unit mass} \qquad \text{... (II)}$$

Processes 1-2 and 3-4 are reversible adiabatic processes, no heat transfer takes place.

$$\text{Net work done} = Q_1 - Q_2$$

$$= C_V (T_3 - T_2) - C_V (T_4 - T_1)$$

$$W = C_V [T_3 - T_2 - T_4 + T_1]$$

$$\text{but} \quad \frac{T_2}{T_1} = \frac{T_3}{T_4} \ , \ T_4 = T_3 \cdot \frac{T_1}{T_2}$$

$$W = C_V \left[ T_3 - T_2 - T_3 \cdot \frac{T_1}{T_2} + T_1 \right]$$

For maximum work output,

$$\frac{dW}{dT_2} = 0, \quad 0 = -1 + \frac{T_1 T_3}{T_2^2}$$

$$\therefore \quad T_2 = \sqrt{T_1 T_3}$$

**Problem 4.4:** Show that the compression ratio for the maximum work to be done per kg of air in an Otto cycle between upper and lower limits of absolute temperatures $T_3$ and $T_1$ is given by

$$R_C = \left(\frac{T_3}{T_1}\right)^{\frac{1}{2(\gamma-1)}}$$

**Solution:** Let us consider P-v diagram of an Otto cycle and also T-s diagram.

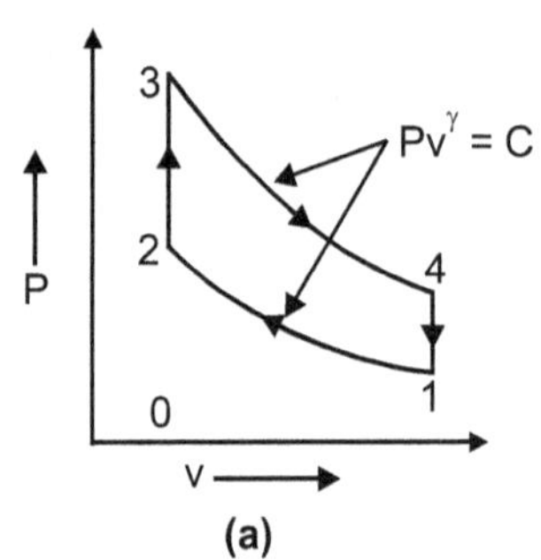


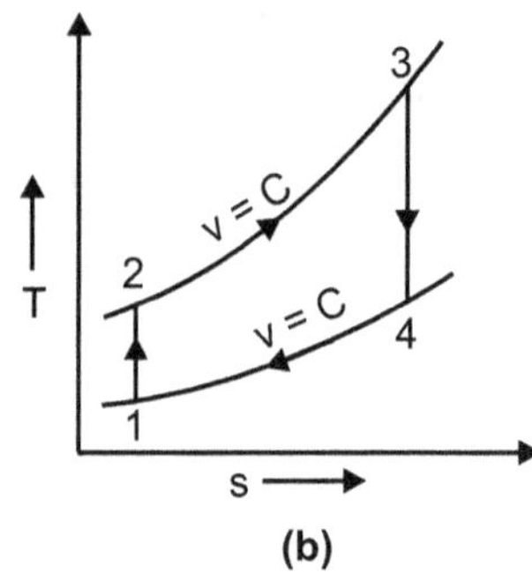


**Fig. 4.6**

Heat added during the process 2-3 is

$$Q_1 = C_V (T_3 - T_2) \text{ for unit mass} \qquad \ldots \text{(I)}$$

Heat rejected during the process 4-1 is

$$Q_2 = C_V (T_4 - T_1) \text{ for unit mass} \qquad \ldots \text{(II)}$$

Processes 1-2 and 3-4 are reversible adiabatic processes, hence no heat transfer occurs.

Net work done,

$$W = Q_1 - Q_2$$
$$= C_V (T_3 - T_2) - C_V (T_4 - T_1)$$
$$= C_V (T_3 - T_2 - T_4 + T_1)$$

But,

$$\frac{T_2}{T_1} = \frac{T_3}{T_4}, \quad T_4 = T_3 \cdot \frac{T_1}{T_2}$$

$$\therefore \quad W = C_V \left(T_3 - T_2 - \frac{T_3 \cdot T_1}{T_2} + T_1\right)$$

For maximum work output, $\dfrac{dW}{dT_2} = 0$.

$$\therefore \qquad 0 = -1 + \frac{T_1 T_3}{T_2^2}$$

$$\therefore \qquad \frac{T_3}{T_2^2} \cdot T_1 = 1$$

Multiply and divide by $T_1$

$$\therefore \qquad \frac{T_3}{T_2^2} \cdot \frac{T_1^2}{T_1} = 1$$

$$\therefore \qquad \frac{T_3}{T_1} = \frac{T_2^2}{T_1^2} \qquad \boxed{\frac{T_2}{T_1} = \left(\frac{v_1}{v_2}\right)^{\gamma-1} = r^{\gamma-1}}$$

$$\frac{T_3}{T_1} = (R_c)^{2(\gamma-1)} \qquad\qquad \text{Let } r = R_c$$

$$\therefore \qquad R_c = \left(\frac{T_3}{T_1}\right)^{\frac{1}{2(\gamma-1)}} \text{ proved.}$$

## 4.3.1 Effect of Compression Ratio on Thermal $\eta$ Highest Temperature and Pressure in the Cycle

The efficiency of an Otto cycle can also be expressed in terms of the highest temperature ($T_3$) and $T_4$ as given below.

$$\text{Now, since } \frac{v_1}{v_2} = \frac{r_3}{v_4} \text{ it follows that,}$$

$$\frac{T_2}{T_1} = \frac{T_3}{T_4} \text{ or } \frac{T_2}{T_3} = \frac{T_1}{T_4}$$

and hence, 
$$1 - \frac{T_2}{T_3} = 1 - \frac{T_1}{T_4} \text{ or } \frac{T_3 - T_2}{T_3} = \frac{T_4 - T_1}{T_4}$$

Therefore,

$$\frac{T_4 - T_1}{T_3 - T_2} = \frac{T_4}{T_3}$$

Hence, we get the equation,

$$\eta = 1 - \frac{T_4}{T_3} = 1 - \frac{T_1}{T_2} \qquad\qquad \text{... (i)}$$

It is seen from equation (iv) that efficiency of Otto cycle is independent of heat supplied, but depends only on the compression ratio 'r' and ratio of specific heat $\gamma$. This is also shown in Fig. 4.7. The efficiency increases with increase in compression ratio and $\gamma$.

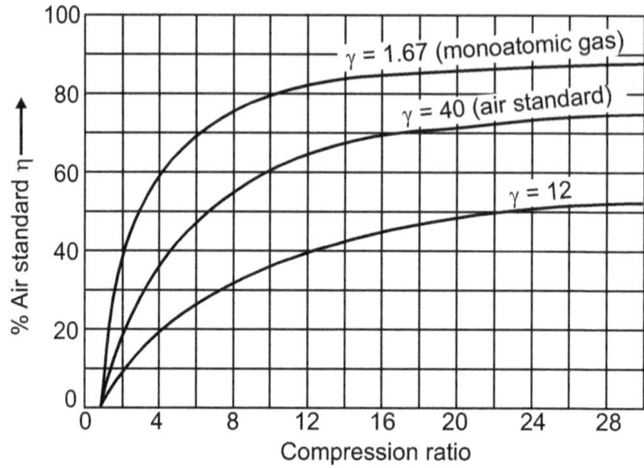


**Fig. 4.7: Otto cycle efficiency at different compression ratios and γ**

The use of monoatomic gases like helium (γ = 1.66) argon (γ = 1.97) instead of air would increase efficiency of Otto cycle.

Fig. 4.7 shows that an increase of compression ratio say from 6 to 10, increases the efficiency substantially but an increase of compression ratio from 10 to 16 increases the efficiency marginally. The efficiency at compression ratio 5 is 47.5 at 10 is 60.2% and at 15 it is 66.1%. See the Table 4.1.

**Table 4.1: Air Standard Efficiency of Otto Cycle for different Compression Ratio**

| Compression ratio | 5 | 6 | 7 | 8 | 9 | 10 | 11 | 12 | 15 |
|---|---|---|---|---|---|---|---|---|---|
| % Efficiency | 47.5 | 51.2 | 54.0 | 56.5 | 58.5 | 62.0 | 62.4 | 63.0 | 66.1 |

The effect of compression ratio on the maximum pressure and maximum temperature of the cycle is shown in Fig. 4.8.

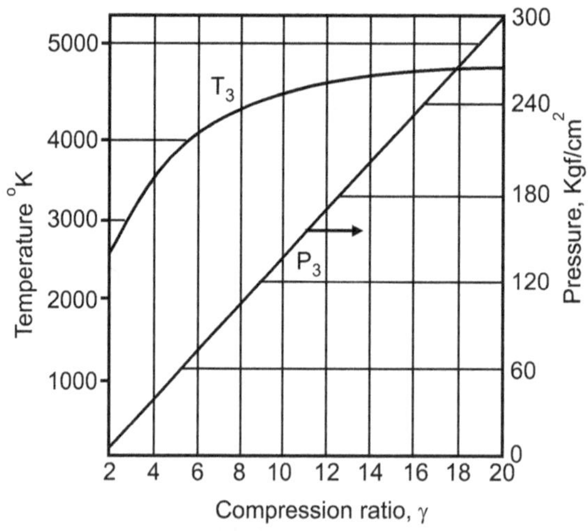


**Fig. 4.8: Effect compression ratio on
maximum pressure ($P_3$) and temperature ($T_3$) of the cycle**

At high compression ratios there is a sharp rise in maximum pressure ($P_3$) and temperature ($T_3$) which introduces problems of knocking, structural strength and bearing reliability.

The specific work transfer and work ratio for Otto cycle are defined as:

$$\text{Specific work transfer, } W = c_v (T_3 - T_4) - c_v (T_2 - T_1)$$

$$\text{and Work ratio, } r_w = \frac{(T_3 - T_4) - (T_2 - T_1)}{(T_3 - T_4)}$$

The specific work transfer in Otto cycle depends on the maximum temperature allowed in the cycle.

# 4.4 THE DIESEL CYCLE                                [May 11, Dec. 11]

It is the thermal cycle for compression-ignition (CI) or diesel engine. The main difference between Otto and Diesel cycles is that heat addition is at constant pressure in Diesel cycle. While the same is at constant volume in Otto cycle. The heat rejection process takes place at constant volume in both the cycles. The Diesel cycle is shown in P-v and T-s diagram in Fig. 4.9.

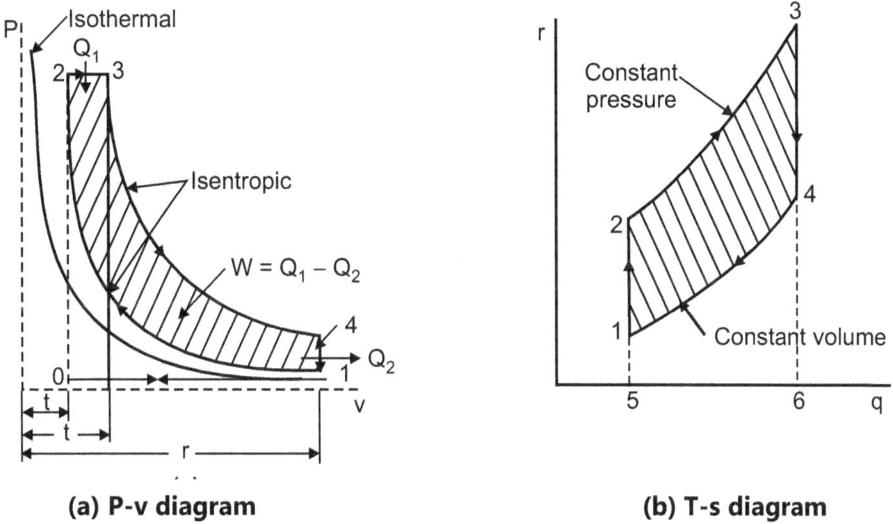


| (a) P-v diagram | (b) T-s diagram |

**Fig. 4.8: The diesel cycle**

**Process 1-2:** It is an isentropic compression (reversible adiabatic compression) of air through the compression ratio $r = \dfrac{v_1}{v_2}$.

The piston moves from bottom dead center (bdc) position to top dead center (tdc) position. No heat transfer takes place during the process.

**Process 2-3:** Heat is added at constant pressure so that state of air changes from point 2 to 3. For unit mass of air,

$$\text{Heat supplied, } Q_s = C_p (T_3 - T_2) \qquad\qquad \ldots \text{(ii)}$$

**Process 3-4:** Isentropic expansion of air takes place. No heat transfer occurs during the process.

**Process 4-1:** Heat is rejected at constant volume. It is assumed that heat rejection takes place instantaneously. For unit mass of air, heat rejected, $Q_r$.

$$Q_r = C_v \cdot (T_4 - T_1) \qquad \ldots \text{(iii)}$$

$$\therefore \quad \text{Work done} = Q_s - Q_r$$

$$= C_p (T_3 - T_2) - C_v (T_4 - T_1) \qquad \ldots \text{(iv)}$$

The thermal efficiency of the Ideal Diesel cycle is given by,

$$\eta = \frac{\text{Heat added} - \text{Heat rejected}}{\text{Head added}}$$

$$= \frac{C_v (T_3 - T_2) - C_v (T_4 - T_1)}{C_v (T_3 - T_2)}$$

$$= 1 - \frac{1}{\gamma}\left(\frac{T_4 - T_1}{T_4 - T_2}\right)$$

$$= 1 - \frac{T_1}{\gamma T_2}\left(\frac{T_4/T_1 - 1}{T_3/T_2 - 1}\right) \qquad \ldots \text{(v)}$$

For isentropic compression and expansion processes:

$$\frac{T_1}{T_2} = \left(\frac{v_2}{v_1}\right)^{\gamma - 1} \text{ and } \frac{T_4}{T_3} = \left(\frac{r_3}{v_4}\right)^{\gamma - 1}$$

For constant pressure heat addition 2-3,

$$\frac{T_3}{T_2} = \frac{v_3}{v_2}$$

Also $\qquad\qquad v_4 = v_1$

$$\text{Thus,} \frac{T_4}{T_1} = \frac{T_3}{T_2}\left(\frac{v_3/v_4}{v_2/v_1}\right)^{\gamma - 1}$$

$$= \frac{v_3}{v_2}\left(\frac{v_3}{v_2}\right)^{\gamma - 1} = \left(\frac{v_3}{v_2}\right)^{\gamma}$$

Substituting these values in equation (v), we get,

$$\eta = 1\frac{1}{\gamma (v_1/v_2)^{\gamma - 1}}\left[\frac{(v_3/v_2)^{\gamma - 1}}{(v_3/v_2) - 1}\right]$$

$$= 1 - \frac{1}{r^{\gamma - 1}}\left[\frac{\rho^{\gamma} - 1}{\gamma (\rho - 1)}\right] \qquad \ldots \text{(vi)}$$

Note that the efficiency of the Diesel cycle differs from that of the Otto cycle only by the bracketed term, which is always greater than unity (except when $\rho = 1$ and there is no heat addition). Thus, the Diesel cycle always has lower efficiency than Otto cycle for the same compression ratio.

## 4.4.1 MEP of Diesel Cycle                                            [May 11]

To derive an equation for mean effective pressure for Diesel cycle, refer Fig. 4.9.

Let clearance volume be unity.

$$\text{Work done} = \text{Area of P-v diagram}$$

$$= P_2 (v_3 - v_2) + \frac{P_3 v_3 - P_4 v_4}{\gamma - 1} - \frac{P_2 v_2 - P_1 v_1}{\gamma - 1}$$

$$= P_2 (\rho - 1) + \frac{P_2 \rho - P_4 r - (P_2 - P_1 r)}{\gamma - 1}$$

$$= \frac{P_2 (\rho - 1) (\gamma - 1) + P_2 (\rho - \rho^\gamma r^{1 - \gamma}) - P_2 (1 - r^{1 - \gamma})}{\gamma - 1}$$

$$= \frac{P_2}{\gamma - 1} \left[ \gamma (\rho - 1) - r^{1 - \gamma} (\rho^\gamma - 1) \right]$$

$$\text{mep} = \frac{\text{Area of the indicator diagram}}{\text{Length of the indicator diagram}}$$

$$= \frac{P_2 \left[ (\rho - 1) - r^{1 - \gamma} (\rho^\gamma - 1) \right]}{(\gamma - 1) (r - 1)}$$

$$= \frac{P_1 r^\gamma \left[ \gamma (\rho - 1) - r^{1 - \gamma} (\rho^\gamma - 1) \right]}{(\gamma - 1) (r - 1)} \qquad \dots \text{(vii)}$$

## 4.4.2 Effect of Compression Ratio on Diesel Cycle Efficiency

The Diesel cycle always has a lower efficiency than the Otto cycle for the same compression ratio which is shown in Fig. 4.10.

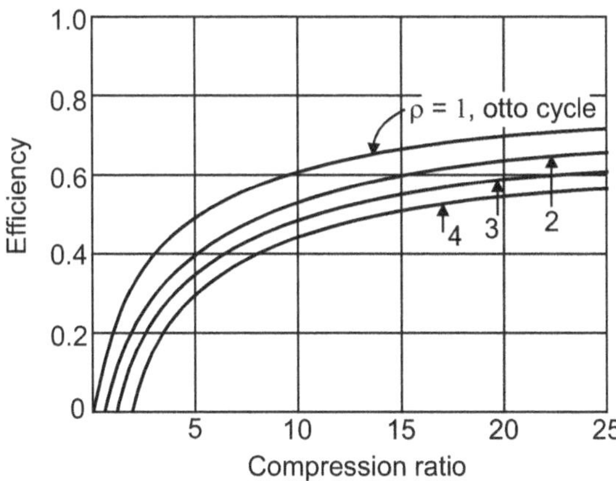


**Fig. 4.10: Efficiency of the diesel cycle for various cut-off and compression ratios**

In Diesel engine the cut-off ratio ($\rho = v_3/v_2$) depends on the load on the engine. It is maximum for maximum load.

The air standard efficiency of Diesel cycle depends on load and increases as the load is decreased and equals as that off Otto cycle efficiency at the limiting condition of zero load.

Diesel engine has normal compression ratio between 15 to 22 and Otto engine has this ratio between 6 to 10. The actual $\eta$ of Diesel engine is higher than that of Otto engine (Petrol engine).

## 4.5 THE DUAL CYCLE OF LIMITED PRESSURE CYCLE

### (The Dual Combustion Cycle)

High speed diesel engines normally work according to the dual cycle (the dual combustion cycle is shown in Fig. 4.11).

In this cycle, port of head addition is at constant volume and remaining at constant pressure.

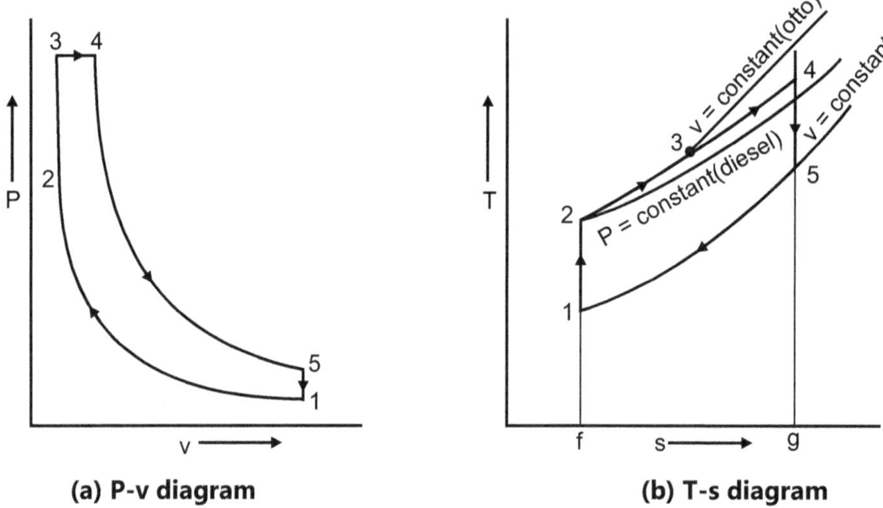


**(a) P-v diagram**                    **(b) T-s diagram**

**Fig. 4.11: Dual or mixed or limited pressure cycle**

The various processes of the cycle are as given below:

**Process 1-2:** It is an isentropic compression of air through the compression ratio $r = \dfrac{V_1}{V_2}$. The piston moves from bdc position to tdc position. No heat exchange takes place during the process.

**Process 2-3:** Partial heat addition at constant volume per unit mass of air,

$$Q_{s1} = C_v (T_3 - T_2) \qquad \text{... (i)}$$

**Process 3-4:** Partial heat, addition at constant pressure per unit mass of air,

$$Q_{s2} = C_p (T_4 - T_3) \qquad \text{... (ii)}$$

**Process 4-5:** Isentropic expansion of air takes place.

No heat exchange takes place during the process.

**Process 5-1:** Heat is rejected at constant volume per unit mass of air,

$$Q_R = C_v (T_5 - T_1) \qquad \text{... (iii)}$$

The efficiency of the cycle may be written as,

$$\eta \;=\; \frac{\text{Heat supplied} - \text{Heat rejected}}{\text{Heat supplied}}$$

$$=\; \frac{C_v\,(T_3 - T_2) + C_v\,(T_4 - T_3) - C_v\,(T_5 - T_1)}{C_v\,(T_3 - T_2) + C_v\,(T_4 - T_2)}$$

$$=\; 1 - \frac{T_5 - T_1}{(T_3 - T_2) + \gamma\,(T_4 - T_3)} \qquad \ldots \text{(iv)}$$

Now, $T_2 = T_1\left(\dfrac{v_1}{v_2}\right)^{\gamma-1} = T_1 r^{\gamma-1},\; T_3 = T_2\dfrac{P_3}{P_2} = T_1 r^{\gamma-1}\,\alpha$

where, $\alpha$ is the pressure ratio $\dfrac{P_3}{P_2}$.

$$T_4 \;=\; T_3\frac{v_4}{v_3}\,T_1\,r^{\gamma-1}\,x\rho$$

and

$$T_5 \;=\; T_4\left(\frac{v_4}{v_5}\right)^{\gamma-1} = T_1 r^{\gamma-1}\cdot\alpha\rho\left(\frac{v_4}{v_5}\right)^{\gamma-1}$$

Now,

$$\frac{v_4}{v_5} = \frac{v_4}{v_1} = \frac{v_4 v_3}{v_3 v_1} = \frac{v_4 v_2}{v_3 v_1},\; \text{etc. since } v_2 = v_3.$$

$\therefore$

$$\frac{v_4}{v_5} \;=\; \frac{\rho}{r} \text{ and hence } T_1 = T_1\,\alpha\rho^{\gamma}$$

Substituting for $T_2$, $T_3$, $T_4$ and $T_5$ into equation (iv), we obtain

$$\eta \;=\; 1 - \frac{1}{r^{\gamma-1}}\left[\frac{\alpha\rho^{\gamma} - 1}{(\alpha - 1) + \alpha\gamma\,(\rho - 1)}\right] \qquad \ldots \text{(v)}$$

If $\alpha > 1$ in the equation (v), gives higher value of efficiency for the given value of $\rho$ and $\gamma$.

Thus, the efficiency of dual cycle is intermediate between those of Otto cycle and Diesel cycle having the same compression ratio.

If one substitutes $\rho = 1$ in equation (v), it becomes Otto cycle and with $\alpha = 1$ it becomes diesel cycle.

The name dual combustion is derived due to the incorporation of features of both Otto cycle and Diesel cycle in dual cycle. Many a times, the world dual cycle can be avoided as it may cause confusion with dual fuel cycle. The heat addition at constant volume increases the cycle efficiency while heat addition at constant pressure limits the maximum pressure in the cycle. Therefore, the dual cycle is usually referred as limited pressure cycle.

## 4.5.1 Mean Effective Pressure of Limited Pressure Cycle

Referring to Fig. 4.11, one can write

$$\text{Work done} \;=\; \text{Area of P-v diagram}$$

$$=\; P_3\,(v_4 - v_2) + \frac{P_4 v_4 - P_5 v_5}{\gamma - 1} - \frac{P_2 v_2 - P_1 v_1}{\gamma - 1}$$

$$=\; P_3\,(\rho - 1) + \frac{P_3\rho - P_5 r - P_2 + P_1 r}{\gamma - 1}$$

$$= P_3 (\rho - 1) + \frac{P_3 (\rho - \rho^\gamma r^{1-\gamma}) - P_2 (1 - r^{1-\gamma})}{\gamma - 1}$$

$$= \frac{P_3 [(\rho - 1)(\gamma - 1) + \rho - \rho^\gamma r^{1-\gamma} - 1/\alpha (1 - r^{1-\gamma})]}{\gamma - 1}$$

$$= \frac{P_3 [\rho^\gamma - \rho - \gamma + 1 + \rho - \rho^\gamma r^{1-\gamma} - 1/x (1 - r^{1-\gamma})]}{\gamma - 1}$$

$$= \frac{P_3 [\alpha\gamma (\rho - 1) + \alpha - \alpha\rho^\gamma r^{1-\gamma} - (1 - r^{1-\gamma})]}{\alpha (\gamma - 1)}$$

$$= \frac{P_3 [\alpha\gamma (\rho - 1) + (\alpha - 1) - r^{1-\gamma} (\alpha\rho^\gamma - 1)]}{\alpha (\gamma - 1)}$$

$$mep = \frac{\text{Area of the indicator diagram}}{\text{Length of the indicator diagram}}$$

$$= \frac{P_2 [\alpha\gamma (C - 1) + (\alpha - 1) - r^{1-\gamma} (\alpha\rho^\gamma - \alpha\rho^\gamma 1)]}{\alpha (r - 1) (\gamma - 1)}$$

$$= \frac{P_1 r^\gamma [\alpha\gamma (\rho - 1) + (\alpha - 1) - r^{1-\gamma} (\alpha\rho^\gamma - 1)]}{(\gamma - 1) (r - 1)} \qquad \ldots \text{(vi)}$$

# 4.6  COMPARISON OF OTTO, DIESEL AND DUAL COMBUSTION (LIMITED PRESSURE) CYCLES  [Dec. 11, 12]

The comparison of the above cycles can be carried out on the basis of various parameters like compression ratio, maximum pressure, maximum temperature, heat input, work output etc.

## 4.6.1 For Same Compression Ratio and Same Heat Input

The three cycles Otto, Diesel and Limited cycle are represented on P-v and T-s diagrams as shown in Fig. 4.12. For all the cycles, the starting point 1 is same and air is isentropically compressed to state 2 as compression ratio is same.

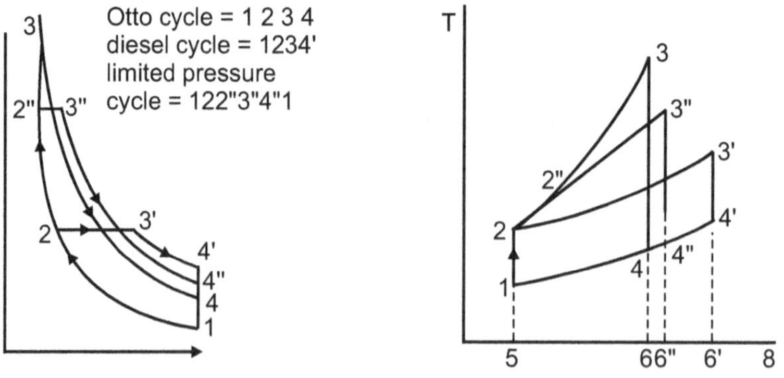


**Fig. 4.12: Otto, diesel and limited-pressure cycle with the same compression ratio and same heat input**

In Otto cycle (1-2-3-4-1), heat is added at constant volume resulting in the highest temperature and pressure.

In Diesel cycle (1-2-3'-4'-1), heat is added at constant pressure resulting in the lowest maximum temperature and pressure.

In limited pressure cycle, the values of maximum temperature and pressures lie between those of Otto and Diesel cycles.

On T-s diagram, the area below the curve 4-1, represents that heat rejected in Otto cycle. The area below the curve 4'-1 on T-s plot represents heat rejected in diesel cycle. Similarly, area below the curve 4"-1, represents heat rejected in limited pressure cycle.

The heat supplied for the three cycles is given by the areas 2-3-6-5, 2-3'-6'-5 and 2-2"-3"-6"-5. These areas are equal to each other.

For same heat input and compression ratio, minimum heat is rejected in the Otto cycle and the maximum heat is rejected in Diesel cycle. Therefore, Otto cycle produces maximum work (maximum area 1-2-3-4-1 on P-v diagram) and highest efficiency. The diesel cycle has the least efficiency, the limited pressure cycle has the $\eta$ between Otto and Diesel cycles. Therefore, in this case the diesel cycle has higher compression ratio $(v_1/v_2)$ than Otto cycle $(v_1/v_2)$. Therefore, diesel cycle gives more/higher expansion than Otto cycle. Hence possesses higher efficiency than Otto cycle. The $\eta$ of limited cycle would fall between these two cycles.

## 4.6.2 For Same Maximum Pressure and Temperature

This parameter is compared in Fig. 4.13 for otto and diesel cycle.

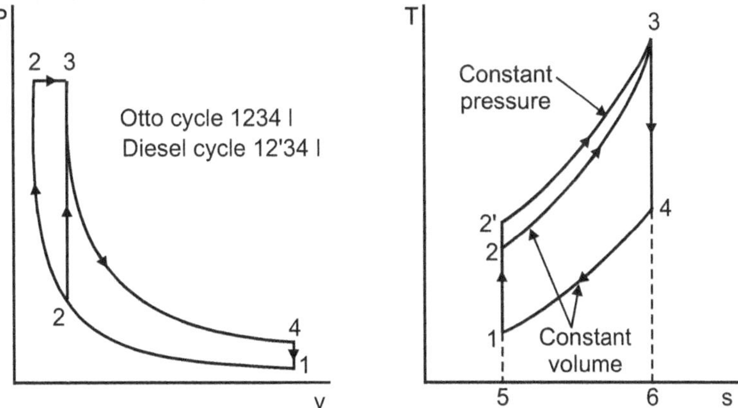



**Fig. 4.13: Otto and Diesel Cycles with the same maximum pressure and same heat input**

From Fig. 4.13, one can conclude that for same maximum pressure and heat input, the heat rejected by both Otto cycle and Diesel cycles is same (area 1-4-6-5-1 on T-s diagram) but the heat supplied to diesel cycle (area 2'-3-6-5-2' on T-s diagram) is more than that of Otto cycle (area 2-3-6-5-2 on T-s diagram).

Therefore, Diesel cycle is more efficient than Otto cycle. Compression ratio is also higher in diesel cycle than Otto cycle.

Limited pressure cycle has the efficiency between Otto and Diesel cycle.

In Otto cycle, the expansion stroke is the longest converting maximum heat into useful work. In Diesel cycle, the expansion stroke is the shortest, converting minimum heat into useful work. The limited pressure cycle stands between these two cycles in this regard.

### 4.6.3 For Constant Maximum Pressure and Same Input                    [Dec. 12]

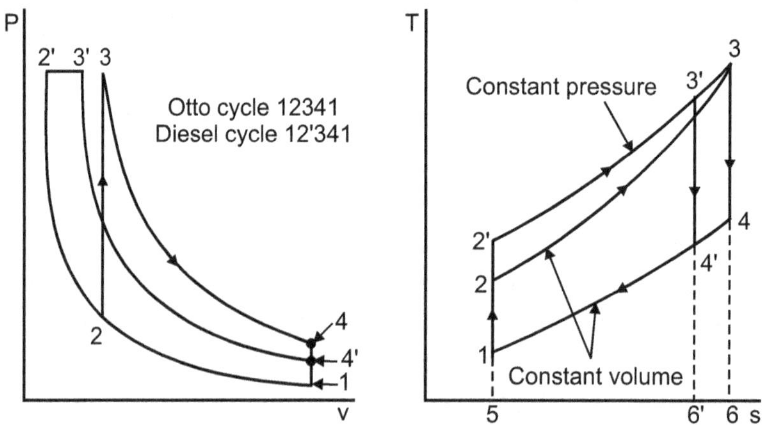


**Fig. 4.14: Otto and Diesel Cycles with the same maximum pressure and temperature**

The two cycles namely Otto and Diesel cycle are compared in Fig. 4.14 for the same maximum pressure and same heat input.

To satisfy the maximum pressure and same heat input:

- The points 3 and 3' must lie on same pressure line in P-v diagram.
- For same heat input the areas 2-3-6-5-2 and 2'-3-6-5-2' must be equal on T-s diagram.

It is clear from the T-s diagram that heat rejected by Otto cycle (area 4-1-5-6-4) is more than that heat rejected by Diesel cycle (area 1-4'-6-5-1). For the condition of same maximum pressure and same heat input.

## 4.7 FOR SAME MAXIMUM PRESSURE AND OUTPUT

The efficiency is given by,

$$\text{Efficiency} = \frac{\text{Work done}}{\text{Heat supplied}} = \frac{\text{Work done}}{\text{Work done} + \text{Heat rejected}}$$

For same maximum pressure and output, the diesel cycle is more efficient than Otto cycle.

## 4.8 BRAYTON CYCLE

The constant pressure or open cycle gas turbine works on Brayton cycle.

- This cycle consists of four reversible processes.
- Two processes are reversible constant pressure and two are isentropic.
- As compressor requires about 70% of turbine output, overall efficiency of cycle is very less.
- Therefore this cycle is not generally used in practice.

- It is used in aeroplanes.

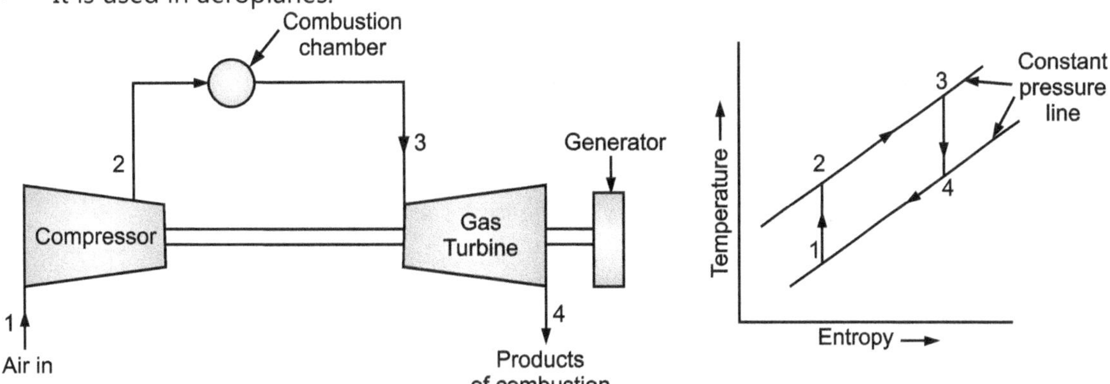


**Fig. 4.15: Constant pressure gas turbine**          **Fig. 4.16: Constant pressure cycle (Joule or Brayton cycle)**

The constant pressure gas turbine works on Joule or Brayton cycle.

**Process 1 – 2  :**  Fresh atmospheric air is drawn into compressor. The compressor is of axial flow type. The air is compressed to 2 to 4 bar. The compression is assumed to be isentropic.

**Process 2 – 3  :**  The compressed air enters the combustion chamber. Here the fuel is injected and ignited by spark plug. The combustion takes place at constant pressure. The temperature rises to @ 2000ºC. The turbine blades cannot withstand such a high temperature, hence products of combustion are cooled by the arrangement shown in Fig. 4.16.

The air passing in the annular space cools the products of combustion and reduces its temperature.

The permissible temperature for turbine blade material is in the range of 730ºC to 930ºC.

**Process 3 – 4  :**  This is an isentropic expansion process. The products of combustion at high temperature and pressure expand isentropically. The pressure energy is converted into kinetic energy.

**Process 4 – 1  :**  The products of combustion after expansion are let off to atmosphere at constant pressure.

The turbine is coupled to the generator and compressor. The compressor absorbs about 60 – 70 % of the turbine output. The remaining power is used to drive the generator.

## 4.8.1 Assumptions for Ideal Cycle Analysis

It is assumed that working fluid in the turbine plant is an ideal gas and following assumptions are made for ideal cycle analysis.

- Compression and expansion are reversible and adiabatic.

- There are no pressure losses in combustion chamber, inlet ducting, exhaust ducting, heat exchangers etc.
- The mass flow of gas is constant throughout the cycle.
- The composition of working fluid does not change throughout the cycle and working fluid is a perfect gas.
- Frictional losses at bearings and windage losses are neglected.
- Between inlet and outlet of each component, change of kinetic energy of working fluid is neglected.

With these assumptions, we will calculate thermal efficiency of the Brayton or Joule cycle.

## 4.8.2 Thermal Efficiency and Work Ratio

Referring to Fig. 4.16, for 1 kg of working fluid,

The heat is supplied during constant pressure process 2 – 3.

$$\text{Heat supplied} = Q_s = h_3 - h_2 = C_p (T_3 - T_2)$$

The heat is rejected during constant pressure process 4 – 1.

$$\text{Heat rejected} = h_4 - h_1 = C_p (T_4 - T_1)$$

$$\text{Net work} = \text{Heat supplied} - \text{Heat rejected}$$

$$= C_p \left[ (T_3 - T_2) - (T_4 - T_1) \right]$$

This net work can also be found from turbine and compressor work

$$\text{Work done by the turbine} = W_t = h_3 - h_4$$

$$= C_p (T_3 - T_4)$$

$$\begin{bmatrix} \text{Work consumed by the} \\ \text{compressor which is supplied} \\ \text{by the turbine} \end{bmatrix} = W_c = h_2 - h_1$$

$$= C_p (T_2 - T_1)$$

$$\text{Net work} = W_T - W_C$$

$$= C_p \left[ (T_3 - T_2) - (T_4 - T_1) \right]$$

$$\text{Thermal efficiency} = \frac{\text{Net work}}{\text{Heat supplied}} = \frac{W_T - W_C}{Q_s}$$

$$= \frac{C_p \left[ (T_3 - T_2) - (T_4 - T_1) \right]}{C_p (T_3 - T_2)}$$

$$= 1 - \frac{T_4 - T_1}{T_3 - T_2} \qquad \text{... (i)}$$

Normally in gas turbine, initial and final pressures are known, hence this equation will be expressed in terms of $P_1$, $P_2$, etc.

Now 1 – 2 and 3 – 4 are isentropic processes.

Hence
$$\frac{T_2}{T_1} = \left(\frac{P_2}{P_1}\right)^{\frac{\gamma-1}{\gamma}}$$

and
$$\frac{T_3}{T_4} = \left(\frac{P_3}{P_4}\right)^{\frac{\gamma-1}{\gamma}}$$

However, as $P_2 = P_3$ and $P_1 = P_4$,

$$\therefore \quad \frac{T_2}{T_1} = \frac{T_3}{T_4} = \left(\frac{P_2}{P_1}\right)^{\frac{\gamma-1}{\gamma}} = (r_p)^m$$

where $m = \dfrac{\gamma-1}{\gamma}$ and $r_p$ = pressure ratio $= \dfrac{P_2}{P_1} = \dfrac{P_3}{P_4}$

$$\therefore \quad \frac{T_1}{T_2} = \frac{T_4}{T_3} = \frac{T_4 - T_1}{T_3 - T_2} \qquad \qquad \dots \text{(ii)}$$

$$\text{But thermal efficiency} = 1 - \frac{T_4 - T_1}{T_3 - T_2} = 1 - \frac{T_1}{T_2}$$

$$\therefore \quad \text{Thermal efficiency} = 1 - \frac{1}{(r_p)^{\frac{\gamma-1}{\gamma}}} \qquad \qquad \dots \text{(iii)}$$

From the above equation we observe that the thermal efficiency of the Brayton or Joule's cycle is function of $r_p$, the pressure ratio.

As pressure ratio increases, thermal efficiency increases. However, pressure ratio cannot increase beyond a certain value. As pressure ratio increases, temperature $T_2$ increases which in turn increase $T_3$. The value of $T_3$ is limited by metallurgical considerations. Normally, a pressure ratio of 2 to 4 is used.

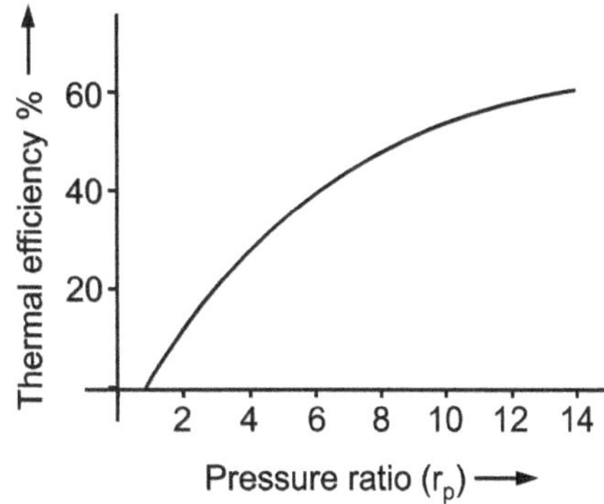


**Fig. 4.17: Pressure ratio Vs thermal efficiency**

Another term normally used is work ratio.

Work ratio is defined as the ratio of the net work to the work developed by the turbine.

$$\text{Work ratio} = r_w = \frac{W_T - W_C}{W_T}$$

Now,
$$W_T - W_C = C_p (T_3 - T_4) - C_p (T_2 - T_1)$$

$$\therefore \quad W_T - W_C = W_n = C_p T_3 \left(1 - \frac{T_4}{T_3}\right) - C_p T_1 \left(\frac{T_2}{T_1} - 1\right)$$

where,
$$W_n = \text{Net work}$$

$$\therefore \qquad W_n = C_p\, T_3\left(1 - \frac{1}{r_p^m}\right) - C_p\, T_1\left(r_p^m - 1\right) \qquad \dots \text{(iv)}$$

Now, $\qquad r_W = \text{Work ratio} = \dfrac{W_T - W_C}{W_T} = 1 - \dfrac{W_C}{W_T}$

$$= 1 - \frac{C_p\,(T_2 - T_1)}{C_p\,(T_3 - T_4)}$$

$$= 1 - \frac{C_p\, T_1\left[\dfrac{T_2}{T_1} - 1\right]}{C_p\, T_3\left(1 - \dfrac{T_4}{T_3}\right)}$$

$$= 1 - \frac{C_p\, T_1\left(r_p^m - 1\right)}{C_p\, T_3\left(1 - \dfrac{1}{r_p^m}\right)}$$

$$= 1 - \frac{T_1\left(r_p^m - 1\right)}{T_3\left(r_p^m - 1\right)} \ \propto\, r_p^m$$

$$= 1 - \frac{T_1}{T_3} \cdot r_p^m \qquad \dots \text{(v)}$$

The work ratio is maximum when $\dfrac{T_1}{T_3} = r_p^m$ is minimum.

This is when $T_1$ is minimum and $T_3$ is maximum for the same $r_p$.

## 4.9 REFRIGERATION CYCLE

### 4.9.1 Refrigeration

**Definition:** Refrigeration is the science of producing and maintaining the temperature below that of the surrounding.

Refrigeration is also defined as a phenomenon of producing cold relative to the surrounding.

The unit of refrigeration is tonne of refrigeration or simply tonne. It is denoted by the symbol TR.

One tonne refrigeration is equivalent to the amount of heat extracted from one tonne of water which is at $0°$ C for converting it to the ice at $0°C$ in one day or 24 hours.

$$1\ TR = 211\ kJ/min$$
$$= 3.5167\ kW$$

## 4.9.2 Reversed Carnot Cycle

It is proved that heat engine based on Carnot cycle is having maximum efficiency (i.e. it converts maximum heat into work).

Similarly, reversed Carnot cycle can be employed as a reversible refrigeration cycle. Such reversible refrigeration cycle gives maximum COP working between the temperature limits $T_L$ and $T_H$.

A reversed Carnot cycle is shown in Fig. 4.18 on T-s diagram and P - v diagram.

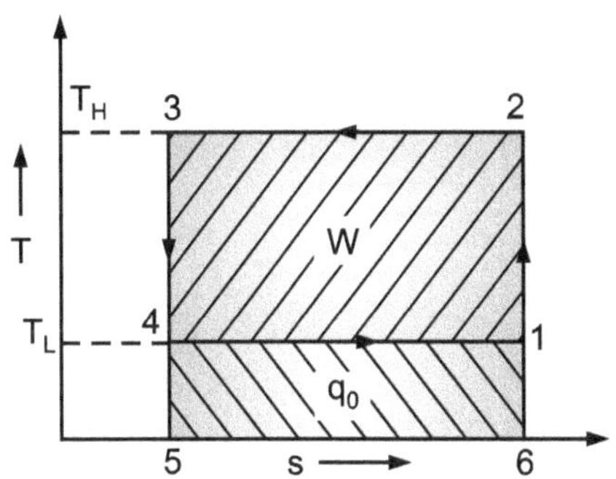


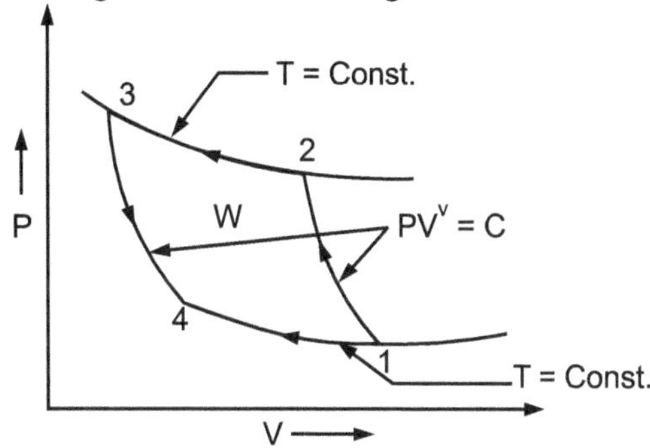


**Fig. 4.18: Reversed Carnot cycle**

The reversed Carnot cycle consists of two isothermal and two isentropic operations as follows:

Process 1 – 2      :      Isentropic compression, $s_1 = s_2$

Process 2 – 3      :      Isothermal heat rejection to the hot reservoir at $T_H$ = constant

Process 3 – 4      :      Isentropic expansion, $s_3 = s_4$

Process 4 – 1      :      Isothermal heat absorption from low temperature body, at $T_L$

(1)   Heat absorbed from cold body,

$$Q_2 = T_L \cdot \Delta s = \text{Area } 1-4-5-6$$

(2)   Heat rejected to hot body,

$$Q_1 = T_H \cdot \Delta s = \text{Area } 2-3-5-6$$

(3)   Work done, $W = Q_1 - Q_2 = (T_H - T_L) \cdot \Delta s \left[\dfrac{Q_1}{Q_2} = \dfrac{T_1}{T_2}\right]$

$$= \text{Area } 1-2-3-4$$

$$\text{COP for cooling} = \frac{Q_2}{W} = \frac{T_L}{T_H - T_L} = \frac{1}{\dfrac{T_H}{T_L} - 1}$$

$$\text{COP for heating} = \frac{Q_1}{W} = \frac{T_H}{T_H - T_L} = \frac{1}{1 - \dfrac{T_L}{T_H}}$$

The Carnot COP depends on operating temperatures $T_H$ and $T_L$ only and not on the properties of working substance (refrigerant) used.

Reversed Carnot cycle is theoretical in its concept but serves as an ideal cycle ever to be achieved in practice.

**Problem 4.5:** A Carnot refrigerator extracts 100 kJ heat per minute from a cold room which is maintained at –15° C and it is discharged to atmosphere which is at 30° C. Find the ideal power required to run the unit.

**Solution:**

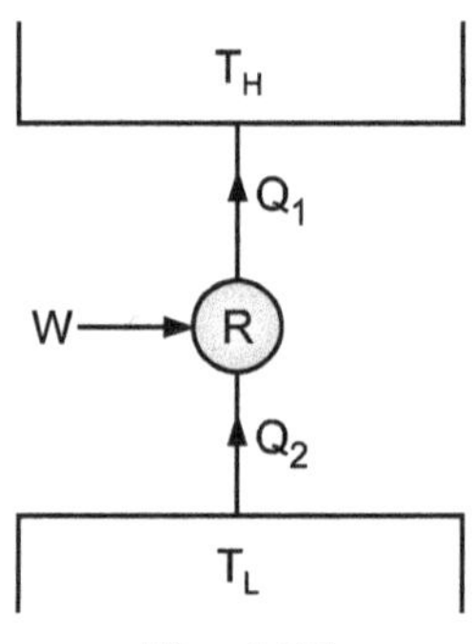


**Fig. 4.19**

**Given:**

$$T_H = 30 + 273 = 303 \text{ K}$$

$$T_L = -15 + 273 = 258 \text{ K}$$

$$Q_2 = \frac{100}{60} = 1.666 \text{ kW}$$

$$\text{COP for cooling} = \frac{T_L}{T_H - T_L} = \frac{258}{(303 - 258)} = 5.73$$

$$\text{COP for cooling} = \frac{Q_2}{W}$$

$$5.73 = \frac{1.666}{W}$$

$$\therefore \quad W = \frac{1.666}{5.73} = 0.29 \text{ kW} \qquad \text{... Ans.}$$

## 4.9.3 Classification of Refrigeration Cycles

Based on the principle of operation, refrigeration cycles are classified as,

(a)   Reversed carnot cycle

(b)   Air refrigeration cycle

(c)   Vapour compression refrigeration cycle

(d)   Vapour absorption refrigeration cycle.

## (a)  Reversed Carnot Cycle:

It has been already discussed in previous Section 4.8.2.

## (b)  Air Refrigerator (Working on Bell - Coleman Cycle):

The flow diagram of the working refrigerator is shown in Fig. 4.20 and its working is represented in Fig. 4.18 on P-v and T-s diagrams.

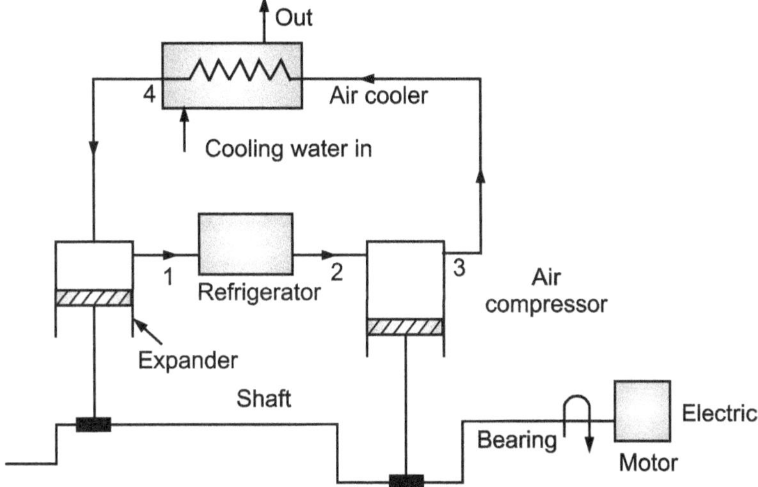


**Fig. 4.20: Air refrigerator working on Bell - Coleman cycle**

This unit consists of (1) Air compressor, (2)  An expander, (3) Air cooler (air pipe immersed in cooling water), (4) Refrigerator (cold space from where heat is to be removed).

The work obtained by the expansion of air in the expander is utilized to drive the compressor.

Air acts as a refrigerant. The cycle is explained as follows: It consists of two isobaric and two isentropic processes.

**Stage 1:** Air from the refrigerator is drawn into the compressor cylinder. It is then compressed adiabatically to state 3. This compression process is shown by the curve 2 – 3. The temperature of the air increases from $T_2$ to $T_3$.

No heat is added or rejected during this process.

**Stage 2:** The hot air enters the cooler (heat exchanger). The air is cooled at constant pressure ($P_3$) in the heat exchanger by the water, shown by curve 3 – 4.

Heat is rejected to the water. This heat rejected / kg of air = $c_p$ ($T_3 - T_4$) kJ.

**Stage 3:** The air at pressure ($P_3$ or $P_4$) enters the expander, where it undergoes expansion process adiabatically (curve 4 – 1).

There is no heat exchange during this process. The temperature of air decreases from $T_4$ to $T_1$.

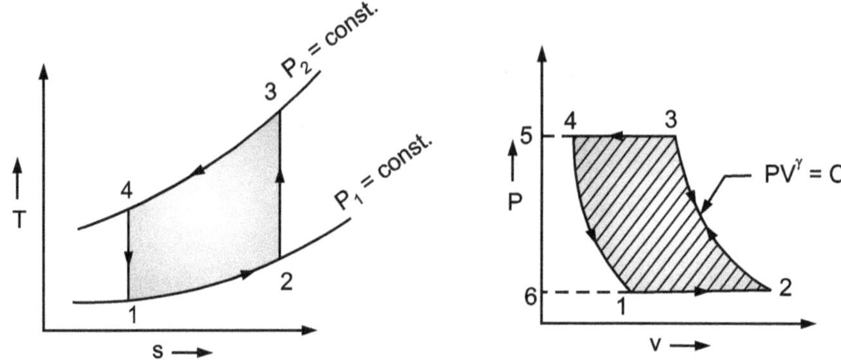



**Fig. 4.21: Bell - Coleman cycle/Reversed Brayton cycle**

**Stage 4:** The cold air at temperature $T_1$ is passed through the refrigerator where it absorbs heat at constant pressure $P_2$ (or $P_1$), shown by curve $1 - 2$.

The heat absorbed by air at pressure $P_2 = c_p (T_2 - T_1)$ kJ.

Advantages and disadvantages of the air - refrigeration system are given below.

**Advantages :**

- The refrigerant air is available free of cost.

- Air is non-flammable, so there is no danger of fire as in case of $NH_3$.

- The system is suitable for air conditioning of aircraft. The compressed air is available in aircraft i.e. initial compression of air is obtained from the RAM effect of high kinetic energy of the ambient air relative to the aircraft.

**Disadvantages:**

- The heat is absorbed by air from the refrigerator in the form of **sensible heat only**. The specific heat of air is very less. Therefore, the amount of air to be circulated is very large compared with vapour compression refrigeration system for the same refrigeration effect.

- Air contains moisture. Freezing of this moisture may block up the valves and pipe lines.

- COP of this system is very low.

- Only applicable where compressed air is available at cheaper rate i.e. in aircraft.

**(c) Vapour Compression Refrigeration Cycle:**

A suitable vapour refrigerant such as $R_{12}$, $R_{22}$, $R_{134a}$, $R_{113}$, etc. is used in this cycle. The refrigerant absorbs heat from the refrigerating space (evaporator) by undergoing a change of phase from liquid to vapour. The refrigerant undergoes a change of phase from vapour to liquid in the condenser.

The refrigerant does not leave the refrigeration system. It is circulated again and again undergoing different processes.

The working of vapour compression refrigeration system can be explained with block diagram (Fig. 4.22) and P - v and P - h diagrams (Fig. 4.20).

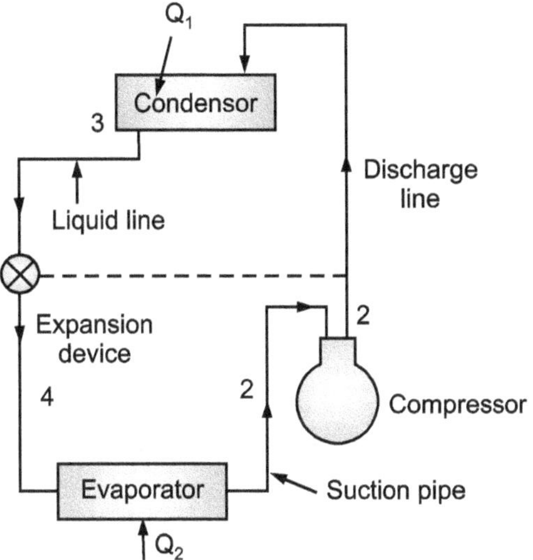


**Fig. 4.22: Vapour compression system**

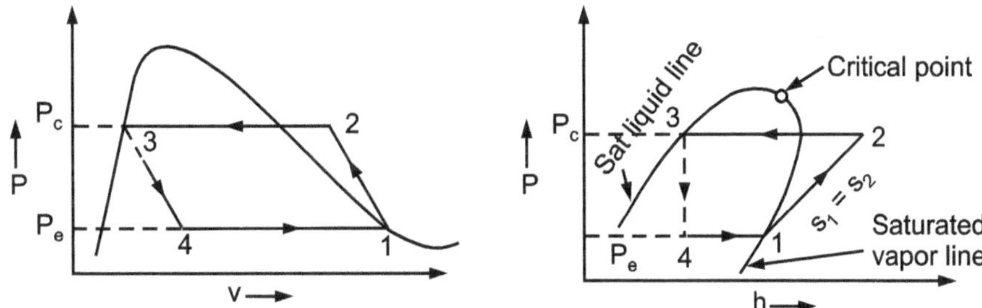


**Fig. 4.23: Vapour compression cycle on P - v and P - h planes**

It consists of two isobaric processes : one isentropic process and one isenthalpic process.

**Process 1 – 2:** The refrigerant vapour is compressed isentropically from dry saturated state 1 to state 2 (to pressure $P_c$ i.e. condensing pressure). During the process, no heat exchange occurs.

**Process 2 – 3:** Heat is rejected from the refrigerant at constant pressure in the condenser. During this process, vapour refrigerant condenses to liquid.

$$Q_2 = \text{Heat rejected} = h_2 - h_3 \text{ kJ/kg}$$

**Process 3 – 4 (Isenthalpic Expansion):** The liquid refrigerant undergoes constant enthalpy expansion process from condensing pressure $P_c$ to evaporator pressure $P_e$. This is a throttling of liquid refrigerant in the capillary tube. The heat exchange during the process is negligible.

**Process 4 – 1:** The refrigerant at state 4 enters the evaporator. It absorbs heat from the refrigerated space, during which it changes its state from liquid to vapour. This process takes place at constant evaporator pressure $P_e$.

$$\text{Heat absorbed} = \text{Refrigerating effect}$$
$$Q_2 = h_1 - h_4$$

$$\therefore \qquad COP = \frac{h_1 - h_4}{h_2 - h_1}$$

$$\text{Compressor work} = (h_2 - h_3) - (h_1 - h_4) = h_2 - h_1 \text{ because } h_3 = h_4.$$

The cycle discussed above is a simple saturation cycle. But practically, there are various losses occurring during each process. Therefore, actual vapour compression refrigeration cycle is quite different from this.

The performance of this system is completely based on the properties of refrigerant. The various refrigerants used are R - 12, R - 11, ammonia, R-22, R-13, $CO_2$, etc.

It has been recently invented that R-12 and R-11 etc. are ozone depleting agents. The release of these refrigerants to atmosphere is now causing holes to the ozone layer in the stratosphere. This has enormous adverse environmental problems. Therefore, these refrigerants R-12, R-11 and R-13 are to be replaced by new refrigerants.

Therefore, at this stage, it is necessary to discuss the properties of ideal refrigerants. It should have the following properties.

**Thermodynamic Properties:**

- It should have lower boiling point at atmospheric pressure. To operate the system at lower evaporating pressure (lower refrigerating temperature), compressor is to work under greater pressure ratio.

| Refrigerants | Normal boiling points | Applications |
| --- | --- | --- |
| $NH_3$ | $-33.3°C$ | Ice plant, air distillation |
| F - 11 | $+23.3°$ C | Air conditioning, foaming |
| F - 134 a | $-26.5°$ C | Used in domestic refrigerator |
| F - 22 | $-41.3°$ C | Air conditioning |

- **Freezing point:** Low freezing point is necessary because the refrigerant should not freeze at evaporator temperature. So the freezing point of a refrigerant must be much below the evaporator temperature.

- **Evaporator and condenser pressures:** Evaporator pressure should be just above atmospheric pressure (it should not be vacuum). The condenser pressure should not be too high for keeping compressor work to minimum possible.

- **Latent heat of refrigerant:** High latent heat of refrigerant at evaporating temperature is desirable because the refrigerating effect per kg of refrigerant will be high.

- **Critical temperature:** The critical temperature is defined as the temperature above which the latent heat becomes zero. This temperature must be much higher than the condensing temperature.

**Safe Working Properties:**

- It should be chemically inert.
- It should be non-flammable, non-explosive and non-toxic.
- It should not react with lubricating oil.

**Physical Properties:**

- **Specific Volume:** Low specific volume of the refrigerant at the suction of compressor is desirable because it reduces the size of compressor for the same refrigerating effect.
- **Specific Heat:** Low specific heat of liquid and high specific heat of vapour are desirable.
- **Thermal Conductivity:** High thermal conductivity of refrigerant in liquid and vapour state is desirable.

**Other Properties:**

- **Odour:** Odour may or may not be advantageous. Distinct odour of refrigerant helps in detecting the leak of the refrigerant. But such odour may spoil the refrigerated products.
- **Refrigerant and oil relationship:** The refrigerant should not react with lubricating oil.
- It should have minimum ozone depletion potential.

**Vapour Absorption Refrigeration System**

Compressor of a vapour compression refrigeration system requires a large mechanical power for its operation. The compressor increases the pressure of large volume of refrigerant from evaporator pressure to condenser pressure.

In vapour absorption system, the compressor is replaced by an absorber and a generator.

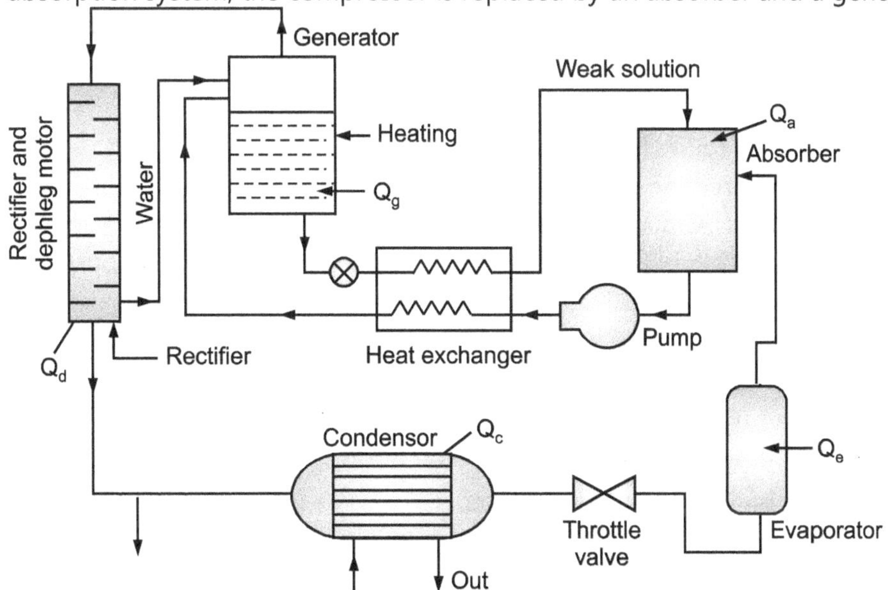


**Fig. 4.24: Ammonia - water absorption system**

Simple ammonia vapour absorption system is shown in Fig. 4.24. The essential components of this system are evaporator, absorber, generator, the condenser, analyzer, rectifier, and heat exchangers.

In this system, water serves as an absorbent and ammonia ($NH_3$) as refrigerant.

Heat is supplied to the generator. Therefore, it produces ammonia vapour and water particles (vapour). The pressure of ammonia in the generator is about 10 bar. It passes through rectifier, where water particles are separated and returned to the generator.

If these particles are carried to the throttle valve through condenser, then they may solidify to ice, blocking the passage.

The ammonia vapour passes through a condenser coil, where it changes changing in phase from vapour to liquid. This liquid ammonia is throttled through the throttle valve to reduce its pressure to evaporator pressure.

The ammonia circulated through the evaporator coil extracts heat producing the refrigeration effect, during which it changes its phase from liquid to vapour.

The ammonia vapour enters the absorber where weak aqua $NH_3$ solution is sprayed. The water absorbs ammonia. The mixture of ammonia and water becomes strong solution. This strong solution is heated by the hot weak solution in the heat exchanger and then supplied to the generator. The heat exchanger serves two purposes : (i) it cools the weak solution, (ii) it heats the strong solution.

The weak solution at lower temperature is desirable in the absorber because absorption process occurs more effectively at lower temperature.

The strong solution is heated in the generator where separated ammonia vapour is taken through rectifier and in this way the cycle repeats.

Other vapour absorption refrigeration systems include (i) Lithium - Bromide absorption refrigeration system, (ii) Electroflux system.

**Comparison of vapour compression refrigeration system with vapour absorption system is done in the following paragraphs.**

- Vapour compression refrigeration system (VCRS) requires a compressor to increase the pressure of vapour refrigerant to condensing pressure while vapour absorption refrigeration system (VARS) uses absorber and generator for this purpose.

- VCRS requires electrical power for the operation of compressor while VARS does not require power for this purpose but may require for the working of pump. VARS is a heat operated system.

- Waste heat (exhaust steam) from steam power plant can be used as heat input to VARS but this is not the case with VCRS.

- The COP of VCRS is badly affected by the load variation, but the COP of VARS remains fairly constant irrespective of load.

- VARS are available commercially with large capacity (more than 400 TR), but such large capacity units of VCRS are not commercially available.

- VCRS systems are available in smaller capacity (even upto 0.25 TR), but smaller capacity units of VARS are not available.
- VARS is complicated, while VCRS is compact.
- Wear and tear problems are absent in VARS, but such problems are unavoidable with VCRS because of moving parts.
- VARS are not useful for domestic purposes because of their large capacity.
- VCRS is noisy in operation while VARS is quiet in operation.

**Remarks:**

(i)   $T_3$ is decided by metallurgical considerations and is limited to @ 1000 K.

(ii)  $T_1$ is atmospheric temperature which is usually 15°C or 288 K.

(iii) $r_w$ = work ratio = $1 - \dfrac{T_1}{T_3} \cdot r_p^m$ is a function of temperature ratio and pressure ratio.

(iv)  Thermal efficiency = $1 - \dfrac{1}{r_p^{\frac{\gamma-1}{\gamma}}}$ is function of pressure ratio only.

**Problem 4.6:** 1 kg of air is circulated in Otto cycle having compression ratio of 6. The initial pressure and temperature of the Otto cycle are respectively 1 bar and 100°C. The maximum pressure in the cycle is 35 bar. Calculate the values of pressure, volume and temperature at the four salient points of the cycle. Also find the ratio of heat supplied to heat rejected.

**Solution:**

**Point 1:**

$$\text{Pressure} = 1 \text{ bar}, \text{Temperature} = 100°C$$

$$P_1V_1 = mRT$$

$$\therefore \quad V_1 = \frac{1 \times 0.287 \times 10^3 \times 373}{1 \times 10^5} = \mathbf{1.07051 \ m^3}$$

**Point 2:**

$$P_1V_1^\gamma = P_2V_2^\gamma$$

$$\therefore \quad P_2 = P_1 (V_1/V_2)^\gamma = 1 \times 6^{1.4}$$

$$= 12.3 \text{ bar}$$

$$V_2 = \frac{V_1}{6} = \frac{1.0705}{6} = 0.1784 \ m^3$$

$$\frac{P_1V_1}{T_1} = \frac{P_2V_2}{T_2}$$

$$\therefore \quad T_2 = \frac{P_2V_2}{P_1V_1} T_1 = \frac{12.3 \times 0.1784 \times 373}{1 \times 1.0705} = 765 \text{ K or } \mathbf{492°C}$$

**Point 3:**

$$V_3 = V_2 = 0.1784 \text{ m}^3$$

$$P_3 = 35 \text{ bar}$$

$$\frac{P_3}{T_3} = \frac{P_2}{T_2}$$

$$\therefore \quad T_3 = \frac{P_3}{P_2} T_2 = \frac{35}{12.3} \times 765 = 2176.83 \text{ or } \mathbf{1802°C}$$

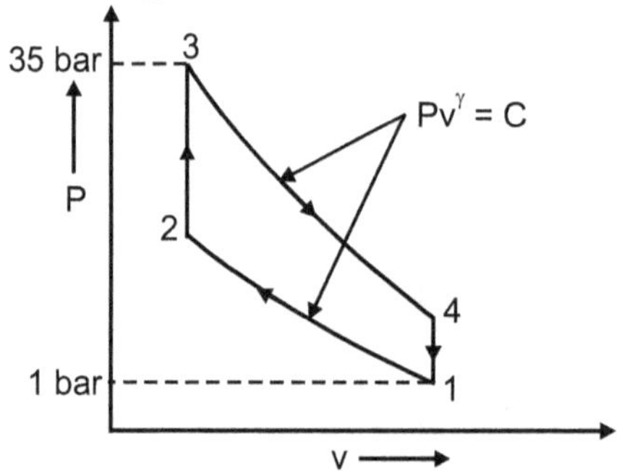

**Fig. 4.25**

**Point 4:**

$$P_3 V_3^\gamma = P_4 V_4^\gamma$$

$$\therefore \quad P_4 = P_3 \left(\frac{V_3}{V_4}\right)^\gamma = 35 \times \left(\frac{1}{6}\right)^{1.4}$$

$$= 2.84 \text{ bar}$$

$$V_4 = V_1 = 1.0705 \text{ m}^3$$

$$\frac{P_4}{T_4} = \frac{P_1}{T_1}$$

$$T_4 = T_1 \frac{P_4}{T_1} = 373 \times \frac{2.84}{1} = 1059.32 \text{ K or } \mathbf{783°C}$$

| | Pressure<br>bar | Volume<br>m³ | Temperature<br>°C |
|---|---|---|---|
| Point 1 | 1.0 | 1.0705 | 100 |
| Point 2 | 12.3 | 0.1784 | 492 |
| Point 3 | 35.0 | 0.1784 | 1802 |
| Point 4 | 2.84 | 1.0705 | 783 |

$$C_v = \frac{R}{(\gamma - 1)} = \frac{0.287}{(1.4 - 1)} = \mathbf{0.7175 \text{ kJ/kg·K}}$$

$$\text{Heat supplied} = C_v (T_3 - T_2)$$
$$= 0.7175 (1802 - 492) = 0.7175 \times 1310 = \textbf{939.9 kJ/kg}$$
$$\text{Heat rejected} = C_v (T_4 - T_1)$$
$$= 0.7175 (783 - 100) = 0.7175 \times 683 = \textbf{490.05 kJ/kg}$$
$$\therefore \quad \frac{\text{Heat supplied}}{\text{Heat rejected}} = \frac{939.9}{490.05} = \textbf{1.92}$$

**Problem 4.7:** 1045 kJ heat is added in Otto cycle having a compression ratio of 8. At the beginning of Otto cycle, the pressure and temperature are respectively 1 bar and 288 K. Determine:

(a)  Maximum temperature in the cycle.

(b)  The air standard efficiency.

(c)  The work done per kg of air.

(d)  The heat rejected.

**Solution:**

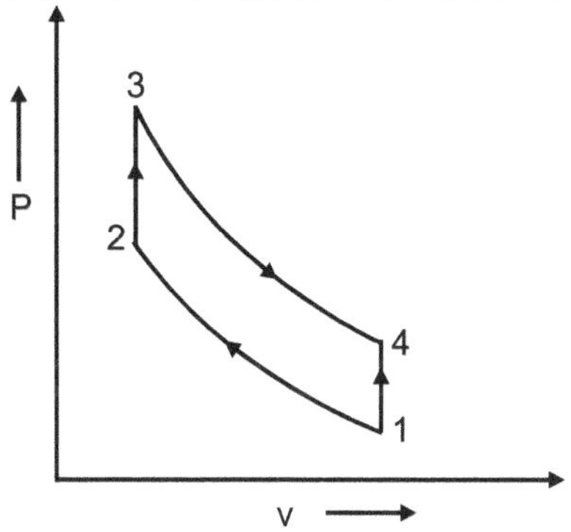

(a) 

$$T_1 = 15 + 273 = 288 \text{ K}$$
$$P_1 = 1 \text{ bar}$$
$$P_2 = P_1 \times \left(\frac{V_1}{V_2}\right)^{\gamma}$$
$$= 1 \times 8^{1.4}$$
$$P_2 = 18.38 \text{ bar}$$
$$T_2 = T_1 \times \left(\frac{V_1}{V_2}\right)^{\gamma - 1}$$
$$= 288 \times 8^{1.4 - 1}$$
$$T_2 = 288 \times 2.3 = \textbf{663 K}$$

$$\text{Heat supplied} = C_v (T_3 - T_2)$$
$$1046 = 0.718 (T_3 - 663)$$
$$T_3 = \left(\frac{1046}{0.718}\right) + 663 = 2119.82 \text{ or } \textbf{1847°C}$$



**Fig. 4.26**

The maximum temperature in the cycle is **1847°C**.                                 ... **Ans.**

(b)  Air standard efficiency

$$= 1 - \frac{1}{r^{\gamma - 1}}$$
$$= 1 - \frac{1}{8^{0.4}} = 1 - \frac{1}{2.3} = 1 - 0.435 = 0.565 = \textbf{56.5\%} \quad ... \textbf{Ans.}$$

(c)                Work done  =  Heat supplied × Efficiency

$$= 1046 \times 56.5$$

$$= \mathbf{590.99 \ kJ}$$

(d)
$$T_4 = T_3 \times \left(\frac{V_3}{V_2}\right)^{\gamma-1} = 2119.82 \times \left(\frac{1}{8}\right)^{1.4-1}$$

$$= \frac{2119.82}{23} = 922.7 \ K$$

$$\text{Heat rejected} = C_v(T_4 - T_1) = 0.718(922.7 - 288)$$

$$0.718 \times 639 = 458.802 \ kJ/kg$$

$$= \mathbf{455.7 \ kg/kJ} \qquad \qquad \dots \textbf{Ans.}$$

**Problem 4.8:** In an Otto cycle air initially at 15°C and 1.05 bar is compressed isentropically until the pressure rises to 15 bara. Heat is added at constant volume until the pressure rises to 35 bara. Calculate: (a) The air standard efficiency, (b) Compression ratio, (c) Mean effective pressure for the cycle.

**Solution:** Refer Fig. 4.27.

$$P_1 V_1^{\gamma} = P_2 V_2^{\gamma}$$

$$\frac{V_1}{V_2} = \left(\frac{P_3}{P_1}\right)^{\frac{1}{\gamma}} \frac{1}{\gamma} = 0.714$$

$$r = \left(\frac{13}{1.05}\right)^{0.714} = 6$$

$$\eta = 1 - \frac{1}{r^{\gamma-1}}$$

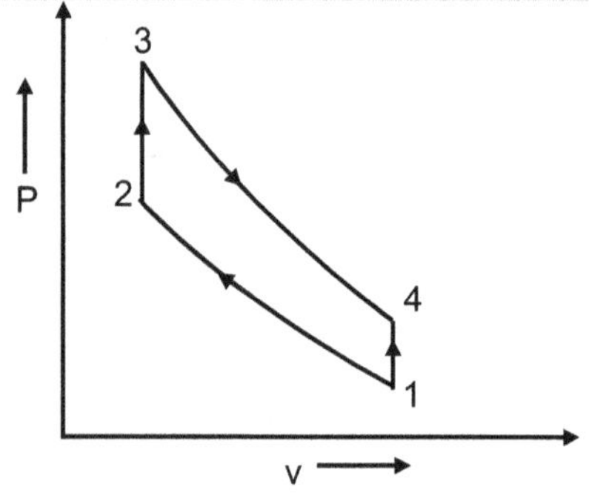


**Fig. 4.27**

$$= 1 - \frac{1}{6^{0.4}}$$

$$= 1 - 0.488$$

$$\eta = \mathbf{51.2\%}$$

$$\frac{P_1 V_1}{T_1} = \frac{P_2 V_2}{T_2}$$

$$\therefore \qquad T_2 = \frac{P_2 V_2}{P_1 V_1} \times T_1 = \frac{13}{1.05} \times \frac{1}{6} \times 288 = \mathbf{594 \ K}$$

Now,
$$\frac{P_3 V_3}{T_3} = \frac{P_2 V_2}{T_2}$$

$$T_3 = \frac{P_3 \times T_1}{P_2} = \frac{35}{13} \times 594 = \mathbf{1600 \ K}$$

$$\text{Heat supplied} = C_v(T_3 - T_2) = 0.718(1600 - 594) = \mathbf{722.308 \ kJ/kg}$$

$$\therefore \qquad \text{Work done} = \eta \times Q_1 = 0.512 \times 722.308 = \mathbf{369.821 \ kJ/kg}$$

To find swept volume,

$$P_1 V_1 = mRT_1$$

$$V_1 = \frac{1 \times 0.287 \times 288}{1.05 \times 10^2} = \mathbf{0.787 \ m^3/kg}$$

$$V_1 - V_2 = \left(\frac{5}{6}\right) \times 0.787 = \mathbf{0.656 \ m^3/kg}$$

$$mep = \frac{W}{V_1 - V_2} = \frac{369.821}{0.656 \times 10^2} = \mathbf{5.6375 \ bar}$$

**Problem 4.9:** Air at 20°C and 1 bar pressure is compressed isentropically in an Otto cycle having compression ratio of 1800 kJ/kg of heat is added at constant volume. Calculate the maximum temperature and pressure for the cycle. Also find temperature at the end of the expansion process. What is the efficiency and mean effective pressure of the cycle. Take $C_v = 0.718$ kJ/kg·K and $\gamma = 1.4$.

**Solution:**

$$\frac{T_2}{T_1} = \left(\frac{V_1}{V_2}\right)^{\gamma - 1} = r^{\gamma - 1}$$

$$\therefore \qquad T_2 = T_1 \, r^{\gamma - 1} = 293 \times 8^{0.41} = \mathbf{687 \ K}$$

Now heat addition during 2-3 $= C_v (T_3 - T_2)$

$$1800 = 0.718 (T_3 - 687)$$

$\therefore$ Maximum temperature $T_3 = \mathbf{3157 \ K}$

Also

$$\frac{P_2}{P_1} = \left(\frac{V_1}{V_2}\right)^{\gamma} = 8^{1.41} = \mathbf{18.8}$$

Hence, $\qquad P_2 = \mathbf{18.8 \ bar}$

From the gas laws with $V_2 = V_3$. We have $\dfrac{P_3}{T_3} = \dfrac{P_2}{T_2}$.

$$\text{Maximum pressure, } P_3 = P_2 \cdot \frac{T_3}{T_2} = 18.8 \times \frac{3157}{687}$$

$$= \mathbf{86.4 \ bar} \qquad\qquad \textbf{... Ans.}$$

At the end of expansion,

$$T_3 = T_4 \, r^{\gamma - 1}$$

Hence, $\qquad T_4 = \dfrac{T_3}{8^{0.41}} = \dfrac{3157}{2.35} = 1344 \ K \qquad\qquad$ **... Ans.**

$$\text{The efficiency is } \eta = 1 - \frac{1}{r^{\gamma - 1}} = 1 - \frac{1}{8^{0.41}}$$

$$= 1 - \frac{1}{2.35} = 0.574 \text{ or } 57.4\% \qquad\qquad \textbf{... Ans.}$$

For the mean pressure, two alternative solutions (a) and (b) are given, (a)　　　　　　$Q_{1-2} = 0 = V_2 - V_1 + W_{12}$

or　　　　　　$W_{12} = V_1 - V_2 = C_v (T_1 - T_2)$

Similarly,　　　$W_{34} = c_v (T_3 - T_4)$

Also,　　　　　$W_{23} = 0 = W_{41}$

$\therefore$　　　　　　$\oint \delta W = C_v \{(T_1 - T_2) + (T_3 - T_4)\}$

[**Note:** Alternatively,　$W = Q_{23} - Q_{12}$]

or　　　　　　$\oint \delta W = 0.718 \times \{(293 - 687) + (3157 - 1344)\}$

　　　　　　　　　$= 0.718 \times 1419 - 687) = \textbf{1018.842 kJ/kg}$

Now,　　　　$P_m (V_1 - V_2) = \oint \delta W$ and from the gas laws

$$V_1 = \frac{RT_1}{P_1} = \frac{0.287 \times 293}{1 \times 10^2} = \textbf{0.84 m}^3\textbf{/kg}$$

Now,　　　　$V_2 = \dfrac{V_1}{8}$ and $V_1 - V_2 = V_1 \left(1 - \dfrac{1}{8}\right)$

Hence,　　　$P_m = \dfrac{1018.842}{0.84} \times \dfrac{8}{7} = \textbf{13.846 bar}$

(b)　　　　　$\oint \delta W = \eta\, q_{2-3} = 0.574 \times 1800$

　　　　　　　　　$= \textbf{1033.2 kJ/kg}$

Hence, $P_m$ is found as in (a) above.

---

**Problem 4.10:** Show that the mean effective pressure of an Otto cycle can be expressed in the form $\dfrac{\eta_{th}\, \Delta P}{(r - 1)(\gamma - 1)}$, where, $\eta_{th}$ is the thermal efficiency of the cycle $\Delta P$ is the pressure rise during the heat transfer to the cycle, r is the compression ratio and $\gamma$ is the ratio of specific heats of the working.

The working substance of a four-stroke reciprocating S.I. engine produces an internal power of 50 kW at 4800 rpm. The stroke and bore of the engine of which has four cylinders is 80 mm. The clearance volume is 50000 mm$^3$. The pressure rise during combustion is 45 bar. Compare the mep of the engine with that of the comparable Otto cycle. In both cases take $\gamma = 1.4$.

**Solution:**

$$\text{Mean effective pressure} = \frac{\text{Area of the p-v diagram}}{\text{Length of the diagram}}$$

$$= \frac{\text{Work done}}{\Delta V} = \frac{\oint P\, dV}{\Delta V}$$

Now,
$$W = \oint P\, dV = \eta_{th} \times \text{Heat transfer to cycle}$$

$$= \eta \times c_v\,(T_3 - T_2) \times m$$

Thus,
$$\text{mep} = \frac{\eta_{th}\, c_v\,(T_3 - T_2)\, m}{\Delta V}$$

Now,
$$V_v = \frac{R}{\gamma - 1}$$

$$T = \frac{PV}{mR}$$

and
$$\Delta V_2 = (\gamma - 1)$$

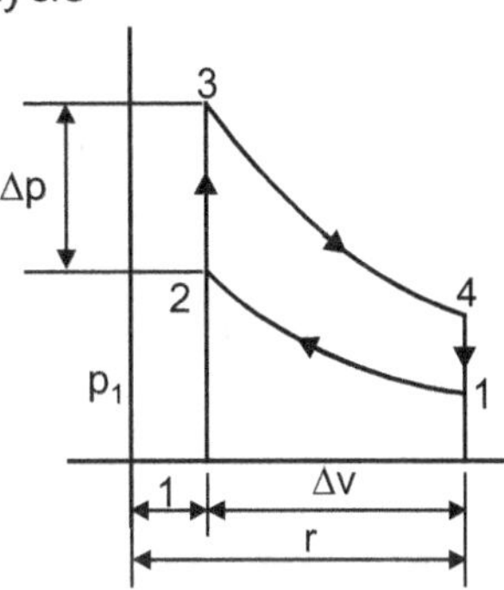

**Fig. 2.28**

$\therefore$
$$\text{mep} = \eta_{th}\left[\frac{R}{\gamma - 1}\right]\left[\frac{P_3 V_3}{mR} - \frac{P_2 V_2}{mR}\right]\frac{m}{V_2\,(R - 1)}$$

Now,
$$V_3 = V_2$$

and
$$P_3 - P_2 = \Delta P$$

$\therefore$
$$\text{mep} = \frac{\eta_{th}\,\Delta P}{(\gamma - 1)\,(r - 1)}$$

For the engine considered compression ratio,

$$r = \frac{\frac{1}{4}\,\pi \times 80^2 \times 80 + 50000}{50000} = \textbf{9.04}$$

and the swept volume,
$$\Delta V = \left(\frac{\pi}{4}\right) \times 80^2 \times 80$$

$$= 0.4 \times 10^{-3}\ \text{m}^3$$

Air standard efficiency
$$\eta = 1 - \frac{1}{(9.04)^{0.4}} = \textbf{0.585}$$

Ideal mep
$$= \frac{0.585 \times 45}{0.4 \times 8.04} = \textbf{8.18 bar} \qquad \qquad \textbf{... Ans.}$$

For the actual engine, the work transfer per cycle per cylinder.

$$= \frac{\text{Power output}}{\text{Number of cylinders} \times \text{Number of working strokes per unit time}}$$

$$= \frac{50}{4 \times \left(\dfrac{4800}{2}\right)} = 0.3125\ \text{kJ}$$

The engine mep
$$= \frac{\text{Work transfer per cycle}}{\text{Swept volume}} = \frac{0.3125 \times 10^3}{0.4 \times 10^{-3} \times 10^5}$$

$\therefore$  Actual mep $= 7.813$ bar $\qquad \qquad$ **... Ans.**

**Problem 4.11:** A petrol engine is supplied with fuel which has calorific value of 10,000 kcal/kg. The pressure in the cylinder at 30% and 70% of the compression stroke are 1.33 bar and 2.66 bar respectively. Assuming that the compression follows the law $PV^{1.33}$ = Constant. Find the compression ratio.

If the relative efficiency of the engine compared with the air standard cycle efficiency is 50%. Calculate the fuel consumption in kg/kWh.

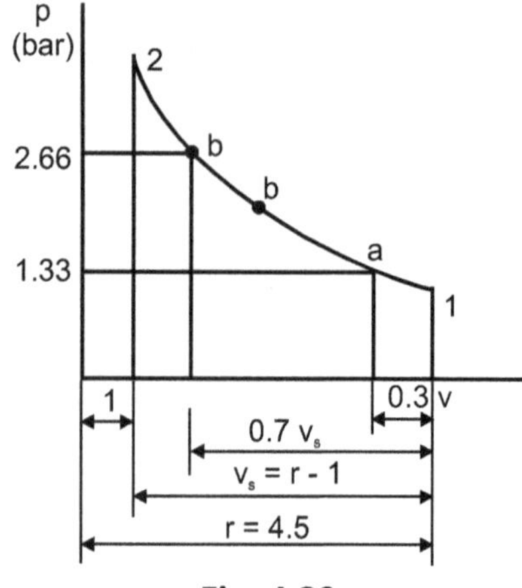


**Fig. 4.29**

**Solution :**

At 30% of compression stroke,

$$V_a \;=\; 1 + 0.7\,(r - 1) = (0.7)\,r + 0.3$$

At 20% of compression stroke,

$$V_b \;=\; 1 + 0.3\,(r - 1) = (0.3)\,r + 0.7$$

Now,

$$\frac{V_1}{V_2} \;=\; \left(\frac{P_2}{P_1}\right)^{\frac{1}{n}} = \left(\frac{2.66}{1.33}\right)^{\frac{1}{1.33}} = 1.684$$

$$1.684 \;=\; \frac{(0.7)\,r + 0.3}{(0.3)\,r + 0.7}$$

or

$$r \;=\; 4.51$$

$$\text{Air standard efficiency} \;=\; 1 - \frac{1}{(4.51)^{0.4}} = 0.453$$

$$\text{Indicated thermal efficiency} = 0.5 \times 0.453 = 0.227$$

$$\text{Heat supplied} \;=\; 15871.32 \text{ kJ/kWh}$$

∴　Indicates specific fuel consumption,

$$\text{isfc} \;=\; \frac{15871.32}{10000 \times 4.184} = 0.38 \text{ kg/kWh}$$

**Problem 4.12:** An air-standard diesel cycle has a compression ratio of 14. The pressure at the beginning of the compression stroke is 1 bar and the temperature is 27°C. The maximum temperature is 2500°C. Determine the thermal efficiency and the mean effective pressure.

**Solution:**

$$T_2 \;=\; T_1 \left(\frac{V_1}{V_2}\right)^{\gamma - 1} = 300 \times (14)^{0.4} = 300 \times 2.88 = \mathbf{864\ K}$$

$$P_2 \;=\; P_1 \left(\frac{T_2}{T_1}\right)^{\frac{\gamma}{\gamma - 1}} = 1 \left(\frac{864}{300}\right)^{3.5} = 1 \times 40.5 = \mathbf{40.5\ bar}$$

Now,
$$\frac{V_3}{V_2} = \frac{T_3}{T_2} = \frac{2773}{864} = 3.21$$

and
$$\frac{T_3}{T_4} = \left(\frac{V_4}{V_3}\right)^{\gamma-1} = \left(\frac{V_4}{V_2} \times \frac{V_2}{V_3}\right)^{\gamma-1} = \left(\frac{14}{3.21}\right)^{0.4} = (4.36)^{0.4} = \mathbf{1.8}$$

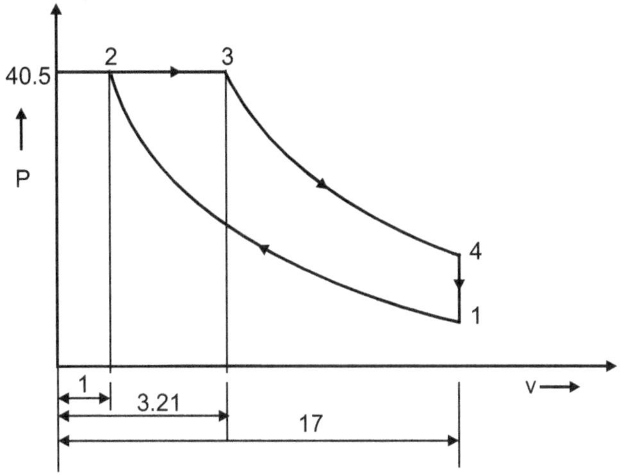

**Fig. 4.30**

$\therefore$
$$T_4 = \frac{T_3}{1.8} = \frac{2773}{1.8} = \mathbf{1540\ K}$$

$$\eta = \frac{C_v\,(T_3 - T_2) - C_v\,(T_4 - T_1)}{C_p\,(T_3 - T_2)}$$

$$= 1 - \frac{T_4 - T_1}{\gamma\,(T_3 - T_2)} = 1 - \frac{1540 - 300}{1.4\,(2773 - 864)}$$

$$\eta = 1 - 0.464 = 0.536 = \mathbf{53.62\%}$$

$$V_1 \text{ for 1 kg} = \frac{RT_1}{P_1} = \frac{0.287 \times 300}{1 \times 10^2}$$

$$= \mathbf{0.861\ m^3/kg}$$

Stroke volume $> V_1 - V_2$
$$= V_1 \left(1 - \frac{1}{14}\right)$$

$$= 0.861 \left(1 - \frac{1}{14}\right) = 0.800\ m^3/kg$$

Mean effective pressure
$$= \frac{\text{Net work/Cycle}}{\text{Stroke volume}}$$

$$= \frac{C_p\,(T_3 - T_2) - C_v\,(T_4 - T_1)}{0.8}$$

$$P_m = \frac{1.005 \times 1909 - 0.718 \times 1240}{0.8}$$

$$P_m = 10.282\ \text{bar} \hspace{3cm} \textbf{... Ans.}$$

**Example 4.13:** Overall compression ratio of an ideal diesel engine is 18. Constant pressure heat addition ceases at 10% of stroke. Intake conditions are 1 bar and 20°C. The air consumption is 100 m³/hr. Determine (a) Maximum temperature and pressure in the cycle, (b) Thermal efficiency of the engine and (c) Indicated power of the engine. Assume $\gamma = 1.4$.

**Solution:**

Let clearance volume = 1.

Swept volume = 18 − 1 = 17.

10% of the swept volume

$$= 17 \times 0.1 = 1.7$$

∴    Constant pressure energy addition ceases at 1 + 1.7 = 2.7

$$\frac{V_3}{V_2} = \rho = \frac{2.71}{1} = 2.7$$

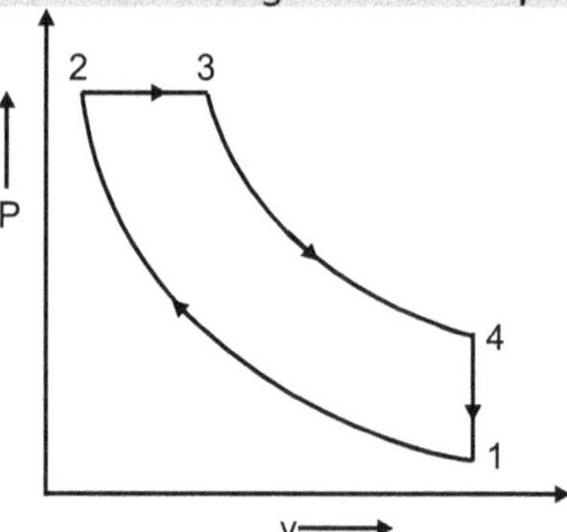

**Fig. 4.31: Diesel Cycle**

Thermal efficiency

$$\eta_{th} = 1 - \frac{1}{r^{\gamma-1}}\left[\frac{\rho^{\gamma-1}}{r\,(\rho-1)}\right]$$

$$= 1 - \frac{1}{(18)^{1.4}-1}\left[\frac{(2.7)^{1.4-1}}{1.4\,(2.7-1)}\right]$$

$$\eta_{th} = 1 - 0.4 = 0.6 \text{ or } 60\% \qquad\qquad \text{... \textbf{Ans.}}$$

$$T_1 = 20 + 273 = 293 \text{ K}, P_1 = 1 \text{ bar}$$

$$P_2 = P_1 \times \left(\frac{V_1}{V_2}\right)^{\gamma} = 1 \times (18)^{1.4} = \textbf{53.6 bar}$$

$$P_3 = P_2 = 53.6 \text{ bar}$$

$$T_2 = T_1 \times \left(\frac{V_1}{V_2}\right)^{\gamma-1} = 293 \times (18)^{1.4-1}$$

$$= 293 \times 3.175 = \textbf{930 K}$$

$$\frac{P_2 V_2}{T_2} = \frac{P_3 V_3}{T_3}$$

$$T_3 = T_2\frac{V_3}{V_2} = 930 \times 2.7 = 2510 \text{ K or } \textbf{2237°C} \qquad\qquad \text{... \textbf{Ans.}}$$

The maximum temperature and pressure of the cycle are 2237°C and 153.6 bar respectively.

Let us consider the cycle for 100 m³ for air

$$\therefore \qquad V_1 - V_2 = 100 \text{ m}^3, V_1 = 18\,V_2 \qquad\qquad (\because r = 18)$$

$$18\,V_2 - V_2 = 100$$

$$\text{or} \qquad V_2 = \frac{100}{17} = 6.13 \text{ m}^3$$

$$V_1 = 100 + 6.13 = \textbf{106.13 m}^3$$

$$V_3 = 2.7\,V_2 = 2.7 \times 6.13 = \textbf{15.9 m}^3$$

$$V_4 = V_2 = \textbf{106.13 m}^3$$

$$P_4 = P_3 \left(\frac{V_3}{V_4}\right)^\gamma = 53.6 \left(\frac{15.9}{106.13}\right)^{1.4}$$

$$= 53.6 \,\frac{1}{14.6} = 3.67 \text{ bar}$$

$$\text{Work done} = P_2 (V_3 - V_2) + \frac{(P_3 V_3 - P_4 V_4) - (P_2 V_2 - P_1 V_1)}{(\gamma - 1)}$$

$$= 53.6\,(15.9 - 6.13) +$$

$$\frac{(53.6 \times 15.9 - 3.67 \times 106.13) - (53.6 \times 6.13 - 1 \times 106.13)}{1.4 - 1}$$

$$= 524 + 602.6 = 1126.5 \times 10^2 \text{ kJ}$$

$$\text{Indicated power} = \frac{1126.5 \times 10^2}{60 \times 60}$$

$$= \textbf{30.67 kW}$$

**Problem 4.14:** An ideal diesel engine has a diameter of 12 cm and stroke 18 cm. The clearance volume is 10% of the swept volume. Determine the compression ratio and the air standard efficiency of the engine if the cut-off takes place at 6% of the stroke.

**Solution:**

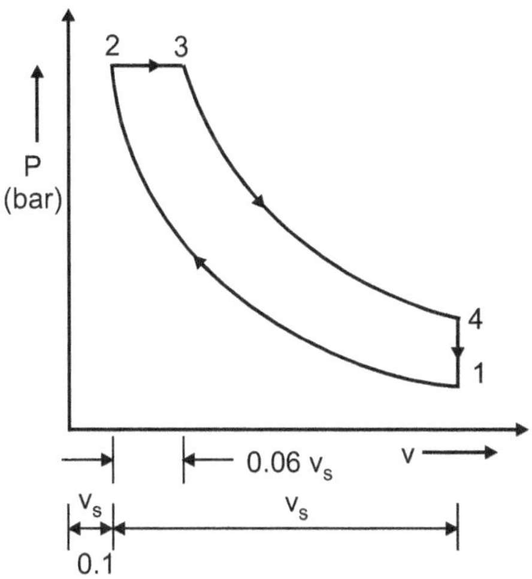


**Fig. 4.32**

$$\text{Stroke volume, V} = \frac{\pi}{4} \times d^2 \times L = \frac{\pi}{4}(12)^2 \times 18$$

$$= \textbf{2035 cm}^3$$

$$\text{Clearance volume, V}_c = 0.1 \times V_a = 0.1 \times 2035 = \textbf{203.5 cm}^3$$

$$\text{Total volume, V}_1 = V_c + V_a = 203.5 + 2035 = \textbf{2239 cm}^3$$

$\therefore$     Compression ratio $= \dfrac{V_1}{V_2} = \dfrac{V_1}{V_c} = \dfrac{2239}{203.5} = \mathbf{11.00}$       **... Ans.**

$$\text{Cut-off ratio, } \rho = \dfrac{V_3}{V_2} = \dfrac{V_2 + (V_3 - V_2)}{V_2}$$

$$= \dfrac{203.5 + 0.06 \times 203.5}{203.5}$$

$$= \mathbf{1.6}$$

$\therefore$    The air standard efficiency of the cycle

$$\eta = 1 - \dfrac{1}{r^{\gamma-1}}\left[\dfrac{\gamma^{\gamma} - 1}{\gamma\,(\rho - 1)}\right]$$

$$= 1 - \dfrac{1}{(11)^{0.4}}\left[\dfrac{(1.6)^{1.4} - 1}{1.4\,(1.6 - 1)}\right]$$

$$\eta = 0.57 \text{ or } 57\% \qquad\qquad \textbf{... Ans.}$$

**Problem 4.15:** A dual combustion cycle has an adiabatic compression volume ratio of 15 : 1. The conditions at the beginning of compression are 1 bar, 25°C and 0.15 m³. The maximum pressure of the cycle is 66 bar and the maximum temperature of the cycle is 1500°C. If $C_v = 0.71$ kJ/kg·K and $\gamma = 1.4$. Calculate the pressure, volume and temperature at the corners of the cycle and the thermal efficiency of the cycle.

**Solution:**

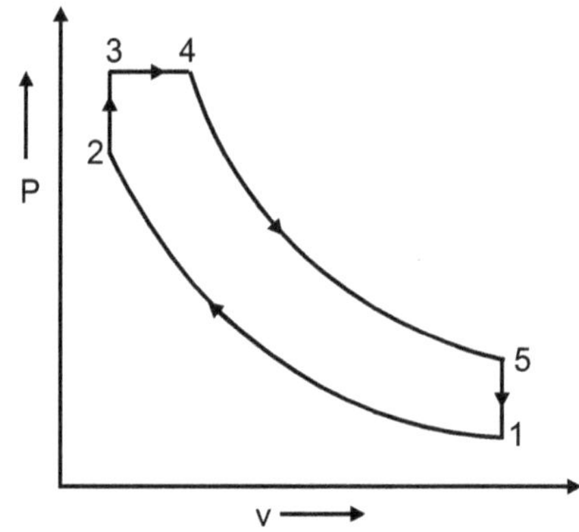


**Fig. 4.33**

$P_1 = 1$ bar, $T_1 = 25 + 273 = 298$ K, $V_1 = 0.1$ m³

$$V_2 = \left(\dfrac{0.1}{15}\right) = 0.01 \text{ m}^3$$

$$P_2 = P_1 \times \left(\dfrac{V_1}{V_2}\right)^{\gamma} = P_1\left(\dfrac{V_1}{V_2}\right)^{\gamma} = 1 \times (15)^{\gamma}$$

$$= 44.2 \text{ bar}$$

$$T_2 \;=\; T_1 \cdot \left(\frac{V_1}{V_2}\right)^{\gamma-1} = 298 \left(\frac{1}{15}\right)^{1.4-1}$$

$$= \textbf{882 K}$$

$$P_3 \;=\; 63 \text{ bar}$$

$$T_3 \;=\; T_2 \cdot \left(\frac{P_3}{P_2}\right) = 882 \times 65 \,(44.2)$$

$$= \textbf{1297 K}$$

$$V_3 \;=\; V_2 = 0.01 \text{ m}^3$$

$$V_4 \;=\; V_3 \left(\frac{T_4}{T_2}\right) = 0.01 \times \frac{(1500 + 273)}{1297}$$

$$= 0.066 \times \frac{1773}{1297} = \textbf{0.0136 m}^3$$

$$P_4 = P_3 \;=\; 65 \text{ bar}$$

$$V_5 = V_1 \;=\; 0.1 \text{ m}^3$$

$$P_5 \;=\; P_4 \left(\frac{V_4}{V_5}\right)^{\gamma} = 16 \times \left(\frac{0.0136}{0.1}\right)^{1.4}$$

$$P_5 \;=\; 0.061 \text{ bar}$$

$$T_5 \;=\; T_4 \left(\frac{V_4}{V_5}\right)^{\gamma-1} = 1773 \left(\frac{0.0136}{0.1}\right)^{1.4-1} = \frac{1773}{2.62}$$

$$= \textbf{798 K or 525°C}$$

|  | Pressure (bar) | Volume (m³) | Temperature (°C) |
|---|---|---|---|
| Point 1 | 1 | 0.15 | 25 |
| Point 2 | 44.2 | 0.01 | 882 |
| Point 3 | 65 | 0.01 | 1297 |
| Point 4 | 63 | 0.0136 | 1500 |
| Point 5 | 0.061 | 0.15 | 525 |

Thermal efficiency,

$$\eta_{th} \;=\; 1 - \frac{T_5 - T_1}{T_3 - T_2 + \gamma (T_4 - T_3)}$$

$$= 1 - \frac{525 - 25}{(1297 - 882) + 1.4\,(1500 - 1297)}$$

$$= 1 - \frac{500}{415 + 1.4 \times 203}$$

$$= \textbf{0.284} \hspace{3cm} \textbf{... Ans.}$$

**Problem 4.16:** A high speed diesel engine working on ideal dual combustion cycle takes in air at a pressure of 1 bar and temperature of 50°C and compresses it adiabatically to 1/15 of its original volume. At the end of the compression the heat is added in such a manner that during the first stage the pressure increases at constant volume to twice the pressure of the adiabatic compression and during the second stage following the constant volume addition, the volume is increased twice the clearance volume at constant pressure. The air is then allowed to expand adiabatically to the end of the stroke where it is exhausted heat being rejected at constant volume. Calculate (a) The temperature at the key points of the cycle and (b) In the ideal thermal efficiency.

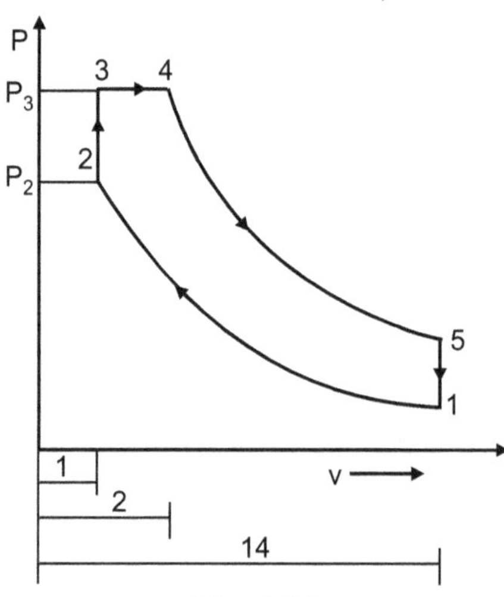


**Fig. 4.34**

**Solution:**

(a)
$$T_2 = T_1 (r)^{\gamma - 1} = 323 (14)^{0.4} = \mathbf{930\ K}$$

$$P_2 = P_1 \left(\frac{V_1}{V_2}\right)^{\gamma} = 1 (15)^{1.4} = \mathbf{44.3\ bar}$$

$$P_2 = 2 \times 44.3 = 88.6\ bar$$

$$T_3 = T_2 \left(\frac{P_3}{P_2}\right) = 930 \times \frac{88.6}{44.3} = \mathbf{1860\ K} \qquad \textbf{... Ans.}$$

$$T_4 = T_3 \left(\frac{V_4}{V_3}\right) = 1860 \times 2 = \mathbf{3720\ K} \qquad \textbf{... Ans.}$$

Now expansion ratio $= \dfrac{V_5}{V_4} = \dfrac{15}{2} = 7.5$

$\therefore$
$$T_5 = \frac{T_4}{\left(\dfrac{V_5}{V_4}\right)^{\gamma - 1}} = \frac{3720}{(7.5)^{0.4}} = \mathbf{1661.5\ K} \qquad \textbf{... Ans.}$$

(b)
$$\text{Heat added} = C_v (T_3 - T_2) + C_p (T_4 - T_3)$$
$$= 0.718 (1860 - 930) + 1.005 (3720 - 1860)$$
$$= 2537\ kJ/kg$$

$$\text{Heat rejected} = C_v (T_5 - T_1) = 0.718 (1661.5 - 323)$$
$$= \mathbf{961.0\ kJ/kg}$$

$$\text{Air standard efficiency} = \frac{2537 - 961}{2537} = 0.621\ or\ \mathbf{62.1\%}$$

## EXERCISE

1.  Define compression ratio. What is its range for (a) the SI engines, (b) the CI engine? What factors limit the compression ratio in each type of engine?
2.  What will be the effect of variables on engine performance viz.
    (i) Compression ratio on thermal efficiency, (ii) Fuel : Air Ratio on thermal efficiency, (iii) Fuel-air ratio on maximum pressure and maximum temperature, (iv) Fuel-air ratio on exhaust gas temperature.
3.  Give limitations of air standard cycle. Explain with suitable graphs, the effect of dissociation on maximum temperature and brake power. How does the presence of CO affects dissociation?
4.  Derive the relation for the percentage variation in air standard efficiency of diesel cycle with percentage variation of $C_v$.
5.  Explain characteristic features of the fuel-air cycle.
6.  What are the effects of operating variables on the performance of the fuel-air cycle?
7.  List the differences between actual cycles and air-standard cycles.
8.  What are the assumptions made in air standard cycle analysis?
9.  What is use of air standard cycle analysis?
10. Define mean effective pressure. What does this criterion indicate for reciprocating engines?
11. Obtain an expression for the air standard efficiency on a volume basis of an engine working on the Otto cycle.
    Hence show that the efficiency of the Otto cycle is lower than that of Carnot cycle.
12. Show by graphs how the efficiency of the Otto cycle varies with compression ratio and the ratio of specific heats of working medium.
13. Derive an expression for the mean effective pressure of the Otto cycle?
14. What is the difference between Otto and Diesel cycle? Derive the formula for the efficiency of the Diesel cycle. Hence show that the efficiency of Diesel Cycle is always lower than the efficiency of the Otto cycle for the same compression ratio.
15. Show by graph how the efficiency of Diesel cycle varies with compression ratio and cut-off ratio.
16. Explain why the higher efficiency of the Otto cycle compared to Diesel cycle for the same compression ratio is not a result of practical importance.
17. Derive an expression for the mean effective pressure of Diesel cycle.
18. Explain the dual combustion cycle? Why this cycle is also called limited pressure cycle? Derive an expression for the air standard efficiency of dual cycle.
19. Compare the Otto, Diesel and limited pressure cycles for the same compressor ratio and same heat input.
20. Compare the Otto and Diesel cycles for:
    (a)  Same constant maximum pressure and same heat input.
    (b)  Same maximum pressure and temperature.
    (c)  Same maximum pressure and output.

## UNIVERSITY QUESTION PAPERS

### DEC. 2013

1. For Dual Cycle define the following by using P–V diagram:　　　　**[6]**
   - (i)　Clearance Volume　　(ii)　Swept Volume
   - (iii)　Compression ratio　(iv)　Cut off ratio
   - (v)　Expansion ratio　　　(vi)　Pressure ratio

### MAY 2014

1. Explain Air standard Otto Cycle on P–V and T–s Diagram. State the formula for Compression ratio in terms of stroke and clearance volume, Expansion ratio, Net work done, Air standard Efficiency.　　　**[6]**

2. A gas turbine power plant operates between pressure ratio of 9.77. Operating temperature limits are 295 K and 1085 K. Determine Turbine work, Compressor work and Thermal efficiency.　　　**[6]**

### DEC. 2014

1. Draw P–v and T–s diagram for Otto cycle and derive the efficiency equation for Otto cycle.　　　**[6]**

### MAY 2015

1. A heat engine working on Carnot cycle absorbs heat from three thermal reservoirs at 1000 K, 800 K and 680 K. The engine does 10 kW of net work and rejects 400 kJ/min. of heat to a heat sink at 300 K. If the heat supplied by the reservoir at 1000 K is 60% of the heat supplied by the reservoir at 600 K, make calculations for the quantity of heat absorbed by each reservoir.　　　**[6]**

2. State the assumptions made for air standard cycle. Derive an expression for the air standard efficiency and mean effective pressure of an Otto cycle.　　　**[6]**

### NOV. 2015

1. Draw P–V and T–S diagram of Otto cycle and derive an expression to find its thermal efficiency.　　　**[6]**

### MAY 2016

1. Derive the relation for efficiency for Otto gas power cycle.　　　**[6]**

# Chapter 5

# AVAILABILITY

## 5.1 INTRODUCTION

It comes to our mind why an engineer has to understand the availability. The answer is to save energy, to consume energy in an optimal way, to reduce energy wastage etc. To achieve these, the engineers have to take a closer look at all the energy conversion devices (e.g. prime movers and energy consuming devices) and to develop new techniques to better utilize the existing limited resources. The first law of thermodynamics deals with conversion of energy from one form to another and tells that energy cannot be created or destroyed. It tells only the conversion of one form of energy to another however, it does not quantify the energy that changes from one form to another. First law is not a sufficient tool to quantify the process inefficiency or thermodynamic irreversibility which are inherently present in all real processes. For Problem, as per first law, throttling process is a constant enthalpy process. The energy content of the fluid before throttling and after throttling remains constant. Throttling is a real expansion process. The real process is always accompanied with process irreversibility. It is the limitation of first law that it could not quantify such process irreversibilities.

The second law of thermodynamics deals with the quality of energy. Second law is concerned with the degradation of energy during a process. It quantifies the process irreversibility and offers an opportunity to obtain maximum work output from a stream while bringing it from high temperature and pressure conditions to the reference temperature and pressure conditions. Therefore, at this stage, it becomes necessary to study available and unavailable energy of a system undergoing through a process.

## 5.2 AVAILABLE AND UNAVAILABLE ENERGY     [May 10, 11]

'**Available energy**' is the maximum portion of the energy which could be converted into useful work and which reduces the system to a 'dead state'. The dead state is one at which the system reaches thermodynamic equilibrium with the surrounding.

When a system is at high pressure than atmospheric pressure, then there is an opportunity to obtain useful work while reducing it to ambient pressure through an expansion device. Similarly, any system which is at higher temperature than ambient temperature, then also there is an opportunity to obtain useful work while reducing its temperature to ambient temperature through a thermodynamic cycle.

Therefore, available energy can be further defined as "the theoretical maximum useful work that can be obtained from a system while changing its state ($p_1$ and $T_1$) to reference state ($p_0$ and $T_0$) through a reversible process".

To obtain a maximum useful work from a system, its state ($p_1$ and $T_1$) has to be reduced to reference state ($p_0$ and $T_0$) through a reversible process. However, in reality, the end state of the system will not be at reference state but little above that state. It means say the system reaches to a state ($p_2$ and $T_2$) which is in between the initial state ($p_1$ and $T_1$) and reference state ($p_0$ and $T_0$). Therefore, the actual work obtained is less than that of maximum possible work (available energy). The portion of the available energy which is not converted to useful work is known as **unavailable energy.**

## 5.3 AVAILABLE ENERGY REFERRED TO A CYCLE

The maximum work output obtainable from a certain heat input in a cyclic heat engine (reversible engine) is called the available energy (AE). The minimum energy that has to be rejected to the sink as per the second law is called the unavailable energy (UE) or the unavailable part of supplied energy.

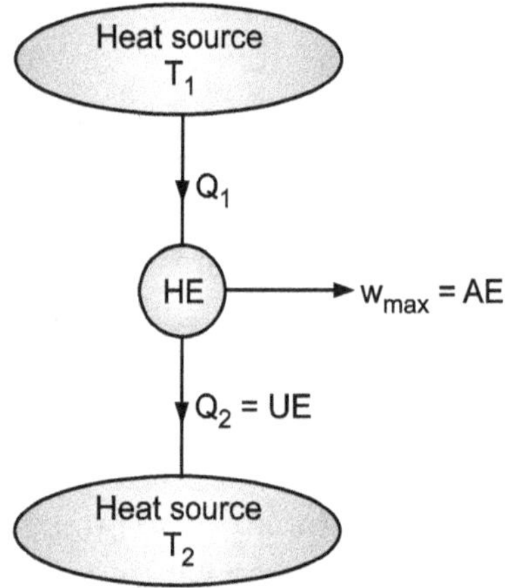


**Fig. 5.1: Available and unavailable energy in a cycle**

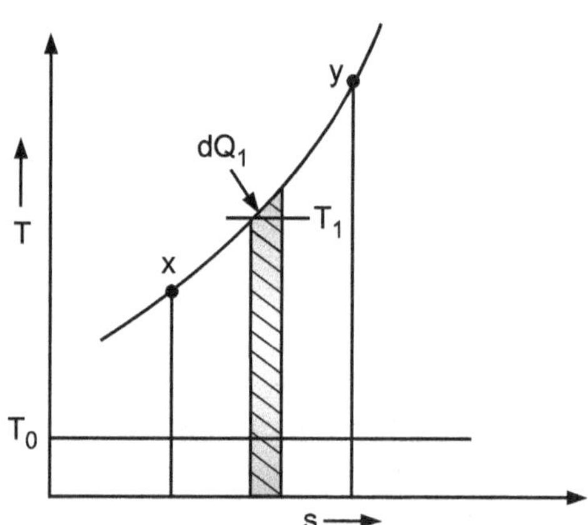


**Fig. 5.2: Availability of energy**

Let $Q_1$ be the heat energy supplied, which consists of two parts (AE and UE).

Therefore,           $Q_1 = AE + UE$           ... (5.1)

$$w_{max} = AE = Q_1 - UE$$

For the heat engine working between $T_1$ and $T_2$,

$$\eta_{rev} = 1 - \frac{T_2}{T_1}$$

For a given source temperature $T_1$, $\eta_{rev}$ will increase with decrease of sink temperature $T_2$. The lowest possible temperature at which heat rejection would take place is the temperature of the surroundings, $T_0$.

$$\eta_{max} = 1 - \frac{T_0}{T_1}$$

$$w_{max} = \left(1 - \frac{T_0}{T_1}\right) Q_1$$

Let us consider a process x-y, during which heat is supplied reversibly to a heat engine as shown in Fig. 5.2. Assuming an elementary cycle, $dQ_1$ is the heat supplied to a reversible heat engine at $T_1$, then

$$dw_{max} = \eta_{rev} \times dQ_1$$

$$= \left(\frac{T_1 - T_0}{T_1}\right) \cdot dQ_1$$

$$= dQ_1 - \frac{T_0}{T_1} dQ_1 = AE$$

The heat engine receiving heat for the whole process x-y and rejecting heat at $T_0$

$$\int_x^y dw_{max} = \int_x^y dQ_1 - \int_x^y \frac{T_0}{T_1} \cdot dQ_1$$

$$\therefore \qquad w_{max} = AE = Q_{xy} - T_0(s_y - s_x) \qquad \qquad \dots (5.2)$$

$$\text{Unavailable energy, } UE = Q_{xy} - w_{max}$$

$$= T_0(s_y - s_x)$$

The unavailable energy is nothing but the product of the lowest temperature of heat sink ($T_0$) and the change of entropy of the system during the process, which is as shown in Fig. 5.3.

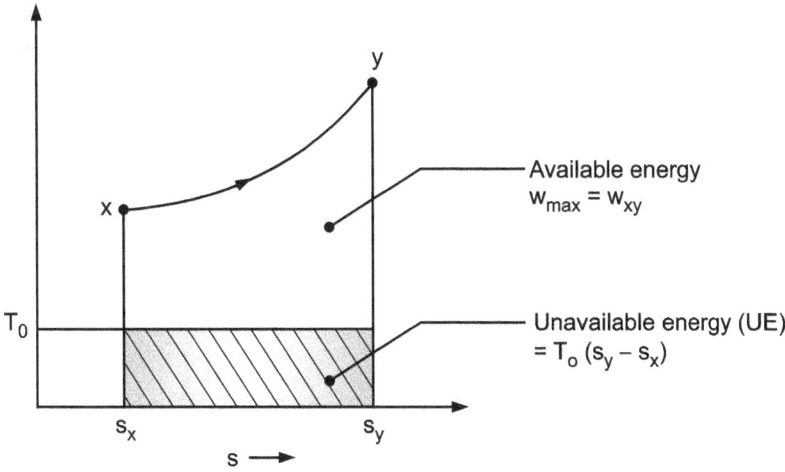


**Fig. 5.3: Unavailable energy according to second law**

The available energy is also known as **energy** and the unavailable energy as **energy.** It may please be note here that energy and energy are the correct words.

## 5.4 DECREASE IN AVAILABLE ENERGY IN A HEAT TRANSFER PROCESS THROUGH A FINITE TEMPERATURE DIFFERENCE

In order to transfer heat from one system to another, a finite temperature difference is needed. To achieve this, there is a decrease in the availability of energy. This can be shown as given below.

Consider a reversible heat engine (Carnot engine) operating between the temperature limits $T_1$ and $T_0$ as shown in Fig. 5.4.

$$\text{Heat supplied, } Q_1 = T \cdot \Delta s$$
$$\text{Heat rejected, } Q_2 = T_0 \cdot \Delta s$$
$$\text{Max. work done, } w = A.E = [T_1 - T_0]\, \Delta s$$

Assume heat $Q_1$ is transferred through a finite temperature difference ($\Delta T$) from the source at $T_1$ to the engine absorbing heat at $T_1'$, lower than $T_1$ (See Fig. 5.5). The availability of $Q_1$ as received by the engine at $T_1'$ can be found by allowing the engine to operate reversibly in a cycle between $T_1'$ and $T_0$ receiving $Q_1$ and rejecting $Q_2'$. Now, the heat supply $Q_1$ takes place at lower temperature.

The heat, $\qquad\qquad Q_1 = T_1 \Delta s = T_1' \Delta s'$

Since $\qquad\qquad T_1 > T_1'$

$\therefore \qquad\qquad \Delta s' = \Delta s$

The heat rejected, $\qquad Q_2 = T_0 \Delta s$

$\qquad\qquad\qquad Q_2' = T_0 \Delta s'$

$\because \qquad\qquad \Delta s' > \Delta s$

$\therefore \qquad\qquad Q_2' > Q_2$

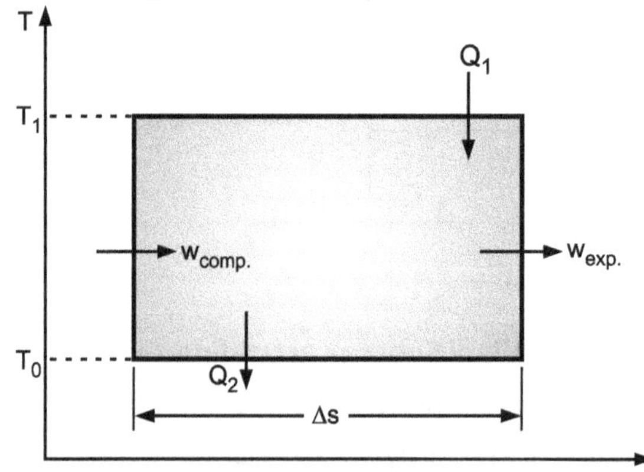


**Fig. 5.4: Reversible (Carnot) engine on T-s diagram**

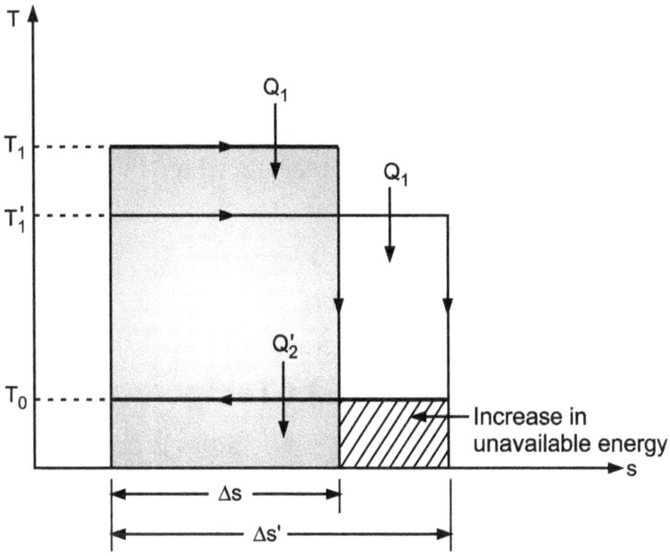

**Fig. 5.5: Increase in unavailable energy due to
heat transfer through a finite temperature difference**

Now, work done in new cycle (with $\Delta T$ at source).

$$w' = Q_1 - Q_2' = T_1' \, \Delta s' - T_0 \, \Delta s'$$

and with no $\Delta T$

$$w = Q_1 - Q_2 = T_1 \, \Delta s - T_0 \, \Delta s$$

$\therefore$

$$w' < w, \text{ because } Q_2' > Q_2$$

The loss of available energy due to irreversible heat transfer through finite temperature difference between the source and the working fluid during the heat addition process is given as,

$$w - w' = Q_2' - Q_2$$

$$= T_0 \, (\Delta s' - \Delta s)$$

i.e. decrease in available energy, A.E.

$$= T_0 \, (\Delta s' - \Delta s) \qquad\qquad \dots (5.3)$$

Hence, the decrease in AE is the product of the lowest feasible temperature of heat rejection ($T_0$) and the additional entropy change in the system while receiving heat irreversibly, compared to the case of reversible heat transfer from the same source. The greater is the temperature difference ($T_1 - T_1'$), the greater is the heat rejection $Q_2'$ and the greater will be the unavailable part of the energy supplied which is shown in Fig. 5.5.

Energy is said to be degraded each time it flows through a finite temperature difference ($\Delta T$). That is, why the second law of thermodynamics is sometimes called the law of degradation of energy.

## 5.5 AVAILABILITY OF HEAT

Consider a certain amount of heat $\delta Q$ is withdrawn from a heat reservoir or from a system of finite size. Now, one has to understand the availability of heat $\delta Q$. To understand this one is required to find out the work that can be obtained when this heat $\delta Q$ is supplied to a reversible cycle which will reject that heat at an environment temperature $T_0$.

The heat $\delta Q$ will be available in two ways:

(i)  Heat $\delta Q$ is withdrawn at constant temperature.

(ii) Heat $\delta Q$ is withdrawn not at constant temperature.

### 5.5.1 Heat $\delta Q$ is withdrawn at Constant Temperature 'T'

**Withdrawal of heat** from a source at constant temperature is possible only when the source must be a thermal reservoir. Fig. 5.6 shows the Carnot cycle on T-s diagram, working between the temperature limits T and $T_0$. Here, it is assumed that heat is supplied to Carnot engine at constant temperature T and rejected to heat sink at $T_0$.

According to first law,

$$(\delta w_{rev})_{cycle} = (\delta Q)_{sup} - (\delta Q)_{rej}$$

or

$$(W_{cycle}) = \int_{1}^{2} \delta Q - \int_{4}^{3} T_0 \, ds$$

$$= Q - T_0 (s_3 - s_4)$$

$$= T \, \Delta s - T_0 \, \Delta s$$

$\therefore$ Availability, $A = w_{rev} = Q - T_0 \, \Delta s$      ... (5.4)

Here, $\Delta s$ represents change of entropy of fluid during unavailability of heat

$$= UA = Q - A = T_0 \cdot \Delta s \qquad \text{... (5.5)}$$

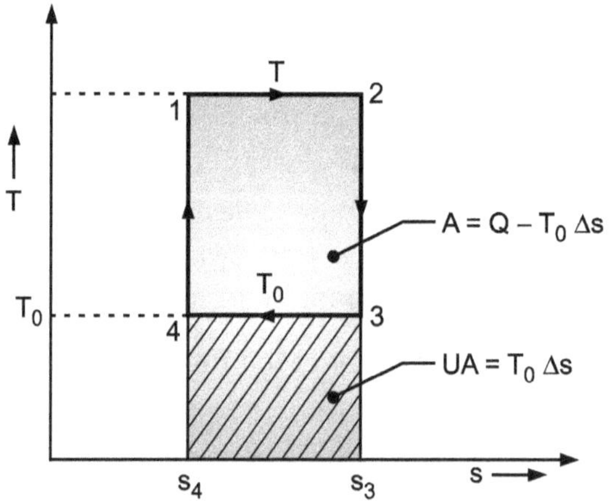

**Fig. 5.6: Availability of heat**

## 5.5.2   Heat $\delta Q$ is withdrawn not at Constant Temperature (Available Energy from a finite Energy Source)

Assume a hot gas of mass $m_g$ at temperature T. Let the gas be cooled at constant pressure from state 1 at T to state 3 at $T_0$ as shown in Fig. 5.7. The heat given up by the gas $Q_1$ be utilized in heating up reversibly a working fluid of mass $m_{wf}$ from state 3 to state 1 along the same path so that $\Delta T$ between the gas and working fluid at any instant is zero and hence the entropy increase of the universe is also zero. The working fluid expands isentropically from state 1 to state 2. Further, it rejects heat $Q_2$ isothermally at $T_0$ to return to the initial state 3 to complete the heat engine cycle.

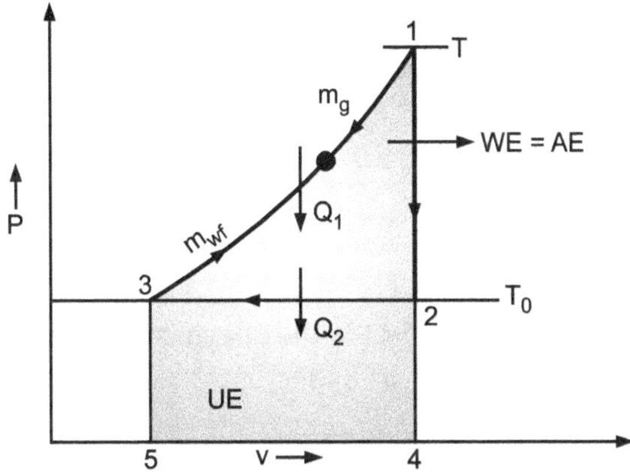


**Fig. 5.7: Available energy of a finite energy source**

$$Q_1 = m_g \cdot c_{pg}\,(T - T_0) = m_{wf} \cdot c_{pwf}\,(T - T_0)$$
$$= \text{Area } 14531$$
$$m_g \cdot c_{pg} = m_{wf} \cdot c_{pf}$$
$$\Delta s_{gas} = \int_{T}^{T_0} m_g \cdot c_{pg}\,\frac{dT}{T} = m_g \cdot c_{pg} \ln\left(\frac{T_0}{T}\right) \text{ negative}$$
$$\Delta s_{wf} = \int_{T_0}^{T} m_{wf} \cdot c_{pwf}\,\frac{dT}{T} = m_{wf} \cdot c_{pwf} \ln\left(\frac{T}{T_0}\right) \text{ positive}$$
$$\Delta s_{univ} = \Delta s_{gas} + \Delta s_{wf} = 0$$
$$Q_2 = T_0 \cdot \Delta s_{wf}$$
$$= T_0 \cdot m_{wf} \cdot c_{pwf} \cdot \ln\left(\frac{T}{T_0}\right)$$
$$= \text{Area } 1231$$

Therefore, the available energy (availability) of a gas of mass $m_g$ at temperature 'T' is given by,

$$AE = m_g \cdot c_{pg} \cdot \left[ (T - T_0) - T_0 \cdot \ln\left(\frac{T}{T_0}\right) \right] \qquad \ldots (5.6)$$

## 5.6 QUALITY OF ENERGY

Availability signifies the quality of energy. In order to demonstrate this consider the case of heat loss from a hot gas flowing through a pipeline as shown in Fig. 5.8. Due to heat loss to the surroundings, the temperature of the gas decreases continuously from inlet at A to the exit at B. Although the process is irreversible, but for the analysis consider a reversible isobaric path between the inlet and exit states of the gas as shown in Fig. 5.9. Now, consider an infinitesimal process on this irreversible isobaric process and for this change in entropy is given by,

$$ds = \frac{mc_p dT}{T}$$

or
$$\frac{dT}{ds} = \frac{T}{mc_p} \qquad \ldots (5.7)$$

where, m is the mass of gas flowing and $c_p$ is the specific heat. The slope dT/ds depends on the gas temperature T. The decrement in T decreases the slope while increment in T will increase the slope.

Let the heat Q be lost to the surroundings during infinitesimal process as the temperature of the gas decreases from $T_1'$ to $T_1''$, $T_1$ being the average of the two. Thus,

$$\text{Heat loss} = Q = mc_p (T_1' - T_1'') = T_1 \Delta s_1 \qquad \ldots (5.8)$$

Available energy loss with this heat at temperature $T_1$ is expressed as,
$$w_1 = A_1 = Q - T_0 \Delta s_1 \qquad \ldots (5.9)$$

During the process the gas temperature has reached $T_2$ ($T_2 < T_1$), assume that the same heat loss Q occurs as the gas temperature decreases from $T_2'$ to $T_2''$, $T_2$ being the average temperature.

$$\text{Heat loss} = mc_p (T_2' - T_2'') = T_2 \Delta s_2 \qquad \ldots (5.10)$$

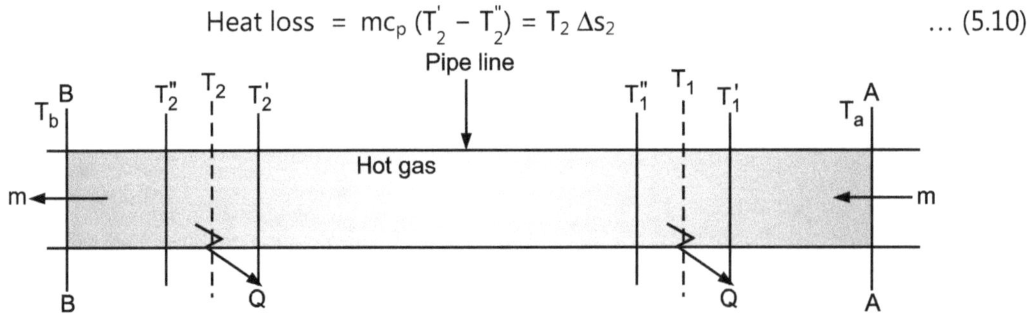


**Fig. 5.8: Heat loss from a hot gas flowing through a pipe line**

Thus, available energy lost with this heat loss at temperature $T_2$ is given by,

$$w_2 = A_2 = Q - T_0\,\Delta s_2 \qquad\qquad \text{... (5.11)}$$

From equations (5.8) and (5.9), we have $\Delta s_1 < \Delta s_2$ as $T_1 > T_2$

Thus, from equations (5.9) and (5.11), we have, $w_1 > w_2$ $\qquad\qquad$ ... (5.12)

The loss of available energy is more, when heat loss occurs at a higher temperature $T_1$ than when the same heat loss occurs at a lower temperature $T_2$. Therefore, a loss of heat of 1 kJ at say 1200°C is more harmful than the same heat loss of 1 kJ at say 200°C. Adequate insulation must be provided for high temperature fluids ($T >>> T_0$) to prevent the heat loss. This may not be so important for low temperature fluids ($T - T_0$), since the loss of available energy such fluids would be low. Similarly, adequate insulation must be provided for very low temperature fluids ($T << T_0$) to prevent heat gain from surroundings.

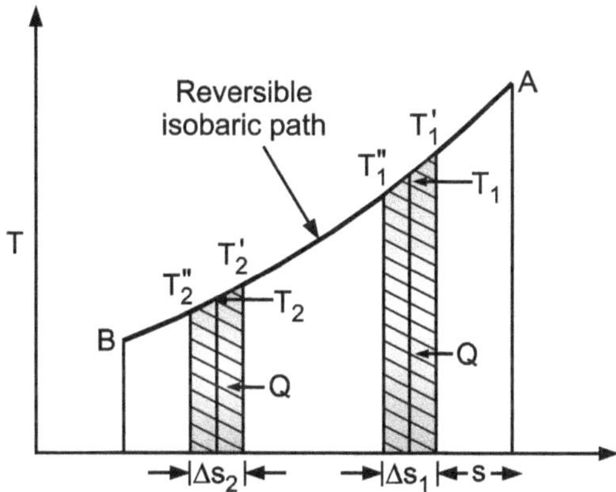


**Fig. 5.9: Concept of energy quality**

It is to be noted that the available energy or energy of a fluid at a higher temperature $T_1$ is more than at a lower temperature $T_2$ and decreases with temperature.

The above discussion tells that the second law affixes a quality of energy of a system at any state. Further, the quality of energy of gas at say 1200°C is much superior to that at, say 200°C, since the gas at 1500°C has the capacity doing more work than that the gas at 200°C, under the same environmental conditions. This clearly suggests that awareness of this energy quality as of energy quantity is essential for the efficient use of our precious energy resources and for energy conversion. Thus, a concept of energy or available energy provides a useful measure of this energy quality for better utilisation of energy sources.

## 5.7 AVAILABILITY IN A NON-FLOW (CLOSED) SYSTEM

**[May 10, Dec. 11, 12]**

Let us consider a system consisting of a fluid in a cylinder-piston arrangement as shown in Fig. 5.10. The fluid expands reversibly from initial condition of $p_1$ and $T_1$ to final atmospheric conditions of $p_0$ and $T_0$. Imagine also the system works in conjunction with a reversible heat engine which receives heat reversibly from the fluid in the cylinder such that the working substance of the heat engine follows the cycle 0-1-3-0 as shown in Fig. 5.11.

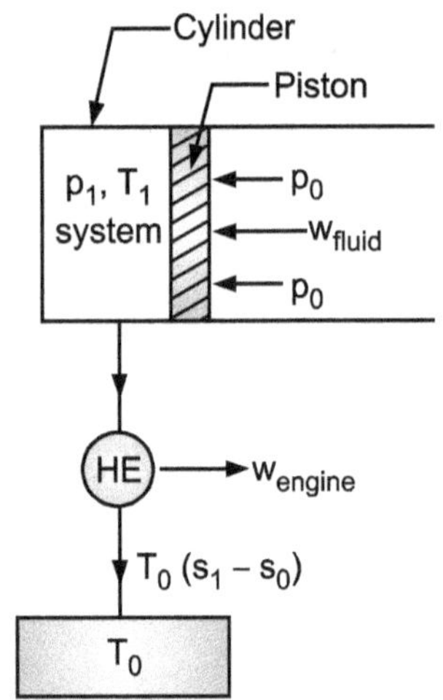
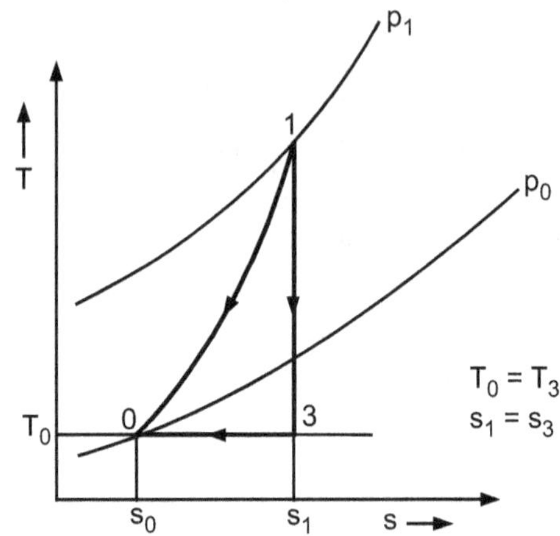

**Fig. 5.10: Closed system conjunction with heat engine**

**Fig. 5.11: Imaginary engine**

The cycle in Fig. 5.11 is possible only if an infinite number of reversible heat engines were arranged in parallel each operating on a Carnot cycle, each one receiving heat at a different constant temperature and each one rejecting heat at $T_0$.

The work done by the engine is given as,

$$W_{engine} = \text{Heat supplied} - \text{Heat rejected}$$

$$= Q - T_0 (s_1 - s_0) \qquad \dots \text{(i)}$$

The heat supplied to the engine is equal to the heat rejected by the fluid in the cylinder. Therefore, we can write for the fluid in the cylinder undergoing the process from state 1 to state 0.

$$-Q = (u_0 - u_1) + W_{fluid}$$

$$W_{fluid} = (u_1 - u_0) - Q \qquad \dots \text{(ii)}$$

Adding equations (i) and (ii), one gets

$$W_{fluid} + W_{engine} = [(u_1 - u_0) - Q] + [Q - T_0 (s_1 - s_0)]$$

$$= (u_1 - u_0) - T_0 (s_1 - s_0) \qquad \dots \text{(5.13)}$$

The piston is pushed towards bds position by the fluid inside the cylinder, against the atmospheric pressure $p_0$. Therefore, the work done by the fluid on the piston is less than the total work done by the fluid.

Work done on atmosphere $= p_0 (v_0 - v_1)$ $\qquad \dots \text{(5.14)}$

Therefore, the maximum work available

$$W_{max} = (u_1 - u_0) - T_0 (s_1 - s_0) - p_0 (v_0 - v_1) \qquad \dots \text{(5.15)}$$

$$W_{max} = (u_1 + p_0 v_1 - T_0 s_1) - (u_0 + p_0 v_0 - T_0 s_0) \qquad \dots \text{(5.16)}$$

$$W_{max} = \alpha_1 - \alpha_2$$

The property, $\alpha = u + p_0 v - T_0 s$ (per unit mass) is called the **non-flow availability function ($\phi$).** The term $u + pv - Ts$ is called Gibb's function. This Gibb's function (G) does involve only properties of the system. The availability function involves the properties of the system and atmosphere.

## 5.8 AVAILABILITY IN STEADY FLOW SYSTEMS

Consider a steady fluid flowing with a velocity $c_1$ from a reservoir in which the pressure and temperature remain constant at $p_1$ and $T_1$ through a device to atmospheric pressure of $p_0$. Let the reservoir be at a height $Z_1$ from the datum, which can be taken at exit from the device i.e. $Z_0 = 0$. For maximum work to be obtained from the device, the exit velocity, $c_0$, must be zero. It can be shown as for a reversible heat engine working between the limits would reject $T_0 (s_1 - s_0)$ units of heat, where $T_0$ is the atmospheric temperature. Thus,

$$w_{max} = \left( h_1 + \frac{c_1^2}{2} + Z_1 g \right) - h_0 - T_0 (s_1 - s_0)$$

In several thermodynamic systems, the kinetic and potential energy terms are negligible i.e.,

$$w_{max} = (h_1 - T_0 s_1) - (h_0 - T_0 s_0)$$
$$= b - b_0$$

The property, $b = h - T_0 s$ (per unit mass) is called the steady-flow availability function.

(In the equation $b = h - T_0 s$; the function 'b' (like the function 'a') is a composite property of a system and its environment; this is known as Keenan function.)

## 5.9 HELMHOLTZ AND GIBB'S FUNCTIONS

The work done in a non-flow reversible system (per unit mass) is given by,

$$w = Q - (u_0 - u_1)$$
$$= T \cdot ds - (u_0 - u_1)$$
$$= T (s_0 - s_1) - (u_0 - u_1)$$

i.e.
$$w = (u_1 - Ts_1) - (u_0 - Ts_0) \qquad \ldots (5.17)$$

The term $(u - Ts)$ is known as Helmholtz function. This gives maximum possible output when the heat Q is transferred at constant temperature.

If work against atmosphere is equal to $p_0 (v_0 - v_1)$, then the maximum work available,

$$w_{max} = w - \text{Work against atmosphere}$$
$$= w - p_0 (v_0 - v_1)$$
$$= (u_1 - Ts_1) - (u_0 - Ts_0) - p_0 (v_0 - v_1)$$
$$= (u_1 + p_0 v_1 - Ts_1) - (u_0 + p_0 v_0 - Ts_0)$$
$$= (h_1 - Ts_1) - (h_0 - Ts_0)$$

i.e.
$$w_{max} = g_1 - g_0 \qquad \ldots (5.18)$$

where, $g = h - T \cdot s$ is known as Gibb's function or Free energy function.

The maximum possible available work when system changes from 1 to 2 is given below.

$$w_{max} = (g_1 - g_0) - (g_2 - g_0) = g_1 - g_2 \qquad \ldots (5.19)$$

Similarly, for steady flow system, the maximum work available is,

$$w_{max} = (g_1 - g_2) + (KE_1 - KE_2) + (PE_1 - PE_2) \qquad \ldots (5.20)$$

where, K.E. and P.E. represent the kinetic and potential energies.

It may be noted that Gibb's function $g = (h - Ts)$ is a property of the system where availability function $a = (u + p_0 v - T_0 s)$ is a composite property of the system and surroundings.

Again,
$$a = u + p_0 v - T_0 s$$
$$b = u + pv - T_0 s$$
$$g = u + pv - Ts$$

When state 1 proceeds to dead state (zero state)
$$a = b = g$$

## 5.10 IRREVERSIBILITY [May 11]

The actual work which a system does is always less than the idealized reversible work. The difference between the maximum possible available work and idealized reversible work is called the irreversibility of the process.

Thus, Irreversibility, $I = w_{max} - w \qquad \ldots (5.21)$

This is also sometimes referred to as 'degradation' or 'dissipation'.

For a non-flow process between the equilibrium states, when the system exchanges heat only with environment, irreversibility (per unit mass),

$$i = [(u_1 - u_2) - T_0 (s_1 - s_2)] - [(u_1 - u_2) + Q]$$
$$= T_0 (s_2 - s_1) - Q$$
$$= T_0 (\Delta s)_{system} + T_0 (\Delta s)_{surr.}$$

i.e., $\qquad i = T_0 [(\Delta s)_{system} + (\Delta s)_{surr.}] \qquad \ldots (5.22)$

$\therefore \qquad i \geq 0$

Similarly, for steady flow-process,

$$i = w_{max} - w \text{ (per unit mass)}$$
$$= \left[ \left( b_1 + \frac{c_1^2}{2} + gZ_1 \right) - \left( b_2 + \frac{c_2^2}{2} + gZ_2 \right) \right]$$
$$- \left[ \left( h_1 + \frac{c_1^2}{2} + gZ_1 \right) - \left( h_2 + \frac{c_2^2}{2} + gZ_2 \right) + Q \right]$$
$$= T_0 (s_2 - s_1) - Q$$
$$= T_0 (\Delta s)_{system} + T_0 (\Delta s)_{surr.}$$

i.e. $\qquad i = T_0 (\Delta s_{system} + \Delta s_{surr.})$

The same expression for irreversibility applies to both flow and non-flow processes.

The quantity $T_0 (\Delta s_{system} + \Delta s_{surr.})$ represents (per unit mass) an increase in unavailable energy (or energy).

## 5.11 SECOND LAW EFFICIENCY OR EFFECTIVENESS

The first law efficiency is the ratio of output energy of a device to input energy of the device.

The first law is concerned only with the quantities of energy and disregards the forms in which the energy exists. Further, it does not also discriminate between the energies available at different temperatures.

The second law of efficiency ($\eta_{II}$) provides a means of assigning a quality index to energy through the concept of available energy or exergy. Improved energy resource utilisation can be realized by reducing unavailable energy within the system and or losses.

### 5.11.1 Effectiveness

The effectiveness of a cycle is defined as the ratio of increase in availability of the surroundings (due to work delivered by the cycle) to the decrease in availability of the surroundings (due to heat supplied to the cycle). Thus,

$$\eta_{II} = \varepsilon = \frac{|\text{Increase in availability of surrounding}|}{|\text{Decrease in availability of surroundings}|} \qquad \ldots (5.23)$$

The algebraic sum of numerator and denominator of equation (5.23) represents the loss of available energy, $E_{x,\,loss}$ because of the irreversibility of cycle.

**(a) Effectiveness of Power Cycle:** The increase in the available energy of the surroundings in the case of power cycle is equal to the work delivered by the cycle and the decrease in the available energy of the surroundings is equal to the availability of heat supplied to the cycle. Thus,

$$\eta_{II} = (\varepsilon)_{\text{Power cycle}} = \frac{|\text{Work delivered by cycle}|}{|\text{Availability of heat supplied}|} = \frac{W_{output}}{(E_x)_{fuel}} \qquad \ldots (5.24)$$

**(b) Effectiveness of Steady Flow Process:** The effectiveness of steady flow process is given by,

$$\eta_{II} = (\varepsilon)_{sf} = \frac{|\text{Increase in availability of surroundings}|}{|\text{Decrease in availability of the flow stream}|} \qquad \ldots (5.25)$$

**(c) Effectiveness of a Turbine:** Fig. 5.12 shows the process path in a turbine on T-s diagram. Due to friction the entropy increases during the expansion process while due to heat losses entropy tends to decrease a little. The effectiveness of a turbine is given by,

$$\eta_{II} = (\varepsilon)_{turbine} = \left|\frac{w}{(\Delta a)_{sf}}\right| = \left|\frac{w}{a_{sf}}\right| \qquad \ldots (5.26)$$

If changes in K.E. and P.E. are negligible, then the work delivered to the surroundings per unit mass is given by,

$$w = (h_1 - h_2) - q$$

Availability of a steady flow system,

$$a_{sf} = w_{max} = (h_1 - h_2) - T_0 (s_1 - s_2)$$

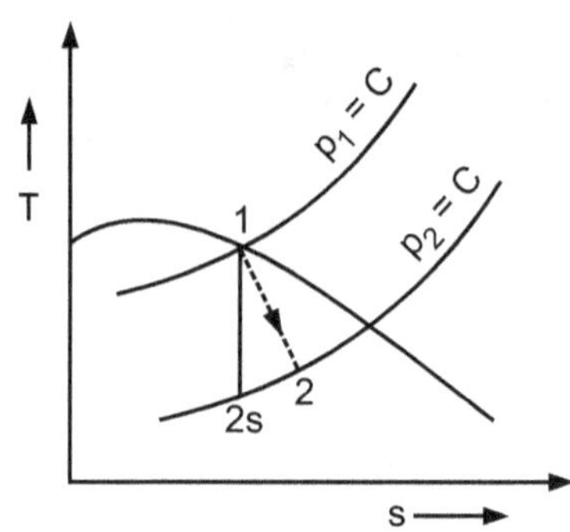


**Fig. 5.12: Expansion through turbine**

$$\eta_{II} = (\varepsilon)_{turbine} = \frac{h_1 - h_2 - q}{(h_1 - h_2) - T_0(s_1 - s_2)} \qquad \ldots (5.27)$$

And, the loss of available energy,

$$I = a_{sf} - w = (h_1 - h_2) - T_0(s_1 - s_2) - (h_1 - h_2) + q$$

or $$\qquad I = q - T_0(s_1 - s_2) \qquad \ldots (5.28)$$

If the expansion process in the turbine is adiabatic, then $q = 0$, hence,

$$\eta_{II} = (\varepsilon)_{turbine} = \left| \frac{h_1 - h_2}{(h_1 - h_2) - T_0(s_1 - s_2)} \right| \qquad \ldots (5.29)$$

and $$\qquad I = T_0(s_2 - s_2) \qquad \ldots (5.30)$$

**(d) Effectiveness of Pump or Compressor:** Since the work is supplied by the surroundings in the case of pump of compressor, there is an increase in available energy of the stream. The effectiveness of a pump or compressor is given by,

$$(\varepsilon)_{pump} = \left| \frac{\text{Increase in available energy of the flow stream}}{\text{Decrease in availability of surroundings}} \right|$$

or $$\qquad \eta_{II} = (\varepsilon)_{pump} = \left| \frac{a_{sf}}{w} \right| \qquad \ldots (5.31)$$

From First law, $w = q - \Delta h$. Taking sign convention of $w$ in consideration,

$$(\Delta a)_{sf} = \Delta h - T_0 \Delta s \text{ if K.E. and P.E.} = 0$$

$$\therefore \qquad \eta_{II} = (\varepsilon)_{pump} = \left| \frac{\Delta h - T_0 \Delta s}{q - \Delta h} \right| \qquad \ldots (5.32)$$

And $$\qquad I = w - a_{sf} = q + T_0 \Delta s$$

If the compression process is adiabatic, $\eta_{II} = (\varepsilon)_{pump} = \left| \dfrac{\Delta h - T_0 \Delta s}{-\Delta h} \right| \qquad \ldots (5.33)$

and $$\qquad I = T_0 \Delta s \text{ per unit mass} \qquad \ldots (5.34)$$

## 5.12 DEAD STATE

If the state of the system ($p_1$, $T_1$) is different from the state of surroundings, then there exists a potential to obtain work while changing the state of the system to that of surroundings (See Fig. 5.13). However, as the system changes its state towards that of the surroundings, this opportunity of producing work diminishes and ceases to exist when the two are equilibrium with each other.

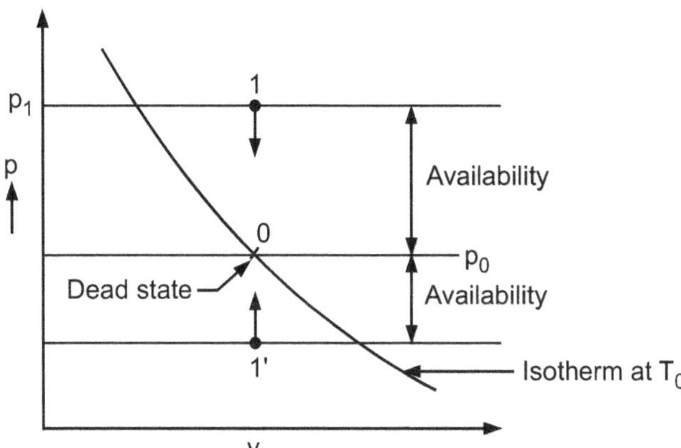


**Fig. 5.13: Availability decreases as the state of the system approaches $p_0$ and $T_0$**

The dead state is one at which the system is in thermodynamic equilibrium (mechanical, thermal and chemical equilibrium) with the surroundings. It means pressure and temperature of the system ($p_1$, $T_1$) and that of surroundings ($p_0$, $T_0$) are one and the same. Also, there is no chemical gradient as such so that a chemical reaction between system and surrounding occurs. All the spontaneous processes terminate at dead state.

## 5.13 CLASSIFICATION OF ENERGY

After studying the degradation of energy which says that the quality of heat energy depends upon its temperature at which it is available.

The sources of energy can be divided into two groups, viz. high grade energy and low grade energy. The high grade energy is fully convertible to useful work. Therefore, work and electrical energy are the two Problems of high grade energy.

Low grade energy are those which cannot be converted fully to useful work. These are heat or thermal energy, heat derived from nuclear fusion or fission and heat derived from combustion of fossil fuel.

## SOLVED PROBLEMS

**Problem 5.1:** A heat of 15000 kJ is withdrawn from a thermal reservoir at 225°C. The heat sink is at 15°C. Calculate the availability and unavailability.

**Solution:** The availability = A = Q − $T_0$ Δs.

Let the heat 15000 kJ is to be transferred reversibly to a cycle at constant temperature of 225°C. The increase in entropy

$$\Delta s = \frac{Q}{T} = \frac{15000}{(225 + 273)} = 30.1 \text{ kJ/K}$$

$$\text{Availability, } A = Q - T_0 \,\Delta s$$
$$= 15000 - 288 \times 30.1$$
$$= \mathbf{6331.2 \text{ kJ}}$$

Unavailable part of energy (heat)

$$= T_0 \,\Delta s = 288 \times 30.1$$
$$= \mathbf{8668.8 \text{ kJ}}$$

**Problem 5.2:** Air initially at 10 bar and 500 K expands in a piston-cylinder arrangement to a final state of $p_2 = 1.5$ bar and $T_2 = 300$ K. Neglect the changes in PE and KE. Assume the environment at $T_0 = 288$ K and $p_0 = 1$ bar. Find the maximum work per kg of air due to its expansion. Also calculate the availability at the initial and final states and as a whole.

**Solution:** For a closed system (non-flow process)

$$W_{rev} = W_{max} = (u_1 - u_2) + p_0 (V_1 - V_2) - T_0 (s_1 - s_2)$$

$$(u_1 - u_2) = c_v (T_1 - T_2) = 0.71 \text{ kJ/kg·K} (500 - 300) = 142 \text{ kJ/kg}$$

$$c_v = 0.71 \text{ kJ/kg}$$

$$p_0 (V_1 - V_2) = p_0 \left( \frac{RT_1}{p_1} - \frac{RT_2}{p_2} \right) = 1 \times 10^5 \left( \frac{287 \times 500}{10 \times 10^5} - \frac{287 \times 300}{1.5 \times 10^5} \right)$$
$$= 14350 - 57400 = -43050 \text{ J/kg}$$
$$= -43.050 \text{ kJ/kg}$$

$$T_0 (s_1 - s_2) = T_0 \left[ R \ln \left( \frac{p_2}{p_1} \right) - c_p \ln \left( \frac{T_2}{T_1} \right) \right]$$
$$= 288 \left[ 287 \times \ln \left( \frac{1.5}{10} \right) - 1005 \ln \left( \frac{300}{500} \right) \right]$$
$$= 288 \,[-544.47 + 513] = -8954 \text{ J/kg}$$
$$= -8.954 \text{ kJ/kg}$$

$$W_{max} = 142 - 43.0 - 8.954 = \mathbf{90.0 \text{ kJ/kg}}$$

The availability at initial state, $a_1$,

$$= (u_1 - u_0) + p_0 (V_1 - V_0) - T_0 (s_1 - s_0)$$

$$= c_v (T_1 - T_0) + p_0 \cdot R \cdot \left( \frac{T_1}{p_1} - \frac{T_0}{p_0} \right) - T_0 \left( c_p \ln \left( \frac{T_1}{T_0} \right) - R \ln \frac{p_1}{p_0} \right)$$

$$= 0.71 \,(500 - 300) + 1 \times 0.287 \left( \frac{500}{10} - \frac{288}{1} \right) -$$

$$288 \left[ 1.005 \ln \frac{500}{300} - 0.287 \ln \left( \frac{10}{1} \right) \right]$$

$$= 142 - 68.3 - 288 \,(1.617 - 0.66)$$

$$= 142 - 68.3 + 42.2 = 115.9 \text{ kJ/kg}$$

The availability at the final state, $a_2$

$$= (u_2 - u_0) + p_0 (V_2 - V_0) - T_0 (s_2 - s_0)$$

$$= c_v (T_2 - T_0) + p_0 R \left(\frac{T_2}{p_2} - \frac{T_0}{p_0}\right) - T_0 \left(c_p \ln \frac{T_2}{T_0} - R \ln \frac{p_2}{p_0}\right)$$

$$= 0.71 (300 - 288 + 1 \times 0.287) \left(\frac{300}{1} - \frac{288}{1}\right)$$

$$- 288 \left(1.005 \ln \frac{300}{288} - 0.287 \ln \frac{1.5}{1}\right)$$

$$= \textbf{4.88 kJ/kg}$$

The availability as a whole, $a = w_{rev} = w_{max}$

$$= a_1 - a_2 = 115.9 - 4.88 = \textbf{111.0 kJ/kg}$$

**Problem 5.3:** Find the availability of air during a non-flow process for the following different cases:

    (a)   $p = 10$ bar, $T = T_0$      (b) $p = p_0$, $T = 400$ K

    (c)   $p = 10$ bar, $T = 150$ K   (d) $p = 0.5\, p_0$, $T = T_0$

**Solution:** Availability for non-flow process, $a_{nf}$

$$a_{nf} = (u + p_0 V - T_0 s) - (u_0 + p_0 V_0 - T_0 s_0) \text{ kJ}$$

For unit mass

$$= (u - u_0) + p_0 (V - V_0) - T_0 (s - s_0)$$

(a)

$$a_{nf} = c_v (T - T_0) + p_0 R \left(\frac{T}{p} - \frac{T_0}{p_0}\right) - T_0 \left(c_p \ln \frac{T}{T_0} - R \ln \frac{p}{p_0}\right)$$

Here, $p = 10$ bar and $T = T_0$.

The above formula reduces to,

$$a_{nf} = T_0 \left[R \ln \left(\frac{p}{p_0}\right)\right] = 288 \left[0.287 \ln \left(\frac{10}{1}\right)\right]$$

$$= \textbf{190.3 kJ/kg}$$

(b)   $p = p_0$ and $T = 400$ K.

$$a_{nf} = c_v (T - T_0) + p_0 R \left(\frac{T}{p_0} - \frac{T_0}{p_0}\right) - T_0 \left(c_p \ln \frac{T}{T_0} - R \ln \frac{p_0}{p_0}\right)$$

$$= c_v (T - T_0) + RT - RT_0 - T_0 \cdot c_p \cdot \ln \left(\frac{T}{T_0}\right)$$

$$= c_v (T - T_0) + R (T - T_0) - T_0 \cdot c_p \ln \left(\frac{T}{T_0}\right)$$

$$= 0.71 (400 - 288) + 0.287 (400 - 288) -$$

$$288 \times 1.005 \ln \left(\frac{400}{288}\right)$$

$$= 79.52 + 32.14 - 95.08 = \textbf{16.57 kJ/kg}$$

(c)
$$a_{nf} = c_v (T - T_0) + \frac{p_0 RT}{p} - \frac{p_0 RT_0}{p_0} - T_0 \left( c_p \ln \frac{T}{T_0} - R \ln \frac{p}{p_0} \right)$$

$p = 10$ bar, $T = 150$

$$= 0.71 (150 - 288) + \frac{0.287 \times 150}{10} - \frac{0.287 \times 288}{1}$$

$$- 288 \left( 1.005 \ln \frac{150}{288} - 0.287 \times \ln \frac{10}{1} \right)$$

$$= -97.98 + 4.30 - 82.65 + 39.5$$

$$= \mathbf{-136.75 \ kJ/kg} \qquad \text{(negative because T is below °C)}$$

(d)  $p = 0.5\, p_0$, $T = T_0$

$$a_{nf} = c_v (T - T_0) + \frac{p_0 RT}{p} - RT_0 - T_0 (s - s_0)$$

$$= c_v (T_0 - T_0) + p_0 R \left( \frac{T}{p} - \frac{T_0}{p_0} \right) - T_0 \left( c_p \ln \frac{T}{T_0} - R \ln \frac{p}{p_0} \right)$$

$$= \frac{p_0 RT}{p} - RT_0 - T_0 \left( 0 - R \ln \frac{0.5\, p_0}{p_0} \right)$$

$$= RT_0 + (RT_0)(-0.693) = (1 - 0.693)\, RT_0 = 0.3068\, RT_0$$

$$= 0.3068 \times 0.287 \times 288 = \mathbf{25.3 \ kJ/kg}$$

**Problem 5.4:** 4 kg of water at 50°C is mixed with 6 kg of water at 80°C in a steady flow process. Determine (a) The temperature of resulting mixture. (b) Is the mixing process isentropic? (c) What is the unavailable energy with respect to the receiver at 50°C?

**Solution:** (a) From first law of thermodynamics,

$$m_1 h_1 + m_2 h_2 = m_3 h_3$$

Assuming specific heat of water constant,

$$m_1 \cdot c_p T_1 + m_2\, c_p\, T_2 = m_3\, c_p\, T_3$$
$$m_1 T_1 + m_2 T_2 = m_3 T_3$$
$$4\, T_1 + 6\, T_2 = 10\, T_3$$
$$4 \times 50 + 6 \times 80 = 10\, T_3$$

$\therefore$ $\qquad\qquad\qquad\qquad \mathbf{T_3 = 68°C}$

(b) Increase in entropy due to mixing process is,

$$\Delta s = m_1\, c_p\, \ln \frac{T_3}{T_1} + m_2\, c_p\, \ln \frac{T_3}{T_2}$$

$$= 4 \times 4.186 \ln \frac{341}{323} + 6 \times 4.186 \ln \frac{341}{353}$$

$$= 0.9080 - 0.8686 = 0.0394 \ kJ/K$$

(c)      Unavailable energy $= T_0\, \Delta s = 288 \times 0.0394 = \mathbf{11.3 \ kJ}$

**Problem 5.5:** One kilogram of air at 1 bar pressure and temperature of 300 K is compressed to 8 bar, 370 K. Determine the irreversibility if the sink temperature is  293 K. Assume $R = 297$ J/kg·K, $Q = 1.004$ kJ/kg·K, $c_v = 716$ J/kg·K.

**Solution:**      Irreversibility, $I = W_{max} - W_{act}$

$$-w_{max} = \text{Change in internal energy} - T_0 \times \text{Change in entropy}$$

or $$-w_{max} = (u_2 - u_1) - T_0 (s_2 - s_1) = w_{rev}$$

or $$-w_{max} = c_v (T_2 - T_1) - T_0 [c_p \ln (T_2/T_1) - R \ln (p_2/p_1)]$$

$$= 0.716 (400 - 300) - 293 \times [1.005 \ln (400/300) -$$

$$0.287 \ln (8/1)]$$

or $$w_{max} = \mathbf{-161.75 \ kJ/kg}$$

(negative sign indicates that work is done on the air)

The index of compression 'n' is given by,

$$\frac{T_2}{T_1} = \left(\frac{p_2}{p_1}\right)^{[(n-1)/n]}$$

or $$\frac{n-1}{n} = \frac{\ln (T_2/T_1)}{\ln (p_2/p_1)} = \frac{\ln (370/300)}{\ln (6.8/1)} = 1$$

or $$n = \mathbf{1.1606}$$

$$w_{actual} = \frac{mR (T_1 - T_2)}{n-1} = \frac{1 \times 0.287 (300 - 370)}{1.123 - 1}$$

$$= -178.7049 \ kJ/kg$$

$$I = w_{rev} - w_{act} = -149.53 - (-163.33) = \mathbf{16.9549 \ kJ/kg}$$

**Problem 5.6:** A system at 600 K receives 8200 kJ/min heat from a source of  1000 K. The temperature of atmosphere is 300 K. Assuming that the temperature of system and source remain constant during heat transfer, find out:

(i)    The entropy produced during heat transfer.

(ii)   The decrease in available energy after heat transfer.

**Solution:** Refer Fig. 5.14.

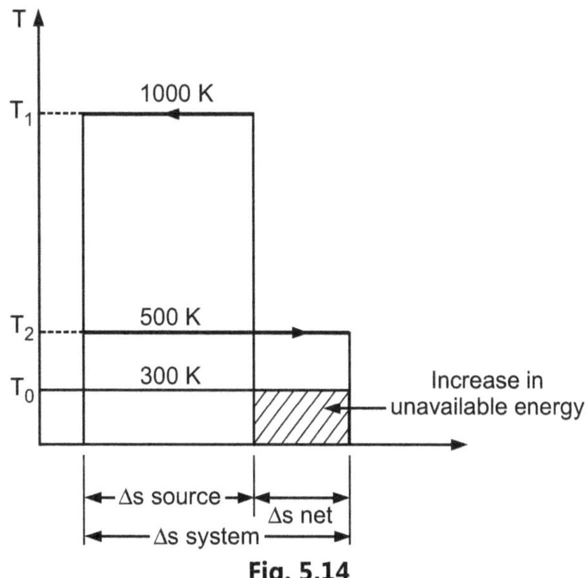


**Fig. 5.14**

$$\text{Temperature of source, } T_1 = 1000 \text{ K}$$
$$\text{Temperature of system, } T_2 = 600 \text{ K}$$
$$\text{Temperature of atmosphere, } T_0 = 300 \text{ K}$$
$$\text{Heat received by the system, } Q = 8200 \text{ kJ/min}$$

**(i) Net change of entropy:**

Change in entropy of the source during heat transfer

$$= \frac{-Q}{T_1} = \frac{-8200}{1000} = -8.2 \text{ kJ/min·K}$$

Change in entropy of the system during heat transfer

$$= \frac{Q}{T_2} = \frac{8200}{600} = 13.67 \text{ kJ/min·K}$$

**The net change of entropy, $\Delta s$ = −8.2 + 13.67 = 5.47 kJ/min·K**

**(ii) Decrease in available energy:**

Available energy with source

$$= (1000 - 300) \times 8.2 = 5740 \text{ kJ}$$

Available energy with the system

$$= (600 - 300) \times 12.67 \text{ kJ} = 4101 \text{ kJ}$$

∴     Decrease in available energy = 5740 − 4101 = **1639 kJ**

Also, increase in available energy

$$= T_0 (s_2 - s_1) = T_0 \, \Delta s$$
$$= 300 \times 5.47 = \textbf{1641 kJ}$$

**Problem 5.7:** 10 kg of air at 550 K and 7.5 bar pressure is enclosed in a closed system. If the atmosphere temperature and pressure are 300 K and 1 bar respectively, determine:

  (i)   The availability if the system goes through the ideal work producing process.

  (ii)  The availability and effectiveness if the air is cooled at constant pressure to atmospheric temperature without bringing it to complete dead state. Take $c_v$ = 0.718 kJ/kg·K; $c_p$ = 1.005 kJ/kg·K.

**Solution:**        Mass of air, m  =  10 kg
$$\text{Temperature, } T_1 = 550 \text{ K}$$
$$\text{Pressure, } p_1 = 7.5 \text{ bar}$$
$$\text{Atmospheric pressure, } p_0 = 1 \text{ bar}$$
$$\text{Atmospheric temperature, } T_0 = 300 \text{ K}$$

For air: $c_v$ = 0.718 kJ/kg·K; $c_p$ = 1.005 kJ/kg·K.

(i)  Change in available energy (for bringing the system to dead state)

$$= m \left[(u_1 - u_0) - T_0 \, \Delta s\right]$$

Also,                    $\Delta s = c_v \log_e \left(\dfrac{T_1}{T_0}\right) + R \log_e \dfrac{V_1}{V_0}$

Using the ideal gas equation,

$$\frac{p_1 V_1}{T_1} = \frac{p_0 V_0}{T_0}$$

$\therefore \qquad \dfrac{V_1}{V_0} = \dfrac{p_1}{p_0} \cdot \dfrac{T_0}{T_1} = \dfrac{7.5}{1} \times \dfrac{300}{550} = 4.0909$

$\therefore \qquad \Delta s = 0.718 \log_e \left(\dfrac{550}{300}\right) + 0.287 \log_e \left(\dfrac{1}{4.0909}\right)$

$$= 0.4352 + (-0.4043) = 0.3088 \text{ kJ/kg·K}$$

$\therefore$   Change in available energy

$$= m \left[(u_1 - u_0) - T_0 \Delta s\right] = m \left[c_v (T_1 - T_0) - T_0 \Delta s\right]$$
$$= 10 \left[0.718 (550 - 300) - 300 \times 0.3088\right] = 1702.36 \text{ kJ}$$

Loss of availability per unit mass during the process

$$= p_0 (V_0 - V_1) \text{ per unit mass}$$

Total loss of availability $= p_0 (V_0 - V_1)$

But, $\qquad\qquad V_1 = \dfrac{mRT_1}{p_1} = \dfrac{10 \times 287 \times 550}{7.5 \times 10^5} = 2.104 \text{ m}^3$

$$\left[\because \ pV = mRT \text{ or } V = \frac{mRT}{p}\right]$$

and $\qquad\qquad V_0 = 4.0909 \times 2.104 = 8.60 \text{ m}^3$

$\therefore \qquad$ Loss of availability $= \dfrac{1 \times 10^5}{10^3} = (8.60 - 2.104)$

$$= \mathbf{649.6\ kJ}$$

(ii) Heat transferred during cooling (constant pressure) process

$$= m \cdot c_p (T_1 - T_0)$$
$$= 10 \times 1.005 (550 - 300) = 2512.5 \text{ kJ}$$

Change in entropy during cooling

$$\Delta s = mc_p \log_e \left(\frac{T_1}{T_0}\right)$$

$$= 10 \times 1.005 \times \log_e \left(\frac{550}{300}\right) = 6.09 \text{ kJ/K}$$

Unavailable energy $= T_0 \Delta s$

$$= 300 \times 6.09 = 1827.49 \text{ kJ}$$

Available energy $= 25125 - 1827.49 = \mathbf{685\ kJ}$

Effectiveness, $\varepsilon = \dfrac{\text{Available energy}}{\text{Change in available energy}}$

$$= \frac{685}{1702.36} = \mathbf{0.402}$$

**Problem 5.8:** In a power station, the saturated steam is generated at 180°C by transferring the heat from hot gases in a steam boiler. Find the increase in total entropy of the combined system of gas and water and increase in unavailable energy due to irreversible heat transfer. The gases are cooled from 900°C to 450°C and all the heat from gases goes to water. Assume water enters the boiler at saturated condition and leaves as saturated steam.

Take: $c_{pg}$ (for gas) = 1.0 kJ/kg·K, $h_{fg}$ (latent heat of steam at 200°C) = 1940.7 kJ/kg.

Atmospheric temperature = 20°C.

Obtain the results on the basis of 1 kg of water.

**Solution:** Refer Fig. 5.15.

$$\text{Temperature of saturation steam} = 180 + 273 = 453 \text{ K}$$
$$\text{Initial temperature of gases} = 900 + 273 = 1173 \text{ K}$$
$$\text{Final temperature of gases} = 900 + 273 = 723 \text{ K}$$
$$\text{For gases: } c_{pg} = 1 \text{ kJ/kg·K}$$
$$\text{Latent heat of steam at 200°C}$$
$$\text{saturation temperature, } h_{fg} = 1940.7 \text{ kJ/kg}$$
$$\text{Atmospheric temperature} = 20 + 273 = 293 \text{ K}$$

Heat lost by gases = Heat gained by 1 kg saturated water when it is converted to steam at 200°C.

$$\therefore \quad m_g c_{pg} (1173 - 723) = 1940.7$$

[where, $m_g$ = Mass of gases, $c_{pg}$ = Specific heat of gas at constant pressure]

$$\text{i.e.} \quad m_g = \frac{1940.7}{1.0 \times (1173 - 723)} = 4.31 \text{ kg}$$

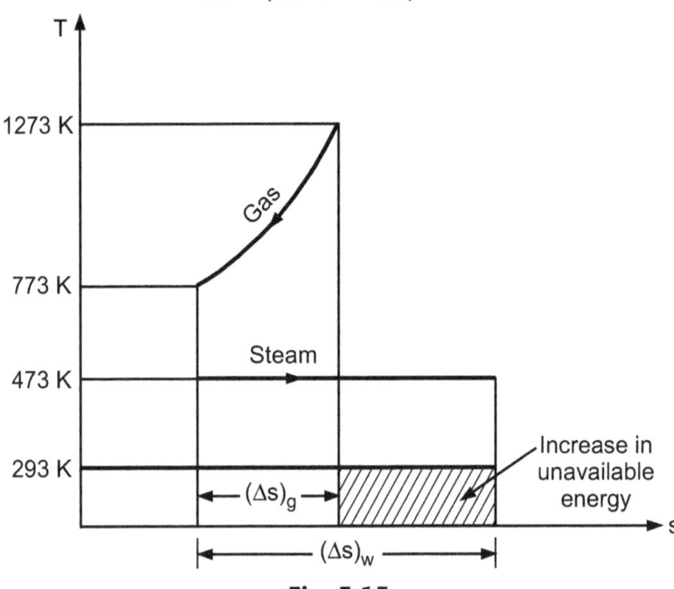


**Fig. 5.15**

Change of entropy of $m_g$ kg of gas,

$$(\Delta s)_g = m_g \, c_{pg} \, \log_e\left(\frac{723}{1173}\right)$$

$$= 3.88 \times 1.0 \times \log_e\left(\frac{723}{1173}\right) = \mathbf{-1.877 \ kJ/K}$$

Change of entropy of water (per kg) when it is converted into steam,

$$(\Delta s)_w = \frac{h_{fg}}{T_s} = \frac{1940.7}{180 + 273} = 4.28 \ kJ/kg{\cdot}K$$

Net change in entropy due to heat transfer

$$= -1.877 + 4.28 = \mathbf{2.40 \ kJ/K}$$

Increase in unavailable energy due to heat transfer

$$= 293 \times 2.40 \ \text{i.e. cross hatched area}$$

$$= \mathbf{705.28 \ kJ \ per \ kg \ of \ steam \ formed}$$

**Problem 5.9:** 5 kg of gas ($c_v$ = 705.28 kJ/kg·K) initially at 3.5 bar and 500 K receives 900 kJ of heat from an infinite source at 1100 K. If the surrounding temperature is 288 K, find the loss in available energy due to above heat transfer.

**Solution:** Refer Fig. 5.16.

$$\text{Mass of gas, } m_g = 5 \text{ kg}$$

$$\text{Initial pressure of gas} = 3.5 \text{ bar}$$

$$\text{Initial temperature, } T_1' = 500 \text{ K}$$

$$\text{Quantity of heat received by gas, } Q = 900 \text{ kJ}$$

$$\text{Specific heat of gas, } c_v = 0.81 \text{ kJ/kg{\cdot}K}$$

$$\text{Surrounding temperature} = 288 \text{ K}$$

$$\text{Temperature of infinite source, } T_1 = 1100 \text{ K}$$

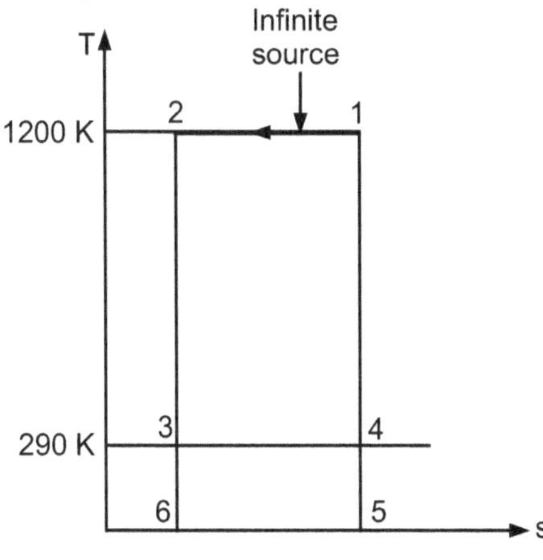


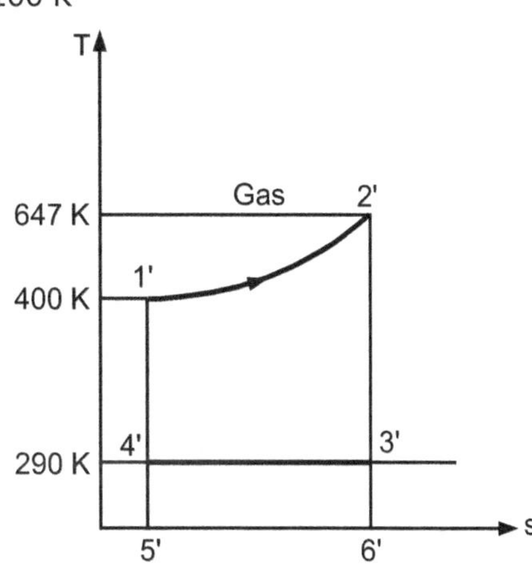


**Fig. 5.16**

Heat received by the gas is given by,

$$Q = m_g\, c_v\, (T_2' - T_1')$$

$$900 = 5 \times 0.81\, (T_2' - 500)$$

$$\therefore \quad T_2' = \frac{900}{5 \times 0.81} + 500 = 722.22 \text{ K}$$

Available energy with the source

$$= \text{Area } 1\text{-}2\text{-}3\text{-}4\text{-}1$$

$$= (1100 - 288) \times \frac{900}{1100} = 664 \text{ kJ}$$

Change in entropy of the gas

$$= m_g c_v\, \log_e \left(\frac{T_2'}{T_1'}\right) = 5 \times 0.81 \times \log_e \left(\frac{722.22}{500}\right) = 1.49 \text{ kJ/K}$$

Unavailability of the gas $= \text{Area } 3' \text{ - } 4' \text{ - } 5' \text{ - } 6' \text{ - } 3'$

$$= 288 \times 1.49 = 428.91 \text{ kJ}$$

Available energy with the gas $= 900 - 428.91 = 471.08$ kJ

$\therefore \quad$ Loss in available energy due to heat transfer

$$= 664 - 471.08 = \textbf{192.91 kJ}$$

**Problem 5.10:** Calculate the unavailable energy in 60 kg of water at 60°C with respect to the surroundings at 288 K, the pressure of water being 1 atmosphere.

**Solution:** Refer Fig. 5.17.

$$\text{Mass of water, } m = 60 \text{ kg}$$

$$\text{Temperature of water, } T_1 = 60 + 273 = 333 \text{ K}$$

$$\text{Temperature of surroundings, } T_0 = 15 + 273 = 288 \text{ K}$$

$$\text{Pressure of water, } p = 1 \text{ atm.}$$

Assume the water is cooled at a constant pressure of 1 atm from 60°C to 6°C. The heat given up may be used as a source for a series of Carnot engines each using the surroundings as a sink. It is assumed that the amount of energy received by any engine is small relative to that in the source and temperature of the source does not change while heat is being exchanged with the engine.

Consider that the source temperature has fallen to T, at which level there operates a Carnot engine which takes in heat at this temperature and rejects heat $T_0$ = 279 K. If $\delta s$ is the entropy change of water, the work obtained is,

$$\delta w = -m\, (T - T_0)\, \delta s$$

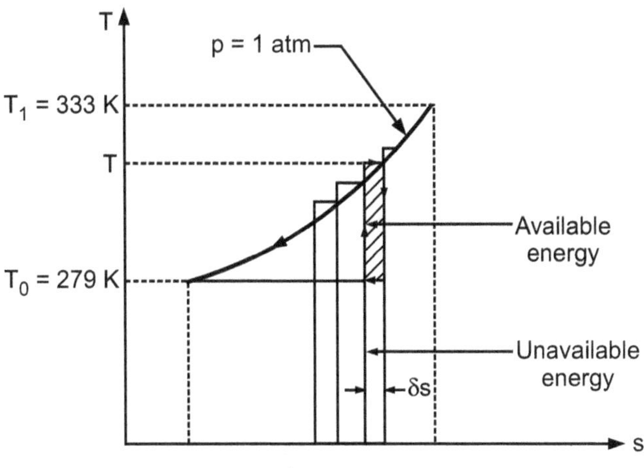



**Fig. 5.17**

where, $\delta s$ is negative.

$$\therefore \qquad \delta w = -60\,(T - T_0)\,\frac{c_p\,\delta T}{T} = -60\,c_p\left(1 - \frac{T_0}{T}\right)\delta T$$

With a large number of engines in the series, the total work (maximum) obtainable when the water is cooled from 333 K to 279 K would be,

$$w_{max} = \text{Available energy}$$

$$= -\lim. \sum_{333}^{288} 60\,c_p\left(1 - \frac{T_0}{T}\right)\delta T$$

$$= \int_{279}^{333} 60\,c_p\left(1 - \frac{T_0}{T}\right)dT$$

$$= 60\,c_p\left[(333 - 288) - 288\,\log_e\left(\frac{333}{288}\right)\right]$$

$$= 60 \times 4.187\,(45 - 41.81) = 801.39\ \text{kJ}$$

Also, $\qquad Q_1 = 60 \times 4.187 \times (333 - 288) = 11304.9\ \text{kJ}$

$\therefore \qquad$ Unavailable energy $= Q_1 - w_{max}$

$$= 11304.9 - 801.39 = \mathbf{10503.51\ kJ}$$

**Problem 5.11:** 10 kg of water is heated in an insulated tank by a churning process from 288 K to 340 K. If the surrounding temperature is 288 K, find the loss in availability for the process.

**Solution:** $\qquad$ Mass of water, $m = 10$ kg

$$\text{Temperature, } T_1 = 340\ \text{K}$$

$$\text{Surrounding temperature, } T_0 = 288\ \text{K}$$

$$\text{Specific heat of water, } c_p = 4.187\ \text{kJ/kg·K}$$

**Loss in availability:**

Work added during churning = Increase in enthalpy of the water

$$= 10 \times 4.187 \times (340 - 288) = 2177.24 \text{ kJ}$$

Now the energy in the water = 2177.24 kJ

The availability out of this energy is given by,

$$m [(u_1 - u_0) - T_0 \, \Delta s]$$

where,
$$\Delta s = c_p \, \log_e \left(\frac{T_1}{T_0}\right)$$

$\therefore$
$$\Delta s = 4.187 \, \log_e \left(\frac{340}{288}\right) = 0.694 \text{ kJ/kg·K}$$

$\therefore$ Available energy $= m [c_v (T_1 - T_0) - T_0 \, \Delta s]$

$$= 10 [4.187 (340 - 288) - 300 \times 0.694] = 95.24 \text{ kJ}$$

$\therefore$ Loss in availability $= 2177.24 - 95.24 = \mathbf{2082 \text{ kJ}}$

This shows that conversion of work into heat is highly irreversible process (since out of 2177.24 kJ of work energy supplied to increase the temperature, only 95.4 kJ will the available again for conversion into work).

**Problem 5.12:** Calculate the decrease in available energy when 15 kg of water at 80°C mixes with 30 kg of water at 30°C, the pressure being taken as constant and the temperature of the surroundings being 288 K.

Take $c_p$ of water as 4.18 kJ/kg·K.

**Solution:** Temperature of surrounding, $T_0 = 15 + 273 = 288$ K

Specific heat of water, $c_p = 4.18$ kJ/kg·K

The available energy of a system of mass, m specific heat $c_p$ and at temperature T, is given by,

$$\text{Available energy, A.E.} = mc_p \int_{T_0}^{T} \left(1 - \frac{T_0}{T}\right) dT$$

Now, available energy of 15 kg of water at 80°C,

$$(\text{A.E.})_{15 \text{ kg}} = 15 \times 4.18 \int_{15 + 273}^{80 + 273} \left(1 - \frac{288}{T}\right) dT$$

$$= 62.7 \left[(353 - 288) - 288 \ln (353/288)\right]$$

$$= 62.7 (65 - 68.61) = 400.65 \text{ kJ}$$

Available energy of 30 kg of water at 30°C,

$$(A.E.)_{30\ kg} = 30 \times 4.18 \int\limits_{(15\ +\ 273)}^{(30\ +\ 273)} \left(1 - \frac{288}{T}\right) dT$$

$$= 30 \times 4.18 \left[(303 - 288) - 288 \log_e \left(\frac{288}{288}\right)\right]$$

$$= 125.4\ (15 - 14.36) = 80.256\ kJ$$

Total available energy,

$$(A.E.)_{total} = (A.E.)_{20\ kg} + (A.E.)_{30\ kg}$$

$$= 400.65 + 80.256 = 480.906\ kJ$$

If T°C is the final temperature after mixing, then,

$$15 \times 4.18 \times (80 - T) = 30 \times 4.18 \times (T - 30)$$

or $\qquad 15\ (80 - T) = 30\ (T - 30)$

$$\therefore \qquad T = \frac{15 \times 80 + 30 \times 30}{15 + 30} = 46.66°C$$

Total mass after mixing = 15 + 30 = 45 kg

Available energy of 45 kg of water at 45.66°C

$$(A.E.)_{50\ kg} = 45 \times 4.18 \left[(319.66 - 288) - 288 \log_e \left(\frac{319.66}{288}\right)\right]$$

$$= 188.1\ (31.66 - 30.03) = \mathbf{306.603}$$

$\therefore$   Decrease in available energy due to mixing

$$= \text{Total energy before mixing} - \text{Total energy after mixing}$$

$$= 480.906 - 306.603 = \mathbf{174.306}.$$

---

**Problem 5.13:** In an heat exchanger (parallel flow type) water enters at 50°C and leaves at 70°C while oil (specific gravity = 0.82, specific heat = 2.6 kJ/kg·K) enters at 250°C and leaves at 80°C. If the surrounding temperature is 27°C, determine the loss in availability on the basis of one kg of oil per second.

**Solution:** Refer Fig. 5.18.

$$\text{Inlet temperature of water, } T_{w1} = 50°C = 323\ K$$

$$\text{Outlet temperature of water, } T_{w2} = 70°C = 343\ K$$

$$\text{Inlet temperature of oil, } T_{01} = 250 = 523\ K$$

$$\text{Outlet temperature of oil, } T_{02} = 80 = 353\ K$$

$$\text{Specific gravity of oil} = 0.82$$

Specific heat of oil $= 2.6$ kJ/kg·K

Surrounding temperature, $T_0 = 27 + 273 = 300$ K

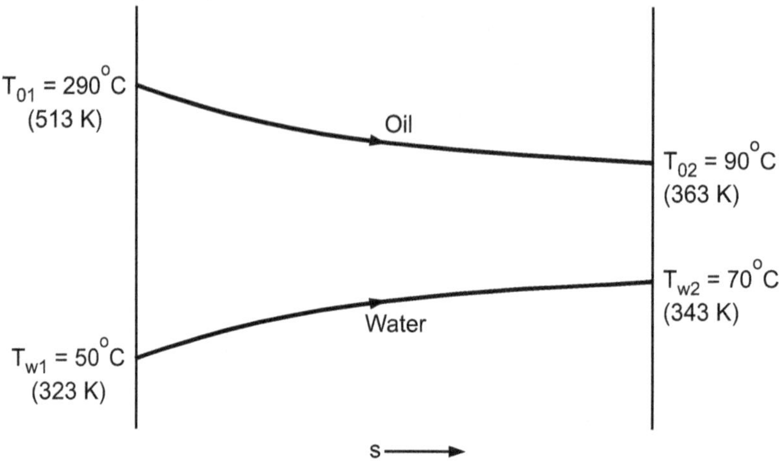


**Fig. 5.18**

### Loss in availability:

Consider one kg of oil.

$$\text{Heat lost by oil} = \text{Heat gained by water}$$

$$m_o \times c_{po} \times (T_{o1} - T_{o2}) = m_w \times c_{pw} \times (T_{w2} - T_{w1})$$

where,

$$c_{po} = \text{Specific heat of oil } (2.6 \text{ kJ/kg·K})$$

$$c_{pw} = \text{Specific heat of water } (4.18 \text{ kJ/kg·K}), \text{ and}$$

$$m_o = \text{Mass of oil } (= 1 \text{ kg})$$

$$m_w = \text{Mass of water } (=?)$$

$\therefore \quad 1 \times 2.6 \times (523 - 353) = m_w \times 4.18 \times (343 - 323)$

or $\quad 442 = 83.6\, m_w$ or $m_w = \mathbf{5.288 \text{ kg}}$

$$\text{Entropy change of water} = m_w\, c_{pw}\, \log_e \frac{T_{w2}}{T_{w1}} = 4.66 \times 4.18 \times \log_e \left(\frac{343}{323}\right) = 1.17 \text{ kJ/K}$$

$$= 5.288 \times 4.18 \times \ln \left(\frac{343}{323}\right) = 1.327 \text{ kJ/K}$$

$$\text{Entropy change of oil} = m_o c_{po}\, \log_e \left(\frac{T_{o2}}{T_{o1}}\right) = 1 \times 2.6\, \log_e \left(\frac{353}{523}\right) = \mathbf{-1.022 \text{ kJ/K}}$$

Change in availability of water

$$= m_w\, [c_{pw}\, (T_{w2} - T_{w1})] - T_o\, (\Delta s)_w$$

$$= 5.28 \times [4.18\,(343 - 323)] - 300 \times 1.327 = \mathbf{43.308 \text{ kJ}}$$

+ve sign indicates an increase in availability.

Change in availability of oil $= m_o [c_{po} (T_{o2} - T_{o1})] - T_0 (\Delta s)_o]$

$$= 1 \times [2.6 (353 - 523) - 300 \times (-1.022)] = \mathbf{-135.41\ kJ/K}$$

(−ve sign indicates the loss).

**Problem 5.14:** 1 kg of ice at 0°C is mixed with 15 kg of water at 30°C. Assuming the surrounding temperature as 15°C, calculate the net increase in entropy and unavailable energy when the system reaches common temperature.

**Given:** Specific heat of water = 4.18 kJ/kg·K; Specific heat of ice = 2.1 kJ/kg·K and enthalpy of fusion of ice (latent heat) = 333.5 kJ/kg.

**Solution:**

$$\text{Mass of ice, } m_{ice} = 1\ kg$$

$$\text{Temperature of ice, } T_{ice} = 0 + 273 = 273\ K$$

$$\text{Mass of water, } m_{water} = 15\ kg$$

$$\text{Temperature of water, } T_{water} = 30 + 273 = 303\ K$$

$$\text{Surrounding temperature, } T_0 = 15 + 273 = 288\ K$$

$$\text{Specific heat of water} = 4.18\ kJ/kg·K$$

$$\text{Specific heat of ice} = 2.1\ kJ/kg·K$$

$$\text{Latent heat of ice} = 333.5\ kJ/kg$$

Let $T_c$ = Common temperature when heat flows between ice and water stops.

$$\text{Heat lost by water} = \text{Heat gained by ice}$$

i.e.,     $15 \times 4.18 (303 - T_c) = 4.18 (T_c - 273) + 333.5$

or          $1899 - 62.8\ T_c = 4.18\ T_c - 1141.14 + 333.5$

or          $66.88\ T_c = 20472.74$

$\therefore$          $T_c = 306.11$ K or 33.11°C

Change of entropy of water $= 15 \times 4.18 \log_e \left( \dfrac{306.11}{300} \right) = \mathbf{+1.264\ K}$

Change of entropy of ice $= 1 \times 4.18 \log_e \left( \dfrac{306.11}{273} \right) + \dfrac{333.5}{273}$

$$= \mathbf{1.70\ kJ/K}$$

Net change of entropy, $\Delta s = +1.264 + 1.7 = 2.964$

Hence, net increase in entropy = **2.964 kJ/K**

Increase in unavailable energy $= T_0 \Delta s = 288 \times 2.964 = \mathbf{853\ kJ}$

**Problem 5.15:** Calculate the decrease in available energy when 25 kg of water at 95°C mix with 35 kg of water at 35°C, the pressure being taken as constant and temperature of the surroundings being 15°C. Take $c_p$ of water = 4.2 kJ/kg·K.

**Solution: Mixing of water:**

25 kg and 95°C.

35 kg and 35°C.

To find temperature of the mixture, we equate enthalpies according to energy balance.

$$m_1 \cdot c_p \cdot T_1 + m_2 \cdot c_p \cdot T_2 = m_3 \cdot c_p \cdot T_3$$

$$\therefore \quad 25 \times c_p \times 95 + 35 \times c_p \times 35 = (35 + 25)\, c_p \cdot T_3$$

$$\therefore \quad T_3 = 60°C = 333\ K$$

Now, change in availability,

$$\Sigma\, \Delta A = (A)_{25} + (A)_{35} - (A)_{60}$$

Available energy of 25 kg water

$$= (AE)_{25} = Q - T_0 \cdot \Delta S$$

$$= mc_p\left[(T_1 - T_0) - T_0 \log_e \frac{T_1}{T_0}\right]$$

$$= 25 \times 4.2 \times \left[(368 - 288) - 288 \log_e \frac{368}{288}\right] = \mathbf{987.5\ kJ}$$

Available energy of 35 kg water

$$= (AE)_{35} = 35 \times 4.2 \times \left[(308 - 288) - 288 \log_e \frac{308}{288}\right] = \mathbf{97.59\ kJ}$$

Available energy of mixture

$$= (AE)_{60} = 60 \times 4.2 \times \left[(333 - 288) - 288 \log_e \left(\frac{333}{288}\right)\right] = \mathbf{803.27\ kJ}$$

$$\text{Decrease in availability} = (AE)_{25} + (AE)_{35} - (AE)_{60}$$

$$= 987.5 + 97.59 - 803.27 = \mathbf{281.82\ kJ}$$

---

**Problem 5.16:** At constant pressure 138 kPa, 5 kg of oxygen is cooled from 500 K to 300 K. The temperature of the surrounding is 277°C. Find the available part of heat removed and entropy increase of universe.

**Solution: Given Data:** m = 5 kg, $p_1$ = 138 kPa, $T_1$ = 500 K, $T_0$ = 277 K,

$p_0$ = 1 bar = 100 kPa.

Initial availability of $O_2$,

$$A_1 = (u_1 - u_0) + p_0 (V_1 - V_0) - T_0 (s_1 - s_0)$$

$$s_1 - s_0 = c_p \cdot \log_e \frac{T_1}{T_0} - R \log_e \frac{p_1}{p_0}$$

$$= 0.9169 \log_e \frac{500}{277} - 0.287 \log_e \frac{138}{100}$$

$$= 0.54151 - 0.09243 = 0.4491 \text{ kJ/kg·K}$$

$$\therefore \quad A_1 = mc_v (T_1 - T_0) + mR\, p_0 \left[\frac{T_1}{p_1} - \frac{T_0}{p_0}\right] - mT_0 \,[0.4491]$$

$$= 5 \times 0.653 \,(500 - 277) + 5 \times 0.287 \times 100 \left[\frac{500}{138} - \frac{277}{100}\right]$$

$$- 5 \times 277 \times 0.4491$$

$$= 728.095 + 122.4325 - 622.00 = \mathbf{228.524\ kJ}$$

Final availability at $T_2 = 300$ K, $T_0 = 277$ K, $p_2 = p_1 = 138$ kPa, $p_0 = 100$ kPa

$$A_2 = mc_v (T_2 - T_0) + mR\, p_0 \left[\frac{T_2}{p_2} - \frac{T_0}{p_1}\right] - mT_0 \,(s_2 - s_0)$$

$$s_2 - s_0 = c_p \cdot \log_e (T_2/T_0) - R \log_e (p_2/p_0)$$

$$= 0.9169 \log_e \left(\frac{300}{277}\right) - 0.287 \log_e \left(\frac{138}{100}\right) = -0.0193 \text{ kJ/kg·K}$$

$$A_2 = 5 \times 0.653 \,(300 - 277) + 5 \times 0.287 \times 100 \left[\frac{300}{138} - \frac{277}{100}\right]$$

$$- 5 \times 277 \,(-0.0193)$$

$$\therefore \quad A_2 = 75.095 + (-85.54) + 26.7305 = 16.287 \text{ kJ}$$

Available part of heat removed = $16.287 - 228.524 = \mathbf{-212.237\ kJ}$

**Problem 5.17:** Two engines have same thermal efficiency as 30%. Their source temperatures are different as shown:

| Temperature | Engine I | Engine II |
|---|---|---|
| Source | 600 K | 1000 K |
| Sink | 300 K | 300 K |

Using second law efficiency, choose best performing engine.

**Solution: Given Data:**

$$\eta_{th} = 30\%$$

For I: $T_H = 600$ K; $T_L = 300$ K

For II: $T_H = 1000$ K; $T_L = 300$ K

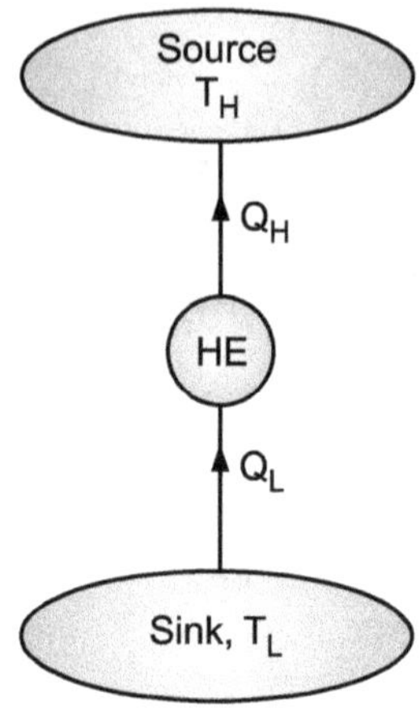


**Fig. 5.19**

According to second law,

$$\text{HE efficiency} = 1 - \frac{T_L}{T_H}$$

$$\text{For Engine I, } \eta = 1 - \frac{T_L}{T_H} = 1 - \frac{300}{600} = \textbf{0.5 or 50\%}$$

$$\text{For Engine II, } \eta = 1 - \frac{T_L}{T_H} = 1 - \frac{300}{1000} = \textbf{0.7 or 70\%}$$

Engine II is more efficient than engine I, according to second law.

**Problem 5.18:** 1 kg of air is contained in a rigid tank at 500 kPa and 700 K. The dead state is taken as 20°C and 100 kPa. Calculate the maximum useful work:

(i)   If the system were to change to dead state.

(ii)  When the air is cooled to 400 K in the tank.

(Take for air, $c_p$ = 1.005 kJ/kg·K, R = 0.287 kJ/kg·K).

**Solution: Given Data:** $p_1$ = 500 kPa, $T_1$ = 700 K, $p_0$ = 100 kPa,

$T_0$ = 20°C = 50 + 273 = 293 K, $c_p$ = 1.005 kJ/kg·K, R = 0.287 kJ/kg·K.

Now,                     $c_p - c_v = R$

∴                        $c_v = c_p - R = 1.005 - 0.287 = 0.718$ kJ/kg·K

**(i) If the system is changed to dead state:**

$$A_1 = w_{max} = (u_1 - u_0) + p_0 (V_1 - V_0) - T_0 (s_1 - s_0)$$

$$= c_v (T_1 - T_0) + Rp_0 \left( \frac{T_1}{p_1} - \frac{T_0}{p_0} \right) - T_0 (s_1 - s_0)$$

Now,          $$s_1 - s_0 = c_p \cdot \log_e \left( \frac{T_1}{T_0} \right) - T \log_e \left( \frac{p_1}{p_0} \right)$$

$$= 1.005 \ln\left(\frac{700}{293}\right) - 0.287 \times \ln\left(\frac{500}{100}\right)$$

$$= \mathbf{0.4133 \ kJ/kg \cdot K}$$

$$\therefore \qquad w_{max} = 0.178 \times (700 - 293) + 0.287 \times \left(\frac{p_0}{p_1} \times T_1 - T_0\right)$$

$$- 293 \times 0.4133$$

$$= 0.718 \times 407 + 0.287 \times \left(\frac{100}{500} \times 700 - 293\right) - 121.0969$$

$$= \mathbf{127.22 \ kJ/kg \cdot K}$$

## (ii) When the system is cooled to 400 K:

The availability in the final state,

$$A_2 = (u_2 - u_0) + p_0 (V_2 - V_0) - T_0 (s_2 - s_0)$$

$$= c_v (T_2 - T_0) + p_0 R \times \left(\frac{T_2}{p_2} - \frac{T_0}{p_0}\right) - T_0 \left(c_p \ln \frac{T_2}{T_0} - R \ln \frac{p_2}{p_0}\right)$$

$$= c_v (T_2 - T_0) + p_0 R \times \left(\frac{T_2}{p_2} - \frac{T_0}{p_0}\right) - T_0 (s_2 - s_0)$$

Now, $\qquad s_2 - s_0 = c_p \log_e\left(\frac{T_2}{T_0}\right) - R \log_e\left(\frac{p_2}{p_0}\right)$

$$= 1.005 \ln\left(\frac{400}{293}\right) - 0.287 \times \ln\left(\frac{500}{100}\right)$$

$$= 0.3128 - 0.462$$

$$= \mathbf{-0.1492 \ kJ/kg}$$

$$\therefore \qquad A_2 = c_v (T_2 - T_0) + R\left(\frac{p_0}{p_2} \times T_2 - T_0\right) - T_0 \times (s_2 - s_0)$$

$$= 0.718 \times (400 - 293) + 0.287 \times \left(\frac{100}{500} \times 400 - 293\right)$$

$$- 293 \times (-0.1492)$$

$$= 76.826 - 61.131 + 43.701$$

$$= \mathbf{59.396 \ kJ/kg}$$

The availability as a whole,

$$a = A_1 - A_2 = 127.22 - 59.396$$

$$= \mathbf{67.824 \ kJ/kg}$$

## EXERCISE

1. Explain the concept of available and unavailable energy. When does the system become dead?
2. Define the term 'availability'.
3. Is the availability function same for a non-flow and a flow process?
4. Define availability function and find the relationship between availability function and change in availability.
5. How are the concepts of entropy and unavailable energy related to each other?
6. Derive an expression for availability in non-flow systems.
7. Derive an expression for availability in steady-flow systems.
8. Differentiate between availability function and Gibb's energy function.
9. Derive an expression for decrease in available energy when heat is transferred through a finite temperature difference.
10. Derive a general expression for irreversibility in (i) Non-flow process, (ii) Steady flow process.
11. What is the effectiveness of a system and how does it differ from efficiency?

## UNIVERSITY QUESTION PAPERS

### DEC. 2013

1. A system at 400 K receives 150 kJ of heat from a heat source at 1200 K. Atmospheric temperature is 300 K. The temperature of both the system and the source are assumed to be constant during the heat transfer process, find the net change in the entropy, available energy of the heat source, available energy of system. **[6]**

### DEC. 2014

1. 1000 kg of heat leaves the hot gases at 1400 deg. C from a fire box and goes to a steam at 250 deg. C. Atmospheric temperature is 20 deg. C. Divide the energy into available and unavailable part as it : (i) Leaves the hot gases  (ii) Enters the system.**[6]**

### MAY 2015

1. A system at 450 K receives 225 kJ/s of heat energy from a source at 1500K, and the temperature of both the system and source remains constant during the heat transfer process. Represent the process on temperature–entropy diagram and determine :
(i)   Net change in entropy      (ii)   Available energy of heat source and system
(iii)   Decrease in available energy.
Take atmospheric temperature equal to 300 K. **[6]**

### NOV. 2015

1. Prove that when heat is transfer through finite temperature difference it causes loss of available energy. **[6]**

# Chapter 6

# PROPERTIES OF PURE SUBSTANCES

## 6.1 INTRODUCTION

Steam is a pure substance. A pure substance is defined as a homogeneous and chemically stable substance eventhough it undergoes a change of phase.

Steam is used in many engineering and chemical industries. It is used as a working substance for steam power plants and is used as a medium for heating in chemical, sugar and textile industries. Therefore, it is essential to study the properties of steam at different conditions.

Substances may exist in different phases. At atmospheric pressure and temperature conditions, copper is a solid, mercury is a liquid and nitrogen is a gas. Under different conditions, each may appear in different phase. So let us discuss the phase transformation of water at constant pressure.

## 6.2 PHASE TRANSFORMATION OF WATER AT CONSTANT PRESSURE [May 11]

1. Assume 1 kg mass of ice at −20°C and 1 atm. pressure in a frictionless piston cylinder arrangement. Weight W is kept on the piston to maintain a pressure of 1 atm. on the ice.

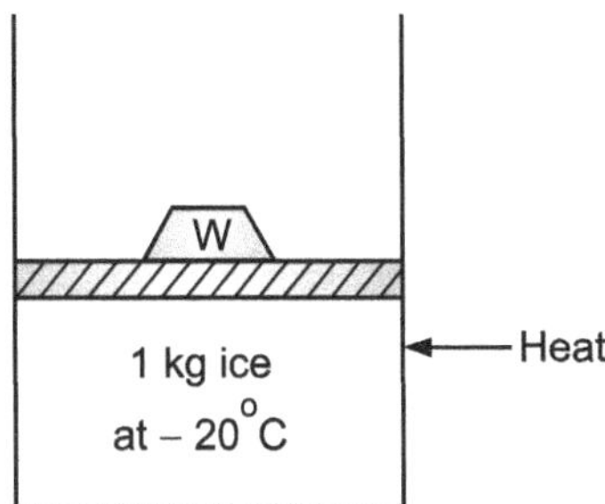


**Fig. 6.1: At 1 atm. pressure and − 20°C, water exists in the solid phase**

2. As we add heat, the temperature of ice will go on increasing till it reaches 0°C. At this stage, ice starts melting and there will be no rise in temperature till all the ice melts. (Process a − b in Fig. 6.7)

3.  The addition of heat will be utilised to increase the temperature of water from 0°C to 100°C (Process c - d in Fig. 6.7).

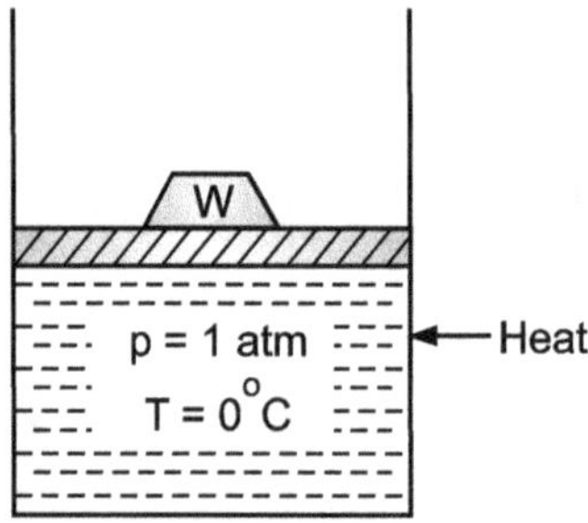


**Fig. 6.2: At 1 atm. pressure and at 0°C, water exists
in the liquid state (compressed liquid)**

4.  Now on further heating, water starts boiling and gets converted into vapour.

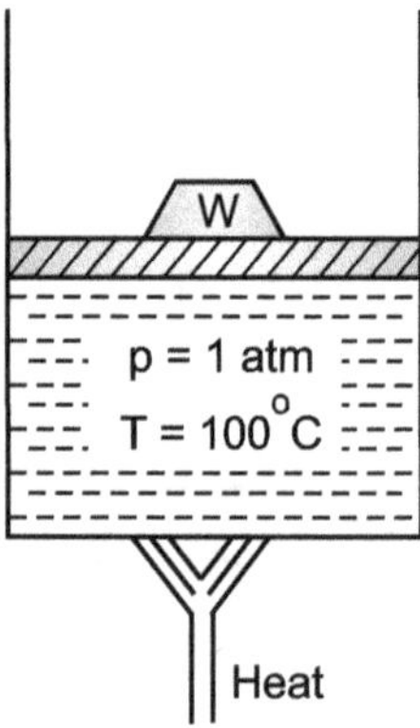


**Fig. 6.3: At 1 atm. pressure and 100°C, water exists as a liquid which is ready to vapourise
(saturated liquid)**

5.  Part of the water is evaporated. Therefore, there is a mixture of water and vapour.

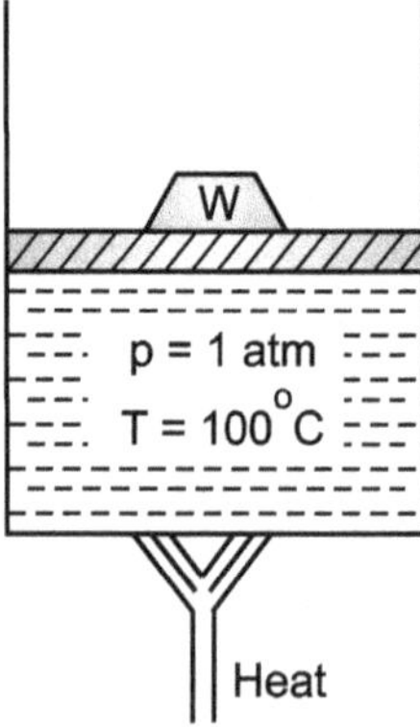


**Fig. 6.4: As more heat is added, part of saturated liquid vapourizes
(saturated liquid–vapour mixture)**

6.  See point 'd' in Fig. 6.7. The entire cylinder is filled with vapour. Any heat loss from this vapour will cause some of the vapour to condense.

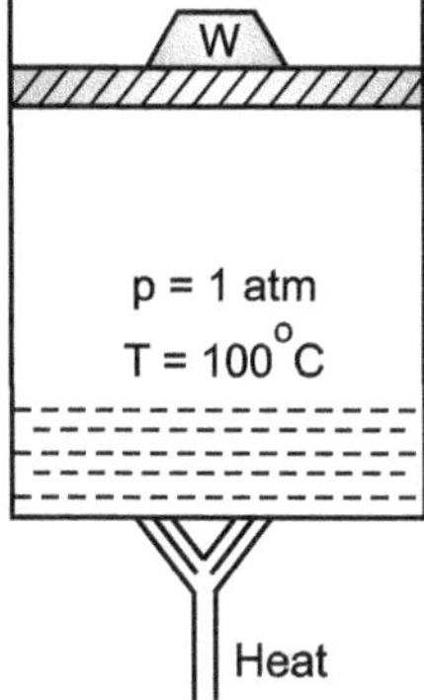


**Fig. 6.5: At 1 atm. pressure, the temperature remains constant at 100°c until the last drop of liquid is vapourised (saturated vapour)**

7.  Further addition of heat will increase the temperature of steam. So, it is called as superheated steam.

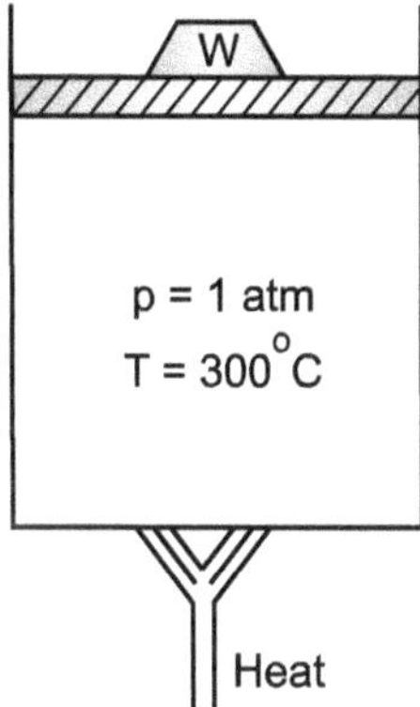


**Fig. 6.6: As more heat is added, the temperature of the vapour starts rising (superheated vapour)**

All the above steps are represented in Fig. 6.7.

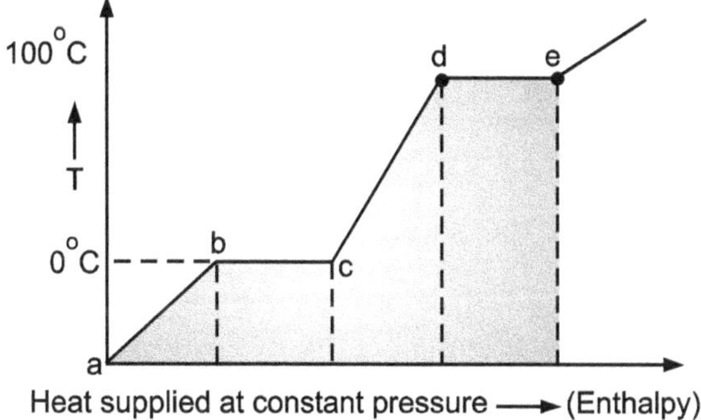


**Fig. 6.7: Temperature - Heat supplied**

In Fig. 6.7,    a – b   →   Sensible heating of ice

b – c   →   Melting of ice

c – d   →   Sensible heating of liquid

d – e   →   Saturated mixture of liquid and vapour

From point e – onwards, superheating of steam.

## 6.3 EFFECT OF PRESSURE ON BOILING POINT

The boiling temperature of water increases with increasing pressure. The 'Boiling Temperature' of water at a particular pressure is known as "saturation temperature" and corresponding pressure is known as 'saturation pressure.'

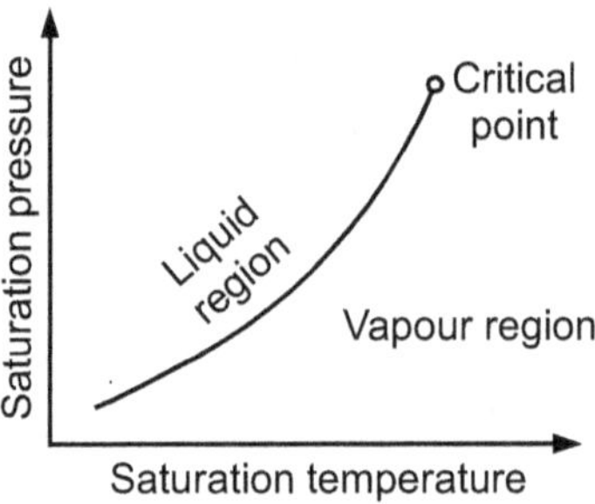


**Fig. 6.8: Relation between saturation pressure and saturation temperature of water**

The critical temperature of steam is defined as the temperature above which it is impossible to liquify the steam by pressure alone, irrespective of the intensity of temperature. At critical point "the change of volume falls to zero".

For water, the properties are:

$$\text{Critical pressure } (p_C) \;=\; 221.2 \text{ bar}$$

$$\text{Critical temperature } (T_C) \;=\; 647.3 \text{ K}$$

$$\text{Critical volume, } (v_C) \;=\; 0.00317 \text{ m}^3/\text{kg}$$

## 6.4 PROPERTY DIAGRAMS

### 6.4.1 p–v Diagram of Water

The p-v diagram of a pure substance is shown in Fig. 6.9.

From Fig. 6.9, it is clear that as the saturation temperature is increased, the volume of saturated liquid increases.

Volume of the saturated liquid is very small compared with the volume of saturated vapour. As the pressure goes on increasing, the volume of vapour goes on decreasing upto critical point.

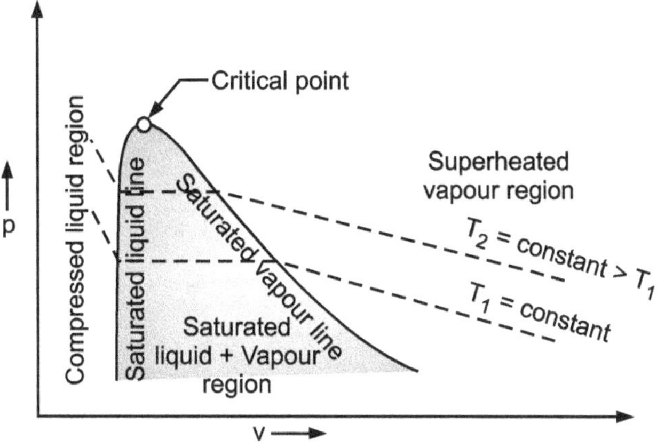


**Fig. 6.9: p-v Diagram of a pure substance**

## 6.4.2 Temperature Specific Volume Diagram of Water

The phase change diagram of water at 1 atm. pressure is described in Article 6.2. The process is repeated for different pressures to draw T-v diagram as shown in Fig. 6.10.

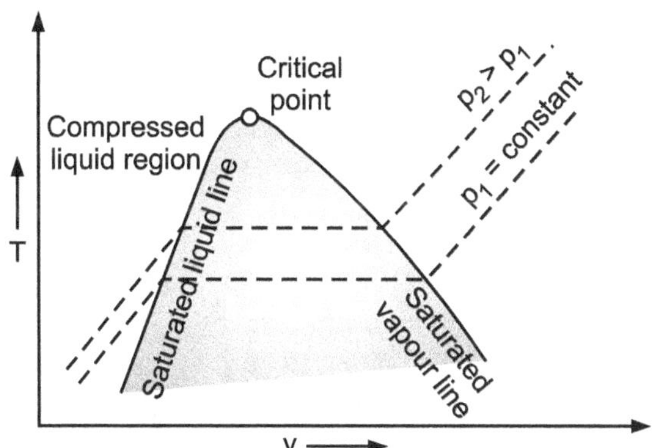


**Fig. 6.10: T-v diagram for pure substance**

From Fig. 6.10, we can draw the following conclusions:

1.   Water starts boiling at a much higher temperature corresponding to higher pressures.

2.   The specific volume of the saturated liquid is larger and the specific volume of saturated vapour is smaller than the corresponding values at 1 atm. pressure. It means, the horizontal line that connects the saturated liquid and saturated vapour states is much shorter.

## 6.4.3 Enthalpy – Entropy (h–s) Diagram of Water

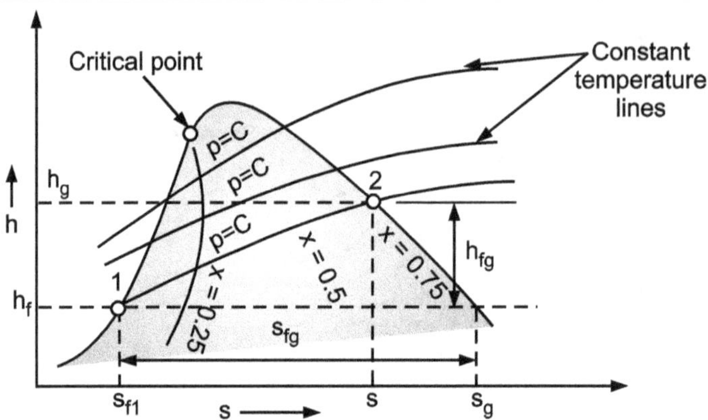



**Fig. 6.11: Enthalpy-Entropy diagram of water (Mollier diagram)**

Fig. 6.11 is the h-s or Mollier diagram indicating only the liquid and vapour phases. As the pressure increases, saturation temperature increases and also slope of the isobar increases. On this diagram, constant volume lines diverging in vapour region, is also shown. As the pressure increases, $h_{fg}$ decreases and reduces to zero ($h_{fg} = 0$) at critical point.

## 6.4.4 T-s Diagram for Water

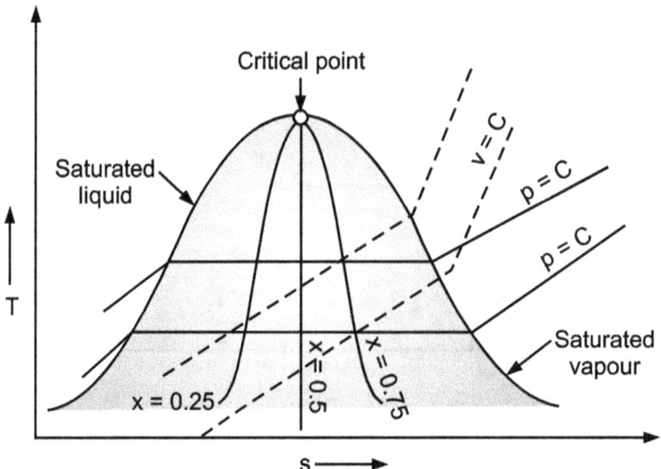



**Fig. 6.12: Temperature-Entropy diagram for water**

For reversible process, the change in entropy is given as:

$$ds = \frac{\partial Q}{T} = \int Tds = \int dQ$$

The area under the curve (T-s) for a process gives the heat transfer.

Fig. 6.12 shows T-s diagram for water. Constant pressure, constant specific volume and constant quality lines are also shown.

# 6.5 PROPERTIES OF STEAM

**(a) Sensible Heat of Water or Enthalpy of Water:** The quantity of heat absorbed by one kg of water to raise its temperature from the freezing point to the boiling point is known as sensible heat.

It is denoted by $h_f$ and calculated as

$$h_f = c_p \, \Delta T \text{ for unit mass} \qquad \ldots (6.1)$$

where,  $c_p$ = Specific heat of water at constant pressure, kJ/kg·K

$\Delta T$ = Temperature rise, °C

$h_f$ = Sensible heat, kJ/kg

The error resulted in the value of $h_f$, calculated by this formula increases as the temperature rises. Therefore, generally $h_f$ is taken from Steam Table.

**(b) Latent Heat (Enthalpy of Evaporation) ($h_{fg}$):** It is the amount of heat required to convert one kg of water at a given saturated temperature $T_s$ and pressure 'P' into steam at the same temperature and pressure conditions. This varies with pressure.

For given temperature or pressure, it can be obtained from steam table.

**Ex.** (i) Find the enthalpy of evaporation at 3.5 kPa pressure.

**Ans.** Referring the steam table based on pressure, $h_{fg}$ = 1753.7 kJ/kg at 3.5 kPa.

**Ex.** (ii) Find enthalpy of evaporation at 150°C.

**Ans.** $h_{fg}$ = 2114.3 kJ/kg at 150°C.

**(c) Enthalpy or Total Heat:** It is the amount of heat required to raise the temperature of one kg of water from freezing point to the boiling temperature, (corresponding to given pressure) and then to convert it into dry saturated steam at the same temperature and pressure.

It is denoted by $h_g$.

$$h_g = h_f + h_{fg} \qquad \ldots (6.2)$$

where,  $h_f$ = Sensible heat, kJ/kg and

$h_{fg}$ = Latent heat, kJ/kg

**(d) Wet Steam:** It is a homogeneous mixture of vapour and fine water particles. This exists in the steam space of boiler.

The quality of wet steam depends on the amount of water particles present in the mixture. The quality of wet steam is defined by the dryness fraction.

The dryness fraction (x) is expressed by the ratio of mass of dry vapour (steam) to the total mass of the mixture of water and steam.

$$\therefore \qquad x = \frac{m_s}{m_w + m_s} \qquad \qquad \text{... (6.3)}$$

where,    $x$  =  Dryness fraction or quality of steam

$m_s$  =  Mass of dry steam, kg

$m_w$  =  Mass of liquid water in the mixture, kg

If dryness fraction of wet steam $(x) = 0.8$, then one kg of steam contains 0.2 kg of water (moisture) and 0.8 kg of dry steam.

(i)   Enthalpy of evaporation or Latent heat of 1 kg of wet steam

$$= \; x \cdot h_{fg} \; \text{kJ/kg} \qquad \qquad \text{... (6.4)}$$

(ii)  Total heat or enthalpy of one kg of wet steam is equal to the sum of the enthalpy of saturated water + enthalpy of evaporation i.e.

$$h_g \; = \; h_f + x h_{fg} \; \text{kJ/kg} \qquad \qquad \text{... (6.5)}$$

$$= \; h_f + x \, (h_g - h_f)$$

(iii) Specific volume: Let us consider 1 kg of water heated at constant pressure (1.01325 bar). This heating process is shown in T-v diagram of Fig. 6.13.

Let point A be on the line 2–3 in vapour region having dryness fraction x. Therefore, each of mixture at 'A' contains x kg of vapour and $(1 - x)$ kg of liquid water. At point 2, the water is at saturated liquid state completely $(x = 0)$. At state point 3, the mixture is completely saturated steam (dry saturated state), therefore, $x = 1$.

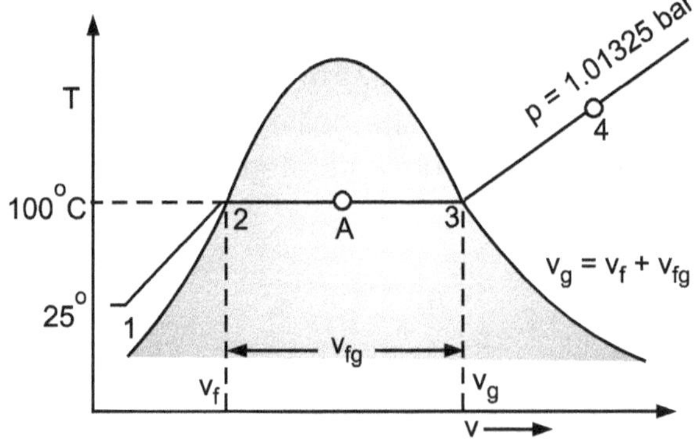


**Fig. 6.13**

If $v_A$ is the specific volume at point A, then,

$$v_A \; = \; (1 - x) \, v_f + x \cdot v_g \qquad \qquad \text{... (6.6)}$$

But        $v_g \; = \; v_f + v_{fg}$

Put in equation (6.6) and simplify

$$v_A \; = \; v_f + x \cdot v_{fg} \; \text{...... } m^3/\text{kg} \qquad \qquad \text{... (6.7)}$$

This is the specific volume of wet steam having dryness fraction x.

**(e)** The specific volume of superheated steam at superheat temperature $T_{sup}$ is calculated by using Charle's law.

$$\frac{v_g}{T_s} = \frac{v_{sup}}{T_{sup}}$$

$$\therefore \quad v_{sup} = \frac{v_g}{T_s} \cdot T_{sup} \qquad \text{... (6.8)}$$

where,

$v_g$ = Specific volume of dry saturated steam

$T_s$ = Temperature of dry saturated steam, K

$v_{sup}$ = Specific volume of superheated steam

**(f) Superheated Steam:** When steam is heated out of contact with water, it will result in increase of temperature. Superheating of the steam occurs at constant pressure. The amount of superheating is measured by the rise in temperature of the steam above its saturation temperature ($t_s$). Greater superheating of the steam will help to acquire the properties of perfect gas.

Enthalpy of superheat

$$= c_p (T_{sup} - T_{sat}) \text{ kJ/kg} \qquad \text{... (6.9)}$$

where, $c_p$ = Mean specific heat of superheated steam at constant temperature

The term ($T_{sup} - T_{sat}$) is known as degree of superheat.

The value of $c_p$ ranges from 2 kJ/kg·K to 2.5 kJ/kg·K

The enthalpy (total heat) of one kg of superheated steam ($H_{sup}$) is

$$h_{sup} = h_f + h_{fg} + c_p (T_{sup} - T_{sat}) \text{ kJ/kg} \qquad \text{... (6.10)}$$

$$= h_g + c_p (T_{sup} - T_{sat}) \qquad \text{... (6.11)}$$

**(g) Internal Energy:** We know that change in enthalpy is

$$dh = du + d (pv)$$

$$h_2 - h_1 = u_2 - u_1 + (p_2 v_2 - p_1 v_1) \text{ for unit mass}$$

$$\therefore \quad u_2 - u_1 = (h_2 - h_1) - (p_2 v_2 - p_1 v_1) \text{ for } m = 1 \qquad \text{... (6.12)}$$

(i)    For wet steam,

Let $x_2$ and $x_1$ be dryness fractions at conditions 2 and 1 respectively.

$$\therefore \quad h_2 = h_{f2} + x_2 \cdot h_{fg_2}$$

and

$$v_2 = x_2 v_{g2}$$

$$h_1 = h_{f_1} + x_1 \cdot h_{fg_1}$$

and
$$v_1 = x_1 \cdot v_{g1}$$

Then, change in internal energy,

$$(u_2 - u_1) = [(h_{f_2} + x_2 h_{fg_2}) - (h_{f_1} + x_1 h_{fg_1})]$$

$$- \left( p_2 \cdot x_2 \cdot v_{g_2} - p_1 x_1 \cdot v_{g_1} \right) \qquad \ldots (6.13)$$

(ii)  Internal energy of superheated steam.

$$h_2 = h_{sup_2} = h_{g_2} + c_p (T_{sup_2} - T_{sat_1})$$

and
$$v_2 = v_{sup_2} = \frac{v_{sat_2}}{T_{sat_2}} \times T_{sup_2}$$

$$\therefore \quad u_2 - u_1 = (h_{sup_2} - h_1) - (p_2 v_{sup_2} - p_1 v_1) \qquad \ldots (6.14)$$

**(h)  Entropy (s):** Entropy of a dry saturated steam can be obtained from steam table corresponding to a pressure or temperature of steam.

(i)  Entropy of wet steam

$$s = (1 - x) s_f + x \cdot s_g$$

or
$$s = s_f + x \, s_{fg}$$

$$= s_f + x \, (s_g - s_f)$$

$$= s_f + x \, s_g \qquad \ldots (6.15)$$

because $x \, s_f$ is very small.

(ii)  Entropy of superheated steam,

$$s_{sup} = s_g + \text{Entropy of superheat kJ/kg·K}$$

$$\text{Entropy of superheat} = c_p \ln \frac{T_{sup}}{T_{sat}}$$

$$\therefore \quad s_{sup} = s_g + c_p \ln \frac{T_{sup}}{T_{sat}} \qquad \text{kJ/kg·K for unit mass} \ldots (6.16)$$

## SOLVED PROBLEMS

**Problem 6.1:** Obtain all the properties of steam in the following cases:

(i)  Steam is dry saturated at 11 bar.

(ii)  Steam has a pressure of 8 bar and dryness fraction 0.9.

(iii)  Steam is superheated having pressure 15 bar and temperature 250°C. Assume $c_p$ for superheated steam.

**Solution:** (i) Dry saturated steam at 11 bar

$$T_{sat} = 184.1°C \text{ from steam table}$$

$$v_g = 0.17739 \text{ m}^3/\text{kg}$$

$$v_f = 0.001133 \text{ m}^3/\text{kg}$$

$$h_f = 781.1 \text{ kJ/kg}$$

$$h_{f_g} = 1998.6 \text{ kJ/kg}$$

$$h_g = h_f + h_{fg}$$

$$= 2779.7 \text{ kJ/kg}$$

$$s_f = 2.179 \text{ kJ/kg·K}$$

$$s_{fg} = \frac{h_{fg}}{T_{sat}}$$

$$= 4.371 \text{ kJ/kg·K}$$

$$s_g = s_f + s_{fg}$$

$$= 6.55 \text{ kJ/kg·K}$$

(ii)　Steam at 8 bar and 0.9 dryness fraction

$\rightarrow$　Wet steam

$$T_{sat} \text{ at 8 bar} = 170.4°C \text{ from steam table}$$

$$v_f = 0.0011150 \text{ m}^3/\text{kg}$$

$$v_x = (1-x)\, v_f + x \cdot v_g$$

$$= (1-0.9) \times 0.001115 + 0.9 \times 0.24026$$

$$= \mathbf{0.21635 \ m^3/kg}$$

$$h_x = h_f + x h_{fg}$$

$$= 720.9 + 0.9 \times 2046.5$$

$$= \mathbf{2562.75 \ kJ/kg}$$

$$s_f = 2.046 \text{ kJ/kg·K}$$

$$s_x = s_f + x \cdot s_{fg}$$

$$= 2.046 + 0.9 \times 4.614$$

$$= \mathbf{6.1986 \ kJ/kg·K}$$

(iii)　Superheated steam at 15 bar and 250°C from steam table, $T_{sat}$ = 198.3°C at 15 bar.

$$v_{sup} = \frac{T_{sup}}{T_{sat}} \cdot v_g$$

$$= \left(\frac{250 + 273}{198.3 + 273}\right) \times 0.13167$$

$$= 0.14611 \text{ m}^3/\text{kg}$$

$$h_{sup} = h_g + c_p (T_{sup} - T_{sat})$$

$$= 2789.9 + 2.1 (250 - 198.3)$$

$$= \mathbf{2898.47 \ kJ/kg}$$

$$s_{sup} = s_g + c_p \cdot \ln\left(\frac{T_{sup}}{T_{sat}}\right)$$

$$= 6.441 + 2.1 \ln\left(\frac{250 + 273}{198.3 + 273}\right)$$

$$= \mathbf{6.6596 \ kJ/kg}$$

**Problem 6.2:** Estimate the condition of the steam in the following cases.

    (i)   $p = 20$ bar,     $h = 2797.2$ kJ/kg

    (ii)  $p = 14$ bar,     $v = 0.13$ m³/kg

    (iii) $p = 12$ bar,     $s = 6.70$ kJ/kg·K

**Solution:**

(i)   For $p = 20$ bar, $h_g = 2797.2$ kJ/kg from steam table. Therefore, $h_g = h$.

    $\therefore$   **Steam is dry and saturated.**

    (**Note:** If $h < h_g$, it would be wet and if $h > h_g$, it would be superheated).

(ii)  $p = 14$ bar, $v = 0.13$ m³/kg,

    From steam table, at $p = 14$ bar, $v_g = 0.14073$ m³/kg

    Comparison of $v$ and $v_g$:

    $v < v_g$ $(0.13 < 0.14073)$

    $\therefore$   **Steam is wet.**

    $\therefore$          $v = v_x = x \, v_g$

    $\therefore$          $x = \dfrac{v_x}{v_g}$

$$= \frac{0.13}{0.14073}$$

$$= \mathbf{0.9237}$$

**Note:** The steam would have been dry saturated if $v = v_g$ and would be superheated if $v > v_g$.

(iii)   $p = 12$ bar, $s = 6.7$ kJ/kg·K

Now $s_g = 6.519$ kJ/kg·K for dry saturated steam (from steam table).

Comparison of $s$ and $s_g$:

$s > s_g$. Therefore steam is superheated.

(**Note:** It would be dry saturated if $s = s_g$ and wet if $s < s_g$)

$$\therefore \qquad s_{sup} = s_g + c_p \ln\left(\frac{T_{sup}}{T_{sat}}\right)$$

$$6.7 = 6.519 + 2.1 \ln\left(\frac{T_{sup}}{188 + 273}\right)$$

$$\therefore \qquad T_{sup} = \mathbf{229.496°C}$$

# 6.6 THERMODYNAMIC PROCESSES

The general energy equations applicable to perfect gases are also applicable to vapours and the procedure for finding the change in internal energy is also same as was adopted in case of gases.

The different processes of expansion and compression of gases are also applicable to vapours but the results obtained may be different.

The equations for the work done by vapour are the same as those used for perfect gases.

## 6.6.1 Constant Volume Heating or Cooling

The process can be represented on p–v and T–s planes (See Fig. 6.14).

It is assumed that wet steam (state 1) is heated at constant volume, till it reaches a superheat condition (state 2).

$$v_1 = v_2 \text{ for constant volume}$$

$$x_1 \cdot v_{g_1} = v_{sup_2}$$

$$x_1 v_{g_1} = \frac{T_{sup_2}}{T_{sup_2}} \cdot v_{sat_2} \qquad\qquad \dots (6.17)$$

(a)   Work done,

$$W_{1-2} = \int_1^2 p\, dv = 0 \text{, as } dv = 0$$

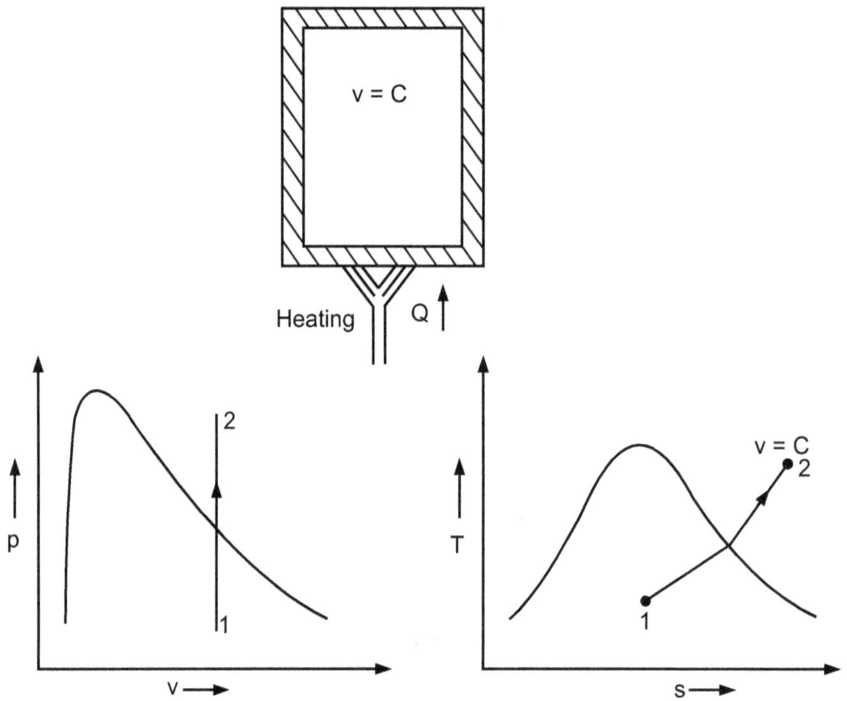


**Fig. 6.14: Heating of vapour at constant volume (assuming state 2 superheated)**

(b)  Heat transferred by first law,

$$\delta Q = du + pdx$$

$$Q_{1-2} = (u_2 - u_1) \text{ as } pdv = 0$$

$$= (h_2 - p_2 v_2) - (h_1 - p_1 v_1) \qquad \qquad \dots (6.18)$$

where,    $h_2 = h_{sup_2}$

$$= h_g + c_p (T_{sup_2} - T_{sat_2}) \text{ kJ/kg}$$

$p_2$ = Pressure at 2 kPa,

$v_2 = v_{sup_2}$ , $m^3/kg$

$h_1 = h_{x_1} = h_{f_1} + x \cdot h_{fg_1}$ kJ/kg

$p_1$ = Pressure at 1, kPa

$v_1 = vx_1$

$$= v_{f_1} + x \cdot v_{fg_1} \ m^3/kg$$

Similar equations are considered if the condition of steam at state 2 is wet.

**Problem 6.3: Constant volume:** A vessel contains 4 kg of steam at 10 bar and 220°C. Find the volume of the vessel. If the vessel is cooled till the steam pressure drops to 3 bar, find the final condition of steam and the heat transfer during cooling.

**Solution:**

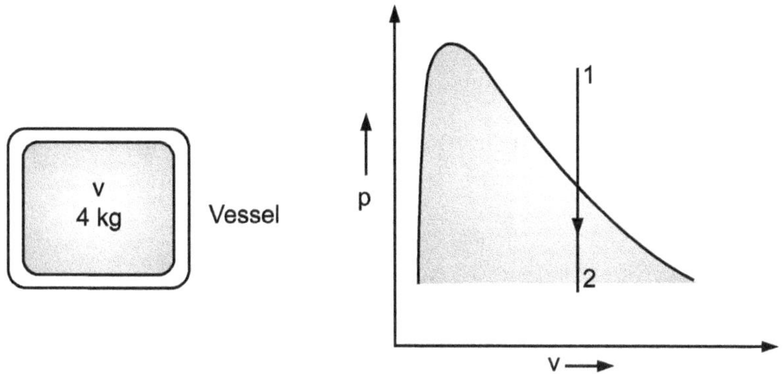


**Fig. 6.15**

**Given**: $p_1 = 10$ bar, $m = 4$ kg, $T_1 = 220°C$ and $p_2 = 3$ bar.

For $p_1 = 10$ bar, $T_{sat_1} = 179.9°C$ from steam table.

$T_1 > T_{sat_1}$, hence steam is super-heated.

$$v_{sup_1} = \frac{T_{sup_1}}{T_{sat_1}} \times v_{g_1} \ m^3/kg$$

$$= \frac{(220 + 273)}{(179.9 + 273)} \times 0.1943$$

$$= \mathbf{0.2115 \ m^3/kg}$$

∴ Volume of vessel,

$$V = m \times v_{sup\ 1}$$

$$= 4 \times 0.2115$$

$$= \mathbf{0.846 \ m^3}$$

The steam undergoes a non-flow constant volume cooling process. If $V_2$ is the final specific volume of steam,

$$\text{Volume of vessel} = v = m \cdot v_2$$

$$\therefore \quad v_2 = \frac{v}{m} = \frac{0.846}{4} = \mathbf{0.2115 \ m^3/kg}$$

Final condition of steam is found by comparing $v_2$ with $v_{g_2}$ at 3 bar.

$$\therefore \quad v_{g_2} = 0.60553 \ m^3/kg \ \text{from steam table}$$

$$v_2 < v_{g_2}, \text{ the steam is wet having dryness fraction } x_2$$

$$v_2 = x_2 \cdot v_{g_2}$$

$$0.2115 = x_2 \times 0.60553$$

$$\therefore \quad x_2 = \mathbf{0.3493}$$

The heat transferred during the non-flow constant volume process can be found from the following equation

$$Q = \Delta u + W_{1-2}$$

$$W_{1-2} = \int_{1}^{2} pdv = 0, \text{ Since } dv = 0$$

$$Q = \Delta u$$

$$= m \ (u_2 - u_1)$$

$$= m \left[ (h_2 - p_2 v_2) - (h_1 - p_1 v_1) \right] \ kJ$$

$$= m \left[ (h_2 - h_1) - v_1 \ (p_2 - p_1) \right] \ kJ$$

$$\therefore \quad h_2 = h_{f_2} + x_2 \cdot h_{fg_2}$$

$$= 561.4 + 0.3493 \times 2163.2$$

$$= \mathbf{1316.96 \ kJ/kg}$$

$$h_1 = h_{g_1} + c_p \ (T_{sup_1} - T_{sat_1})$$

$$= 2776.2 + 2.1 \ (220 - 179.9)$$

$$= \mathbf{2860.4 \ kJ/kg}$$

$$\therefore \quad Q = \text{Heat transfer}$$

$$= 4 \left[ (1316.96 - 2860.4) - 0.2115 \ (3 - 10) \times 100 \right]$$

$$= \mathbf{-5581.58 \ kJ \ rejected.}$$

---

**Problem 6.4:** A closed vessel of 0.75 m³ capacity contains dry saturated steam at 0.35 MPa. The vessel is cooled until the pressure is reduced to 0.2 MPa. Calculate

(i)   Mass of steam in the vessel.

(ii)  The final dryness fraction of steam.

(iii) The amount of heat transferred during the cooling process.

**Extract from steam table**

| Pressure in MPa | $T_s$ °C | $v_f$ m³/kg | $v_g$ m³/kg | $h_f$ kJ/kg | $h_{fg}$ kJ/kg | $h_g$ kJ/kg |
|---|---|---|---|---|---|---|
| 0.18 | 116.9 | 0.001057 | 0.978 | 491 | 2211 | 2702 |
| 0.20 | 120.2 | 0.001061 | 0.886 | 505 | 2202 | 2702 |
| 0.3 | 133.5 | 0.001073 | 0.605 | 561 | 2163 | 2724 |
| 0.35 | 138.9 | 0.001078 | 0.524 | 584 | 2148 | 2732 |
| 0.40 | 143.6 | 0.001084 | 0.462 | 605 | 2134 | 2739 |

**Solution: Given**: Volume of vessel, $V = 0.75$ m³, $p_1 = 0.35$ MPa.

At this pressure, specific volume, $v_{g_1} = 0.524$ m³/kg.

(i) Mass of steam in the vessel

$$= \frac{V}{v_{g_1}} = \frac{0.75}{0.524} = \textbf{1.431 kg}$$

(ii) The volume of vessel, $V = m \cdot v_2$

$$v_2 = \frac{V}{m} = \frac{0.75}{1.431} = \textbf{0.524 m³/kg}$$

At pressure $p_2 = 0.2$ MPa, volume of steam (dry saturated) $= v_{g_2} = 0.8860$.

$v_2 < v_{g_2}$. Therefore it is a wet steam.

$$\therefore \qquad x_2\, v_{g_2} = v_2$$

$$\therefore \qquad x_2 = \frac{v_2}{v_{g_2}} = \frac{0.524}{0.886} = 0.589$$

(iii) Heat Transfer,

$$Q = \Delta u + \int_1^2 p\, dv \quad \text{where} \quad \int_1^2 p\, dv = 0$$

$$\therefore \quad Q = \Delta u$$

$$= m\left[(h_2 - p_2 v_2) - (h_1 - p_1 v_1)\right]$$

$$h_2 = h_{f_2} + x \cdot h_{fg_2}$$

$$= 505 + 0.589 \times 2202 = \textbf{1801.9 kJ/kg}$$

$$V_2 = x \cdot v_{g_2} = 0.589 \times 0.886$$

$$= \textbf{0.524 m³/kg}$$

$$p_2 = 0.2 \text{ MPa} = 200 \text{ kPa}$$

$$h_1 = h_{g_1} = 2732 \text{ kJ/kg}$$

$$\mathbf{p_1 = 350 \text{ kPa}}$$

$$v_1 = v_{g_1} = 0.524$$

$$Q = 1.431 \,[(1801.9 - 200 \times 0.524) - (2732 - 350 \times 0.524)]$$

$$= 1.431 \,[1697.1 - 2548.6]$$

$$\mathbf{= -1218.5 \text{ kJ}}$$

## 6.6.2 Constant Pressure Process               [Dec. 11, May 11]

The process is represented on p-v and T-s planes (See Fig. 6.16).

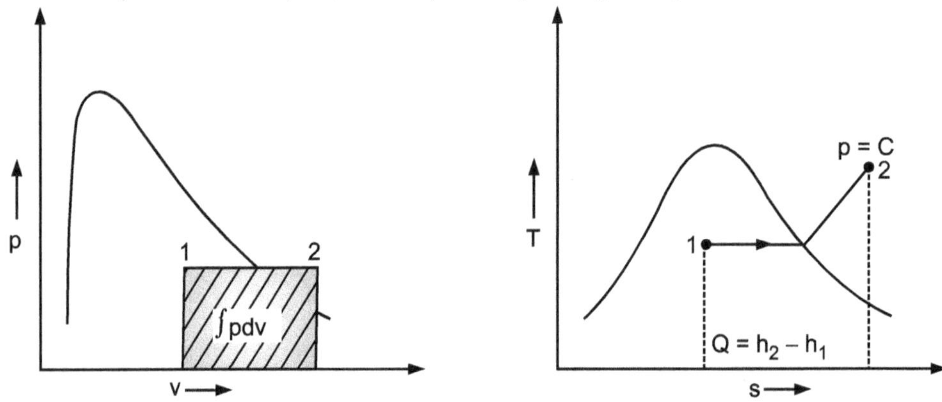


**Fig. 6.16: Constant pressure process on p–v and T–s planes**

(a)  Work done:

$$W_{1-2} = \int pdv = p \int dv$$

$$= p\,(v_2 - v_1) \text{ kJ/kg} \qquad \qquad ... (6.19)$$

p is in kN/m² and v in m³/kg

$$v_2 = v_{sup_2}$$

$$= \frac{T_{sup}}{T_{sat}} \times v_g \qquad \qquad ... (6.20)$$

$$v_1 = x_1 \cdot v_{g_1} \text{ at pressure } p_1 \text{ and dryness fraction } x_1$$

(b) Heat transfer:

$$Q_{1-2} = (u_2 - u_1) + \int_1^2 pdv$$

$$= (u_2 - u_1) + p\,(v_2 - v_1) \text{ kJ/kg}$$

where p is in kN/m² and v in m³/kg

$$p \ = \ p_1 = p_2$$

$$\therefore \qquad Q_{1-2} \ = \ h_2 - h_1 \qquad\qquad\qquad \dots (6.21)$$

(c)  Change in internal energy:

$$u_2 - u_1 \ = \ (h_2 - h_1) - (pv_2 - pv_1) \ \text{kJ/kg} \qquad \dots (6.22)$$

$$= \ (h_2 - h_1) - p \, (v_2 - v_1) \ \text{kJ/kg} \qquad \dots (6.23)$$

$v_2$ and $v_1$ are to be determined depending upon the condition.

**Problem 6.5: Constant Pressure Process:** Steam at 10 bar and 230°C is cooled under constant pressure until the quality of steam becomes 80% dry. Find (a) the work done, (b) change in enthalpy and heat transfer, if the process is non-flow.

**Solution:**

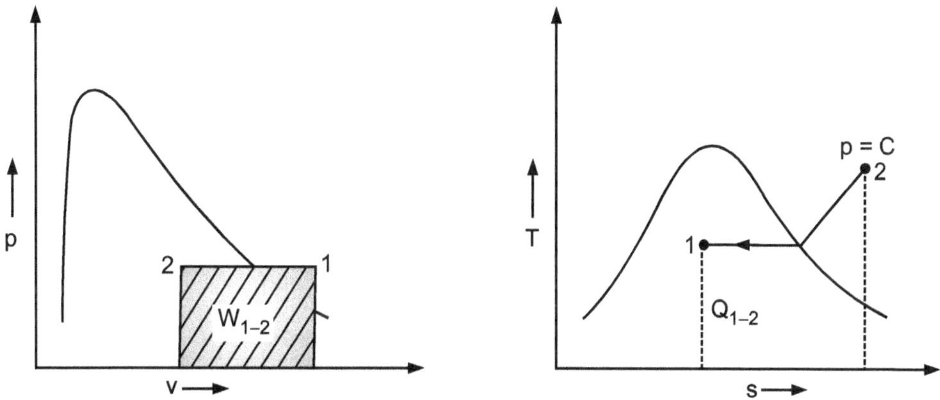


**Fig. 6.17: p-v and T-s diagrams**

For 10 bar pressure,

$T_s$ = 179.9°C, $v_f$ = 0.001127 m³/kg , $v_g$ = 0.194,

$h_f$ = 763 kJ/kg, $h_{fg}$ = 2015 kJ/kg

(i)  Work done,  $\qquad\qquad W_{1-2} \ = \ \displaystyle\int_{1}^{2} pdv$

$$W_{1-2} \ = \ p \, (v_2 - v_1) \ \text{for m = 1}$$

As $T_s$ = 179.9°C, but given temperature at state 1 is 230°C. Therefore steam is superheated at state 1.

$$\therefore \qquad v_{sup_1} \ = \ \frac{v_{sup_1}}{v_{sat_1}} \times v_{sat_1}$$

$$= \ \frac{(230 + 273)}{(179.9 + 273)} \times 0.194$$

$$= \ \mathbf{0.2154 \ m^3/kg}$$

Therefore, steam is in wet condition at state 2.

Therefore $\quad v_2 = x_2 \cdot v_{g_2}$

$$= 0.8 \times 0.198$$

$$= \mathbf{0.1584 \ m^3/kg}$$

$$W_{1-2} = \frac{10 \times 10^5}{10^5} \times (0.1584 - 0.2154)$$

$$= \mathbf{-\ 57 \ kJ/kg}$$

Negative sign indicates that work is done on the steam.

(ii)  Change in enthalpy = Heat transfer

$$= h_2 - h_1$$

$$= \left(h_{f_2} + x_2 \, h_{fg_2}\right) - \left(h_{f_1} + h_{fg_1} + c_p \left(T_{sup_1} - T_{sat_1}\right)\right)$$

But $\qquad h_{f_2} = h_{f_1}$

$\therefore$  Change in enthalpy $= (x_2 - 1) \, h_{fg_1} + c_p \left(T_{sup_1} - T_{sat_1}\right)$

$$= (0.8 - 1) \times 2015 + 2.1 \,(230 - 179.9)$$

$$= \mathbf{-\ 297.8 \ kJ/kg}$$

Negative sign indicates that heat is lost by the steam (system).

## 6.6.3 Constant Temperature (Isothermal) Process

For wet steam, a constant temperature process is also a constant pressure process. As soon as the steam becomes superheated, it behaves as a perfect gas and follows isothermal process. This is shown on p-V and T-s planes (See Fig. 6.18).

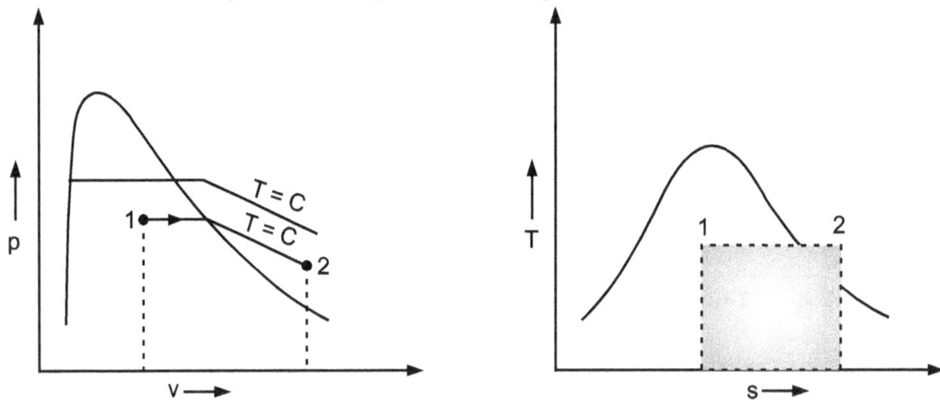


**Fig. 6.18: Isothermal process**

(a)  Isothermal law can be applied to the process 1-2 as,

$$p_1 v_1 = p_2 v_2$$

i.e. $\qquad p_1 \cdot (x_1 v_{g_1}) = p_2 \,(v_{sup_2}) \qquad\qquad \dots (6.24)$

because of the condition that steam is wet at state 1 and it is superheated at state 2 (See Fig. 6.18).

$\therefore$ From above equation, $x_1$ is determined. The state 2 may not be necessarily superheated, but may be wet also.

It follows that,

$$h_1 \;=\; h_{f_1} + x_1\, h_{fg_1}$$

$$h_2 \;=\; h_{f_2} + x_2\, h_{fg_2} \text{ if final condition of steam is wet.}$$

$$h_2 \;=\; h_{f_2} + h_{fg_1} + k_p\,(T_{sup_2} - T_{sat_2}) \text{ if steam is superheated at point 2.}$$

(b) Work done: By first law

$$Q_{1-2} \;=\; \Delta u + W_{1-2}$$

$$\therefore \qquad W_{1-2} \;=\; Q_{1-2} - \Delta u$$

$$=\; Q_{1-2} - (u_2 - u_1)$$

$$=\; Q_{1-2} - (u_1 - u_2) \qquad\qquad \text{for unit mass ... (6.25)}$$

This $W_{1-2}$ can also be obtained by

$$W_{1-2} \;=\; p_1 v_1 \ln \frac{v_2}{v_1}$$

$$\therefore \qquad \frac{v_2}{v_1} \;=\; r = \frac{p_1}{p_2}$$

$$=\; p_1 \left( x_1 \cdot V_{g_1} \right) \ln r \qquad\qquad\qquad \text{... (6.26)}$$

(c) Heat transfer

$$Q_{1-2} \;=\; W_{1-2} + (u_2 - u_1)$$

$$=\; p_1 \cdot x_1 V_{g_1} \log_e r + (u_2 - u_1) \text{ per unit mass.} \qquad \text{... (6.27)}$$

---

**Problem 6.6:** A reciprocating steam engine receives dry saturated steam at 14 bar. Expansion takes place hyperbolically to a pressure of 4 bar. Calculate the final condition of steam at the end of expansion and the work done per kg of steam during expansion.

**Solution:** Let us represent the process on p-v and T-s diagrams.

The expansion is being hyperbolic, $p_1 v_1 = p_2 v_2$. The volume of dry saturated steam at 14 bar pressure is $v_{g_1} = 0.1633$ m³/kg.

The specific volume of dry saturated steam at pressure of 4 bar is $v_{g_2} = 0.4625$ m³.

$$\therefore \qquad p_1 v_1 \;=\; p_2 v_2$$

---

$$v_2 = \frac{p_1 v_1}{p_2} = \frac{14}{4} \times 0.1633 = \mathbf{0.49 \ m^3/kg}$$

$$\therefore \qquad v_2 > v_{g_2}$$

$\therefore$ Steam is superheated state at point 2.

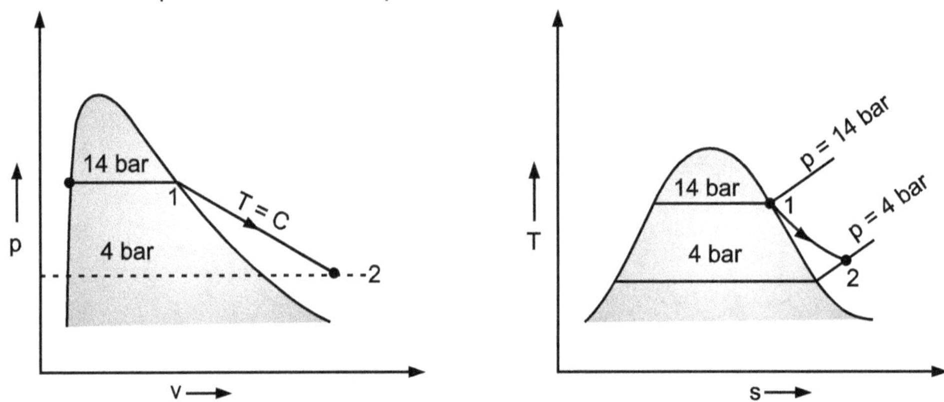



**Fig. 6.19: p-v and T-s diagrams**

Work done, 
$$W_{1-2} = p_1 v_{g_1} \ln \frac{v_2}{v_1} = p_1 v_{g_1} \ln \frac{p_1}{p_2}$$

$$= \frac{14 \times 10^5}{1000} \times 0.1633 \times \log \frac{12}{4}$$

$$= \mathbf{251.1 \ kJ/kg}$$

## 6.6.4 Polytropic Process                    [Dec. 10]

This process is stated by the law $pv^n = c$, where n = polytropic index. For different values of 'n', each process discussed earlier can be obtained. But for vapour, pv = RT does not apply.

The process is shown in Fig. 6.20.

In Fig. 6.20, state 1 is assumed as superheated state and state 2 as wet condition.

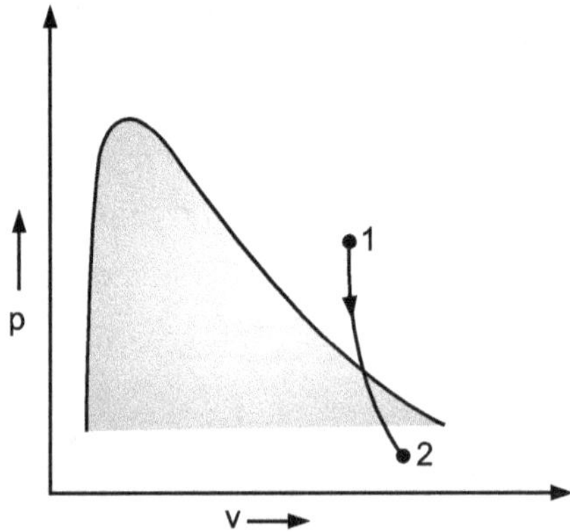



**Fig. 6.20: Polytropic process on p-v plane**

(a)   Work done for non-flow process,

$$W_{1-2} \;=\; \int_1^2 p\,dv = \frac{p_1 v_1 - p_2 v_2}{n - 1} \qquad\qquad \text{... (6.28)}$$

(b)   Heat transfer during the non-flow process.

$$Q_{1-2} \;=\; (u_2 - u_1) + \frac{p_1 v_1 - p_2 v_2}{n - 1}$$

$v_1$ and $v_2$ are calculated for the steam depending upon its state.

**Problem 6.7:** Steam at a pressure of 14 bar with 50°C superheat expands according to $pv^{1.25} = C$ to a pressure of 4 bar in a cylinder-piston arrangement. Determine (1) work done per kg of steam, (2) heat transferred.

**Solution:** At pressure of 14 bar, the properties of dry saturated steam are: $T_{sat}$ = 195.04°C, $v_{g_1}$ = 0.14072 m³/kg, $h_{f_1}$ = 830 kJ/kg, $h_{fg_1}$ = 1957.7 kJ/kg, $h_{g_1}$ = 2787.8 kJ/kg.

Similarly, at 4 bar pressure,

$v_{g_2}$ = 0.46222 m³/kg, $h_{f_2}$ = 604.67 m³/kg, $h_{fg_2}$ = 2133 kJ/kg, $h_{f_2}$ = 2737.6 kJ/kg.

$T_1$ = 195.04 + 50 = 244.04°C.

As the steam is superheated by 50°C,

$$v_{sup_1} \;=\; \frac{T_{sup_1}}{T_{sat_1}} \times v_{sat_1}$$

$$=\; \frac{(244.04 + 273)}{(195.04 + 273)} \times 0.14072$$

$$=\; \mathbf{0.15545 \ m^3/kg}$$

(a)          $W_{1-2} \;=\; \dfrac{p_1 v_1 - p_2 v_2}{n - 1}$

$$=\; \frac{p_1 v_1}{n - 1} \left[ 1 - \left( \frac{P_2}{P_1} \right)^{\frac{n-1}{n}} \right]$$

$$=\; \frac{14 \times 10^5}{1000} \times \frac{0.15545}{(1.25 - 1)} \left[ 1 - \left( \frac{4}{14} \right)^{\frac{1.25 - 1}{1.25}} \right]$$

$$=\; \mathbf{192.9 \ kJ/kg}$$

The work done can also be calculated as

$$W_{1-2} = 100 \frac{p_1 v_1 - p_2 v_2}{n-1}; \ p \text{ in bar}$$

$$192.9 = 100 \times \frac{(14 \times 0.15545 - 4 \times v_2)}{1.25 - 1}$$

$$v_2 = 0.423 \text{ m}^3/\text{kg}$$

but $\quad v_{g_2} = 0.4622$

$\therefore \qquad v_{g_1} > v_2 \therefore$ Steam is wet.

Dryness fraction $x_2 = ?$

$$p_1 v_1^{\frac{1}{n}} = p_2 v_2^{n}$$

$$14 \times (0.15545) = 4 \times (x_2 \cdot v_{g_2})^n$$

$\therefore \qquad$
$$(x_2)^n = \frac{14}{4} \times \left(\frac{0.15545}{0.4622}\right)^n$$

$$x_2 = \left(\frac{14}{4}\right)^{\frac{1}{n}} \times \frac{0.15545}{0.4622} = \mathbf{0.916}$$

(b)　Heat transferred,

$$Q_{1-2} = (u_2 - u_1) + W_{1-2}$$

$$u_1 = h_1 - 100 \, p_1 v_1 \text{ at 14 bar, } p_1 \text{ in bar}$$

$$h_1 = h_{g_1} + c_p \log\left(\frac{T_{sup_1}}{T_{sat_1}}\right)$$

$$= 2787.8 + 2.1 \log (50) = \mathbf{2796 \ kJ/kg}$$

$$u_1 = 2796 - 100 \times 14 \times 0.15545$$

$$= \mathbf{2578.3 \ kJ/kg}$$

$$u_2 = (h_2 - 100 \, p_2 v_2)$$

$$u_2 = h_{f_2} + x_2 \cdot h_{f_2} - 100 \times p_2 v_2$$

where $v_2 = x_2 \cdot v_{g_2}$

$\therefore$
$$u_2 = (604.04 + 0.916 \times 2133) - 100 \times 4 \times (0.916 \times 0.4622)$$

$$u_2 = 2388.8 \text{ kJ/kg}$$

$$W_{1-2} = 192.9$$

$\therefore$
$$Q_{1-2} = (2388.8 - 2578.3) + 192.9$$

$$= \mathbf{2.97 \ kJ/kg}$$

## 6.6.5 Adiabatic Process

Reversible adiabatic process is an isentropic process. The process is stated by the law $pV^\gamma = c$, where $\gamma$ = adiabatic index. This is represented on T-s and h-s planes.

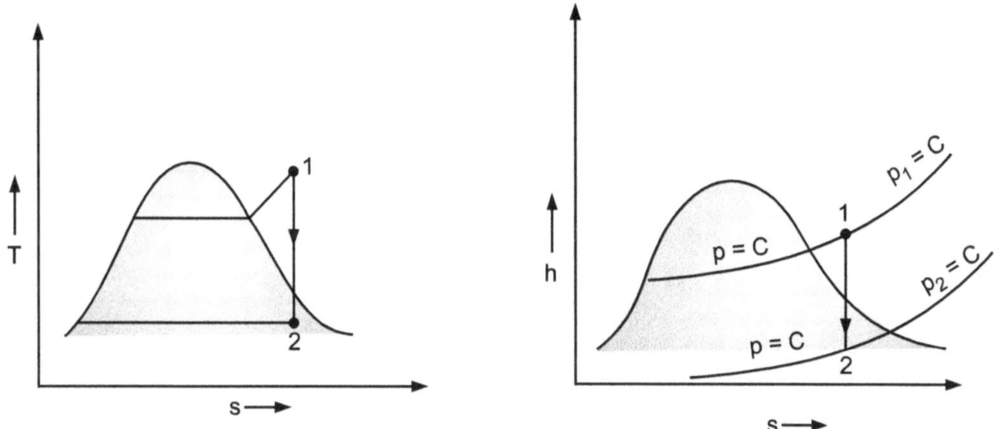



**Fig. 6.21: Adiabatic process on T-s and h-s planes**

(a) Work done $\qquad Q_{1-2} = u_2 - u_1 + W_{1-2}$

For reversible adiabatic process, heat transfer

$$Q_{1-2} = 0$$

$\therefore \qquad W_{1-2} = -(u_2 - u_1)$

**Problem 6.8:** Steam initially at 1.5 MPa and 300°C expands reversibly and adiabatically in a steam engine to 40°C. Determine (a) condition of steam after expansion, (b) work done/kg of steam.

**Solution:** The reversible adiabatic expansion of steam in a turbine is a steady flow isentropic process.

**Data:** $p_1 = 15$ bar, $T_1 = 300°C$, $T_2 = 40°C$, $p_2 = p_{sat}$ at 40°C and $s_2 = s_1$.

Now, $\qquad s_1 = s_{g_1} + c_p \ln\left(\dfrac{T_1}{T_{sat}}\right)$ kJ/kg·K

$$= 6.441 + 2.1 \ln\left(\frac{300 + 273}{198.3 + 273}\right)$$

$$= \mathbf{6.85732\ kJ/kg·K} = s_2 \text{ at } p_2$$

From steam table,

$$p_2 = 0.07375 \text{ bar at } T_2 = 40°C.$$

and $\qquad s_{g_2} = 8.258$ kJ/kg·K at 40°C

$$s_2 < s_{g_2}$$

Therefore steam after expansion is wet.

$$s_2 = 6.85132$$

$$= s_{x_2}$$

$$= s_{f_2} + x_2 \cdot s_{fg_2}$$

$$6.85732 = 0.572 + x_2 \times 7.686$$

$\therefore \qquad x_2 = \mathbf{0.81698}$

Adiabatic expansion process is represented on h-s diagram (See Fig. 6.22).

(b)  Work done ($W_{1-2}$):

By first law,

$$Q_{1-2} = u_2 - u_1 + W_{1-2}$$

$$Q_{1-2} = 0 \text{ for adiabatic process}$$

$\therefore \qquad W_{1-2} = u_1 - u_2$

$$= (h_1 - h_2) - (p_1 v_1 - p_2 v_2) \qquad\qquad \text{... (1)}$$

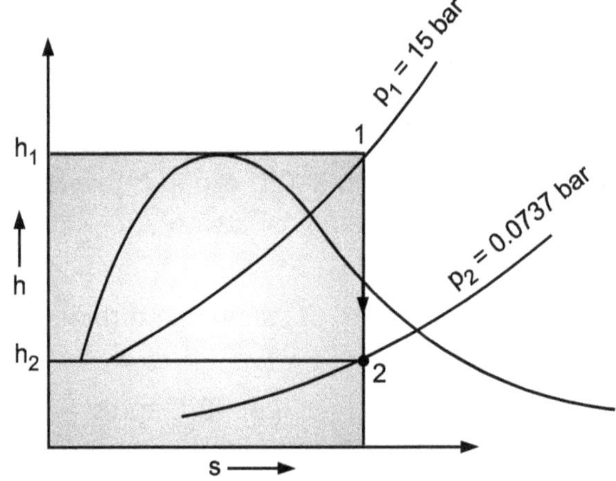


**Fig. 6.22: h-s diagram**

Now, $\qquad h_1 = h_{g_1} + c_p \cdot \ln\left(\dfrac{T_{sup_1}}{T_{sat_1}}\right)$

$$= 2789.9 + 2.1 \ln\left(\frac{300 + 273}{198.1 + 273}\right)$$

$$= \mathbf{2790.3 \ kJ/kg}$$

$$h_2 = h_{f_2} + x_2 h_{fg_2}$$

$$= 167.45 + 0.81698 \times 2406.9$$

$$= \textbf{2133.8 kJ/kg}$$

$$v_1 = v_{sup_1} = \frac{T_{sup_1}}{T_{sat_1}} \times v_{sat_1}$$

$$= \frac{(300 + 273)}{(198.1 + 273)} \times 0.13166$$

$$= \textbf{0.160 m}^3\textbf{/kg}$$

$$v_2 = v_{x_2} = v_{f_2} + x_2 v_{g_2}$$

$$= 0.0010078 + 0.81698 \times 19.546$$

$$= \textbf{15.9697 m}^3\textbf{/kg}$$

Put all these in equation (1)

$$W_{1-2} = (2790.3 - 2133.8) - (15 \times 100 \times 0.160 - 0.07375 \times 100 \times 15.9697)$$

$$= \textbf{533.0 kJ/kg}$$

$$\therefore \textbf{ Work is obtained}$$

## 6.6.6 Throttling Process

When a fluid passes through small aperture (opening), it is said to be throttled and enthalpy of the fluid remains constant during throttling.

Throttling is a steady flow process, therefore, apply steady flow energy equation.

$$Q = \Delta h + \Delta KE + \Delta PE + W$$

Since $Q = 0$, $W = 0$. If $\Delta PE$ and $\Delta KE$ are neglected, then $\Delta h = 0$ i.e. $h_1 = h_2$.

It is represented on T-s and h-s planes (See Fig. 6.23). Throttling is an irreversible process. Hence shown by dotted lines.

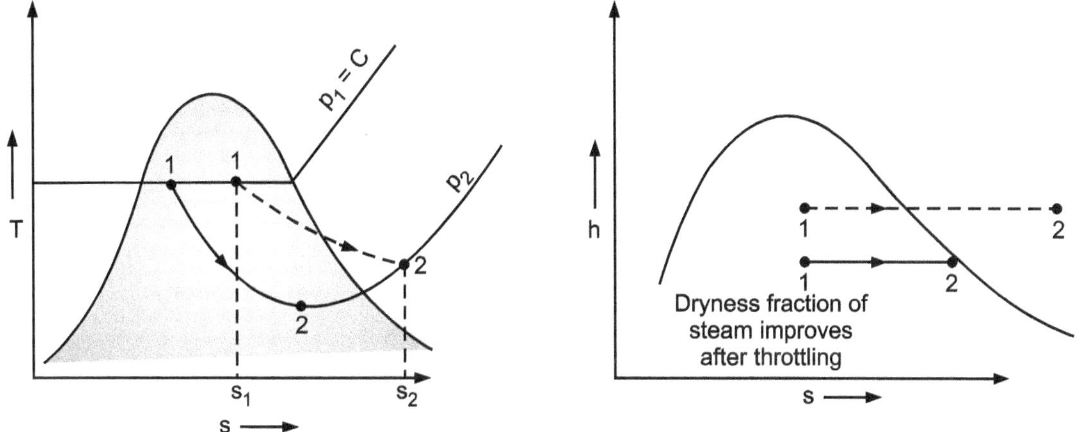


**Fig. 6.23: Throttling process**

**Problem 6.9:** Steam is throttled from 6 bar and 0.98 dryness fraction to a final pressure at 1 bar. Find the final condition of steam.

**Solution:** Throttling is irreversible and constant enthalpy process,

$$h_1 = h_{x_1} = h_{f_1} + x_1 h_{fg_1}$$

$$= 670.4 + 0.98 \times 2085$$

$$= 2713.7 \text{ kJ/kg}$$

$$= h_2 \text{ kJ/kg}$$

Now $\quad h_{g_2} = 2675.4$ kJ/kg at 1 bar.

$h_2 > h_{g_2}$, hence steam after throttling is superheated

$$h_2 = h_{sup_2} = 2713.7$$

$$h_{sup_2} = h_{g_2} + c_p (T_{sup_2} - T_{sat_2})$$

$$2713.7 = 2675.4 + 2.1 (T_{sup_2} - 99.63)$$

$$\therefore \quad T_{sup_2} = \mathbf{117.87}$$

The final condition of steam after throttling can also be found from Mollier diagram shown below.

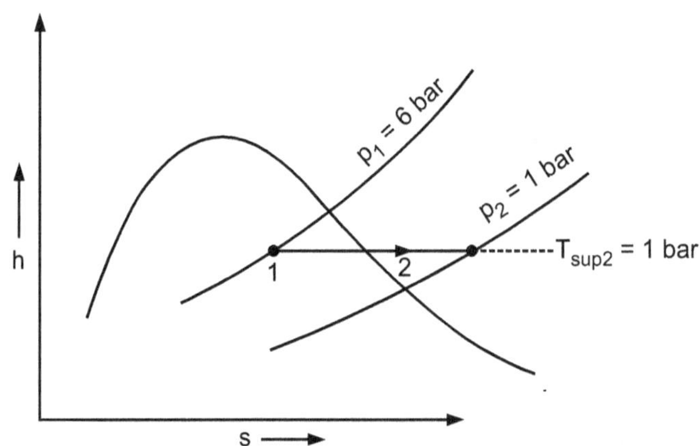


**Fig. 6.24: h-s diagram**

If the steam is expanded from state 1 (wet condition) to state 2 (wet condition)

$$\therefore \quad h_{f_1} + x_1 h_{fg1} = h_{f_2} + x_2 h_{fg2} \qquad \ldots (6.29)$$

If the steam becomes superheated after throttling as shown by dotted line 1-2, then

$$h_{f_1} + x_1 h_{fg1} = h_{f_2} + x_2 h_{fg2} + c_{ps} (T_{sup2} - T_{s_2})$$

$$= h_g + c_{ps}(T_{sup2} - T_{s2}) \qquad \text{... (6.30)}$$

During throttling, the pressure always falls.

$$\therefore \qquad p_2 < p_1$$

$$\therefore \qquad h_{f_1} > h_{f_2} \quad \text{and} \quad h_{fg1} < h_{fg2}$$

If the sensible heat difference $(h_{f_1} - h_{f_2}) = h_1$ is greater than $(h_{fg1} - h_{fg2}) = h_2$ then the heat $(h_1 - h_2)$ is utilized to dry out the steam or to even superheat which depends upon the initial condition of steam $(x_1)$ and final pressure after throttling. The throttling process is used for:

- Determining the dryness fraction of steam,

- Controlling the speed of the engine and turbine,

- In refrigeration system to reduce the pressure and temperature of the liquid refrigerant from the condenser condition to the evaporator condition.

## 6.7 MEASUREMENT OF DRYNESS FRACTION OF STEAM

Knowledge of the state of steam is necessary in many applications of the steam. Let the steam be flowing through a pipe. The pressure and temperature of steam through pipe be directly measured with the help of pressure gauge and thermometer. Based on the T and P of the steam, its condition can be determined referring the steam table. If the measured temperature is above the saturation temperature of steam (known from the steam tables as pressure is known), then it is also known that the vapour is in superheated condition. On the other hand, if the measured temperature corresponds to the saturated temperature of steam at the measured pressure, then the steam may be saturated or even it may be in wet condition, state may be anything from saturated liquid to dry and saturated steam.

The quality of steam is designated by the dryness fraction of the steam and it is experimentally measured.

The dryness fraction of the steam is defined as the ratio of the mass of dry steam present in the total mass of steam.

$$\therefore \qquad x = \frac{m_s}{m_s + m_w} \qquad \text{... (6.31)}$$

where, $m_s$ and $m_w$ are the masses of steam and water in the mixture of $(m_s + m_w)$.

The dryness fraction of the steam is measured experimentally with the help of steam calorimeters. There are four types of calorimeters used for measuring the dryness fraction of steam.

### 6.7.1 Barrel or Tank Calorimeter

- The dryness fraction of steam can be found with the help of a barrel calorimeter. The arrangement of this calorimeter is known in Fig. 6.25.

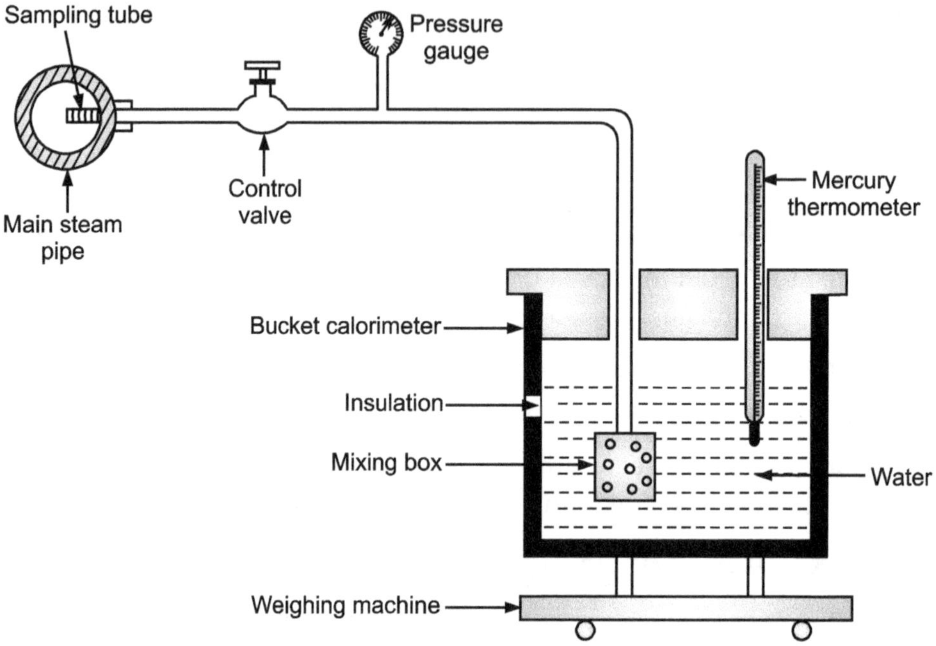


**Fig. 6.25 : Tank calorimeter**

- A known quantity of steam is passed through a known mass of water and steam is completely condensed.

- The heat lost by steam is equal to heat gained by the water.

- The weight of calorimeter with water before mixing the steam and after mixing the steam are obtained by weighing.

- The temperature of water before and after mixing the steam are measured by mercury thermometer.

- The pressure of steam passed through the sample tube is measured with the help of pressure gauge.

    Let      $p_s$ = Gauge pressure of steam (kPa)

             $p_a$ = Atmospheric pressure (kPa)

             $T_s$ = Saturation temperature of steam known from the steam table at pressure $(p_s + p_a)$

             $h_{fg}$ = Latent heat of steam, kJ/kg

             $x$ = Dryness fraction of steam

             $m_c$ = Mass of calorimeter in kg

             $m_1$ = Mass of calorimeter and water in kg

             $m_w$ = $(m_1 - m_c)$ = Mass of water in calorimeter, kg

$m_2$ = Mass of calorimeter, water and condensed steam, kg

$m_s$ = ($m_2 - m_1$) = Mass of steam condensed in calorimeter in kg

$T_1$ = Temperature of water and calorimeter before mixing the steam in °C

$T_2$ = Temperature of water and calorimeter after mixing the steam in °C

The heat lost by steam is equal to the heat gained by water and calorimeter, so

$$(m_s) [xh_{fg} + (T_s - T_2)] \; = \; (m_w) c_{pw} (T_2 - T_1) + m_c c_{pc} (T_2 - T_1)$$

$$(m_2 - m_1) [xh_{fg} + (T_s - T_2)] \; = \; (m_1 - m_c) c_{pw} (T_2 - T_1) + m_c c_{pc} (T_2 - T_1)$$

where, $c_{pw}$ and $c_{pc}$ are the specific heats of water and calorimeter respectively.

$$x \; = \; \frac{(c_{pw} m_w + c_{pc} m_c) (T_2 - T_1) - m_s (T_s - T_2)}{m_s h_{fg}} \qquad \text{... (6.32)}$$

The $m_c c_{pc}$ is known as water equivalent of calorimeter.

The losses due to convection and radiation are not taken into account. Hence, certain error is involved while determining the dryness fraction. The calculated value of dryness fraction neglecting losses is always less than the actual value of the dryness.

## 6.7.2 Separating Calorimeter                    [Dec. 11, May 11]

One important assumption is made here that all the water particles are removed in separating section and the steam entering in the bucket calorimeter is completely dry. The arrangement of the calorimeter is shown in Fig. 6.26.

This calorimeter is used to measure the probable value of dryness fraction of steam when the steam is very wet. The steam is passed through a sample tube as shown in the figure. The moisture is separated mechanically from the steam. Steam is passed through perforated trays and water particles are separated due to inertia of the droplets. The outgoing steam is condensed in the bucket calorimeter as discussed earlier.

Let $\qquad m_w$ = Mass of water separated from the steam

$\qquad\qquad m_s$ = Mass of steam condensed in the bucket calorimeter

$$x \; = \; \frac{m_s}{m_s + m_w} \qquad \text{... (6.33)}$$

The only advantage of this method is the quick determination of the dryness fraction of very wet steam. In practice, it is not possible to remove all the water particles from the steam by this mechanical process and therefore, the dryness fraction obtained by this calorimeter will not be very accurate. The dryness fraction calculated by its method is always greater than the actual. This calorimeter can also be used in combination with throttling calorimeter.

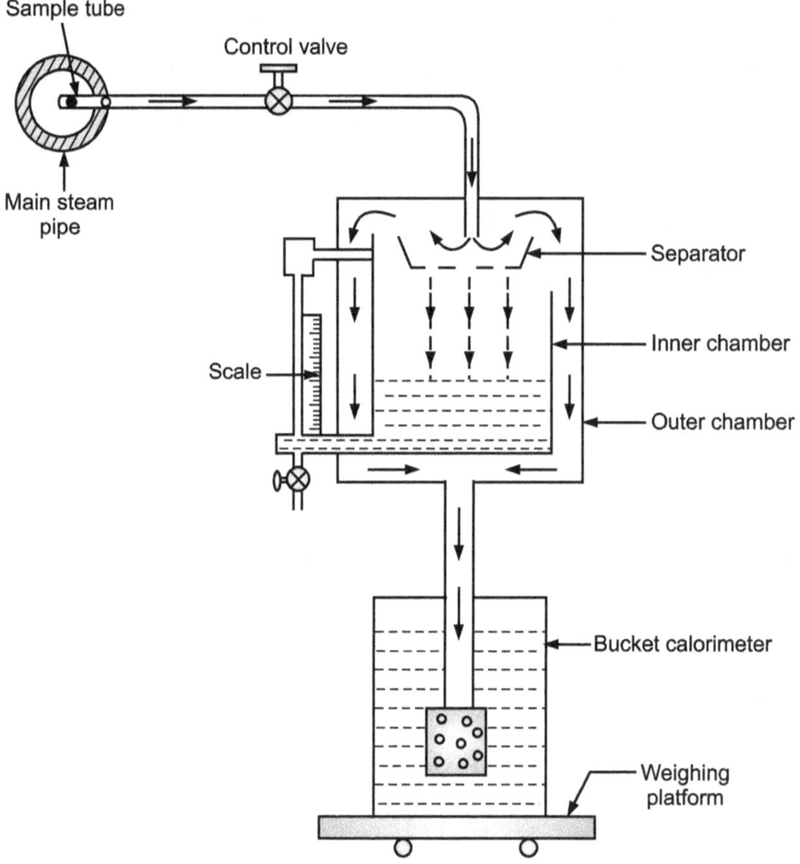


**Fig. 6.26: Separating calorimeter**

## 6.7.3 Throttling Calorimeter        [May 11]

The arrangement of this calorimeter is shown in Fig. 6.27.

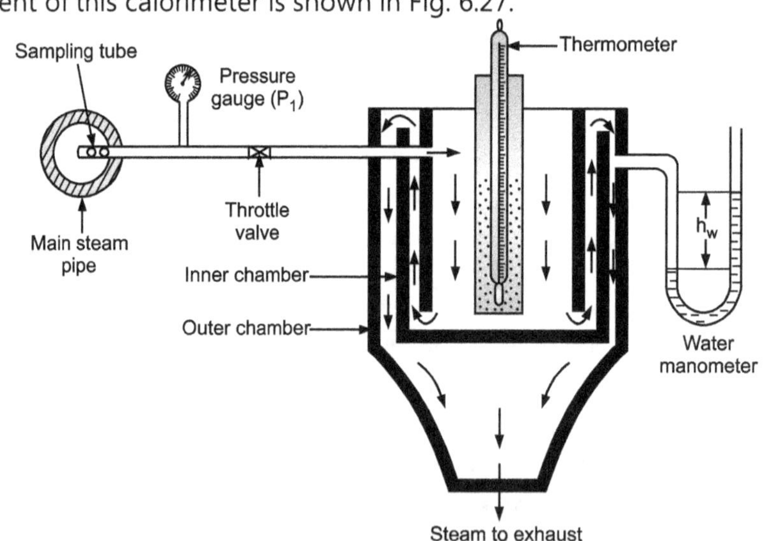


**Fig. 6.27: Throttling Calorimeter**

The steam whose dryness fraction is to be determined is taken into the calorimeter through a sample tube and passed through a throttle valve as shown in Fig. 6.27.

The steam is allowed to throttle down to a lower pressure until it comes out in superheated condition. The pressure and temperature of steam coming out of the throttling valve are measured with the help of a manometer and a thermometer.

Let $\quad p_1$ = Gauge pressure of steam in bar

$\qquad x_1$ = Dryness fraction of steam

$\qquad p_a$ = Atmospheric pressure in a bar

$\qquad T_{s1}$ = Saturation temperature of steam at a pressure of $(p_1 + p_a)$ known from steam tables

$\qquad h_{fg1}$ = Latent heat of steam at pressure $(p_1 + p_a)$

$\qquad h_w$ = Manometer reading in cm of water above atmospheric pressure

$\therefore$ Absolute pressure of steam after throttling

$$p_2 = \left[ p_a + \frac{h_w}{13.6} \times \frac{1.03}{76} \right] \text{bar}$$

$\qquad T_{s2}$ = Saturation temperature of steam at pressure $p_2$

$\qquad h_{fg2}$ = Enthalpy of saturated steam at pressure $p_2$

$\qquad c_{ps}$ = Specific heat of superheated steam

$\qquad T_{sup2}$ = Temperature of steam after throttling

The enthalpy of steam remains constant during throttling process.

Enthalpy of steam before throttling = Enthalpy of steam after throttling

$\therefore \qquad h_{f_1} + x_1 h_{fg1} = h_{f2} + h_{fg2} + c_{ps}(T_{sup2} - T_{s2}) = h_{g2} + c_{ps}(T_{sup2} - T_{s2})$

$\therefore \qquad x_1 = \dfrac{[h_{g2} + c_{ps}(T_{sup2} - T_{s2})] - h_{f_1}}{h_{fg1}} \qquad \ldots (6.34)$

The condition for the successful operation of this calorimeter is that the steam must be superheated after throttling. This condition requires a high dryness fraction of the steam before throttling. This calorimeter cannot be used if the dryness fraction of the steam is above 0.96. The minimum dryness fraction of the steam that can be measured by throttling calorimeter depends upon the initial pressure of the steam as the pressure after throttling virtually remains near atmospheric.

## 6.7.4 Separating and Throttling Calorimeter                    [Dec. 10]

The dryness fraction measured with the help of separating calorimeter is always higher than the actual. This is because of incomplete separation of moisture by mechanical means. The arrangement of a separating and throttling calorimeter is shown in Fig. 6.28.

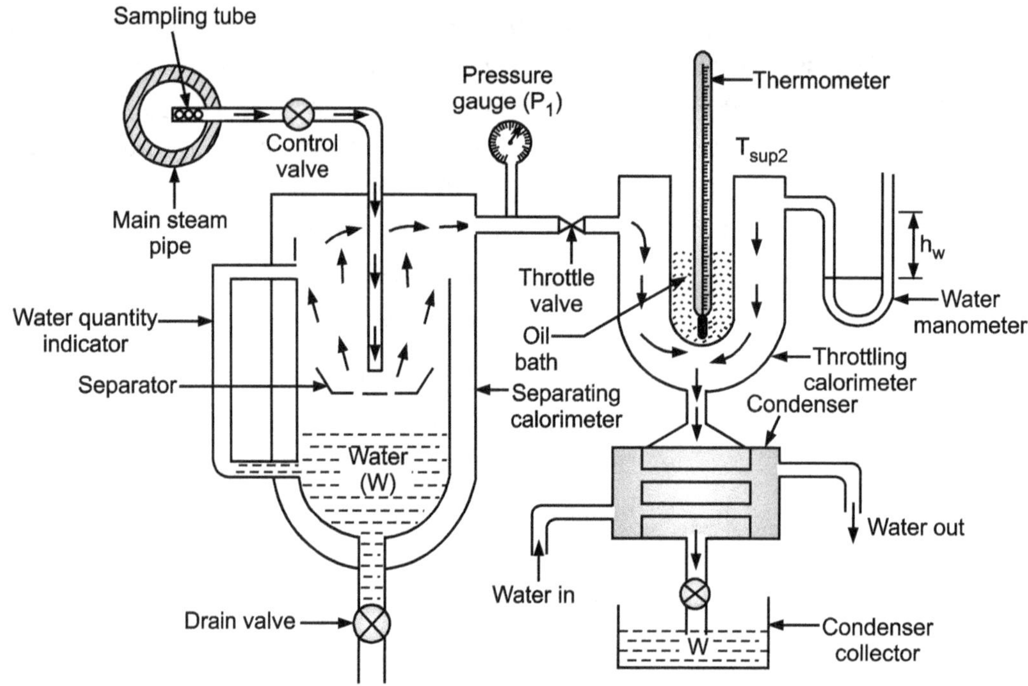



**Fig. 6.28: Separating and throttling calorimeter**

The mass of the water separated in separating calorimeter and the pressure and temperature of the steam leaving the throttle valve are recorded with the help of water manometer and mercury in gall thermometer.

Let  $m_s$  =  Mass of steam condensed and collected from condenser

$m_w$  =  Mass of water collected from separating calorimeter

$x$  =  Actual dryness fraction of steam in main pipe

$x_1$  =  Apparent dryness fraction of steam measured by separating calorimeter assuming that the steam coming out of separating calorimeter is completely dry

$x_2$  =  Actual dryness fraction of steam entering into the throttling calorimeter

The apparent dryness fraction is given by $x_1 = \dfrac{m_s}{m_s + m_w}$   ... (6.35)

Amount of water carried by the steam before entering into the calorimeter

$$= (1 - x)(m_s + m_w) \qquad \text{... (6.36)}$$

Amount of water separated in separating calorimeter

$$= (1 - x_1)(m_s + m_w) \qquad \text{... (6.37)}$$

The amount of water carried by the steam into the throttling calorimeter

$$= (1 - x_2) m_s \qquad \text{... (6.38)}$$

The mass of water in the steam given by the equation (6.36) must be equal to the quantities of water given by equations (6.37) and (6.38).

$$\therefore \quad (1 - x)\,(m_s + m_w) = (1 - x_1)\,(m_s + m_w) + (1 - x_2)\,m_s$$

$$\therefore \quad 1 - x = (1 - x_1) + (1 - x_2)\,\frac{m_s}{m_s + m_w}$$

But 
$$\frac{m_s}{m_s + m_w} = x_1$$

Substituting this valve in the above equation,

$$(1 - x) = (1 - x_1) + (1 - x_2) \times x_1 = 1 - x_1 + x_1 - x_1 x_2$$

$$x = x_1 x_2 \qquad \qquad \dots (6.39)$$

This calorimeter gives very accurate value of the dryness fraction of the steam when it is considerably wet and which cannot be measured accurately by any other method discussed earlier.

**Problem 6.10:** A vessel with a partition in it contains initially 2 kg of dry and saturated steam at 7.0 bar in one compartment and 1 kg of steam with dryness fraction 0.8 at 3.5 bar in the other compartment. After the partition is removed, the pressure of mixture is found to be 5 bar. Neglecting the volume of water, find the dryness fraction of the mixture.

**Solution:**

| **Part A** | **Part B** |
|---|---|
| 2 kg | 1 kg |
| dry saturated | 0.8 dry |
| 7 bar | 3.5 bar |

**Properties from steam tables:**

| p (bar) | $v_g$ m³/kg | $h_f$ kJ/kg | $h_{f_g}$ kJ/kg |
|---|---|---|---|
| 3.5 | 0.52397 | 584.3 | 2147.3 |
| 5 | 0.37466 | 640.1 | 2107.4 |
| 7 | 0.2727 | 697.1 | 2064.9 |

Volume of compartment A,

$$V_A = m_A \cdot v_{g_A}$$

$$= 2 \times 0.2727$$

$$= \mathbf{0.5454 \ m^3}$$

Volume of compartment B,

$$V_B = m_B \times \left( v_{g_B} \times x_B \right)$$

$$= 1 \times 0.52397 \times 0.8$$

$$= \mathbf{0.419176 \ m^3}$$

Total volume of the vessel = 0.5454 + 0.419176 = **0.9645 m³**

After removal of partition, two steams will mix each other. The pressure of mixture is 5 bar.

∴   Specific volume of mixture at 5 bar is 0.37466 m³/kg.

∴   Total volume of mixture

$$= v_{mix} \times m_{mix}$$

$$= 0.37466 \times 3 = 1.1241 \ m^3$$

∴   Dryness fraction of mixture $= \dfrac{\text{Total volume of vessel}}{\text{Volume of mixture at 5 bar}}$

$$= \frac{0.9645}{1.1241} = \mathbf{0.8580}$$

---

**Problem 6.11:** A steam turbine obtains steam from a boiler at a pressure of 15 bar and 0.98 dry. It was observed that steam looses 25 kJ of heat per kg as it flows through the pipe line, while pressure remains constant. Calculate dryness fraction of steam at turbine end of pipe line.

**Solution:**

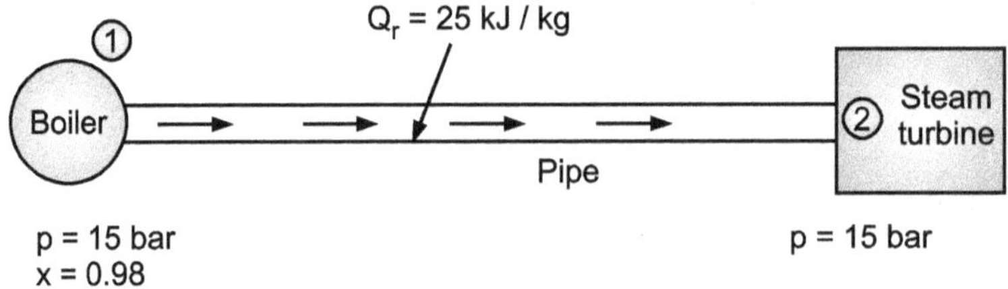


**Fig. 6.29: Block diagram**

At 15 bar, $h_f$ = 844.6 kJ/kg, $h_{fg}$ = 1945.3 kJ/kg

Enthalpy of steam at the boiler outlet,

$$h_1 = h_{f_1} + x_1 h_{fg_1}$$

---

$$= 844.6 + 0.98 \times 1945.3$$

$$= \mathbf{2750.994 \ kJ/kg}$$

Enthalpy of steam at inlet to turbine,

$$h_2 = h_{f_2} + x_2 \, h_{fg_2} \qquad h_{f_1} = h_{f_2}, \ h_{fg_1} = h_{fg_2}$$

$$\therefore \qquad h_2 = 844.6 + x_2 \times 1945 - 3$$

Equating the enthalpies at point 1 and point 2, considering the heat lost to the surrounding from the pipe,

$$2750.994 - 25 = 844.6 + x_2 \times 1945.3$$

$$\therefore \qquad x_2 = \mathbf{0.967}$$

**Problem 6.12:** Find enthalpy, internal energy and specific volume in the following cases:

(i)  mass = 5 kg, p = 10 bar, quality = 95%

(ii)  mass = 2 kg, p = 20 bar, volume = 0.35 m³

**Solution:** (i) **Given:** For p = 10 bar, m = 5 kg, quality = 95%

$$h_f = 762.6 \ kJ/kg$$

and

$$h_{f_g} = 2013.6 \ kJ/kg$$

$$v_g = 0.19430 \ m^3/kg$$

$$h = h_f + x \cdot h_{fg}$$

$$= 762.6 + 0.95 \times 2013.6$$

$$= \mathbf{2675.52 \ kJ/kg}$$

$$\text{Total enthalpy, } H = m \cdot h$$

$$= 5 \times 2675.52$$

$$= \mathbf{13377.6 \ kJ}$$

$$v_x = \text{specific volume of wet steam}$$

$$= x \cdot v_g$$

$$= 0.95 \times 0.19430$$

$$= \mathbf{0.184585 \ m^3/kg}$$

$$\text{Total volume} = m \cdot v_x$$

$$V = 5 \times 0.184585$$

$$= \mathbf{0.9223 \ m^3}$$

$$h = u + pv$$

$$u = h - pv$$

$$= 13377.6 - 10 \times 100 \times 0.9223$$

$$\text{Internal energy} = \mathbf{12454.6 \ kJ}$$

(ii) $m = 2$ kg, at 20 bar, $h_f = 908.59$ kJ/kg, $h_{fg} = 1888.6$ kJ/kg,

$v_g = 0.099536$ m³/kg, $h_g = 2797.19$ kJ/kg.

Given volume is $\qquad V = \mathbf{0.35 \ m^3}$

Volume of 2 kg dry saturated steam

$$= 0.099536 \times 2$$

$$= \mathbf{0.19907 \ m^3}$$

$\therefore$ Steam is superheated.

$$h = h_g + c_p \log \frac{v_{sup}}{v_{sat}}$$

$$= 2797.19 + 2.1 \log \frac{0.35}{0.19907}$$

$$= \mathbf{2798.3 \ kJ/kg}$$

$\therefore \qquad$ Total enthalpy $H = 2 \times 2798.3$

$\therefore \qquad\qquad\qquad H = 5596.75$ kJ

$\qquad\qquad\qquad\qquad H = u + pv$

$\qquad\quad 5596.75 = u + 20 \times 100 \times 0.35$

$\qquad\qquad\qquad\quad u = $ Internal energy $= \mathbf{4896.75 \ kJ}$

---

**Problem 6.13:** Find the condition of steam and determine enthalpy from the following table:

(i)    $p = 40$ bar, $\qquad\qquad v = 0.062$ m³/kg

(ii)   $p = 30$ bar, $\qquad\qquad t = 260°C$

(iii) $p = 40$ bar, $\quad$ heat added $= 2400$ kJ/kg

(iv) $p = 30$ bar, $\qquad\qquad v = 0.0666$ m³/kg

**Solution:**

(i)    $p = 40$ bar, $v = 0.062$ m³/kg

From steam table, at 40 bar,

$$v_g = 0.049749 \text{ m}^3/\text{kg}$$

$$T_{sat} = 250.3°C$$

$$h_g = 2800.3$$

As given volume, $v > v_g$, steam is in superheated condition

$$T_{sup} = \frac{T_{sat}}{v_{sat}} \times v_{sup}$$

$$= \frac{(250 + 273)}{0.049749} \times 0.062 = \textbf{651.7 K}$$

$\therefore$    Degree of superheat $= 651.7 - (250 + 273)$

$$= \textbf{128.79 K}$$

$$h_{sup} = h_g + c_p (651.7 - 523.3)$$

$$= 2800.3 + 270.45$$

$$= \textbf{3070.7 kJ/kg}$$

(ii)   $p = 30$ bar and $t = 260°C$

At 30 bar, $t_{sat} = 233.8°C$

$h = 2802.3$ kJ/kg

$t > t_{sat}$, therefore, steam is superheated.

$\therefore$

$$h_{sup} = h_g + c_p \ln \frac{T_{sup}}{T_{sat}}$$

$$= 2802.3 + 2.1 (533 - 506.8)$$

Enthalpy $= \textbf{2858.3 kJ/kg}$

(iii)   $p = 40$ bar, $Q = 2400$ kJ/kg, $h_f = 1087.4$ kJ/kg

At 40 bar, $h_g = 2800.4$ kJ/kg, $h_{f_g} = 1712.9$,

$Q = \Delta h = h - h_0$ kJ/kg But $h_0 = 0$

$Q < h_g$ $\therefore$ steam is wet.

$$h = h_f + x \cdot h_{fg}$$

$$2400 = 1087.4 + x \times 1712.9$$

$\therefore$    $x = $ dryness fraction $= 0.7665$

Enthalpy $= h = h_f + x \cdot h_{fg}$

$$= 1087.4 + 0.7665 \times 1712.9$$

$$= \textbf{2400 kJ/kg} \text{ already given}$$

(iv)   $p = 30$ bar, $v = 0.066$ m$^3$/kg

From steam table, $v_g = 0.0666$ m$^3$/kg at 30 bar.

$\therefore$ $\qquad\qquad\qquad\qquad\qquad v = v_g \therefore$ Steam is dry saturated

$\qquad\qquad$ Enthalpy $= h_g = $ **2802.3 kJ/kg**

---

**Problem 6.14:** Steam at 10 bar and 0.925 dry is contained inside a vessel having a capacity of 1 m³. The delivery valve is opened and the steam is blown off. The period of blowing is so regulated that pressure drops at 5 bar. The delivery valve is then closed and the vessel is cooled until the pressure becomes 4 bar. Estimate,

   (i)    Mass of steam blown off.

   (ii)   Dryness fraction of steam in the vessel after cooling.

**Solution: Extract from steam table**

|  | Specific volume, m³/kg | $h_f$ kJ/kg | $h_{f_g}$ kJ/kg |
|---|---|---|---|
| 10 | 0.1943 | 762.5 | 2013.5 |
| 5 | 0.3737 | 640.1 | 2107.4 |
| 4 | 0.4622 | 604.6 | 2133.0 |

(i)   Initial mass of steam in the vessel

$$= \frac{V}{v_x}$$

$$= \frac{1}{(0.925 \times 0.1943)}$$

$$= \textbf{5.56 kg}$$

Total heat before blowing $=$ Total heat after blowing

$$h_{f_1} + x_1\, h_{fg_1} = h_{f_2} + x_2 \cdot h_{fg_2}$$

$$762.5 + 0.925 \times 2013.5 = 640.1 + x_2 \times 2107.4$$

$$\therefore \qquad\qquad x_2 = 0.94$$

Mass of steam after blowing $= \dfrac{V}{v_{x_2}} = \dfrac{1}{0.94 \times 0.3737}$

$$= \textbf{2.87 kg}$$

Mass of steam blown off $= 5.56 - 2.87 = 2.69$ kg

(ii)  Dryness fraction after cooling

$$x_3\,(m \cdot v_{g_3}) = V$$

$$x_3 = \frac{V}{m \cdot v_{g_3}}$$

$$= \frac{1}{2.87 \times 0.4622}$$

$$= \textbf{0.755}$$

**Problem 6.15:** 2.5 kg of steam at a pressure of 1 bar and with a dryness fraction of 0.96 is compressed hyperbolically to a pressure of 8.0 bar. Determine:

   (i)    The final condition of steam.

   (ii)   The heat transferred during compression.

**Solution: Given:** $m = 2.5$ kg.

$p_1 = 1$ bar, $x_1 = 0.96$

(i)   Properties of steam at 1 bar are:

$$v_{g_1} = 1.694 \text{ m}^3/\text{kg}$$

$$h_{f_1} = 417 \text{ kJ/kg}$$

$$h_{fg_1} = 2258 \text{ kJ/kg}$$

$$h_{g_1} = 2675 \text{ kJ/kg}$$

$$\therefore \qquad \text{Mass of steam} = \frac{\text{Volume of steam}}{\text{Specific volume of steam}}$$

$$2.5 = \frac{V_1}{1.694 \times 0.96}$$

$$\therefore \qquad V_1 = 4.0656 \text{ m}^3$$

$\therefore$ Apply hyperbolic law to the compression process.

$$p_1 V_1 = p_2 V_2$$

$$\therefore \qquad v_2 = \frac{p_1 V_1}{p_2}$$

$$= \frac{1}{8} \times 4.0656 = 0.5082 \text{ m}^3$$

Let $x_2$ be the dryness fraction after compression.

$$x_2 = \frac{V_2}{m \cdot V_{g_2}}$$

$$= \frac{0.5082}{2.5 \times 0.24030}$$

$$= 0.846$$

$$V_{g_2} = 0.24030 \text{ at 8 bar pressure}$$

Properties of dry steam at 8 bar pressure

$$T_{sat_2} = 170.4°C$$

$$v_{g_2} = 0.2403$$

$$h_{f_2} = 721 \text{ kJ/kg}$$

$$h_{fg_2} = 2048$$

(ii)   Heat transfer during the compression

$$= h_2 - h_1$$

$$h_1 = m\left(h_{f_1} + x_1 h_{fg_1}\right)$$

$$= 2.5\,(417 + 0.96 \times 2258)$$

$$= \textbf{6461.7 kJ}$$

$$h_2 = \text{Total enthalpy at point 2 (after compression)}$$

$$= m\left(h_{f_2} + x_2 h_{fg_2}\right)$$

$$= 2.5\,(721 + 0.846 \times 2048)$$

$$= \textbf{6134 kJ}$$

$$\therefore \qquad Q = h_2 - h_1$$

$$= 6134 - 6461.7$$

$$= -327.68 \text{ kJ is lost by steam during compression.}$$

---

**Problem 6.16:** Determine the volume occupied by 1 kg of steam at a pressure of 0.7 MN/m$^2$ and having dryness fraction of 0.97.

This is expanded adiabatically to a pressure of 0.12 MN/m$^2$, the law of expansion being $pv^{1.13}$ = Constant. Determine

 (i) The dryness fraction of steam

 (ii) The change of internal energy of the steam during expansion.

| P | $T_{sat}$ | kJ/kg | | | $v_g$ |
|---|---|---|---|---|---|
| MN/m$^2$ | °C | $h_f$ | $h_{fg}$ | $h_g$ | m$^3$/kg |
| 0.12 | 104.8 | 439.4 | 2244.1 | 2683.4 | 1.428 |
| 0.70 | 165 | 697 | 2064.9 | 2762 | 0.273 |

**Solution:** m = 1 kg, $p_1$ = 0.7 MN/m$^2$ = 7 bar, $x_1$ = 0.97, $p_2$ = 1.2 bar.

(i)  Volume of steam, $V_1 = m \cdot x_1 \cdot v_{g_1}$

$$= 1 \times 0.97 \times 0.273$$

$$= \mathbf{0.2645 \ m^3}$$

$$p_1 v_1^n = p_2 v_2^n$$

$$7 \times (0.2645)^{1.13} = 1.2 \times v_2^{1.13}$$

$$\therefore \qquad v_2 = 1.2591 \ m^3/kg$$

$$\text{because } m = 1$$

$$\text{At } p_2 = 1.2 \text{ bar}, \ v_{g_2} = 1.481 \ m^3/kg$$

$$\therefore \quad v_{g_2} > v_2 \ \therefore \text{ Steam is wet}$$

$$\text{Dryness fraction, } x_2 = \frac{v_2}{v_{g_2}}$$

$$= \frac{1.2591}{1.481} = \mathbf{0.88}$$

(ii)  Change in internal energy $(\Delta u) = u_2 - u_1$

$$u_1 = h_1 - p_1 v_1$$

$$= \left( h_{f_1} + x_1 \, h_{fg_1} \right) - 100 \times 7 \times 0.2645$$

$$= (697 + 0.97 \times 2064.9) - 700 \times 0.2645$$

$$= \mathbf{2514 \ kJ/kg}$$

$$u_2 = h_2 - p_2 v_2$$

$$= \left( h_{f_2} + x_2 \cdot h_{fg_2} \right) - 100 \times p_2 \times v_2$$

$$= (489.4 + 0.88 \times 2244.1)$$

$$- 100 \times 1.2 \times (0.88 \times 1.428)$$

$$= 2307.8 \ kJ/kg$$

$$\therefore \qquad \Delta u = (2307.8 - 2514)$$

$$= \mathbf{-206.2 \ kJ/kg \ (decreases)}$$

---

**Problem 6.17:** Dry saturated steam at a pressure of 1.25 MN/m$^2$ flows along a steam pipe of 150 mm diameter with velocity of 24 m/sec.

Find:

(i)   Volume flow in m$^3$/sec.

(ii)  Mass flow in kg/min.

(iii) Final temperature if steam is throttled to 0.12 MN/m$^2$.

Take $\qquad c_p = 2$ kJ/kg·K $\hfill$ **(P.U. May 2007)**

---

**Solution: Given:** Dry saturated steam.

$$p_1 = 1.25 \text{ MN/m}^2 = 12.5 \text{ bar}$$
$$D = 150 \text{ mm} = 0.15 \text{ m}$$
$$c = 24 \text{ m/sec}$$

(i) Volume flow rate

$$= A \times c$$

$$= \frac{\pi}{4} D^2 \times c$$

$$= \frac{\pi}{4} (0.15)^2 \times 24$$

$$= \mathbf{0.424 \ m^3/sec.}$$

(ii)  Mass flow rate:

At 12.5 bar, from steam table,

$$v_1 = 0.15693 \text{ m}^3/\text{kg}$$

$\therefore \qquad \rho_1 = \dfrac{1}{v_1} = 6.37 \text{ kg/m}^3$

$\therefore \quad$ Mass flow rate $=$ Volume flow rate $\times$ Density

$$= 0.424 \times 6.37$$
$$= 2.7 \text{ kg/sec}$$
$$= 162.11 \text{ kg/min}$$

(iii)  Final temperature after throttling $(T_2)$

From steam table, at 12.5 bar,

$$h_1 = h_g = 2784.1 \text{ kJ/kg}$$

For throttling process,

$$h_2 = h_1 = 2784.1 \text{ kJ/kg}$$

From superheated steam table, at $p_2 = 1.2$ bar,

$$h_2 = 2784.1 \text{ kJ/kg}$$

| Temperature | h |
|---|---|
| 150 | 2774.8 |
| y | $h_2$ = 2784.1 |
| 200 | 2874.4 |

By interpolation,

$$\frac{200 - 150}{y - 150} = \frac{2874.4 - 2774.8}{2784.1 - 2774.8}$$

$\therefore \qquad y - 150 = 4.6686$

$$\therefore \qquad y = 154.67°C$$

The final temperature of steam after throttling is,

$$T_2 = 154.67°C$$

**Problem 6.18:** The following data were obtained in a test on a combined separating and throttling calorimeter:

Pressure of steam sample = 15 bar, Pressure of steam at exit = 1 bar, Temperature of steam at the exit = 150°C, Discharge from separating calorimeter = 0.5 kg/min, Discharge from throttling calorimeter = 10 kg/min. Determine the dryness fraction of the sample steam.

**Solution: Given data:**

Pressure of steam sample, $p_1 = p_2 = 15$ bar

Temperature of steam at the exit, $t_{sup3} = 15°C$

Pressure of steam at the exit, $p_3 = 1$ bar

Discharge from separating calorimeter, $m_w = 0.5$ kg/min

Discharge from throttling calorimeter, $m_s = 10$ kg/min

From steam tables,

at $p_1 = p_2 = 15$ bar; $h_{f_2} = 844.7$ kJ/kg, $h_{fg2} = 1945.2$ kJ/kg

at $p_3 = 1$ bar and 150°C; $h_{sup3} = 2776.4$ kJ/kg

$$\text{Also,} \, h_2 = h_3$$

$$\therefore \qquad h_{f2} + x_2 \, h_{fg2} = h_{sup3}$$

$$844.7 + x_2 \times 1945.2 = 2776.4$$

$$\therefore \qquad x_2 = \frac{2776.4 - 844.7}{1945.2} = \mathbf{0.993}$$

$\therefore$ Quality of steam supplied,

$$x_1 = \frac{x_2 \cdot m_s}{m_s + m_w} = \frac{0.993 \times 10}{10 + 0.5} = \mathbf{0.946}$$

**Problem 6.19:** Two boilers one with superheater and other without superheater are delivering equal quantities of steam into a common main. The pressure in the boilers and the main is 15 bar. The temperature of the steam from a boiler with a superheater is 300°C and temperature of the steam in the main is 200°C. Determine the quality of steam supplied by the other boiler. **(P.U. Dec. 2007)**

**Solution: Boiler B1** = 15 bar and 300°C

$$\text{Enthalpy, } h_1 = h_{g1} + c_{ps} (T_{sup} - T_s)$$

$$= 2789.9 + 2.25 (300 - 198.3)$$

$$= \mathbf{3018.725 \text{ kJ/kg}} \qquad \qquad \dots \text{(i)}$$

**Boiler B2:** 15 bar (temperature not known)

$$h_2 = h_{f_2} + x_2 \times h_{fg_2}$$

$$= 844.7 + x_2 \times 1945.2 \qquad \qquad \dots \text{(ii)}$$

**Main:** 15 bar, 200°C

Total heat of 2 kg of steam in the steam main

$$= 2\,[h_g + c_{ps}\,(T_{sup} - T_s)]$$

$$= 2\,[2789.9 + 2.25 \times (200 - 198.3)]$$

$$= 5587.45 \text{ kJ} \qquad \qquad \dots \text{(iii)}$$

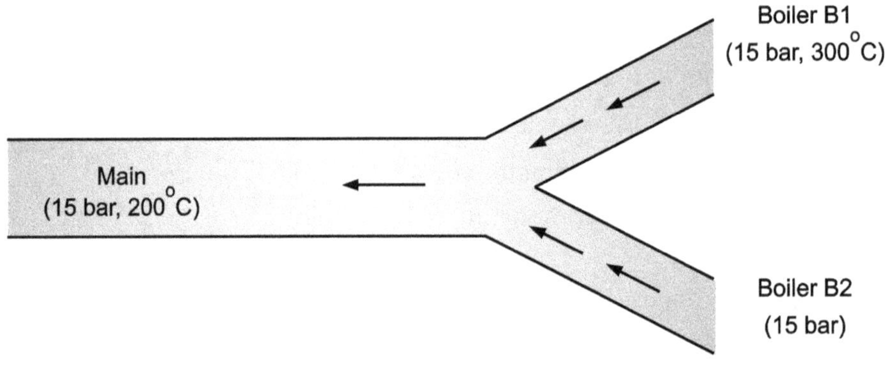


**Fig. 6.30**

Adding (i) and (ii) and equating with (iii)

$$3018.725 + 844.7 + x_2 \times 1945.2 = 5587.45$$

$$x_2 = \textbf{0.8863}$$

Hence, quality of steam supplied by the other boiler = 0.8863.

**Problem 6.20:** A closed vessel of 0.6 m³ capacity contains dry steam at 360 kPa. The vessel is cooled till pressure drops upto 200 kPa. Find out:

    (i)    Mass of steam

    (ii)   Final dryness of steam

**Solution: Given:**          $V = 0.6 \text{ m}^3$

    Dry steam,            $p_1 = 360 \text{ kPa} = 3.6 \text{ bar}$

                        $p_2 = 200 \text{ kPa} = 2 \text{ bar}$

    Mass of steam:

(i)    At 3.6 bar, from steam table,

$$v_1 = v_g$$

$$= \textbf{0.51032 m}^3\textbf{/kg}$$

Total volume of vessel,

$$V = m \cdot v_1$$

$$\therefore \quad m = \frac{V}{v_1} = \frac{0.6}{0.51032} = 1.176 \text{ kg}$$

$$\therefore \quad m = \mathbf{1.176 \text{ kg}}$$

(ii) Find dryness fraction of steam:

Volume remains constant,

$$v_1 = v_2 = v_{f_2} + x_2 \cdot v_{fg_2}$$

$$0.51032 = 0.0010608 + x_2 \times 0.88544$$

$$\therefore \quad x_2 = \mathbf{0.575}$$

# EXERCISE

1. Explain phase transformation of water at constant pressure with the help of T-s diagram.
2. What is the effect of pressure on boiling point?
3. Draw p-v, T-v, h-s and T-s diagrams for water.
4. What is meant by sensible heat, latent heat and enthalpy of water?
5. What is dryness fraction? How do you calculate specific volume, enthalpy and entropy of wet steam?
6. How do you find enthalpy and specific volume of superheated steam?
7. What is internal energy? How do you calculate it for a wet steam and superheated steam?
8. Represent the following processes on p-v and T-s diagrams.

    (a) Constant volume      (b) Constant pressure

    (c) Hyperbolic           (d) Isentropic

# EXAMPLES FOR PRACTICE

1. A closed vessel of 0.75 m$^3$ capacity contains dry saturated steam at 0.35 MPa. The vessel is cooled until the pressure is reduced to 0.2 MPa. Calculate:

    (a) The mass of steam in the vessel.

    (b) The final dryness fraction of steam.

    (c) The amount of heat transferred during the cooling process.

    **(Ans.** (a) 1.431 kg, (b) 0.591, (c) 927.9 kJ/kg**)**

2. A steam engine obtains steam from a boiler at a pressure of 30 bar and 0.98 dry. It was observed that when steam flows through a pipe, heat lost to the surroundings is 50 kJ/kg and pressure remains constant. Calculate the dryness fraction of steam at engine end of pipe line.                    **(Ans.** $x = 0.95$**)**

3. A vessel of 1.2 m$^3$ capacity contains steam of 1.0 MPa and 0.92 dryness fraction. Steam is blown off until the pressure drops to 0.5 MPa. The valve is then closed. Determine the mass of steam blown off.                    **(Ans.** 3.31 kg**)**

4.  A quantity of steam at a pressure of 2.1 MN/m$^2$ and 0.9 dry occupies a volume of 0.427 m$^3$. It is expanded according to pv$^{1.25}$ = constant, to a pressure of 0.7 MN/m$^2$. Determine:

(a) Mass of steam

(b) The work transfer

(c) The change in internal energy

(d) The heat exchange between the steam and the surroundings, stating the direction of heat flow.                     **(Ans.** m = 5 kg, Δu = –322.6 kJ/kg, W = 143.4 kJ/kg, dQ = –179.24 kJ/kg**)**

# UNIVERSITY QUESTION PAPERS

## DEC. 2013

1.  Steam at 1.5 MPa and 0.7 dry is throttled to 0.1 MPa. Find the condition of the steam after throttling. Show the process on Mollier chart.                                     **[6]**

2.  State different methods to determine the dryness fraction of steam. Explain working of any one Calorimeter with neat sketch for estimating the dryness fraction.     **[6]**

## DEC. 2014

1.  Define dryness fraction. Explain throttling calorimeter with neat diagram for estimating the dryness fraction.                                                               **[6]**

## MAY 2015

1.  Sketch and explain the construction and working of a separating and throttling calorimeter used for determining the dryness fraction of steam in a boiler.          **[6]**

## NOV. 2015

1. A sample of steam generated in a boiler at a pressure of 12 bar is passed through separating and throttling calorimeter to measure its dryness fraction. The following observations were recorded during the test :                                               **[6]**

(i)   Pressure of steam after throttling – 1.2 bar,

(ii)  Temperature of steam after throttling – 120°C

(iii) Mass of steam collected after throttling – 1 kg

(iv)  Mass of water collected through separating calorimeter – 15 gm.

Find the quality of steam generated by boiler.

Assume Cp of superheated steam 2.1 kJ/kgK.

## MAY 2016

1.  Discuss the principle and working of Throttling Calorimeter with neat labelled diagram and show the prbtess on h–s diagram.                                              **[6]**

**Unit - IV**

# Chapter 7

# THERMODYNAMIC VAPOUR CYCLE

## 7.1 INTRODUCTION

Thermal power plants use fossil fuels to generate the power. The steam power plant is one of the most successful thermal power plants for the conversion of heat energy into mechanical work. The sequences of various processes that occur in steam power plant are as listed below.

- Heat energy released by the combustion of fuel or by atomic fission is utilized to vaporize water into steam.

- The steam thus produced is expanded in a steam engine or turbine to obtain useful work or power.

- The vapour leaving the turbine is normally condensed and pumped back to its initial state constituting a cycle.

- Thus, the working fluid changes from liquid to vapour and back to its original state.

- This succession of processes is designated as vapour cycle to recognize the state of the working substance during the work output process.

Steam turbines power plants from 1 MW upto 1000 MW units resulting in about 35% to 38% overall thermal efficiency are in current use all over the world. Now a days, combined (gas and steam turbine) cycle plant is gaining popularity as it yields about 55 to 60% overall thermal efficiency.

The power developed from steam turbine plant is costlier than hydel-power plant. But one cannot meet the power demand only through hydel power plants, therefore, it is necessary to go for this plant. Also it takes a short time to set up (three to four years) as compared to the hydel which takes nearly ten years and needs a lot of preparatory work in the selection of site.

Carnot vapour cycle is the ideal cycle and which consists of the various ideal processes involved to generate the power from thermal energy.

## 7.2 THE CARNOT VAPOUR CYCLE

The Carnot vapour cycle consists of four fundamental elements namely:

(i) Boiler (Steam generator)

(ii) Turbine

(iii) Condenser

(iv) Feed pump handling a two phase mixture-water and its vapour

Fig. 7.1 shows a steam power plant operating on the Carnot cycle. The processes of the working fluid (steam, i.e. water) are represented on p-v and T-s diagrams as shown in Fig. 7.2.

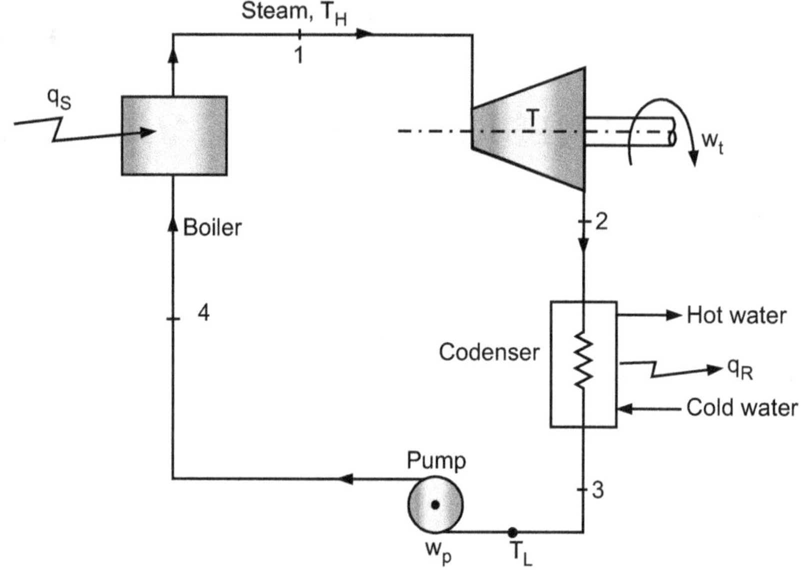


**Fig. 7.1: A steam power plant operating on Carnot cycle**

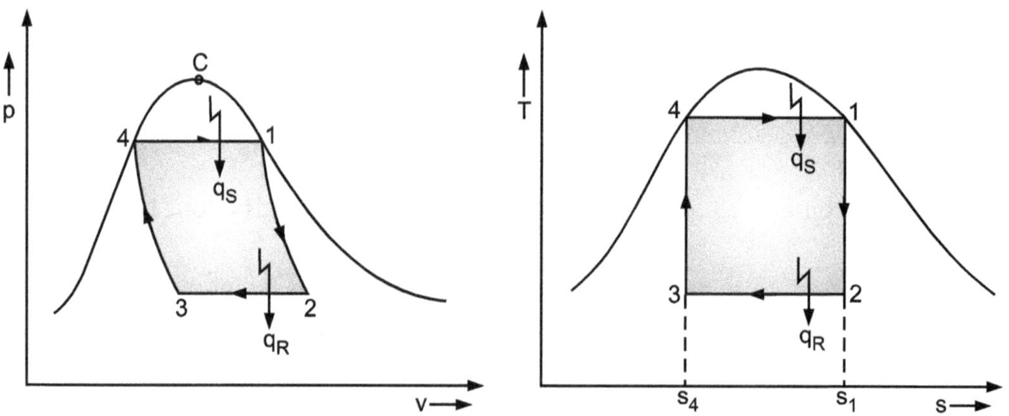


**Fig. 7.2: Carnot vapour cycle on p-v and T-s diagrams**

Water is heated at constant pressure in the boiler to produce steam. It means heat ($q_S$) is supplied to the boiler. The condition of steam at the outlet of boiler is at saturated state (represented by point 1 on p-v and T-s diagrams) in Carnot cycle. However, in practice the condition of steam may be superheated one. It is assumed that the condition of water at the outlet of condenser is at point 3. It means a mixture of water and vapour. The mixture is pressurized in the pump such that the condition of water is saturated (point 4). This saturated water is converted to steam in the boiler where it gains (receiver) heat from the burnt gases. The analysis of Carnot cycle is given below assuming a unit mass of working substance.

Heat supplied in the boiler, $q_s = h_1 - h_{f4}$

Heat rejected in the condenser, $q_R = h_2 - h_3$.

Work is obtained through turbine, where steam expands from its pressure $p_1$ to pressure $p_2$.

$$\text{Work, } w_1 = h_1 - h_2$$

$$\text{Work obtained} = \text{Heat supplied} - \text{Heat rejected}$$

$$= (h_1 - h_{f4}) - (h_2 - h_3)$$

$$\text{Thermal efficiency, } \eta_{th} = \frac{\text{Work done}}{\text{Heat supplied}}$$

$$= \frac{(h_1 - h_{f4}) - (h_2 - h_3)}{h_1 - h_{f4}} \qquad \text{... (7.1)}$$

Thermal efficiency may also be obtained from turbine and pump work.

For turbine, $\qquad w_t = h_1 - h_2$

For pump, $\qquad w_p = w_{3-4} = h_{f4} - h_3$

$$w_{net} = w_t - w_p = (h_1 - h_2) - (h_{f4} - h_3)$$

$$= (h_1 - h_{f4}) - (h_2 - h_3)$$

$$\therefore \qquad \eta_{th} = \frac{(h_1 - h_{f4}) - (h_2 - h_3)}{h_1 - h_{f4}}$$

Thermal efficiency of a Carnot cycle may be expressed in terms of temperature.

Referring T-s diagram, heat supplied,

$$q_s = T_H (s_1 - s_4)$$

$$\text{Heat rejected, } q_R = T_L (s_1 - s_4) = T_L (s_2 - s_3)$$

$$\therefore \qquad \eta_{th} = \frac{q_s - q_R}{q_s} = \frac{T_H - T_L}{T_H} \qquad \text{... (7.2)}$$

## Limitations of Carnot Vapour Cycle:

- The condition of working substance at the outlet of condenser is a wet steam. It is a mixture of water and water vapour. The condition of this mixture from state point 3 (p-v and T-s diagram) is to be changed to state 4 (p-v and T-s diagram). This process is carried out through a pump. There is not pump which would handle a mixture of water and water vapour. Therefore, a complete condensation of water vapour in the condenser is desirable.

  Further, the pump has to work in such a way that the condition of water at the outlet of pump is saturated (point 4 in p-v and T-s plots). This is also difficult to achieve in practice.

- The saturated steam is expanded in the turbine. The quality of steam decreases while passing through the turbine, therefore, it is also difficult to carry out the expansion of wet steam in the turbine.

## 7.3 RANKINE CYCLE

Carnot cycle is not a theoretical cycle for steam power plant because it is difficult to build a pump which can pump a mixture of water and vapour and deliver it at a saturated condition. This difficulty is overcome in the Rankine cycle with complete condensation of steam in the condenser. Rankine cycle is the theoretical cycle for steam power plant.

A diagrammatic of Rankine cycle steam turbine power plant is shown in Fig. 7.3. The power plant consists of four basic elements: (i) boiler, (ii) steam turbine, (iii) condenser and (iv) feed pump.

**(i)  Boiler:** In the boiler, steam is produced from water at the operating pressure. Fuel is burnt, the heat released is supplied to the water at constant pressure.

**(ii)  Steam turbine:** Here, the steam from the boiler pressure expands and thus performs mechanical work.

**(iii) Condenser:** In the condenser, the exhaust steam from the turbine gives up heat to the cooling water which otherwise cannot be converted into work and is rejected. The condenser enables the exhaust steam to be used as a working fluid of the boiler again. There is a cooling system for condenser consisting of cooling tower and cooling pump. This is not shown in Fig. 7.3.

**(iv) Feed pump:** The feed pump is used to pump the condensate from the hot-well (in which the condensate is collected) to the boiler at the boiler pressure.

The various processes of the Rankine cycle on p-v, T-s and h-s diagrams are shown in Figs. 7.4, 7.5 and 7.6 respectively. The various processes are:

**Process 3-4:**  The water which is at low pressure $p_2$ is pumped isentropically into the boiler at high pressure $p_1$.

**Process 4-5:**  Water is first heated up to the saturation temperature or evaporation temperature $T_1$ in the boiler and during this process the state point moves along the curve 4-5 called the sensible heating. The heat supplied during the process is $(h_{f5} - h_{f4})$ and is represented by the area L-3-4-5-M on T-s diagram, i.e., the sensible heat of water. Many times point 5 is not shown in power plants because it is the intermediate point in steam generation.

**Process 5-1:**  At constant pressure $p_1$ and temperature $T_1$, water is completely vaporized into steam. The heat added in this process is equal to $(h_1 - h_{f5})$ and is represented by M-5-1-N on T-s diagram, i.e. the latent heat of vaporization. The state point 1 shows the dry and saturated condition of steam.

**Process 1-2:**  It is an isentropic expansion of steam in turbine from pressure $p_1$ to $p_2$.

**Process 2-3:**  At constant pressure $p_2$ and temperature $T_2$, the exhaust steam is condensed in the condenser giving latent heat to cooling water.

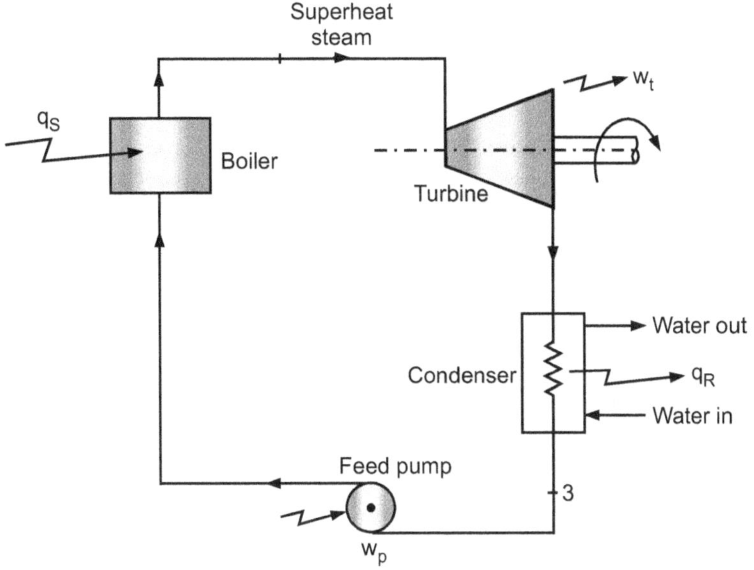


**Fig. 7.3: Rankine cycle steam power plant**

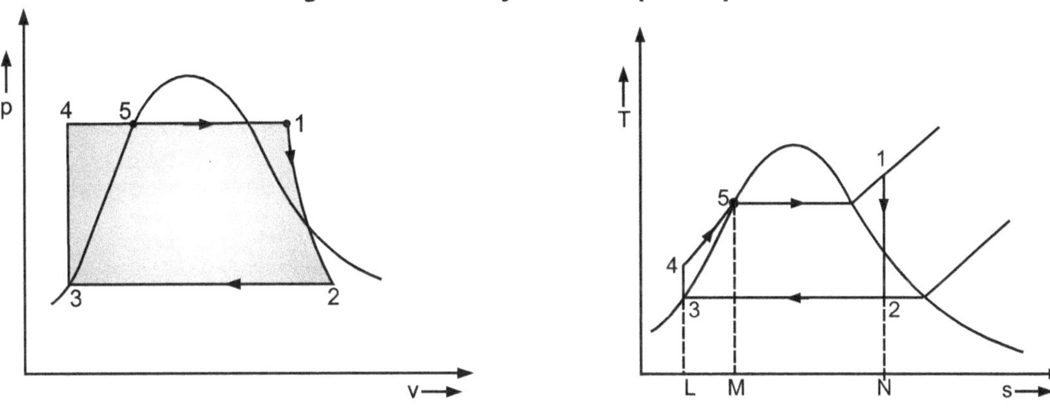


**Fig. 7.4: Rankine cycle on p-v diagram**          **Fig. 7.5: Rankine cycle on T-s diagram**

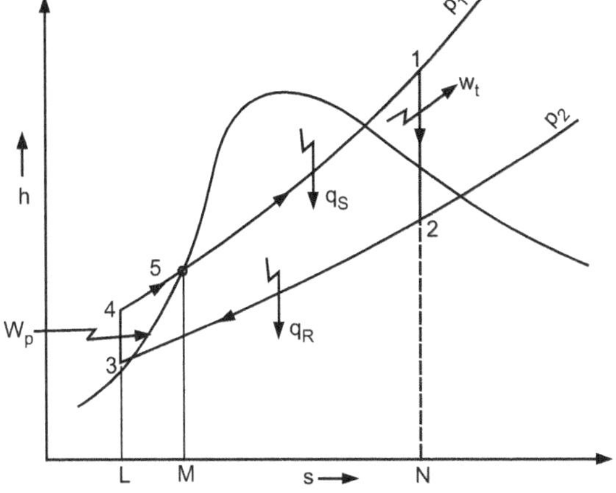


**Fig. 7.6: Rankine cycle on h-s diagram**

It is possible that steam leaving the boiler may be dry and saturated, wet or superheated. To obtain thermal efficiency of the Rankine cycle, the assumptions made are:

- Steady flow.
- Negligible kinetic and potential energy changes.
- One kg of working fluid flows through the various elements of the cycle.

First law of thermodynamics is applied separately to each of the four components of the Rankine cycle. Let us assume that, from **first law**, $\delta q - \delta u = dh$ or $q - w = \Delta h$.

Heat supplied in the boiler, process 4-1, $\qquad q_{4-1} = q_s = q_1 - h_{f4}$

Heat rejected in the condenser, process 2-3, $\qquad q_{2-3} = q_R = h_2 - h_{f3}$

Work obtained through turbine, 1-2, $\qquad w_{1-2} = w_t = h_1 - h_2$

Work supplied to the pump, 3-4, $\qquad w_{3-4} = w_p = h_{f4} - h_{f3}$

Pump work, $w_p$ is also given by, $\qquad w_p = h_{f4} - h_{f3} = v_{f3}(p_1 - p_3) =$

$$v_{f2}(p_1 - p_2)$$

where $h_{f2}$ and $h_{f4}$ are the enthalpy of water at pressures $p_2$ and $p_1$ respectively. $v_{f2}$ is the specific volume of water in $m^3/kg$ at final pressure $p_2$.

The net work = Turbine work − Pump work

or $\qquad w_{net} = w_t - w_p = (h_1 - h_2) - (h_{f4} - h_{f3})$ kJ/kg

or $\qquad w_{net} = (h_1 - h_2) - v_{f2}(p_1 - p_2)$ kJ/kg

While determining the net work from the plant, the work at the pump is to be subtracted from the turbine work output.

$$\eta_{th} = \frac{\text{Net work}}{\text{Head added}} = \frac{w_{net}}{q_A} = \frac{(h_1 - h_2) - (h_{f4} - h_{f3})}{(h_1 - h_{f4})} \qquad \ldots (7.3)$$

Thermal efficiency may also be calculated from heat supplied $q_A$ and heat rejected $q_R$.

$$w_{net} = q_s - q_R = (h_1 - h_{f4}) - (h_2 - h_{f2}) - (h_1 - h_2) - (h_{f4} - h_{f3})$$

$\therefore \qquad$ 
$$\eta_{th} = \frac{w_{net}}{q_A} = \frac{(h_1 - h_2) - (h_{f4} - h_{f3})}{(h_1 - h_{f4})}$$

or $\qquad$
$$\eta_{th} = \frac{(h_1 - h_2) - (h_{f4} - h_{f3})}{(h_1 - h_{f3}) - (h_{f4} - h_{f3})} = \frac{(h_1 - h_2) - w_p}{(h_1 - h_{f2}) - w_p} \qquad \ldots (7.4)$$

Many times the capacity of steam power plant is expressed in terms of **steam rate**. **Steam rate** is the rate of steam flow (kg/hr) required to produce unit shaft power (1 kW). Therefore,

$$\text{Steam rate} = \frac{1}{w_t - w_p} \times \frac{kg}{kJ} \times \frac{1 \text{ kJ/sec}}{1 \text{ kW}}$$

$$= \frac{1}{w_t - w_p} \cdot \frac{kg}{kW \ sec} = \frac{3600}{w_t - w_p} \cdot \frac{kJ}{kWh}$$

Cycle efficiency is expressed many times as heat rate which is the rate of heat input ($Q_s$) required to produce work output (1 kW).

$$\text{Heat rate} \;=\; \frac{3600\,Q_s}{w_t - w_p} \;=\; \frac{3600\ \text{kJ}}{\eta_{cycle} \cdot \text{kWh}}$$

Compared to turbine work, pump work is infinitesimally small and it may be neglected because the specific volume of water is very small. Here, we have

$$w_p \;=\; 0 \ \text{or} \ h_{f4} = h_{f3} = h_{f2}$$

$$\therefore \qquad \eta_{th} \;=\; \frac{h_1 - h_2}{h_1 - h_{f3}} \;=\; \frac{h_1 - h_2}{h_1 - h_{f2}} \qquad\qquad \text{... (7.5)}$$

The thermal efficiency of the Rankine cycle may also be expressed in terms of areas on T-s diagram. Referring to Fig. 7.5,

$$\eta_{th} \;=\; \frac{\text{area } 123451}{\text{area } L3451NL} \ \text{and neglecting pump work,}$$

$$\eta_{th} \;=\; \frac{\text{area } 123451}{\text{area } L351NL}$$

The overall thermal efficiency of a steam power plant varies from 35% to 38%.

In the above analysis, it is assumed that heat additions and rejection take place reversibly. This is, however, not possible in actual power plants. A substantial temperature difference exists between the hot flue gases and working fluid. But the irreversibility associated with this difference is reduced and the thermal efficiency of the cycle is increased by operating a steam generator at a pressure above the critical.

The efficiency of the Rankine cycle is shown on T-s plot in Fig. 7.7.

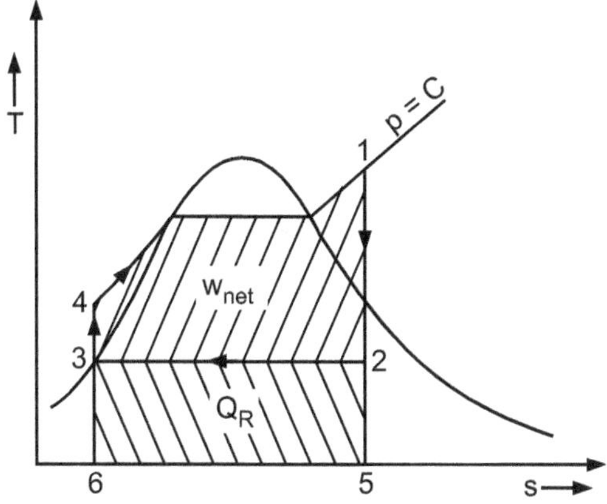


**Fig. 7.7: w_net and Q_R are proportional to areas**

The heat supplied $Q_s$ is proportional to area 1-5-6-4-1, $w_{net}$ proportional to area 1-2-3-4-1 and the heat rejection $Q_s$ proportional to area 2-5-6-3-2.

## 7.4 COMPARISON OF RANKINE AND CARNOT CYCLES

Carnot cycle has the maximum possible efficiency operating between the limits of temperature. But it is not suitable in steam power plant. Carnot cycle and Rankine cycle are shown in Fig. 7.8 and Fig. 7.9 respectively with the help of T-s plots.

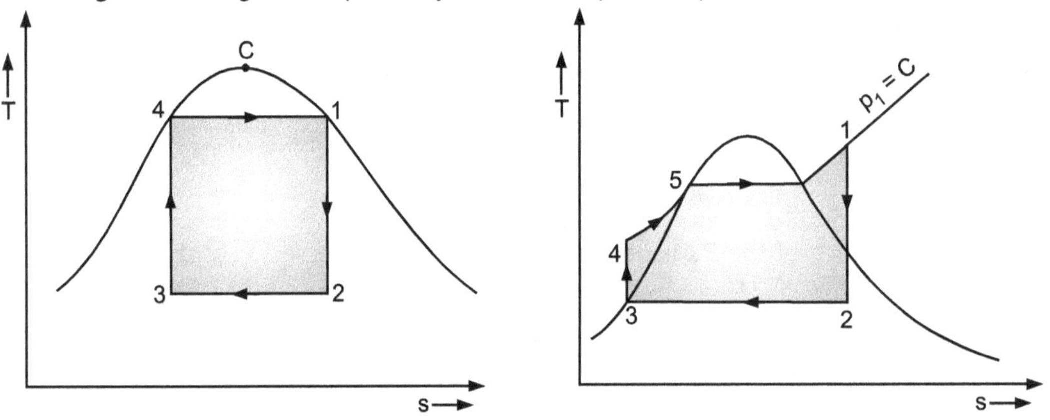

Fig. 7.8: Carnot cycle　　　　　Fig. 7.9: Rankine cycle

The reversible adiabatic expansion in the turbine, the constant temperature heat rejection in the condenser, and the reversible adiabatic compression in the pump are similar characteristic features of both Rankine and Carnot cycles.

- The reversible heat addition takes place at constant temperature (process 4-1) in Carnot cycle; while it is at constant pressure (process 4-5-1) in Rankine cycle.

- The heat supplied per kg of water is more in Rankine cycle than that in Carnot cycle. The heat rejection in condenser of both the cycles is same per unit mass operating between the same temperature limits. Therefore, thermal efficiency of Rankine cycle is less than that of Carnot cycle.

- In Carnot cycle, it is difficult to control the quality of steam to state 3, so that at the end of isentropic compression, it reaches saturated liquid state. But there is a complete condensation of steam in Rankine cycle.

## 7.5 IMPROVING THE EFFICIENCY OF THE RANKINE CYCLE

Steam power plants are responsible for the production of most of the electric power in the world. A small increase in the thermal efficiency will lead to a large saving in the fuel requirement. Therefore, every effort is made to improve the efficiency of the cycle on which steam power plants operate.

Thermal efficiency of a power cycle would be increased by two ways:

- Increase the average temperature at which heat is transferred to the working fluid in the boiler, or

- Decrease the average temperature at which heat is rejected from the working fluid in the condenser.

Next we discuss three ways of accomplishing this for the simple ideal Rankine cycle.

## 7.5.1 Lowering the Condenser Pressure (Lowers $T_{low, av}$)                    [Dec. 10]

Lowering the operating pressure of the condenser automatically lowers the temperature of the steam and thus the temperature at which heat is rejected. Steam exists as a saturated mixture in the condenser at the saturation temperature corresponding to the pressure inside.

- The effect of lowering the condenser pressure on the Rankine cycle efficiency is illustrated on T-s diagram in Fig. 7.10.

- For comparison purposes, the turbine inlet state is maintained the same.

- The colored area on this diagram represents the increase in net work output as a result of lowering the condenser pressure from $p_4$ to $p_4'$.

- The increase in the input requirements is represented by the area under curve 2'-2, but this increase is very small. Thus the overall effect of lowering the condenser pressure is an increase in the thermal efficiency of the cycle.

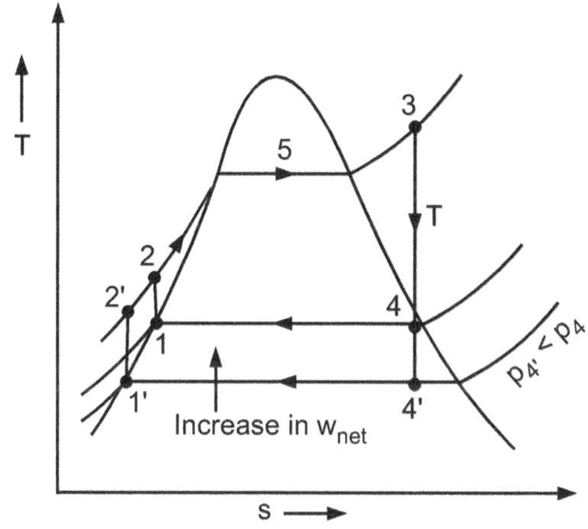


**Fig. 7.10: The effect of lower condenser pressure on Rankine cycle**

The condensers of steam power plants usually operate well below the atmospheric pressure which increases the efficiency. Vapour power cycles operate in a closed loop therefore, the vacuum pressure in the condenser does not present a major problem. However, there is a lower limit on the condenser pressure that can be used. It cannot be lower than the saturation pressure corresponding to the temperature of the cooling medium. Let us take an example of a condenser is to be cooled by water at 15°C. Allowing a temperature difference of 8°C for effective heat transfer, the steam temperature in the condenser must be above 23°C, thus the condenser pressure must be above 3.5 kPa, which is the saturation pressure at 23°C.

Lowering the condenser pressure it creates the problem of air leakage into the condenser. More importantly, it increases the moisture content of the steam at the last stages of the turbine, as highly undesirable in turbines because it decreases the turbine efficiency and erodes the turbine blades.

## 7.5.2 Superheating the Steam to High Temperature (Increases $T_{high,\,av}$)

The average temperature at which heat is added to the steam can be increased without increasing the boiler by superheating the steam to high temperatures.

- The effect of superheating on the performance of vapour power cycles is illustrated on a T-s diagram in Fig. 7.11.

- The colored area on this diagram represents the increase in the heat input.

- Thus both the net work and heat input increase as a result of superheating the steam to a higher temperature.

- The overall effect is an increase in thermal efficiency, however, since the average temperature at which heat is added increases.

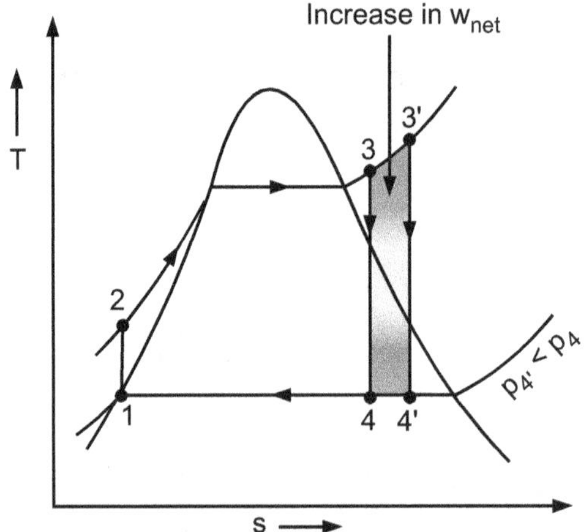


**Fig. 7.11: The effect of superheating the steam to higher temperature on the ideal Rankine cycle**

Superheating the steam to higher temperature decreases the moisture content of the steam at the turbine exit, as can be seen from the T-s diagram (the quality at state 4' is higher than that at state 4). This is desirable effect.

The temperature to which steam can be superheated is limited, however, by metallurgical considerations. Presently the highest steam temperature allowed at the turbine inlet is about 620°C. This value depends on improving the present materials or finding new ones that can withstand higher temperatures. Ceramics are very promising in this regard.

## 7.5.3 Increasing the Boiler Pressure (Increases $T_{high,\,av}$)

Another way of increasing the average temperature during the heat addition process is to increase the operating pressure of the boiler. This, in turn, raises the average temperature at which heat is added to the steam and thus raises the thermal efficiency of the cycle.

- The effect of increasing the boiler pressure on the performance of vapour B power cycles is illustrated on a T-s diagram in Fig. 7.12.

- For a fixed turbine inlet temperature, the cycle shifts to the left and the moisture content of steam at the turbine exit increases.

- This undesirable side effect can be corrected, however, by reheating the steam, as discussed in the next section.

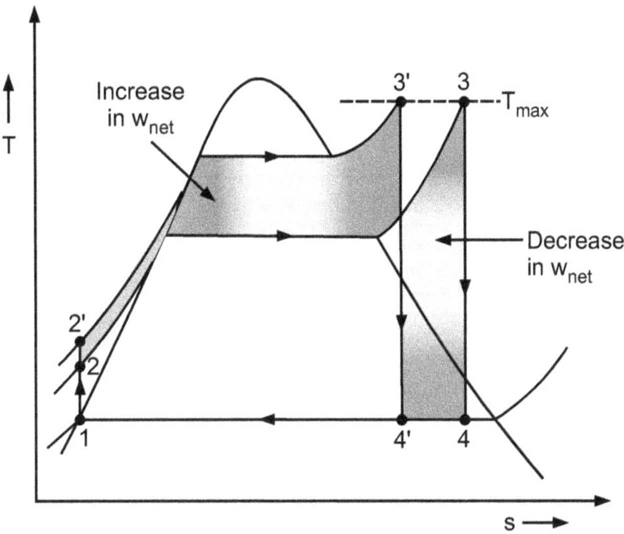


**Fig. 7.12: Effect of increasing boiler pressure on ideal Rankine cycle**

Operating pressures of boilers have gradually increase over the years from about 2-7 bar in 1922 to over to 300 bar today. Today many modern steam power plants operate at supercritical pressures (P > 22.09 MPa) and have thermal efficiencies of about 40 percent for fossil-fuel plants and 34 percent for nuclear power plants is due to the lower maximum temperatures used in those plants for safety reasons.

# SOLVED PROBLEMS

**Problem 7.1:** A simple Rankine cycle works between pressure of 25 bar and 0.05 bar. The initial condition of steam is dry saturated. Calculate the cycle efficiency, work ratio and specific steam consumption.

| Sat. Temp. °C | Sat. Pr. bar | $v_f$ m³/kg | $v_g$ m³/kg | $h_f$ kJ/kg | $h_g$ kJ/kg | $s_f$ kJ/kg·K | $s_g$ kJ/kg·K |
|---|---|---|---|---|---|---|---|
| 223.9 | 25 | 0.001197 | 0.0799 | 961.9 | 2800.9 | 2.554 | 6.254 |
| 32.9 | 0.05 | 0.001005 | 28.195 | 137.8 | 2561.6 | 0.476 | 8.396 |

**Solution:** The cycle is represented on T-s diagram as shown in Fig. 7.13.

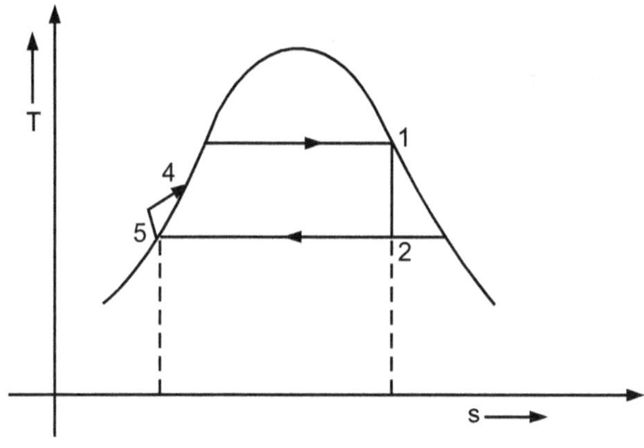

**Fig. 7.13**

The turbine process being 1-2

From tables,

$$h_1 = 2800.9 \text{ kJ/kg}$$

$$s_1 = 6.254 \text{ kJ/kg·K}$$

$$\text{The pump work} = v_f \left[ p_4 - p_3 \right]$$

$$= 0.001197 \left[ 25 + 0.05 \right] \times 10^5 \text{ J} = 5.9 \text{ kJ/kg}$$

As $\qquad s_1 = s_2 = s_{f2} + x_2 \left( s_{g2} - s_{f2} \right)$

$\therefore \qquad x_2 = \dfrac{6.254 - 0.476}{8.396} = 0.6881$

$\therefore \qquad h_2 = h_{f2} + x h_{fg2} = 137.8 + 0.688 \times 2561.1 = 1812.15 \text{ kJ/kg}$

$\therefore \qquad \text{Turbine work} = 2800.9 - 1812.15 = 988.75 \text{ kJ/kg}$

$$\text{Cycle efficiency} = \frac{(h_1 - h_2) + (h_4 - h_3)}{(h_1 - h_{f4})}$$

$$= \frac{988.75 - 5.9}{2800.9 - (137.8 + 5.9)}$$

$$= \textbf{0.3698 or 36.98\%}$$

$$\text{Work ratio} = \frac{\text{Net work}}{\text{Turbine work}} = \frac{982.85}{988.75} = \textbf{0.994}$$

$$\text{Specific steam consumption} = \frac{1}{W} \times 3600 = \frac{3600}{988.75}$$

$$= \textbf{3.64 kg/kWh}$$

**Problem 7.2:** A steam power plant based on simple Rankine cycle works between 50 bar and 0.1 bar. If the steam supplied is dry saturated find (a) Cycle efficiency, and (b) Specific steam consumption.

**Solution:** The Rankine cycle is shown in Fig. 7.14. The following values are taken from steam tables.

| P (sat) bar | T (°C) | $v_f$ m³/kg | $v_g$ m³/kg | $h_f$ kJ/kg | $h_g$ kJ/kg | $s_f$ kJ/kg·K | $s_g$ kJ/kg·K |
|---|---|---|---|---|---|---|---|
| 50 | 263.9 | 0.001286 | 0.039 | 1154.4 | 2794.2 | 2.921 | 5.974 |
| 0.1 | 45.83 | 0.00101 | 14.67 | 191.8 | 2584.8 | 0.649 | 8.151 |

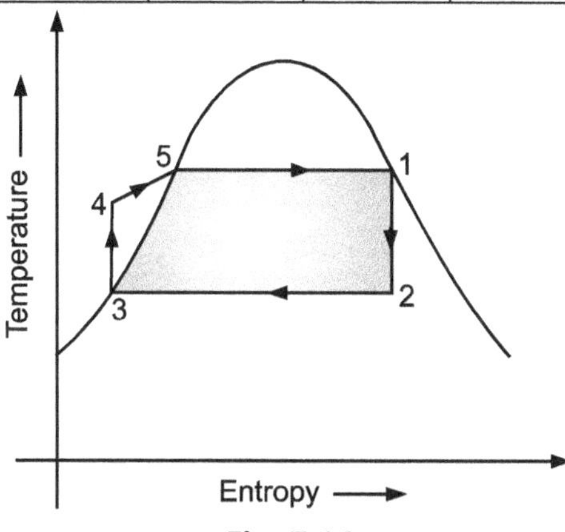


**Fig. 7.14**

As process 1-2 is isentropic expansion,

$$s_1 = s_2$$

$\therefore \quad s_{f1} + s_{fg1} = s_{f2} + x s_{fg2}$

$$2.921 + 3.053 = 0.649 + x_2 \times 7.502$$

$\therefore \quad x_2 = 0.706$

$$h_{g1} = h_{f1} + h_{fg1}$$
$$= 1087 + 1713 = 2794.2 \text{ kJ/kg}$$

$\therefore \quad h_{g2} = h_{f2} + x_2 h_{fg2}$
$$= 191.8 + 0.906 \times 2392.9 = 1881.19 \text{ kJ/kg}$$

Work done by the pump, $w_p = v_{sw1}(p_4 - p_3)$

$$= \frac{0.00101\,(50 - 0.1) \times 10^5}{1000}$$

$$= \mathbf{5.014 \text{ kJ/kg}}$$

Net work done per kg of steam

$$w_n = h_{g1} - h_{g2} - w_p = 2794.2 - 1881.19 - 5.014 = 907.996 \text{ kJ/kg}$$

$$\eta_{rankine} = w_n/(h_{g1} - h_{f4}) = 907.9/[2794.2 - (191.8 + 5.014)]$$

$$= \mathbf{34.8\%}$$

Specific steam consumption $= 1 \text{ kW} - \text{hr}/[w_{net}] \text{ kJ/kg} = 3600/907.9$

$$= \mathbf{3.965 \text{ kg/kW-hr.}}$$

**Problem 7.3:** In a Rankine cycle, the steam at inlet to turbine is saturated at a pressure of 25 bar and the exhaust pressure is 0.1 bar. Determine: (i) The pump work, (ii) Turbine power, (iii) The Rankine efficiency, (iv) The condenser heat flow and (v) The dryness at the end of expansion. Assume flow rate of 10 kg/s.

**Solution:** From the steam tables:

| P (sat) bar | T (sat) °C | $v_f$ m³/kg | $v_g$ m³/kg | $h_f$ kJ/kg | $h_g$ kJ/kg | $s_f$ kJ/kg·K | $s_g$ kJ/kg·K | $v_f$ m³/kg | $v_g$ m³/kg |
|---|---|---|---|---|---|---|---|---|---|
| 25 | 223.9 | 0.001197 | 0.0799 | 961.9 | 1839 | 2800.9 | 2.554 | 3.699 | 6.254 |
| 0.1 | 45.83 | 0.00101 | 14.67 | 191.8 | 2392.9 | 2584.8 | 0.649 | 7.502 | 8.151 |

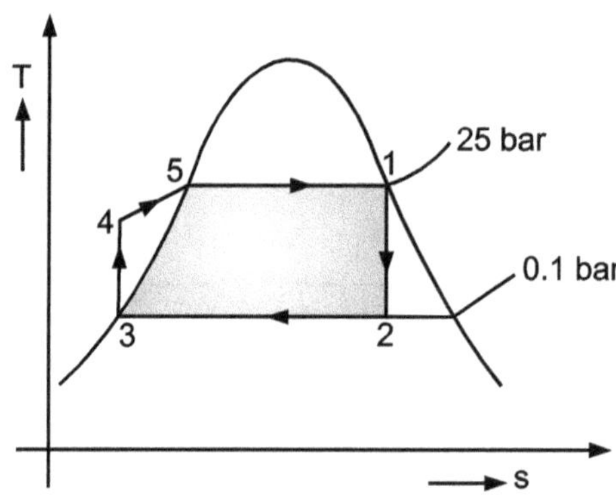


**Fig. 7.15**

$$h_1 = h_{g1} = 2800.9 \text{ kJ/kg}$$

$$h_3 = h_{f3} \text{ at 0.1 bar} = \textbf{191.8 kJ/kg}$$

(i)
$$\text{The pump work} = m\,(p_4 - p_3)\,v_f$$
$$= 1 \times 10^5\,(25 - 0.1) \times 0.00101$$
$$= 2.514 \text{ kJ}$$

$$\text{As } v_f \text{ at 0.1 bar} = 0.00101 \text{ m}^3/\text{kg}$$

$$h_4 = h_3 + 3 \text{ kJ/kg}$$
$$= 191.8 + 2.514 \text{ kJ/kg}$$

$$\text{The power required for the pump} = \frac{10 \times 2.514 \text{ kJ}}{\text{sec}} = \frac{25.14 \text{ kJ}}{\text{sec}} = \textbf{25.14 kW}$$

(ii)  The isentropic enthalpy drop is found using

∴
$$s_1 = s_2 = s_{f2} + x_2\,(s_{g2} + s_{f2})$$

From steam tables,

$$s_1 = 6.254 \text{ kJ/kg·K}$$
$$s_{f2} = 0.649 \text{ kJ/kg·K}$$
$$s_{g2} = 8.151 \text{ kJ/kg·K}$$

∴     Dryness at the outlet of expansion process

$$x_2 = \frac{s_1 - s_{f2}}{s_{g2} - s_{f2}} = \frac{6.254 - 0.649}{8.151 - 0.649} = 0.747$$

∴         $h_2 = h_{f2} + x_2 h_{fg2} = 1979.2 \text{ kJ/kg}$

∴         Turbine power $= m (h_1 - h_2)$

$$= 10 (2800.9 - 1979.2) \text{ kJ/s}$$

$$= \textbf{8127 kW}$$

Compared to this the pumping power of 30 kW is very small.

(iii)  Rankine efficiency:     $= \dfrac{(h_1 - h_2) - (h_4 - h_3)}{(h_1 - h_4)}$

$$= \frac{(2800.9 - 1979.2) - (191.8 - 189.3)}{(2800.9 - 191.8)}$$

$$= 0.3139 \text{ or } \textbf{31.39\%}$$

(iv)  The heat flow in the condenser $= m (h_2 - h_3) = 10 (1979.2 - 189.3)$

$$= \textbf{17899 kW}$$

(v)   Dryness at the end of expansion $= \textbf{0.747 or 74.7\%}$

---

**Problem 7.4:** A steam power plant operating on ideal Carnot cycle uses steam at 5 bar and 90% dryness at the end of the isothermal expansion process. The pressure during isothermal compression is 3 bar. Find the thermal efficiency of the cycle.

Also find the power developed by the engine if the engine uses 1 kg of steam per cycle and makes 200 cycles/min. Assume that the liquid is saturated at the beginning of isothermal expansion (evaporation).

**Solution:** The cycle is shown on T-s diagram as shown in Fig. 7.16. From steam table, $T_1$ and $T_2$ are obtained.

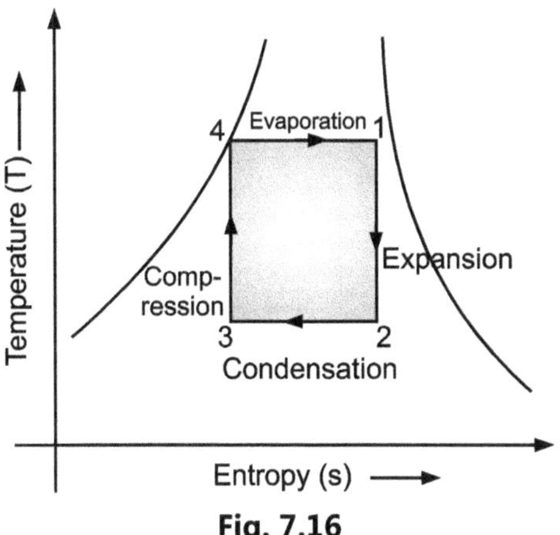


**Fig. 7.16**

Sat. temp. $T_1$ at 5 bar $= 151.9°C = 424.9 \text{ K}$

---

$$\text{Sat. temp. } T_2 \text{ at 3 bar} = 133.5°C = 406.5 \text{ K}$$

$$\eta_{th} = \frac{T_1 - T_2}{T_1} = \frac{424.9 - 406.5}{424.9} \times 100 = 4.3\%$$

Input during the isothermal expansion per cycle $= m_s \cdot x h_{fg}$

where,                              $m_s$ = Mass of steam per cycle

$x$ = Dryness fraction of steam at 10 bar

$h_{fg}$ = Latent heat of steam at 10 bar

$\therefore$                              Input $= 1 \times 0.9 \times 2163.2 = 1446.8$ kJ/cycle

where,                              $h_{fg} = 2163.2$ kJ

$\therefore$                    Output/cycle $= 906 \times 0.043 = 83.715$

$\therefore$          Output per minute $= 83.715 \times 200 = $ **16743.168 kJ/m**

$\therefore$                    Power $= \dfrac{16743.168}{60} = $ **279.05 kW**

---

**Problem 7.5:** A steam turbine operates on ideal Carnot cycles using dry saturated steam at 15 bar. The exhaust takes place at 0.05 bar into a condenser. Assume that the expansion and compression are isentropic and liquid enters the boiler as saturated liquid. Find the (a) Power developed by the turbine if the steam consumption is 20 kg/min. and (b) The efficiency of the operating cycle.

**Solution:** $h_1$ = Enthalpy of dry saturated steam at 15 bar (from steam tables).

| Sat. Temp °C | $v_f$ m³/kg | $v_g$ m³/kg | $h_f$ kJ/kg | $h_g$ kJ/kg | $s_f$ kJ/kg·K | $s_g$ kJ/kg·K | $v_f$ m³/kg |
|---|---|---|---|---|---|---|---|
| 198.3 | 15 bar | 0.001154 | 0.13167 | 144.6 | 2789.9 | 2.314 | 6.441 |
| 32.90 | 0.05 bar | 0.001005 | 28.194 | 137.8 | 2561.6 | 0.476 | 8.396 |

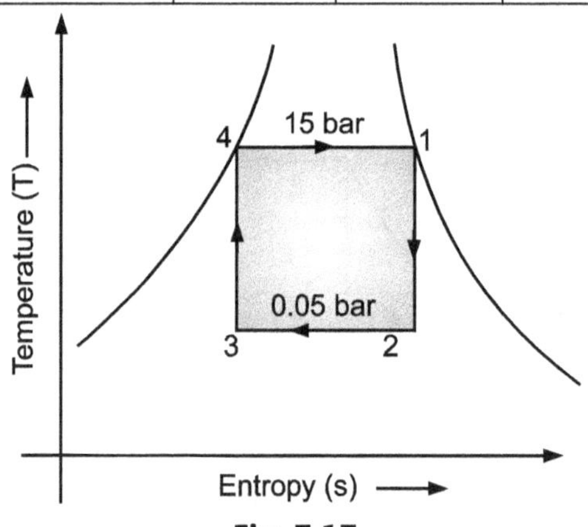


**Fig. 7.17**

$$h_1 = h_g = 2789.9 \text{ kJ/kg}$$

The expansion 1-2 is isentropic.

$$s_1 = s_2$$

$$s_1 = s_{g1} = s_{f2} + x_2\, s_{fg}$$

Substituting the values from steam tables,

$$6.441 = 0.476 + x_2\,(7.92)$$

$$\therefore \qquad x_2 = 0.753$$

$$h_2 = h_{f2} + x_2\, h_{fg2}$$

$$\therefore \qquad (\text{at } 0.05 \text{ bar}) = 137.8 + 0.753 \times 2561.6 = \mathbf{2066.68\ kJ/kg}$$

For isentropic compression process 3-4,

$$\therefore \qquad s_3 = s_4 = s_{f4} \text{ as point 4 is on saturated liquid line}$$

$$s_3 = s_{f3} + x_3\, s_{fg3}$$

Substituting the values from steam tables,

$$0.476 + x_3\,(7.920) = 2.314$$

$$\therefore \qquad x_3 = 0.232$$

$$h_3 = h_{f3} + x_3\, h_{fg3} = 137.8 + 0.232 \times 2423.8 = \mathbf{700.12\ kJ/kg}$$

Work of expansion is given by,

$$w_e = h_1 - h_2 = 2789.9 - 2066.68 = \mathbf{723.22\ kJ}$$

Work of compression is given by,

$$w_c = h_4 - h_3 = h_{f4} - h_3$$

$$= 844.6 - 700.12 = \mathbf{144.48\ kJ/kg}$$

$$w_n \text{ (Net work done)} = w_e - w_c$$

$$= 723.22 - 144.48 = \mathbf{578.74\ kJ/kg}$$

$$\therefore \qquad \text{Work done per minute} = 578.74 \times 20 = \mathbf{11574.8\ kJ/min}$$

$$\therefore \qquad \text{Power developed by the engine} = \frac{11574.8}{60} = \mathbf{192.91\ kW}$$

$$\text{Heat supplied} = h_1 - h_4 = h_1 - h_{f4}$$

$$= 2789.9 - 844.6 = \mathbf{1945.3\ kJ/kg}$$

$$\therefore \qquad \text{Cycle efficiency} = \frac{578.74}{1945.3} = 0.2975 = \mathbf{29.75\%}$$

The Carnot efficiency is also given by

$$= \frac{T_1 - T_2}{T_1}$$

where, $T_1$ saturation temperature of steam at 15 bar = (273 + 198.3) K and $T_2$ (saturation temperature of steam at 0.05 bar = 273 + 33) K.

$$\therefore \qquad \text{Carnot efficiency} = \frac{(198.3 + 273) - (33 + 273)}{(198.3)} = \frac{165.3}{471.3}$$

$$= 0.3507 \text{ or } \mathbf{35.07\%}$$

**Problem 7.6:** A boiler feed pump works on the (full admission) non-expansive cycle. Steam is supplied at 12 bar and dry saturated condition. The exhaust takes place at 1 bar. Draw the cycle of operation on p-v and T-s diagrams and find:

(a)　The steam consumption per kW-hour

(b)　Theoretical efficiency of the cycle.

(c)　Heat removed in the condenser per kg of steam.

(d)　If the feed pump supplies 50 kg of water per minute to the boiler, find the power required to run the pump.

**Solution:** Non-expansive cycle means that there is no expansion of the steam in the cylinder, and high pressure steam is admitted throughout the stroke.

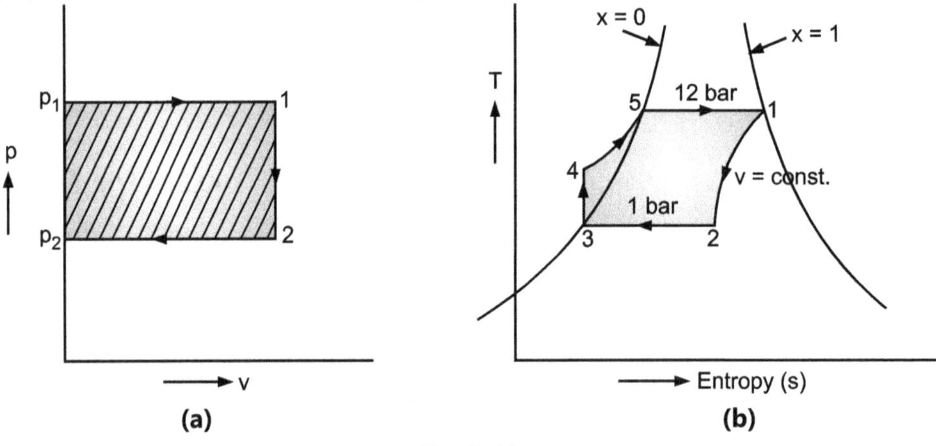


**Fig. 7.18**

(a)　Work done per kg of steam:

$$w = \frac{(p_1 - p_2)\, v_1}{J}$$

where,　　　　　　　　$v_1 = v_{s1}$ (as dry steam is supplied)

$$= \frac{[(12 - 1) \times 10^5] \times 0.16321}{1000} = \textbf{179.53 kJ/kg}$$

Pump work per kg of steam:

$$w_p = \frac{v_s\, (p_1 - p_2)}{J}$$

where, $v_s$ is the specific volume of saturated water at 1 bar.

∴　　　　　　　　$$w_p = \frac{0.001043\,(12 - 1) \times 10^5}{1000} = \textbf{1.1473 kJ/kg}$$

Net work available is,

$$w_n = 179.53 - 1.1473 = 178.38 \text{ kJ/kg}$$

$$\text{Steam consumption per kWh} = \frac{3600}{178.38} = \textbf{20.18 kg/kWh}$$

(b)  Heat supplied per kg of steam is

$$h_s = h_1 - h_{f4}$$
$$= h_1 - (h_{f3} + w_p)$$
$$h_1 = 2782.7$$

$\therefore$    $h_2 = 2782.7 - (417.5 + 1.1473) = 2364.05$ kJ/kg

The cycle efficiency $= \dfrac{178.38}{2364.05} \times 100 = \mathbf{7.54\%}$

(c)  Heat removed in the condenser per kg of steam

$$= h_2 - h_{f3} = (h_1 - w_n) - h_{f3}$$
$$= 2782.7 - 178.38 - 417.5 = \mathbf{2186.82 \ kJ/kg}$$

(d)  Power required to run the feed pump $= \left(\dfrac{100}{60}\right) \times w_p = \left(\dfrac{100}{60}\right) \times 1.1473 = \mathbf{1.912 \ kW.}$

**Problem 7.7:** Dry saturated steam at 12 bar is supplied to a steam turbine. The exhaust takes at 1 bar. Determine the following: (a) Rankine efficiency, (b) Steam consumption per kWh if the efficiency ratio is 0.65, (c) Carnot efficiency for the given pressure limit using steam as a working fluid. (d) If the exhaust pressure is reduced to 0.1 bar by introducing a jet condenser, find the percentage increase in Rankine efficiency and percentage decrease in specific steam consumption. Neglect the pump work.

**Solution:** Enthalpy of dry saturated steam at 12 bar.

From steam table, $h_g = 2782.7$ kJ/kg.

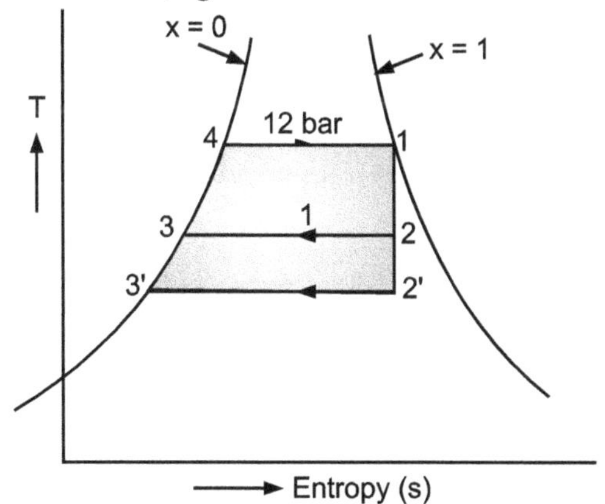


**Fig. 7.19**

The isentropic expansion from 12 bar to 1 bar is represented by 1-2.

$\therefore$    $S_{g1} = S_{f2} + x_2 \, S_{fg2}$

$\therefore$    $6.519 = 1.303 + x_2 \times 6.057$

$\therefore$    $x_2 = 0.8611$

Similarly, for exhaust pressure 0.1 bar, the process is 1-2.

$$\therefore \qquad s_{g1} = s'_{f2} + x'_2 \times s'_{fg2}$$

$$\therefore \qquad 6.519 = 0.649 + x'_2 \times 7.502$$

$$\therefore \qquad x'_2 = 0.7824$$

The enthalpies at 2 and 2' are calculated as,

$$h_2 = h_{f2} + x_2 \, h_{fg2} = 417.5 + 0.8611 \times 2257.9 = 2361.77 \text{ kJ/kg}$$

$$h'_2 = h'_{f2} + x'_2 \, h'_{fg2} = 191.8 + 0.7824 \times 2392.9 = 2064.0 \text{ kJ/kg}$$

(a)  Rankine efficiency when exhaust pressure is 1 bar is,

$$\eta_r = \frac{h_1 - h_2}{h_1 - h_{f2}} = \frac{2782.7 - 2361.77}{2782.7 - 417.5} = \frac{420.93}{2365.2} = 0.1779 = 17.79\%$$

Rankine efficiency when exhaust pressure is 0.1 bar is,

$$\frac{h_1 - h'_2}{h_1 - h'_{f2}} = \frac{2782.7 - 2064}{2782.7 - 191.8} = \frac{718.7}{2590.9} = 0.2773 = 27.73\%$$

(b)  Efficiency ratio $= \dfrac{\text{Indicated thermal efficiency}}{\text{Rankine efficiency}}$

(i)  When exhaust pressure is 1 bar

Indicated thermal efficiency, $\eta_i = 0.1779 \times 0.65 = 0.115635$

Indicated thermal efficiency, $\eta_i = \dfrac{3600}{m_s \, (h_1 - h_{f2})}$

where, $m_s$ is specific steam consumption in kg/kWh.

$$0.115635 = \frac{3600}{m_s \, (2782.7 - 417.5)}$$

$$\therefore \qquad m_s = \frac{3600}{0.115635 \times 2365.2} = 13.08 \text{ kg/kWh}$$

(ii)  When the exhaust pressure is 0.1 bar, then $\eta_i$ (indicated thermal efficiency)

$$= 0.2773 \times 0.65 = 0.18024$$

$$\therefore \qquad m_s = \frac{3600}{\eta'_i \, (h_1 - h'_{f2})} = \frac{3600}{0.18024 \, (2782.7 - 191.8)}$$

$$= \mathbf{7.709 \ kg/kWh}$$

$\therefore$   Percentage decrease in specific steam consumption

$$= \frac{13.08 - 7.709}{13.08} \times 100 = 41.06\%$$

(c)   Carnot efficiency when exhaust pressure is 1 bar

$$= \frac{T_1 - T_2}{T_1} = \frac{188 - 100}{188 + 273} = \frac{88}{461.0}$$

$$= 0.190 = 19.08\%$$

Carnot efficiency when exhaust pressure is 0.1 bar

$$= \frac{T_1 - T_2}{T_1} = \frac{188 - 46}{188 + 273}$$

$$= \frac{142}{461} = 0.3080 = 30.80\%$$

Percentage increase in Carnot efficiency

$$= \frac{30.80 - 19.8}{19.8} = 0.3571 = 35.71\%$$

| Exhaust pressure | Carnot efficiency | Rankine efficiency |
|---|---|---|
| 1 bar | 19.08 | 17.79 |
| 0.1 bar | 30.80 | 27.73 |

**Problem 7.8:** In a Rankine engine, the specific steam consumption is 6 kg/kWh. The enthalpy of steam supplied is 2000 kJ/kg and condensate is at a temperature of 60°C. Find thermal efficiency of the engine.

**Solution:** The Rankine engine working on Rankine cycle is shown in Fig. 7.20.

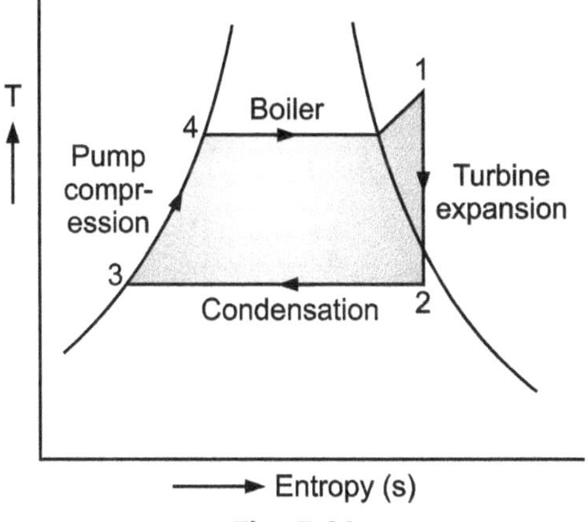


**Fig. 7.20**

$$h_1 = 2500 \text{ kJ/kg}$$
$$h_{f3} = 4.2 \times (60 - 0) = 252 \text{ kJ/kg}$$

The thermal efficiency is given by,

$$\eta = \frac{kW}{m'_s \,(h_1 - h_{f3})}$$

where, $h_1$ and $h_{f3}$ are in kJ and $m'_s$ is steam consumption per second.

$$\therefore \quad \eta = \frac{kW \times 3600}{3600 \; m_s' \; (h_1 - h_{f3})} = \frac{kW \times 3600}{m_s \; (h_1 - h_{f3})}$$

where, $m_s$ is steam consumption per hour.

$$\eta = \frac{3600}{\dfrac{m_s}{kW} (h_1 - h_{f3})} = \frac{3600}{\dot{m} \; (h_1 - h_{f3})}$$

where, $\dot{m}_s$ is the steam consumption per kW per hour which is known as specific steam consumption.

$$\therefore \quad \eta = \frac{3600}{6 \; (2000 - 252)} = 0.34 = \mathbf{34\%}$$

**Problem 7.9:** Dry saturated steam is supplied to a turbine at 16 bar. The isentropic expansion continues to 1.1 bar. Determine (i) The Rankine efficiency, (ii) How is the Rankine efficiency affected if the exhaust is sent to condenser where pressure is maintained at 0.3 bar?

**Solution:** Refer to Fig. 7.21.

(i)   The Rankine efficiency is,

$$\eta_r = \frac{h_1 - h_2}{h_1 - h_{f2}}, \; h_1 = h_g = 2791$$

$$h_1 = 2791.7 \; kJ/kg$$

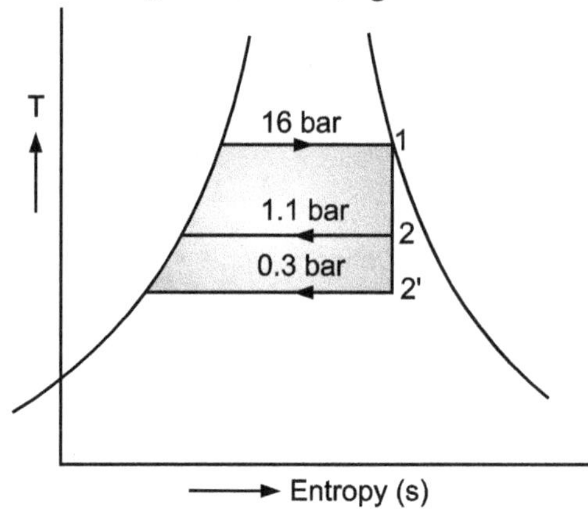


**Fig. 7.21**

As expansion 1-2 is isentropic,

$$\therefore \quad s_1 = s_2$$

$$s_{g1} = s_{f2} + x_2 \, s_{fg2} \text{ (values are taken from steam table)}$$

$$6.418 = 1.33 + x_2 \times 5.9947$$

$$\therefore \quad x_2 = 0.8482$$

$$\therefore \quad h_2 = h_{f2} + x_2 \, h_{fg2} = 428.84 + 1 + 2250.8 = 2680.64 \; kJ/kg$$

$$\eta_r = \frac{2791.7 - 2346.5}{2791.7 - 428.84} = 0.1884 = \mathbf{18.8\%}$$

(ii) When the expansion is continued to 0.3 bar, then,

$$s_1 = s_2' = s_{f2}' + x_2' \, h_{fg2}'$$

$$\therefore \qquad 6.44 = 0.944 + x_2' \times 6.825$$

$$\therefore \qquad x_2' = 0.805$$

$$\therefore \qquad h_2' = h_{f2}' + x_2' \cdot h_{fg2}' = 289.3 + 0.805 \times 2336.1 = 2169.86 \text{ kJ/kg}$$

$$\therefore \qquad \eta_r' = \frac{h_1 - h_2'}{h_1 - h_{f2}'} = \frac{2791.7 - 2169.86}{2791.7 - 289.3} = \frac{621.84}{2502.4} = 0.248 = \mathbf{24.84\%}$$

Alternately, $h_2$ and $h_2'$ can also be directly obtained from h-s chart after drawing vertical line from point '1' and making the points 2 and 2' which is more easy than this method.

**Problem 7.10:** The enthalpy of steam at inlet to a turbine of a power plant is 3000 kJ/kg and enthalpy of steam leaving the turbine is 2600 kJ/kg.

   (a)   If the temperature of saturated condensate is 50°C, find (i) Rankine efficiency and (ii) Specific steam consumption.

   (b)   If the highest temperature of steam supplied in the above power plant is 400°C, what would be the maximum possible efficiency of the plant?

   (c)   If the mass flow rate of steam in the above power plant is 1 kg/sec. find

(i) Power developed by the turbine, (ii) Heat transfer in the condenser, (iii) Work required for he feed pump if the boiler pressure is 10 bar, (iv) Heat supplied in the boiler.

**Solution:** Refer to Fig. 7.22.

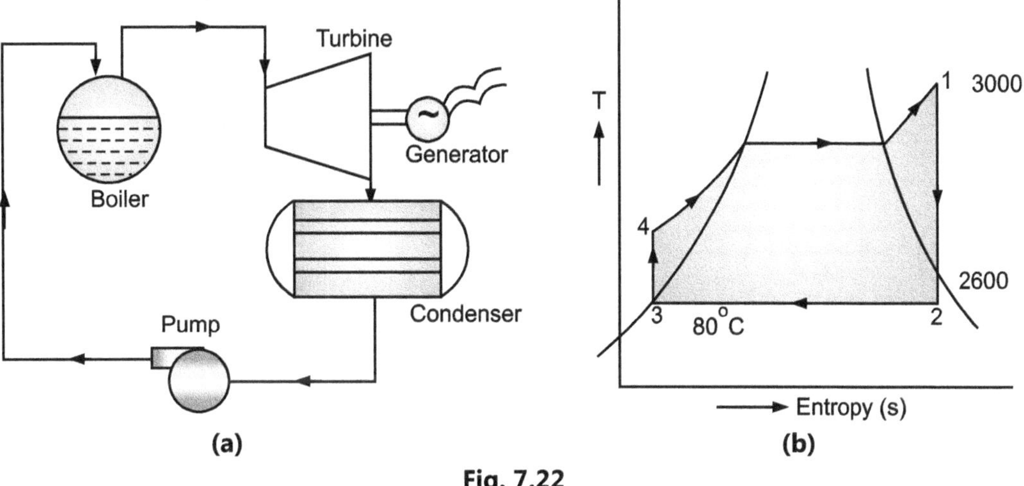


**Fig. 7.22**

Rankine efficiency is given by,

$$\eta_r = \frac{h_1 - h_2}{h_1 - h_{f2}} = \frac{3000 - 2600}{3000 - 50} = \frac{400}{2950} = 0.1355 = 13.55\%$$

$$\eta_r = \frac{3000}{\dot{m}_s\,(h_1 - h_{f3})} = \frac{3000}{\dot{m}_s\,(3000 - 50)} \quad \text{where, } \dot{m}_s \text{ is in kg/kW-hr.}$$

$$\dot{m}_s = \frac{3000}{0.1355 \times 2950} = 7.505 \text{ kg/kW-hr}$$

(b)  The highest possible efficiency is as per Carnot efficiency

$$\therefore \qquad \eta_c = \frac{T_1 - T_2}{T_1} = \frac{400 - 50}{400 + 273} = \frac{350}{673} = 0.52 = \mathbf{52\%}$$

(c)  (i)   Power developed by the turbine $= 1 \times (3000 - 2600) = 400$ kW

(ii)  Heat transfer in the condenser per kg of steam

$$= h_2 - h_{f2} = 2600 - 50 = \mathbf{2550 \text{ kJ/kg}}$$

(iii)  Work required to run pump $= (v_w \cdot dp)\, m_w$

where, $v_w$ is specific volume of saturated water at 50°C

$$= \frac{0.001012 \times (10 - 0.12335) \times 10^5 \times (1)}{10^3} \text{ kW} = \mathbf{1 \text{ kW}}$$

(iv)  Heat supplied in the boiler per kg of steam

$$= h_2 - h_{f3} = 3000 - 50 = \mathbf{2950 \text{ kJ/kg}}$$

**Problem 7.11:** A steam turbine plant operates on the Rankine cycle. Steam is delivered from the boiler to the turbine at a pressure of 3.5 MN/m$^2$ and with a temperature of 350°C. Steam from the turbine exhausts into a condenser at a pressure of 10 kN/m$^2$ condensate from the condenser is returned to the boiler by means of a feed pump.

Determine:

(i)   The dryness fraction of the steam entering the condenser.

(ii)  Rankine efficiency.

Draw T-s diagram.

**Solution: Given Data: Rankine cycle**

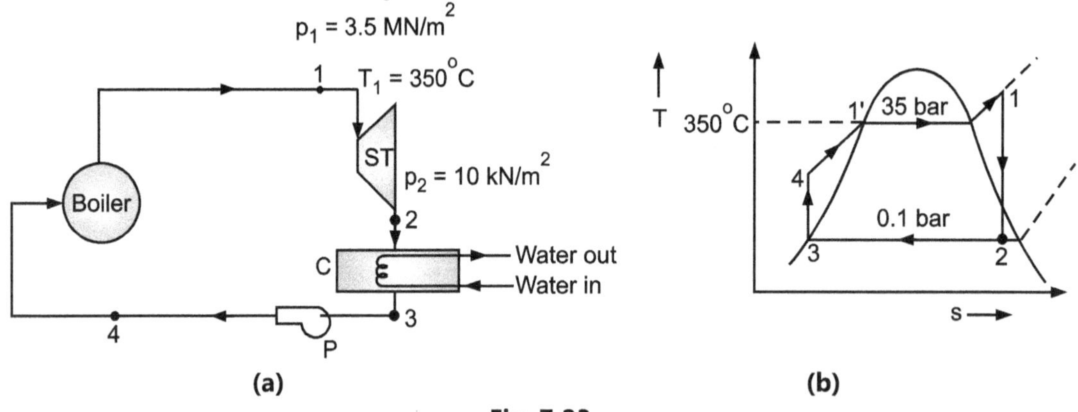


**Fig. 7.23**

Determine:

  (i)   Dryness fraction of steam at point 2.

  (ii)  Rankine efficiency.

At 35 bar and 350°C from steam table (superheated),

$$h_1 = 3106.45 \text{ kJ/kg}$$

$$s_1 = 6.663 \text{ kJ/kg·K}$$

To find $h_2$, from isentropic expansion process 1-2,

$$s_1 = s_2$$

$$= s_{f2} + x_2 \cdot s_{fg2}$$

$\therefore \qquad\qquad 6.663 = 0.649 + x_2 \times 7.502 \qquad\qquad\qquad \text{... (at 0.1 bar)}$

$\therefore \qquad\qquad x_2 = \dfrac{6.663 - 0.649}{7.502} = 0.8016$

Now, $\qquad\qquad h_2 = h_{f2} + x_2 \cdot h_{fg2}$

$$= 191.8 + 0.8016 \times 2392.9 \qquad\qquad \text{... (at 0.1 bar)}$$

$$h_2 = 2110.075 \text{ kJ/kg}$$

From steam table, at 0.1 bar,

$$h_3 = h_{f2} = 191.8 \text{ kJ/kg}$$

Also, $\qquad$ Pump $(w_p)$ work $= v_4 (p_4 - p_3)$

$$= 0.001010 \times (35 - 0.1) \times 10^2 \text{ kJ/kg}$$

$$= 3.5249 \text{ kJ/kg}$$

$\therefore \qquad\qquad h_4 - h_3 = 3.5249$

$\therefore \qquad\qquad h_4 = h_3 + 3.5249 = 191.8 + 3.5249$

$$h_4 = \textbf{195.3249 kJ/kg}$$

Now, Rankine cycle efficiency $(\eta_R)$:

$$= \frac{\text{Turbine work} - \text{Pump work}}{\text{Heat supplied}} = \frac{(h_1 - h_2) - w_p}{h_1 - h_4}$$

$$= \frac{(3106.45 - 2110.075) - 3.5249}{(3106.45 - 195.3249)}$$

$$= \frac{992.85}{2911.1251} = 0.341 \text{ or } \textbf{34.1\%}$$

**Problem 7.12:** The feed water to a boiler enters an economiser at 32°C and leaves at 120°C, being fed into the boiler at this temperature. The steam leaves the boiler 0.95 dry at 2 MPa and passes through a superheater where its temperature is raised to 250°C without change of pressure. The steam output is 8.2 kg/kg of coal burned and the calorific value of the coal is 28000 kJ/kg. Determine the energy received per kilogram of water and steam in: (i) The economiser, (ii) The boiler, (iii) The superheater expressing the answers as percentages of the energy supplied by the coal.

**Solution:**

Heat released per kg of coal = $Q$ = 28000 kJ/kg

Energy received per kg of water in economiser = $Q_1$

$$= c_{pw}\,(T_{w2} - T_{w1}) = 4.18 \times (120 - 32) = 367.84 \text{ kJ/kg}$$

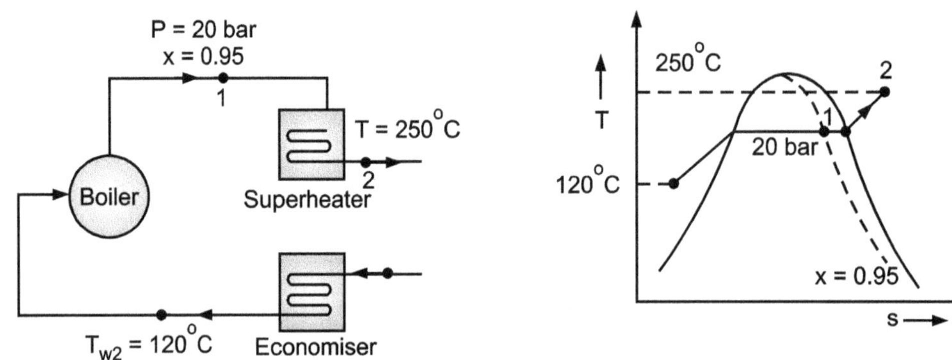


**Fig. 7.24**

Energy received per kg of water in boiler = $Q_2$

$$= h_1 - h_{f\,(at\ 120°C)}$$
$$= (h_{f1} + x h_{fg1}) - h_{f\,(at\ 120°C)}$$
$$= (908.6 + 0.95 \times 1888.6) - 504.1$$
$$= \textbf{2198.67 kJ/kg} \qquad\qquad ... \text{(7.85\% of Q)}$$

Energy received per kg of steam in superheater = $Q_3$

$$= (h_2 - h_1) = (2902.4 - 2702.77)$$
$$= \textbf{199.63 kJ/kg} \qquad\qquad ... \text{(0.713\% of Q)}$$

**Problem 7.13:** A steam power plant is operated at a boiler pressure of 7 MPa and the condenser pressure of 20 kPa. Calculate:

(i)  Pump work

(ii)  Turbine work

(iii)  Heat added

(iv)  Rankine cycle efficiency

(v)  Net power produced in MW if the steam is produced at the rate of 37.8 kg/sec and at 550°C.

**Solution: Rankine cycle:**

Steam pressure at inlet to turbine = $p_1$ = 7 MPa = 70 bar

Steam temperature at inlet to turbine = $T_2$ = 550°C

Steam pressure at exit of turbine = $p_2$ = 20 kPa = 0.2 bar

Mass flow rate of steam = $m_s$ = 37.8 kg/sec

Calculate:

(i)  Pump work = $w_p$, (ii) Turbine work = $w_T$, (iii) Heat added = $Q_A$, (iv) Rankine cycle efficiency = $\eta_{cycle}$, (v) Net power produced in MW.

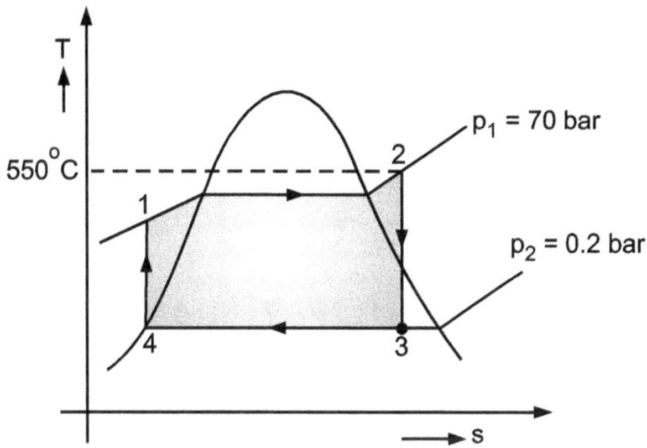


**Fig. 7.25**

The following properties are taken from superheat steam table.

At $p_1$ = 70 bar and $T_1$ = 550°C.

Enthalpy of steam at point 2 = $h_2$ = 3530.9 kJ/kg.

Entropy of steam at point 2 = $s_2$ = 6.9486 kJ/kg·K

From saturated steam table,

At $p_3$ = 0.2 bar,

$$\text{Entropy of steam at point 3} = s_3 = s_{f3} + x_3 \cdot s_{fg3}$$
$$= 0.8320 + x_3 \cdot (7.0766)$$

For, isentropic expansion (2-3) process,

$$s_2 = s_3$$
$$\therefore \quad 6.9486 = 0.8320 + x_3 \cdot (7.0766)$$
$$\therefore \quad x_3 = 0.864$$

Now, Enthalpy of steam at exit of turbine = $h_3 = h_{f3} + x_3 \cdot h_{fg3}$
$$= 251.4 + 0.864 \times 2358.3$$
$$= 2288.96 \text{ kJ/kg}$$

Enthalpy at point 4 = $h_4 = h_{f3} = 251.4$ kJ/kg

For finding '$h_1$',

$$\text{Pump work} = w_p = v_f \cdot (p_1 - p_2)$$
$$\therefore \quad h_1 - h_4 = v_f (p_1 - p_2)$$
$$\therefore \quad h_1 = v_f (p_1 - p_2) + h_4$$
$$= (0.001017)(70 - 0.2) \times 10^2 + 251.4$$
$$h_1 = 258.881 \text{ kJ/kg}$$

(i)　　　　　Pump work $= w_p = v_f (p_1 - p_2)$

$$= 0.001017 \times (70 - 0.2) \times 10^2 = \textbf{7.48256 kJ/kg}$$

(ii)　　　　　Turbine work $= w_T = h_2 - h_3$

$$= 3530.9 - 2288.97 = \textbf{1241.93 kJ/kg}$$

(iii)　　　　　Heat supplied $= Q_s = h_2 - h_1$

$$= 3530.9 - 258.88 = \textbf{3272.02 kJ/kg}$$

(iv)　　　Rankine cycle efficiency $= \eta_{cycle}$

$$= \frac{w_T - w_p}{Q_A}$$

$$= \frac{1241.93 - 7.48256}{3272.02} = \textbf{0.3773 or 37.73\%}$$

(v)　Net power developed:

　　　　Net work done $= w_T - w_p$

$$= 1241.93 - 7.48256 = \textbf{1234.45 kJ/kg}$$

Given that,

　　　　Steam flow rate $= m_s = 37.8$ kg/sec

$\therefore$　　　　Net power developed $=$ Net work done $\times m_s$

$$= 1234.45 \times 37.8$$

$$= 46662.113 \text{ kJ/sec or kW}$$

$$= \textbf{46.66 kW}$$

---

**Problem 7.14:** A steam power plant operates between boiler pressure of 30 bar and condenser pressure of 0.04 bar with dry saturated steam supplied at inlet to the turbine. Calculate:

(i)　The cycle efficiency

(ii)　Specific steam consumption

(iii)　Work ratio

(iv)　Plot the cycle on T-s diagram.

**Solution: Given:**

　　　　Boiler pressure, $p_1 = 30$ bar

　　　Condenser pressure $= p_2 = 0.04$ bar

At inlet to turbine, dry saturated steam.

Calculate:

(i)　The cycle efficiency $= \eta_{cycle}$

(ii)　Specific steam consumption $=$ S.S.C.

(iii)　Work ratio

(iv)　Plot the cycle on T-s diagram.

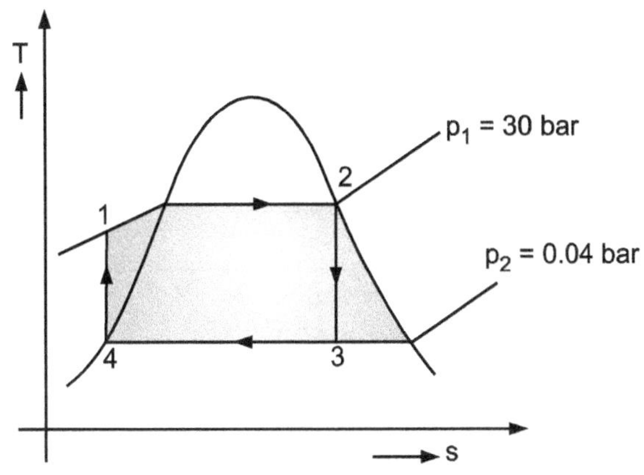


**Fig. 7.26**

At pressure, $p_1$ = 30 bar

Enthalpy at inlet of turbine = $h_2 = h_g$ = 2804.2 kJ/kg

Entropy at inlet of turbine = $s_2 = s_g$ = 6.1869 kJ/kg

For process 2-3:

$$s_2 = s_3$$
$$\text{at 30 bar} = \text{at 0.04 bar}$$

∴
$$s_2 = s_{f3} + x_3 \cdot s_{fg3}$$

∴
$$6.1869 = 0.4226 + x_3 \times 8.0520$$
$$x_3 = 0.7159$$

Now,

$$\text{Enthalpy at point 3} = h_3 = h_{f3} + x_3 \cdot h_{fg3}$$
$$= 121.46 + 0.7159 \times 2432.9 = 1863.1 \text{ kJ/kg}$$
$$\text{Enthalpy at point 4} = h_4 = h_{f3} = 121.46 \text{ kJ/kg}$$

For finding $h_1$:

$$\text{Pump work} = w_p = h_1 - h_4$$

∴
$$v_f (p_1 - p_4) = h_1 - h_4 \qquad \qquad \text{... (1)}$$

At 0.04 bar,
$$v_f = 0.001004 \text{ m}^3/\text{kg}$$

Then equation (1) becomes,

$$(0.001004) \times (30 - 0.04) \times 10^2 = h_1 - 121.46$$

∴
$$h_1 = 124.47 \text{ kJ/kg}$$

(i)    Rankine cycle efficiency $= \eta_{cycle} = \dfrac{(h_2 - h_3) - (h_1 - h_4)}{(h_2 - h_1)}$

$$= (2804.2 - 1863.135) - \dfrac{(124.47 - 121.46)}{(2804.2 - 124.47)}$$

$$= \dfrac{(941.065 - 3.01)}{2679.73} = \textbf{0.35 or 35\%}$$

(ii)    Specific steam consumption (SSC):

$$S.S.C = \frac{3600}{w_{net}} \text{ kg/kW-hr.}$$

$$= \frac{3600}{(w_T - w_p)}$$

$$= \frac{3600}{(h_2 - h_3) - (h_1 - h_4)}$$

$$= \frac{3600}{(941.065 - 3.01)} = \mathbf{3.84}$$

(iii)   Work Ratio (WR):

$$WR = \frac{w_{net}}{w_T}$$

$$= \frac{(h_2 - h_3) - (h_1 - h_4)}{(h_2 - h_3)}$$

$$= \frac{941.065 - 3.01}{941.065} = \mathbf{0.997}$$

(iv)  Cycle on T-s diagram is shown in Fig. 7.31.

**Problem 7.15:** A steam turbine receives superheated steam at 100 bar and 600°C. It is exhausted at 2 bar and then used for process of humidity control. If the steam flow rate is 7200 kg/hr, find the ideal cycle efficiency of the plant. Also find the input in kW and specific steam consumption.

**Solution: Given Data:** $p_2$ = 100 bar, $T_2$ = 600°C, $p_3$ = 2 bar, $m_s$ = 7200 kg/hr

From steam table,

At 100 bar, $T_2$ = 600°C

$$h_2 = 3622.7 \text{ kJ/kg}$$
$$s_2 = 6.9013 \text{ kJ/kg·K}$$

At 2 bar,

$$s_f = 1.5301$$
$$s_{fg} = 5.5967 \text{ kJ/kg·K}$$

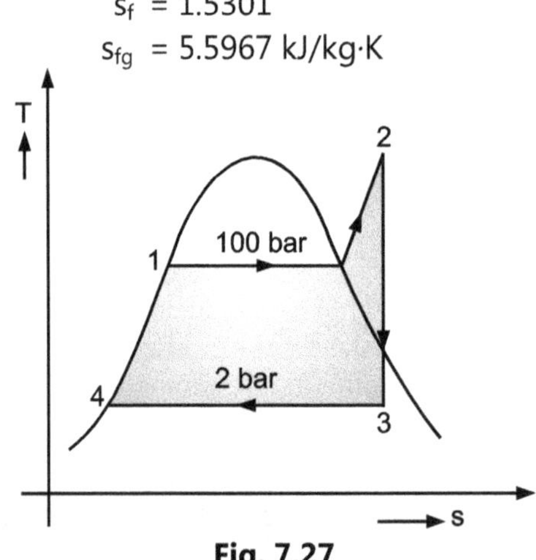


**Fig. 7.27**

Adiabatic expansion 2-3,

$$s_2 = s_3$$
$$6.9013 = s_f + x_3\, s_{fg}$$
$$6.9013 = 1.5301 + x_3 \times 5.5967$$
$$x_3 = 0.9591$$

The enthalpy of steam at point '3'

$$h_3 = h_f + x_3\, h_{fg} \text{ at 2 bar}$$
$$= 504.7 + 0.9591 \times 2201.6 = 2617.59 \text{ kJ/kg}$$

$$\text{Heat supplied} = h_2 - h_1$$
$$= 3622.7 - 1408.04 = 2214.66 \text{ kJ/kg}$$

$$\text{Turbine work} = h_2 - h_3$$
$$= 3622.7 - 2617.59 = 1005.11 \text{ kJ/kg}$$

$$\text{Ideal cycle efficiency} = \frac{\text{Turbine work}}{\text{Heat supplied}}$$

$$= \frac{1005.11}{2214.66} = \textbf{45.38\%}$$

$$\text{Output in kW} = 1005.11 \times \frac{7200}{3600} = \textbf{0.2010.2 kW}$$

$$= \textbf{2010.22 kW}$$

$$\text{Specific steam consumption} = \frac{7200}{2010.22} = \textbf{3.582 kg/kW-h}$$

---

**Problem 7.16:** Steam of mass 10 kg and pressure 1000 kPa, 0.85 dry, is heated at constant pressure till the volume is doubled. Determine:

   (i)    Final quality of steam.

   (ii)   Heat added.

   (iii)  Change in internal energy.

**Solution: Given Data:** $m = 10$ kg, $p_1 = 1000$ kPa, $x = 0.85$, $v_2 = 2v_1$

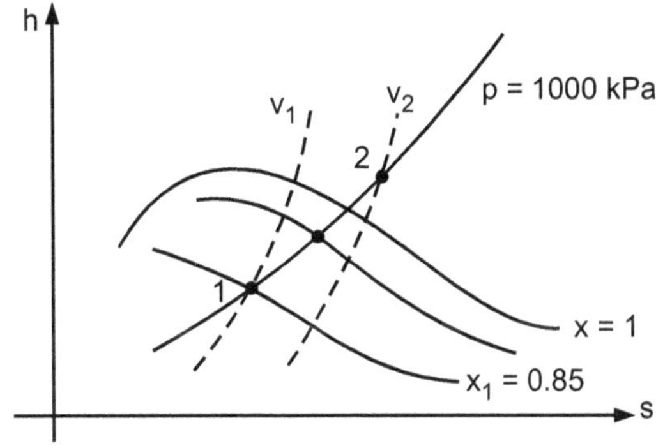


**Fig. 7.28**

At 10 bar pressure,

$$v_g = 0.19429 \ m^3/kg$$
$$T_s = 179.88°C$$
$$v_1 = x \times 0.19429$$
$$= 0.85 \times 0.19429$$
$$v_1 = \mathbf{0.1651465}$$

The specific volume at point 2 (after heating),

$$v_2 = 2 \times v_1 = 2 \times 0.1651465$$
$$= 0.3303 \ m^3/kg$$

But, $v_2 > v_g$ at 10 bar pressure.

Therefore, steam is in superheat state.

$\therefore$      Final quality of steam is **superheated**.

From superheat steam table,

At $v_2 = 0.3303 \ m^3/kg$, $p_2 = 1000 \ kPa$

$$T_2 = 450.11°C$$

Now, 
$$h_1 = h_{f1} + xh_{fg}$$
$$= 762.61 + 0.85 \times 2013.6 = 2474.17 \ kJ/kg$$
$$(\because \text{ at 10 bar})$$

and 
$$h_2 = 3371.35 \ kJ/kg \qquad \dots (\because \text{ at } T_2 = 450.11°C)$$

$$\text{Heat added} = h_2 - h_1 = 3371.35 - 2475.17$$
$$= 897.18 \ kJ/kg$$
$$= 897.18 \times 10 \ kJ = \mathbf{8971.8 \ kJ}$$

Change in internal energy,

$$u_2 - u_1 = (h_2 - h_1) + (p_1v_1 - p_2v_2)$$
$$= 8971.8 + 10 \times 1000 \times (0.1651465 - 0.3303)$$
$$= \mathbf{7320.335 \ kJ}$$

(i)      Final quality of steam = Superheated steam with temperature 450.11°C.

(ii)      Heat added = 8971.8 kJ.

(iii)      Change in IE = 7320.335 kJ.

---

**Problem 7.17:** A Carnot steam cycle operates between a source temperature of 311.06°C for a boiler pressure of 10 MPa and a sink temperature of 32.88°C (condenser pressure 5 kPa). Determine the ratio of net work to turbine work and the thermal efficiency of the cycle when all processes are reversible. Also determine specific steam consumption.   **(P.U. May 2006)**

**Solution: Given Data: Carnot cycle**

$$T_1 = 311.06°C = 311.06 + 273 = 584.06 \ K$$
$$T_2 = 32.88°C = 32.88 + 273 = 305.88 \ K$$

---

$p_1$ = 10 MPa = 100 bar

$p_2$ = 5 kPa = 0.05 bar

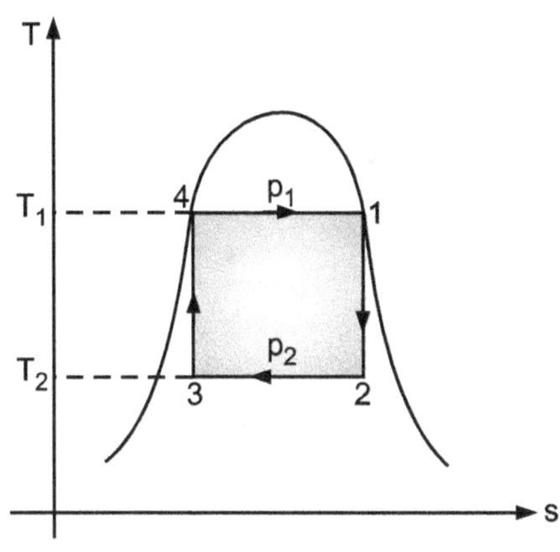

**Fig. 7.29**

At 100 bar pressure, from steam table,

$$T_s = 310.96°C$$
$$h_1 = h_g = 2727.70 \text{ kJ/kg}$$
$$h_4 = h_f = 1407.04 \text{ kJ/kg}$$
$$s_1 = s_g = 5.6198 \text{ kJ/kg·K}$$
$$s_4 = s_f = 3.3605 \text{ kJ/kg·K}$$

At 0.05 bar pressure,

$$T_s = 32.898°C, \ h_f = 137.77 \text{ kJ/kg}$$
$$h_{fg} = 2423.8 \text{ kJ/kg}$$
$$s_f = 0.4763 \text{ kJ/kg·K}$$
$$s_{fg} = 7.9197 \text{ kJ/kg·K}$$

To find dryness fraction at point 2, equate entropies at point 1 and point 2.

$$s_1 = s_{f2} + x_2 s_{fg2}$$
$$5.6198 = 0.4763 + x_2 \times 7.9197$$
$$x_2 = 0.64945$$
$$h_2 = h_{f2} + x_2 h_{fg2}$$
$$= 137.77 + 0.64945 \times 2423.8 = 1711.9 \text{ kJ/kg}$$

To find dryness fraction at point '3', equate entropies at point 4 and point 3.

$$s_4 = s_{f3} + x_3 s_{fg3}$$
$$\therefore \quad 3.3605 = 0.4763 + x_3 \times 7.9197$$
$$\therefore \quad x_3 = 0.3642$$
$$\therefore \quad h_3 = h_{f3} + x_3 h_{fg3}$$
$$= 137.77 + 0.3642 \times 2423.8 = 1020.7 \text{ kJ/kg}$$

$$\text{Turbine work} = w_T = h_1 - h_2 = 2727.70 - 1711.92 = 1015.78 \text{ kJ/kg}$$

$$\text{Pump work} = w_p = h_4 - h_3 = 1408.04 - 1020.67 = 387.37 \text{ kJ/kg}$$

$$\text{Heat supplied} = Q_s = h_1 - h_4 = 2727.70 - 1408.04 = 1319.66 \text{ kJ/kg}$$

$$\text{Net work} = w_{net} = w_T - w_p = 1015.78 - 387.37 = 628.41 \text{ kJ/kg}$$

$$\text{Work ratio} = \frac{w_T - w_p}{w_T} = \frac{w_{net}}{w_T} = \frac{628.41}{1015.78} = \textbf{0.6186}$$

$$\text{Thermal efficiency} = \eta_{th} = \frac{w_{net}}{Q_s} = \frac{628.41}{1319.66} = \textbf{0.4762 or 47.62\%}$$

$$\text{Specific steam consumption} = \frac{3600}{w_{net}} = \frac{3600}{628.41} = \textbf{5.729 kg/kW-hr}$$

**Problem 7.18:** A steam power plant operating on Rankine cycle receives steam from a boiler at 3.5 MPa and 350°C. It is exhausted to condenser at 10 kPa. Calculate:

(i)   Energy supplied per kg of steam generated in a boiler.

(ii)  Quality of steam entering the condenser.

(iii) Rankine cycle efficiency considering feed pump work.

(iv)  Specific steam consumption.

**Solution: Given:**

$$p_1 = 3.5 \text{ MPa} = 35 \text{ bar}$$
$$T_1 = 350°C$$
$$p_2 = 10 \text{ kPa} = 0.1 \text{ bar}$$

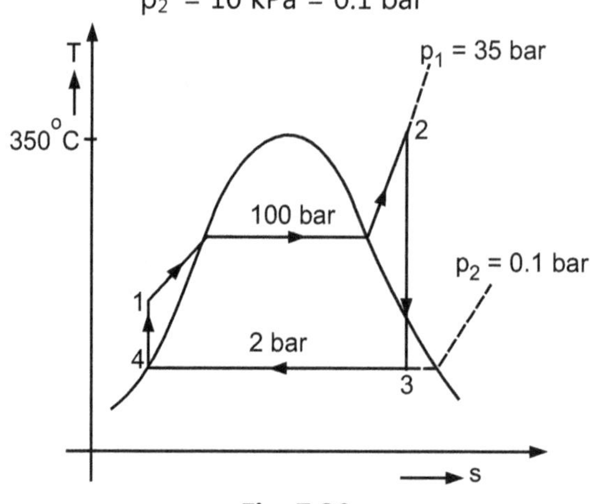


**Fig. 7.30**

From steam table, at 0.1 bar,

$$h_4 = h_f = 191.8 \text{ kJ/kg}$$

$$w_p = \frac{p_1 - p_2}{10} = 3.49 \text{ kJ/kg} = h_1 - h_4$$

$\therefore \qquad\qquad h_1 = 195.29 \text{ kJ/kg}$

and $h_2$ corresponding to 35 bar and 350°C = 3106.45 kJ/kg

For isentropic process,　　　　$s_2 = s_3$

$$s_2 = s_{f3} + x_3\, s_{fg3}$$

$s_2$ at 35 bar and 350°C $= 6.663$ kJ/kg by interpolation.

$\therefore$　　　　$6.663 = 0.649 + x_3 \times 7.502$

$\therefore$　　　　$x_3 = 0.8016$

and　　　　$h_3 = h_{f3} + x_3\, h_{fg3}$

$$= 191.8 + 0.8016 \times 2392.9 = 2110.075$$

$$= 2110.075 \text{ kJ/kg}$$

$\therefore$　　Heat supplied $= h_2 - h_1 = 2911.16$ kJ/kg

Work of turbine $= w_T = h_2 - h_3$

$$= 3106.45 - 2110.075 = \textbf{996.375 kJ/kg}$$

Rankine efficiency $= \eta_{rankine} = \dfrac{w_T - w_p}{\text{Heat supplied}}$

$$= \frac{996.375 - 3.49}{2911.6} = \textbf{0.3410 or 34.10\%}$$

Specific steam consumption $= 55 = \dfrac{3600}{w_{net}} = \dfrac{3600}{992.88} = \textbf{3.63 kg/kW-hr}$

---

**Problem 7.19:** A steam plant using Rankine cycle generated steam at 10 bar and 380°C. Condensation occurs at 0.06 bar. Find out Rankine efficiency. What will be Carnot efficiency? Neglect feed pump work.

**Solution:** Rankine cycle,

$$p_1 = 10 \text{ bar, } T_{sup3} = 380°C,$$
$$p_b = 0.06 \text{ bar}$$

Neglecting pump work,

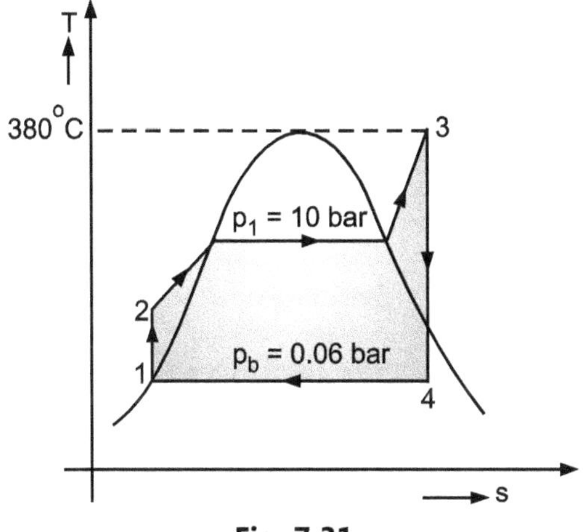


**Fig. 7.31**

At $p_1$ = 10 bar, $T_{sup3}$ = 380°C from steam table,

$$h_3 = 3240 \text{ kJ/kg}$$
$$s_3 = 7.4 \text{ kJ/kg·K}$$
$$T_{s3} = 179.88°C$$

At $p_b$ = 0.06 bar,

$$h_1 = h_{f4} = 151.50 \text{ kJ/kg}$$
$$h_{fg4} = 2416 \text{ kJ/kg}$$
$$s_{f4} = 0.5209 \text{ kJ/kg}$$
$$s_{fg4} = 7.8103 \text{ kJ/kg}$$
$$T_{s4} = 36.183°C$$

For isentropic process 3-4,

$$s_3 = s_4$$
$$s_3 = s_4$$
$$\therefore \quad 7.4 = s_{f4} + x_4\, s_{fg4}$$
$$\therefore \quad 7.4 = 0.5209 + x_4 \times 7.8103$$
$$\therefore \quad x_4 = 0.881$$
$$\therefore \quad h_4 = h_{f4} + x_4 \cdot h_{fg4}$$
$$= 151.50 + 0.881 \times 2416$$
$$h_4 = 2279.996 \text{ kJ/kg}$$

$$\text{Turbine work} = w_T = h_3 - h_4$$
$$= 3240 - 2279.996$$
$$= \textbf{960 kJ/kg}$$

$$\text{Heat supplied} = Q_s = h_3 - h_1$$
$$= 3240 - 151.50$$
$$= \textbf{3088.5 kJ/kg}$$

$$\text{Rankine efficiency} = \frac{w_T}{Q_s} = \frac{960}{3088.5}$$
$$= 0.3108$$
$$= \textbf{31.08\%}$$

$$\text{Carnot efficiency} = \frac{T_1 - T_2}{T_1}$$
$$= \frac{T_{s3} - T_{s4}}{T_{s3}}$$
$$= \frac{179.88 - 36.183}{179.88}$$
$$= 0.7988$$
$$= \textbf{79.88\%}$$

**Problem 7.20:** In a Rankine cycle, the steam at inlet to turbine is saturated at a pressure of 35 bar and the exhaust pressure is 0.2 bar.

Determine:

- (i)    Pump work
- (ii)   Turbine work
- (iii)  Rankine efficiency
- (iv)   Condenser heat flow
- (v)    Dryness at the end of expansion.

Assume flow rate of 9.5 kg/s.

**Solution:** Pressure and conditions of steam, at inlet to the turbine,

$$p_1 = 35 \text{ bar}$$
$$x = 1$$

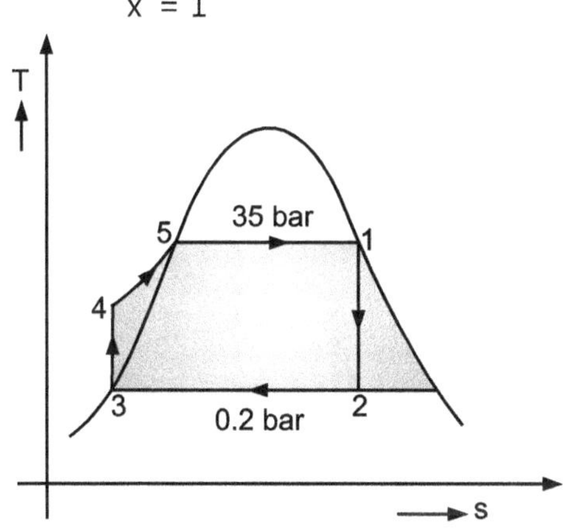


**Fig. 7.32**

Exhaust pressure, $p_2 = 0.2$ bar

Flow rate, $\dot{m} = 9.5$ kg/sec

From steam table,

At 35 bar, $h_1 = h_{g1} = 2802$ kJ/kg

$$c_{g1} = 6.1228 \text{ kJ/kg·K}$$

At 0.2 bar, $h_f = 251.5$ kJ/kg

$$h_{fg} = 2358.4 \text{ kJ/kg}$$

$$v_f = 0.001017 \text{ m}^3/\text{kg}; \ s_f = 0.8312 \text{ kJ/kg·K}$$

$$s_{fg} = 7.0773 \text{ kJ/kg·K}$$

**(i)   The pump work:**   Pump work $= (p_4 - p_3) \, v_f = (35 - 0.2) \times 10^5 \times 0.001017$

$$= 3.54 \text{ kJ/kg}$$

$\therefore$   Power required to drive the pump $= 9.5 \times 3.54$ kJ/sec

$$= 33.63 \text{ kW}$$

**(ii) The turbine work:**

$$s_1 = s_2 = s_{f2} + x_2 \cdot s_{fg2}$$
$$6.1228 = 0.8321 + x_2 \times 7.0773$$
$$x_2 = 0.747$$

$\therefore$
$$h_4 = h_{f2} + x_2 \cdot h_{fg2}$$
$$= 251.5 + 0.747 \times 2358.4 = 2013 \text{ kJ/kg}$$

$\therefore$ Turbine work $= \dot{m}\,(h_1 - h_2) = 9.5 \times (2802 - 2013)$
$$= \mathbf{7495.5 \text{ kW}}$$

**(iii) Rankine efficiency:**

$$\eta_{Rankine} = \frac{h_1 - h_2}{h_1 - h_{f2}} = \frac{2802 - 2013}{2802 - 251.5}$$

$$= \frac{789}{2550.5} = \mathbf{0.3093 \text{ or } 30.93\%}$$

**(iv) Condenser heat flow:**

The condenser heat flow $= \dot{m}\,(h_2 - h_{f3})$
$$= 9.5 \times [(2013) - 251.5]$$
$$= \mathbf{16734.25 \text{ kW}}$$

**(v) The dryness at the end of expansion, $x_2$:**

$$x_2 = 0.747 \text{ or } 74.7\%$$

---

**Problem 7.21:** Steam at 20 bar and 360° expands in a steam turbine to 0.08 bar. It is then condensed in a condenser to saturated water. The pump feeds back the water to the boiler. Assume ideal Rankine cycle and determine:

(i)    The net work done per kg of steam.

(ii)   The Rankine efficiency.

**Solution:**

**Given Data:**

$$p_1 = 20 \text{ bar}$$
$$T_1 = 360°C$$
$$p_b = 0.08 \text{ bar}$$

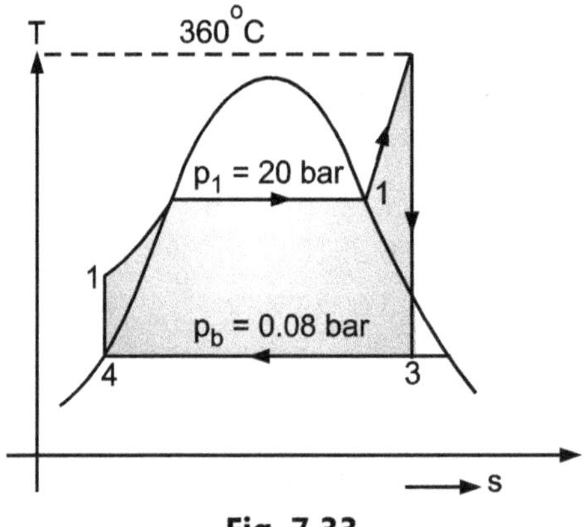

**Fig. 7.33**

From steam tables corresponding to condenser pressure of 8 bar,

$$h_4 = h_f = 173.86 \text{ kJ/kg}$$

We have,

$$w_p = \left[\frac{p_1 - p_b}{10}\right] \text{kJ/kg} = h_1 - h_4$$

$$= \frac{20 - 0.08}{10}$$

$$= 1.992 \text{ kJ/kg} = h_1 - h_4$$

$$\therefore \quad h_1 = w_p + h_4 = 1.992 + 173.86$$

$$h_1 = 175.852 \text{ kJ/kg}$$

$\therefore$ $h_2$ corresponding to 20 bar and 360°C = 3160.62 kJ/kg

At 350°C = 3138.6 kJ/kg and at 400°C = 3248.7 kJ/kg

$$\text{Difference is } \frac{110.1}{50°C} = 2.202 \text{ kJ/kg}$$

$$\therefore \quad 2.202 \times 10 = 22.02 \text{ kJ/kg}$$

$$\therefore \quad \text{At } 360°C = 3138.6 + 22.02$$

$$= 3160.62 \text{ kJ/kg}$$

Now, for isentropic process 2-3:

Entropy before expansion $s_2$ = Entropy after expansion $s_3$

To find $\quad s_2 = 7.1296$ at 400°C

6.9596 at 350°C

$$\frac{0.17}{50} = 0.0034 \text{ kJ/kg·K}$$

$$0.0034 \times 10 = 0.034 \text{ kJ/kg·K}$$

$$6.9596 + 0.034 = 6.9936 \text{ kJ/kg·K}$$

$$\therefore \quad 6.9936 = s_{f3} + x_3 \cdot s_{fg3} \text{ at condenser pressure}$$

$$= 0.5925 + x_3 \times 7.6371$$

$$\therefore \quad x_3 = 0.8382$$

$$h_3 = h_{f3} + x_3 \cdot h_{fg3} \text{ at condenser pressure}$$

$$= 173.86 + 0.8382 \times 2403.2$$

$$= 2188.15 \text{ kJ/kg}$$

$$\therefore \quad \text{Work done} = w_s = w_T - w_p = (h_2 - h_3) - w_p$$

$$= (3160.62 - 2188.15) - 1.992$$

$$= 970.478 \text{ kJ/kg}$$

and

$$\eta_{\text{Rankine}} = \frac{w_s}{q_i} = \frac{970.478}{h_2 - h_1}$$

$$= \frac{970.478}{3160.62 - 175.852} = \textbf{32.51\%}$$

## 7.6 REFRIGEARTION CYCLE

Refrigeration Engineering is by itself a very important branch of the very wide field of Mechanical Engineering and is nearer to and well acknowledged by the people whom it directly serves. We all know that in the scorching hot months of April and May, we like to take cold water and like to sit in air-conditioned building so as to derive maximum comfort. These benefits are directly bestowed by the science of refrigeration.

The term **Refrigeration** has come from the word **freeze** meaning to convert the state of the body from liquid to solid through the process of extracting the sensible heat by lowering the temperature and then the latent heat by changing the state of the body.

Thus the term **Refrigeration may be defined as a thermodynamic cyclic process whereby cold is produced or a temperature less than atmosphere or surroundings is produced.**

A machine that produces temperature less than that of the surroundings is called a **Refrigerator.**

**Refrigeration is the technique of producing cold and keeping temperature below those of the immediate surroundings.**

**Refrigeration means reduction of the temperature of a body below the general level of temperature of the surroundings.** It further implies the maintenance of the temperature of the body at a lower level of temperature than the surrounding.

## 7.7 TERMS AND DEFINITIONS IN REFRIGERATION

Before getting on the topic "Refrigeration", a few terms and conditions are required to be considered, since they are the ground work for what is to come.

1.    **Refrigeration** is the cooling of the selected space or object by the removal of heat from the space or object, thus lowering the temperature. This may be accomplished by natural means viz. using of ice, snow etc. or by mechanical refrigeration.

2.    **Refrigerants** are chemical compounds that are alternately compressed and condensed or cooled and then permitted to expand and evaporate extracting heat from the space or body thus producing low temperature.

3.    **Mechanical refrigeration** is the utilization of mechanical components and power for producing refrigeration.

4.    **Unit of refrigeration or Ratings for refrigeration :** The BTU is too small unit to be convenient in rating commercial refrigerating plants. The larger unit used in refrigerating practice is roughly defined as the number of BTU required to freeze 1 ton of water at 32°F (0°C) into ice at 32°F (0°C). The heat of fusion of ice is very nearly 144 BTU/lb. [80 kcal/kg $\approx$ 335 kJ/kg]. 1 ton of water is a smaller ton used in refrigeration practice and is equal to 2000 lbs. Therefore, to freeze 2000 lbs, there must be abstracted $2000 \times 144 = 288000$ BTU. This precise unit 288000 BTU is the definition of a **standard ton** of refrigeration.

To specify capacity, we must know how long it takes to perform a particular amount of refrigeration. One **standard commercial ton of refrigeration** is defined as 288000 BTU absorbed at a uniform rate during 24 hours. When the engineer speaks of a ton of refrigeration, he generally means a standard commercial ton. Thus, for capacity, a ton refrigeration is

$$\frac{288000}{24} = 12000 \text{ BTU/hr}$$

or

$$\frac{12000}{60} = 200 \text{ BTU/min.}$$

$$= 210 \text{ kJ/min. in S.I. units.}$$

$$= 3.516 \text{ (kJ/sec.} = \text{kW)}$$

$$\simeq 3.52 \text{ kW approx.}$$

**5.  Refrigerating effect :**  It is the amount of heat extracted from a body for the purpose of cooling a body or space. It is denoted by N or $Q_A$.

**6.  Heating load :**  It is defined as the amount of heat energy supplied to the body or space to be heated up by a heat pump.

It is denoted by (H) or $Q_R$.

Here,

$$H = N + \text{(Work supplied to compressor)}$$

$$= N + W$$

or

$$Q_R = Q_A + W$$

**7.  Coefficient of Performance (C.O.P) :** Two factors mentioned above are of great importance in deciding which of the refrigerants should be used for a given project of heat removal or addition.

The two factors that determine the coefficient of performance of a refrigerant are refrigerating effect and heat of compression.

Coefficient of performance is defined as the ratio of the desired effect to the energy supplied to get that effect.

$\therefore$

$$(C.O.P.)_R = \frac{\text{Desired effect}}{\text{Work or energy to compressor}}$$

$$= \frac{\text{Refrigerating effect}}{\text{Compressor work}}$$

$$= \frac{N}{W}$$

Similarly,

$$(C.O.P.)_H = \frac{H}{W} = \frac{N + W}{W} = 1 + \frac{N}{W}$$

$$= 1 + (C.O.P.)_R$$

The C.O.P. is therefore a rate or a measure of the efficiency of a refrigeration cycle or a heating cycle in the utilization of the expended energy during the compression process.

As seen from the above equations, the less energy expended in the compression process, the larger will be the C.O.P. of the refrigeration system and heating system (heat pump). Therefore, the refrigerant having the highest C.O.P. would probably be selected providing other qualities and other factors are equal.

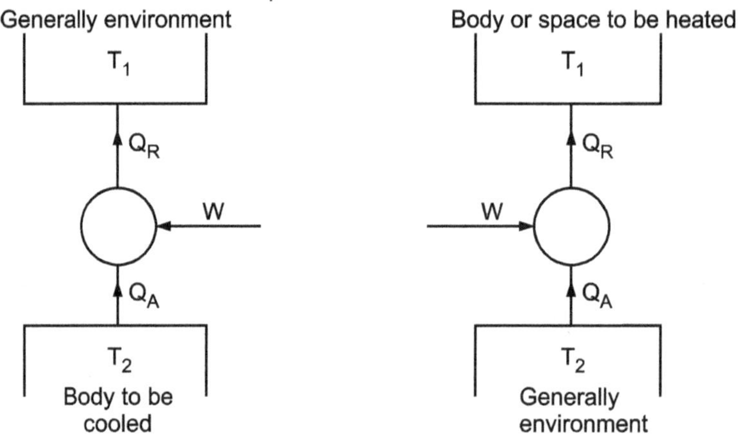


**Fig. 7.34**

Fig. 7.34 shows the two cases discussed above.

**8. Refrigeration load** : Once the temperature of the body is lowered below that of the surroundings, it will be natural that heat will flow from the surroundings to the refrigerated body. Consequently, it means that to maintain the temperature of the refrigerated body, the continuous extraction of heat from a body whose temperature is below the temperature of the surroundings, is essential.

The heat to be extracted from a body by a machine called refrigerator, to maintain the temperature of the body at the required level, is called **Refrigeration load.** This heat to be extracted from a body is also called as **Refrigerating effect.**

In general, the heat sources in a refrigerator may be classified in accordance with the following items :

- Heat transmission (Conduction, Convection and Radiation),
- Air leakage and ventilation,
- Product heat itself,
- Miscellaneous internal sources.

In a refrigerator, heat is being virtually pumped from the lower level to the higher level of temperature and is rejected at the high level of temperature. This process according to the second law of Thermodynamics, can only be performed by the aid of external work. Hence, a supply of power from an external source is required to operate a refrigerating machine.

## 7.8 VAPOUR COMPRESSION CYCLE

The modern refrigerating plants work on the vapour compression system. In this type of plant, the working fluid is a vapour which readily evaporates and condenses. This is the most common method of securing refrigeration. This refrigerating system is a closed system in which the fluid or refrigerant does not leave the system. It is circulated over and over again through the system, alternately condensing and evaporating. While evaporating, it absorbs heat from the cold body which is used as its latent heat, and it is converted into vapour from liquid. In condensing it rejects heat to the external hot body which is used to cool it. The refrigerator is, therefore, a latent heat pump, as it pumps its latent heat from the cold body and delivers it to the cooling medium.

Vapour compression system has several inherent advantages over air refrigeration, the principal ones being smaller size for a given refrigerating capacity, higher coefficient of performance i.e. lower power requirements for a given capacity and less complexity in both design and operation. The major disadvantages of the vapour compression system are being largely eliminated by improvements in design, which result in greater safety and prevention of leaks, and by the development of non-toxic, non-flammable vapour for use as refrigerants.

Let us take a look at, in general, what happens in a simple refrigeration cycle - vapour compression cycle, and the major components of which it is made. See Fig. 7.35.

Two different pressures exist in the cycle - the evaporating or low pressure in the "low side" and the condensing, or high pressure, in the "high side". These pressure areas are separated by two dividing points, one is the metering device where the refrigerant flow is controlled, and the other is at the compressor, where the vapour is compressed.

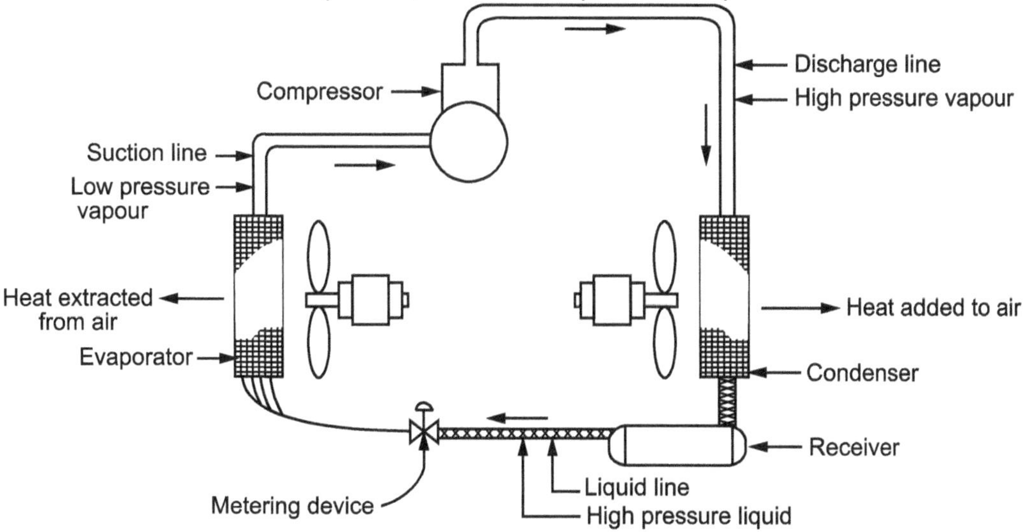


**Fig. 7.35 : Simple refrigeration system**

The **metering device** is a good place to start the trip through the cycle. This may be an expansion valve, a capillary tube, or other device to control the flow of the refrigerant into the **evaporator,** or cooling coil, as a low-pressure, low-temperature  refrigerant. The expanding refrigerant evaporates (changes state) as it goes through the cooling coil, where it removes the heat from the space in which the evaporator is located.

Heat will travel from the warmer air to the coils cooled by the evaporation of the refrigerant within the system, causing the refrigerant to **'boil'** and evaporate, changing it to a vapour.

Now this low-pressure, low-temperature vapour is drawn to the compressor, where it is compressed into a high-temperature, high-pressure vapour. The compressor discharges it to the **condenser,** so that it can give up the heat that it picked up in the cooling coil or evaporator. The refrigerant vapour is at a higher temperature than that of the air passing across the condenser (air-cooled condenser); therefore heat is transferred from the warmer refrigerant vapour to the cooler air.

In this process, as heat is removed from the vapour, a change of state takes place and the vapour is condensed back into a liquid, at a high pressure and a high temperature.

The liquid refrigerant now travels to the metering device where it passes through a small opening or orifice where a drop in pressure and temperature occurs, and then it enters the evaporator or cooling coil. As the refrigerant makes it way into the larger opening of the tubing or coil, it vaporizes, ready to start another cycle through the system.

Thus the major components of the vapour compression cycle are :

- Compressor,
- Condenser,
- Throttle or expansion valve (metering device), and
- Evaporator.

The mechanical refrigeration system described above is essentially the same whether the system be a **domestic refrigerator, a low-temperature freezer or a comfort air conditioning system**. Refrigerants will be different and size of equipment will vary greatly, but the principle of operation and the refrigeration cycle remains the same.

## 7.8.1 Flow Diagram

The devices necessary to carry out the vapour compression cycle are simple and are represented diagrammatically in Fig. 7.36.

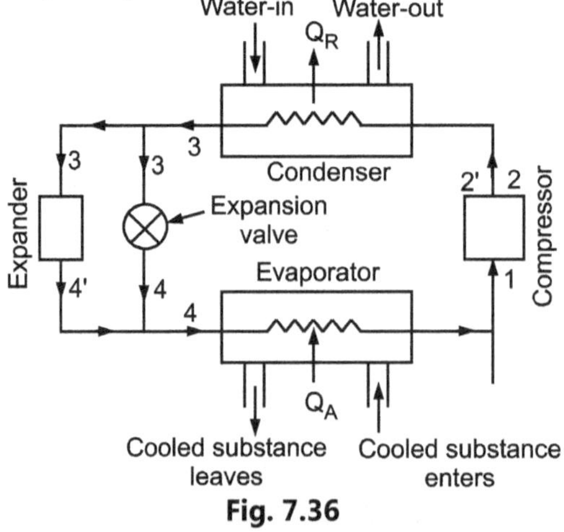


**Fig. 7.36**

In the ideal study here we will assume all flow is without friction, except flow through the expansion valve, and all processes except those in the condenser and evaporator (cold room) are adiabatic or isentropic.

Fig. 7.37 shows the reversed idealized vapour cycle 1-2-3-4 on the T-S diagram with numbers corresponding to those in Fig 7.36.

Starting from state 1, the vaporous refrigerant enters the compressor, which may be either a rotating or a reciprocating machine. The refrigerant is at a lower temperature and pressure as it enters the compressor. Ideally, this compression is reversible adiabatic or isentropic denoted by a vertical line 1-2 on T-S diagram. Actual compression process may not be isentropic but adiabatic with friction and is shown by 1-2' on the diagram of Fig. 7.37. This compression increases the pressure to $p_2$, say, thereby increasing the saturation temperature of the refrigerant at $p_2$. This temperature will be above the normal sink temperature $T_O$.

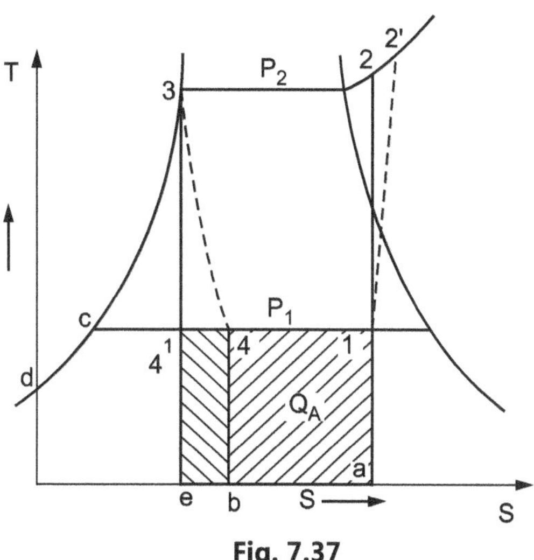


**Fig. 7.37**

After compression, the vapour at a higher pressure and higher temperature either at 2 or at 2' - enter the condenser. These condensers are either water-cooled condensers (large plants) or air-cooled condensers (small units like household refrigerator). The condenser removes the superheat if any, the latent heat of vaporization at higher pressure $p_2$. Thus, the vapours reject the heat to the cooling medium – either water or air. This condensation takes place at constant pressure $p_2$. After the heat rejection, the liquid is at the saturation temperature only - ideally and this state is shown by the point 3. Thus 2-3 is the heat rejection process.

In the state 3, liquid refrigerant either enters expander as in case of air cycle or it enters an expansion valve, which is a throttling valve separating the region of higher pressure from that of lower pressure. Expansion through an expander is again ideal - an isentropic - shown by a vertical line 3-4'. Expansion through an expansion valve is an isenthalpic process or constant enthalpy process and is shown by 3-4.

At 4, the very wet mixture of vapour and liquid enters the evaporator, absorbing heat $Q_A$ (doing refrigeration) from the surroundings, process 4-1. When expander is used, the condition of liquid is given by state 4' so that 4'-1 is the heat addition or refrigeration process. The surroundings may be a cold room, as the inside to the household refrigerator, or another substance. In commercial ice manufacture, cold brine circulates about the cans containing water, taking heat from the water for the purpose of freezing it. The brine then flows through the evaporator, where it is cooled again, hence to return to pick up more heat from the water in the cans. When air is to be cooled, it generally circulates directly about the evaporator coils. Thus, 4-1 or 4'-1 is the heat absorption process.

Thus, the cycle is complete and is repeated.

## 7.8.2  Analysis of Vapour compression cycle

The energy diagram is shown in Fig. 7.37. Considering ideal cycle i.e. isentropic compression, for the cycle, we have

$$Q_A - Q_R = W \text{ as usual.}$$

If the system is operating in a steady flow, with $\Delta K = 0$ and $W_{sf} = 0$ in the condenser, and in the evaporator, we can write,

$$Q_A = h_1 - h_4 \text{ or } h_1 - h_4' \text{ (for expander)}$$

and
$$Q_R = h_2 - h_3$$

$$\therefore \quad W = Q_A - Q_R = (h_1 - h_4) - (h_2 - h_3)$$
$$= (h_1 - h_2) - (h_4 - h_3) \text{ kJ/kg.}$$

or
$$= (h_1 - h_2) - (h_4' - h_3) \text{ kJ/kg.}$$

When expansion valve is used,

$$h_3 = h_{4=} h_4' \text{ as expansion or throttling is isenthalpic process.}$$

$\therefore$   When expansion valve is used,

$$W = \text{Work} = (h_1 - h_2) \text{ and is } -ve.$$

Negative sign indicates that the work is supplied from outside. Or the positive quantity is $= (h_2 - h_1)$.

$$\therefore \qquad \text{Work} = h_2 - h_1$$

When expander cylinder is used,

$$\text{Work of expansion} = h_3 - h_4'$$

$\therefore$   Net work=Work of compression – Work of expansion

$$= (h_2 - h_1) - (h_3 - h_4')$$
$$= W_c - W_e \text{ kJ/kg.}$$

From the study of T–S diagram, we have

Net work done (when expansion valve is used),

$$W = h_2 - h_1$$
$$= \text{Area 1-2-3-4-1}$$

and when expander is used,

$$W = \text{Net work done} = (h_2 - h_1) - (h_3 - h_4')$$
$$= [\text{Area 1-2-3-4-1}] - [\text{Area 3-4-4'-3}]$$
$$= \text{Area 1-2-3-4'-1}$$

Again, when expansion valve is used,

$$N = \text{Refrigerating effect} = h_1 - h_4$$

$$N = \text{Area a-1-4-b-a}$$

and when expander is used,

$$N = \text{Refrigerating effect} = h_1 - h_4'$$

$$= \text{Area a-1-4'-e-a}$$

Thus, the **coefficient of performance** of the ideal cycle for refrigeration is given by

$$\text{C.O.P.} = \frac{h_1 - h_4}{h_2 - h_1} = \frac{h_1 - h_3}{h_2 - h_1} \quad \text{(with expansion valve)}$$

$$= \frac{h_1 - h_4'}{(h_2 - h_1) - (h_3 - h_4')} \quad \text{(with expander)}$$

Cycle analysis done above is on the basis of unit mass of refrigerant.

∴   Mass flow rate of refrigerant per x ton refrigeration is

$$m_R = \frac{3.516 \, x}{\text{Refrigeration per kg}} \quad \text{kg/sec.}$$

where                $m_R$ = Mass of refrigerant kg/sec.

If $x_1$ is the dryness fraction of vapour at inlet to compressor and N is the speed of compressor in rpm, then,

$$V = x_1 \, V_{g_1} \text{ is volume of 1 kg}$$

$$= V_{g_1} \text{ is volume if } x_1 = 1$$

$$= V_{g_1} \times \frac{T_1}{T_{sat_1}} \text{ is volume if superheated.}$$

If d and *l* are the diameter and stroke of the compressor, swept volume and dimensions d and *l* are related as

$$m_R \, V = \left(\frac{\pi}{4} d^2 \, l\right) \times \frac{N}{60} \quad \text{for single acting.}$$

If $\eta_{vol.}$ is the volumetric efficiency of the compressor then,

$$m_R \, V = \frac{\pi \, d^2 \, l}{4} \times \eta_{vol.} \times \frac{N}{60}$$

### 7.8.3 Pressure-Enthalpy (Total heat) Chart

In the earlier treatment, the vapour compression cycle is represented on T-S diagram or chart for the vapour. That was necessary to understand the basic conception of the cycle. The pressure-total heat, or pressure-enthalpy chart is probably the most convenient chart for refrigerator calculations. This is the chart recommended by the refrigeration sub-committee of the Institution of Mechanical Engineers. The pressure is represented on the y-axis (ordinate) and enthalpy on the x-axis (abscissa). As on other charts the two main lines of saturated vapour and liquid are available. Fig. 7.38 shows a typical pressure-enthalpy (p-h) chart.

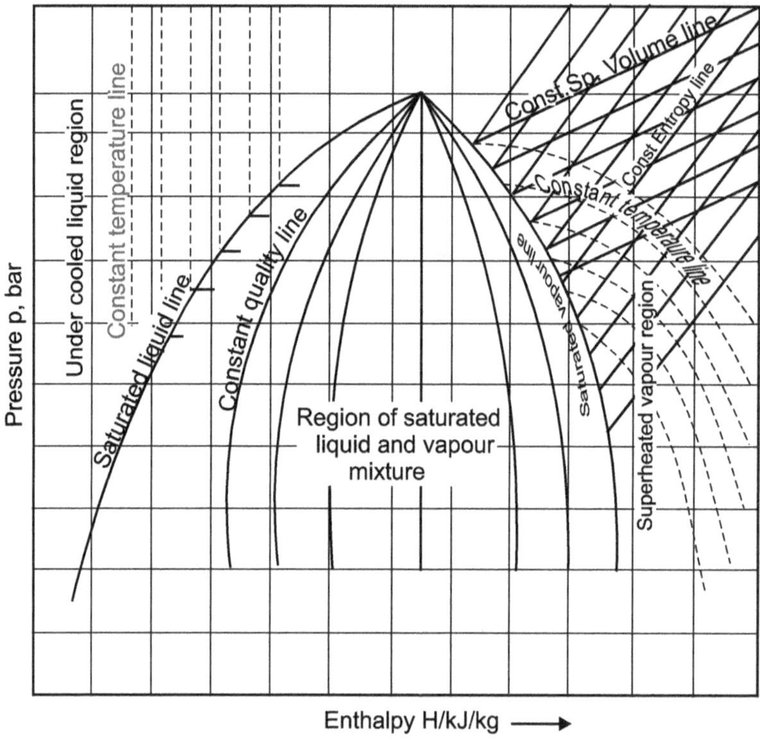


**Fig.7.38 : Typical p-h diagram for a refrigerant**

The portion of the diagram between the saturation liquid and saturated vapour represents equilibrium states of mechanical mixture of saturated liquid with saturated vapour. In this region, pressure and temperature are not independent variables. The region to the left of saturated liquid line is called undercooled liquid region. The undercooling takes place at constant pressure with decrease in temperature. The region to the right of saturated vapour line is termed as superheated vapour region. It is the result of heating saturated vapour at constant pressure, with increase in temperature and specific volume. In this region, lines of constant temperature and constant specific volume are drawn. Lines of constant entropy are also shown to facilitate plotting of isentropic compression. Except for liquid-vapour mixture region, a knowledge of any two properties will suffice to determine the state of the fluid at any point on the chart and hence permit evaluation from the chart of all other properties. Pressure, specific volume, temperature, enthalpy and entropy are given on the chart; internal energy is usually not plotted but can be readily calculated once the pressure, specific volume and enthalpy are known.

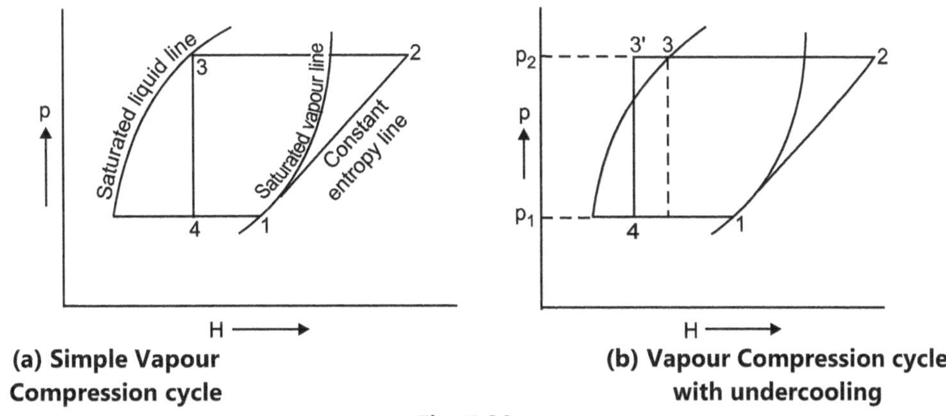


**(a) Simple Vapour Compression cycle**

**(b) Vapour Compression cycle with undercooling**

**Fig. 7.39**

The simple vapour compression cycle is represented on p-h chart in Fig. 7.39 (a). The vapour compression cycle with undercooling or subcooling is shown in Fig. 7.39 (b). Here the compressor draws dry saturated vapour from the evaporator at lower pressure $P_1$ corresponding to the lower temperature limit $T_1$ of the cycle. The vapour is then compressed to the upper pressure limit $P_2$ isentropically to 2. Hence 1-2 is the compression curve represented on a constant entropy line passing through point 1. Since, the vapour is dry and saturated at the beginning of compression, the vapour becomes superheated at the end of compression as represented by point 2. Then 2-3 is the condensation at the end of which all vapour is reduced to saturated liquid which is then throttled through the expansion valve along 3-4. [At 3, the saturated liquid is undercooled to the temperature less than saturated temperature corresponding to $P_2$. This undercooling takes place at constant pressure $P_2$. The undercooled liquid refrigerant is then throttled through the expansion valve along 3'-4']. At 4 or 4' we have the mixture of some vapour and rest liquid which is sent to the evaporator. The refrigerant takes its latent heat from the brine or the body or space to be cooled and forms dry and saturated vapour represented by point 1. Thus, cycle is completed.

The work done = $W = h_2 - h_1$

The heat extracted/refrigerating effect = $N = h_1 - h_4 = h_1 - h_3$

$\therefore$     Coefficient of performance = C.O.P. =    $h_1 - h_4 / h_2 - h_1$

The values of $h_1$, $h_2$, $h_3$ and $h_4$ can directly be read from the chart by projecting the points 1, 2, 3, 4 etc. on the abscissa.

# 7.9 PROPERTIES OF REFRIGERANTS

Refrigerants have to be non-toxic and non-flammable. Thermodynamically, there is no working substance which could be called an ideal refrigerant. Different substances seem to satisfy different requirements. A refrigerant which is ideally suited in a particular application may be a complete failure in the other application. In general, a refrigerant may be required to satisfy requirements which may be classified as thermodynamic, chemical and physical. The selection of refrigerant for a particular application, therefore, depends on satisfying its essential requirements.

**(i) Normal Boiling Temperature :**  The boiling temperature of the refrigerant at atmospheric pressure should be low. If the boiling temperature of the refrigerant is high at atmospheric pressure, the compressor should be operated at high vacuum. The high boiling temperature reduces capacity and operating cost of the system.

**(ii) Freezing Temperature :** The freezing temperature of refrigerant should be well below the operating evaporator temperature. Since the freezing temperatures of most of the refrigerants are below – 35°C, therefore this property is taken into consideration only in low temperature operation. Freezing temperature of water is 0°C and hence it can be used only in air-conditioning applications (above 0°C).

**(iii) Evaporator and Condenser Pressure :** The evaporator pressure should be positive and as near atmospheric as possible. If it is too low, it would result in a large volume of the suction vapour. If it is too high, overall high pressures, including condenser pressure, would result necessitating higher construction and consequently, higher cost of equipment. A positive pressure is required in order to eliminate the possibility of the entry of air and moisture into the system. The normal boiling point of the refrigerant should, therefore, be preferably lower than the refrigeration temperature.

**(iv) Critical Temperature and Pressure :** For high C.O.P. the critical temperature should be very high so that the condenser temperature line on p-h diagram is far removed from the critical point. This ensures reasonable refrigerating effect which becomes too small if the state of the liquid before expansion is near the critical point. Also, the critical pressure should be low so as to result in low condensing pressures.

The critical temperature of a refrigerant is the highest temperature at which it can be condensed to a liquid, regardless of a high pressure. It should be above the highest condensing temperature that might be encountered. If the critical temperature of a refrigerant is too near the designed condensing temperature, the excessive power consumption results.

Except of carbon dioxide for which the critical temperature is 31°C for most of the common refrigerants, critical temperature is much above the normal condensing temperature.

**(v) Volume of Suction Vapour :** The volume of the suction vapour required per unit is an indication of the size of the compressor. Reciprocating compressors are used with refrigerants with high pressures and small volumes of suction vapour. Centrifugal compressors are used with refrigerants with low pressure and large volumes of the suction vapour. The rotary compressors are used with refrigerants having intermediate pressures and volumes of suction vapour.

**(vi) Latent heat of vaporisation :** A refrigerant should have high latent heat of vaporisation at the evaporator temperature. The high latent heat results in high refrigerating effect per kg of refrigerant which reduces the mass of refrigerant to be circulated per ton of refrigeration.

**(vii) C.O.P. and Power Requirements :** For an ideal refrigerant operating between –15°C and 30°C condenser temperature, the theoretical C.O.P. or the reversed Carnot C.O.P. is 5.47. R-11 has the C.O.P. 5.09 which is closest to Carnot value. Practically, all common refrigerants have approximately the same C.O.P. and power requirement. C.O.P. of $CO_2$ is 2.56 and is due to the fact that its critical temperature is too low and the condensing temperature is very close to it. KW/TR value for R-11 is 0.694, while for $CO_2$ is 1.372.

## 7.9.1 Refrigerant-134a

The blended refrigerant-134a is an HFC and mainly has a zero ozone depletion potential and a low green house effect. It is a nonflammable and nonexplosive and is an excellent refrigerant to replace R-12 in many of the applications employing this R-12 refrigerant. Main drawback with this is refrigerant has a relatively high affinity of water or moisture. It has become the new industry-standard refrigerant for automotive airconditioning and refrigerator/freezer appliances. R-134a refrigerating performance suffers at lower temperatures (below −10°F). Some traditional R-12 applications have used alternatives other than R-134a for lower temperatures.

R-134a requires *polyolester* (POE) lubricants. Traditional mineral oils and alkyl benzenes do not mix with HFC refrigerants and their use with R-134a may cause operation problems or compressor failures. In addition, automotive AC systems may use poly alkaline glycols (PAGs), which are typically not seen in stationary equipment. Both POEs and PAGs will absorb moisture, and hold onto it, to a much greater extent than traditional lubricants. The moisture will promote reactions in the lubricant as well as the usual problems associated with water corrosion and acid formation. The best way to dry a wet HFC system is to rely on the filter drier. Deep vacuum will remove "free" water, but not the water that has been absorbed into the lubricant.

The physical and thermodynamic properties of R-134a approach those of R-12 closely enough to provide similar levels of performance in systems with evaporator temperature of −7°C and above. Heat transfer coefficient is higher than R-12. Refrigerant-134a has a miscibility problem with mineral oils normally used with halocarbon refrigerants. But, when the mineral oils are replaced with ester-based synthetic lubricants, the miscibility problem is eliminated.

These refrigerants are primarily used for air conditioning and have replaced R22 in many applications. R134a has a relatively low pressure and therefore about 50% larger compressor displacement is required when compared to R22, and this can make the compressor more costly. Also larger tubing and components result in higher system cost. R134a has been very successfully used in screw chillers where short pipe lengths minimize costs associated with larger tubing. R134a also fi nds a niche where extra high condensing temperatures are needed and in many transport applications.

Comparative numericals for R-12 and R-134a are as follows :

| Suction Temperature | Pressure | | Ref. Effect kJ/kg | |
|---|---|---|---|---|
| | R-12 | R-134a | R-12 | R-134a |
| 40°F (4.44°C) | 3.51 atm | 3.3846 atm | 215.84 | 264.45 |
| 20°F (−6.67°C) | 2.4326 | 2.255 | 206.54 | 252.811 |
| 0°F (−17.78°C) | 1.6242 | 1.4426 | 197.00 | 240.83 |
| − 20°F (−28.89°C) | 1.0853 | 0.8812 | 187.20 | 227.69 |
| − 40°F (−40°C) | 0.4300 | 0.5176 | 177.28 | 216.00 |

Properties of R 134a are given in below

**Properties of R 134a**

| Temp. T°C | Sat. Pre., $P_{sat}$ kPa | Specific volume, m³/kg | | Internal energy kJ/kg | | | Enthalpy kJ/kg | | | Entropy, kJ/kg.K | | |
| | | Sat. liquid, $V_f$ | Sat vapor, $V_g$ | Sat liquid $u_f$ | Evap., $u_{fg}$ | Sat vapor, $u_g$ | Sat liquid $h_f$ | Evap., $h_{fg}$ | Sat vapor, $h_g$ | Sat liquid $s_f$ | Evap., $S_{fg}$ | Sat. vapor, $S_g$ |
|---|---|---|---|---|---|---|---|---|---|---|---|---|
| −40 | −51.25 | 0.0007050 | 0.36081 | −0.036 | 207.40 | 207.37 | 0.30 | 225.86 | 225.86 | 0.00000 | 0.96866 | 0.96866 |
| −38 | 56.86 | 0.0007083 | 0.32732 | 2.475 | 206.04 | 208.51 | 2.515 | 224.61 | 227.12 | 0.01072 | 0.95511 | 0.96584 |
| −36 | 62.95 | 0.0007112 | 0.29751 | 4.992 | 204.67 | 209.66 | 5.037 | 223.35 | 228.39 | 0.02138 | 0.94176 | 0.96315 |
| −34 | 69.56 | 0.0007142 | 0.27090 | 7.517 | 203.29 | 210.81 | 7.566 | 222.09 | 229.65 | 0.03199 | 0.92859 | 0.96058 |
| −32 | 76.71 | 0.0007172 | 0.24711 | 10.05 | 201.91 | 211.96 | 10.10 | 220.81 | 230.91 | 0.04253 | 0.91560 | 0.95813 |
| −30 | 84.43 | 0.0007203 | 0.22580 | 12.59 | 200.52 | 213.11 | 12.65 | 219.52 | 232.17 | 0.05301 | 0.90278 | 0.95579 |
| −28 | 92.76 | 0.0007234 | 0.20666 | 15.13 | 199.12 | 214.25 | 15.20 | 218.22 | 233.43 | 0.06344 | 0.89012 | 0.95356 |
| −26 | 101.73 | 0.0007265 | 0.18946 | 17.69 | 197.72 | 215.40 | 17.76 | 216.92 | 234.68 | 0.07382 | 0.87762 | 0.95144 |
| −24 | 111.37 | 0.0007297 | 0.17395 | 20.25 | 196.30 | 216.55 | 20.33 | 215.259 | 235.92 | 0.08414 | 0.86527 | 0.94941 |
| −22 | 121.72 | 0.0007329 | 0.15995 | 22.82 | 194.88 | 217.70 | 22.91 | 214.26 | 237.17 | 0.09441 | 0.85307 | 0.94748 |
| −20 | 132.82 | 0.0007362 | 0.14729 | 25.39 | 193.45 | 218.84 | 25.49 | 212.91 | 238.41 | 0.10463 | 0.84101 | 0.94564 |
| −18 | 144.69 | 0.0007396 | 0.13583 | 27.98 | 192.01 | 219.98 | 28.09 | 211.55 | 239.64 | 0.11481 | 0.82908 | 0.94389 |
| −16 | 157.38 | 0.0007430 | 0.12542 | 30.57 | 190.56 | 221.13 | 30.69 | 210.18 | 240.87 | 0.12493 | 0.81729 | 0.94222 |
| −14 | 170.93 | 0.0007464 | 0.11597 | 33.17 | 189.09 | 222.27 | 33.30 | 208.79 | 242.09 | 0.13501 | 0.80561 | 0.94063 |
| −12 | 185.37 | 0.0007499 | 0.10736 | 35.78 | 187.62 | 223.40 | 35.92 | 207.38 | 243.30 | 0.14504 | 0.79406 | 0.93911 |
| −10 | 200.74 | 0.0007535 | 0.099516 | 38.40 | 186.14 | 224.54 | 38.55 | 205.96 | 244.51 | 0.15504 | 0.78263 | 0.93266 |
| −8 | 217.09 | 0.0007571 | 0.092352 | 41.03 | 184.64 | 225.67 | 41.19 | 204.52 | 254.72 | 0.16498 | 0.77130 | 0.93629 |
| −6 | 234.44 | 0.0007608 | 0.085802 | 43.66 | 183.13 | 226.80 | 43.84 | 203.07 | 246.91 | 0.17489 | 0.76008 | 0.93497 |
| −4 | 252.85 | 0.0007646 | 0.079804 | 46.31 | 181.61 | 227.92 | 46.50 | 201.60 | 248.10 | 0.18476 | 0.74896 | 0.93372 |
| −2 | 272.36 | 0.0007684 | 0.074304 | 48.96 | 180.08 | 229.24 | 49.17 | 220.11 | 249.28 | 0.19459 | 0.73794 | 0.93253 |
| 0 | 293.01 | 0.0007723 | 0.069255 | 51.63 | 178.53 | 230.16 | 51.86 | 198.60 | 250.45 | 0.20439 | 0.72701 | 0.93139 |
| 2 | 314.84 | 0.0007763 | 0.064612 | 54.30 | 176.97 | 231.27 | 54.55 | 197.07 | 251.61 | 0.21415 | 0.71617 | 0.93031 |
| 4 | 337.90 | 0.0007804 | 0.060338 | 56.99 | 175.39 | 232.38 | 57.26 | 195.51 | 252.77 | 0.22387 | 0.70540 | 0.92927 |
| 6 | 362.23 | 0.0007845 | 0.056398 | 59.68 | 173.80 | 233.48 | 59.97 | 193.94 | 253.91 | 0.23356 | 0.69471 | 0.92828 |
| 8 | 387.88 | 0.0007887 | 0.052762 | 62.39 | 172.19 | 234.58 | 62.69 | 192.35 | 255.04 | 0.24323 | 0.68410 | 0.92733 |
| 10 | 414.89 | 0.0007930 | 0.049403 | 65.10 | 170.56 | 235.67 | 65.43 | 190.73 | 256.16 | 0.25286 | 0.67356 | 0.92641 |
| 12 | 443.31 | 0.0007975 | 0.046295 | 67.83 | 168.92 | 236.75 | 68.18 | 189.09 | 257.25 | 0.26246 | 0.66308 | 0.92554 |
| 14 | 473.19 | 0.0008020 | 0.043417 | 70.57 | 167.26 | 237.83 | 70.95 | 187.42 | 258.37 | 0.27204 | 0.65266 | 0.92470 |
| 16 | 504.58 | 0.0008066 | 0.040748 | 73.32 | 165.58 | 238.90 | 73.70 | 185.73 | 259.46 | 0.28159 | 0.64230 | 0.92389 |
| 18 | 537.52 | 0.0008113 | 0.038271 | 76.08 | 163.88 | 239.96 | 76.52 | 184.01 | 260.53 | 0.29112 | 0.63198 | 0.92310 |

| Temp. T°C | Sat. Pre., $P_{sat}$ kPa | Specific volume, m³/kg | | Internal energy kJ/kg | | | Enthalpy kJ/kg | | | Entropy, kJ/kg.K | | |
|---|---|---|---|---|---|---|---|---|---|---|---|---|
| | | Sat. liquid, $V_f$ | Sat vapor, $V_g$ | Sat liquid $u_f$ | Evap., $u_{fg}$ | Sat vapor, $u_g$ | Sat liquid $h_f$ | Evap., $h_{fg}$ | Sat vapor, $h_g$ | Sat liquid $s_f$ | Evap., $s_{fg}$ | Sat. vapor, $s_g$ |
| 22 | 608.27 | 0.0008210 | 0.033828 | 81.64 | 160.42 | 241.06 | 82.14 | 180.49 | 262.64 | 0.31011 | 0.61149 | 0.92160 |
| 24 | 646.18 | 0.0008261 | 0.031834 | 84.44 | 158.65 | 243.10 | 84.98 | 178.69 | 263.67 | 0.31958 | 0.60130 | 0.92088 |
| 26 | 685.84 | 0.0008313 | 0.029978 | 87.26 | 156.97 | 244.12 | 87.33 | 176.85 | 264.68 | 0.32903 | 0.59115 | 0.92018 |
| 28 | 727.31 | 0.0008366 | 0.28242 | 90.09 | 155.05 | 245.14 | 90.69 | 174.99 | 265.68 | 0.33846 | 0.58102 | 0.91948 |
| 30 | 770.64 | 0.0008421 | 0.026622 | 92.93 | 153.22 | 246.14 | 93.58 | 173.08 | 266.66 | 0.34789 | 0.57091 | 0.91879 |
| 32 | 815.89 | 0.0008478 | 0.024108 | 95.79 | 151.35 | 247.14 | 96.48 | 171.14 | 267.62 | 0.35730 | 0.56082 | 0.91811 |
| 34 | 863.11 | 0.0008586 | 0.023691 | 98.66 | 149.46 | 248.12 | 99.40 | 169.17 | 268.57 | 0.36670 | 0.55074 | 0.91743 |
| 36 | 912.36 | 0.0008595 | 0.022364 | 101.55 | 147.54 | 249.08 | 102.33 | 167.16 | 269.49 | 0.37609 | 0.54066 | 0.91675 |
| 38 | 963.68 | 0.0008657 | 0.021119 | 104.45 | 145.58 | 250.04 | 105.29 | 165.10 | 270.39 | 0.38548 | 0.53058 | 0.91606 |
| 40 | 1017.1 | 0.0008720 | 0.019952 | 107.38 | 143.60 | 250.97 | 108.26 | 163.00 | 271.27 | 0.39486 | 0.5209 | 0.91536 |
| 42 | 1078.8 | 0.0008786 | 0.018855 | 110.32 | 141.58 | 251.89 | 111.26 | 160.86 | 272.12 | 0.40425 | 0.51039 | 0.91464 |
| 44 | 1130.7 | 0.0008854 | 0.017825 | 113.28 | 139.52 | 252.80 | 114.28 | 158.67 | 272.95 | 0.41363 | 0.50027 | 0.91391 |
| 46 | 1191.0 | 0.0008924 | 0.016853 | 116.26 | 137.42 | 253.68 | 117.32 | 156.43 | 273.75 | 0.42302 | 0.49012 | 0.91315 |
| 48 | 1253.6 | 0.0008996 | 0.015939 | 119.26 | 135.29 | 254.55 | 120.39 | 154.14 | 274.53 | 0.43242 | 0.47993 | 0.91236 |
| 52 | 1386.2 | 0.0009150 | 0.014265 | 125.33 | 130.88 | 256.21 | 126.49 | 149.39 | 275.98 | 0.45126 | 0.45941 | 0.91067 |
| 56 | 1529.1 | 0.0009317 | 0.12771 | 131.49 | 126.28 | 257.77 | 132.91 | 144.39 | 277.30 | 0.47018 | 0.43863 | 0.90880 |
| 60 | 1682.8 | 0.0009498 | 0.011434 | 137.76 | 121.46 | 259.22 | 139.36 | 139.10 | 278.46 | 0.48920 | 0.41749 | 0.90669 |
| 65 | 1891.0 | 0.0009750 | 0.009950 | 145.77 | 115.05 | 260.82 | 147.62 | 132.02 | 279.64 | 0.51320 | 0.39039 | 0.90359 |
| 70 | 2118.2 | 0.0010037 | 0.004642 | 154.01 | 108.14 | 262.15 | 156.13 | 124.32 | 280.46 | 0.53755 | 0.36227 | 0.89982 |
| 75 | 2365.8 | 0.0010372 | 0.007480 | 162.53 | 100.60 | 263.13 | 164.98 | 115.85 | 270.82 | 0.56241 | 0.33272 | 0.89512 |
| 80 | 2635.3 | 0.0010772 | 0.006435 | 171.40 | 92.23 | 263.63 | 174.24 | 106.35 | 280.59 | 0.58800 | 0.30111 | 0.88912 |
| 85 | 2928.2 | 0.0011270 | 0.005486 | 180.77 | 82.67 | 263.44 | 184.07 | 95.44 | 279.51 | 0.61473 | 0.26644 | 0.88117 |
| 90 | 3246.9 | 0.0011932 | 0.004599 | 190.79 | 71.29 | 262.18 | 194.76 | 92.35 | 277.11 | 0.64336 | 0.22674 | 0.87010 |
| 95 | 3594.1 | 0.0012933 | 0.003726 | 202.40 | 46.47 | 258.87 | 207.05 | 65.21 | 272.26 | 0.67578 | 0.17711 | 0.85289 |
| 100 | 3975.1 | 0.0015269 | 0.002630 | 118.72 | 29.19 | 247.91 | 224.79 | 3359 | 258.37 | 0.72217 | 0.08999 | 0.81215 |

**Problem 7.22:** A Refrigeration circuit is to cool a room at 0°C using outside air at 30°C to reject the heat. The refrigerant is R134a. The temperature difference at the evaporator and the condenser is 5 K. Find the Carnot COP for the process, the Carnot COP for the refrigeration cycle and the ideal vapour compression cycle COP when using R134a.The temperature at the end of compression is $40^0$C.

**Solution:**

$$\text{Carnot COP for 0°C (273 K) to 30°C (303 K)} = \frac{273}{(303-273)}$$

$$= 9.1$$

Refrigeration cycle evaporating –5°C, condensing 35°C,

$$\text{Carnot COP} = \frac{268}{(308-268)}$$

$$= 6.7$$

For R134a

| Temp. T (°C) | Sat liquid $h_f$ | Evap., $h_{fg}$ | Sat vapor, $h_g$ | $c_p$ |
|---|---|---|---|---|
| | | kJ/kg | | kJ/kg K |
| –6 | 43.84 | 203.07 | 246.91 | 0.87104 |
| –4 | 46.50 | 201.60 | 248.10 | 0.8796 |
| 34 | 99.40 | 169.17 | 268.57 | 1.0954 |
| 36 | 102.33 | 167.16 | 269.49 | 1.1114 |

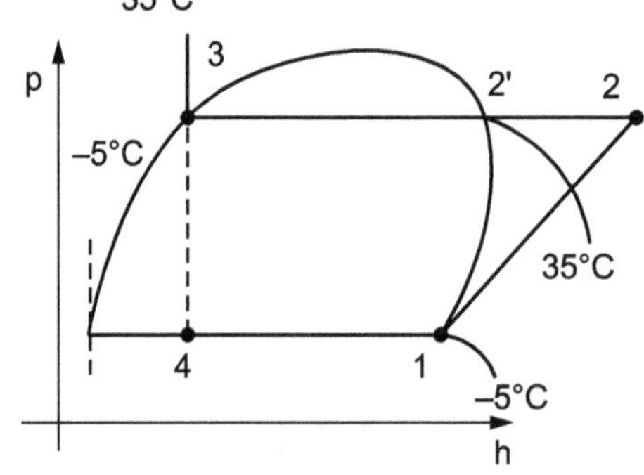


**Fig. 7.40**

The properties at $-5^0$ C and $35^0$ C are calculated from the tables using interpolation.

e.g.
$$h_1 = \frac{(246.91+248.10)}{2}$$

$$= 247.505 \text{ kJ/ kg}$$

$$h_2 = h_g + c_p\,(\,T_{sup} - T_{sat})$$

$$= 269.03 + 1.1034\,(40 - 35)$$
$$= 274.547\ \text{kJ/ kg}$$
$$h_3 = h_4 = 100.865\ \text{kJ/ kg}$$

| Temp. T (°C) | Sat liquid $h_f$ | Evap., $h_{fg}$ | Sat vapor, $h_g$ | $c_p$ |
|---|---|---|---|---|
| | kJ/kg | | | kJ/kg K |
| −5 | 45.17 | 202.335 | 247.505 | 0.87532 |
| 35 | 100.865 | 168.165 | 269.03 | 1.1034 |

$$\text{Cooling effect} = h_1 - h_4$$
$$= 146.64\ \text{kJ/kg}$$
$$\text{Compressor energy input} = h_2 - h_1$$
$$= 274.547 - 247.505$$
$$= 27.042\ \text{kJ/kg}$$

Ideal R134a vapour compression cycle

$$\text{COP} = \frac{146.64}{27.042} = 5.42$$

**Problem 7.23:** An ideal refrigeration cycle operates with R134a as the working fluid. The temperature of refrigerant in the condenser and evaporator are 40°c and -20°c respectively. The mass flow rate of refrigerant is 0.1 kg/s. Determine the cooling capacity and cop of the plant. Take enthalpy of refrigerant vapour at the end of compression as 276 kJ/kg.

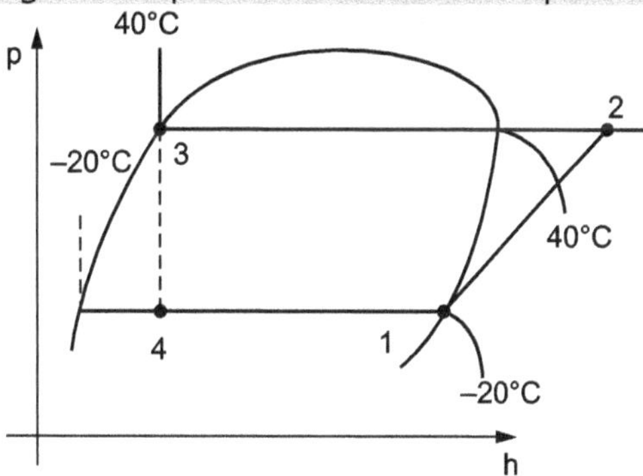


**Fig. 7.41**

**Solution:**

The properties at -20$^0$ C and 40$^0$ C are taken from the tables.

| Temp. T (°C) | Sat liquid $h_f$ | Evap., $h_{fg}$ | Sat vapor, $h_g$ |
|---|---|---|---|
| | kJ/kg | | |
| −20 | 25.49 | 212.91 | 238.41 |
| 40 | 108.26 | 163.00 | 271.27 |

$$h_1 = 238.41 \text{ kJ/kg}$$
$$h_2 = 276 \text{kJ/kg}$$
$$h_3 = h_4 = 108.26 \text{ kJ/kg}$$
$$\text{Refrigerating Effect} = h_1 - h_4$$
$$= 238.41 - 108.26$$
$$= 130.15 \text{kJ/kg}$$
$$\text{Compression Work} = h_2 - h_1 = 37.59 \text{kJ/kg}$$
$$\text{COP} = \frac{\text{Refrigerating Effect}}{\text{Compression Work}}$$
$$= \frac{130.15}{37.59} = 3.46$$
$$\text{Cooling Capacity} = \text{Refrigerating Effect} \times \text{Mass Flow Rate of Refrigerant}$$
$$= 130.15 \times 0.1$$
$$= \mathbf{13.015 \ kW}$$
$$= \mathbf{13.015 / 3.516}$$
$$= \mathbf{3.7 \ TR}$$

**Example 7.24 :** *A R-134a refrigeration system produces 10 TR at evaporating temperature – 10 ℃ and the condensing temperature of 40 ℃. The absolute pressure measured at the inlet and outlet of evaporator are 2 bar and 1.7 bar respectively. Considering there are no superheat and subcooling effects, calculate the following parameters with or without drop in pressure in the evaporator.*

*(i)  Refrigerating effect.*

*(ii)  Mass flow rate.*

*(iii)  Power required in kW/TR.*

*(iv)  COP.*

**Solution :** Capacity 10 TR = **35.16 kW**

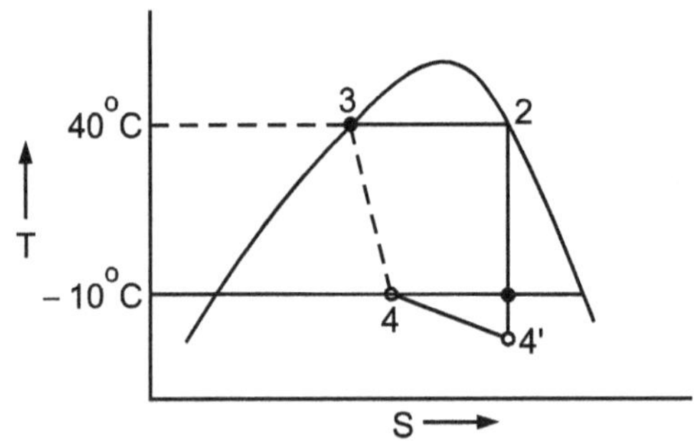


**Fig. 7.42**

**(I) Without drop in pressure :** Assuming dry and saturated condition after compression,

$$h_2 = 419.58 \text{ kJ/kg},$$

$$S_2 = 1.7115 \text{ kJ/kgK}$$

$$S_1 = 0.9509 + x_1 (1.7337 - 0.9509)$$

$$x_1 = \frac{1.7115 - 0.9509}{0.7828} = \frac{0.7606}{0.7828} = 0.9716$$

$$\therefore \quad h_1 = 186.78 + 0.9716 \times (392.75 - 186.78)$$

$$= \textbf{386.9 kJ/kg}$$

$$\therefore \quad \text{Work done/kg} = h_2 - h_1$$

$$= 419.58 - 366.9$$

$$= \textbf{32.68 kJ/kg}$$

$$\text{Refrigerating effect/kg} = h_1 - h_4 = h_1 - h_3$$

$$= 386.9 - 256.35$$

$$= \textbf{130.55 kJ/kg} \qquad \text{... Ans.}$$

$$\text{Mass flow rate} = \frac{35.16}{130.55} = \textbf{0.2693 kg/sec} \qquad \text{... Ans.}$$

$$\text{Power required} = m_r (h_2 - h_1)$$

$$= 0.2693 (419.58 - 386.9)$$

$$= \textbf{8.8 kW} \qquad \text{... Ans.}$$

$$\text{C.O.P.} = \frac{N}{W} = \frac{130.75}{32.68} = 3.995 \approx \textbf{4} \qquad \text{... Ans.}$$

**Example 7.25 :** *A R-134a refrigeration system works with evaporator temperature of -10 $^0$ C and condenser temperature of 40 $^0$.Estimate COP of simple saturation cycle if enthalpy at the end of compression is 290 kJ/ kg.Also find mass flow rate of refrigerant for a plant of capacity 10 TR if the actual COP is 50 % of the theoretical.*

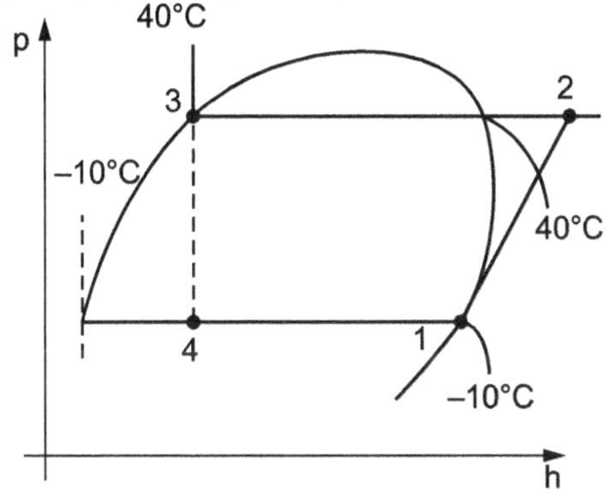


**Fig. 7.43**

### Solution:

The properties at $-10^0$ C and $40^0$ C are taken from the tables.

| Temp. T (°C) | Sat liquid $h_f$ | Evap., $h_{fg}$ | Sat vapor, $h_g$ |
|---|---|---|---|
| | | kJ/kg | |
| −10 | 38.55 | 205.96 | 244.51 |
| 40 | 108.26 | 163.00 | 271.27 |

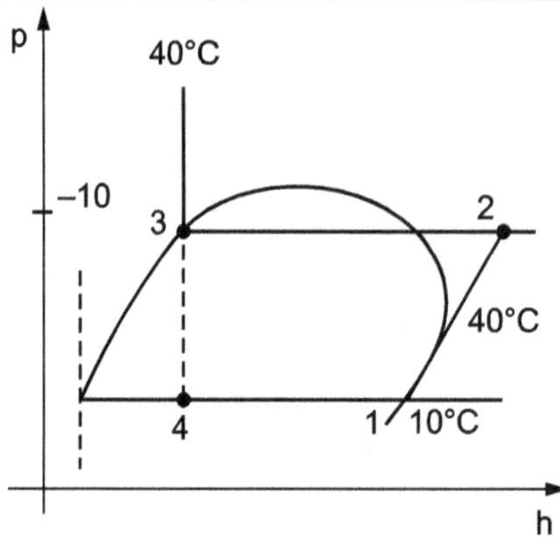


**Fig. 7.44**

$$h_1 = 244.51 \text{kJ/kg}$$
$$h_2 = 290 \text{kJ/kg}$$
$$h_3 = h_4$$
$$= 108.26/\text{kg}$$

$$\text{Refrigerating Effect} = h_1 - h_4$$
$$= 244.51 - 108.26$$
$$= 136.25 \text{ kJ/kg}$$

$$\text{Compression Work} = h_2 - h_1$$
$$= 45.49 \text{ kJ/kg}$$

$$\text{COP} = \frac{\text{Refrigerating Effect}}{\text{Compression Work}} = \frac{136.25}{45.49} = 2.995$$

$$\text{Cooling Capacity} = \text{Refrigerating Effect} \times \text{Mass Flow Rate of Refrigerant}$$
$$= \textbf{Actual COP} \times \text{Compression Work} \times \text{Mass Flow Rate of Refrigerant}$$
$$10 \times 3.516 = 0.5 \times 2.995 \times 45.49 \times m_r$$
$$m_r = \textbf{0.516 kg/s}$$

**Example 7.26 :** *A R-134a refrigeration system works with evaporator temperature of -10 $^0$ C and condenser temperature of 40 $^0$.Calculate diameter and stroke of a single cylinder reciprocating compressor if L/D = 1.2,capcity of the plant is 2 TR and actual COP is 75 % of the* *theoretical. Temperature of the refrigerant at the end of compression is 47 $^0$C. Take $c_p$ = 1.145 kJ/ kg K.The compressor runs at 400 rpm.*

**Solution:**

The properties at $-10^0$ C and $40^0$ C are taken from the tables.

| Temp. T (°C) | Sat liquid $h_f$ | Evap., $h_{fg}$ | Sat vapor, $h_g$ | Specific volume, m³/kg | |
|---|---|---|---|---|---|
| | | kJ/kg | | Sat. liquid, $V_f$ | Sat vapor, $V_g$ |
| −10 | 38.55 | 205.96 | 244.51 | 0.0007535 | 0.099516 |
| 40 | 108.26 | 163.00 | 271.27 | 0.0008720 | 0.019952 |

$$h_1 = 244.51 \text{kJ/kg}$$
$$h_3 = h_4 = 108.26/\text{kg}$$
$$h_2 = h_g + c_p (T_{sup} - T_{sat})$$
$$= 271.27 + 1.145 ( 47 - 40 )$$
$$= 279.285 \text{ kJ/ kg}$$
$$COP = \frac{h_1 - h_4}{h_2 - h_1} = \frac{(244.51 - 108.26)}{(279.285 - 244.51)}$$
$$= 3.918$$
$$\text{Actual COP} = 0.75 \times 3.918$$
$$= 2.9385$$
$$\text{Actual COP} = \frac{\text{Refrigerating Effect}}{\text{Compression}}$$
$$2.9385 = 2 \times 3.516 / m_r (279.285 - 244.51)$$
$$m_r = 0.068815 \text{ kg/s}$$
$$\text{Cylinder Volume} \times \text{Speed (rps)} = m_r \times v_1$$
$$\frac{22}{7} \times D^2 \times L \times \frac{400}{60} = 0.68815 \times 0.099516$$
$$\frac{22}{7} \times 1.2 \times D^3 = 0.68815 \times 0.099516$$
$$D = 0.263 \text{ m}$$
$$L = 0.316 \text{ m}$$

# EXERCISE

1. What are the four basic components of a steam power plant?
2. What is the reversible cycle that represents the simple steam power plant? Draw the flow rate, p-v, T-s and h-s diagrams of this cycle.
3. What do you understand by steam rate and heat rate? What are their units?
4. Why is Carnot cycle not practicable for a steam power plant?
5. What do you understand by the mean temperature of heat addition?
6. For a given $T_2$, show how the Rankine cycle efficiency depends on the mean temperature of heat addition.

7.   What is metallurgical limit?

8.   Explain how the quality at turbine exhaust gets restricted.

9.   How are the maximum temperature and maximum pressure in the Rankine cycle fixed?

10.  When is reheating of steam recommended in a steam power plant? How does the reheat pressure get optimized?

11.  What is the effect of reheat on (a) the specific output, (b) the cycle efficiency, (c) steam rate, and (d) heat rate, of a steam power plant?

12.  Give the flow and T-s diagrams of the ideal regenerative cycle. Why is the efficiency of this cycle equal to Carnot efficiency? Why is this cycle not practicable?

13.  What is the effect of regeneration on the (a) specific output, (b) mean temperature of heat addition, (c) cycle efficiency, (d) steam rate and (e) heat rate of a steam power plant?

14.  How does the regeneration of steam carnotite the Rankine cycle?

15.  What are open and closed heaters? Mention their merits and demerits.

16.  Why is one open and closed heaters used in a steam plant? What is it   called?

17.  How are the number of heaters and the degree of regeneration get optimized?

18.  Draw the T-s diagram of an ideal working fluid in a vapour power cycle.

19.  Discuss the desirable characteristics of working fluid in a vapour power  cycle.

20.  Mention a few working fluids suitable in the high temperature range of a vapour power cycle.

21.  What is a binary vapour cycle?

22.  What are topping and bottoming cycles?

23.  Show that the overall efficiency of two cycles coupled in series equals the sum of the individual cycle efficiencies minus their product.

24.  What is a back pressure turbine? What are its applications?

25.  What is a cogeneration plant? What are the thermodynamic advantages of such a plant?

26.  What is the biggest loss in a steam plant? How can this loss be reduced?

27.  What is a pass-out turbine? When is it used?

28.  Express the overall efficiency of a steam plant as the product of boiler, turbine, generator and cycle efficiencies.

29.  What are the limitations of air refrigeration?

30.  Explain the working of a simple vapour compression cycle machine

31.  Explain simple VCR cycle on p-h and T-s diagram.

32.  Write a note on Reversed carnot Cycle.

33.  Define : (i) COP, (ii) Refrigerating Effect.

34.  Write a note on refrigerant R 134a.

# Chapter 8

# STEAM GENERATORS

## 8.1 INTRODUCTION

Thermal energy is a basic form of energy which is required for heating and power production. It is produced by burning fuels such as wood, coal and fuels from petroleum. Nuclear energy is also used to produce heat. The nuclear fuel does not *'burn'* as such and hence it is outside the scope of oxidation process. This chapter deals with combustion of fuels in air and hence only organic (hydrocarbon) fuels are relevant for discussion in this chapter.

A fuel may be defined as a substance which liberates sufficient thermal energy (also called heat) on oxidation. A fuel mainly consists of the elements: carbon and hydrogen with smaller proportion of sulphur, oxygen, nitrogen and metallic compounds. Carbon, hydrogen and sulphur are called combustibles since they oxidise and produce heat. The metallic compounds are called non-combustibles and produce ash. The combustibles along with nitrogen from air produce products of combustion which are heated to a high temperature during the process. These high temperature gases are used as a source of heat in many apparatus like boilers, furnaces, ovens, I.C. engines, etc. As the temperature of the gases decreases, they transfer less heat and are finally released to the atmosphere. Except carbon dioxide and water vapour in the products of combustion, all other constituents are harmful to the environment and are called pollutants.

## 8.2 CALORIFIC VALUE OF A FUEL

The amount of thermal energy produced per unit quantity of fuel when completely burned is called its calorific value (CV). For solid and liquid fuels, the unit quantity is kilogram and calorific value is given in *kilojoules per kilogram, abbreviated as kJ/kg in S.I. system.* The unit quantity for gaseous fuels is one cubic metre at a certain pressure and temperature. The calorific value for gaseous fuels is stated in *kilojoules per cubic metre, abbreviated as kJ/m³.*

### Higher Calorific Value

The heat liberated from the fuel is initially used to heat the products of combustion, which give up their heat to the apparatus. If all of the heat of products of combustion is to be realised, they should be cooled down to room temperature. The heating value of the fuel in such a case is called Higher Heating Value (HHV) or Higher Calorific Value (HCV) or sometimes Gross Calorific Value (GCV). The *Higher Calorific Value* is defined as the heat

---

released by burning unit quantity of fuel completely to its final products when the products of combustion are cooled down to the room temperature.

In short, the calorific value is called the higher calorific value when the moisture in the products is in the liquid form.

**Lower Calorific Value**

The products of combustion contain water vapour formed due to oxidation of hydrogen fraction of the fuel and also free moisture from the fuel and the air. This moisture evaporates during combustion process and takes away enthalpy of evaporation. When the products of combustion do not cool to room temperature, this hidden heat is not released. The heating value in this case is less than the higher heating value and is called the Lower Heating Value (LHV). It is also called the Lower Calorific Value (LCV) or the Net Calorific Value (NCV). The *Lower Calorific Value* is defined as the amount of heat released by burning the unit quantity of a fuel completely to its final products which leave the apparatus at a higher temperature without condensing the moisture.

It is called lower calorific value when the moisture remains in the vapour form. The HCV and LCV are related by the following formula:

$$\text{LCV} = \text{HCV} - \left\{\begin{array}{l}\text{Mass of moisture per}\\ \text{unit quantity of fuel}\end{array}\right\} \times \left\{\begin{array}{l}\text{Specific enthalpy}\\ \text{of evaporation}\end{array}\right\}$$

For general calculations the moisture formed is taken from the hydrogen content of the fuel and free moisture of the fuel, neglecting the vapour from supply air. If H is the hydrogen fraction of the fuel, water formed from this hydrogen is 9H kg/kg fuel. The specific enthalpy of evaporation ($h_{fg}$) should be taken at the partial pressure of the water vapour in the products of combustion. Since the pressure is not precisely known, the value of $h_{fg}$ may be taken from the steam table at room temperature.

For ash-fired fuel there will be some moisture present. Let M = Mass fraction of fuel moisture, then,

$$\text{LCV} = \text{HCV} - (9H + M) \times h_{fg} \text{ at room temperature.}$$

For dry fuel,

$$\text{LCV} = \text{HCV} - (9H) \times h_{fg} \text{ at room temperature}$$

The determination of calorific value of fuels is carried out in specially designed calorimeters. In the case of solid and liquid fuels, the calorific value is usually determined in a bomb calorimeter whereas that of gaseous fuels and some liquid fuels it is determined in a gas calorimeter.

All fuels for determining calorific value should be dry so that the HCV can be stated as 'on dry basis'. This is necessary because moisture content of a fuel varies. In addition, it is also stated as 'on ash-free basis' since ash content of a fuel widely varies. Let a fuel have A and M as ash and moisture fractions (kg/kg fuel) respectively and HCV be available for dry and ash-free sample.

Then HCV for ash received sample = HCV for dry and ash-free sample × (1 – M – A)

Most tables list higher calorific values for coal because lower calorific value for each value of moisture content will be different. LCV can be obtained by calculation taking into account the moisture and hydrogen content of the fuel.

If an experiment value is not available, it can be estimated for better grades of coal by **Dulong's** formula viz.

$$HCV \ = \ 34000\ C + 144000 \left( H - \frac{O}{8} \right) + 9400\ S \ kJ/kg$$

where C, H, O and S are mass fractions of carbon, hydrogen, oxygen and sulphur respectively in fuel. The mass fractions may be for actual sample or for dry ash-free sample and the value of HCV obtained is for corresponding sample.

The Dulong's formula is not very accurate as it assumes that all the combustible elements are in their free state. Considerable energy is required to break up the chemical structure of the elements and hence the actual calorific value realised is less than that calculated by Dulong's formula.

## 8.3 STOICHIOMETRIC COMBUSTION EQUATION

In a combustion process, combustion is said to be complete when the fuel is completely oxidized, the elements of the fuel are completely converted to their oxides. e.g. carbon in fuel is burned to carbon dioxide, hydrogen to water vapour and sulphur to sulphur dioxide, alongwith production of heat. If the combustion process is incomplete, hydrogen and sulphur usually burn completely while a part of carbon burns to carbon monoxide and the rest to carbon dioxide. With incomplete combustion, heat evolved during the process is less and hence attempt is always made to effect complete combustion of fuel. The purpose of combustion chemistry is to determine the air required for combustion and finding out the products of combustion quantitatively.

The combustion reaction is written in the form of a chemical equation expressing the conservation of mass in terms of conservation of atoms.

For complete combustion of carbon in fuel, the equation is

$$C + O_2 \ \rightarrow \ CO_2 + \text{Heat energy}$$

Above equation means that one molecule of carbon reacts with one molecule of oxygen to produce one molecule of carbon dioxide along with heat. The quantity of heat may not be written every time. **The amount of oxygen given by the above equation is just enough for complete combustion of carbon. Such a balanced equation with the minimum oxygen requirements is called *stoichiometric equation*.** Since the oxygen for combustion is invariably supplied from air the stoichiometric equation is useful to determine the theoretical or minimum air required for combustion. It may be noted that the number of carbon and oxygen atoms are the same before and after the reaction.

The minimum quantity of air needed for complete combustion of fuel is known as stoichiometric air.

The above equation can be interpreted in different ways as follows:

**(a) On molar basis:**

1 mol of carbon + 1 mol of oxygen $\rightarrow$ 1 mol of carbon dioxide.

Note that mols before and after the reaction are different i.e. mols are not conserved during combustion reaction.

**(b) On volume basis:**

1 volume of carbon + 1 volume of oxygen $\rightarrow$ 1 volume of carbon dioxide.

The volume of carbon (a solid) is too small in comparison with the volume of oxygen (a gas) and hence one volume of oxygen with negligible volume of carbon produces one volume of carbon dioxide. Again note that volumes are not conserved during combustion.

**(c) On mass basis:**

The chemical equation on mol or volume basis can be converted to mass basis by multiplying the number of mols (or volumes) by the respective atomic mass. Hence oxidation of carbon can be written as

$1 \times 12$ kg of carbon + $1 \times 32$ kg of oxygen $\rightarrow 1 \times 44$ kg of carbon dioxide.

Thus the total mass of reactants (12 + 32 = 44 kg) equals the mass of the products (conservation of mass theorem).

Since air is supplied for combustion, nitrogen is simultaneously supplied to the process. Although nitrogen does not contribute to the oxidation reaction, it affects the composition of products of combustion and leaves the reaction at a much higher temperature, taking away sensible heat from the reaction.

Air contains 21% of oxygen and 79% of nitrogen by volume (or mol). Hence each mol of oxygen is accompanied by 79/21 = 3.76 mols of nitrogen and 100/21 = 4.76 mols of air.

i.e. 1 mol of $O_2$ + 3.76 mols of $N_2 \rightarrow$ 4.76 mols of air.

Thus stoichiometric equation for complete oxidation of carbon can be written on mol basis as:

1 mol of C + 1 mol of $O_2$ + 3.76 mols of $N_2 \rightarrow$ 1 mol of $CO_2$ + 3.76 mols of $N_2$

On mass (or gravimetric) basis, composition of air is oxygen 23.2% and nitrogen 76.8%. Hence each kg of oxygen is accompanied by 76.8/23.2 = 3.31 kg of nitrogen and 100/23.2 = 4.31 kg of air.

i.e. 1 kg of $O_2$ + 3.31 kg of $N_2 \rightarrow$ 4.31 kg of air.

Hence stoichiometric equation for complete oxidation of carbon can be written on mass basis as:

12 kg of C + 32 kg of $O_2$ + (3.31 × 28) kg of $N_2$ → 44 kg of $CO_2$ + (3.31 × 28) kg of $N_2$

Usually composition of air may be taken on mass basis as $O_2$ = 23% and $N_2$ = 77%.

The mass of $N_2$ associated with unit mass of $O_2$ is therefore

$$\frac{77}{23} \ = \ 3.35 \text{ kg } N_2/\text{kg } O_2$$

and $\qquad$ Mass of air $\ = \ \dfrac{100}{23} = 4.35 \ \dfrac{\text{kg}}{\text{kg } O_2}$

**Note:** Amount of nitrogen may not be always written in the equation.

## 8.4 MINIMUM AIR REQUIREMENT ON MASS BASIS

Any fuel contains carbon, hydrogen, sulphur and oxygen along with nitrogen and non-combustibles called as ash. Combustion equations are written for complete oxidation of combustible elements and net oxygen requirements are determined. From this minimum air required for combustion is calculated. The minimum air is also called as theoretical or stoichiometric air.

For carbon, we have,

$$C + O_2 \ \rightarrow \ CO_2$$

$$12 \text{ kg C} + 32 \text{ kg } O_2 \ \rightarrow \ 44 \text{ kg } CO_2$$

Dividing both sides of the equation by 12, we get,

$$1 \text{ kg of C} + \frac{32}{12} \text{ kg of } O_2 \rightarrow \ \frac{44}{12} \text{ kg of } CO_2$$

i.e. $\ 1$ kg of C + 2.67 kg of $O_2$ → 3.67kg of $CO_2$ $\hfill ... (8.1)$

Thus the mass of oxygen required for complete combustion of carbon is 2.67 times that of carbon producing 3.67 times its mass, the mass of carbon dioxide. For oxidation of hydrogen,

$$2H_2 + O_2 \ \rightarrow 2H_2O$$

i.e. $2 × 2$ kg of $H_2$ + 32 kg of $O_2$ → $2 × 18$ kg of water vapour.

Dividing both sides by 4, we get,

$$1 \text{ kg of } H_2 + 8 \text{ kg of } O_2 \ \rightarrow 9 \text{ kg of } H_2O \hfill ... (8.2)$$

Hence the mass of oxygen required for complete combustion of hydrogen is 8 times that of hydrogen, producing 9 times its mass, the final product of water vapour.

For combustion of sulphur, the following equation can be written,

$$S + O_2 \ \rightarrow \ SO_2$$

$$32 \text{ kg of S} + 32 \text{ kg of } O_2 \rightarrow 64 \text{ kg of } SO_2$$

Dividing both sides by 32, we get,

$$1 \text{ kg of S} + 1 \text{ kg of } O_2 \rightarrow 2 \text{ kg of } SO_2 \qquad \qquad \text{... (8.3)}$$

It means that the mass of oxygen required for complete combustion of sulphur equals the mass of sulphur and produces sulphur dioxide of twice its mass.

Let a fuel contain C mass fraction of carbon, H mass fraction of hydrogen, S mass fraction of sulphur and O, the mass fraction of oxygen. From equations (8.1), (8.2) and (8.3), we can write the minimum oxygen required for complete combustion = 2.67 C + 8 H + S for combustible elements. Since the fuel already contains 'O' kg mass per kg fuel, actual oxygen to be supplied externally,

i.e.         Minimum $O_2$  =  2.67 C + 8 H + S − O kg/kg fuel

Minimum air necessary for complete combustion would be in the proportion 100/23.2 = 4.31 per kg oxygen

∴         Minimum air  =  4.31 (2.67 C + 8 H + S − O) kg/kg fuel         ... (8.4)

A fuel may contain some non-combustibles for which no oxygen is required and hence their account should not be taken for calculation of minimum air.

**Important Note:**

1. **The formula for minimum air is useful when ultimate analysis of fuel is given.** When fuel is given by a chemical formula, stoichiometric equation should be written each time for calculating minimum air.

Suppose the fuel is methane ($CH_4$) for which minimum air is to be calculated. Stoichiometric equation for methane is

$$\text{Fuel + Oxygen} \rightarrow \text{Products of combustion}$$
$$CH_4 + 2O_2 \rightarrow CO_2 + 2H_2O$$

i.e. (12 + 4) kg of methane + (2 × 32) kg of oxygen

$$\rightarrow 44 \text{ kg of } CO_2 + (2 \times 18) \text{ kg of } H_2O$$

Dividing both sides by 16, we have

1 kg of $CH_4$ + 4 kg of oxygen  → 2.75 kg of $CO_2$ + 2.25 kg of $H_2O$

∴   Minimum air required per kg methane

$$= 4.31 \times \text{Minimum oxygen required/kg methane}$$
$$= 4.31 \times 4 = 17.24 \text{ kg}$$

The complete oxidation reaction discussed above takes place under ideal conditions. If a fuel particle finds insufficient air, it will partly burn to carbon monoxide which may or may not oxidize to carbon dioxide depending on the availability of oxygen in the latter part of combustion process. In case of premixed combustible mixture, hydroxyls get converted to aldehydes first which then completely oxidize. If for some reason, oxygen is not available for their burning, aldehydes become a part of combustion products. Also at temperatures above 1200°C, some of the molecules dissociate. Some such reactions are the following:

$$O_2 \rightarrow 2O, \ N_2 \rightarrow 2N \text{ and } 2CO_2 \rightarrow 2CO + O_2$$

The dissociated elements are very active and they may again associate at low temperatures. But if the conditions do not permit they may form other products such as nitrogen oxides.

The non-ideal conditions described for the combustion process lead to reduced heat of combustion as well as emission of products of incomplete combustion to the atmosphere. These products are harmful to the environment and are called as atmospheric pollutants.

## 8.5 ACTUAL AIR

Combustion of fuel seldom completes with stoichiometric air since all the conditions mentioned are not available for each particle of fuel. Air may not be evenly distributed with respect to fuel for which reason actual air supplied for combustion should exceed the minimum air. The difference in the actual air supplied and the minimum air calculated is called as *excess air*. All the values of air quantity are generally taken in kg air/kg fuel. The ratio of excess air to the minimum air when stated on percent basis is called as percent excess air. The ratio of actual air to the minimum air is called as excess air coefficient ($\alpha$) or dilution coefficient. The above mentioned definitions may be summarised as follows:

$$\text{Excess air, } A_{excess} = (\text{Actual air supplied} - \text{Minimum air required})$$

$$= (A_{act} - A_{min})\ \frac{kg}{kg\ fuel}$$

$$\%\ \text{Excess air} = \frac{\text{Excess air}}{\text{Minimum air}} \times 100$$

$$= \left(\frac{\text{Actual air} - \text{Minimum air}}{\text{Minimum air}}\right) \times 100$$

$$= \left(\frac{A_{act}}{A_{min}} - 1\right) \times 100 = (\alpha - 1) \times 100$$

$$\text{where Excess air coefficient } (\alpha) = \frac{\text{Actual air (kg/kg fuel)}}{\text{Minimum air (kg/kg fuel)}}$$

If say, 20% excess air is supplied, actual air is 120% of minimum air or 1.2 times the minimum air and $\alpha = 1.2$. The mass of excess air on unit basis is

$$k = 1.2 - 1 = 0.2\ (\alpha - 1) \times \text{Minimum air} = (k) \times \text{Min air.}$$

## 8.6  AIR : FUEL RATIO

This is a parameter which gives the relative proportion of air and fuel on mass basis. It is defined as the ratio of mass of air to the mass of fuel for combustion i.e.

$$\text{Air to fuel ratio (A : F)} = \frac{\text{Mass of air (kg)}}{\text{Mass of fuel (kg)}} = \frac{m_a}{m_f} = \frac{A}{m_f}$$

The ratio may be taken either for minimum air (i.e. on stoichiometric basis) or for actual air and accordingly, we may write,

$$\text{Minimum air to fuel ratio, } (A:F)_{min} \ = \ \frac{\text{Mass of minimum air (kg)}}{\text{Mass of fuel (kg)}} = \frac{A_{min}}{m_f}$$

$$\text{Actual air to fuel ratio, } (A:F)_{act} \ = \ \frac{\text{Mass of actual air (kg)}}{\text{Mass of fuel (kg)}} = \frac{m_f}{A}$$

The reciprocal of air to fuel ratio is called fuel to air ratio (F: A) i.e.,

$$(F:A) \text{ ratio} \ = \ \frac{1}{(A:F)} = \frac{\text{Mass of fuel (kg)}}{\text{Mass of air (kg)}} = \frac{m_f}{m_a} = \frac{m_f}{A}$$

## 8.7 INCOMPLETE COMBUSTION

Although incomplete combustion of fuel is undesirable and uneconomical for a power plant, it also leads to pollution. When carbon oxidizes to carbon dioxide, it releases 33900 kJ of heat per kg while carbon burning to carbon monoxide heat released is only 10000 kJ/kg. Thus nearly 70% heat is wasted due to incomplete combustion and also carbon monoxide produced is irritant and poisonous. Incompleteness of combustion is due to non-uniform relative distribution of fuel and air and non-ideal conditions in the combustion chamber. Even with sufficient excess air, combustion may not be complete due to these reasons and high amount of excess air does not solve the problem. Air less than the stoichiometric quantity definitely results in incomplete combustion.

The composition of the products of combustion due to incompleteness of combustion depends on the proportion of air. If deficient air is supplied to a hydrocarbon fuel, the products would consist of $CO_2$, CO, $H_2O$ and $N_2$. In case of excess air and incomplete combustion, the products would consist of $CO_2$, CO, $H_2O$, $O_2$ and $N_2$. As stated earlier, hydrogen and sulphur having high reactivity with oxygen would always oxidise completely and carbon would partly burn to CO and partly to $CO_2$. Thus a balance of oxygen supplied and oxygen utilized as well as that of carbon is necessary to solve the problem of incomplete combustion.

## 8.8 EFFECT OF AIR : FUEL RATIO ON PRODUCTS OF COMBUSTION

With stoichiometric air: fuel ratio, all the carbon burns to carbon dioxide and it results in the maximum percentage of $CO_2$ in flue gases under ideal conditions. Neither CO nor $O_2$ are then be present in the flue gas. If excess air is supplied, excess oxygen appears as a product of flue gases; higher the amount of excess air, higher is the $O_2$ content of flue gas. This results in lowering the content of $CO_2$. Thus with A : F ratios greater than stoichiometric, there is an increase in $O_2$ content and a reduction of $CO_2$ content of flue gas.

On the contrary when air supplied is less than the stoichiometric proportion, incomplete combustion of part of carbon produces carbon monoxide. There is no oxygen in flue gases then. As proportion of air decreases, CO part of flue gases increases, due to which, $CO_2$ decreases.

The effect of A : F ratio variation on the content of flue gases is shown by the graph of Fig. 8.1.

The use of this graph can be made to estimate how best are the conditions in the combustion chamber. For a given fuel, the maximum $CO_2$ content of flue gas under ideal conditions of working is known. If $CO_2$ content of flue gases falls, it can be inferred that conditions have departed from ideal. Depending on whether $O_2$ or CO percent has increased in flue gas, one can predict the actual A : F ratio used for combustion.

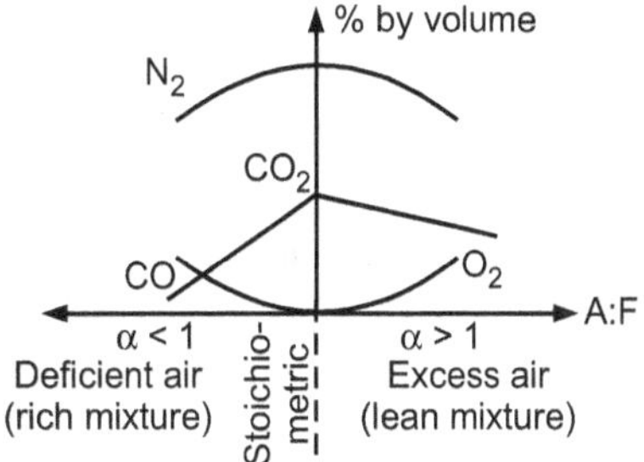


**Fig. 8.1: Deficient air and excess air**

## 8.9  STEAM GENERATORS

A steam generator or boiler is a closed vessel to transfer the heat produced by the combustion of fuel (solid, liquid or gaseous) to water and ultimately to generate steam. The steam produced may be supplied:

- To steam engines and turbines.
- At low pressures for industrial work in cotton mills, sugar factories, breweries, printing, textile industry etc.

## 8.10 SELECTION OF A STEAM BOILER

While selecting a boiler, following factors should be considered.

- The power and the working pressure required,
- The rate at which steam is to be generated,
- The fuel type and water available,
- Comparative initial cost,
- The probable load factor,
- The geographical position of the power house,
- Operating and maintenance cost,
- Erection facilities.

## 8.11 ESSENTIALS OF A GOOD STEAM BOILER

A good boiler should possess following features:

- It should produce quantity of steam efficiently as per requirements,
- It should be capable of quick starting,
- It should be light in weight,
- It should occupy a small space,
- The tubes should not accumulate soot or water deposits and should have a reasonable margin of strength to allow for wear or corrosion,

- It should rapidly meet the fluctuation of the demand,
- It should be easy for inspection and repair,
- It should comply with safety regulations as laid down in the Boilers Act,
- It should be easy to install,
- Boiler components should be transferable without difficulty,
- It should need less attention during operation.

## 8.12 IMPORTANT TERMS FOR STEAM BOILERS

Following are important terms used in steam boilers.

1. **Boiler shell:** It is made from metal plates bent into cylindrical form. The ends of the shell are closed by means of end plates. A boiler shell is designed to have sufficient capacity to contain water and steam as per requirement.

2. **Combustion chamber:** It is the space, meant for burning fuel in order to produce hot gases or flues which transfer heat to water.

3. **Grate:** It is a platform, in the combustion chamber, on which fuel (coal or wood) is burnt. The grate consists of cast iron bars which are spaced apart so that air required for combustion can pass through them.

4. **Furnace:** It is the space, above the grate in which the fuel is actually burnt. The furnace is also called fire box.

5. **Mountings:** These are the essential fittings which are mounted on the boiler for its proper functioning. e.g. Water level indicator, pressure gauge, safety valve etc. A boiler cannot function safely without mountings.

6. **Accessories:** These are the devices which improve efficiency of boiler. They are not essential for the operation of boiler but play an important role to run boiler efficiently. e.g. Superheater, economiser, feed pump etc.

## 8.13 CLASSIFICATION OF STEAM BOILERS

The boilers may be classified as follows:

1. **According to the Position of Water and Hot Gases:**

   (a) **Fire Tube Boiler:** In fire tube steam boilers, the flues and hot gases pass through the tubes which are surrounded by water. The heat is conducted through the walls of the tubes from the hot gases to the surrounding water.

   **Examples:** Simple vertical boiler, Cochran boiler, Lancashire boiler, Cornish boiler, Scotch marine boiler, Locomotive boiler, etc.

   (b) **Water Tube Boilers:** In water tube steam boilers, the water is contained inside the tubes (called water tubes) which are surrounded by flues and hot gases from outside.

   **Examples:** Babcock and Wilcox boiler, Stirling boiler, La-Mont boiler, Benson boiler etc.

2.  **According to the Position of the Furnace:**
    (a) **Internally Fired Boilers:** In these boilers, the furnace is located inside the boiler shell. Most of the fire tube steam boilers are internally fired.
    (b) **Externally Fired Boilers:** In these boilers, the furnace is located outside the boiler shell. Water tube steam boilers are externally fired.
3.  **According to Circulation Method of Water and Steam:**
    (a) **Natural Circulation Steam Boilers:** Here, the circulation of water is by natural convection currents, set up during the heating of water. Most of the steam boilers use a natural circulation of water.
    **Examples:** Babcock and Wilcox boilers.
    (b) **Forced Circulation Boilers:** In forced circulation steam boilers, circulation of water is by using a pump. Forced circulation is used in high pressure boilers.
    **Examples:** La-Mont boiler, Benson boiler, Loeffler boiler etc.
4.  **According to the Number of Tubes:**
    (a) **Single Tube Boilers:** In single tube steam boilers, there is only one fire tube or water tube.
    **Examples:** Simple vertical boiler and Cornish boiler.
    (b) **Multitubular Boilers:** In multitubular steam boilers, there are two or more fire tubes or water tubes.
    **Examples:** Lancashire boiler, Locomotive boiler, Babcock and Wilcox boiler etc.
5.  **According to the Mobility:**
    (a) **Stationary Boilers:** The stationary steam boilers are used in power plants and in industrial process work. They do not move from one place to another.
    **Examples:** Babcock and Wilcox boiler.
    (b) **Mobile Boilers:** The mobile steam boilers are those which move from one place to another.
    **Examples:** Locomotive and Marine boilers.
6.  **According to the Axis of the Shell:**
    (a) **Horizontal Boilers:** In horizontal steam boilers, the axis of the shell is horizontal.
    **Examples:** Lancashire boiler, Locomotive boiler, Babcock and Wilcox boiler etc.
    (b) **Vertical Boilers:** In these boilers, the axis of the shell is vertical.
    **Examples:** Simple vertical boiler, Cochran boiler, etc.

## 8.14 FIRE TUBE BOILERS

The various fire tube boilers are described below.

## 8.14.1 Simple Vertical Boiler

- This boiler is suitable to produce small quantity of steam at low pressure where limited space is available.
- It consists of a cylindrical shell in which fire box and grate are placed near to the bottom as shown in Fig. 8.2. Fire box is surrounded by water in the boiler shell.

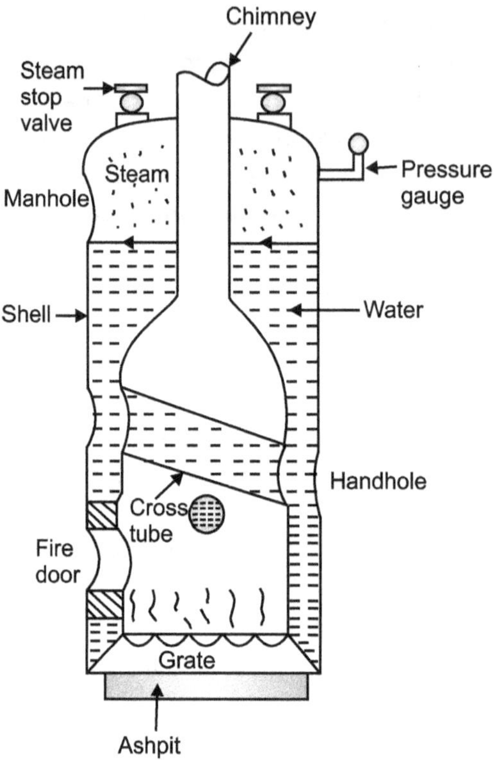


**Fig. 8.2: Simple vertical boiler**

- Two or more cross tubes are fitted in fire box. These tubes are made inclined to improve water circulation and to increase heating area.

- A vertical tube is used to connect fire box with chimney at the top of fire box.

- Through the manhole, the boiler attendant can enter inside the boiler shell for cleaning, inspection and or maintenance.

- For draining out the mud and sediments settled at the bottom, a mud hole is provided.

- Its construction is simple, but efficiency of this boiler is less.

## 8.14.2 Cochran Boiler

- It is also a simple form of vertical fire tube boiler. It consists of the fire brick layer which prevents the overheating of the boiler shell. The hot gases pass through a large number of fire tubes surrounded by water as shown in Fig. 8.3 and convert it into steam. Then steam goes up to steam space.

- The crown of the boiler shell and grate are both hemispherical in shape.

- The waste gases entering the smoke box are released through the chimney. The amount of waste gases leaving the chimney is controlled by means of a damper manually.

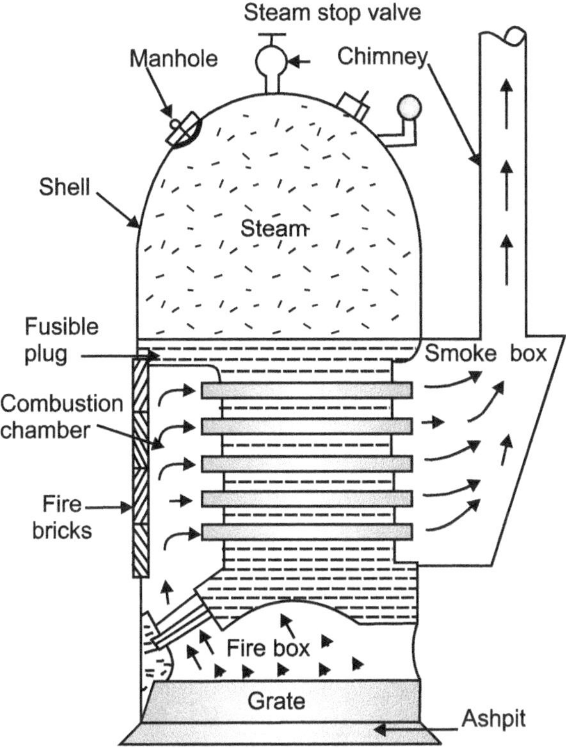


**Fig. 8.3: Cochran boiler**

- When the damper is partly closed, amount of waste gases leaving the chimney will be reduced. Due to this action of the damper, the amount of air entering the grate will also be reduced and obviously, only limited fuel can be burnt and the amount of steam generated also will be reduced. Thus, the damper controls the rate of steam generated.

- Through the manhole, the boiler attendant can enter inside the boiler shell for cleaning.

- By opening the door in the smoke box, the fire tubes and the smoke box can be cleaned by a wire brush.

- The diameter of the boilers varies from 1 to 3 m and the height of the boiler varies from 2 to 6 m depending on the steam requirement. The evaporative capacity of the boiler ranges from 20 to 3000 kg/h.

## 8.14.3 Lancashire Boiler

The Lancashire boiler is a fire tube, stationary, horizontal, internally fired, two tubular, natural circulation boiler. Fig. 8.4 shows constructional details of a Lancashire boiler.

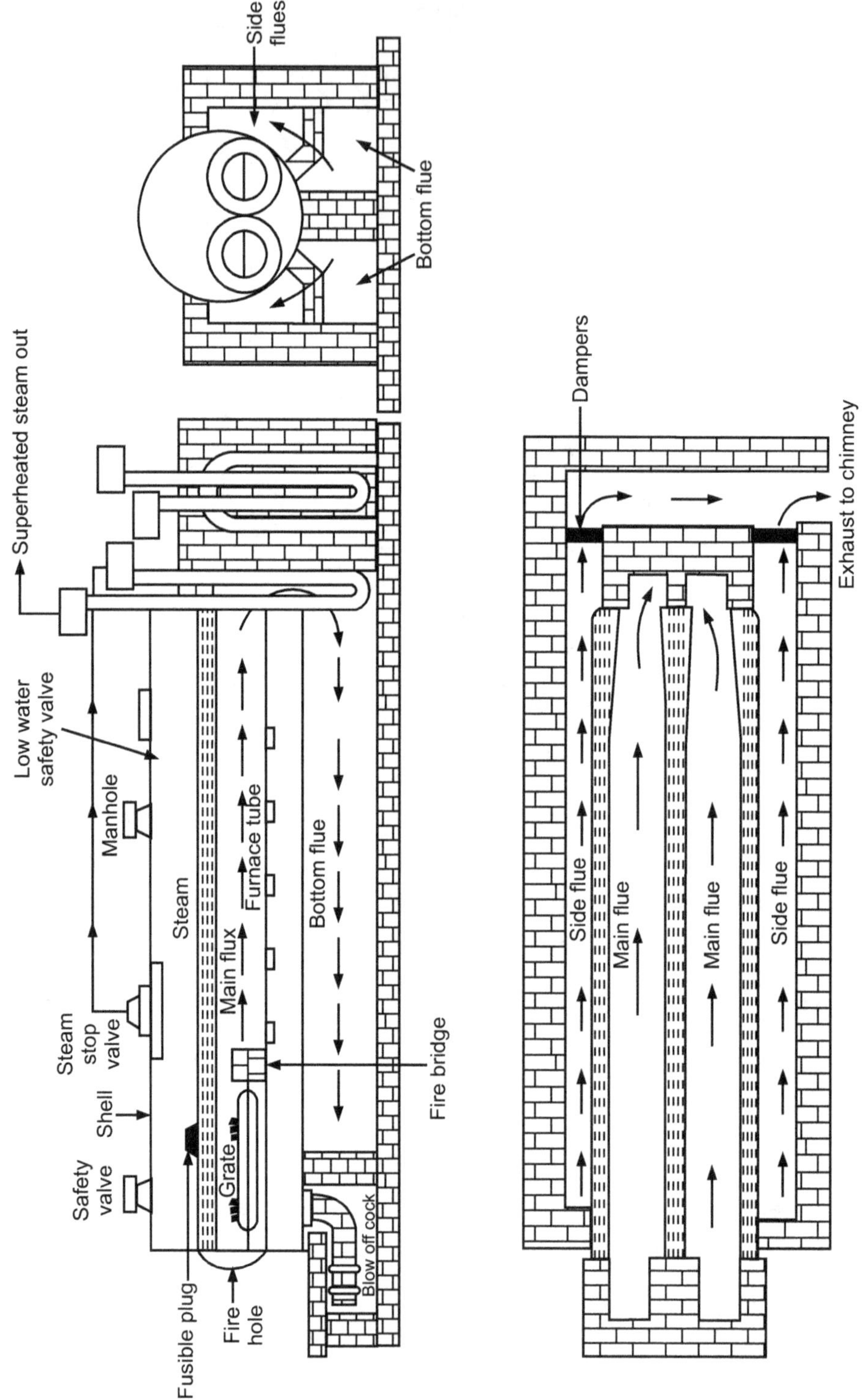


**Fig. 8.4: Lancashire boiler**

- This boiler consists of a cylindrical shell usually of 2 m in diameter and 8-10 m in length. It has two large internal flue tubes having diameters between 0.8-1 m in which grate is situated at the front end of the main flue. The coal is fed to the grate through the fire doors.

- The internal flue tubes are reduced in diameter at the back end to provide access to the lower part of the boiler. One bottom flue and two side flues are formed by brick setting.

- A low fire brick bridge is provided at the end of the grate to prevent the flow of coal and ash particles into the interior of the furnace tubes. The dampers operated by chain in the form of sliding doors are placed at the end of side flues to control the flow of gases. The damper regulates the combustion rate as well as steam generation rate.

- Then all mountings required for safe working of boiler are fitted and are shown in Fig. 8.4.

**Working:**

- These hot gases from the grate pass up to the back end of the tubes (main flue) and then in the downward direction.

- Then they move through bottom passage from back end to the front of the boiler (bottom flue).

- At front end they are divided and pass through two side passages (side flues).

- Then they move along two side flues and come to the chimney.

- This particular arrangement increases the heating surface to large extent.

# 8.14.4 Cornish Boiler

- In construction it is similar to Lancashire boiler in all respect, except it has one main flue passage instead of two, as shown in Fig. 8.5.

- Its cylindrical shell is usually of 1 to 2 m in diameter and 5-7.5 m in length. The diameter of flue tube may be about 0.6 times that of the shell.

- The steam generating capacity and pressure of a Cornish boiler is low as compared to Lancashire boiler.

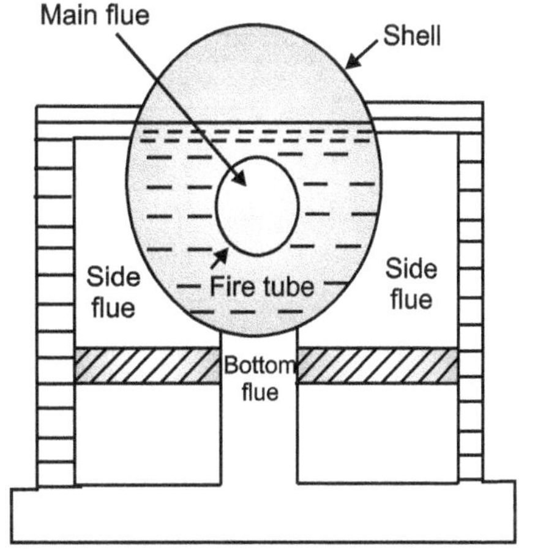


**Fig. 8.5: Cornish boiler**

## 8.14.5 Locomotive Boiler

- It is a horizontal fire tube type mobile boiler. It consists of a shell having 1.5 m in diameter and 4 m in length. Fuel is fed into the fire box through the fuel door and air enters through the damper and the slots in the grate plate.

- The rate of combustion and the amount of steam generated is controlled by the dampers. The fire brick arch deflects the hot gases and improves the combustion efficiency.

- The hot gases pass through large number of fire tubes and enter the smoke box. The circulation of air and hot gases is improved by means of induced draft produced in the smoke box.

- Waste steam from the engine enters the smoke box through the blast pipe and expands.

- Due to the expansion, it produces a partial vacuum which improves the movement of hot gases and air.

- Waste gases go out through a short chimney. A door is provided in the smoke box for inspection and cleaning.

- To remove the moisture from the wet steam and to increase the temperature of steam, it is superheated as shown in Fig. 8.6.

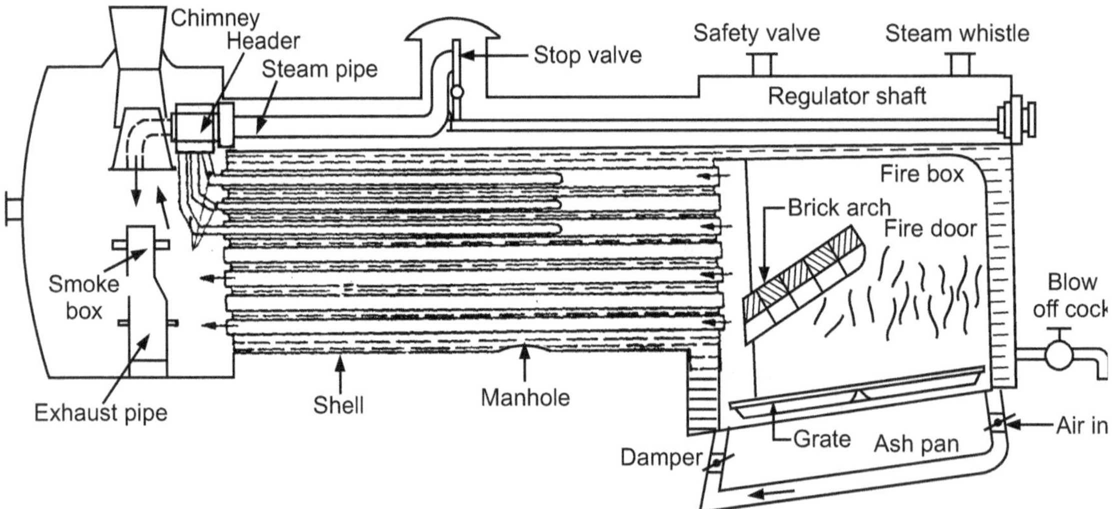


**Fig. 8.6: Locomotive boiler**

- The wet steam through the regulator enters the wet steam header, passes through large number of superheated tubes and finally comes to the superheater header. Then the superheated steam goes to the engine. To accommodate the superheater tubes, some of the fire tubes are larger in diameter.

- There are about 160 fire tubes of 47.5 mm diameter and 24 fire tubes of 130 mm diameter. By superheating, the heat energy per unit mass of steam is increased and the thermal efficiency of the steam plant is considerably increased.

## 8.15  WATER TUBE BOILERS

### 8.15.1 Babcock and Wilcox Boiler

- This boiler consists of a steam water drum mounted on fire brick work. Hot gases from the furnace (placed below water tubes) follow zig-zag path through the fire brick baffles before going to the chimney through the damper.

- The damper controls the rate of burning and thereby the steam generation. The damper is operated by a chain passing through a set of pulleys.

- Water from the steam water drum comes down to the downtake header and then goes to the uptake header through a large number of water tubes, inclined at about 15° for better circulation as shown in Fig. 8.7.

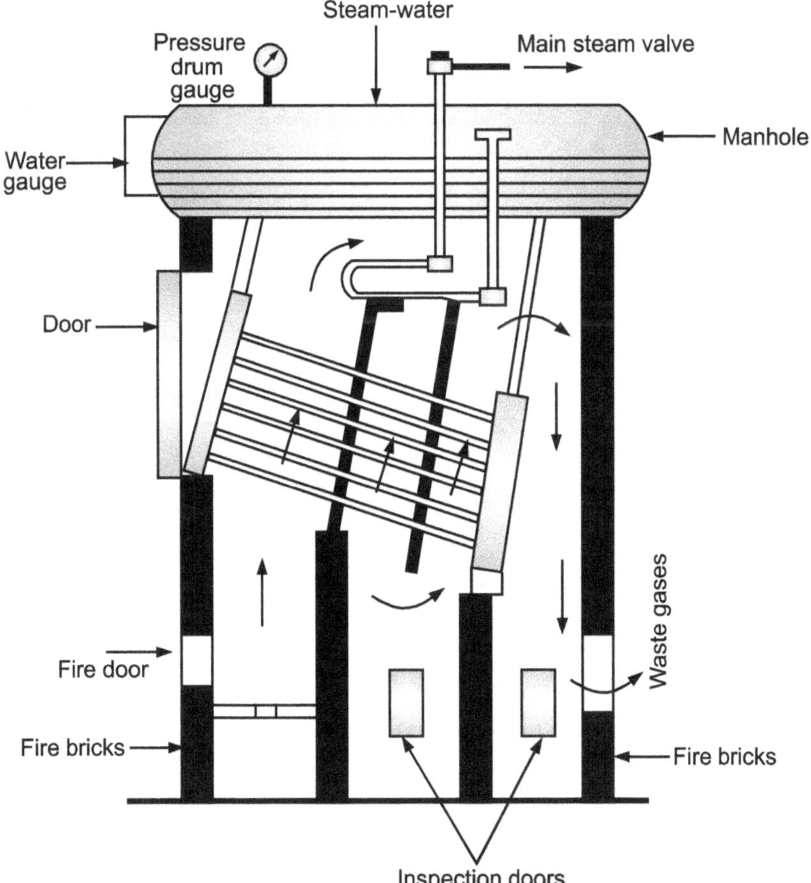


**Fig. 8.7: Babcock and Wilcox boiler**

- The wet steam comes to the wet steam header through an anti-priming pipe. The anti-priming pipe removes some moisture from the steam.

- Then, it passes through a large number of superheater tubes and reaches the superheater header. From the superheater header, it goes to the main steam valve and finally to the steam turbine.

- At the end of the downtake header, a mud drum is connected from where impurities can be removed. Boiler is provided with two inspection doors and other mountings such as the water gauge, the pressure gauge and the safety valve.

- Compared to a fire tube boiler, evaporative capacity, the pressure of steam and the thermal efficiency of this boiler will be higher.

## 8.16  DIFFERENCE BETWEEN WATER TUBE AND FIRE TUBE BOILERS

| Water Tube Boiler | Fire Tube Boiler |
|---|---|
| 1. The water circulates inside the tubes surrounded by hot gases. | 1. The hot gases pass through the tubes which are surrounded by water. |
| 2. The rate of generation of steam is high. | 2. The rate of generation of steam is low. |
| 3. Overall efficiency is upto 90%. | 3. Its overall efficiency is only 75%. |
| 4. For a given power, the floor area required for the generation of steam is less. | 4. The floor area required is more. |
| 5. It can generate steam at a higher pressure. | 5. It can generate steam only upto 25 bar. |
| 6. The direction of water circulation is well defined. | 6. The water does not circulate in a definite direction. |
| 7. It is used for large power plants. | 7. It is not suitable for large plants. |
| 8. It can be transported and erected easily as its various parts can be separated. | 8. The transportation and erection is difficult. |

## 8.17 HIGH PRESSURE BOILERS

The modern high pressure boilers are used for power generation having capacities 30 to 650 tonnes/hour with pressure upto 160 bar and maximum steam temperature of about 540°C.

### 8.17.1 Features of High Pressure Boilers

The unique features of high pressure boilers are as described below:

- **Method of Water Circulation:**

In all modern high pressure boiler plant, forced circulation is used for water circulation. Circulation of water is maintained by using pump which forces the water through boiler plant. The use of natural circulation is limited to subcritical boilers due to its limitations.

- **Type of Tubing**

Most of high pressure boilers are water tube boilers. In these boilers, if the flow takes place through one continuous tube, the large pressure drop takes place due to friction. This loss is reduced by arranging the flow through parallel tube set system. This also results in better steam quality.

- **Method of Heating**

High pressure boiler uses following heating methods to increase heat transfer.

- Superheated steam is mixed with water during heating. This gives high heat transfer coefficient.
- Heat transfer coefficient is improved by increasing water velocity.
- By maintaining gas velocity above sonic speed, heat transfer coefficient is improved.
- Heat is saved by evaporating water above critical pressure of the steam.

## 8.17.2 Advantages of High Pressure Boilers

- Heat of combustion is used more effectively by using tubing set of small diameter.
- The efficiency of the plant is increased upto 40 to 44 percent by using high pressure and high temperature steam.
- All parts are uniformly heated. It reduces overheating and simplifies thermal stress problem.
- Compact in size and requires less floor space.
- Quick response to load change without complicated control devices.
- Use of pump ensures positive water circulation and increases evaporative capacity.
- No scale formation because of high water velocity.
- Use of high pressure and high temperature steam is economical.

## 8.18 BOILER MOUNTINGS

As per IBR Act, following mountings should be provided on a boiler:

- Water Level Indicator
- Pressure Gauge
- Safety Valves
- Stop Valve
- Blow off Cock
- Feed Check Valve
- Fusible Plug
- Man and Mud Holes

## 8.18.1 Water Level Indicator

- This indicates the water level inside the boiler to the operator. They are two in numbers and fitted infront of the boiler.

- It consists of three cocks and a glass tube. Steam cock $C_1$ keeps the glass tube in connection with the steam space. Water cock $C_2$ puts the glass tube in connection with the water in the boiler. Drain cock $C_3$ is used at frequent intervals to ascertain that the steam and water cocks are clear.

- In the working of a steam boiler and for the proper functioning of the water level indicator, the steam and water cocks are opened and the drain cock is closed. The rectangular passage at the ends of the glass tube contains two balls.

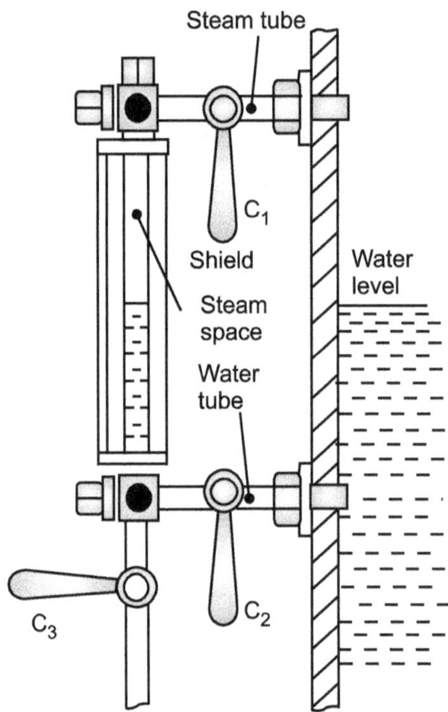


**Fig. 8.8: Water level indicator**

- If the glass tube breaks, the two balls are carried along its passage to the ends of the glass tube, and water and steam will not escape. The glass tube can be easily replaced by closing the steam and water cocks and opening the drain cock.

## 8.18.2 Pressure Gauge

- A pressure gauge is used to measure the pressure of the steam inside the steam boiler shell. It is fixed infront of the steam boiler shell.

- Bourdon type pressure gauge is commonly used in steam boiler.

- It consists of an elliptical elastic bronze tube bent into an arc of a circle, as shown in Fig. 8.9.

- One end of the tube gauge is fixed and connected to the steam space in the boiler. The other end is connected to a sector through a link.

- The steam, under pressure, flows into the tube and causes tube ends to straighten.

- With the help of a simple pinion and sector arrangement, the pointer moves over a calibrated scale, to indicate the gauge pressure.

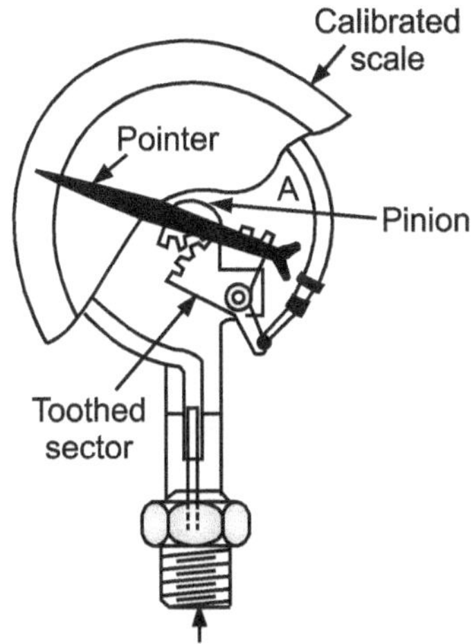


**Fig. 8.9: Bourdon type pressure gauge**

## 8.18.3 Safety Valves

These are the devices attached to the steam chest for preventing explosions due to excessive internal pressure of steam. A steam boiler is usually provided with two safety valves. The function of a safety valve is to blow off the steam when the pressure of steam inside the boiler exceeds the working pressure. The following are the four types of safety valves:

1. Lever safety valve
2. Dead weight safety valve
3. High steam and low water safety valve and
4. Spring loaded safety valve.

**1.    Lever Safety Valve:**

A lever safety valve used for boilers is shown in Fig. 8.10.

- A lever safety valve consists of a valve body. The valve seat is screwed to the body. By using the valve and seat of the same material (bronze), rusting is considerably reduced.

- The thrust on the valve is transmitted by the strut. The guide keeps the lever in a vertical plane. The load is properly adjusted at the other end of the lever.

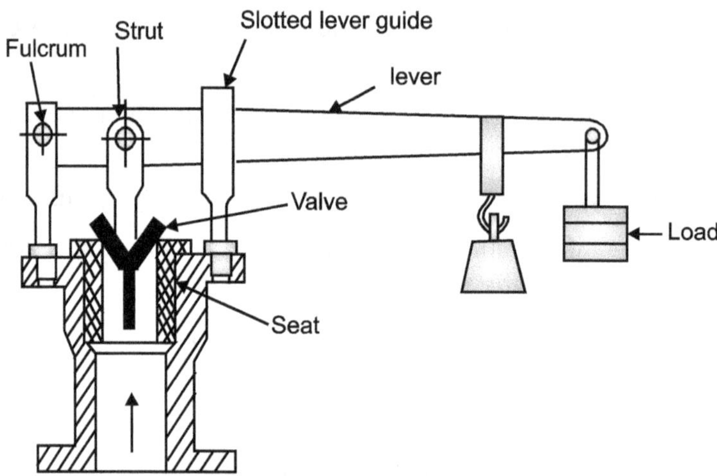


**Fig. 8.10: Lever safety valve**

- When the pressure of steam exceeds the safe limit, the upward thrust of steam lifts the valve from its seat. This allows the steam to escape till the pressure falls back to its normal value. The valve then returns back to its original position.

2. **Dead Weight Safety Valve**

- A dead weight safety valve is shown in Fig. 8.11.

- The valve is made of gun metal, and rests on its gun metal seat. It is fixed to the top of a steel pipe. This pipe is bolted to the mountings block, riveted to the top of the shell.

- Both the valve and the pipe are covered by a case which contains weights. These weights keep the valve on its seat under normal working pressure. The case hangs freely over the valve to which it is secured by means of a nut.

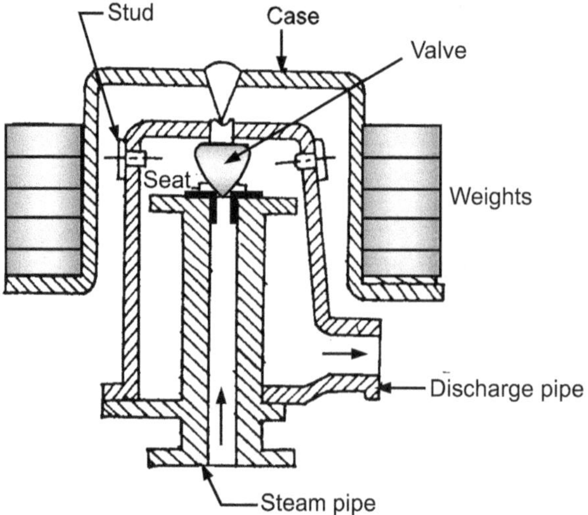


**Fig. 8.11: Dead weight safety valve**

- When the pressure of steam exceeds the normal pressure, the valve as well as the case (along with the weights) are lifted up from its seat. This causes the steam to escape through the discharge pipe, which carries the steam outside the boiler house.

**Advantage:**

It cannot be readily tempered because any added weight must be equal to the total increased pressure of steam on the valve.

**Disadvantage:**

Need heavy load and this load is carried by valves.

### 3.  High Steam Low Water Safety Valve

- This valve is a combination of two valves, one of which is the lever safety valve which blows off steam when the working pressure of steam exceeds, and the second valve operates by blowing off the steam when the water level becomes too low.

- The lever safety valve rests on its seat. In its centre, a seat for a hemispherical valve is formed for low water operation. This valve is loaded directly by the dead weights attached to the valve by a long rod. There is a lever, which has its fulcrum at O.

- The lever has a weight W suspended at the end B. When it is fully immersed in water, it is balanced by a weight F at the other end of the lever, as shown in Fig. 8.12.

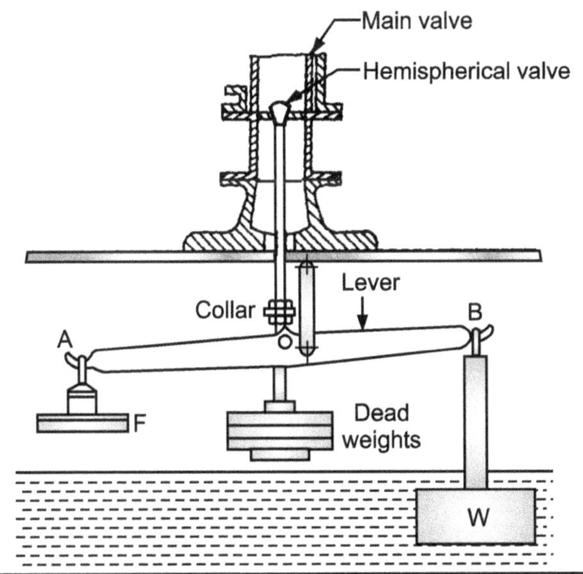


**Fig. 8.12: High steam low water safety valve**

- When the water level falls, the weight W comes out of water and the weight F will not be sufficient to balance weight W. Therefore, weight W comes down. When weight W comes down, the hemispherical valve is lifted up and the steam escapes with a loud noise, which warns the operator.

- This type of valve is generally used in Lancashire and Cornish boilers.

### 4.  Spring Loaded Safety Valve:

This valve is loaded with helical spring instead of weights.

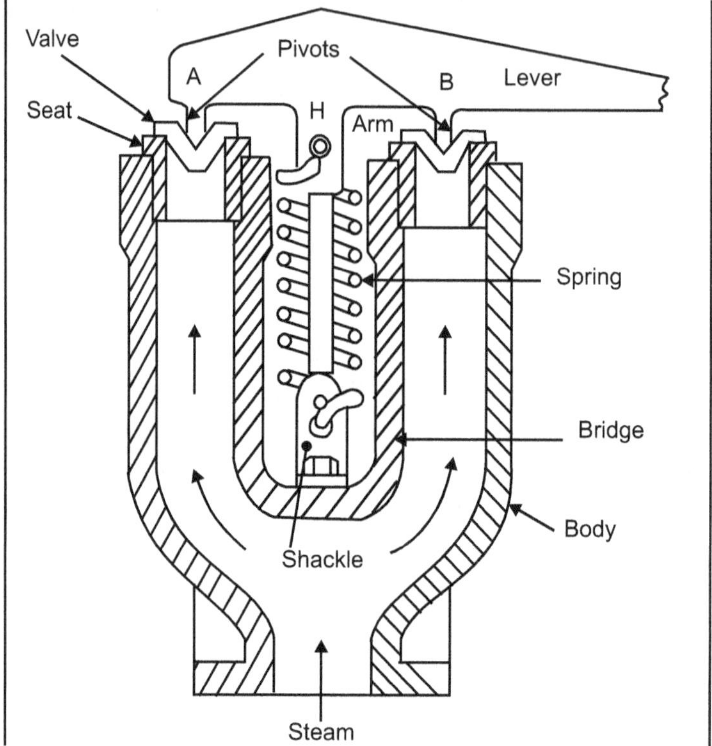


**Fig. 8.13: Spring loaded safety valve**

- A spring loaded safety valve is shown in Fig. 8.13. It consists of a C.I. body connected to the top of a boiler.

- It has two separate valves of the same size. These valves have their seatings in the upper ends of two hollow valve chests. These valve chests are united by a bridge and a base. The base is bolted to a mounting block on the top of a boiler over the fire box.

- The valves are held down by means of a spring and a lever. The lever has two pivots at B and B. The pivot A is joined by a pin to the lever, while the pivot B is forged on the lever. These pivots rest on the centres of the valves.

- The upper end of the spring is hooked to the arm H, while he lower end to the shackle, which is secured to the bridge by a nut. The spring has two safety links, one behind the other, or one on either side of the lever connected by pins at their ends. The lower pin passes through the shackle while the upper one passes through slot in arm H of the lever.

- The lever has an extension, which projects into the driver's cabin. By pulling or raising the lever, the driver can release the pressure from neither valve separately.

- This valve is used in marine and locomotive boilers.

## 8.18.4 Steam Stop Valve

This valve is fitted to the highest part of the shell by means of a flange as shown in Fig. 8.14. The basic functions of a stop valve are:

1.  To control the flow of steam from the boiler to the main steam pipe.

2.  To shut off the steam completely when required.

- The body of the stop valve is made of cast iron and the valve, valve seat and the but through which the valve spindle works, are made of brass or gun metal.

- The spindle passes through a gland and stuffing box. The spindle is rotated by means of a hand wheel. The upper portion of the spindle is screwed and made to pass through a nut in a cross head carried by two pillars. The pillars are screwed in the cover of the body as shown in Fig. 8.14.

- The boiler pressure acts under the valve, so that the valve must be closed against the pressure. The valve is, generally, fastened to the spindle which lifts it up.

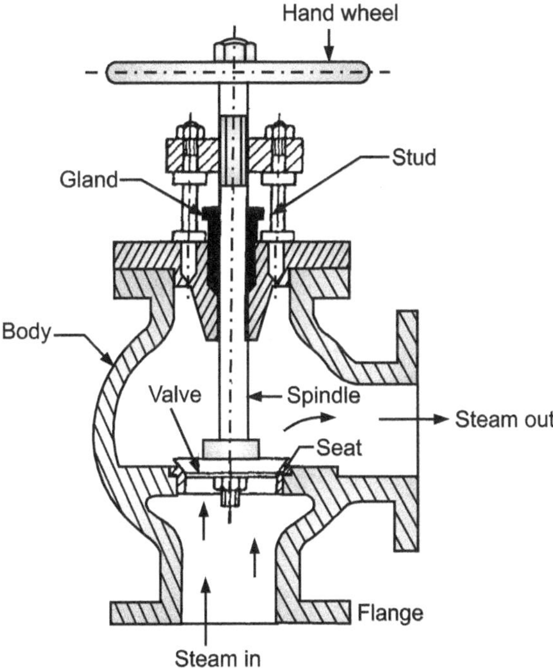


**Fig. 8.14: Steam stop valve**

## 8.18.5 Blow-off Cock

The functions of a blow-off cock are as follows:

1.  To empty the boiler whenever required.

2.  To discharge the mud, scale or sediments which are accumulated at the bottom of the boiler.

- The blow-off cock is fitted to the bottom of a boiler drum and consists of a conical plug fitted to the body or casing. The casing is packed, with asbestos packing, in grooves round the top and bottom of the plug. The asbestos packing is made tight and plug bears on the packing.

- The shank of plug passes through a gland and stuffing box in the cover. The plug is held down by a yoke and two stud bolts. The yoke forms a guard on it. There are two vertical slots on the site of a guard for the box spanner to be used for operating the cock.

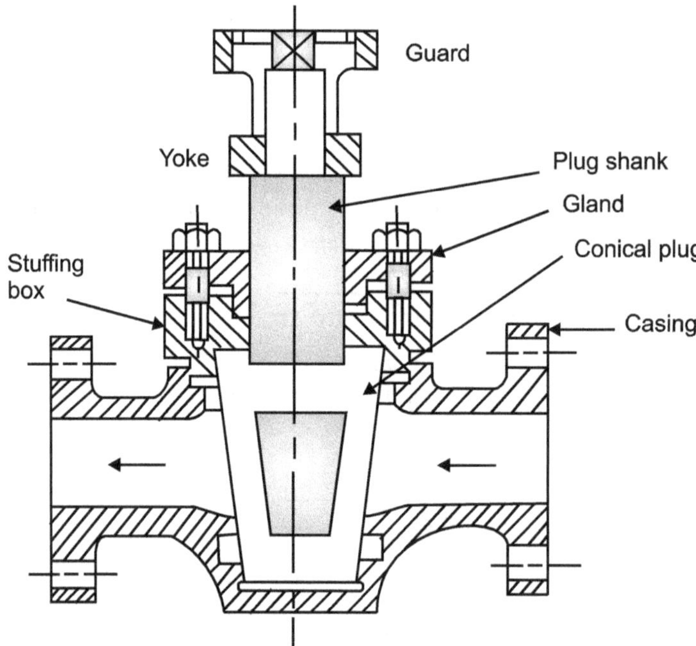


**Fig. 8.15: Blow-off cock**

## 8.18.6 Feed Check Valve

- It is a non-return valve, and its function is to regulate the supply of water, which is pumped into the boiler, by the feed pump.

- This valve must have its spindle lifted before the pump is started. It is fitted to the shell slightly above the normal water level of the boiler.

- It consists of a valve whose lift is controlled by a spindle and hand wheel.

- The body of the valve is made of brass casting and except spindle, its every part is made of brass. The spindle is made of muntz metal. A flange is bolted to the end of boiler at a point from which perforated pipe leads the feed water. This pipe distributes the water in the boiler uniformly.

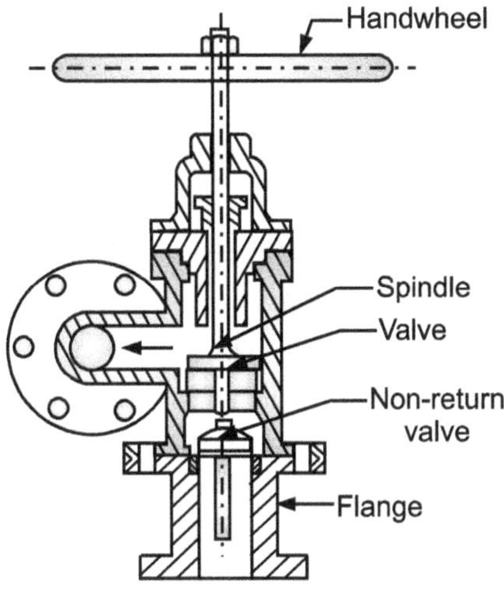



**Fig. 8.16: Feed check valve**

## 8.18.7 Fusible Plug

- It is fitted to the crown plate of the furnace or the fire.

- Its object is to off the fire in the furnace of the boiler when the level of water in the boiler falls limit below safe limit. This avoids the explosion which may take place due to overheating of the furnace plate.

- A fusible plug consists of a hollow gun metal plug as shown in Fig. 8.17 screwed to the furnace crown. A second hollow gun metal plug B is screwed to the first plug. There is also a third hollow gun metal plug C separated from A by a ring of a fusible metal. The inner surface of B and outer surface of C are grooved so that when the fusible metal is poured into the plug, B and C are locked together. A hexagonal flange is provided on plug A to take a spanner for fixing or removing the plug. There is a hexagonal flange on plug B for fixing or removing it. The fusible metal is protected from fire by the flange on the lower end of the plug B. There is also a contact at the top between B and C, so that the fusible metal is completely enclosed.

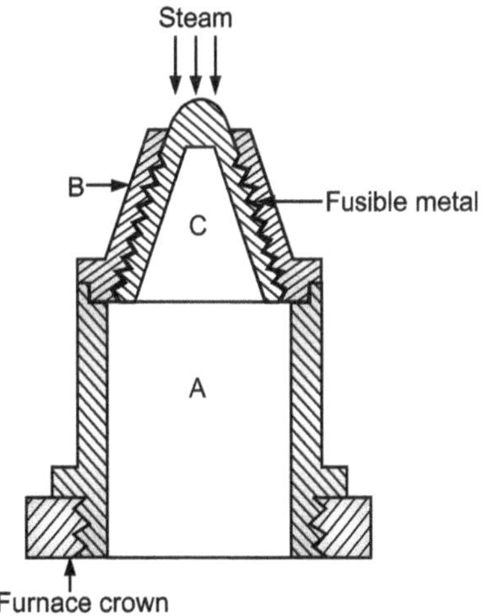



**Fig. 8.17: Fusible plug**

- The fusible plugs must be kept in a good condition and replaced annually.

- A fusible plug must not be refilled with anything except fusible metal.

## 8.19 BOILER ACCESSORIES

### 8.19.1 Superheater

- The purpose of superheater is to increase the temperature of saturated steam without raising its pressure.

- It is placed in the path of hot flue gases from the furnace. The heat, given up these flue gases, is used in superheating the steam.

- A commonly used superheater with Lancashire boiler is shown in Fig. 8.18. It consists of two mild steel boxes or heaters from which hangs a group of solid drawn tubes bent to U-form. The ends of these tubes are expanded into the headers.

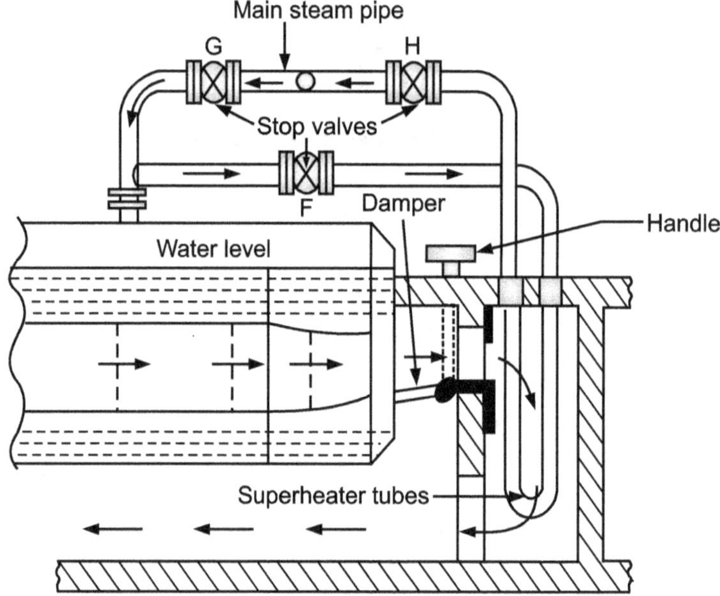


**Fig. 8.18: Superheater**

- The tubes are arranged in groups of four and one pair of header generally carries ten of these groups or fourty tubes in all. The outside of the tubes can be cleaned through the space between the headers. This space is closed by covers.

- The steam enters at one end of the rear header and leaves at the opposite end of the front header. The overheating of superheater tubes is prevented by the use of a balanced damper which is operated by the handle. The superheater is in action when the damper is in a position as shown in Fig. 8.18. If the damper is in vertical position, the gases pass directly into the bottom flue without passing over the superheater tubes. In this way, the superheater is out of action. By placing the damper in intermediate position, some of the gases will pass over the superheater tubes and the remainder will pass directly to the bottom flue. It is thus obvious, that required degree of heat for superheating may be obtained by altering the position of the damper.

- When the superheater is in action, the stop valves G and H are opened and F is closed. When the steam is taken directly from the boiler, the valves G and H are closed and F is open.

## 8.19.2 Economiser

- An economiser is used to heat feed water by utilising the exhaust flue gases before leaving through the chimney.

- It consists of a large number of vertical pipes or tubes placed in an enlargement of the flue gases between the boiler and chimney as shown in Fig. 8.19.

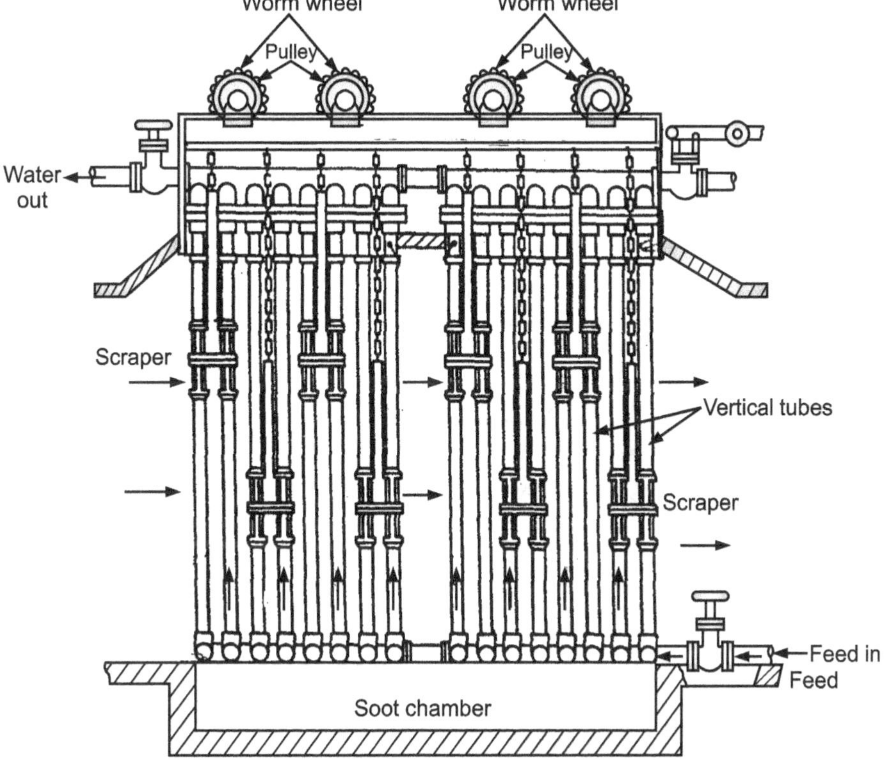


**Fig. 8.19: Economiser**

- The economiser is built-up of transverse section. Each section consists of generally six or eight vertical tubes. These tubes are joined in horizontal pipes or boxes at the top and bottom respectively. The top boxes of the different sections are connected to the pipe $P_T$ while the bottom boxes are connected to pipe $P_B$. These pipes are outside the brickwork enclosing the economiser.

- The feed water is pumped into the economiser at P and enters the pipe $P_B$. It then passes into the bottom boxes and then into the top boxes through the tubes.

- There is a blow-off cock opposite to the feed inlet to remove mud or sediment deposited in the bottom boxes.

- It is essential that the vertical tubes may be kept free from deposits of soot, which greatly reduce the efficiency of the economiser. Each tube is provided with scraper for this purpose. The scrapers of two adjoining sections of tubes are grouped together, and coupled by rods and chains to the adjacent group of scrapers. These are kept in motion continuously when the economiser is in use.

- If the temperature of feed is less than 35°C, then there is a danger of corrosion due to the moisture in the flue gases being deposited in cold tubes.

**Advantages of using an Economiser**

- There is about 15 to 20% of fuel saving.

- It increases the steam raising capacity of a boiler.

- It prevents formation of scale in boiler water tubes.

- Since the feed water entering the boiler is hot, therefore, strains due to unequal expansion are minimised.

## 8.19.3 Air Preheater

- An air preheater is used to recover heat from the exhaust flue gases.

- It is installed between the economiser and the chimney. The air required for the purpose of combustion is drawn through the air preheater when its temperature is raised.

- It is then passed through ducts to the furnace.

- The air is passed through the tubes of the heater internally while the hot flue gases are passed over the outside of the tubes.

**Advantages of using an Air preheater**

1. The preheated air gives the higher furnace temperature which results in more heat transfer to the water and thus increases the evaporative capacity per kg of fuel.

2. There is an increase of about 2% in the boiler efficiency for each 35-40°C rise in temperature of air.

3. It enables a low grade fuel to be burnt with less excess air.

## 8.20 INDIAN BOILER REGULATIONS (IBR) ACT

- IBR stands for The Indian Boiler Regulations Act. It is an Act of Indian National Law.

- It governs the manufacture, installation, operation and maintenance of steam boilers.

- The IBR is not a "type" approval, in which once a certain type of design is approved. It is a specific approval for each and every unit – every boiler, every valve, every trap, every pipe and so on.

- Every item used in an IBR steam system has to be manufactured, installed, tested, operated and maintained under inspection of local inspector.

- The Act defines anything connected to an IBR Boiler as an IBR system i.e. all boiler mountings, steam distribution pipes, valves, traps, strainers etc. are all under IBR.

## 8.21 IBR BOILER AND NON-IBR BOILERS

- A steam boiler is defined in the IBR Act as a vessel containing greater than 22.5 litres of water which is used to generate steam.

- Generally, any boiler above 1000 kg/hr capacity is an IBR boiler.

- Non-IBR boilers are coil type water tube boilers, available in a capacity of 200-850 kg/hr.

- The pressure of steam is dropped below 3.5 $kg/cm^2$, the system becomes Non-IBR. So most process plants use 3.5 $kg/cm^2$ as process steam.

- At the last valve before the process equipment (the process equipment is again Non-IBR).

- Condensate is not steam. It is water and is therefore, exempted from IBR.

- Steam traps on the main lines have to be IBR, but traps installed on the process equipment are Non-IBR.

## 8.22 EVAPORATIVE CAPACITY

The evaporative capacity of a boiler is the quantity of steam produced per hour at full load. It is also known as evaporation rate. The evaporative capacity of a boiler may be expressed in terms of:

- kg of steam/hr

- kg of steam/hr/$m^2$ of heating surface.

- kg of steam/hr/$m^3$ volume of furnace.

- kg of steam/kg of fuel fired.

As per need boilers are producing steam of different qualities (wet, dry or super heated) at different pressure and temperature conditions. Their operating specifications such as temperature of feed water, fuel quality, firing methods, draught type are also different. In such conditions, it is not good to measure their performance in terms of quantity of steam produced per hour. Thus, a more logical method to express evaporation capacity, known as *equivalent evaporation* to compare steam generators has become popular.

## 8.23 EQUIVALENT EVAPORATION

Equivalent evaporation is defined as the *amount of water evaporated from water at 100 °C to dry and saturated steam at 100 °C.*

As per standard conditions, 1 kg of water at 100°C requires 2256.9 kJ $\cong$ 2257 kJ to get converted into steam at 100°C.

Consider a boiler generating $m_s$ kg of steam per hour at a pressure p and temperature T.

Let, h = Enthalpy of steam per kg under the generating conditions

Then,

For dry saturated steam at pressure p,

$$h = h_f + h_{fg}$$

For wet steam at pressure p with dryness fraction x,

$$h = h_f + x \cdot h_{fg}$$

For superheated steam at pressure p and temperature $T_{sup}$,

$$h = h_g + c_p (T_{sup} - T_s)$$

If $h_{f_1}$ = Specific enthalpy of water at given feed water temperature

Then, the heat gained by the steam from the boiler per unit time

$$= m_s (h - h_{f_1}) \text{ kJ}$$

The equivalent evaporation is given by,

$$m_e = \frac{m_s (h - h_{f_1})}{2257} = m_s \times F_e$$

where,

$$F_e = \frac{h - h_{f_1}}{2257} \text{ is known as } \textbf{factor of evaporation}$$

and its value is always greater than unity for all boilers.

It is defined as the *ratio of heat received by 1 kg of water under working conditions to that received by water from and at 100 °C.*

## 8.24 BOILER EFFICIENCY

Boiler efficiency is the ratio of actual heat used in producing the steam to the heat liberated in the furnace. It is also termed as thermal efficiency of the boiler.

Boiler efficiency or thermal efficiency,

$$\eta = \frac{\text{Actual heat used in producing steam}}{\text{Heat liberated in the furnace}}$$

$$= \frac{m_s (h - h_{f_1})}{m_f \times C.V.}$$

where,

$$m_s = \text{Mass of steam generated in kg/hr}$$

$$m_f = \text{Mass of fuel burned in kg/hr}$$

$$C.V. = \text{Calorific value of fuel in kJ/kg}$$

If a boiler consisting of an economizer, and superheater is considered as a single unit, then its efficiency is known as **overall efficiency** of the boiler.

## 8.24.1 Factors Influencing Boiler Efficiency

Factors influencing boiler efficiency can be categorised into two groups:

(1) Fixed factors and (2) Variable factors.

1. **Fixed Factors:**
   - Boiler design which includes the shape and volume of the furnace, the flues arrangement, water and steam circulation arrangement, efficiency of heating surfaces,
   - Properties of fuel burnt,
   - Flue gas and ash heat losses.

2. **Variable Factors:**
   - The condition of heat absorbing surfaces,
   - Humidity and temperature of combustion air,
   - Effectiveness in combustion,
   - Excess air fluctuations,
   - Actual firing rate,
   - Change in draught from rated, due to atmospheric conditions.

## 8.25 BOILER TRIAL

The main objectives of conducting a trial on an existing steam boiler are as follows:

- To determine the efficiency and capacity of the boiler.
- To check the performance with the rated performance.
- To prepare account of the heat energy input and output including various losses for the purpose of corrective steps to improve efficiency.

## 8.25.1 Heat Losses in a Boiler Plant

The following heat losses occur in an boiler plant.

- Heat loss through dry flue gases.
- Heat carried away by steam in flue gases.
- Heat loss due to unburnt fuel.
- Heat loss due to incomplete combustion.
- Heat loss due to radiation.

## SOLVED PROBLEMS

**Problem 8.1:** 5500 kg of steam is produced per hour at a pressure of 7.6 bar in a boiler with dryness fraction 0.98. The feed water temperature is 51°C. The amount of coal burnt per hour is 650 kg of calorific value 30500 kJ/kg. Determine the boiler efficiency and equivalent evaporation.

**Solution:**

**Given:** $m_s$ = 5,500 kg/hr, p = 7.6 bar, x = 0.98, $T_1$ = 51°C, $m_f$ = 650 kg/hr, C.V. = 30500 kJ/kg.

$$\text{Steam generated per kg of coal} = \frac{5,500}{650} = 8.461 \text{ kg/kg of fuel}$$

Enthalpy of feed water at 51°C from steam table,

$$h_{f_1} = 213.70 \text{ kJ/kg}$$

Enthalpy of steam at 7.6 bar from steam table

$$h_f = 711.68 \text{ kJ/kg}$$
$$h_{fg} = 2053.7 \text{ kJ/kg}$$
$$h = h_f + x\, h_{fg}$$
$$= 711.67 + 0.98 \times 2053.7$$
$$= 2724.296 \text{ kJ/kg}$$

**Boiler efficiency,**

$$\eta = \frac{m_s\,(h - h_{f_1})}{m_f \times \text{C.V.}} = \frac{5500 \times (2724.29 - 231.7)}{650 \times 30500}$$
$$= 0.6965 = \mathbf{69.65\%}$$

**Equivalent evaporation,**

$$m_e = \frac{m_s\,(h - h_{f_1})}{2257}$$
$$= \frac{8.461 \times (2724.29 - 213.7)}{2257}$$
$$= \mathbf{9.42 \text{ kg/kg of coal}}$$

---

**Problem 8.2:** The following observations were recorded during a boiler trial of 1 hr duration. 700 kg of coal of calorific value 30,000 kJ/kg is used to produce 5,250 kg of steam at a pressure of 12 bar. Dryness fraction of steam is 94%. Temperature of steam leaving the superheater is 250°C and temperature of hot well is 45°C.

Calculate:

(i)   Equivalent evaporation.

(ii)  Thermal efficiency of boiler.

(iii) Heat added in superheater.

**Solution:**

**Given:** $m_s$ = 5,250 kg/hr, p = 12 bar, C.V. = 30,000 kJ/kg, x = 0.94, $T_{sup}$ = 250°C, $T_1$ = 45°C, $m_f$ = 700 kg/hr

**(i) Equivalent evaporation**

From steam table corresponding to feed water temperature 45°C, we can find,

$$h_{f_1} = 188.45 \text{ kJ/kg}$$

and corresponding to steam pressure of 12 bar,

$$h_f = 798.43 \text{ kJ/kg}$$
$$h_{fg} = 1984.3 \text{ kJ/kg}$$

For wet steam,

$$h = h_f + x \cdot h_{fg}$$
$$= 798.43 + 0.94 \times 1984.3$$
$$= 2663.37 \text{ kJ/kg}$$

Equivalent evaporation,

$$m_e = \frac{m_s (h - h_{f_1})}{2257} = \frac{5250 \times (2663.37 - 188.45)}{2257}$$
$$= 5757.61 \text{ kg/hr}$$

Mass of water evaporated per kg of coal,

$$m_e = \frac{5757.61}{700} = \mathbf{823 \text{ kg/kg of coal}}$$

**(ii) Boiler efficiency**

$$\eta = \frac{m_s (h - h_{f_1})}{m_f \times C.V.}$$
$$= \frac{5250 \times (2663.37 - 188.45)}{700 \times 30000}$$
$$= 0.6187 = \mathbf{61.87\%}$$

**(iii) Heat added in superheater**

Heat added in superheater = Enthalpy of superheated steam − Enthalpy of wet steam

$$= (h_{sup} - h)$$

From steam table corresponding to a steam pressure of 12 bar, we find that,

$$h_g = 2782.7 \text{ kJ/kg}$$

and $\quad T = 188°C$

$\therefore \quad h_{sup} = h_g + c_p (T_{sup} - T)$

$$= 2782.7 + 2.1 (250 - 188) \qquad \text{(Taking } c_p = 2.1 \text{ kJ/kg·K)}$$
$$= 2912.9 \text{ kJ/kg}$$

Heat added to superheater = 2912.9 − 2663.37

$$= \mathbf{249.53 \text{ kJ/kg}}$$

**Problem 8.3:** The following observations were made on a boiler plant during one hour test.

$$\text{Steam generated} \quad = \quad 37500 \text{ kg at 20 bar and } 260°C$$

Temperature of water entering the economiser

$$= \quad 15°C$$

Temperature of water leaving the economiser

$$= \quad 90°C$$

$$\text{Fuel used} \quad = \quad 4400 \text{ kg}$$

$$\text{Energy of combustion of fuel} \quad = \quad 31000 \text{ kJ/kg}$$

Calculate:

(i)   The equivalent evaporation per kg of fuel.

(ii)  The thermal efficiency of the plant.

(iii) The percentage heat energy of the fuel energy utilised by the economiser.

**Solution:**

**Given:** $m_s$ = 37500 kg/hr, p = 20 bar, $T_{sup}$ = 260°C, $T_{ei}$ = 15°C, $T_{eo}$ = 90°C, $m_f$ = 4000 kg/hr, C.V. = 31000 kJ/kg.

**(i)   Equivalent evaporation per kg of fuel:**

Here boiler and economiser is considered as a single unit, so feed water temperature is 15°C and corresponding to this temperature from steam table,

$$h_{f_1} \quad = \quad 62.9 \text{ kJ/kg}$$

Also at steam pressure of 20 bar,

$$h_g \quad = \quad 2797.2 \text{ kJ/kg}$$

and

$$T \quad = \quad 212.37 \text{ °C}$$

For superheated steam,

$$h \quad = \quad h_g + c_p \, (T_{sup} - T)$$

$$= \quad 2797.2 + 2.1 \times (260 - 212.37)$$

$$= \quad 2897 \text{ kJ/kg}$$

$\therefore$   Equivalent evaporation in kg/hr

$$m_e \quad = \quad \frac{m_s \, (h - h_{f_1})}{2257} \quad = \quad \frac{37500 \times (2897 - 62.9)}{2257}$$

$$= \quad 47088.50 \text{ kg/hr}$$

Equivalent evaporation in kg/kg of fuel,

$$m_e \quad = \quad \frac{47088.50}{4400} = \textbf{10.70 kg/kg of fuel}$$

**(ii)  Thermal efficiency of the plant:**

$$\eta \;=\; \frac{m_s\,(h - h_{f_1})}{m_f \times C.V.} \;=\; \frac{37500 \times (2897 - 62.9)}{4400 \times 31000}$$

$$=\; \mathbf{0.7792 = 77.92\%}$$

**(iii)  Percentage heat energy of the fuel energy utilised by the economiser:**

From steam table, at 90°C,

$$h_{f_2} \;=\; 376.80 \text{ kJ/kg}$$

Heat utilised by economiser,

$$Q_e \;=\; m_s\,(h_{f_2} - h_{f_1})$$

$$=\; 37500 \times (376.8 - 62.9)$$

$$=\; 11.77 \times 10^6 \text{ kJ/hr}$$

$$=\; \frac{11.77 \times 10^6}{4400} \text{ kJ/kg of fuel}$$

$$=\; 2675.38 \text{ kJ}$$

$$\text{\% heat utilised by economiser} \;=\; \frac{2675.38}{31000} \times 100 = \mathbf{8.63\%}$$

---

**Problem 8.4:** The following data was recorded during a test performed on a steam plant consisting of a Lancashire boiler, economiser and a superheater.

$$\text{Steam generated} \;=\; 5{,}000 \text{ kg/hr at 14 bar pressure}$$

$$\text{Mass of coal burnt} \;=\; 670 \text{ kg/hr}$$

$$\text{Calorific value of coal} \;=\; 29500 \text{ kJ/kg}$$

Temperature of feed water at entry and exit of economiser = 30°C and 130°C respectively.

Temperature of steam leaving the superheater = 320°C.

Dryness fraction of steam leaving the boiler = 0.97

$$c_p \text{ (superheated steam)} \;=\; 2.3 \text{ kJ/kg·K}$$

$$c_p \text{ (water)} \;=\; 4.18 \text{ kJ/kg·K}$$

Calculate:

(1)  Factor of evaporation.

(2)  Overall efficiency of the plant.

(3)  The percentage of available heat utilised in the boiler, economiser and superheater respectively. Hence, determine percentage of heat lost.

**Solution:**

**Given:** $m_s$ = 5000 kg/hr, p = 14 bar, $m_f$ = 670 kg/hr, C.V. = 29500, $T_{ei}$ = 30°C, $T_{eo}$ = 130°C, $T_{sup}$ = 320°C, x = 0.97.

**1. Factor of evaporation:**

Mass of steam per kg of coal, $\dot{m}_s = \dfrac{5000}{670}$ = 7.46 kg/kg of fuel

From steam table, enthalpy of feed water at 30°C,

$$h_{f_1} \;=\; 125.68 \text{ kJ/kg}$$

and for steam at 14 bar pressure,

$h_f$ = 830.07 kJ/kg, $h_{fg}$ = 1957.7 kJ/kg, $h_g$ = 2787.8 kJ/kg and T = 195°C.

Enthalpy of superheated steam,

$$
\begin{aligned}
h \;&=\; h_g + c_p\,(T_{sup} - T) \\
&=\; 2787.8 + 2.3 \times (320 - 195) \\
&=\; 3075.3 \text{ kJ/kg}
\end{aligned}
$$

Factor of evaporation, $F_e \;=\; \dfrac{h - h_{f_1}}{2257} \;=\; \dfrac{3075.3 - 125.68}{2257} \;=\; \mathbf{1.307}$

**2. Overall efficiency of the plant:**

$$
\begin{aligned}
\eta \;&=\; \frac{\dot{m}_s\,(h - h_{f_1})}{\text{C.V.}} \;=\; \frac{7.46 \times (3075.3 - 125.68)}{29500} \\
&=\; 0.7459 \\
&=\; \mathbf{74.59\%}
\end{aligned}
$$

**3. Percentage of available heat utilised:**

**(a) Heat utilised in boiler:**

Water enters in boiler at 130°C and steam leaves boiler at 14 bar pressure (x = 0.97)

$\therefore$ $\quad Q_B \;=\;$ Enthalpy of steam at boiler outlet – Enthalpy of water at boiler inlet

$$
\begin{aligned}
&=\; \dot{m}_s\,[(h_f + x\,h_{fg}) - h_{f_2}] \qquad (h_{f_2} \text{ at 130°C} = 546.3 \text{ kJ/kg}) \\
&=\; 7.46\,[(830.6) + 0.97 \times (957.7) - 546.3] \\
&=\; 16283.23 \text{ kJ}
\end{aligned}
$$

% Heat utilisation in boiler $= \dfrac{Q_B}{Q_s} \times 100 \;=\; \dfrac{16283.33}{29500} \times 100 = \mathbf{55.197\%}$

**(b) Heat utilised in economiser:**

$$
\begin{aligned}
Q_e \;&=\; \dot{m}_s \cdot c_{pw}\,(T_{eo} - T_{ei}) \\
&=\; 7.46 \times 4.18 \times (130 - 30)
\end{aligned}
$$

$$= 3118.28 \text{ kJ}$$

$$\% \text{ Heat utilisation in economizer} = \frac{Q_e}{Q_s} \times 100 = \frac{3118.28}{29500} \times 100$$

$$= \mathbf{10.570\%}$$

**(c) Heat utilisation in superheater:**

$$Q_{sup} = \dot{m}_s \{[h_g + c_p (T_{sup} - T)] - [h_f + x \, h_{fg}]\}$$

$$= 7.46 \{[2787.8 + 2.3 (320 - 195)]$$

$$- [830.01 + 0.97 \times 1957.7]$$

$$= 2396.90 \text{ kJ}$$

$$\% \text{ Heat utilised in superheater} = \frac{Q_{sup}}{Q_s} \times 100$$

$$= \frac{2396.90}{29500} \times 100$$

$$= \mathbf{8.125\%}$$

**(d) Percentage heat loss:** 100 − % heat utilised in boiler, economiser and superheater

$$= 100 - (55.197 + 10.57 + 8.125)$$

$$= \mathbf{26.108\%}$$

---

**Problem 8.5:** In an experiment on a small oil-fired boiler, the steam is produced at 6 bar pressure, with dryness fraction 0.96. The 75 litres of water is converted into steam in 9.5 minutes. Then 10 litres of fuel oil with specific gravity 0.85 and calorific value 43125 kJ/kg is consumed in 11 minutes 25 seconds. The feed water temperature is 35°C. Determine the boiler efficiency and equivalent evaporation.

**Solution:**

**Given:** p = 6 bar, x = 0.6, water = 75 litres, 10 litres oil, C.V. = 43125 kJ/kg, $T_1$ = 35°C.

Mass of steam = 75 × 1 = 75 kg in 9.5 min.

$$\text{Mass of steam per hour} = 75 \times \frac{60}{9.5}$$

$$m_s = 473.684 \text{ kg/hr}$$

$$\text{Mass of oil} = 10 \times 0.85$$

$$= 8.5 \text{ kg in 11 min. 25 sec.}$$

$$= 8.5 \text{ kg in 685 sec}$$

$$\text{Mass of oil per hour} = 8.5 \times \frac{3600}{685}$$

$$m_f = 44.671 \text{ kg}$$

Mass of steam per kg oil $(\dot{m}_s)$ $= \dfrac{473.684}{44.67} = 10.60 \text{ kg/kg of oil}$

Enthalpy of feed water at 35°C from steam table,

$$h_{f_1} = 146.56 \text{ kJ/kg}$$

and for steam at 6 bar from steam table,

$$h_f = 670.42 \text{ kJ/kg}$$

$$h_{fg} = 2085.0 \text{ kJ/kg}$$

$$h = h_f + x\, h_{fg}$$

$$= 670.42 + 0.96 \times 2085$$

$$= 2672.02 \text{ kJ/kg}$$

Efficiency of boiler, $\quad \eta = \dfrac{\dot{m}_s\,(h - h_{f_1})}{\text{C.V.}}$

$$= \dfrac{10.60 \times (2672.02 - 146.56)}{43125}$$

$$= 0.6207$$

$$= \mathbf{62.07\%}$$

Equivalent evaporation, $m_e = \dfrac{\dot{m}_s\,(h - h_{f_1})}{2257}$

$$= \dfrac{10.60 \times (2672.02 - 146.56)}{2257}$$

$$= \mathbf{11.86 \text{ kg/kg of oil}}$$

## 8.26 ENERGY BALANCE

- In a boiler, heat is produced by burning of fuel in the furnace. But all heat is not utilised for generation of steam. Some heat is lost by different ways.

- A systematic representation of heat release and heat distribution on minute, hour or per kg of fuel basis is known as energy balance sheet or heat balance sheet.

- The procedure to draw heat balance sheet on kJ/min basis is explained below:

**(A) First of all compute heat release by the fuel.**

**Heat released by the fuel,**

$$Q_s = m_f \times \text{C.V.}$$

where,

$$m_f = \text{Mass flow rate of fuel in kg/min}$$

$$C.V. \ = \ \text{Calorific value of fuel in kJ/kg}$$

**(B) Calculate heat distribution in different ways.**

**1. Heat utilised to form steam**

$$Q_1 \ = \ m_s \, (h - h_{f_1})$$

where,

$$m_s \ = \ \text{Mass of steam generated per minute}$$

$$h \ = \ \text{Enthalpy of steam generated, kJ/kg}$$

$$h_f \ = \ \text{Enthalpy of water, kJ/kg}$$

**2. Heat lost through dry flue gases**

$$Q_2 \ = \ m_g \, c_{pg} \, (T_g - T_a)$$

where,

$$m_g \ = \ \text{Mass of dry flue gas per minute}$$

$$c_{pg} \ = \ \text{Specific heat of flue gases, kJ/kg·K}$$

$$T_g \ = \ \text{Flue gas temperature, °C (K)}$$

$$T_a \ = \ \text{Temperature of air entering combustion chamber °C (K)}$$

**3. Heat carried away by steam (moisture) in flue gases**

$$Q_3 \ = \ m_m \, [h_g + c_{ps} \, (T_{sup} - T_s) - h_{f_2}]$$

where,

$$m_m \ = \ \text{Mass of moisture per min.}$$

$$c_{ps} \ = \ \text{Mean specific heat of superheated steam in flue gases}$$

$$T_{sup} \ = \ \text{Temperature of steam leaving the superheater}$$

Sometimes steam formed by combustion of hydrogen is added to above mass.

$$\text{Mass of steam formed} = \ 9H_2$$

where, $H_2 \ = \ \text{Mass of hydrogen present per kg of fuel}$

**4. Heat loss due to unburnt fuel**

$$Q_4 \ = \ m_{fu} \times C.V.$$

$$m_{fu} \ = \ \text{Mass of unburnt fuel per minute}$$

**5. Heat loss due to incomplete combustion of carbon to carbon monoxide**

$$Q_5 \ = \ m_2 \times CV_C$$

where, $m_2 \ = \ \text{Mass of carbon or CO in flue gases/min}$

$$CV_C \ = \ \text{Calorific value of carbon or CO}$$

**6.   Heat lost due to radiation**

$$Q_6 \;=\; Q_5 - (Q_1 + Q_2 + Q_3 + Q_4 + Q_5)$$

**(C)  Above calculated values are placed in a table as following:**

| Heat supplied | kJ/min | % | Heat utilised | kg/min | % |
|---|---|---|---|---|---|
| Heat released by the fuel | $Q_s$ | 100 | 1.  Heat used to form steam | $Q_1$ | $\dfrac{Q_1}{Q_s} \times 100$ |
| | | | 2.  Heat lost through dry flue gases | $Q_2$ | $\dfrac{Q_2}{Q_s} \times 100$ |
| | | | 3.  Heat carried a way by steam in flue gases | $Q_3$ | $\dfrac{Q_3}{Q_s} \times 100$ |
| | | | 4.  Heat loss due to unburnt fuel | $Q_4$ | $\dfrac{Q_4}{Q_s} \times 100$ |
| | | | 5.  Heat loss due to incomplete combustion | $Q_5$ | $\dfrac{Q_5}{Q_s} \times 100$ |
| | | | 6.  Heat loss due to radiation | $Q_6$ | $\dfrac{Q_6}{Q_s} \times 100$ |
| | $Q_s$ | 100 | | $Q_u$ | 100 |

## PROBLEMS ON ENERGY BALANCE

**Problem 8.6:** The following observations were recorded during a boiler trial.

$$\text{Steam produced} \;=\; 540 \text{ kg/hr at 10 bar}$$
$$\text{Fuel used} \;=\; 65 \text{ kg/hr}$$
$$\text{Moisture in fuel} \;=\; 2\% \text{ by mass}$$
$$\text{Mass of dry flue gases} \;=\; 9 \text{ kg/kg of fuel}$$
$$\text{Lower calorific value of fuel} \;=\; 32000 \text{ kJ/kg}$$
$$\text{Temperature of flue gases} \;=\; 325°C$$
$$\text{Temperature of boiler house} \;=\; 28°C$$
$$\text{Feed water temperature} \;=\; 50°C$$
$$\text{Mean specific heat of flue gases} \;=\; 1 \text{ kJ/kg·K}$$
$$\text{Dryness fraction of steam} \;=\; 0.95$$
$$\text{Specific heat for superheated steam} \;=\; 2.3 \text{ kJ/kg·K}$$

Prepare the energy balance sheet for the boiler.

**Solution:**

**Given:** $m_s$ = 540 kg/hr, p = 10 bar, $m_f$ = 65 kg/hr, $m_m$ = 0.02 kg/kg of fuel, $m_g$ = 9 kg/kg of fuel, C.V. = 32000 kJ/kg, $T_g$ = 325°C, $T_a$ = 28°C, $T_1$ = 50°C, $c_{pg}$ = 1 kg/kg·K, x = 0.95

**(A) Heat released by the fuel per kg:**

$$Q_s \quad = \quad \text{Mass of fuel} \times \text{C.V.}$$

$$= \quad (1 - 0.02) \times 32000 \qquad (\because \ 2\% \text{ moisture in the fuel})$$

$$= \quad \textbf{31360 kJ}$$

**(B) Calculation for heat distribution:**

1.  Heat utilised to form steam per kg of fuel.

Steam produced per kg of fuel, $\dot{m}_s = \dfrac{\dot{m}_s}{m_f} = \dfrac{540}{65}$

$$= \textbf{8.31 kg.}$$

From steam table at 50°C,

$$h_{f_1} \quad = \quad 209.26 \text{ kJ/kg}$$

and at 10 bar pressure,

$$h_f \quad = \quad 762.61 \text{ kJ/kg}$$

$$h_{fg} \quad = \quad 2013.6 \text{ kJ/kg}$$

Now, $\qquad\qquad h \quad = \quad h_f + x\, h_{fg}$

$$= \quad 762.61 + 0.95 \times 2013.6$$

$$= \quad \textbf{2675.53}$$

$$Q_1 \quad = \quad \dot{m}_s\,(h - h_{f_1}) = 8.31 \times (2675.53 - 209.26)$$

$$= \quad \textbf{20494.70 kJ}$$

2.  Heat lost through dry flue gases,

$$Q_2 \quad = \quad m_g \cdot c_{pg} \cdot (T_g - T_a)$$

$$= \quad 9 \times 1 \times (325 - 28)$$

$$= \quad \textbf{2673 kJ}$$

3.  Heat carried away by moisture in flue gases.

From steam table at 1.03 bar,

$$h_g \quad = \quad 2776.0 \text{ kJ/kg}$$

and $\qquad\qquad T \quad = \quad 100°C$

at 28°C $\qquad h_{f_2} \quad = \quad 117.3 \text{ kJ/kg}$

$$Q_3 \quad = \quad m_m\,(h_g + c_{ps}\,(T_{sup} - T_s) - h_{f_2})$$

$$= \quad 0.02\,(2676.0 + 2.3\,(325 - 100) - 117.3)$$

$$= \quad \textbf{61.524 kJ}$$

4.   Heat lost due to radiation,

$$Q_4 = Q_s - (Q_1 + Q_2 + Q_3)$$
$$= 31360 - (20494.7 + 2673 + 61.524)$$
$$= \mathbf{8130.78 \ kJ}$$

**(C)  Heat balance sheet on per kg fuel basis:**

| Heat supplied | kJ | % | Heat utilised | kJ | % |
|---|---|---|---|---|---|
| Heat supplied by 1 kg of fuel | 31360 | 100 | 1.  Heat used to form steam | 20494.7 | 65.36 |
| | | | 2.  Heat lost through dry flue gases | 2673.0 | 8.52 |
| | | | 3.  Heat carried away by moisture in flue gases | 61.524 | 0.19 |
| | | | 4.  Heat lost by radiation | 8130.78 | 25.93 |
| $Q_s$ = 31360 | 100 | | | $Q_u$ = 31360 | 100.00 |

**Problem 8.7:** The following data was recorded during a test on a boiler:

$$\text{Mass of feed water} = 650 \text{ kg/hr}$$

Temperature of water at entry and exhaust of the economiser = 30°C and 50°C respectively.

$$\text{Steam pressure} = 11 \text{ bar}$$
$$\text{Fuel used} = 60 \text{ kg/hr}$$
$$\text{Calorific value of fuel} = 45000 \text{ kJ/kg}$$
$$\text{Temperature of flue gases} = 300°C$$
$$\text{Dryness fraction of steam} = 0.97$$
$$\text{Boiler room temperature} = 32°C$$
$$c_p \text{ for gases} = 1.05 \text{ kJ/kg·K}$$
$$c_p \text{ for superheated steam} = 2.2 \text{ kJ/kg·K}$$
$$c_p \text{ for water} = 1.05 \text{ kJ/kg·K}$$

The composition of fuel used by mass,

$H_2$ = 12%, C = 84% and remaining is ash.

The dry flue gas analysis by volume $CO_2$ = 13%, $O_2$ = 5%, $N_2$ = 82%.

Steam partial pressure in exhaust gases is 0.07 bar.

Draw heat balance sheet on the basis of one kg of fuel.

**Solution:**

**Given:** $m_s$ = 650 kg/hr, $m_f$ = 60 kg/hr, $\dot{m}_s$ = 650/60 = 10.83 kg/kg of fuel, p = 11 bar, C.V. = 45000 kJ/kg, $T_g$ = 300°C, x = 0.97, $T_a$ = 32°C, $c_{pg}$ = 1.05 kJ/kg·K,  $c_{ps}$ = 2.2 kg/kg·K, $c_{pw}$ = 4.18 kJ/kg·K, Steam partial pressure = 0.07 bar.

**(A) Heat supplied by 1 kg of fuel:**

$$Q_s = 45000 \text{ kJ/kg}$$

**(B) Calculation of heat distribution:**

1. Heat used to form steam per kg of fuel from steam table at 50°,

$$h_{f_1} = 209.26 \text{ kJ/kg}$$

and at 11 bar pressure, $\quad h_f = 781.12 \text{ kJ/kg}$

$$h_{fg} = 1998.5 \text{ kJ/kg}$$

Now, $\quad h = h_f + x\, h_{fg}$

$$= 781.12 + 0.97 \times 1998.5$$

$$= \mathbf{2719.665 \text{ kJ/kg}}$$

and $\quad Q_1 = \dot{m}_s\,(h - h_{f_1})$

$$= 10.833 \times (2719.665 - 209.26)$$

$$= \mathbf{27195.21 \text{ kJ/kg of fuel}}$$

2. Heat utilised in superheater,

$$Q_2 = \dot{m}_s \cdot c_{pw}\,(T_{eo} - T_{ei})$$

$$= 10.833 \times 4.18 \times (50 - 30)$$

$$= \mathbf{905.64 \text{ kJ}}$$

3. Heat lost through dry flue gases:

   Air required to burn 1 kg of fuel

$$= \frac{N_2 \times C}{33 \times (CO + CO_2)} = \frac{82 \times 84}{33 \times (0 + 13)} = \mathbf{16.056 \text{ kg}}$$

   Dry gases formed per kg of fuel,

$$m_g = 16.056 + 0.84 = \mathbf{16.896 \text{ kg}}$$

   Then, heat lost through dry flue gases,

$$Q_3 = m_g \cdot c_{pg} \cdot (T_g - T_a)$$

$$= 16.896 \times 1.05 \times (300 - 32)$$

$$= \mathbf{4754.52 \text{ kJ/kg of fuel}}$$

4. Heat carried away by moisture in flue gases:

   The moisture formed per kg of fuel,

$$m_m = 9 \times H_2 = 9 \times 0.12 = 1.08 \text{ kg}$$

   From steam table at 0.07 bar,

$$h_g = 2572.6 \text{ kJ/kg}, \quad T_s = 39.025°C$$

and at 32°C

$$h_{f_2} = 134.02°C$$

Then,

$$Q_4 = m_m [h_g + c_{ps}(T_{sup} - T_s) - h_{f_2}]$$
$$= 1.08 \times [2572.6 + 2.2 \times (300 - 39.025) - 134.02]$$
$$= \mathbf{3253.743 \text{ kJ}}$$

5.　Heat lost due to radiation.

$$Q_5 = Q_s - (Q_1 + Q_2 + Q_3 + Q_4)$$
$$= 45000 - (27195.21 + 905.64 + 4754.52 + 3253.743)$$
$$= \mathbf{8890.88 \text{ kJ}}$$

**(C)　Heat balance sheet on per kg of fuel basis:**

| Heat supplied | kJ | % | Heat utilised | kJ | % |
|---|---|---|---|---|---|
| Heat supplied by 1 kg of fuel | 45,000 | 100 | 1.　Heat used to form steam | 27195.21 | 60.43 |
| | | | 2.　Heat used by superheater | 905.64 | 2.01 |
| | | | 3.　Heat lost through dry flue gases | 4754.52 | 10.57 |
| | | | 4.　Heat carried away by moisture in flue gases | 3253.743 | 7.23 |
| | | | 5.　Heat lost by radiation | 8890.88 | 19.76 |
| **$Q_s$ = 45000** | **100** | | | **$Q_u$ = 45000** | **100.00** |

**Problem 8.8:** The following results were obtained from a boiler trial.

$$\begin{aligned}
\text{Feed water/hr} &= 700 \text{ kg} \\
\text{Feed temperature} &= 27°C \\
\text{Steam pressure} &= 8 \text{ bar} \\
\text{Dryness} &= 0.97 \\
\text{Coal consumption} &= 100 \text{ kg/hr (C.V. = 25000 kJ/kg)} \\
\text{Unburnt coal collected} &= 7.25 \text{ kg/hr (C.V. = 2000 kJ/kg)} \\
\text{Flue formed/kg of fuel} &= 17.3 \text{ kg} \\
\text{Flue temperature} &= 325°C
\end{aligned}$$

$$c_{pg} = 1.025 \text{ kJ/kg·K}$$

Room air temperature $= 16°C$

Draw up heat balance sheet on kg/min basis. From the heat balance sheet, write the value of boiler efficiency.

**Solution:**

**Given:** $m_s = 700$ kg/hr, $T_1 = 27°C$, $p = 8$ bar, $x = 0.97$, $m_f = 100$ kg/hr. (C.V. = 25000 kJ/kg·K), $m_{fu} = 7.25$ kg/hr, (C.V. = 2000 kJ/kg), $m_g = 17.3$ kg/kg of fuel, $T_g = 325°C$, $c_{pg} = 1.025$ kg/kg·K, $T_a = 16°C$.

Here heat balance sheet on minute basis is required. So first do following conversions.

$$m_s = 700 \text{ kg/hr} = \frac{700}{60} \text{ kg/min} = \textbf{11.67 kg/min}$$

$$m_f = \frac{100}{60} = \textbf{1.67 kg/min}$$

$$m_{fu} = \frac{7.25}{60} = \textbf{0.121 kJ/min}$$

**(A) Heat supplied/released by fuel per minute:**

$$\begin{aligned} Q_s &= m_f \times \text{C.V.} \\ &= 1.67 \times 25000 \\ &= \textbf{41750 kJ/min} \end{aligned}$$

**(B) Calculation for heat utilization:**

1. Heat used for steam formation

   From steam table at 27°C heat in water,

   $$h_{f_1} = 113.13 \text{ kJ/kg}$$

and at 8 bar for steam,

$$h_f = 720.9 \text{ kJ/kg}$$

$$h_{fg} = 2046.5 \text{ kJ/kg}$$

Now,
$$\begin{aligned} h &= h_f + x\, h_{fg} \\ &= 720.9 + 0.97 \times 2046.5 \\ &= 2706.005 \text{ kJ/kg} \end{aligned}$$

Then,
$$\begin{aligned} Q_1 &= m_s\,(h - h_{f_1}) = 11.67 \times (2706.005 - 113.13) \\ &= \textbf{30258.21 kJ/min} \end{aligned}$$

2. Heat loss through dry flue gases,

$$Q_2 = m_g \cdot c_{pg}\,(T_g - T_a)$$

$$= \ 17.3 \times 1.67 \times 1.025 \times (325 - 16)$$

$$(\because \ 1.67 \text{ kg fuel burnt per minutes})$$

$$= \ \textbf{9150.50 kJ/min}$$

3.  Heat loss due to unburnt fuel

$$Q_3 \ = \ m_{fu} \times C.V.$$

$$= \ 0.121 \times 2000$$

$$= \ \textbf{242 kJ/kg}$$

4.  Heat loss due to radiation

$$Q_4 \ = \ Q_s - (Q_1 + Q_2 + Q_3)$$

$$= \ 41750 - (30258.21 + 9150.50 + 242)$$

$$= \ \textbf{2099.29 kJ/min}$$

**(C)  Heat balance sheet on minute basis:**

| Heat supplied | kJ/min | % | Heat utilised | kJ/min | % |
|---|---|---|---|---|---|
| Heat supplied per min | 41750 | 100 | 1.  Heat used for steam formation | 30258.21 | 72.47 |
| | | | 2.  Heat loss through dry flue gases | 9150.5 | 21.92 |
| | | | 3.  Heat loss because of unburnt fuel | 242.0 | 0.58 |
| | | | 4.  Heat loss due to radiation | 2099.29 | 5.03 |
| $Q_s$ = 41750 | 100 | | | $Q_u$ = 41750 | 100.00 |

From heat balance sheet,

Efficiency of boiler, $\eta$  =  **72.47%**

**Problem 8.9:** 20000 kg of feed weater at 25°C is supplied to a boiler during a trial of 8 hours. At the end of trial, 800 kg of water at 55°C is drained from boiler. Pressure of steam produced by the boiler was recorded as 12 bar with dryness fraction 0.95. The 2520 kg of coal is consumed during trial period with calorific value 30000 kJ/kg.

Calculate the actual evaporation rate, equivalent evaporation and prepare the energy balance sheet for the given data.

**Solution:**

**Given:** Water supplied = 20000 kg, $T_1$ = 25°C, p = 12 bar, x = 0.95, Coal burned = 2520 kg, C.V. = 30000 kJ/kg.

Total steam produced in 8 hours = Water supplied – Water drained

$$= 20000 - 800 = 19200 \text{ kg}$$

$$\therefore \quad \text{Evaporation rate per hour} = \frac{19200}{8} = 2400 \text{ kg/hr}$$

$$\text{Fuel consumed} = \frac{2520}{8} = 315 \text{ kg/hr}$$

$$\text{Mass of steam per kg of coal, } \dot{m}_s = \frac{2400}{315} = 7.619 \text{ kg per kg of fuel}$$

Heat in feed water at 25°C from steam table,

$$h_{f_1} = 108.77 \text{ kJ/kg}$$

Heat in steam at 12 bar pressure,

$$h_f = 798.43 \text{ kJ/kg}$$

$$h_{fg} = 1984.3 \text{ kJ/kg}$$

$$h = h_f + x\, h_{fg} = 798.43 + 0.95 \times 1984.3 = \mathbf{2649.315}$$

$$\text{Equivalent evaporation, } m_e = \frac{\dot{m}_s (h - h_{f_1})}{2257}$$

$$= \frac{7.619 \times (2649.315 - 108.77)}{2257}$$

$$= \mathbf{8.576 \text{ kg/kg of fuel}}$$

Heat supplied during 8 hours,

$$Q_s = 2520 \times 30000 = 75.60 \times 10^6 \text{ kJ}$$

Heat used to form steam for 8 hours,

$$Q_1 = 19200 \times (h - h_{f_1})$$

$$= 19200 \times (2649.315 - 108.77)$$

$$= \mathbf{48.778 \times 10^6 \text{ kJ}}$$

Heat taken by 800 kg of water = (Heat content at 55°C − Heat content at 25°C) × 800

$$= 800 \times (230.17 - 108.77)$$

$$= \mathbf{97.120 \times 10^3 \text{ kJ}}$$

$$\text{Unaccounted heat} = 75.0 \times 10^6 - (48.778 \times 10^6 + 97.120 \times 10^3)$$

$$= 26.724 \times 10^6 \text{ kJ}$$

$$\text{Boiler efficiency, } \eta = \frac{48.778 \times 10^6}{75.0 \times 10^6}$$

$$= 0.64 = \mathbf{64\%}$$

## 8.27 DRAUGHT

It is necessary to force the fresh air in combustion chamber and to exhaust the gases produced by combustion. This flow is possible by maintaining pressure difference. The pressure difference which causes flow of gas is called as draught.

**Classification of Draught:**

There are basically two methods of producing draught:

1.  Natural or Chimney Draught.

2.  Artificial Draught.

    (a)  Steam Jet Draught

        (i) Induced Draught   (ii) Forced Draught

    (b)  Mechanical Draught

        (i) Induced Fan Draught  (ii) Balanced Draught  (iii) Forced Fan Draught

## 8.28 NATURAL DRAUGHT

Natural draught is also known as **chimney draught** because chimney is used to produce this draught. A chimney is a vertical tubular structure built either of concrete, steel or masonry. The draught produced by chimney is due to density difference between the column of hot gases inside the chimney and the outside cold air (cold compared to hot gases).

Fig. 8.20 shows schematic arrangement of a chimney of height H metres above the grate.

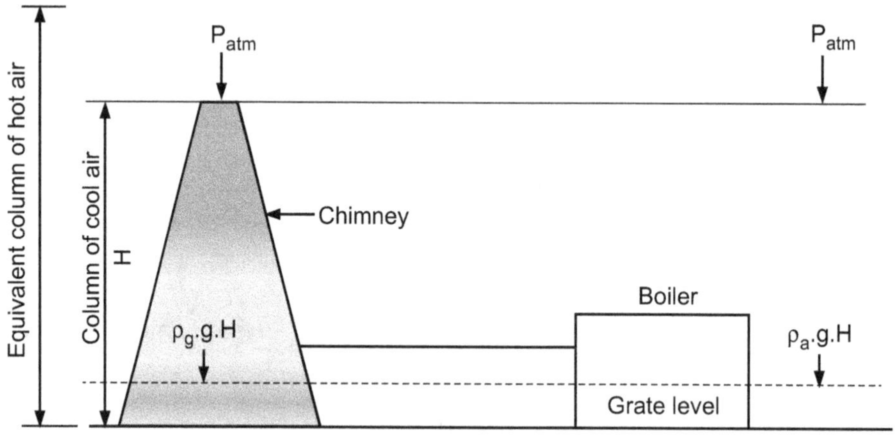


**Fig. 8.20**

Let,

$$H \;=\; \text{Height of chimney above the grate in m}$$

$$h \;=\; \text{Draught required in terms of mm of water}$$

$$p_a \;=\; \text{Atmospheric pressure at chimney top}$$

$$\rho_g \quad = \quad \text{Average mass density of hot gas}$$

$$\rho_a \quad = \quad \text{Mass density of air outside the chimney}$$

Now, pressure at the grate level (chimney side) (because of hot gases)

$$p_1 \quad = \quad p_a + \rho_g \cdot gH$$

and pressure acting on grate on opposite side (because of cold outside air),

$$p_2 \quad = \quad p_a + \rho_a \cdot gH$$

$\therefore$ Net pressure difference causing the flow through the combustion chamber,

$$\Delta p \quad = \quad p_2 - p_1 = (\rho_a - \rho_a)\, gH$$

This difference of pressure causing the flow of gases is known as ***static draught***. Its value is measured by a water manometer and generally less than 12 mm of water.

## 8.28.1 Height of Chimney

The amount of draught depends upon the height of chimney, therefore, its height should be such that it can produce a sufficient draught.

Let,
$$H \quad = \quad \text{Height of chimney above the grate in m}$$

$$H_w \quad = \quad \text{Draught required in terms of mm of water}$$

$$T_a, T_g \quad = \quad \text{Absolute temperature of outside air and flue gas}$$
$$\text{respectively in K}$$

$$V_a, V_g \quad = \quad \text{Volume of outside air and flue gas in } m^3/kg \text{ at}$$
$$\text{temperatures } T_a \text{ and } T_g \text{ respectively}$$

$$m_a \quad = \quad \text{Mass of air supplied per kg of fuel}$$

$$m_a + 1 \quad = \quad \text{Mass of flue gases per kg of fuel}$$

$$V_o, T_o, p_o \quad = \quad \text{Volume, temperature and pressure at N.T.P. conditions}$$

$$p_o \quad = \quad 1.013 \text{ bar} = 1.013 \times 10^5 \text{ N/m}^2$$

$$T_o \quad = \quad 0°C = 273 \text{ K}$$

Volume of outside air per kg of fuel at N.T.P.

$$V_o \quad = \quad \frac{mRT_o}{p_o} \qquad\qquad (\because\, pV = mRT)$$

$$= \quad \frac{m \times 287 \times 273}{1.013 \times 10^5} \qquad\qquad (\because R = 287 \text{ J/kg·K})$$

$$= \quad \textbf{0.773 m m}^3\textbf{/kg of fuel}$$

We know,

$$\frac{V_o}{T_o} \quad = \quad \frac{V_a}{T_a}$$

For outside air,

$\therefore$ Volume of outside air at temperature $T_a$,

$$V_a = \frac{V_o \times T_a}{T_o} = \frac{0.773\, m_a \times T_a}{273}$$

$$= \frac{m_a T_a}{353}\ m^3/kg \text{ of fuel}$$

Density of outside air at temperature $T_a$,

$$\rho_a = \frac{Mass}{Volume} = \frac{m_a}{\dfrac{m_a T_a}{353}} = \frac{353}{T_a}\ kg/m^3$$

Now, for hot flue gases,

$$V_g = \frac{m_a T_g}{353}\ m^3/kg \text{ of fuel} \qquad\qquad (\because \text{ similar to } V_a)$$

Density of flue gases at $T_g$,

$$\rho_g = \frac{Mass}{Volume} = \frac{m_a + 1}{\dfrac{m_a T_g}{353}}$$

$$= \frac{353\,(m_a + 1)}{m_a T_g}\ kg/m^3$$

Draught is produced due to pressure difference. The draught pressure,

$$p = \rho_a - \rho_g$$

$$= \rho_a \cdot g \cdot H - \rho_g \cdot g \cdot H \qquad\qquad (\because\ p = \rho g H)$$

$$= \frac{353}{T_a} \cdot g \cdot H - \frac{353\,(m_a + 1)}{m_a T_g} \cdot g \cdot H$$

$$= 353 \cdot g \cdot H \left( \frac{1}{T_a} - \frac{m_a + 1}{m_a T_g} \right) N/m^2 \qquad\qquad \dots (8.1)$$

Draught pressure in terms of mm of water as indicated by a manometer,

$$h_w = 353\, H \left[ \frac{1}{T_a} - \frac{m_a + 1}{m_a T_g} \right] mm \text{ of water}$$

$$\left( \because\ 1 \text{ mm of water} = 9.81\ \frac{N}{m^2} \right)$$

Assume that draught pressure (p) produced is equivalent of $H_1$ metre height of burnt gases.

$$\therefore \qquad p = \rho_g \cdot g \cdot H_1 = 353 \left[ \frac{m_a + 1}{m_a} \right] \frac{1}{T_g} \cdot H_1 \qquad\qquad \dots (8.2)$$

Equating equations (8.1) and (8.2),

$$H_1 = H \left( \frac{m_a}{m_a + 1} \cdot \frac{T_g}{T_a} - 1 \right) \qquad\qquad \dots (8.3)$$

## 8.28.2 Chimney Diameter

Assuming no loss, the velocity of the gases passing through the chimney is given by,

$$C = \sqrt{2gH_1} \qquad \text{... (8.4)}$$

If the pressure loss in the chimney is equivalent to a hot gas column of h' metre, then,

$$C = \sqrt{2g\,(H_1 - h')} = 4.43\sqrt{1 - \frac{h'}{H_1}} \cdot \sqrt{H_1}$$

$$= K \cdot \sqrt{H_1}$$

where,
$$K = 4.43\sqrt{1 - \frac{h'}{H_1}}$$

and its value,

$$K = 0.825 \qquad \text{... For brick chimneys}$$

$$= 1.1 \qquad \text{... For steel chimneys}$$

The mass of gases flowing through chimney at any cross-section is given by,

$$m_g = \rho_g \cdot A \cdot C \text{ kg/sec} \qquad \text{... (8.5)}$$

Equation (8.4) is used to determine diameter of chimney.

## 8.28.3 Condition for Maximum Discharge through a Chimney

The chimney draught is most effective when the maximum weight of hot gases is discharged in a given time.

Velocity of gas through the chimney,

$$C = \sqrt{2gH_1}$$

$$= \sqrt{2gH\left[\left(\frac{m_a}{m_a + 1}\right)\frac{T_g}{T_a} - 1\right]} \qquad \text{... [$H_1$ from equation (8.3)]}$$

The density of hot gas is given by,

$$\rho_g = \frac{p}{R \cdot T_g} \qquad (\because \text{ From } pV_g = RT_g)$$

The mass of gas delivered per second,

$$m_g = \rho_g \cdot A \cdot C$$

$$= \frac{p}{RT_g} \cdot A \cdot \sqrt{2gH\left[\left(\frac{m_a}{m_a + 1}\right) \cdot \frac{T_g}{T_a} - 1\right]}$$

$$= \frac{p \cdot A \cdot \sqrt{2gH}}{RT_g}\sqrt{\left(\frac{m_a}{m_a + 1}\right) \cdot \frac{T_g}{T_a} - 1}$$

$$= \frac{K}{T_g} \cdot \sqrt{M \cdot T_g - 1}$$

where,
$$K = \frac{p \cdot A \cdot \sqrt{2gH}}{R} \quad \text{and} \quad M = \frac{m_a}{m_a + 1} \cdot \frac{1}{T_a}$$

$\therefore$
$$m_g = K \sqrt{\frac{M \cdot T_g}{T_g^2} - \frac{1}{T_g^2}}$$

$$= K \left( \frac{M}{T_g} - \frac{1}{T_g^2} \right)^{\frac{1}{2}}$$

For maximum discharge differentiating $m_g$ with respect to $T_g$ and equating to zero,

$$\frac{dm_g}{dT_g} = \frac{d}{dT_g} \left[ K \left( \frac{M}{T_g} - \frac{1}{T_g^2} \right)^{\frac{1}{2}} \right] = 0$$

$\therefore$
$$\left( -\frac{M}{T_g^2} + \frac{2}{T_g^2} \right) K = 0$$

$\therefore$
$$\frac{2}{T_g} - M = 0$$

$$\frac{2}{T_g} = M = \frac{m_a}{m_a + 1} \cdot \frac{1}{T_a}$$

$\therefore$
$$\frac{T_g}{T_a} = 2 \left( \frac{m_a + 1}{m_a} \right)$$

Substituting above value of $\dfrac{T_g}{T_a}$ to get $(H_1)_{max}$,

$$(H_1)_{max} = H \left[ \left( \frac{m_a}{m_a + 1} \right) \cdot 2 \left( \frac{m_a + 1}{m_a} \right) - 1 \right]$$

$$(H_1)_{max} = H$$

The draught in mm of water column for maximum discharge,

$$(h_w)_{max} = 353 H \left( \frac{1}{T_a} - \frac{1}{2T_a} \right) = \frac{353 H}{2T_a}$$

---

## PROBLEMS ON BOILER DRAUGHT

**Problem 8.10:** In a boiler plant, it is required to produce draught equivalent of 15 mm of water. The ambient and hot gases temperatures are 20°C and 250°C respectively. The amount of air required for combustion is 18 kg per kg of fuel. Determine the height of chimney.

---

**Solution:**

**Given:** $h_w$ = 15 mm of water, $T_a$ = 20 + 273 = 293 K, $T_g$ = 250°C = 250 + 273 = 525 K

$$h_w = 353\,H\left[\frac{1}{T_a} - \frac{m_a + 1}{m_a \cdot T_g}\right]$$

$$15 = 353 \times H \times \left[\frac{1}{293} - \frac{19}{18 \times 523}\right]$$

$\therefore$     $H$ = **30.5 m**

**Problem 8.11:** A boiler having a chimney of 32 m height. The air-fuel ratio needed in combustion chamber is 20. Temperature of air at the grate entry is 28°C. Find minimum temperature of flue gases required to produce a draught of 18 mm.

**Solution:**

**Given:** H = 32 m, A : F = 20, $T_a$ = 28°C, $h_w$ = 18 mm

$$h_w = 353 \cdot H \cdot \left[\left(\frac{1}{T_a} - \frac{1}{T_g}\frac{m_a + 1}{m_a}\right)\right]$$

$$18 = 353 \times 32 \times \left[\frac{1}{301} - \frac{1}{T_g}\left(\frac{21}{20}\right)\right]$$

$$T_g = 607.37 \text{ K}$$
$$= 607.37 - 273$$
$$= \mathbf{334.37°C}$$

**Problem 8.12:** A boiler uses 20 kg of air per kg of fuel. The fuel consumption is 33 kg/sec and actual draught required is 18 mm of water taking into account all losses.

Determine the chimney height and its diameter if the actual velocity of flue gases is 0.38 times the theoretical velocity due to friction. The surrounding is at 25°C and flue gases temperature is 230°C.

**Solution:**

**Given:** $m_a$ = 20 kg/kg of fuel, $m_f$ = 33 kg/sec, $h_w$ = 18 mm of water, $C$ = $0.38\sqrt{29\,H}$,
     $T_a$ = 25°C = 25 + 273 = 298 K, $T_g$ = 230°C = 230 + 273 = 503 K

**Height of chimney,**

$$h_w = 353 \cdot H \cdot \left(\frac{1}{T_a} - \frac{m_a + 1}{m_a \cdot T_g}\right)$$

$$18 = 353 \times H \times \left(\frac{1}{298} - \frac{20 + 1}{520 \times 503}\right)$$

$$H = \mathbf{40.21\ m}$$

Now,     $H_1 = H \cdot \left(\frac{m_a}{m_a + 1} \cdot \frac{T_g}{T_a} - 1\right) = 40.21 \times \left(\frac{20}{20 + 1} \times \frac{503}{230} - 1\right)$

$$= \mathbf{43.54\ m}$$

The actual velocity of gas,

$$C = 0.38 \times \sqrt{2g\,H_1}$$

$$= 0.38 \times \sqrt{2 \times 9.81 \times 43.54}$$

$$= \textbf{11.109 m/sec}$$

Density of flue gas,

$$\rho_g = \frac{353\,(m_a + 1)}{m_a \cdot T_g} = \frac{353 \times (20 + 1)}{20 \times 503}$$

$$= \textbf{0.7369 kg/m}^3$$

Mass of gas per sec, $\quad m_g = (m_a + 1) \times m_f$ in kg/sec

$$= (20 + 1) \times 33$$

$$= \textbf{693 kg/sec}$$

Also, $\qquad m_g = \rho_g \cdot A \cdot C$

$$\therefore \qquad 693 = 0.7369 \times \frac{\pi}{4} \times D^2 \times 11.109$$

$$\therefore \qquad D^2 = 107.78$$

$$\therefore \qquad D = 10.38 \text{ m} \simeq 10.5 \text{ m}$$

$$\text{Diameter of chimney} = \textbf{10.4 m}$$

---

**Problem 8.13:** To provide natural draught, a chimney of height 16 m is used. Calculate,

(i)  The draught in mm of water when the temperature of chimney gases is such that the mass of the gases discharged is maximum.

(ii) If the temperature of flue gases does not exceed 350°C, find air supplied per kg of fuel for maximum discharge.

Take atmospheric temperature as 20°C.

**Solution:**

**Given:** H = 16 m, $T_g$ = 350 + 273 = 623 K, $T_a$ = 20 + 273 = 293 K.

**(i)  Draught:**

$$(h_w)_{max} = \frac{353 \cdot H}{2T_a}$$

$$= \frac{353 \times 16}{2 \times 293}$$

$$= \textbf{9.64 mm of water}$$

**(ii) Air supplied for maximum discharge:**

The condition for maximum discharge is

$$\frac{T_g}{T_a} = 2\left(\frac{m_a + 1}{m_a}\right)$$

$$\frac{623}{293} = 2\left(\frac{m_a + 1}{m_a}\right)$$

$$\therefore \qquad m_a = \textbf{15.87 kg/kg of fuel}$$

---

**Problem 8.14:** At a location for installing a boiler plant, height of chimney is limited to 45 m. The temperature of flue gases and ambient air are 220°C and 25°C respectively. Pressure loss at grate is 8 mm of water. Also pressure loss in bends and chimney are 3 mm and 4 mm respectively. Determine diameter of the chimney, if a fuel burnt per second is 18 kg.

**Solution:**

**Given:** $H = 45$ m, $T_g = 220°C = 220 + 273 = 493$ K, $T_a = 25°C = 25 + 273 = 298$ K.

Pressure required to overcome losses $= 8 + 3 + 4 = 15$ mm of water

We know,

$$h_w = 353\, H \left( \frac{1}{T_a} - \frac{m_a + 1}{m_a \cdot T_g} \right)$$

$$15 = 353 \times 45 \times \left( \frac{1}{298} - \frac{m_a + 1}{m_a \times 493} \right)$$

$$\frac{15}{353 \times 45} = \frac{1}{298} - \frac{m_a + 1}{m_a \times 493}$$

$$\frac{m_a + 1}{m_a \times 493} = \frac{1}{298} - \frac{15}{353 \times 45} = 2.41 \times 10^{-3}$$

$$m_a + 1 = 2.41 \times 10^{-3} \times 493 \times m_a$$

$$1 = 10188\, m_a - m_a = 0.188$$

$\therefore \qquad m_a = 5.32$ kg

Now,

$$H_1 = H \left( \frac{m_a}{m_a + 1} \cdot \frac{T_g}{T_a} - 1 \right)$$

$$= 45 \times \left( \frac{5.32}{5.32 + 1} \times \frac{493}{298} - 1 \right)$$

$$= \mathbf{17.61\ m}$$

Density of flue gases,

$$\rho_g = \frac{353\,(m_a + 1)}{m_a \cdot T_g}$$

$$= \frac{353 \times (5.32 + 1)}{5.32 \times 493}$$

$$= \mathbf{0.85\ kg/m^3}$$

Velocity of gas,

$$C = \sqrt{2gH_1} = \sqrt{2 \times 9.87 \times 17.61}$$

$$= \mathbf{18.59\ m/sec}$$

Mass of gas per second,

$$m_g = (m_a + 1) \times m_f$$

$$= (5.32 + 1) \times 0.18$$

$$= \mathbf{113.76\ kg/sec.}$$

Also,
$$m_g = \rho_g \cdot A \cdot C$$

$$113.76 = 0.85 \times \frac{\pi}{4} D^2 \times 18.59$$

$$\therefore \qquad D = 3.02 \cong \mathbf{3\ m}$$

## 8.29 DRAUGHT LOSSES

The loss in draught may be due to the reasons mentioned below.

(a)  Frictional losses offered by the flues and gas passages to the flow of gases.

(b)  Loss near bends in the gas flow circuit.

(c)  Loss due to friction head in equipments like grate, economiser, super heater etc.

(d)  Loss due to imparting velocity to the flue gases.

The draught loss in a chimney is twenty percent of the total draught produced by it.

## 8.30 ARTIFICIAL DRAUGHT

For modern boilers static draught required is varying between 30 to 350 mm of water column. It may not be possible to build a chimney high enough to produce such large draught. To meet this requirement, artificial draught is used.

### 8.30.1 Forced Draught

- In this system, a blower is fitted near the base of the boiler (before grate) and the air is forced to pass through various elements as shown in Fig. 8.21.

- As air pressure throughout the system is maintained above atmospheric pressure, the system is known as positive draught system.

- Here function of chimney is to release gases at a height into atmosphere for better dispersion of ash particles and pollutants.

- Height of chimney is less than natural draught system.

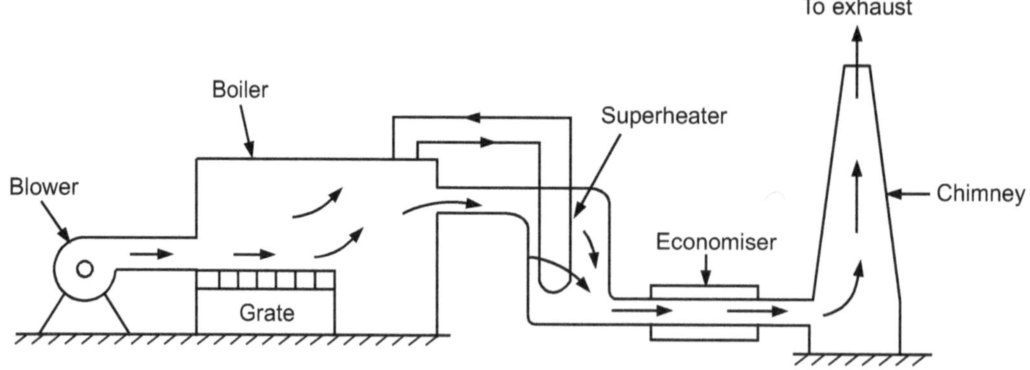


**Fig. 8.21: Forced draught**

## 8.30.2 Induced Draught

- In this system, blower is located near the base of the chimney.

- The air sucked into the system by reducing the pressure below the atmospheric pressure.

- By creating partial vacuum in the furnace and flues, the products of combustion are drawn from the main flue and they pass upto the chimney.

- This draught is used when economiser and preheaters are used in the system.

- The draught is similar in action to natural draught.

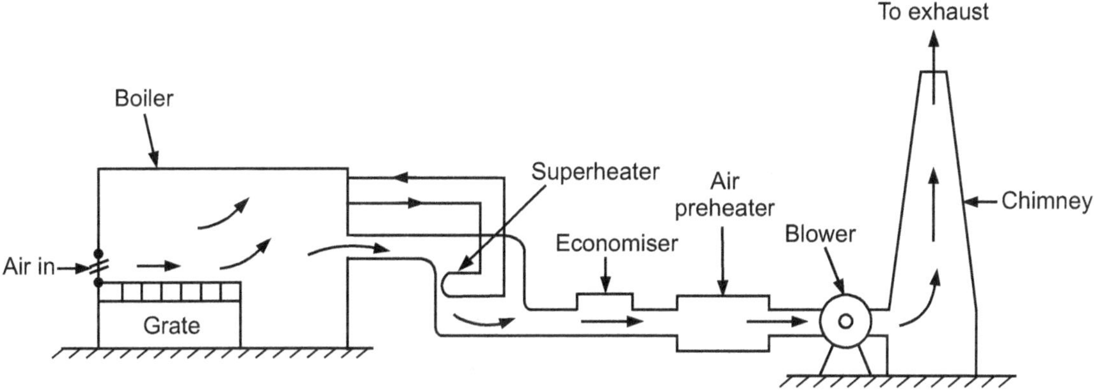


**Fig. 8.22: Induced draught**

## 8.30.3 Difference between Forced and Induced Draught

| Forced Draught | Induced Draught |
|---|---|
| 1. Blower is placed near the base of the boiler and is forced to pass through various elements of system. | 1. Blower is placed near the base of chimney and air sucked to pass through various elements of system. |
| 2. Comparatively less power is required for forced draught fan. | 2. More power is required for induced draught fan. |
| 3. No chance of air leakage in the furnace. | 3. In this system, continuous air leakage takes place. |
| 4. Flow of air is more uniform. | 4. Air flow is not so uniform. |
| 5. Does not require water cooled bearing. | 5. Water cooled boring are required for induced draught. |
| 6. Small fan size is required for same draught. | 6. Big fan size is required for same draught. |

## 8.30.4 Balanced Draught

- It is a combination of forced and induced draught system.

- In this system, forced draught fan overcomes the resistance in air preheater and chain grate stocker while the induced draught fan overcomes draught losses through boiler, economiser, air preheater and connecting flues.

## 8.30.5 Steam Jet Draught

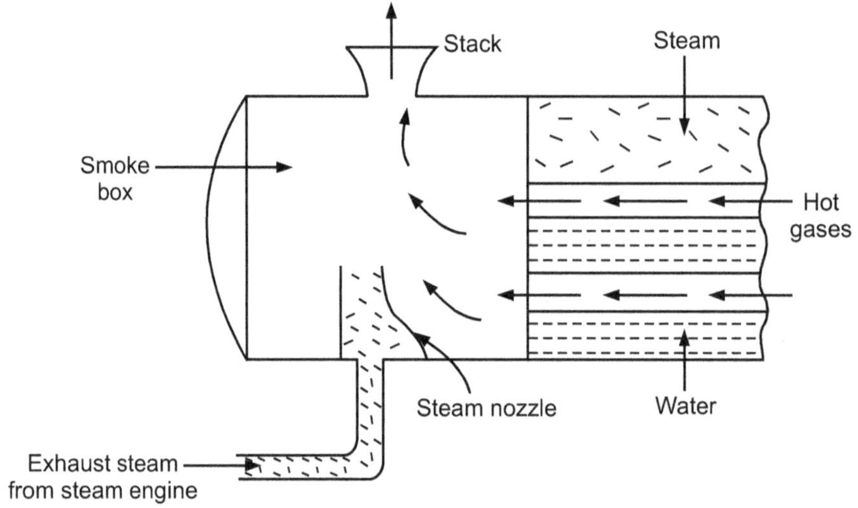


**Fig. 8.23: Steam jet draught**

- Steam jet draught is a simple and easy method of producing artificial draught.

- It may be forced type or induced type.

p Here steam jet directed into the smoke box near the stack induces flow of gases through the tubes, ash pit grates and flues.

The steam jet draught entails following advantages:

(i)   It is simple and economical.

(ii)  Occupies minimum space.

(iii) Maintenance cost is nil, very low attention is required.

Only disadvantage is, it needs high pressure steam for starting.

## 8.31 DIFFERENCE BETWEEN MECHANICAL DRAUGHT AND NATURAL DRAUGHT

| Mechanical Draught | Natural Draught |
|---|---|
| **Advantages** | **Disadvantages** |
| 1. The rate of combustion is more as the available draught is more. | 1. The rate of combustion is low as the available draught is limited. |
| 2. The height of chimney used is less and independent of draught needed. | 2. The height of chimney used is more and designed by draught needed. |
| 3. Fuel consumption per kW is 15% less than for natural draught. | 3. Flue consumption per kW is more. |
| 4. The efficiency of artificial draught is 6 to 8%. | 4. The efficiency of chimney draught is about 1%. |
| 5. Fuel burning capacity of grate is more. | 5. Fuel burning capacity of grate is less. |
| 6. Low capital cost. | 6. High capital cost. |
| 7. The running and maintenance cost is practically nil. | 7. High running and maintenance cost of fan used. |

## EXERCISE

1. Which factors you will consider while selecting a steam boiler?
2. How boilers are classified?
3. Differentiate water tube boilers with fire tube boilers.
4. Explain a fire tube boiler with neat sketch.
5. Explain a water tube boiler with neat sketch.
6. Explain following mountings with neat sketch:
   (a) Water level indicator
   (b) Pressure gauge
   (c) Dead weight safety valve
   (d) Feed check valve
   (e) Fusible plug
7. Explain different accessories used in steam boilers with neat sketch.
8. What features of high pressure boilers are comparing with low pressure boilers?
9. Describe IBR and Non-IBR boilers in brief.
10. Explain the following terms with their significance:
    (a) Evaporative capacity　　(b) Equivalent evaporation　　(c) Boiler efficiency

11.　What are the different sources of heat loss in a boiler plant?

12.　Explain procedure to draw heat balance sheet for a boiler plant.

13.　Compare natural draught with artificial draught.

14.　Explain necessity of producing draught in boiler.

15.　Differentiate between forced and induced draught.

## PROBLEMS FOR PRACTICE

1.　A boiler evaporates 3.6 kg of water per kg of coal into dry saturated steam at 10 bar. Find the equivalent evaporation if the feed water temperature is 32°C.

**(Ans.** 4.2 kg/kg of coal**)**

2.　Two kg of coal is required to produce 8 kg of steam ($x = 0.98$) at a pressure of 10.5 bar. Temperature of feed water is 45°C. Determine equivalent evaporation.

**(Ans.** 4.2 kg/kg of coal**)**

3.　A boiler produces 9 kg of steam per kg of coal at 10 bar from water at 15°C. The dryness fraction of steam is 0.9. Determine efficiency of the boiler when calorific value of coal is 32 000 kJ/kg.　　　　　　　　**(Ans.** 70.65%**)**

4.　The following observations were made in a test on a boiler :

$$
\begin{aligned}
\text{Coal burnt per / hr} &= 480 \text{ kg} \\
\text{Steam generated / hr} &= 4375 \text{ kg at 3 MN/m}^2 \\
\text{Feed water temperature} &= 95°C \\
\text{Temperature of steam leaving the boiler} &= 260°C \\
\text{Calorific value of coal} &= 30\ 700 \text{ kJ/kg} \\
\text{Cp for superheated steam} &= 2.093 \text{ kJ/kg K}
\end{aligned}
$$

Calculate:

(i) The equivalent evaporation from and at 100°C in kg steam/hr.

**(Ans.** 4768 kg/hr**)**

(ii) The efficiency of the boiler　　　　　　　　　　　**(Ans.** 73%**)**

5.　A chimney of 60 m height is used in a boiler plant. The temperature of atmospheric air is 27°C and 15 kg of air is required to burn 1 kg of air. For maximum discharge of hot gases, determine the draught pressure in mm of water. Also find temperature of hot gases.　　　　　　　**(Ans.** 35.3 mm of water, 327°C**)**

6.　A 30 m high chimney is used to produce a natural draught of 15 mm of water. The temperature of atmospheric air is 27°C and that of hot gases in the chimney is 287°C. Calculate mass of the air used per kg of fuel.　　　　**(Ans.** 15.6 kg/kg of fuel**)**

## UNIVERSITY QUESTION PAPERS

### DEC. 2013

1. Explain the Classification of boilers with example.                                    **[6]**

2. In a boiler test 1250 kg of coal is consumed in 24 hours, mass of water evaporated is 13000 kg and boiler pressure of 7 bar. Feed water temperature was 40°C and heating value of coal is 30000 kJ/kg. Find equivalent evaporation per kg of coal and boiler efficiency. (Take enthalpy of 1 kg of steam at boiler exit as 2570 kJ/kg).                                    **[7]**

3. What are the desirable characteristics of a good boiler (6 valid points).               **[6]**

4. A boiler uses 1000 kg of coal per hour. The temperature of the hot gases inside the chimney is 650 K and outside air temperature is 300 K. The draught produced by the chimney of 25 of height is 15 mm of water column. Determine the air supplied per kg of fuel burnt, draught in terms of hot gases, mass flow rate of hot gases and the area of the chimney required if the coefficient of the velocity is 0.4.          **[7]**

### MAY 2014

1. Explain with neat sketch working and operation of Fusible plug.                         **[6]**

2. The following results were obtained from boiler trial:                                  **[7]**

    (a)  Feed water per hour = 700 kg at 27°C,

    (b)  Steam pressure = 8 bar of dryness 0.97.

    (c)  Coal consumption = 100 kg/hr.

    (d)  C. V. Of Coal = 25000 kJ/kg.

    (e)  Unburnt coal collected = 0.6 kg/hr.

    (f)  Flue gas formed per kg of fuel = 17.3 kg at 327 °C (Cp of flue gas 1.025 kJ/kg K).

    (g)  Room Temperature = 16°C.

    Draw the heat balance sheet on kJ/min basis and boiler efficiency.

3. Explain function and location of different boiler mountings and accessories  (three each) with the help of line sketch or block diagram.                                        **[6]**

4. Determine the A: F ratio for an oil fired steam with following data,                    **[7]**

    (a)  Chimney height = 40 m.

    (b)  Draught = 25 mm of water column.

    (c)  Mean Chimney gas temperature = 367 °C.

(d)   Ambient outside temperature = 20 °C.

Also calculate draught in terms of hot gas column and velocity of the flue gases.

## DEC. 2014

1.   Show block diagram of a boiler plant showing location of air–preheater, superheater, economizer clearly indicating the air and water circuit flow.                    **[6]**

2.   The following particulars refer to a steam power plant consisting of a boiler, superheater and economizer :

Steam pressure = 20 bar, Mass of steam generated = 10000 kg/hr, Mass of coal used = 1300 kg/hr, CV for coal 29000 kJ/kg, Temperature of feed water entering the economizer = 35 deg. C, temperature of feed water leaving the economizer = 105 deg. C. Dryness fraction of the steam leaving the boiler = 0.98. Temperature of steam leaving the superheater = 350 deg. C.

Determine :

-   Overall efficiency of the boiler plant.

-   Equivalent evaporation of the given boiler from and at 100 deg. C in kg of steam generated/kg of coal burnt and

-   Percentage of heat utilised in economizer, boiler and super-heater.          **[7]**

3.   Define equivalent evaporation and boiler efficiency. Explain heat balance sheet for boiler.                                                                            **[7]**

4.   How must air per kg of coal is burnt in a boiler having chimney height of  32.3 m to create a draught of 19 mm of water column when the temperature of the flue gases leaving chimney is 370 deg C and temperature of boiler house is 29.5 deg. C. Also calculate the draught produced in terms of hot gas column.                    **[6]**

## MAY 2015

1.   Describe briefly the advantages which you would expect to be gained from incorporating an economizer, air preheater, and a superheated in a steam generating plant. By line diagram, indicate the position of these accessories in a typical boiler plant.                                                               **[6]**

2.   The following data relates to a trial on boiler using economizer, air preheater and superheater :

Condition of steam at exit of boiler = 20 bar, 0.96 dry

Temperature of steam at exit of superheater = 300°C

Steam evaporation rate/kg of fuel = 12 kg

Room temperature, $t_0$ = 25°C

Temperature of feed water at exit of economizer, $t_1$ = 50°C, Temperature of air at exit of air preheater, $t_a$ = 70°C The temperature of flue gases at inlet to superheater, economizer, air preheater and exit of air preheater are respectively 650°C, 430°C, 300°C and 180°C respectively.

Assume that air supplied is 19 kg/kg of fuel of calorific value of 45,000 kJ/kg, find :

(i)    Equivalent evaporation with and without economizer, from and at 100°C.

(ii)   Thermal efficiency of the boiler with and without economizer.

(iii)  Thermal efficiency of superheater, economizer and air preheater.    **[7]**

3.    Define steam generator and write down the classification of boilers.    **[6]**

4.    In a certain boiler installation, a steel chimney of 30 m height produces and natural draught equivalent to 17.75 mm of water column. The mean temperature of the boiler house is 298 K and that of hot gases leaving the chimney is 633 K. If the boiler uses 1350 kg of coal per hour, make calculations for :

(i)    Air supplied per kg of coal burnt on the grate,

(ii)   Draught in terms of column of hot flue gases,

(iii)  Density and mass flow rate of hot gas.    **[7]**

## NOV. 2015

1.    With the help of suitable diagram explain the construction and working of Cochron boiler.    **[6]**

2.    Determine the air–fuel ratio for an oil fired steam generator with the following data :

Chimney height–32 m,

Chimney draught–12 mm of water column,

Flue gas temperature through chimney–297'C

Ambient air temperature, 27°C

Also calculate the velocity of flue gas through chimney neglecting gas losses in the flow of flue gas through chimney.

3.    Write the function and locations of the following boiler mountings :    **[6]**

(i)    Blow off cock

(ii)   Fusible plug

(iii)  Steam safety valve.

4. The following readings were recorded during boiler trial of 6 hour duration :

Pressure of steam generated – 12 bar,

Mass of steam generated – 40000 kg

Dryness fraction of steam generated – 0.85

Feed water temperature – 30°C,

Coal used – 4000 kg.

Calorific value of coal – 33400 kJ/kg,

Find :

(i)   Factor of equivalent evaporation

(ii)  Equivalent evaporation from and at 100°C

(iii) Efficiency of boiler.                                                  **[7]**

### MAY 2016

1. Discuss the Boiler plant layout indicating loation of various accessories and water, air and flue gas circuit.                                           **[6]**

2. 5400 kg of steam is produced per hour at a pressure of 750 kPa in a boiler when feed water is at 41.5 deg. C. The dryness fraction of the steam is 0.98. The amount of the coal burnt per hour is 670 kg with CV of 31000 kJ/kg. Determine the boiler efficiency and equivalent evaporation.                              **[7]**

3. Show in tabular form boiler heat balance sheet and the formulas involved for estimating each component.                                                **[6]**

4. A boiler is equiped with a chimney of 24 m height. The ambient temperature is 25 deg. The temperature of flue gases passing through the chimney is 300 deg. C. If the air flow through the combustion chamber is 20 kg/kg of fuel burned, find

(i)   The theoretical draught in cm of water column and

(ii)  The velocity of the flue gases passing through the chimney
     if 50% of the head is lost in friction.                               **[7]**

# Chapter 9

# PSYCHROMETRY

## 9.1 INTRODUCTION : AIR CONDITIONING

Air Conditioning is as old as man himself. The primitive people who wore the skins of animals, were in a crude sense controlling the escape or containment of their own body heat and effecting a change in their personal comfort. Seeking shelter from the sun or finding refuge in caves from cold or heat were basically actions that changed their environment. The discovery and use of fire was perhaps the most important advent in that area.

Later history shows the ruling class – kings – used slaves equipped with palm branches to fan their masters. Thus, the art of evaporative cooling provided some relief from the desert or tropical heat. History also recalls the Romans, who engineered ventilation and panel heating into their famous baths. The Romans also brought ice from the northern mountains to chill wine, and possibly also to chill water for bathing or drinking.

Moving into the middle ages, the remarkable Leonardo da Vinci built a water-driven fan to ventilate rooms of a house. Other early innovations included rocking chairs with bellows action to produce spot ventilation for the occupant and clock mechanisms that activated fan devices above beds.

By todays' standards, these Problems of comfort conditioning seem rather crude, and perhaps, if fully explored, some would be humorous.

Early texts on Refrigeration discussed the applications of using ice for preservation of food and the initial development of the concept of mechanical / chemical refrigeration in 1748 in Scotland by Dr. William Cullen.

It was in 1844 that Dr. John Gorrie (1803 – 55) described his new refrigeration machine. In 1851, he was granted US Patent 8080. This was the first commercial machine in the world built and used for refrigeration and air conditioning.

The real **"father of air-conditioning" was Willis H. Carrier (1876 – 1950)** as noted by many industry professionals and historians. Throughout his brilliant career, Carrier contributed more to the advancement of the developing industry than any other individual. In 1911, he presented his epoch-making paper dealing with the properties of air. These assumptions and formulae formed the basis for the first psychrometric chart and became the authority for all fundamental calculations in the air conditioning industry.

Carrier died in 1950, having witnessed the real turning point in the industry's growth. These were only a few of the steps along the way towards development of modern air conditioning as we know it today.

**Mr. Willis Carrier**

Meaning of air conditioning depends on what point of view is being considered. Ask the man on the street and he would most probably answer "keeping cool". Ask the owner of a printing plant and he would respond with a statement that might mean closely controlling temperature and humidity so that the behaviour of the paper could be held within certain tolerances. One answer is from the standpoint of human comfort, and the other is about a commercial consideration.

A dictionary definition might read **"the process that heats, cools, cleans and circulates air, and controls the moisture content on a continuous basis"** or "Air conditioning means conditioning the air for maintaining specific conditions of temperature, humidity (moisture content in air), dust level inside an enclosed space, and ventilation of air". The need for which the conditioned space is asked for, dictates the conditions to be maintained. Air conditioning, thus, is classified as 'comfort air conditioning', and 'industrial air conditioning'.

## 9.2  COMFORT AIR-CONDITIONING

The human body is a heat generating device. Its normal temperature is 37°C. It can regulate or control this condition by four methods :

    (i)     Convection,

    (ii)    Radiation,

    (iii)   Conduction, and

    (iv)   Evaporation.

When in an environment where room conditions are too warm, but less than 37°C, it will transfer heat to the air passing over the skin by convection. Simultaneously, it gives up heat by conduction to clothing, bedding or whatever is in contact with the skin. Additionally, it throws off heat by means of radiation to the cooler surrounding objects. If these three are not sufficient, sweat glands will open, allowing skin moisture to evaporate. This change of state from water to vapour absorbs much heat. Thus, temperature change and air motion are important elements.

In colder surroundings, radiation, conduction and convection take place more rapidly, thus, requiring clothing to insulate and hold body heat. Evaporation becomes minimal and the amount of the skin perspiration decreases.

When the outside environment is warm – temperature greater than 37°C – the heat from the objects will come to the skin by radiation, convection and conduction, increasing the skin temperature. Now the sweat glands are opened and the sweat or skin moisture to evaporate taking heat from the skin, thus the skin temperature reduces.

Evaporative loss is a function of the difference in vapour pressure between the water on the skin and that of the ambient air. It also depends on the relative velocity of air flow over the wet surface. Insensible perspiration results from the body fluids oozing through skin under osmotic pressure and hence, humidity in air is required to be controlled.

The body is also sensitive to impurities. Dust, smoke, plant pollen, etc. cause irritation to the nose, lungs and eyes, so this indicates another need for the clean air.

Finally, the body requires 'fresh air' to renew its oxygen supply or to dilute undesirable odours.

Stated simply, the body should have a comfortable and healthful atmosphere, and five properties of air must be treated :

- Temperature (heating or cooling).
- Moisture content (humidifying or dehumidifying).
- Movement of the air (circulation).
- Cleanliness of the air (filtering).
- Ventilation (introduction of outside air).

Human beings are born into a hostile environment, the degree of hostility varies with the season of the year and with the geographical locality.

The design specifications for a comfort conditioning system is intended to be the framework for providing a comfortable environment for human beings throughout the year, in the presence of sensible heat gains in summer and sensible heat losses in winter. Dehumidification would be achieved in summer in humid atmosphere and humidification would be achieved in tropical summer.

The essential feature of comfort air conditioning is that it aims to produce an environment which is comfortable to the majority of the occupants. The ultimate in comfort can never be achieved, but the use of individual automatic control for individual rooms helps considerably in satisfying most people.

Comfort conditioning requirements are :

| | | |
|---|---|---|
| Temperature | – | 22 to 26°C |
| Relative humidity | – | 20 to 60% |
| Circulation of air | – | Not to exceed 0.15 m/sec. |

## 9.3  INDUSTRIAL AIR CONDITIONING

Commerce and Industry have used air conditioning in several ways :  first to increase personal productivity and second to provide space process cooling for specific needs.

A distinction should be made between comfort air conditioning and industrial air conditioning. As we have seen in the previous article, comfort air conditioning plants are applied to those plants which are used for residences, stores, theatres, restaurants etc. where the main object is to produce comfortable and healthy conditions for the occupants.

Industrial air conditioning, on the other hand, refers to the air conditioning in the manufacturing institutions where varying temperature and humidity conditions may affect the manufacturing processes or the products. Thus, healthy conditions which are essential for the best results to be produced and maintained even if they may not entirely agree with those required for human comfort.

Few people may know that air conditioning was used until about 1925, almost exclusively in manufacturing plants.

Worker productivity in air conditioned areas has improved, in terms of less absenteeism, less labour turnover, less noise distraction, less trips to the water fountains, more efficient production, fewer mistakes, and less time lost due to heat fatigue and accidents. In general, better morale and better relationships between employer and employee result.

Benefits to the worker's health and comfort are incidental in industrial air conditioning, but often the design conditions can be adjusted to be as near the comfort conditions as possible.

## 9.4 PSYCHROMETRY

**Psychrometry** is study of properties of moist air.Atmospheric air cosists of dry air and water vapour i. e. steam at low pressure. The mixture is known as moist air. Psychrometric is the state of atmosphere with reference to the moisture in the air.

**Basic Terms :**

The air around us is composed of a mixture of dry gases and water vapour. The gases contain approximately 77% nitrogen and 23% oxygen with the other gases totalling less than 1%. Water vapour exists in small quantities.

Before proceeding further, we will define some of the terms, with reference to air-vapour mixture, used very often in air-conditioning study.

**(a)  Saturated and superheated water vapour :**

When a mixture of air and water vapour contains the maximum amount of water that it can hold, at the given temperature, it is said to be saturated. If the  temperature of the mixture of air and water vapour is higher than the saturation temperature, the vapour is said to be superheated. If the temperature of air drops down below its saturation temperature, some of the vapour will be condensed.

## (b)  Dry Bulb Temperature (DBT) :

It is the true temperature of moist air at rest, measured by an ordinary thermometer. It is written many times as $t_{db}$ or simply $t_d$.

## (c)  Web Bulb Temperature (WBT) :

It is the temperature of air indicated by a thermometer whose bulb is covered by a piece of the wet muslin or silk, which is dipped in a small basin of water. This keeps the bulb moistened or wet. Hence, the temperature indicated by such a thermometer is called **Wet Bulb Temperature** denoted by $t_{wb}$ or $t_w$.

If there is much water vapour present in the atmosphere, there will be little evaporation of the moisture from the bulb of the thermometer and a small cooling effect will be produced. With the dry air, more rapid evaporation will take place and more cooling effect will lower the temperature more. Hence, the difference in dry bulb temperature and wet bulb temperature is the measure of the moisture content in the air, and is called Wet Bulb Depression.

**Thermodynamic Wet Bulb Temperature :**

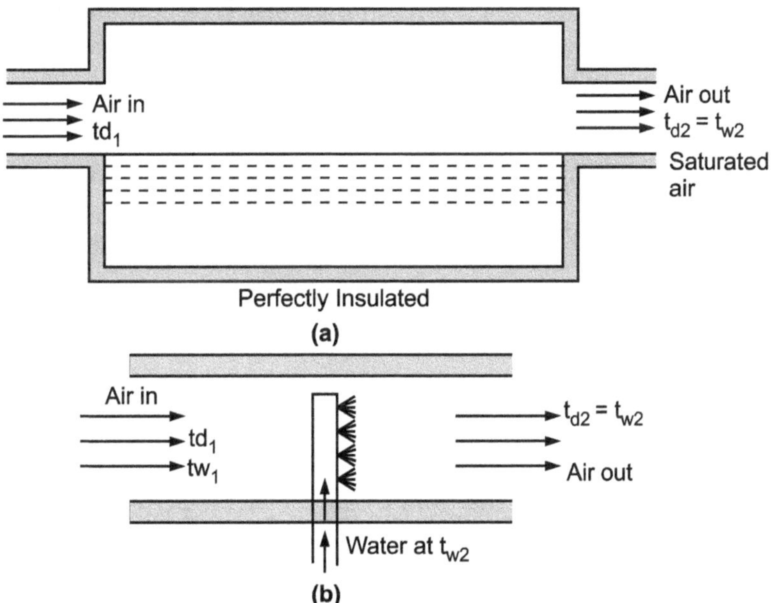


**Fig. 9.1: Thermodynamic wet bulb temperature**

Adiabatic saturation temperature is that temperature at which water by evaporating into air, can bring the air to saturation adiabatically.

Thermodynamic wet bulb temperature is this adiabatic saturation temperature.

Consider the system as shown in Fig. 9.1 (a).

The system shown provides adiabatic saturation of air. It consists of a chamber considered to be infinite in length (a concept only) containing water at temperature $t_2$ which is the wet-bulb temperature of air entering the system. The system is perfectly insulated. The total quantity of water present in the chamber could be very large compared to that added to the air in a given length of time.

For any state of moist air, there exists a temperature $t°$ at which liquid water may be evaporated into air to bring it to saturation at exactly this same temperature.

Fig. 9.1 (b) shows another system in which there is a chamber into which the water at the wet bulb temperature is sprayed and the evaporation of water brings the air to saturation adiabatic saturation.

### (d)  Dew Point Temperature (DPT) :

The saturation temperature at which the condensation of water vapour to visible water takes place, is called as dew point temperature. It is written many time tdp.

As the air is cooled, the relative humidity increases. If the temperature is lowered sufficiently, thereafter a point will be reached at which the relative humidity would be 100%, or the air will be fully saturated. **The temperature at which the given moisture or water vapour saturates the air is called the Dew Point Temperature.** A further lowering of the temperature of the air below the dew point temperature, causes water vapour to condense in the form of water particles. An Problem is the sweating on a glass of ice water. The cold glass reduces the air temperature below its dew point, and the moisture that condenses forms beads on the glass surface.

### (e)  Absolute humidity :

The actual weight of water vapour contained in a unit volume 1 cu.m of air is called the absolute humidity. It is expressed in FPS system as grains (7,000 grains per pound) / ft$^3$, or in MKS / SI units as kg per cu.m of air.

### (f)  Relative humidity (RH) :

The ratio of the actual amount of moisture present in one cu.m of air at a certain temperature to the amount of moisture needed to saturate it at that temperature is called **relative humidity (RH).** This ratio is expressed as a percentage.

Relative humidity is also defined as the ratio of actual partial pressure of vapour in a space to the saturation pressure of pure water at the same temperature.

$$\phi \; = \; \frac{\text{Mass of water vapour / cu.m}}{\text{Mass of water vapour at saturation}}$$

$$= \; \frac{m_v}{m_s}$$

$$= \; \frac{\dfrac{p_v \times \text{volume}}{R_v \times T}}{\dfrac{p_s \times \text{volume}}{R_v \times T}}$$

$$= \frac{p_v}{p_s} = \frac{\text{Actual vapour pressure}}{\text{Vapour pressure at saturation}}$$

$$\boxed{\phi = \frac{p_v}{p_s}}$$

where,

$$m_v = \text{mass of vapour}$$

$$m_s = \text{mass of vapour at saturation}$$

$$R_v = \text{specific gas constant for actual water vapour}$$

$$p_v = \text{vapour pressure}$$

$$p_s = \text{vapour pressure at saturation}$$

Relative humidity is also defined as the ratio of actual mol fraction to the mol fraction at saturation at the same temperature.

$$\therefore \qquad RH \; \phi = \frac{\text{Actual mol fraction of vapour}}{\text{Mol fraction at saturation}}$$

$$= \frac{p_v \times \text{vol.}/R_v T}{p_s \times \text{vol.}/R_v T}$$

$$= \frac{p_v}{p_s}$$

## (g) Specific humidity or Humidity ratio (w)

It is the weight of water vapour present in 1 kg of dry air (kg/kg of dry air).

When air is cooled or heated, its specific volume varies and hence for accuracy and simplification of calculations, the weight of air handled is used. The moisture content is expressed as so many kg of water vapour in one kg of dry air.

$$\text{Specific humidity} = \frac{\text{Actual weight of vapour}}{\text{kg. of dry air}}$$

$$w = \frac{m_v}{m_a}$$

$$= \frac{p_v \times \text{vol.} / R_v \times T}{p_a \times \text{vol.} / R_a \times T}$$

$$= \frac{p_v \times R_a}{p_a \times R_v}$$

$$= \frac{p_v}{p_a} \times \frac{287}{8314.4/18.015}$$

$$= \frac{0.622 \times p_v}{p_a}$$

$$= \frac{0.622 \times p_v}{p - p_v}$$

where,    $p$ = Atmospheric pressure

= Partial pressure of dry air + Partial pressure of vapour

= $p_a + p_v$

$\therefore$    $p_a = p - p_v$

$\therefore$

$$\boxed{w = \frac{0.622\, p_v}{p - p_v}}$$

## (h)  Degree of saturation (μ)

It is defined as the ratio of moisture actually contained per kg of dry air to the moisture required to saturate one kg of dry air at the same dry bulb temperature. This is also called as percentage of humidity. It is denoted by $\mu$.

$\therefore$

$$\mu = \frac{w}{w_s} = \frac{0.622\, p_v / (p - p_v)}{0.622\, p_s / (p - p_s)}$$

$$= \frac{p_v}{p_s} \times \frac{p - p_s}{p - p_v}$$

$$= \phi \times \frac{p\,(1 - p_s / p)}{p\,(1 - p_v / p)}$$

$$= \phi \times \frac{1 - \dfrac{p_s}{p}}{1 - \dfrac{p_v}{p}}$$

$$= \phi \times \frac{1 - p_s/p}{1 - \dfrac{\phi\, p_s}{p}}$$

Solving we get,

$$\boxed{\phi = \frac{\mu}{1 - (1 - \mu)\dfrac{p_s}{p}}}$$

## (i)  Psychrometer

It is an instrument for finding the humidity or hygrometric state of the atmosphere.

## 9.5  SLING THERMOMETER OR PSYCHROMETER

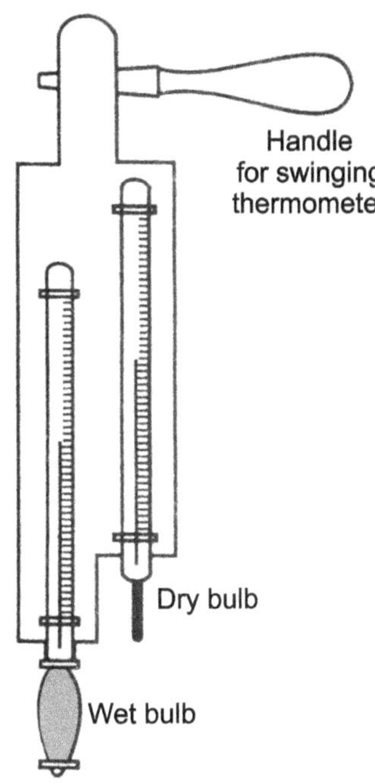


**Fig. 9.2: Sling thermometer**

The sling thermometer consists of the dry and wet-bulb thermometers fixed side by side on a wooden or metal plate. Humid air, due to the evaporation of water from the wet wick, can stagnate around the wet bulb and this can give a wrong wet bulb reading. So it is necessary to have moving air over the wet bulb. For obtaining this, the plate with the thermometers is attached to a wooden handle through a swivel connection so that the complete assembly can be easily rotated or whirled. Since the dry bulb and the wet bulb thermometers are mounted side by side, stray water particles from the wet wick can affect the dry bulb reading. To avoid this, the wet bulb thermometer is fixed on the plate at a lower level than the dry bulb thermometer. The water used for wetting the wick should be clean. Dirt can accumulate on the wet wick and thus give a wrong reading. So the wick should be clean. A dirty wick should be replaced. Everytime, a reading is taken, it should be ensured that the wick is wet. Before taking the readings of the dry and wet bulbs the psychrometer should be whirled round rapidly for about a minute. This should be repeated a number of times until the reading on the wet bulb becomes steady.

## 9.6  PRESSURE OF AIR-VAPOUR MIXTURE

We know that Dalton's Law states that the pressure of a mixture of gases is the sum of the partial pressures of each constituents and that each constituent occupies the entire volume of the mixture and temperature of each constituent is the temperature of the mixture.

As atmospheric air contains dry air and water vapour, the total mixture pressure is the sum of partial pressure of dry air ($p_a$) and partial pressure of vapour ($p_v$).

$\therefore$ 

$$p = \text{Total mixture pressure}$$
$$= \text{Barometric pressure}$$
$$= p_a + p_v$$

There are many equations for calculating the partial pressure of the water vapour. Dr. Carrier's equation presented in 1911, is probably most widely used in ordinary problems when charts are not available.

Original equation in F.P.S. system is given as

$$p_v = p_{wb} - \frac{(p - p_{wb})\,(t_{db} - t_{wb})}{2800 - 1.3\,t_{wb}}$$

or $$= p_{wb} - \frac{(p - p_{wb})\,(t_{db} - t_{wb})}{2830 - 1.44\,t_{wb}}$$

In this equation,

$$p_{wb} = \text{saturation pressure at } t_{wb} \text{ in inches of Hg.}$$

$$p_v = \text{partial pressure of vapour in inches of Hg.}$$

$$p = \text{barometric pressure in inches of Hg.}$$

and $t_{db}$ and $t_{wb}$ are the temperatures in °F.

This equation for $p_v$ may, now, be written in MKS system as

$$p_v = p_{wb} - \frac{(p - p_{wb})\,(t_{db} - t_{wb})}{1527.4 - 1.3\,t_{wb}}$$

where pressures are in mm of Hg and temperatures are in °C.

## 9.7   TOTAL HEAT OR ENTHALPY

The total heat content of the air and water vapour mixture is also known as enthalpy. It is the sum of both sensible and latent heat values, expressed in kJ/kg of dry air.

The total heat of air containing aqueous vapour is the sum of the heat in the air and the heat of vapour. If it were necessary to know the absolute total heat or enthalpy, then it would be necessary to include all heat above the absolute zero; but for air conditioning work, it is more practicable to choose another reference above which the total heat is calculated. Fortunately, air conditioning involves only a calculation of changes in enthalpy. It follows that such changes may be readily determined if a datum level of enthalpy is adopted for its expression. Thus, we are really always dealing in relative enthalpy, although we may not refer to it as such.

The total heat, as originally defined by Dr. Carrier and hereafter referred to as Carrier total heat or enthalpy, consists of (a) the heat in the air above zero degree of centigrade, (b) the heat of vapour in the air.

The enthalpy, h, used in psychrometry is defined by the equation

$$h = h_a + \mu\,h_g$$

where, $$h_a = \text{enthalpy of 1 kg dry air} - \text{kJ/kg}$$

$$h_g = \text{enthalpy of water vapour} - \text{kJ/kg}$$

$$\mu = \text{degree of saturation}$$

The value of temperature chosen for zero enthalpy is 0°C for both dry air and water. The relationship between the enthalpy of dry air and its temperature is not quite linear and values taken from NBS circular No. 564, for the standard atmospheric pressure of 101.325 kPa and suitably modified for the chosen zero, for the basis of the tables of properties of humid air. An approximate equation for the enthalpy of dry air over the range 0°C to 60°C is

$$h_a = 1.007\,t - 0.026$$

and for lower temperatures down to –10°C, the approximate equation is

$$h_a = 1.005\,t$$

Values of $h_g$ for the enthalpy of vapour over water have been taken from steam tables, slightly increased to take account of the influence of barometric pressure and modified to fit the zero datum.

The enthalpy of vapour over ice, however, is based on the information in the ASHRAE Handbook of Fundamentals (1967).

For the purpose of approximate calculations, without recourse to the psychrometric tables, we may assume that, in the range of 0°C to 60°C, the vapour is generated from water at 0°C and that the specific heat of superheated steam is constant. The following equation can then be used for the enthalpy of water vapour

$$h_g = 2501 + 1.84\,t$$

These equations can be combined to give us an approximate expression for the enthalpy of humid air at a barometric pressure of 101.325 kPa.

$$h = h_a + w\,h_g$$

$$= (1.007\,t - 0.026) + w\,(2501 + 1.84\,t)$$

or $\qquad h = 1.005\,t_{db} + w\,(2501 + 1.84\,t_{db})$

$$\boxed{h = 1.005\,t_{db} + w\,(2501 + 1.84\,t_{db})}$$

We can find specific humidity from adiabatic saturation system.

Referring to Fig. 9.1 (a), let unsaturated air enter the system at point 1. Its psychrometric properties are :

$$\text{Enthalpy} = h_1$$

$$\text{DBT} = t_{db_1}$$

$$\text{Specific humidity} = w_1$$

$$\text{Total pressure} = p$$

Let saturated air leave the system at 2. Its corresponding properties are

$$\text{Enthalpy} = h_2 = h_{2s}$$

$$\text{DBT} = \text{WBT} = t_{wb_2}$$

$$\text{Specific humidity} = w_{2s}$$

Total pressure $= p$

Water at $t_{wb_2}$, which is supplied, has liquid enthalpy $h_{w_2}$. System is adiabatic.

$$\therefore \quad h_1 + (w_{2s} - w_1)\, h_{w_2} = h_{2s}$$

$$\therefore \quad h_1 - w_1 \times h_{w_2} = h_{2s} - w_{2s}\, h_{w_2}$$

Here,
$$h_1 = h_{a_1} + w_1 \times (\text{Enthalpy of superheated vapour at } t_{db_1} \text{ per kg})$$

$$= h_{a_1} + w_1 \times h_{v_1}$$

$$w_{2s} = \text{sp. humidity corresponding to } t_{wb_2} \text{ (saturation condition)}$$

$$w_1 = \text{sp. humidity at point 1}$$

$$h_{w_2} = \text{sensible heat of water at } t_{wb_2}$$

$$h_{2s} = \text{enthalpy of 1 kg air at } t_{wb_2}$$

$$+ w_{2s} \,(\text{Enthalpy of saturated vapour at } t_{wb_2} \text{ per kg vapour})$$

$$= h_{a_2} + w_{2s} \times h_{v_2}$$

Substituting these values, we get

$$h_{a_1} + w_1\, h_{v_1} + (w_{2s} - w_1)\, h_{wb_2} = h_{a_2} + w_{2s}\, h_{wb_2}$$

$$\therefore \qquad w_1 = \frac{(h_{a_2} - h_{a_1}) + w_{2s}\,(h_{v_2} - h_{wb_2})}{h_{v_1} - h_{wb_2}}$$

$$= \frac{w_{2s}\,(h_{v_2} - h_{wb_2}) - (h_{a_1} - h_{a_2})}{h_{v_1} - h_{wb_2}}$$

$$= \frac{w_{2s}\,(h_{fg_2} = L_2) - 1.005\,(t_{db_1} - t_{db_2})}{h_{v_1} - h_{wb_2}}$$

$$= \frac{w_{2s}\, L_{2s} - 1.005\,(t_{db_1} - t_{db_2})}{h_{v_1} - h_{wb_2}}$$

Here
$$t_{db_2} = t_{wb_2}$$

$$\boxed{\; w_1 = \frac{w_{2s}\, L_{2s} - 1.005\,(t_{db_1} - t_{db_2})}{h_{v_1} - h_{wb_2}} \;}$$

## 9.8 PSYCHROMETRIC TABLE

Psychrometric properties of Air at Standard Barometric Pressure of 760 mm of Hg or 1.01325 bar are tabulated for temperatures from $-10°C$ to $60°C$.

The columns that are given in the table are shown below.

**Table 9.1 Properties of Air**

| | Properties of Water and Steam | | | | | Properties of dry air at 760 mm of Hg | | Properties of mixture of dry air and saturated steam i.e. $(1 + w)$ kg at 760 mm of Hg. | | |
|---|---|---|---|---|---|---|---|---|---|---|
| Tempera-ture | Saturation pressure of water and steam $p_s$ | | Enthalpy of saturated water $h_f$ or $h_w$ | Enthalpy of saturated steam $h_g$ | Specific volume of saturated steam $v_g$ | Specific volume $v_a$ | Enthalpy $h_a$ | Volume of mixture $(1 + w)$ kg per kg of dry air – $V_{as}$ | Enthalpy of mixture $(1 + w)$ kg per kg of dry air $h_{as}$ | Specific humidity per kg of dry air $w_s$ |
| $t^oC$ | mm of Hg | bar | kJ/kg | kJ/kg | $m^3$/kg | $m^3$/kg | kJ/kg | $m^3$/kg | kJ/kg | kg/kg |

By applying fundamental procedures of statistical mechanics, Goff and Gratch calculated accurate thermodynamic properties of moist air for standard sea level conditions (Total pressure 760 mm of Hg).

Calculations for specific volume, specific enthalpy and specific entropy of **unsaturated moist air** are approximately given closely by the following relations :

$$v = v_a + \mu (v_{as} - v_a)$$

$$h = h_a + \mu (h_{as} - h_a)$$

$$s = s_a + \mu (s_{as} - s_a)$$

# 9.9 PSYCHROMETRIC CHART

In the articles 9.4, 9.5 and 9.6 above we studied the properties of air and moisture mixtures as applicable to air conditioning. Since, the air conditioning is treating or conditioning air to alter its temperature and moisture content to suit specific requirements, it is necessary to know how exactly air behaves when it is subjected to cooling, heating, humidifying etc. The changes occurring in air as it is subjected to these air conditioning processes, can be traced, analysed and predicted through the use of psychrometric tables or psychrometric charts. The tables are more accurate, but the chart is accurate enough for practical purposes and is much easier to use. Many calculations can be saved by using psychrometric chart. Once understood, the chart is quite simple to use, inspite of the innumerable lines and curves that appear on the chart.

The chart shows the relationship between the following :

- Dry bulb temperature (DBT).
- Wet bulb temperature (WBT).
- Relative humidity (RH).
- Dew point temperature.

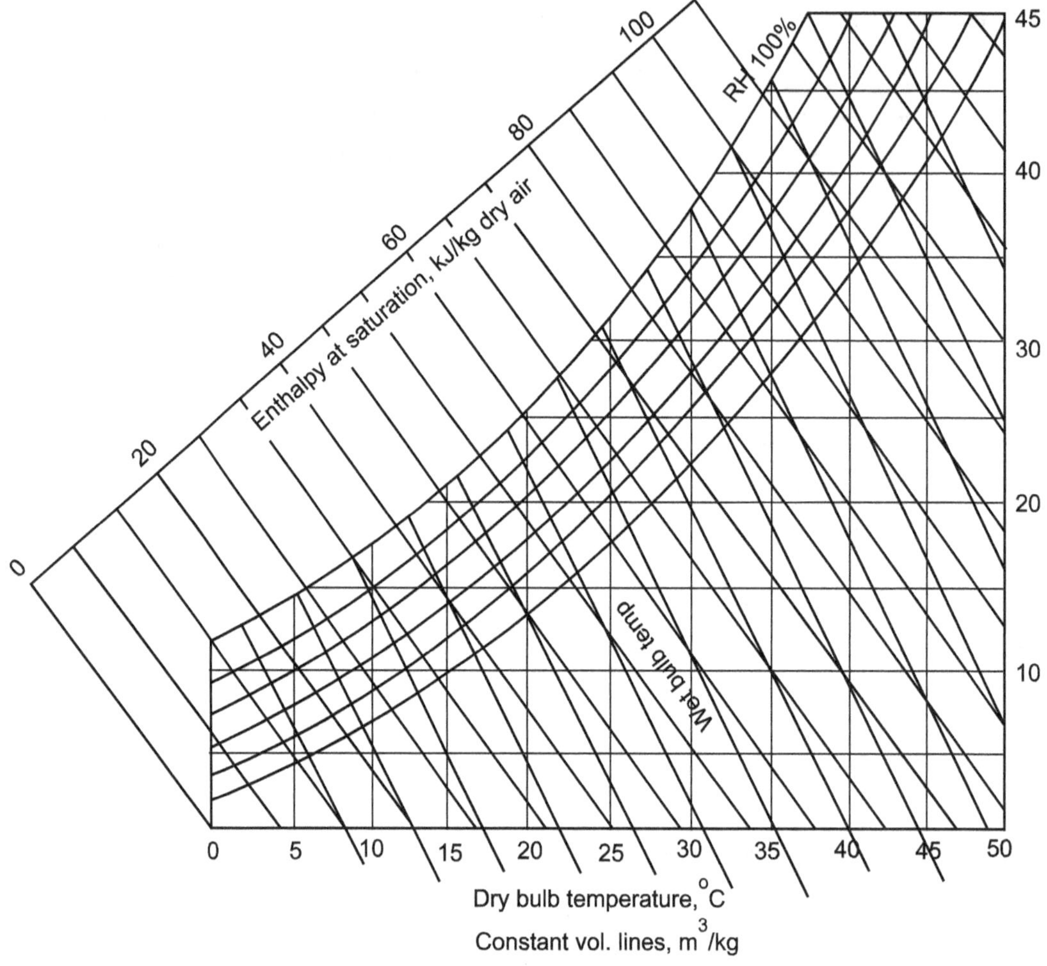



**Fig. 9.3: Psychrometric chart**

If any of the two factors are known, the remaining two can be ascertained from the chart. Other details, such as enthalpy, moisture content, specific volume etc. can also be found from the chart, once any two of the four factors are known.

The following description will serve to understand the psychrometric chart and its use.

**Dry Bulb Temperature (DBT) :**

The dry bulb temperature scale is laid horizontally at the bottom of the chart. The vertical lines extending from the bottom scale to the top are constant temperature lines, i.e. all points on one given line have the same dry bulb temperature as indicated in the DB scale.

**Wet Bulb Temperature (WBT) :**

The wet bulb temperature scale is laid along the outer curve of the left side of the chart. From the points on this curve, constant wet bulb lines run diagonally downwards to the right hand side of the chart. All points on one given WB line are at the same WB temperature.

**Relative Humidity (RH) % :**

The curve lines starting from left and extending upwards and to the right side of the chart are constant relative humidity lines, marked in percentages. The outer curved line on the left, is the 100% RH line or the saturation curve. Since dry bulb, wet bulb and dew point temperatures are the same only when the air is saturated with moisture, any point on this 100% or saturation curve is indicative of all the three temperatures.

The constant RH curves decreases in values, moving from the saturation curve (100% curve) to the right.

**Dew point temperature :**

The constant dew point lines run horizontally starting from the saturation curve to the right side end. All points on one given dew point line have the same dew point temperature. Since the wet bulb and dew point temperatures will be the same at 100% RH, the WB scale marked on the saturation curve is also the dew point scale.

**Moisture content :**

At the right end of the dew point lines, the vertical scale is the specific humidity scale i.e. grammes or kg per kg of dry air. Constant dew point temperature lines are also constant specific humidity lines.

**Enthalpy or Total Heat :**

We know that the total heat content of air is purely dependent upon the wet bulb temperature, i.e. air samples having a different dry bulb temperature but the same wet bulb temperature have the same total heat or enthalpy - only the proportion of sensible heat and latent heat in the constant total heat varies.

**Specific volume :**

The weight of air has to be taken for calculation purposes. But in the field work, we deal with volume of air (handled by fan, cooled and dehumidified by cooling coils etc.). The ratings of fan and cooling and heating coils etc. are given in terms of the volume of air handled in cu-m per minute or hour. Therefore, in the psychrometric chart, specific volume lines are given to find the volume of air per unit weight of dry air. Specific volume of air changes with temperature. Specific volume lines are shown on the chart and marked cu-m/kg dry air.

## 9.10  METHOD OF USING PSYCHROMETRIC CHART

**(a)  When dry bulb and wet bulb temperatures are given :**

Vertical line at dry bulb temperature, say 30°C, will meet wet bulb temperature line, say 25°C, at the point A. Horizontal line from A towards right to meet specific humidity scale line to get w-sp-humidity. The same horizontal line on the left of A will meet 100% RH curve to give dew point temperature, say x. Extension of constant wet bulb temperature line of 25°C to meet  the enthalpy scale to give enthalpy of air at A say h. Through the point A, one constant relative humidity curve will pass and that will be the relative humidity, say Y%, at the point A. Similarly, point A will lie on any one constant specific volume line to give the specific volume, say z m³/kg dry air, at the point A. Thus, all the unknown properties are obtained when DBT and WBT are given.

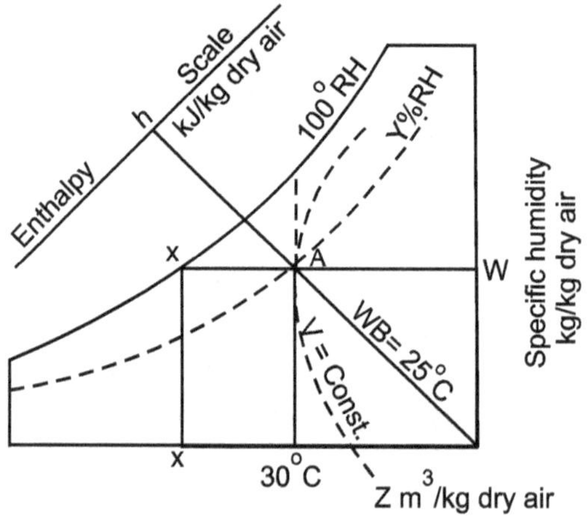


**Fig. 9.4**

**(b) When dry bulb temperature and relative humidity are given :**

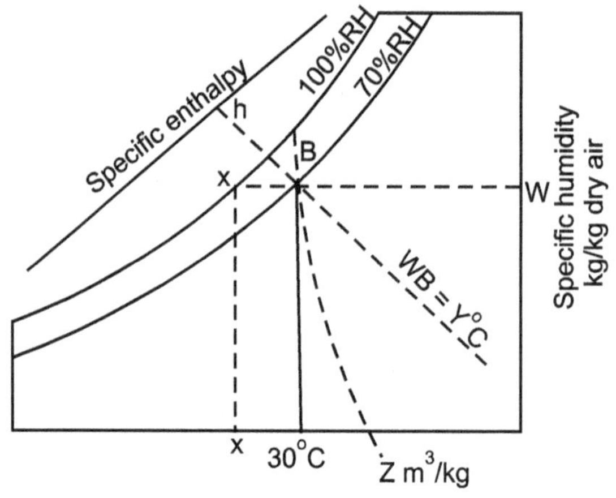


**Fig. 9.5**

Vertical line at dry bulb temperature, say 30°C, will meet a constant relative humidity, say 70% RH, curve in point say B. Fig. 9.5 gives the procedures to be followed to get specific humidity w, specific volume z, wet-bulb temperature Y and specific enthalpy h kJ/kg dry air and dew point temperature x.

**(c) When dry bulb temperature and dew point temperature are given :**

Draw the vertical line at dry bulb temperature, say 30°C. Let the dew point temperature given as 20°C. Draw a vertical line at 20°C DBT to meet 100% RH curve in P. From P draw a horizontal line to meet the vertical line at DBT = 30°C in point C. Then we can find WBT, h, w and specific volume as shown in Fig. 9.6.

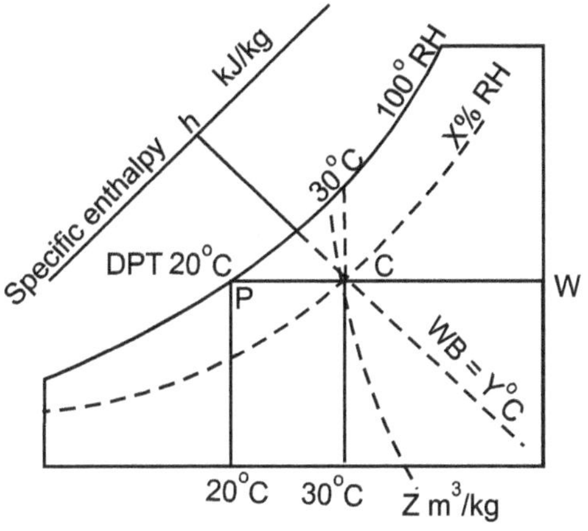


**Fig. 9.6**

Similarly, once any two properties or conditions are given, we can get the state point and once the state point is obtained, we can read all other quantities given in the chart.

# 9.11  PSYCHROMETRIC PROCESSES

Conditioning of air to the conditions of human comfort or of the optimum control of an industrial process requires certain processes to be carried out on the outside air available. The processes affecting the psychrometric properties of air are called as **psychrometric processes.**  These processes involve :

    (a)   Mixing of air streams (adiabatic mixing)

    (b)   Heating (sensible)

    (c)   Cooling (sensible)

    (d)   Humidifying

    (e)   Dehumidifying

    (f)   Evaporative cooling (adiabatic saturation) and mostly the combinations of these various processes.

We will now study one by one of these processes.

**(a)  Mixing of air streams :**

Very often air having different conditions are mixed in the air-conditioned system, such as the mixing of return air (for recirculation) with fresh air before it enters the cooling coil, mixing of cooled - dehumidified air with bypass air etc. The psychrometric chart can be used to find the resulting condition of the mixture.

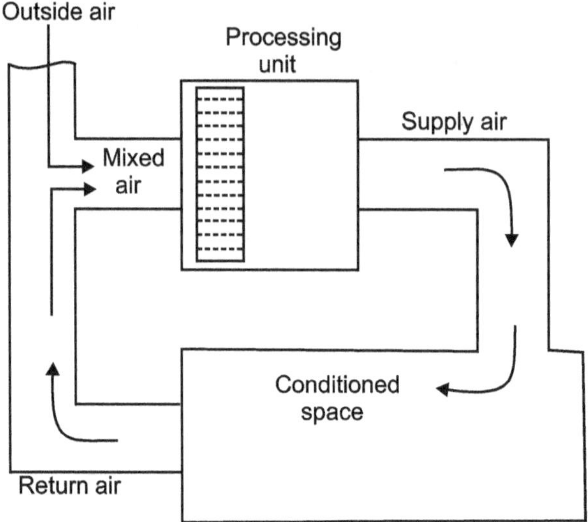


**Fig. 9.7: Mixing of air streams**

The schematic diagram in Fig. 9.7 shows the mixing of ventilation air from outdoors mixed with room air returning for recirculation.

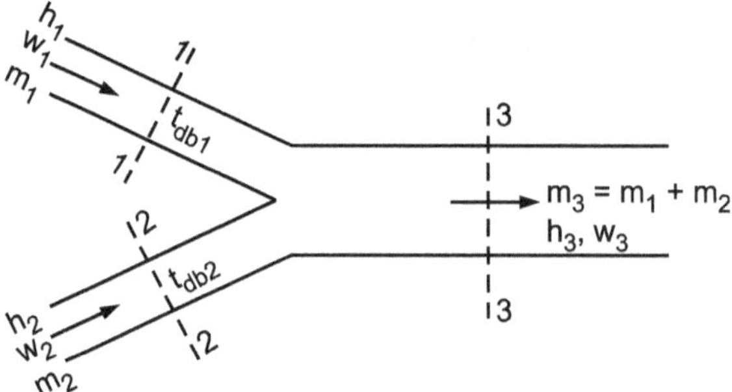


**Fig. 9.8: Adiabatic mixing**

The two air streams of masses $m_1$ and $m_2$, humidity ratios $w_1$ and $w_2$ and enthalpies $h_1$ and $h_2$ respectively, when mixed without addition or rejection of heat and moisture, say, results in a stream of mass $m_3$, humidity ratio $w_3$ and specific enthalpy $h_3$.

∴　We have　　　$m_3 = m_1 + m_2$

$$m_3 w_3 = m_1 w_1 + m_2 w_2$$

$$m_3 h_3 = m_1 h_1 + m_2 h_2$$

Eliminating $m_3$ and rearranging the above equations, we have

$$m_1 w_1 + m_2 w_2 = w_3 (m_1 + m_2)$$

$$m_1 (w_1 - w_3) = m_2 (w_3 - w_2)$$

and　　　$m_1 (h_1 - h_3) = m_2 (h_3 - h_2)$

$$\text{or} \qquad \frac{m_1}{m_2} = \frac{w_3 - w_2}{w_1 - w_3} = \frac{h_3 - h_2}{h_1 - h_3}$$

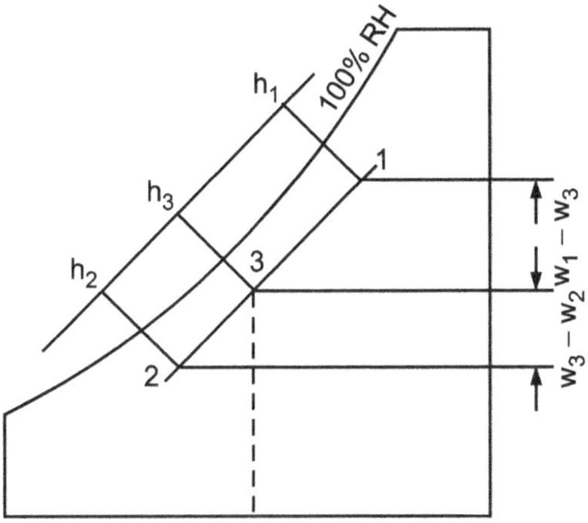

**Fig. 9.9: Adiabatic mixing**

The final condition of the mixture can be found with the help of chart as follows :

First find or determine the percentage of ventilation air in the mixture. Let it be x%. Therefore, the recirculated air percentage will be $(100 - x)$.

Then locate the two points 1 and 2 from the given conditions of two streams. Join $1 - 2$. Next step is very important. Multiply the dry bulb temperature of each air by its percentage in the mixture. If $t_{db_1}$ = 30°C and the percentage of air stream 1 is x%, it contributes $(30 \times x)$ DB degrees to the mixture. Similarly, if $t_{db_2}$ = 25°C, so second stream contributes $(100 - x) \times 25$ DB to the mixture. The dry bulb temperature of the mixture will be $[30x + 25 (100 - x)]$°C. Thus, point 3 can be found on the chart, or point 3 divides the distance AB (measured with scale) inversely proportional to the quantities of the two air mixing. In other words, if the quantities of air at points 1 and 2 are mixing in the ratio 9 : 1 of the total air, the resultant point 3 will lie on the line $1 - 2$, dividing it in the ratio of 1 : 9.

Once the point 3 is located, we can get from the chart other properties.

**(b) Sensible heating only :**

By sensible heating we mean adding heat to air, which raises the temperature of air. No moisture is added or removed and hence the vapour content or specific humidity remains the same. In this case, the dew point temperature remains the same. The wet bulb temperature, however, has increased and the relative humidity has decreased. This explains why the relative humidity in the early morning is high but decreases as the day goes warmer.

Heating is usually done by electric resistance heating coil, or steam coils or hot air / gas coils. The heat added represents sensible heat addition only.

The sensible heat added per kg of dry air

$$h_1 - h_2 = C_{p_a}(t_{db_2} - t_{db_1}) + w\, C_{p_v}(t_{db_2} - t_{db_1})$$

$$= (C_{p_a} + w\, C_{p_v})(t_{db_2} - t_{db_1})$$

This process is shown in Fig. 9.10.

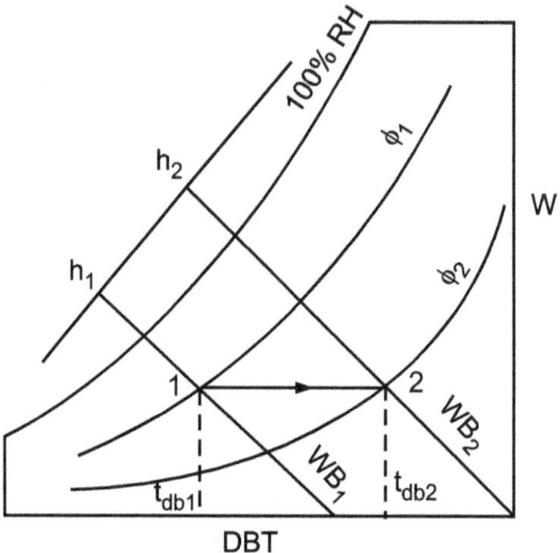


**Fig. 9.10: Sensible heating**

## (c) Sensible cooling only :

The word only is used to signify that the process is only sensible cooling and there is no latent heat removal. Latent heat removal from air occurs when some moisture contained in the air is condensed, thus bringing down the amount of moisture contained in the air. Specific humidity remains constant in sensible cooling. The dew point temperature remains constant.

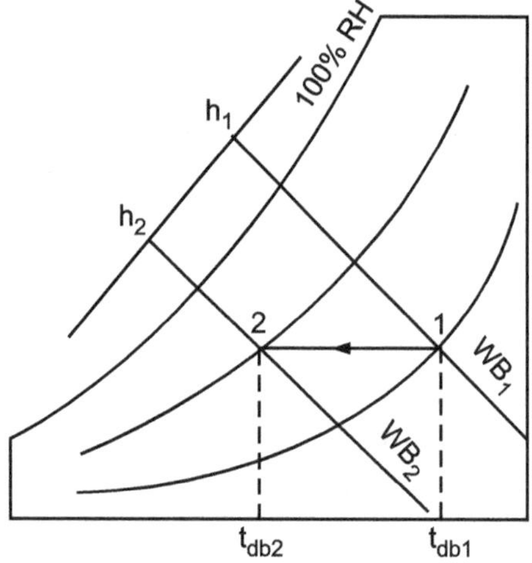


**Fig. 9.11: Sensible cooling**

Cooling of air is usually done by means of cooling coils through which cold water is circulated and the temperature of this water will be higher than the dew point temperature.

In sensible cooling, the wet bulb temperature decreases and the dew point temperature remains constant. This is shown in Fig. 9.11.

The sensible heat removed per kg of dry air

$$h_1 - h_2 = C_{p_a}(t_{db_1} - t_{db_2}) + w\, C_{p_v}(t_{db_1} - t_{db_2})$$

$$= (C_{p_a} + w\, C_{p_v})(t_{db_1} - t_{db_2})$$

## By-pass Factor (BF) :

If $t_c$ is the temperature of the heating or cooling coil, then in passing the air through the heating coil and cooling coil apparatus, it is expected that the air after the process should be at the coil temperature. But this does not happen due to the effect of 'by-pass' in the heating/cooling coil apparatus.

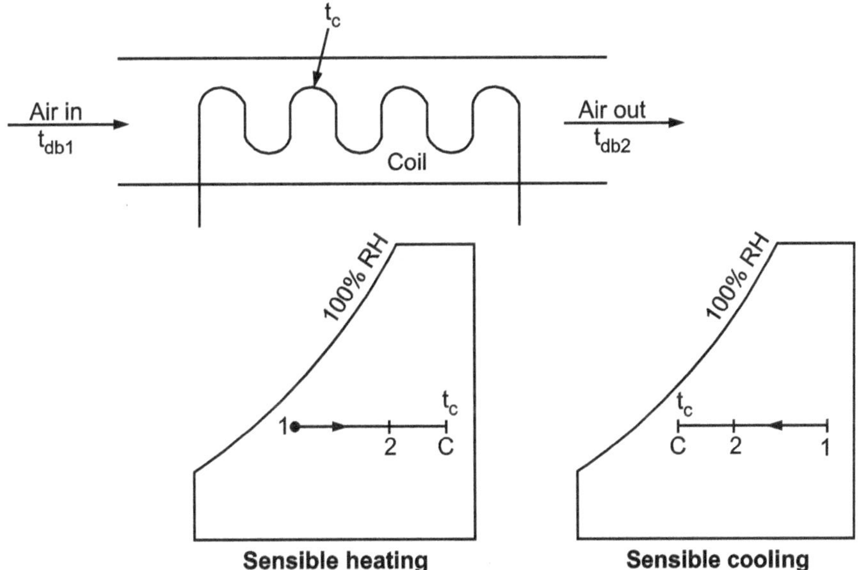


**Fig. 9.12: By-pass factor**

Consider the cooling apparatus as a cooling coil in which chilled water is circulated or as the cooling coil of a refrigeration plant. The air passing over the cooling coil and fins gets cooled. All the air cannot come in contact with the coil and fins. Some air passing between the fins will not get direct contact with the cold surface of the coil and fins and we can say that this part of the air 'by-passes' the cooling surface of the cooling coil and comes out of the cooling surface of the cooling coil and comes out of the cooling apparatus at the same condition as if entered and mixes with the cooled air, thus giving a condition of a mixture of cooled and initial air. The amount of by-pass depends upon :

- Number of fins per unit length on the coil or gas between the fins or pitch of the fins.

- Velocity of air over the coil.

- Number  of rows of coil pipes in the direction of air flow.

The by-pass factor (1) increases as the velocity of air over coil increases, (2)  decreases as the pitch of the fins decreases and (3)  decreases as the number of rows of the coil increases.

In an ideal case, $t_{db_2} = t_c$ (reversible heating or cooling). The efficiency of heating or cooling processes can be expressed as a by-pass factor BF.

$$\text{By-pass factor} \ = \ \frac{t_c - t_{db_2}}{t_c - t_{db_1}} \ \text{for heating}$$

$$= \ \frac{t_{db_2} - t_c}{t_{db_1} - t_c} \ \text{for cooling.}$$

If we consider the total mass m of dry air, as divided in two fractions $m_1$ and $m_2$ and assume that $m_1$ by-pass the coil and mixes with the mass $m_2$ which comes in complete contact with coil and attains the temperature $t_c$.

$$\therefore \qquad \frac{m_1}{m} = \frac{t_c - t_{db_2}}{t_c - t_{db_1}} \quad \text{Fraction of the mass by-pass = BF.}$$

$$\therefore \qquad (1 - BF) = \frac{m_2}{m} = \frac{t_{db_2} - t_{db_1}}{t_c - t_{db_1}} \quad \begin{array}{l}\text{Fraction of mass actually}\\ \text{coming in contact with the coil}\end{array}$$

In an actual process there is no separation of the masses as assumed; but this assumption gives a very convenient method of analysing the process.

Assume the constant rate of change of wet bulb temperatures with a dry bulb temperature, along a process line, a convenient expression for by-pass factor is

$$BF \ = \ \frac{t_{db_2} - t_{w_2}}{t_{db_1} - t_{w_1}}$$

### (d)  Humidifying and dehumidifying only :

Adding or removing moisture at constant dry bulb temperature can be represented by a vertical line on a psychrometric chart.

Pure humidifying process is possible only when heat of vaporisation is supplied from a source other than air without affecting the dry bulb temperature. This happens when water at the dry bulb temperature of the entering air is sprayed in a chamber whose temperature is maintained at the air DB temperature.

Let,              c   represent the condition of spray water,

a   represent the condition of entering air,

b   depend on the amount of moisture sprayed per kg of dry air flowing,

$h_b - h_a$ is heat that is to be supplied for evaporation of moisture.

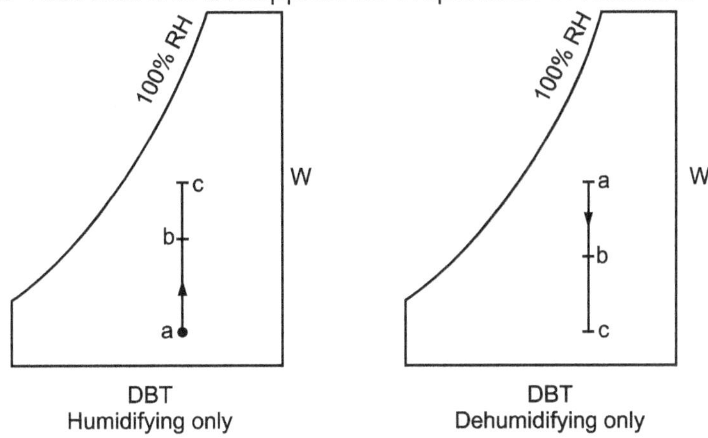


DBT
Humidifying only

DBT
Dehumidifying only

**Fig. 9.13: Humidifying and dehumidifying**

Pure dehumidification occurs without the change of dry bulb temperature of air, when air is passed over chemical absorbing moisture and heat evolved when moisture is absorbed, is removed immediately by the surrounded walls, which are maintained at the dry bulb temperature of air. The chemicals are also maintained at the dry bulb temperature of air. The process of pure dehumidification is shown in Fig. 9.13.

Pure humidification and dehumidification processes are not found in practice and are always accompanied by heating and cooling.

Heat added or subtracted is purely due to change of moisture content and hence is equal to the latent heat change.

$$Q_L = \Delta W \times L$$

**(e) Cooling and Dehumidification :**

This process involves not only sensible cooling but also latent heat removal or reduction of moisture content or dehumidification. Therefore, the air will have to be cooled below its dew point temperature.

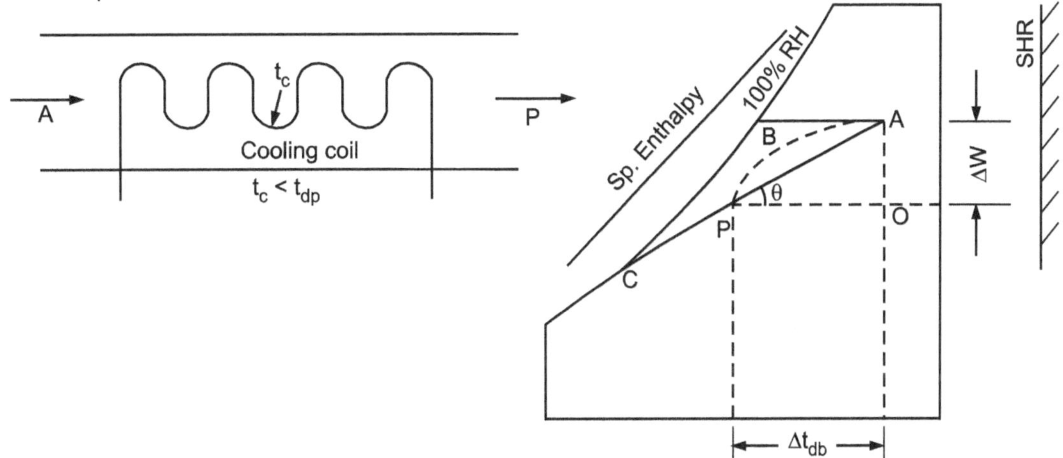


**Fig. 9.14: Cooling and Dehumidification**

Thus, when air is passed over a coil whose temperature $t_c$ is below the dew point temperature of air passing over it, the moisture condenses out and dehumidification results. Such a process is represented on psychrometric chart along ABC as shown in Fig. 9.14.

In passing through the cooling apparatus, it is to be expected that the air after the process should be at the saturated condition given by C. But this does not happen due to the effect of 'by-pass' in the cooling apparatus. For simplicity of understanding, this process can be considered as two distinct processes, namely,

(1)  Cooling from A to its dew point B i.e. sensible cooling, represented by AB and

(2)  Cooling and dehumidifying from B to C represented by BC.

Part of the air which comes in contact with the coil surface is cooled and dehumidified to the condition C and the remaining air which does not come in contact with the coil surface, by-passes the coil and then mixes with the air at C and the final condition of air coming out of the apparatus is shown by P. The actual process taking place in the apparatus is given by a dotted line AP and not ABC.

When the temperature of the coil is below the dew point temperature, $t_{dp}$, of the air passing over it, the coil temperature is called the **'Apparatus Dew Point'** (ADP) temperature.

Then the by-pass factor is given by

$$BF = \frac{t_p - ADP}{t_A - ADP}$$

Efficiency of the coil is $1 - BF$. As the final condition obtained is independent of the path of the process followed, the process may be assumed to have followed the path AO and OP i.e first dehumidification only, followed by sensible cooling OP.

$\therefore \qquad\qquad\quad h_A - h_p = (h_A - h_o) + (h_o - h_p)$

Here, $\qquad\qquad h_A - h_o = $ Latent heat removal

$$= Q_L = L \times \Delta W$$

and $\qquad\qquad h_o - h_p = $ sensible heat removal

$$= Q_s$$

$$= C_{p_a} \,(\Delta t_{db}) + C_{p_v} \times \Delta t_{db}$$

$\therefore \quad$ Total heat removal $Q_t = Q_s + Q_L$

The ratio $\dfrac{Q_s}{Q_t}$ is called the Sensible Heat Ratio (SHR) or Sensible Heat Factor (SHF).

$$\therefore \qquad\qquad SHR = \frac{Q_s}{Q_t} = \frac{Q_s}{Q_s + Q_L}$$

$$= \frac{1}{1 + \dfrac{Q_L}{Q_S}}$$

$$= \frac{1}{1 + \dfrac{L}{(C_{p_a} + C_{p_v})} \tan \theta}$$

where,  $\tan \theta = \dfrac{\Delta w}{\Delta t_{db}}$

$\tan \theta$ = slope of the line AP.

## Dehumidifiers

1. Refrigerator evaporator coil or chilled water coils.

2. Chemical dehumidifiers

   (a) absorbent-type

   (b) adsorbent-type

Sensible heat ratio slopes are given on the psychrometric chart and if SHR is known for a given process, the process line can be drawn on the chart from the initial given condition at the slope given by SHR on the chart.

## (f) Cooling and Humidification :

By spraying water at a temperature higher than the dew-point temperature, $t_{dp}$, of the air and lower than the dry bulb temperature $t_{db}$, into the air path, cooling and humidification can be achieved.

Cooling and humidification process is called evaporative cooling process. Air is passed through a fresh water air washer. The water is neither cooled nor heated. The continuously recirculating water through the spray banks in the air washer will soon attain a temperature equal to the wet bulb temperature of the air entering the air washer.

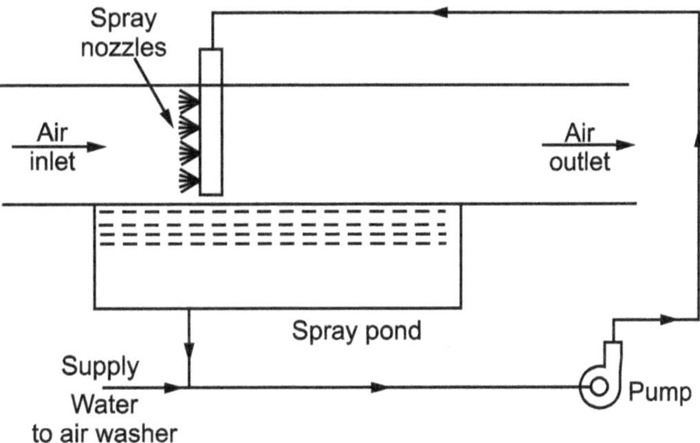


**Fig. 9.15: Cooling and humidification**

The temperature of water will then remain constant as long as the wet bulb temperature of the entering air does not change. Since the wet bulb temperature of the air is always higher than its dew point, the spray water temperature (equalling the wet bulb temperature of the air) will be higher than the dew point temperature of the air. Since the water temperature does not change, it can neither add nor remove heat from the air. However, the water temperature is higher than the air dew point temperature, this means that the vapour pressure of the air washer water is higher than that of the vapour in the air. Hence, the evaporation of water takes place, adding moisture to the air stream. Since the water temperature is lower than the dry bulb temperature of air, there is some sensible cooling and a drop in the dry bulb temperature of the air. But the heat lost by the air in the sensible cooling is equal to the latent heat gained by the air by the addition of water vapour to the air. This means that the air has surrendered its sensible heat to evaporate the water and thus gain back whatever heat has been surrendered in the form of latent heat. Thus, there is no change in the total heat content of the air in passing through the air washer though the proportion of sensible heat and latent heat changes. Because the total heat content does not change, the wet bulb temperature of entering air and leaving air will be the same. The dry bulb temperature drops down, dew point temperature and relative humidity RH goes up as shown in Fig. 9.16.

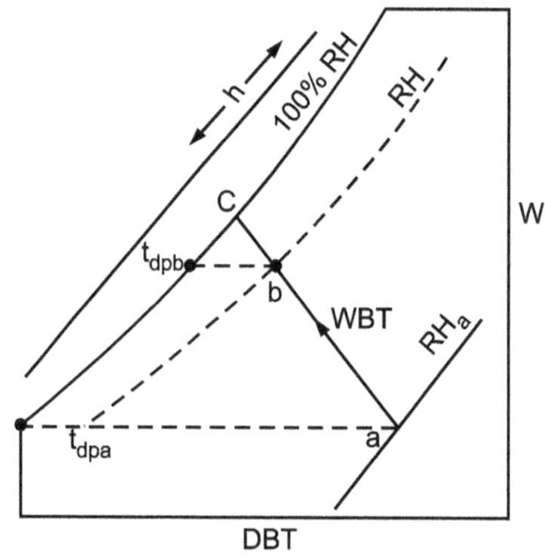


**Fig. 9.16**

Theoretically, air passing through the air washer should be cooling down to its own wet bulb temperature. In other words, the difference between the dry bulb temperature of the entering and leaving air should be equal to the wet bulb depression of the entering air [i.e. $(t_{db_a} - t_{db_2}) = (t_{db_a} - t_{wb_a})$]. But no air washer is 100% efficient. The efficiency of an air washer, therefore, is the ratio of the actual drop in the dry bulb temperature of air in passing through the air washer to the wet-bulb depression of the entering air.

$$\therefore \quad \text{Air washer efficiency} = \frac{t_{db_a} - t_{db_b}}{t_{db_a} - t_{db_c} \text{ or } (t_{wb_a})}$$

The condition b at the outlet of the washer will depend on the by-pass factor of the spray.

### (g) Heating and Humidification :

If air is heated and moisture is added to it, the process is called heating and humidification. This process can be considered as two distinct processes, viz.

- Heating from $t_{db_a}$ to $t_{db_b}$ and

- Addition of moisture (equal to $w_c - w_b$).

So in the chart, line AB will represent the heating and BC the humidification process and line AC will be the representation of the combined effect of heating and humidification. See Fig. 9.17.

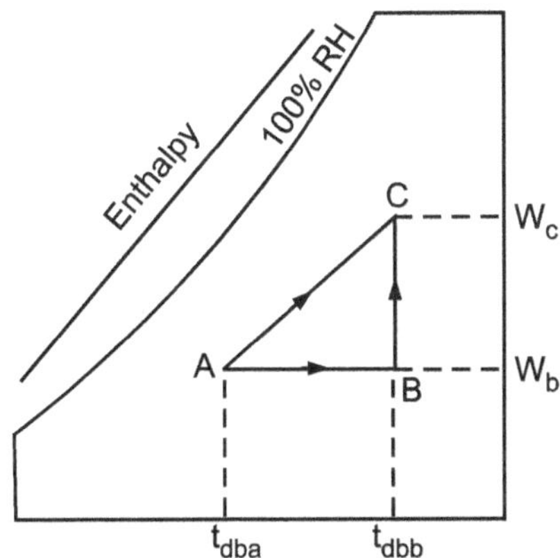


**Fig. 9.17: Heating and Humidification**

When the air is passed through a humidifier, in which hot water is sprayed at a temperature higher than the dry bulb temperature of air, the unsaturated air gets saturated and the latent heat of evaporation is taken from the water itself. As a result, air is heated and humidified and spray water is cooled. The maximum outlet condition of air corresponds to saturation at spray water temperature and minimum temperature to which the spray water is cooled, corresponds to the wet bulb temperature of inlet air. Cooling beyond this temperature will upset the equilibrium condition at inlet, and more sensible heat flow from air to water than required by latent heat of evaporation will raise the water temperature and prevent its further fall.

This process has industrial application in cooling towers and evaporative condensers and also in winter air conditioning.

**Different types of humidifiers (without any description with sketch) are :**

- Pan-type humidifiers.
- Rotating type humidifiers.
- Atomizing humidifiers.
- Centrifugal wheel-type humidifier.

- Wetted element humidifier.
- Plenum power type humidifier.
- By-pass humidifier.

**Humidistat :**

Where close control of humidity is desired, a humidistat may be used to energize or deenergize the water solenoid relay.

A humidistat is a switch mechanism actuated by changes in moisture. The sensing or hygroscopic element of a typical residential humidistat is composed of tightly strung human hair or a Teflon strip that will contract or expand under varying relative humidity conditions. This movement is sufficient to open or close an electric current.

Some humidistats are wall mounted, but others are made for duct mounting and may be equipped with a sail switch to sense air movement in the duct.

## (h)  Heating and Dehumidification :

Simultaneous heating and dehumidification can be accomplished by passing air over a solid adsorbent surface or through a liquid absorbent spray. Dehumidification results from the lower water vapour pressure of the absorbent other than that of air. Moisture is condensed out of air and latent heat of condensation is liberated which heats the air sensibly. Thus, this process is inverse of adiabatic saturation and follows constant wet bulb temperature line downwards on psychrometric chart.

Solid adsorbents, such as silica gel, or activated alumina and liquid absorbents such as solutions of inorganic salts (brine, lithium chloride) or organic compounds like ethylene glycol are used.

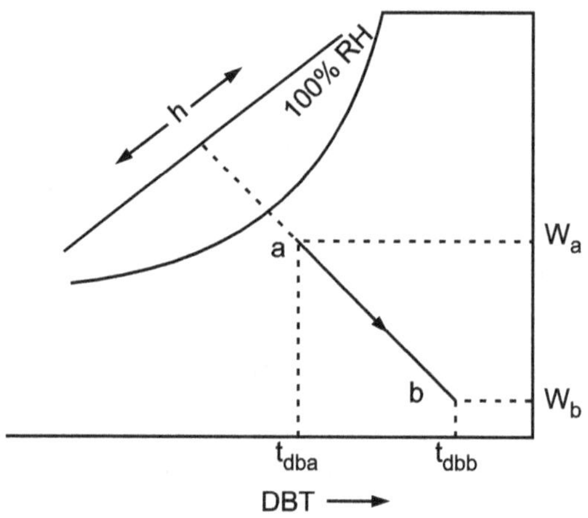


**Fig. 9.18 : Heating and dehumidification process**

In practice, all kinds of air conditioning systems employ one process combined with other, or combinations of psychrometric processes are used to give the required conditions for comfort and even industrial air conditioning applications.

## 9.12 APPLICATIONS OF AIR CONDITIONING

Air-Conditioning, as we have seen, is mainly divided into two types :

1.   Comfort air conditioning and

2.   Industrial air conditioning.

We will enumerate the applications accordingly.

1. **Comfort air conditioning :**

Following are the applications for comfort air conditioning.

- Comfort air conditioning had its first major use in **motion picture theaters.** (Early 1920s).

- At the end of the decade came the introduction of the first **self-contained room air-conditioner**.

- Multiroom office buildings

- Hotels, restaurants and night clubs

- Apartments

- Hospitals

- Departmental stores

- Drug store

- Dress shops

- Barbar shops

- Grocery stores

- Banks

- Dance halls and skating rinks

- Transportation : Trains, Air planes, Buses and trollys, automobiles.

and many more applications can be listed.

2. **Industrial air conditioning applications :**

Here human comfort element is not considered. Following are some of the applications of industrial air conditioning.

- **Textile industry :** The two chief processes used are referred to as **viscose** and **acetate** or as wet and dry spinning, respectively, both of which are 24-hour per day operations and required reliable air-conditioning equipment. An increase in relative humidity increases the length, weight, elongation, softness, flexibility, pliability and limpidity of yarns but decreases their strength. A decrease in relative humidity will have the opposite effect.

- **Printing industry :** Variations in weather cause distorting, curling and buckling of papers, static electricity, misregister of colour printing, ink off-set, ink misting, troubles with composition rolls and distortion of wooden cut mounts. Most of these results are from the reactions of the hygroscopic materials involved.

- Candy and Gum

- Drugs and Chemicals

- Libraries and Museums

- Metal working

- Laboratories and Cabinets

and many more applications can be listed.

## 9.13 EVAPORATIVE COOLING

Liquid will evaporate if there is a difference between the vapour pressure in the air and the saturation pressure of liquid (water) at the water temperature. The larger the difference between the vapour pressure and saturation pressure, the rate of evaporation is higher. The evaporation of water will have a cooling effect on water and thus reduce its temperature. Then the saturation pressure will reduce and the rate of evaporation will reduce. This will continue till some kind of quasi-steady operation is reached. This phenomenon, thus, explains why the water temperature is always less than the surrounding air particularly in dry climate like summer.

We, therefore, conclude that the air at the water surface will always be saturated because of the direct contact with water, and thus the vapour pressure.

Then, the natural tendency of water to evaporate in order to achieve pressure equilibrium, forms the basis for the operation of the **evaporative cooler** – sometimes called the swamp coolers. Air coolers available in the market work on this evaporative cooling principle. In these coolers, hot and dry outdoor air is forced to flow through a wet cloth/felt before entering the building or space - some of the water evaporates by absorbing heat from the air, and thus cooling it. Evaporative coolers are commonly used in dry climates (tropical regions) and provide effective cooling. These coolers are much cheaper to run than air conditioners since they are not costly to buy and the remaining cost of the fan of evaporative cooler is much less than that for compressor of an air conditioner.

## 9.14 AIR WASHER

Air washer is an equipment used for

- Cooling and dehumidification.

- Cooling and humidification.

- Heating and humidification.

- Humidification.
- Adiabatic saturation.
- Cooling.

**Process in air conditioning systems :** The schematic diagram for air washer is shown in Fig. 9.19.

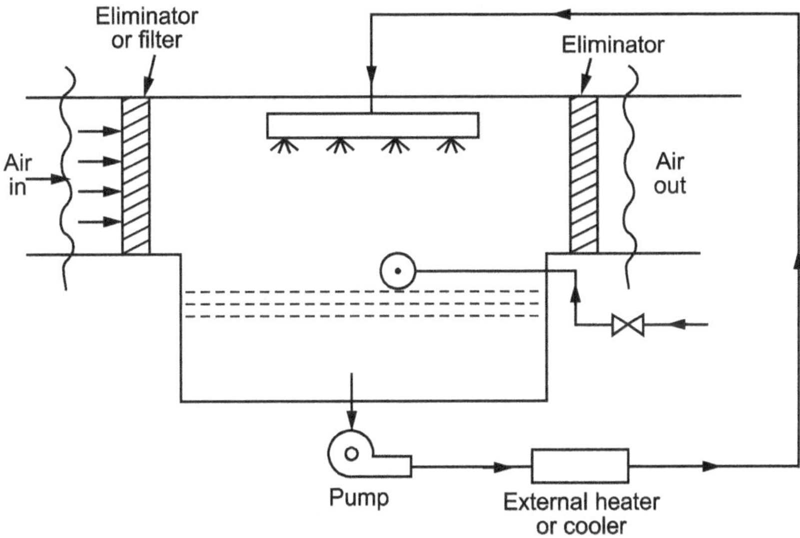


**Fig. 9.19: Air washer**

The process that can be carried out with the type of the washer shown, can be represented on the psychrometric chart as shown in Fig. 9.20.

(a) **Cooling :** In this case the temperature of the water will be equal to the dew point of the air entering. It is represented by 1 – 2a.

(b) **Adiabatic saturation :** If the water sprayed is at a temperature equal to the dew point temperature of the air, then we get saturation of air and it follows the WBT line. It is represented by the line 1 – 2b.

(c) **Cooling and dehumidification :** Here, if the temperature of spray water is less than dew point temperature of entering air, we get this type of the process 1 – 2c.

(d) **Cooling and humidification :** In this case, temperature of spray water is greater than entering air and dew point temperature of air. This is shown by 1 – 2d. If the temperature of spray water is greater than dew point temperature but less than wet bulb temperature of the entering air, this is shown as 1 – 2d'.

(e) **Humidification :** In this process, the mean surface temperature of water is equal to the dry bulb temperature of air. The enthalpy of air increases and the external heat is required to heat water. This is shown by a vertical line 1 – 2e.

(f) **Heating and humidification :** In this case, the temperature of water is greater than the temperature of entering air. External heating is necessary for water. This is shown by 1 – 2f.

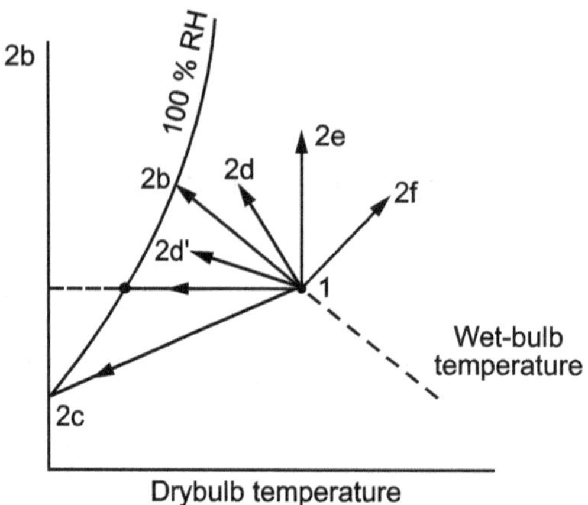



**Fig. 9.20**

In comparison with cooler coil, the washer suffers from a number of disadvantages :

- It is more bulky.

- Maintenance is more expensive.

- Corrosion is a greater risk.

- As it uses an open chilled water circuit, the deposition of scale, rust, etc. in the water chillier take place. Naturally the heat transfer efficiency is reduced and the cost of refrigeration plant is increased.

It is true that the washer allows the humidification of air, we can always think of steam injection for humidification as it dispenses with the need for extensive water works and is perfectly safe.

There is one point strongly in favour of air washers and sprayed cooler coils, viz., the presence of the large mass of water in the sump tank and spray chamber gives a thermal inertia to the system, smoothing out fluctuations in the state of air leaving the coil or water, and adding stability to the operation of the automatic controls.

Now-a-days, the air washers are very much out of fashion because of the four points mentioned and the more efficiency of the coil.

**There are three different types of air washers. They are :**

(a)    Spray-type air washer.

(b)    High-velocity spray-type air washer.

(c)    Cell-type air washer.

**(a)    Spray-type air washer :** Spray-type air washer consists of a chamber or casing containing a spray-nozzle system, a tank to collect the spray-water as it falls and an eliminator section for removal of the entrained drops of water from the air. A pump recirculates water at a rate greater than the evaporation rate. Intimate contact between the spray water and the air flow causes heat and mass transfer between air and water. Washers are commonly available from 0.9 to 118 $m^3$/sec capacity. No standardisation exists.

The simplest design has a single bank of spray nozzles with a casing of 1.2 to 2.1 m long. This type of washer is used primarily as an evaporative cooler or humidifier. It is sometimes used as an air cleaner when the dust is wettable. Two or three spray banks are generally used when a very high degree of saturation is necessary.

Essential requirements in the air washer operations are :

- Uniform distribution of the air across the spray chamber.

- An adequate amount of spray water broken-up in fine droplets.

- Good spray distribution across the air stream.

- Sufficient length of travel through the spray and the wetted surfaces.

- The elimination of free moisture from the outlet air.

**(b) High-velocity spray-type air washer :** High-velocity air washers generally operate at air velocities in the range of 6 to 9 m/sec and in some cases of 12 m/s. 6 to 8 m/s is the most accepted range for optimum operation.

Units of upto 70 $m^3$/s capacity are available in one piece including spray systems, eliminators, pump, fan, dampers filters and other functional components. Such units are self-housed, prewired, prepiped and ready for hoisting into place.

High velocity washers are rectangular in cross-section, and except for the eliminators, are similar in appearance and construction to conventional lower velocity types. These washers are available either as free-standing separate devices for incorporation into field-built central stations or in complete preassembled central stations packages from the factory.

**(c) Cell-type air washers :** These washers obtain intimate air-water contact by passing the air through cells packed with glass, metal or fibre screens. Water passes over the cells arranged in tiers. Behind the cells are blade-type or glass-mat eliminators. Most cell-type washers are arranged for concurrent air and water flow. They are also constructed for special duty with counter-current flow characteristics or in a combination of both arrangements. Cell washers come to many sizes of insulated or uninsulated construction - standard washers are available upto 10 cells high by 12 cells wide with a capacity of upto 100 $m^3$/s.

Atomisation of the spray water is not required in cell-type washers, but good water distribution over the face of the cell is essential. A saturation effectiveness of 90 to 97% is possible.

The Dynel/polyster-mat type of cell washer operates at a basic spray rate of 0.1 litre/sec of water per $m^3$/sec.

## 9.15 FOGGED AIR

Under certain conditions saturated air can hold additional moisture in the form of minute water droplets.

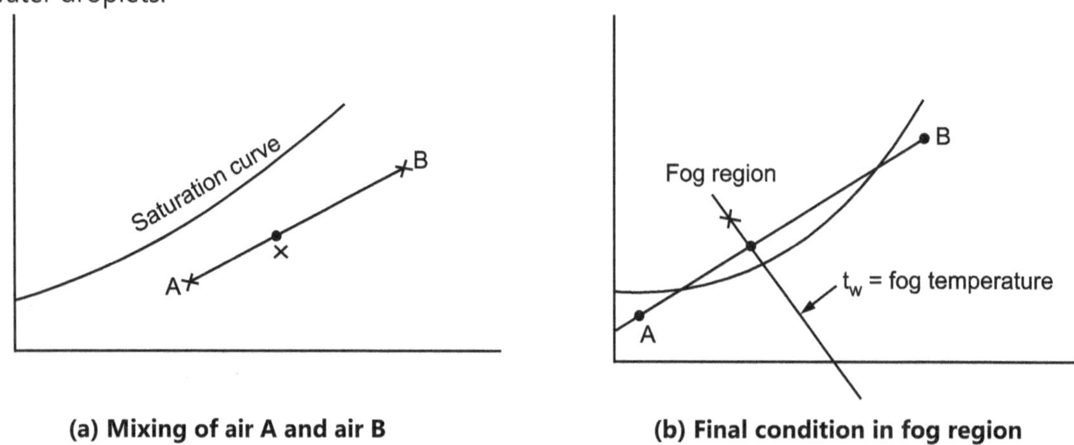

| **(a) Mixing of air A and air B** | **(b) Final condition in fog region** |

**Fig. 9.21**

The area to the left or above the saturation curve on the psychrometric chart represent conditions of fogged air. Such an atmospheric condition can be created in more than one manner. When warm humid air is mixed with cold air, the resulting mixture will be a fog if the state of the final mixture lies in the fog region of the psychrometric chart. Illustrates this condition where equal amounts of air at conditions A and B are mixed. The final condition will be represented by X. The temperature of the fog is that of the extended wet-bulb line through X.

Fog can also result when steam or a very fine water spray is injected into air in a quantity greater than that necessary to saturate air. Lesser quantities incompletely mixed with the air can result in part fog and part unsaturated air.

To clear fog : (1) Heating the fog, (2) Mixing the fog with warmer unsaturated air and (3) mechanically separating the water droplets from the air.

## 9.16 THERMODYNAMICS OF HUMAN BODY

Man and many other living creatures may be compared in some respects with an automatically controlled stoker-fired furnace. Food consisting mainly of carbon, hydrogen, oxygen, nitrogen and certain minerals, which likewise are the main elements in coal, is taken periodically just as coal is fed into the hopper. Air is continually drawn in, and the oxygen combines with the carbon to form carbon dioxide, which is exhaled. Oxygen, also, combines with hydrogen to form water vapour which is also exhaled. Some water also leaves through the sweat glands and evaporates from the skin surface as a part of the marvelous control system that maintains our body temperature at about 37°C (96.6°F). Heat evolved from this oxidation process, termed **metabolism**, as it is from the oxidation or combustion process in the furnace.

# 9.17 COMFORT-PHYSIOLOGICAL CONSIDERATIONS

The ASHRAE handbook of fundamentals (3) gives the exhaustive details of physiological principles of human **thermal** comfort. Only essential details are given here.

The amount of heat generated and dissipated by the human body varies considerably with activity and age as well as with size and gender. The body has a complex regulating system acting to maintain the deep body temperature of about 37ºC (96.6ºF) regardless of the environmental conditions. A normal, healthy person generally feels most comfortable when the environment is maintained at conditions where the body can easily maintain a thermal balance with the surroundings. ASHRAE specifies conditions in which 80% or more of the occupants will find the environment thermally acceptable.

The environmental factors that affect a person's thermal balance and therefore which influence thermal comfort are :

- The dry bulb temperature of the surrounding air.
- The humidity of the surrounding air.
- The relative velocity of the surrounding air.
- The temperature of any surface that can directly view any part of the body and thus exchange radiation.

In addition, the **personal variables** that influence thermal comfort are **activity** and **clothing.**

The basic mechanisms that the body uses to control body temperatures are metabolism, blood circulation near the surface of the skin (cutaneous blood circulation), respiration and sweating. **Metabolism** determines the rate at which energy is converted from chemical to thermal form within the body, and **blood circulation** controls the rate at which the thermal energy is carried to the surface of the skin. In **respiration**, air is taken in at ambient conditions but leaves saturated with moisture and very near the body temperature. **Sweating** has a significant effect on the rate at which energy can be carried away from the skin by heat and mass transfer.

Heat is exchanged between the body and its environment by four modes :

(1) Evaporation (E), (2) Radiation (R), (3) Convection (C) and (4) Positive or negative storage of heat (S) in the body that would cause the deep tissue temperature to rise or fall. For a normally clothed, healthy human being in a comfortable condition or environment and engaged in a non-strenous activity, S = 0 and the thermo-regulatory system of the body is able to modify the losses by radiation and convection to maintain a stable, satisfactory temperature. Evaporative losses occur in three ways : by exhalation of saturated water vapour from the lungs, by a continual normal process of insensible perspiration, and by an emergency mechanism of sweating.

Insensible perspiration results from the body fluids oozing through skin under osmatic pressure and forming microscopic droplets on the surface which, because of their small size, evaporate virtually instantaneously, not being felt or seen and hence termed insensible.

If the body temperature tends to rise, the thermo-regulatory system increases the evaporative loss by operating sweat-glands selectively and flooding strategic surfaces. In extreme cases the body is entirely covered with sweat that must evaporate on the skin to give a cooling effect. If the sweat rolls off or is absorbed by clothing, its cooling effect will be reduced.

At the end we write the thermal energy balance in the equation form as –

$$M - W = E + R + C + S$$

where,  $M$ = Thermal energy generated by metabolism

$W$ = Work or energy spent in during the activity

## 9.18  HUMAN REQUIREMENTS OF COMFORT

For a common person, to feel comfortable, the following conditions are desirable :

- Dry bulb temperature should be between 22°C and 26°C.

- The relative humidity should be between 20% and 60%.

- The average air velocity in the room should preferably not to exceed 0.15 m/sec.

- The temperature difference between the feet and the head should be as small as possible, normally not exceeding 1.5°C and never more than $3^\circ$C.

- The carbon dioxide content should not exceed about 0.1%.

Not all these variables are directly amenable to regulation and no air-conditioning system is able to achieve control over all of them. The two most important are dry bulb temperature and air velocity.

## 9.19  HUMAN COMFORT AND EFFECTIVE TEMPERATURE

It is logical to ask what the desired temperature-humidity relationship is. The answer is that there is no one specific condition. People react differently to different conditions.

Many attempts have been made with considerable success, to correlate the four environmental factors – dry bulb temperature, velocity of air, relative humidity and mean radiant temperature – that contribute to the comfort of human beings by influencing bodily thermal equilibrium. Five scales of comforts have been established :

(a)  Equivalent temperature

(b)  Effective temperature

(c)  Corrected effective temperature

(d)   New effective temperature and

(e)   Resultant temperature.

Losses occur by radiation if the skin temperature exceeds that of the surrounding surface and by convection if it is greater than the ambient dry bulb temperature. The average temperature of the surrounding surfaces is termed **the mean radiant temperature $T_m$** and is defined as the surface temperature of that sphere which, if it surrounded the point in question, would radiate to it the same quantity of heat as the room surfaces around the point actually do.

Yaglau and others using a survey of the responses of the people to a relatively short term exposure in different environments founded the scale of **Effective temperature,** defined as the temperature of still, saturated air that gives a feeling of comfort similar to that of another combination of three relevant environmental variables. It was considered to over emphasis the influence of humidity and more recently it has been recognised that with a longer term occupancy of an environment, importance of humidity is less when the body is in comfortable thermal equilibrium. Skin temperature and the ratio of evaporative heat loss from the skin to the maximum possible evaporative loss are regarded as of significance and a new effective temperature scale has been introduced by ASHRAE.

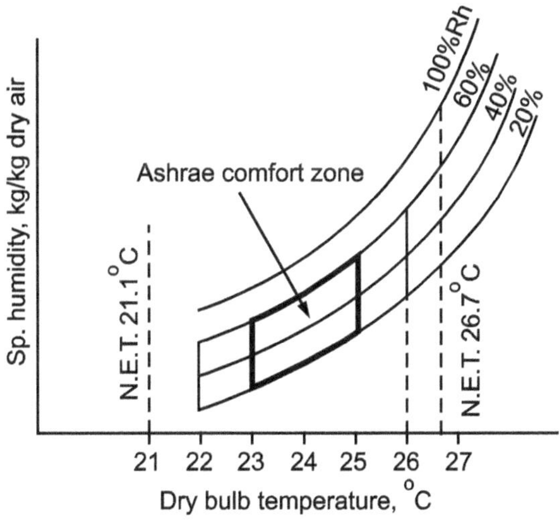


**Fig. 9.22**

Fig. 9.22 shows the new comfort zone as recommended by ASHRAE comfort standard. It refers to an environment occupied for about one hour where the dry-bulb temperature is approximately equal to the mean radiant temperature and the air velocity is less than 0.23 m/sec. The comfort zone lies within about 23°C and 25°C, between approximately 20% and 60% saturation (Relative humidity).

From the above discussions, it is clear that effective temperature is the index of sensations of warmth produced by the combined effect of air temperature, humidity and air motion. Sensations of warmth depends not only on the temperature of the surrounding air as shown by ordinary thermometer, but also upon the wet bulb temperature i.e. humidity, air movement and radiation effects. Effective temperature cannot be measured directly by dry-bulb thermometer but from the effective temperature chart after knowing DBT, WBT and air velocity. To illustrate, the effective temperature of an air conditioning plant is 15ºC, when the conditioned air produces a sensation of warmth or comfort like that experienced in slow moving air – 6 m/min or 0.1 m/sec – at 15ºC.

The energy generated by a person's metabolism varies considerably with that person's activity. A unit to express the metabolic rate per unit of body surface area is **MET**, defined as the metabolic rate of a sedentary person (seated, quiet). 1 MET = 56.2 $W/m^2$. Typical metabolic heat generation for various activities are given in the table. The average adult is assumed to have an effective surface area for heat transfer of 1.83 $m^2$ and therefore dissipate approximately 106 W when functioning in a quiet, seated manner.

The other personal variable that affects comfort is the type and amount of clothing that a person is wearing. Clothing insulation is usually described as a single equivalent uniform layer over the whole body. Its insulating value is expressed in terms of clo units : 1 clo = 0.155 $m^2$-C/W.

In addition to the definition of **effective temperature** above, the most common environmental index with the widest range of application, the **effective temperature ET** is the temperature of an environment at 50 percent relative humidity that results in the same total heat loss from the skin as in the actual environment. It combines temperature and humidity into a single index so that two environments with the same effective temperature should produce the same thermal response even though the temperatures and humidities may not be the same. Also **effective temperature** depends on clothing and activity, therefore, it is not possible to generate a universal chart utilizing the parameter. Calculations of **ET** are tedious and  usually involve computer routines, and a **standard effective tempeature (SET) has  been defined for typical indoor conditions. These conditions are :**

$$\text{Clothing insulation} \quad = \quad 0.6 \text{ clo}$$

$$\text{Moisture permeability index} \quad = \quad 0.4$$

$$\text{Metabolic activity level} \quad = \quad 1.0 \text{ met}$$

$$\text{Air velocity} \quad < \quad 6 \text{ m/min}$$

$$\text{Ambient temperature} \quad = \quad \text{Mean radiant temperature}$$

## Table 9.2 :  Typical metabolic heat generation for various activities

Met → Metabolic rate of a person seated quiet

| | W/m$^2$ | met |
|---|---|---|
| **1. Resting** | | |
| Sleeping | 41 | 0.7 |
| Reclining | 47 | 0.8 |
| Seated quiet | 56 | 1.0 |
| Standing relaxed | 69 | 1.2 |
| **2. Walking (on level)** | | |
| 0.89 m/s | 117 | 2.0 |
| 1.34 m/s | 151 | 2.6 |
| 1.79 m/s | 221 | 3.8 |
| **3. Office activities** | | |
| Reading, seated | 56 | 1.0 |
| Writing | 56 | 1.0 |
| Typing | 63 | 1.1 |
| Filing seated | 69 | 1.2 |
| Filing standing | 92 | 1.4 |
| Walking about | 98 | 1.7 |
| Lifting and packing | 123 | 2.1 |
| **4. Driving/flying** | | |
| Car | 56 - 117 | 1-2 |
| Aircraft, routine | 69 | 1.2 |
| Aircraft, in landing | 104 | 1.8 |
| Aircraft, combat | 139 | 2.4 |
| Heavy vehicle | 186 | 3.2 |
| **5. Miscellaneous activities** | | |
| Cooking | 91 - 117 | 1.6 - 2.0 |
| House cleaning | 117 - 199 | 2 - 3.4 |
| Seated, heavy limb movement | 129 | 2.2 |
| Machine work | | |
| Sawing (table saw) | 104 | 1.8 |
| Light machine work | 117 – 139 | 2.0 - 2.4 |
| Heavy machine work | 234 | 4.0 |
| Handling 50 kg bags | 234 | 4.0 |
| Pick and shovel work | 278 | 4.8 |

| 6. Miscellaneous leisure | | |
|---|---|---|
| Dancing-social | 139 – 256 | 2.4 - 4.4 |
| Exercise | 173 - 234 | 3 - 4 |
| Tennis, singles | 208 - 234 | 3.6 - 4 |
| Basket-ball | 284 - 442 | 5 - 7.6 |
| Wresting competitive | 411 - 506 | 7 - 6.7 |

The **operative temperature** is the average of the mean radiant and ambient air temperatures, weighted by their respective heat transfer coefficients. For the usual practical applications, it is the mean of the radiant and dry bulb temperatures and is sometimes referred to as the **adjusted dry bulb temperature**. It is the uniform temperature of an imaginary enclosure with which an individual exchanges the same heat by radiation and convection as in the actual environment. **The effective temperature and the operative temperature are used in defining comfort conditions.**

In the study of comfort, stress caused by heat and cold and the reaction of the human body to various environmental conditions are the important factors to be considered.

The **wind chill index WCI** is an empirical index for the combined effect of wind and low temperature. For wind velocities less than 80 km/hr, the index seems to reliably express subjective discomfort due to cold. An index derived from the WCI is the **equivalent wind chill temperature**, the ambient temperature that would produce, in a calm wind, the same WCI as the actual combination of air temperature and the wind velocity.

## 9.20 COMFORT ZONE AND COMFORT CHART

We have seen above that there is no one specific condition in which a human feels comfortable. People react differently to different conditions. A research study was conducted over many years, checking the reactions of large number of people to establish a range of combined temperatures, humidities and air movement that provided the most comfort. This is known as the **comfort zone**. Each combination, as we have defined above, of dry-bulb temperature, humidity (relative humidity for that purpose) and air velocity, is known as **effective temperature ET**. It was found, for Problem, that with a given air velocity, a number of different combinations of dry-bulb temperatures and relative humidity readings would give the same feeling of comfort to over 90% of the people involved. Thus, a comfort zone could be constructed. From the shaded zone of effective temperatures, it can be determined what dry-bulb temperature and relative humidity will produce the desirable effect of comfort. Note one obvious fact :  **the higher the relative humidity, the lower the dry-bulb temperature can be**.

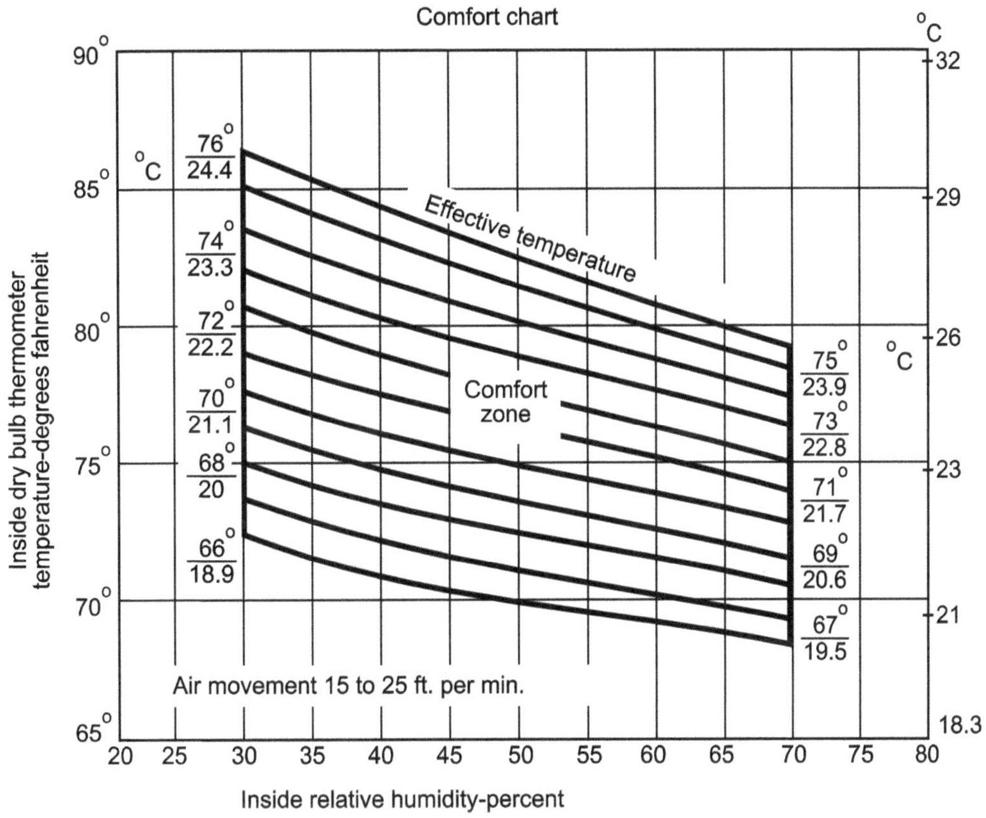


**Fig. 9.23 : Comfort zone and chart**

The comfort zone chart is a good selling point with average people, since it explains how temperature and humidity should be controlled and thus shows the need for year round air conditioning. The chart is representative of the conditions found in homes, theaters, offices, etc. where periods of long occupancy occur. However, it is not completely accurate for conditions in retail stores, banks, drug stores and similar situations, where short duration of occupancy coupled with rapid temperature changes and air motion will indeed change the experienced effective temperature. Therefore, while designing systems, one must take into consideration all these factors.

## 9.21 COMFORT CONDITIONS

ASHRAE Standard 55 gives the conditions for an acceptable thermal environment. For this ASHRAE established **thermal scale** which describes the thermal sensations to a corresponding scale. These numbers and corresponding sensations are :

| | |
|---|---|
| + 3 | Hot |
| + 2 | Warm |
| + 1 | Slightly warm |
| 0 | Neutral |
| − 1 | Slightly cool |
| − 2 | Cool |
| − 3 | Cold |

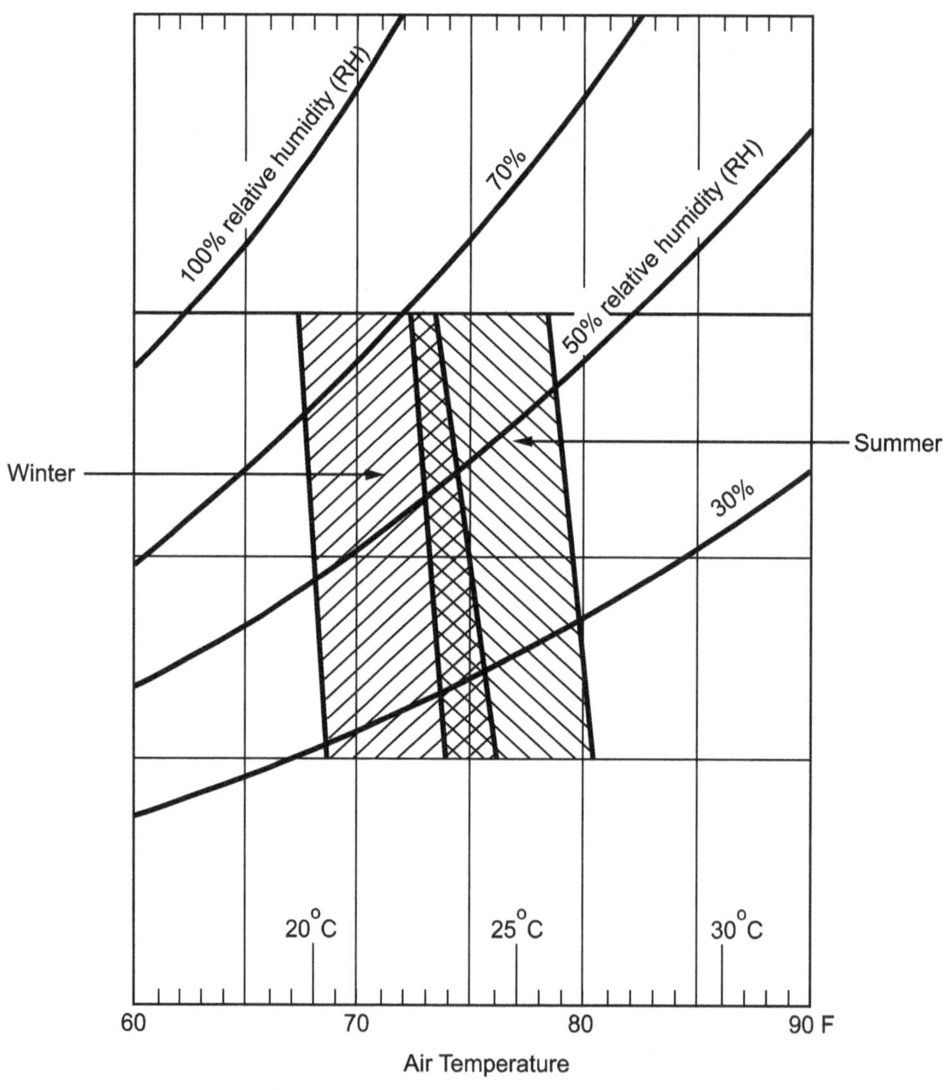


**Fig. 9.24 : Other form of comfort-zone chart**

The co-ordinates of the comfort zones are :

**Winter :** Operative temperature $t_o$ = 20 to 23.5°C at 18°C wet bulb temperature and $t_o$ = 20.5 to 24.5°C at 2°C dew point temperature. The slanting side boundaries of the winter zone correspond to 20 and 23.5°C effective temperature lines and are loci of constant comfort or thermal sensations.

**Summer :** Operative temperature $t_o$ = 22.5 to 26°C at 20°C wet bulb temperature and $t_o$ = 23.5 to 27°C at 2°C dew-point temperature. The slanting side boundaries of the summer zone correspond to 23 and 26°C ET lines.

In this figure, the upper and lower humidity limits are based on considerations of dry skin, eye irritation, respiratory health, microbial growth and other moisture related phenomena.

In can be seen that the winter and summer comfort zones overlap. In this region people in summer dress tend to approach a slightly cool sensation, but those in winter clothing would be near a slightly warm sensation.

Table 9.3 gives the operative temperature range for sedentary persons in minimal clothing. Air speeds are less than 0.15 m/s and 50 percent relative humidity. For sedentary persons it is necessary to avoid the discomfort of drafts, but active persons are less sensitive.

**Table 9.3**

| Season | Clothing type | clo | Optimum operative temperature, °C | Operative temperature (10% disfaction) |
|---|---|---|---|---|
| Winter | Heavy slacks, long sleeve shirts and sweater | 0.9 | 22°C | 20 – 23.5°C |
| Summer | Light slacks and short sleeve shirts | 0.5 | 24.5 | 23 – 26°C |
| | Minimal | 0.005 | 27 | 26 – 29°C |

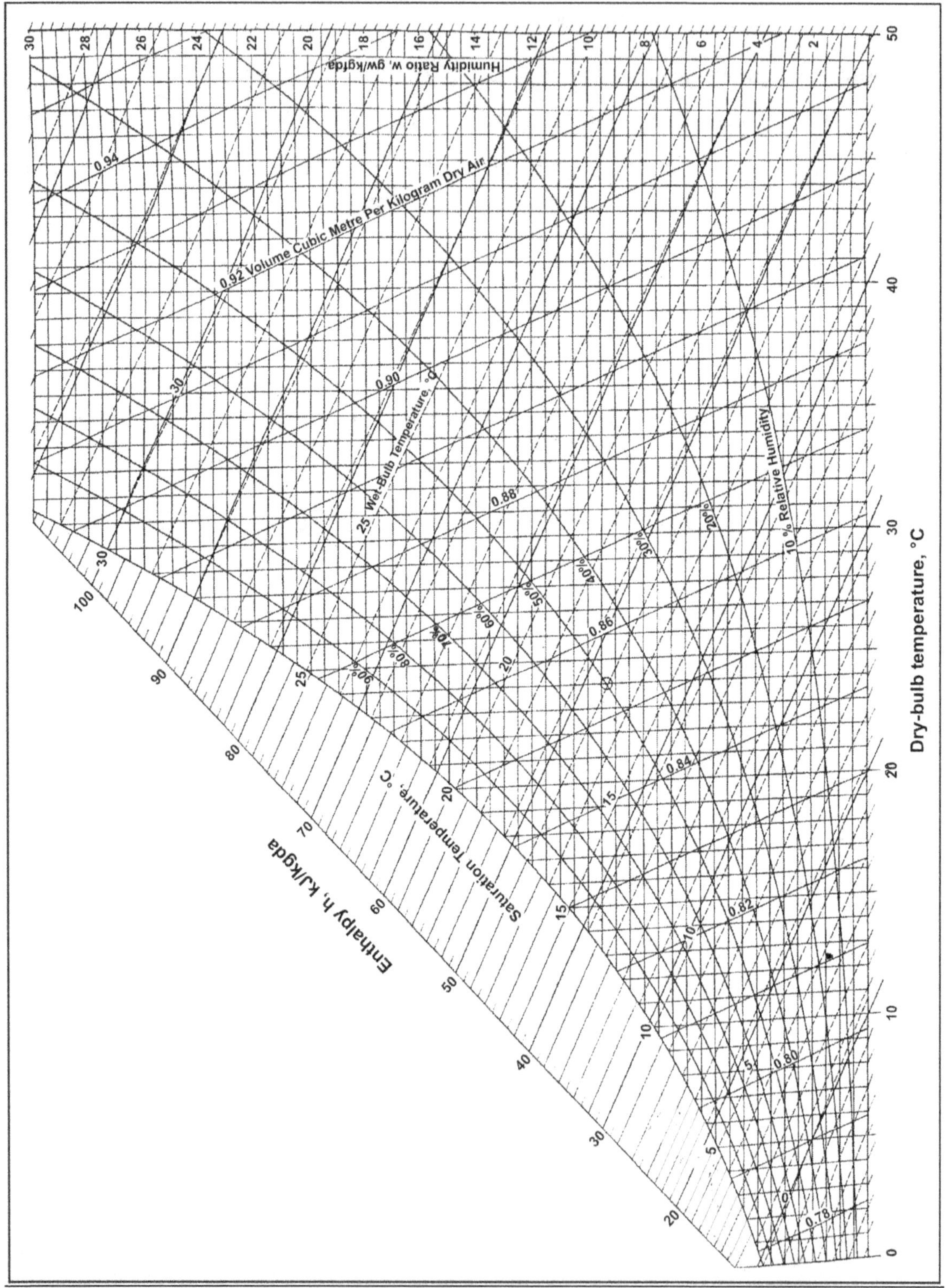

Humidity Ratio w, gw/kgfda
Volume Cubic Metre Per Kilogram Dry Air
Wet-Bulb Temperature, °C
Relative Humidity
Saturation Temperature, °C
Enthalpy h, kJ/kgda
Dry-bulb temperature, °C

# SOLVED PROBLEMS

**Problem 9.1 :** *The air in a auditorium has a dry bulb temperature of 24°C and wet bulb temperature of 16°C. Assuming a barometric pressure of 1 bar, determine (a) the specific humidity, (b) the relative humidity and (c) the dew point temperature.*

**Solution :**  (a)  DBT = 24°C,  WBT = 16°C

From tables we get the saturation pressures as :

$$p_s = 22.37 \text{ mm of Hg}$$

$$p_w = 13.628 \text{ mm of Hg}$$

$$\therefore \quad p_v = p_w - \frac{(p - p_w)(t_d - t_w)}{1527.4 - 1.3\, t_w}$$

$$= 13.628 - \frac{(750.062 - 13.628) \times (24 - 16)}{1527.4 - 1.3 \times 16}$$

$$= 13.628 - \frac{736.434 \times 8}{1527.4 - 20.8}$$

$$= 13.6280 - 3.8998$$

$$= \textbf{9.7282 mm of Hg.}$$

$$\therefore \quad \text{Specific humidity} = \frac{0.622\, p_v}{(p - p_v)}$$

$$= \frac{0.622 \times 9.7282}{75.0620 - 9.7282} = \frac{6.051}{65.3338}$$

$$= \textbf{0.09262 kg/kg of dry air} \qquad \textbf{... Ans.}$$

$$(b) \quad \text{Relative humidity :} \quad \phi = \frac{p_v}{p_s} = \frac{9.7282}{22.37}$$

$$= \textbf{0.4349} \text{ or } \textbf{43.49 \%} \qquad \textbf{... Ans.}$$

**Problem 9.2 :** *For moist air at 35°C, obtain the relative humidity if dew point is given as 290°K. The total pressure is 1 bar.*

**Solution :** Saturated pressure of vapour at 35°C $t_{db}$ is given as 42.17 mm of Hg and the actual vapour pressure corresponding to dew point temperature is 14.524 mm of Hg. These pressures are obtained either from psychrometric tables or steam tables.

$$\therefore \quad \text{Relative humidity} = \frac{p_v}{p_s} = \frac{14.524}{42.17}$$

$$= \textbf{0.3444} = \textbf{34.44\%} \qquad \textbf{... Ans.}$$

$$= \text{DBT of the mixture}$$

**Problem 9.9 :** *In an industrial air conditioning system, 20 cu-m of air at 30°C DBT, 75% RH is first cooled and dehumidified and then heated to obtain 20°C DBT and 60% RH.*

*Show the process on the psychrometric chart and find :*

1. *Cooling coil capacity in TR,*
2. *Capacity of the heating coil in kW,*
3. *Amount of water removed from air.*

**Solution :** The process is shown in Fig. 9.25.

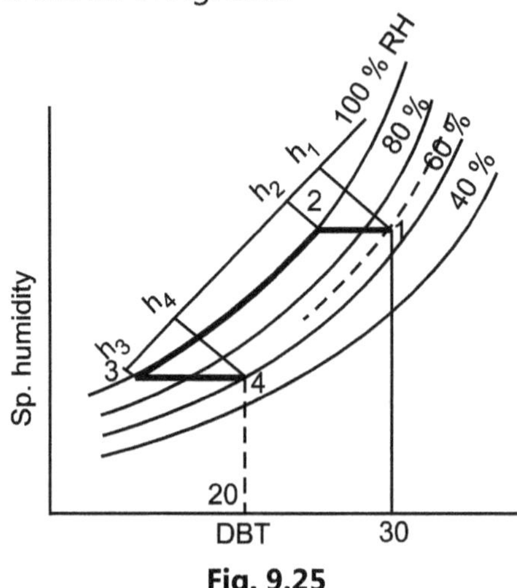


**Fig. 9.25**

With reference to chart, specific volume at inlet conditions = 0.8875 m³/kg

$$\therefore \quad \text{Mass of air circulated/min} \;=\; \frac{20}{0.8875}$$

$$= \textbf{22.5352 kg/min}$$

From the chart,

$$h_1 = 82 \text{ kJ/kg}$$

$$h_3 = 34 \text{ kJ/kg}$$

$$h_4 = 43 \text{ kJ/kg}$$

$$w_1 = w_2 = 20.4 \text{ gm/kg of dry air}$$

$$w_3 = w_4 = 6.6 \text{ gm/kg of dry air}$$

**1. Cooling coil capacity in TR :**

$$\text{Capacity in TR} = \frac{m\,(h_1 - h_3)}{60 \times 3.516}$$

$$= \frac{22.5352}{60} \times \frac{(82 - 34)}{3.516}$$

$$= \textbf{5.1275 TR} \qquad\qquad \text{... Ans.}$$

**2. Heating coil capacity in kW :**

$$\text{Capacity in kW} = \frac{m\,(h_4 - h_3)}{60}$$

$$= \frac{22.5352}{60} \times (43 - 34)$$

$$= \textbf{3.38 kJ/sec, kW} \qquad \textbf{... Ans.}$$

### 3. Amount of water removed from air :

$$\text{Water removed} = m (w_1 - w_3)$$

$$= 22.5352 \times 60 \times (20.4 - 6.6) \text{ gm/hour}$$

$$= \frac{22.5352 \times 60 \times 11.8}{1000} \text{ kg/hour}$$

$$= \textbf{15.955 kg/hour} \qquad \textbf{... Ans.}$$

**Problem 9.12 :** *Air supplied to the room is at 17°C DBT and has a relative humidity of 60%. If this air is passed at the rate of 0.5 m³/sec. over a cooling coil which is at a temperature of 6ºC, calculate the amount of vapour which will be condensed in one hour.*

**[P.U. May 1996]**

**Solution :** Condition of air supplied to room is shown by point 1.

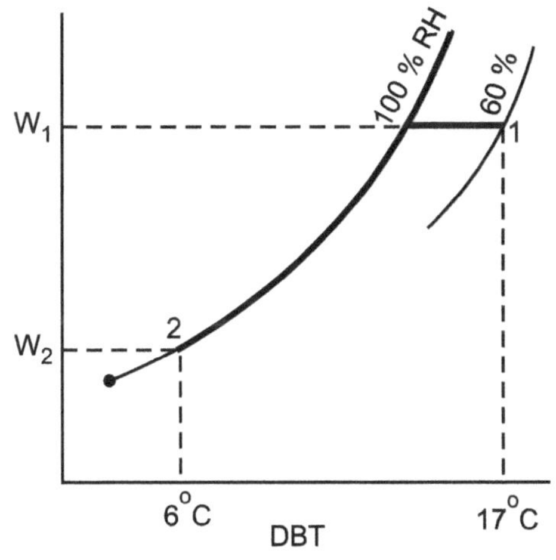


**Fig. 9.26**

Specific humidity $w_1$ = **0.007215 kg/kg of dry air**     **... Ans.**

Specific Volume at state 1 = **0.83118 m³/kg of dry air**

∴  Mass of air flowing per hour

$$= \frac{0.5 \times 3600}{0.83118}$$

$$= \textbf{2165.6 kg/hour}$$

Specific humidity $w_2$ = 0.005818 kg/kg of dry air.

∴  Amount of vapour condensed/hour

$$= 2165.6 \times (0.007215 - 0.005818)$$

$$= \textbf{3.025 kg/hour} \qquad\qquad \textbf{... Ans.}$$

**Problem 9.18 :** *(a) Define and explain the following terms used in air conditioning.*

*(1) Psychrometry, (2) DPT, (3) WBT, (4) RH.*

*(b)  What is Comfort Air Conditioning ? Recommend suitable psychrometric processes for following atmospheric conditions. Show the processes on handmade psychrometric chart.*

*(1) 35 ℃ DBT, 65% RH, (2) 40 ℃ DBT 10% RH.*

*(c)  Atmospheric air at 30 ℃ DBT and 60% RH is passed over a cooling coil with bypass factor of 0.15 at the rate of 200 m³/min. The coil surface temperature is 14 ℃. Find supply air DBT, cooling coil capacity in TR and amount of moisture separated per hour.*

**Solution :**

(b)  Assume comfort conditioning requirements as –

DBT = 22°C; RH = 40%

**(i)  Fig. 9.33 shows the processes.**

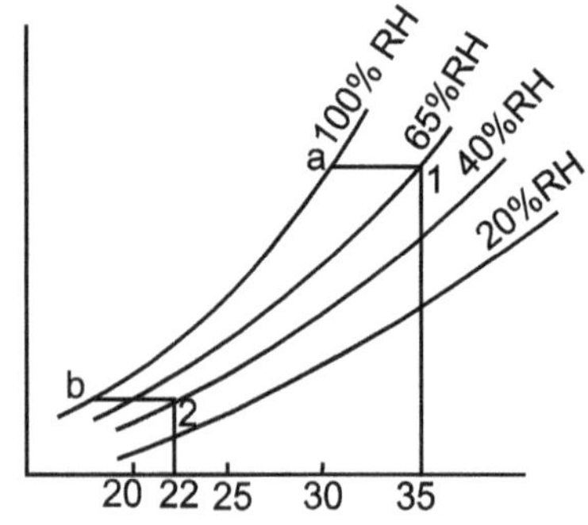


**Fig. 9.27**

1 is atmospheric condition of air. 2 is required condition of air. Processes recommended : 1-a-sensible cooling. a-b : condensation or separation of moisture and b-2 is sensible heating.

**(ii)  Fig. 9.34 shows the processes.**

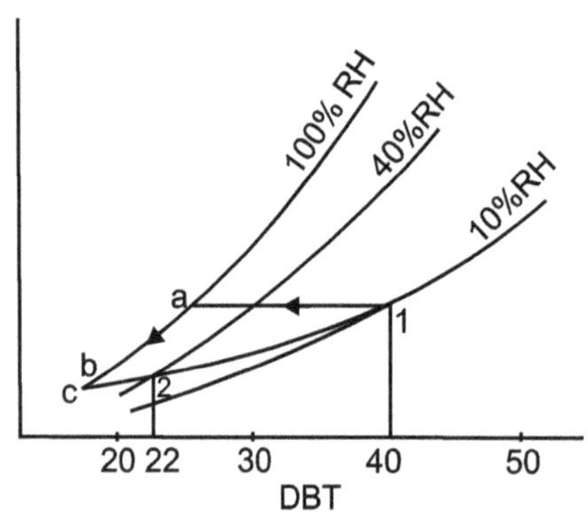


**Fig. 9.28**

1 is atmospheric condition.

2 is required condition.

To achieve 2, we proceed as

1-a sensible cooling

a-b moisture removal or condensation.

b-2 sensible heating or use a cooling coil having surface temperature $t_c$ having a bypass factor $BF = \dfrac{2-c}{1-c}$.

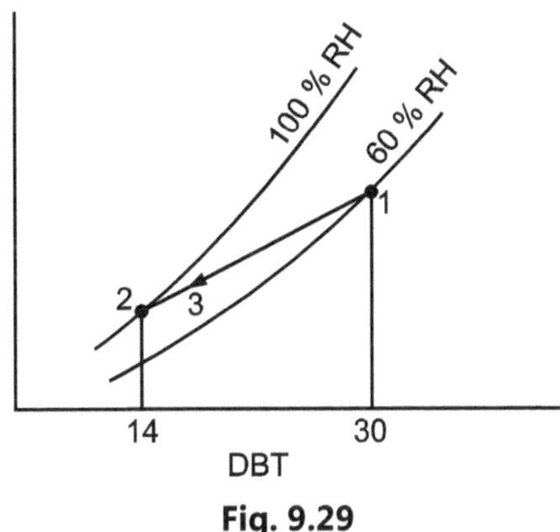



**Fig. 9.29**

**(c) Fig. 9.35 shows the processes.**

1 is the condition of atmospheric air. 2 is the condition if the air is passed over the cooling coil having 100% efficiency or zero bypass factor.

1-2 is measured from chart. This is $2\frac{3''}{8}$ or $\frac{19''}{8}$ or 6 cm approximately. Cooling coil has BF = 0.15. Then point 3 is located on the chart and from chart DBT of the supply air is found to be 16.4°C approximately.

Specific volume of atmospheric air is 0.88 cu-m/kg. (from chart).

$$\therefore \quad \text{Mass of air flowing} = m_a = \frac{200}{0.88}$$

$$= \textbf{226.273 kg/min.}$$

$$\text{From chart, } h_1 = 71 \text{ kJ/kg.; } W_{H_1}$$

$$= 0.016 \text{ kg/kg of dry air}$$

$$h_3 = 44 \text{ kJ/kg.; } W_{H_3}$$

$$= 0.0108 \text{ kg/kg of dry air}$$

$$\therefore \quad \text{Moisture separated/hour} = (W_{H_1} - W_{H_3}) \times \text{Mass of air/hr.}$$

$$= (0.016 - 0.0108) \times 226.273 \times 60$$

$$= 0.0052 \times 226.273 \times 60$$

$$= \textbf{70.91 kg/hour} \qquad \textbf{... Ans.}$$

$$\text{Also heat removed from air/sec.} = (h_1 - h_3) \times \text{Mass of air/sec.}$$

$$= (71 - 44) \times \frac{227.273}{60}$$

$$= \frac{27 \times 227.273}{60}$$

$$= \textbf{102.273 (kJ/sec = kW)} \qquad \textbf{... Ans.}$$

$$= \text{Capacity of the cooling air.}$$

**Problem 9.19 :** *(a) 100 m³/min. of air at 15°C DBT and 80% RH is heated until its temperature is 25°C. Find the following :*

    *(i)    Heat added to the air in kJ/min.*

    *(ii)   RH of the heated air.*

    *Assume air pressure as 100 kPa.*

*(b)  Define the following :*

    *(i)    Effective temperature.*

    *(ii)   Adiabatic saturation temperature.*

*(c)  Compare central air conditioning system with unit air conditioning system.*

**Solution :** (a) From chart,      $h_1 = 36.5$ kJ/kg of dry air

Heating is sensible heating i.e. humidity ratio is to be same. Therefore, this heating process will be shown as a horizontal line on psychrometric chart.

$$h_2 = 47 \text{ kJ/kg of dry air}$$

$\therefore$    Heat added per kg of dry air $= h_2 - h_1$

$$= 47 - 36.5$$

$$= 10.5 \text{ kJ/kg of dry air}$$

Specific volume of air $= v_1 = 0.8282$ cu-m/kg.

$\therefore$    Mass of air $= \dfrac{100}{0.8282}$

$$= \textbf{120.744 kg/min.}$$

$\therefore$    Heat added per minute $= 120.744 \times 10.5$

$$= \textbf{1266.81 kJ/min} \qquad \textbf{... Ans.}$$

From chart,    RH of heated air $= \textbf{43\%}$        **... Ans.**

**Problem 9.21 :** *Air at 10°C DBT and 90% RH is to be heated and humidified to 35°C DBT and 22.5°C WBT. The air is preheated sensibly before passing to the air washer in which water is circulated. The relative humidity of air coming out of the air washer is 90%. Find :*

*(1)  The temperature to which the air should be preheated.*

*(2)  The total heating required.*

*(3)  Make-up water required in the air washer.*

*(4)  The humidifying efficiency of the air washer.*

*(Use of psychrometric chart is expected while solving the problem).*

**Solution :**

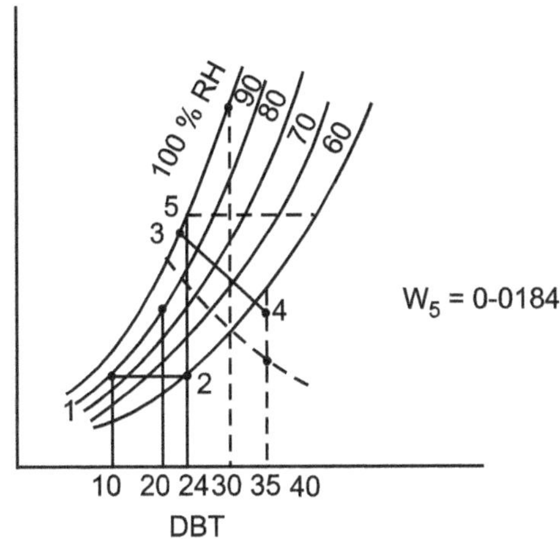


**Fig. 9.30**

1 - 2   Sensible heating  $h_1 = 26.2$,  $h_2 = 42$ kJ/kg

2 - 3   Sensible humidifying  $h_3 = 66.5$ kJ/kg

3 - 4   Heating and dehumidifying $h_4 = 66.5$ kJ/kg

$W_1 = W_2 = 0.00712$,  $W_3 = 0.0168$,  $W_1 = 0.0122$

Referring to the diagram,

(1)   The temperature to which the air should be preheated = $T_2$ = **24°C**          **... Ans.**

(2)   The total heating required

$$= h_3 - h_1 = 66.5 - 26.2$$

$$= \textbf{39.3 kJ/kg}$$          **... Ans.**

(3)   Make-up water in the air washer

$$= w_3 - w_2$$

$$= 0.01680 - 0.00712$$

$$= \textbf{0.00968 kg/kg of dry air}$$          **... Ans.**

(4)   Humidifying efficiency of the washer

$$\eta_H = \frac{w_3 - w_2}{w_5 - w_2}$$

$$= \frac{0.01680 - 0.00712}{0.01840 - 0.00712}$$

$$= \frac{0.00968}{0.01128}$$

$$= 0.8581$$

$$= \mathbf{85.81\%} \qquad \qquad \textbf{... Ans.}$$

**Problem 9.23 :** (a) *Define and discuss the significance of following terms :*

(1)   *Dew point temperature.*

(2)   *Specific humidity.*

(3)   *Degree of saturation.*

(4)   *Relative humidity.*

(b)   *For a hall to be air conditioned,*

   *Outdoor conditions : DBT = 40 °C, WBT = 20 °C*

   *Required conditions : DBT = 20 °C, RH = 60%*

   *Seating capacity of hall = 1500.*

   *Amount of outdoor air supplied = 0.3 m³/min/person.*

*If required conditions are achieved first by adiabatic humidification and then by cooling, estimate :*

(a)   *Capacity of cooling coils in tonnes (TR).*

(b)   *Capacity of humidifier in kg/hr.*

**Solution :**

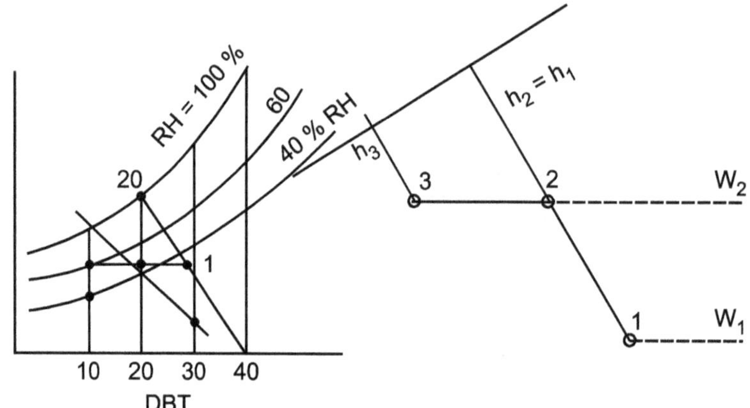


**Fig. 9.31**

From psychrometric chart,

$$h_1 = h_2 = 56.5 \text{ kJ/kg of dry air}$$

$$h_3 = 42.5 \text{ kJ/kg of dry air}$$

$$w_1 = 0.0066 \text{ kg/kg of dry air}, \quad w_2 = 0.0086 \text{ kg/kg of dry air}$$

1-2 – Adiabatic humidification process.

This is along the WBT line.

2-3 – Sensible cooling.

Specific volume/kg of dry air at inlet $= $ **0.893 cu.m./kg**

$$\therefore \quad \text{Mass of air supplied/min} = \frac{1500 \times 0.3}{0.893} \frac{m^3/min}{m^3/kg}$$

$$= \textbf{503.92 kg/min}$$

**(a) Capacity of cooling coil in TR :**

$$\text{Capacity of cooling coil/sec} = m_a (h_2 - h_3)$$

$$= \frac{503.92}{60} \times (56.5 - 42.5)$$

$$= \frac{503.92 \times 15}{60}$$

$$= 125.98 \ (kJ/sec = kW)$$

$$1 \ TR = 3.516 \ kW$$

$$\therefore \quad \text{Capacity in TR} = \frac{125.98}{3.516}$$

$$= \textbf{35.83 TR} \hspace{4cm} \textbf{... Ans.}$$

**(b) Capacity of humidifier in kg/hr :**

Capacity of humidifier/kg of dry air supplied

$$= w_2 - w_1$$

$$= 00086 - 0.0066$$

$$= 0.002 \ kg/kg \ of \ dry \ air$$

$$\therefore \quad \text{Capacity in kg/hr} = 0.002 \times 503.92 \times 60$$

$$= \textbf{60.47 kg/hour} \hspace{3cm} \textbf{... Ans.}$$

**Problem 9.24 :** *(a) An air conditioning system is designed under following conditions :*

*Outdoor conditions : DBT = 30°C, RH = 75%*

*Required indoor conditions : DBT = 22°C, RH = 70%.*

*Free air circulated = 3.33 m³/s*

*Coil dew point temperature = 14°C*

*The required conditioning is achieved by cooling and dehumidification first and then by heating.*

*Find :*

*(i)    Capacity of cooling coil in tonnes.*

*(ii)   Capacity of heating coil in kW.*

*(iii)  Amount of water vapour removed.*

*(b)    Explain summer air conditioning system for hot and humid weather.*

*(c)    Discuss the process of chemical dehumidification.*

**Solution :** (a) The process is shown in psychrometric chart.

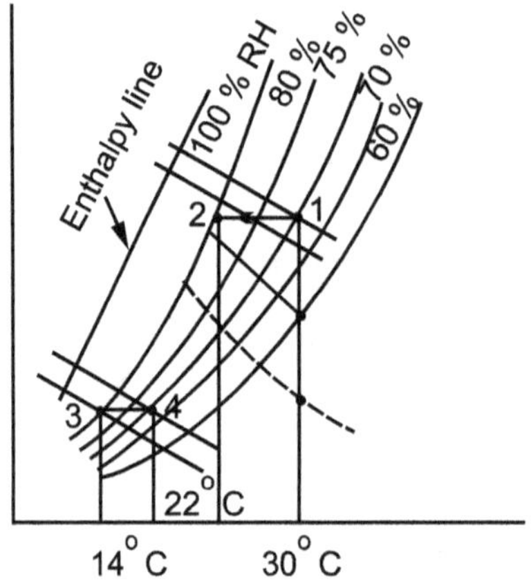


**Fig. 9.32**

1-2  –  Sensible cooling

2-3  –  Dehumidification

3-4  –  Sensible heating to 22°C and 70%

From chart,    $w_1 = w_2 = 0.0202$ kg/kg of air

$w_3 = w_4 = 0.0114$ kg/kg of air

$h_1 = 81.5$,  $h_2 = 76.5$,   $h_3 = 45.5$,

$h_4 = 51$ kJ/kg of dry air

Specific volume at 1 $= \dfrac{8}{28} \times 0.02 + 0.88$

$= 0.88 + 0.00571$

$= 0.88571$ m$^3$/kg

Free air is assumed to be at inlet conditions :

∴     Mass of air circulated/sec $= \dfrac{3.33}{0.88571}$

$= $ **3.76 kg/s**

### (a) Capacity of cooling coil in tonnes :

$$\text{Capacity} = (h_1 - h_3)\, m_a = 3.76 \times (81.5 - 45.5)$$

$$= 3.76 \times 36$$

$$= 135.36 \text{ kJ/s} = \text{ kW}$$

$$= \frac{135.36}{3.516} \text{ TR}$$

$$= \mathbf{36.5\ TR} \qquad\qquad \text{... Ans.}$$

### (b) Capacity of heating coil in kW :

$$\text{Heating coil capacity} = m_a\,(h_4 - h_3)$$

$$= 3.76 \times (51 - 45.5) = 3.76 \times 5.5$$

$$= \mathbf{20.68\ kJ/s\ =\ kW} \qquad\qquad \text{... Ans.}$$

### (c) Amount of water removed/min :

$$\text{Amount of water removed/min} = (m_a \times 60)\,(w_1 - w_4)$$

$$= (3.76 \times 60) \times (0.0202 - 0.0114)$$

$$= 3.76 \times 60 \times 0.0088$$

$$= \mathbf{1.9853\ kg/min} \qquad\qquad \text{... Ans.}$$

**Problem 9.25 :** *(a) Discuss the thermal balance mechanism of a human body. List the factors influencing human comfort. Explain the significance of effective temperature.*

*(b) The atmospheric air at 25°C DBT and 12°C WBT flows at the rate of 100 cmm through a duct. Dry saturated steam at 100°C is injected into the air stream at the rate of 72 kg/hour. Calculate the specific humidity and enthalpy of air leaving the duct. Also find DBT, WBT and RH of air. Show the process on psychrometric chart.*

*(c) 200 cmm of saturated air at 10°C DBT and 100% RH is mixed adiabatically with 200 cmm of air at 30°C and 95% RH. Determine the final DBT, RH of air after mixing. Also find moisture separated, if any, during the process. Sketch the process on psychrometric chart.*

**Solution :** (b)

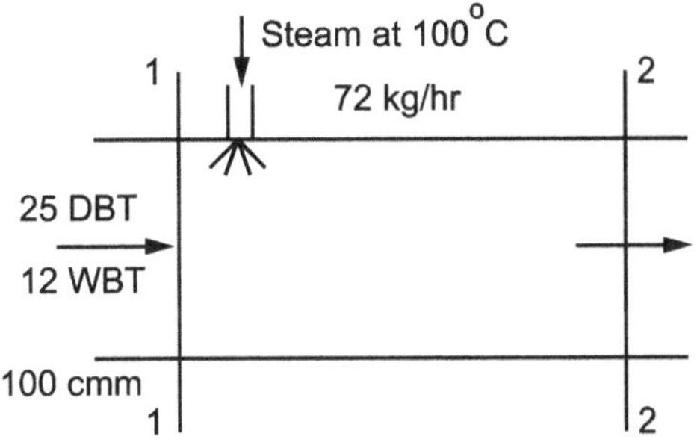


**Fig. 9.33**

From chart :

$$w_1 = 0.003346$$

$$h_1 = 34.179 \text{ kJ/kg}$$

$$v_1 = 0.84901 \text{ m}^3/\text{kg}$$

$$\therefore \quad m_1 = \frac{100}{0.84901} = 116.78 \text{ kg/min}$$

$$\text{Enthalpy of steam at } 100°C = 2676 \text{ kJ/kg}$$

$$= \frac{2676}{60} \times \frac{72}{1} = 3211.2 \text{ kJ/min}$$

$$m_1 w_1 + w_2 = m_3 w_3$$

$$116.78 \times 0.003346 + 1.2 = (116.78 + 1.2)\, w_3$$

$$0.3941 + 1.2 = 1.5941$$

$$w_3 = \frac{1.5941}{118.98}$$

$$= 0.0134 \text{ kg/kg of dry air} \qquad \textbf{... Ans.}$$

$$\therefore \quad \text{Specific humidity} = \textbf{0.0134 kg/kg of dry air} \qquad \textbf{... Ans.}$$

$$m_1 h_1 + m_2 h_2 = (m_1 + m_2)\, h_3$$

$$116.78 \times 34.179 + 1.2 \times 2676 = (116.78 + 1.2)\, h_3$$

$$4025.6 + 2676 \times 1.2 = 116.98\, h_3$$

$$4025.6 + 3211.2 = 7236.8 = 116.98\, h_3$$

$$h_3 = \frac{7236.8}{118.98}$$

$$= \textbf{60.82 kJ/kg} \qquad \textbf{... Ans.}$$

$$= 1.005\, t_d + w\,(2501 + 1.82\, t_d)$$

$$= 1.005\, t_d + 0.0134 \times (2501 + 1.82 \times t_d)$$

$$= 1.005\, t_d + 33.513 + 0.02439\, t_d$$

$$= 1.02939\, t_d + 33.513$$

$$60.820 - 33.513 = 26.307 = 1.02939\, t_d$$

$$t_d = \frac{27.307}{1.02939}$$

$$= \textbf{26.53°C} \qquad \textbf{... Ans.}$$

From table, $\quad WBT = 21°C \qquad$ **... Ans.**

$$RH = 61.5\,\% \qquad \textbf{... Ans.}$$

(c)

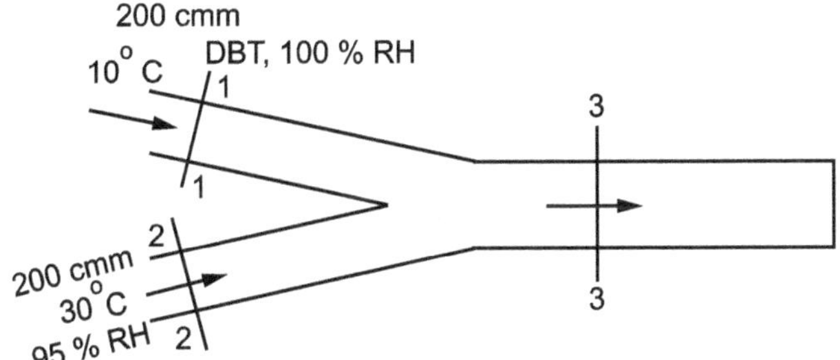


**Fig. 9.34**

From chart and tables :

$$w_1 = 0.007661 \text{ kg/kg of dry air}$$

$$h_1 = 29.348 \text{ kJ/kg of dry air}$$

$$v_1 = 0.8116 \text{ cu.m./kg of dry air}$$

∴   Weight of air flowing through section 1-1

$$m_1 = \frac{200}{0.8116} = 246.43 \text{ kg/min}$$

Again section 2-2 :

$$w_2 = 0.026 \text{ kg/kg of dry air}$$

$$h_2 = 96.5 \text{ kJ/kg of dry air}$$

$$w_{s_2} = 0.027329$$

∴   $$\mu = \text{Degree of saturation} = \frac{0.026}{0.02729} = 0.9527$$

∴   $$v_2 = v_a + \mu (v_{as} - v_a) \text{ approx.}$$

$$= 0.8586 + 0.9527 [0.8962 - 0.8586]$$

$$= 0.8586 + 0.9527 \times 0.0376 = 0.8586 + 0.03582$$

$$= 0.89442 \text{ cu.m./kg}$$

∴   Weight  of air flowing through section 2-2,

$$m_2 = \frac{200}{0.89442} = \textbf{223.6 kg/min}$$

∴   $$m_1 w_1 + m_2 w_2 = m_3 w_3$$

∴   $$246.43 \times 0.007661 + 223.6 \times 0.026 = (246.43 + 223.6) + w_3$$

∴   $$6.7015 = 470.03 \times w_3$$

$$w_3 = \frac{7.7015}{470.03} = \mathbf{0.01638 \ kg/kg \ of \ dry \ air}$$

Similarly,
$$m_1 h_1 + m_2 h_2 = m_3 h_3$$
$$246.43 \times 29.348 + 223.6 \times 96.5 = (246.43 + 223.6) \, h_3$$
$$7232.23 + 21576.4 = 470.03 \, h_3$$

$\therefore$
$$h_3 = \frac{28809.63}{470.03} = 61.2932 \ kg/kg \ of \ dry \ air$$

We have,
$$h_3 = C_p t_{db} + w_3 (2501 + 1.82 \, t_{db})$$
$$= 1.005 \, t_{db} + 0.01638 \times (2501 + 1.82 \, t_{db})$$
$$61.2932 = 1.005 \, t_{db} + 40.97 + 0.0298 \, t_{db}$$
$$= (1.005 + 0.0298) \, t_{db} + 40.97$$
$$= 1.0348 \, t_{db} + 40.97$$

$\therefore$
$$t_{db_3} = \frac{61.2932 - 40.97}{1.0348} = \frac{20.3232}{1.0348}$$
$$= \mathbf{19.64°C} \qquad \text{... Ans.}$$

Assume for calculation purpose, $t_{db} = $ DBT $ = 20°C.$

$\therefore$
$$w_{s_3} = 0.014758$$
$$p_{s_3} = 16.53 \ mm \ of \ Hg$$
$$w_3 = \frac{0.622 \, p_{v_3}}{p - p_{v_3}}$$

$\therefore$
$$0.01638 = \frac{0.622 \, p_{v_3}}{760 - p_{v_3}}$$

$\therefore$
$$\frac{p_{v_3}}{760 - p_{v_3}} = \frac{0.01638}{0.622} = 0.02633$$
$$p_{v_3} = 20.01 - 0.02633 \, p_{v_3}$$
$$1.02633 \, p_{v_3} = 20.01$$
$$p_{v_3} = \frac{20.01}{1.02633}$$
$$= \mathbf{19.5 \ mm \ of \ Hg}$$

All these calculations show that air at the particular temperature cannot have specific humidity greater than saturated air at that temperature.

$\therefore$ In practice, $0.01638 - 0.014758 = 0.001622$ kg/kg of dry air is condensed.     **... Ans.**

$\therefore$ The air after mixing is 100% saturated and the relative humidity is 100%.     **... Ans.**

**Problem 9.26 :** *10 cmm of air at DBT = 30°C and 55% RH is mixed adiabatically with 2.5 cmm of outside air. Outside conditions are DBT = 5°C and WBT = 1°C. The mixture is further passed over the steam coil whose surface temperature is 100°C and 70% of mass of air is in contact with coil surface. Find :*

*(i)   The outlet condition of air.*

*(ii)  Total amount of heat absorbed.*

*(iii) Represent the process on psychrometric chart.*

**Solution :** Air A 10 cmm, DBT = 30°C, 55%, $V_A = 0.878$ m$^3$/kg

$\qquad$ B  2.5 cmm, DBT = 5°C,  WBT = 1°C, $V_B = 0.796$ m$^3$/kg.

$\therefore \quad M_A = \dfrac{10}{0.878} =$ **11.39 kg,**

$\qquad M_B = \dfrac{2.5}{0.796} =$ **3.14 kg**

For adiabatic mixing, $M_C = M_A + M_B$

$$\dfrac{11.39}{14.53} \times t_{dA} + \dfrac{3.14}{14.53} \times t_{dB} = \dfrac{14.53}{14.53} \times t_{dC}$$

$$\dfrac{11.39}{14.53} \times 30 + \dfrac{3.14}{14.53} \times 5 = \dfrac{14.53}{14.53} \times t_{dC}$$

$$23.52 + 1.08 = t_{dc} = \textbf{24.6°C}$$

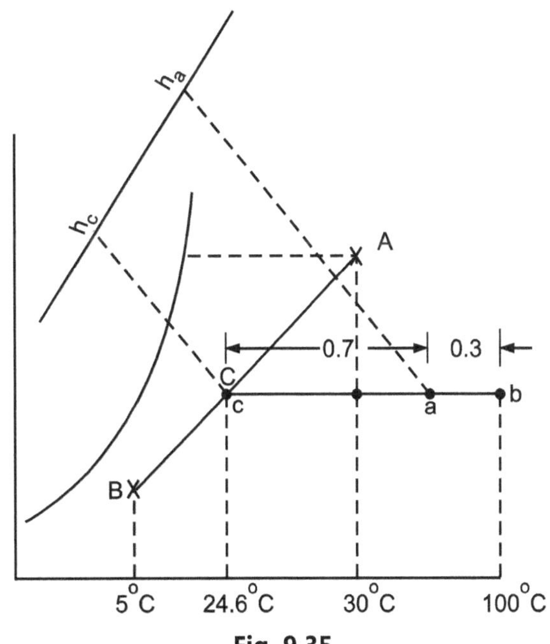


**Fig. 9.35**

Bypass factor $= 0.3$

$$= \dfrac{t_b - t_a}{t_b - t_c} = \dfrac{100 - t_a}{100 - 24.6} = \dfrac{100 - t_a}{75.4}$$

$\therefore \qquad 0.3 \times 75.4 = 100 - t_a = 22.62$

$\therefore$            $t_a$ = outlet condition of air (temperature)

(i)            $t_a$ = $100 - 22.62$

           = $76.38°C$      ... **Ans.**

(ii) **Total amount of heat absorbed :**

Total heat absorbed/kg = $h_a - h_c$ kJ/kg

= $C_{p_a} \, (76.38 - 24.6)$

= $1.005 \times 52.78$

= **53.04 kJ/kg**

Total mass of the mixture = $11.39 + 3.14$

= **14.53 kg**

$\therefore$    Total heat absorbed = $53.04 \times 14.53$ = **770.73 kJ**      ... **Ans.**

**Problem 9.29 :** *250 kg/hour of air saturated at 2°C is mixed with 50 kg/hour of air at 30°C and 55% RH. Determine the final state of air.*

**Solution :**

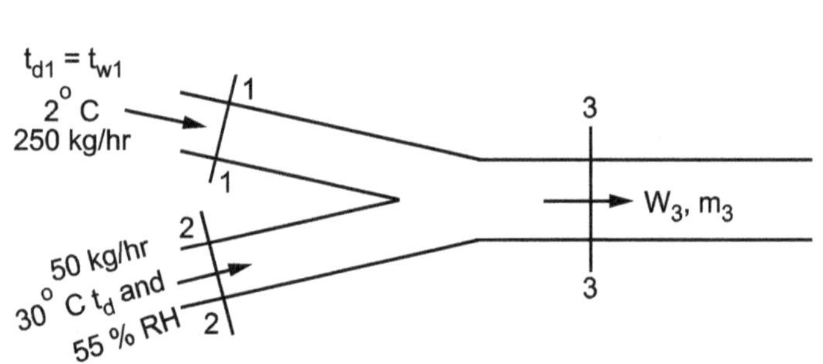


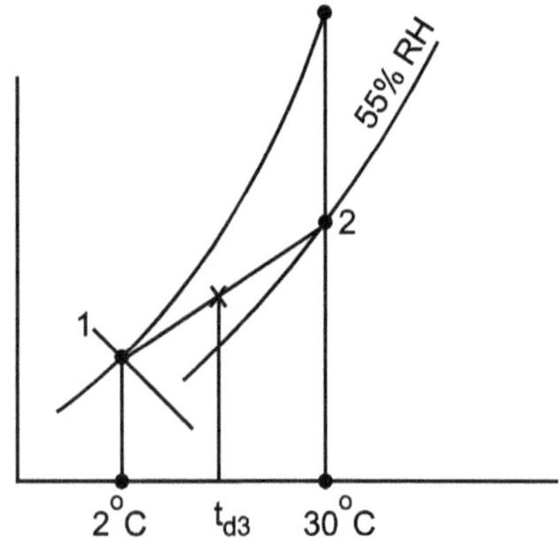


**Fig. 9.36**

Dry bulb temperature of the mixture $t_{d_3}$ is calculated as

$$m_1 t_{d_1} + m_2 t_{d_2} = m_3 t_{d_3}$$

$$\frac{250}{300} \times 2 + \frac{50}{300} \times 30 = \frac{300}{300} \times t_{d_3}$$

$$500 + 1500 = 300 \, t_{d_3} = 2000$$

$\therefore$        $t_{d_3} = \dfrac{2000}{300}$ = **6.67°C**      ... **Ans.**

Again,        $W_1 = 0.004381$ kg/kg dry air

$$W_2 = 0.01466 \text{ kg/kg dry air}$$

$\therefore \qquad W_3 = \dfrac{250 \times 0.004381 + 50 \times 0.01466}{300}$

$\qquad\qquad = \dfrac{1.0953 + 0.7328}{300}$

$\qquad\qquad = \dfrac{1.8281}{300} = 0.0061 \text{ kg/kg dry air}$   **... Ans.**

$\therefore \qquad h_2 = 66.62 \text{ kJ/kg dry air}$

$\qquad\qquad h_1 = 12.982 \text{ kJ/kg dry air}$

$\therefore \qquad h_3 = \dfrac{250 \times 12.982 + 50 \times 67.62}{300} = \dfrac{3245.5 + 338.1}{300}$

$\qquad\qquad = \mathbf{22.088 \ kJ/kg \ dry \ air}$   **... Ans.**

**Problem 9.30 :** *Air at 20 °C DBT and 19 °C DPT enters a heating and humidifying apparatus, from which it leaves at 35 °C DBT and 28 °C DPT. Moisture is supplied as liquid water at 25 °C to humidify the air. Find the quantity of heat and moisture that must be added per kg of dry air through the apparatus. Draw the process on psychrometric chart.*

**Solution :**

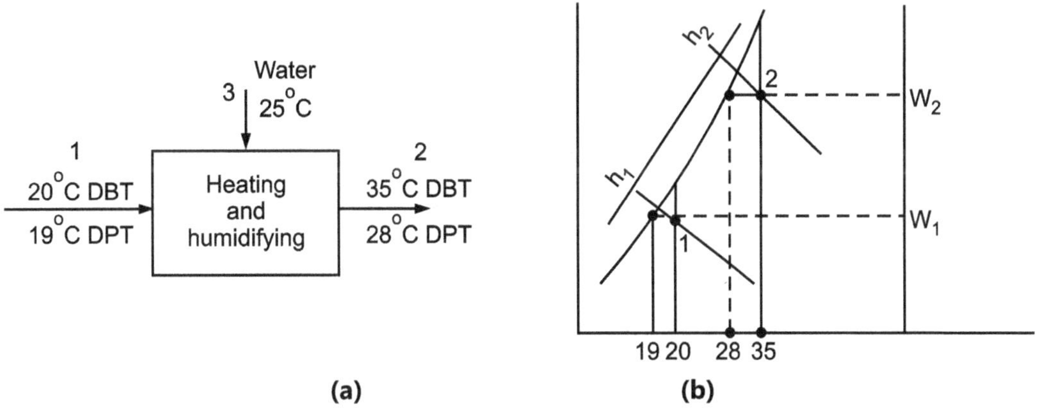


**Fig. 9.37**

**At inlet :** DPT = 19°C,

$\therefore \qquad W_1 = 0.013848 \text{ kg/kg dry air}$

**At outlet :** DPT = 28°C,

$\qquad\qquad W_2 = \text{Weight of moisture per kg dry air}$

$\qquad\qquad\quad = 0.024226 \text{ kg/kg dry air}$

$\therefore \quad$ Weight of moisture added in the humidifier

$\qquad\qquad = W_2 - W_1 = 0.024226 - 0.013848$

$$= 0.010378 \text{ kg/kg dry air} \qquad \text{... Ans.}$$

The process is shown in Fig. 9.39.

$$h_1 = 55.264 \text{ kJ/kg dry air}$$

Similarly, enthalpy of 1 kg air at outlet of humidifier

$$h_2 = 96.368 \text{ kJ/kg dry air}$$

$\therefore$     Heat added per kg of dry air

$$= h_2 - h_1$$

$$= 96.368 - 55.264$$

$$= 42.104 \text{ kJ/kg dry air} \qquad \text{... Ans.}$$

**Problem 9.32 :** *If at a site, barometer reads 750 mm of Hg, air is at 40 ℃ DBT and 20 ℃ DPT, obtain the values of following psychrometric properties by first principle.*

*(1)  Specific humidity.*

*(2)  Specific enthalpy.*

*(3)  Specific volume.*

*(4)  RH.*                                                  **(Dec. 2005)**

**Solution :**

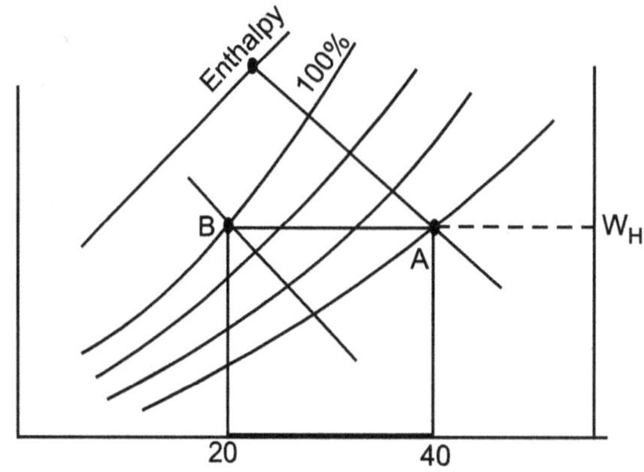


**Fig. 9.38**

**The condition is represented by state A which is located by intersection of a vertical through 40°C on x axis and horizontal through 20°C from saturation curve.**

(1)         Specific humidity $= W_A$

$$= 0.014758 \text{ kg/kg dry air} \qquad \text{... Ans.}$$

**(2) Specific enthalpy :** Specific enthalpy is given by

$$h_A = 76.249 \text{ kJ/kg dry air} \qquad \text{... Ans.}$$

**(3)  Specific volume :** Specific volume is given by

$$V_A = \mathbf{0.9080 \ m^3/kg \ dry \ air} \qquad \text{... Ans.}$$

**(4)  Relative humidity :**

$$RH = 0.2957$$

$$= \mathbf{29.57\%} \qquad \text{... Ans.}$$

**Problem 9.34 :** *Air at 10°C DBT and 90% RH is to be heated and humidified to 35°C DBT and 22.5°C WBT. The air is preheated sensibly before passing to the air washer in which water is circulated. The relative humidity of air coming out of air washer is 90%.  Find :*

*(i)   the temperature to which the air should be preheated,*

*(ii)  the total heating required,*

*(iii) make-up water required in the air washer, and*

*(iv)  the humidifying efficiency of the air washer.*

*(Use of psychrometric chart is expected while solving the problem.)*

**Solution :**

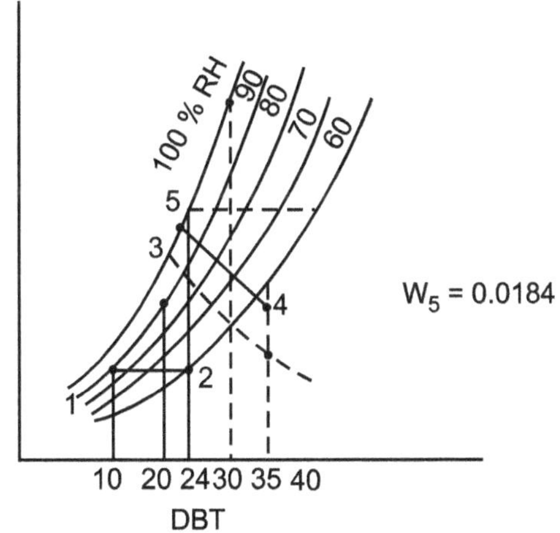


**Fig. 9.39**

1-2 sensible heating,  $h_1 = 26.2$, $h_2 = 42$ kJ/kg

2-3 sensible humidifying, $h_3 = 66.5$ kJ/kg

3-4 heating and dehumidifying, $h_4 = 66.5$ kJ/kg.

$\quad W_1 = W_2 = 0.00712$, $W_3 = 0.0168$, $W_4 = 0.0122$ kJ/kg

Referring to the diagram :

(i)   The temperature to which the air should be preheated = $T_2$ = **24°C**          ... Ans.

(ii)   The total heating required

$$= h_3 - h_1 = 66.5 - 26.2 = \textbf{39.3 kJ/kg} \qquad \textbf{... Ans.}$$

(iii)  Make-up water in the air washer

$$= W_3 - W_2 = 0.01680 - 0.00680$$

$$= \textbf{0.01000 kg/kg dry air} \qquad \textbf{... Ans.}$$

(iv)   Humidifying efficiency of the washer

$$\eta_H = \frac{W_3 - W_2}{W_5 - W_2}$$

$$= \frac{0.01680 - 0.0068}{0.01840 - 0.0068}$$

$$= \frac{0.00968}{0.01128} = \textbf{0.8581}$$

$$= \textbf{85.81\%} \qquad \textbf{... Ans.}$$

**Problem 9.36 :** *(a) Define and discuss the significance of the following terms :*
*(1) Dew point temperature, (2) Specific humidity, (3) Degree of saturation,*
*(4) Relative humidity.*
*(b) For a hall to be air conditioned.*
*Outdoor conditions – dbt = 40 °C, wbt = 20 °C*
*Required conditions – dbt = 20 °C, RH = 60%.*
*Seating capacity of hall = 1500.*
*Amount of outdoor air supplied = 0.3 m³/min person*
*If required conditions are achieved first by adiabatic humidification and then by cooling, estimate*
*(a) Capacity of cooling coils in tones (TR).*
*(b) Capacity of humidifier in kg/hr.*           *(Nov. 2003)*

**Solution :**

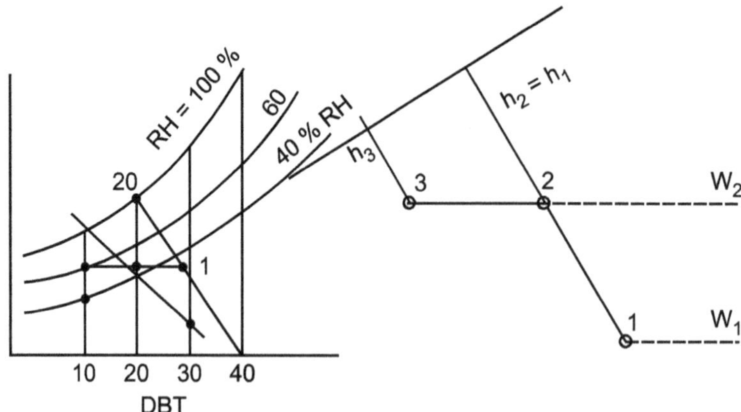


**Fig. 9.40**

From psychrometric chart,

$$h_1 = h_2 = 56.5 \text{ kJ/kg dry air}$$
$$h_3 = 42.5 \text{ kJ/kg dry air}$$
$$W_1 = 0.0066 \text{ kg/kg dry air}$$
$$W_2 = 0.0086 \text{ kg/kg dry air}$$

1-2  Adiabatic humidification process

This is along the WBT line.

2-3  Sensible cooling.

Specific volume/kg dry air at inlet

$$= 0.893 \text{ cu.m./kg}$$

$\therefore$  Mass of air supplied/min

$$= \frac{1500 \times 0.3}{0.893} \frac{\text{m}^3/\text{min}}{\text{m}^3/\text{kg}}$$

$$= \mathbf{503.92 \ kg/min}$$

**(a)  Capacity of cooling coil in TR :**

Capacity of cooling coil/sec $= m_a \, (h_2 - h_3)$

$$= \frac{503.92}{60} \times (57.5 - 42.5) \ = \ \frac{503.92 \times 15}{60}$$

$$= 125.98$$

$$1 \text{ TR} = 3.516 \text{ kW}$$

$\therefore$  Capacity in TR $= \dfrac{125.98}{3.516} = \mathbf{35.83 \ TR}$                         **... Ans.**

**(b)  Capacity of humidifier kg/hr :**

Capacity of humidifier/kg dry air supplied

$$= W_2 - W_1 = 0.0086 - 0.0066$$
$$= 0.002 \text{ kg/kg dry air}$$

$\therefore$  Capacity in kg/hr $= 0.002 \times 503.92 \times 60$

$$= \mathbf{60.47 \ kg/hour}$$                         **... Ans.**

**Problem 9.37 :** *(a) An air conditioning system is designed under following conditions :*

*Outdoor conditions (i) BT = 30 °C, RH = 75%.*

*Required indoor conditions DBT = 22 °C, RH = 70%*

*Free air circulated = 3.33 m³/s*

*Coil dew point temperature = 14 °C.*

*The required conditioning is achieved by cooling and dehumidification first and then by heating. Find :*

*(i)  Capacity of cooling coil in tonnes.*

*(ii)  Capacity of heating coil in kW.*

*(iii)  Amount of water vapour removed.*

*(b)  Explain summer air conditioning system for hot and humid weather.*

*(c)  Discuss the process of chemical dehumidification.*

**Solution :** (a)  The processes are shown on psychrometric chart.

   1-2 sensible cooling

   2-3 dehumidification

   3-4 sensible heating to 22°C and 70%

From chart,

$W_1 = W_2 = 0.0202$ kg/kg air

$W_3 = W_4 = 0.0114$ kg/kg air

$h_1 = 81.5$, $h_2 = 76.5$, $h_3 = 45.5$,

$h_4 = 51$ kJ/kg dry air

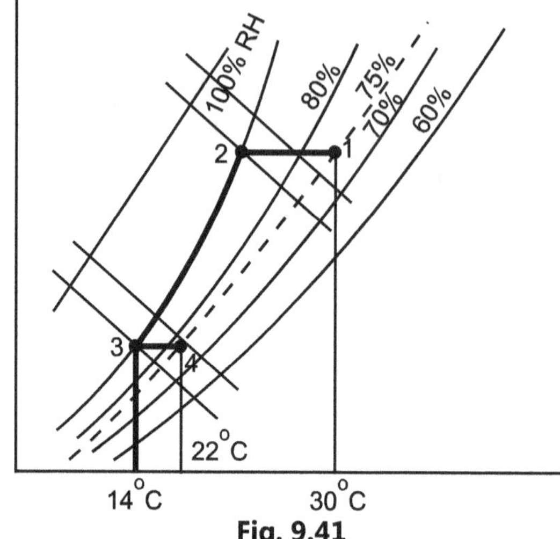


**Fig. 9.41**

$$\text{Specific volume at 1} = \frac{8}{28} \times 0.02 + 0.88$$

$$= 0.88 + 0.00571$$

Free air is assumed to be at inlet conditions.

$$\therefore \quad \frac{\text{Mass of air}}{\text{circulated/sec}} = \frac{3.33}{0.88571} = \textbf{3.76 kg/s}$$

**(a)  Capacity of cooling coil in tonnes :**

$$\text{Capacity} = (h_1 - h_3)\, m_a = 3.76\,(81.5 - 45.5)$$

$$= 3.76 \times 36 = \textbf{135.36 kJ/s = kW}$$

$$= \frac{135.36}{3.516}\, TR = \textbf{36.5 TR} \qquad \text{... Ans.}$$

**(b)  Capacity of heating coil kW :**

$$\text{Heating coil capacity} = m_a\,(h_4 - h_3)$$

$$= 3.76\,(51 - 45.5)$$

$$= 3.76 \times 5.5$$

$$= \textbf{20.68 kJ/s = kW} \qquad \text{... Ans.}$$

**(c)  Amount of water removed/min :** Amount of water removed/min

$$= (m_a \times 60)\,(W_1 - W_4)$$

$$= (3.76 \times 60)\,(0.0202 - 0.0114)$$

$$= 3.76 \times 60 \times 0.0088$$

$$= \textbf{1.9853 kg/min} \qquad \text{... Ans.}$$

---

**Problem 9.42 :** *In an industrial air conditioning system, 20 cu.m. of air at 30°C DBT, 75% RH is first cooled and dehumidified and then heated to obain 20°C DBT, 60% RH.*

*Show the processes on the psychrometric chart provided and find :*

*(i)   Cooling coil capacity in TR*

*(ii)  Capacity of the heating coil in kW.*

*(iii) Amount of water removed from air.*

*You are advised to attach the psychrometric chart, duly completed, along with the answer book.*

**Solution :**

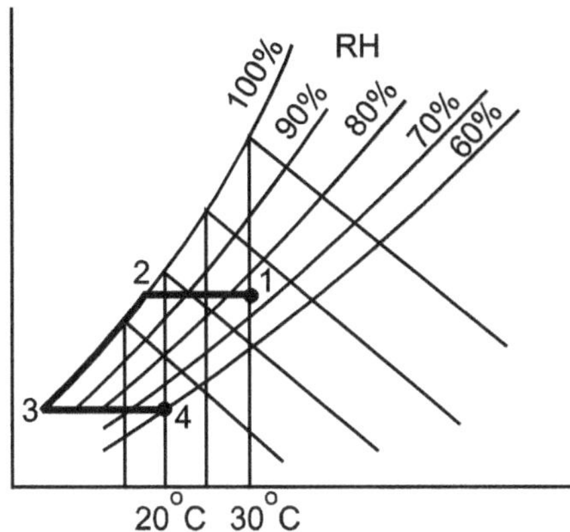


**Fig. 9.42**

With reference to chart, specific volume at inlet conditions = 0.8875 cu.m./kg.

$$\therefore \quad \text{Mass of air circulated/min} = \frac{20}{0.8875} = 22.5352 \text{ kg/min}$$

The processes are shown on the chart.

From the chart, $\quad h_1 = 82$ kJ/kg

$\qquad\qquad h_3 = 34$ kJ/kg, $\ h_4 = 43$ kJ/kg

$W_1 = W_2 = 20.4$ gm/kg, $\ W_3 = W_4 = 6.6$ gm/kg.

(1) Cooling coil capacity in TR

$$= m(h_1 - h_3) = \frac{22.5352}{60} \times \frac{(82 - 34)}{3.516}$$

$$= \textbf{5.1275 TR} \qquad\qquad\qquad\qquad \textbf{... Ans.}$$

(2) Capacity of heating coil in kW

$$= m(h_4 - h_3) = \frac{22.5352}{60} \times (43 - 34)$$

$$= \textbf{3.38 kJ/sec i.e. kW} \qquad\qquad \textbf{... Ans.}$$

(3) Amount of water removed from air

$$= m(W_1 - W_3)$$

$$= \frac{22.5352}{60}[20.4 - 8.6] = \textbf{4.432 gm/sec}$$

$$= 0.004432 \text{ kg/sec}$$

$$= \textbf{15.96 kg/hour} \qquad\qquad\qquad \textbf{... Ans.}$$

## EXERCISE

1. What do you understand by the term "Air Conditioning" ? How will you classify the different air conditioning systems ?

2. Distinguish clearly between comfort air conditioning and industrial air conditioning.

3. What are the applications of air conditioning ?

4. In what way an industrial air conditioning is applied in practice ? Give Problems.

5. What are the factors on which comfort air conditioning depends ? Explain.

6. How the human body responds to the following different environmental conditions ?
   (1) Dry hot weather
   (2) Humid and hot weather and
   (3) Cold weather.

6. Define the following terms as applied in air conditioning language :
   (a) Dry bulb temperature (DBT)
   (b) Wet bulb temperature (WBT)
   (c) Dew point temperature (DPT)
   (d) Humidity, specific humidity and absolute humidity
   (e) Relative humidity
   (f) Degree of saturation
   (g) Saturated air
   (h) Enthalpy of air.

6. What do you understand by the terms "Adiabatic saturation temperature" and "Thermodynamic Wet Bulb Temperature" ?

9. Are the dry bulb temperature and dew point temperature are same ? When they are same ?

10. When dry bulb temperature, wet bulb temperature and dew point temperature are numerically same ?

11. Define and explain the terms "Effective temperature" and "Comfort zone".

12. Will "Cooling of air" mean air conditioning ? Explain.

13. What is evaporative cooling ? Under what conditions it will take place ?

14. What is the best Problem of evaporative cooling in air conditioning systems ?

15. What are psychrometric tables and psychrometric charts ?

16. How will you construct psychrometric chart ?

16. Enumerate the different psychrometric processes that are taking place.

16. Explain with neat sketch/diagram each of these processes and show them on the hand-drawn psychrometric chart.

19. For the given state of air, how will you find dew-point temperature with the help of psychrometric chart and psychrometric table ?

20. What is a by-pass factor ?  Explain and define. Where this factor is considered ?

21. Distinguish clearly the central air conditioning system and unitary air conditioning system.

22. Explain with a neat sketch the working of "Window Air Conditioner". Can this be called as unitary air conditioning system ?

23. What do you understand by 'Split Unit' air conditioner ? What are the advantages and disadvantages of this unit ?

24. What is DX type central air conditioning system ? Explain.

25. What is an air washer ? Explain the different types of air washers.

26. Where chilled water air washer will be used ? Explain.

26. Explain the 'recirculation of air' in air conditioning system. Is there any advantage for this recirculation ?

26. Find the relative humidity and specific humidity for air at 30°C and having dew point temperature of 15°C.       (**Ans. :** RH = $\phi$ = 40.169%, $w_H$ = 0.010783 kg /kg of dry air)

29. Air is supplied to a room at 17°C and 60% RH. If the barometer reads 1.01325 bar, calculate the specific humidity and dew point of the air.

(**Ans. :**  $w_H$ = 0.007213 kg/kg of dry air, DPT = 9.18°C)

30. One kg of air at 40°C DBT and 50% RH is mixed with 2 kg of air at 20°C DBT and 20° DPT. Calculate temperature and specific humidity of the mixture.

(**P.U. Dec. 1995**)  (**Ans. :**  $T_3$ = 27°C, $w_3$ = 0.0179)

31. Outside air at 760 mm of Hg pressure has its DBT and WBT as 30°C and 20°C respectively. Determine its specific humidity, relative humidity, vapour density, DPT and enthalpy of air.       (**Ans. :** w = 0.01048, $\phi$ = 39.56%, $p_a$ = 0.01199 kg/m³;

DPT = 14.75°C, h = 56.9 kJ/kg of dry air)

32. Outside air flowing at the rate of 2 kg/sec at 30°C DBT, 21°C WBT mixes adiabatically with return air stream flowing at the rate of 3 kg/sec at 21°C DBT and 50% RH. Determine the DBT, WBT, w and h of the mixed stream.

(**Ans :**  h = 49.5 kJ/kg; 0.0092; DBT = 24.6°C; WBT = 16.6°C)

33. Air at 30°C DBT and 60% RH is passed through a cooling coil at the rate of 200 kg/min. The surface temperature of the coil is 14°C and by-pass factor is 0.12. Find the DBT, cooling coil capacity in TR, moisture condensed.

(**Ans. :** 15.95°C;  TR = 52.3; 1.08 kg/min)

34. 45 m³/min of air at 20°C and 75% RH is heated till its DBT becomes 30°C. Calculate the mass flow rate of air, RH and heat added per hour.

(**Ans. :** 53.3 kg/min; $\phi$ = 41%; Q = 33.42 kJ/hour)

35. A small room requires 6 m³/min of conditioned air at 20°C DBT and 60% RH, while the surrounding conditions in winter are 12°C DBT and 10°C WBT. Conditioned air is obtained by first heating the air-heating coil having a by-pass factor 0.4 and then by adiabatic humidifying. Determine the surface temperature of coil and the capacity of the humidifier. (**Ans. :** ADP = 32.75°C; 0.76 kg/hr)

36. 50 cu-m/min. of air at 15°C DBT and 80% RH is heated until its temperature becomes 22°C. Find :

(1) Heat added per hour

(2) RH of the heated air.

Assume barometer reads 760 mm of Hg. (**Ans. :** (1) 26126.9 kJ/hr; (2) RH = 51.7%)

36. Outside air at 12°C and 75% RH is to be conditioned to a temperature of 22°C DBT and 60% RH. Amount of air supplied is 100 m³/min.

The required condition is achieved first by heating and then by adiabatic humidifying. Find the following :

(1) Quantity of steam required per hour. Steam at 2 bar and 0.96 dry.

(2) Quantity of water required per hour in the humidifier. You can use chart.

(**Ans. :** (1) 156.4 kg/hr, (2) 25 kg/hr.)

36. Atmospheric air – 760 mm of Hg at 40°C DBT and 60% RH is passed through the conditioning system wherein 10 gm of water per kg of dry air are removed. Find :

(a) Relative humidity

(b) Wet bulb temperature and

(c) Dew point temperature. (**Ans. :** (a) 69%, (b) 25.2°C, (c) 23.6°C)

39. Outside air –760 mm of Hg – at 30°C DBT and 25°C WBT is heated to 40°C. If the air supply is 150 m³/min, find the amount of heat added and RH, WBT of the air.

(**Ans. :** 1762.73 kJ/min; 36.8%; 26.75 °C)

40. Cold air at 10°C and at 60% RH is required for an industrial processes at the rate of 100 cu-m/hr. When the outside conditions are 41°C DBT and 25°C WBT, the required conditions are achieved first by cooling and dehumidifying and then by heating. Determine :

(a) Heat removed from the air per minute,

(b) Relative humidity and wet bulb temperature.

**Time : 2 Hours**  |  **End Sem (Theory) Examination**  |  **Max. Marks : 50**

---

**1. (a)** Define the following terms with example. **[6]**

    (i) Intensive and extensive properties

    (ii) Zeroth law of thermodynamics

    (iii) Heat Sink and Heat Source

**(b)** 25 kg of copper block, $C_p$ = 0.386 kJ/kg K at 95°C is dropped in 25 litres of water at 27°C. Assume perfect heat transfer, and no heat lost to the surrounding. Find the final equilibrium temperature reached for water and copper block and entropy generation. **[6]**

**OR**

**2. (a)** What are the Kelvin–Planck and Clausius statements of second law of thermodynamic ? Also establish their equivalence. **[6]**

**(b)** In an I.C. Engine during the compression stroke heat rejected to the cooling water is 45 kJ/kg and work input is 90 kJ/kg. Calculate the change in internal energy of the working fluid stating that whether it is gain in internal energy or loss of internal energy. **[6]**

**3. (a)** Steam at 1.7 MPa and 0.7 dry is throttled to 0.2 MPa. Find the condition of the steam after throttling. Show the process on Mollier chart. **[6]**

**(b)** Draw P–v and T–s diagram for Otto cycle and derive the efficiency equation for Otto cycle. **[6]**

**OR**

**4. (a)** Discuss the principle and working of Throttling Calorimeter with diagram and show the process on h-s diagram. **[6]**

**(b)** 900 kg of heat leaves the hot gases at 1350°C from a fire box and goes to a steam at 230°C. Atmospheric temperature is 15°C. Divide the energy into available and unavailable part as it : **[6]**

    (i) Leaves the hot gases   (ii) Enters the system.

**5. (a)** Give the classification of steam boilers. **[6]**

**(b)** 4500 kg of steam is produced per hour at a pressure of 7.6 bar in a boiler with dryness fraction 0.96. The feed water temperature is 49°C. The amount of coal burnt per hour is 650 kg of calorific value 28500 kJ/kg. Determine the boiler efficiency and equivalent. **[7]**

---

**OR**

**6. (a)** Define draught. Give classification of it. Explain natural draught and artificial draught.   **[7]**

**(b)** A boiler uses 18 kg of air per kg of fuel. The fuel consumption is 30 kg/sec and actual draught required is 16 mm of water taking into account all losses. Determine the chimney height and its diameter if the actual velocity of flue gases is 0.38 times the theoretical velocity due to friction. The surrounding is at 25 °C and flue gases temperature is 220 °C.   **[6]**

**7. (a)** Explain the working of sling thermometer with neat diagram.   **[6]**

**(b)** The air in a auditorium has a DBT of 24 °C and WBT of 16 °C . Assuming a barometric pressure of 1 bar, determine the specific humidity, relative humidity and dew point temperature.   **[7]**

**OR**

**8. (a)** What are the types of air washers? Explain them in detail.   **[6]**

**(b)** Air at 18°C DBT and 20°C DPT Enters a heating and humidifying apparatus, from which it leaves at 35°C DBT and 28°C DPT. Moisture is supplied as liquid water at 24°C TO humidify the air. Find the quantity of heat and moisture that must be added per kg of dry air through the apparatus. Draw the process on psychrometric chart.   **[7]**

**Time : 2 Hours**  **Max. Marks : 50**

**1.** **(a)** Define any three and give suitable example wherever necessary:  **[6]**
   (i)   Enthalpy  (ii)   Intensive and extensive properties
   (iii)   Quasi–static Process.  (iv)   Zeroth law of thermodynamics
   (v)   Heat Sink and Heat Source

**(b)** A reversible heat engine operates between three isothermal heat reservoirs. The engine receives 4000 kW heat from reservoir A at 1000 K produces work output of 1600 kW. Heat source reservoir B and Heat sink reservoir C are at  300 K and 400 K respectively. Calculate the heat transfer with the reservoir B and C using Clausius inequality theorem. Also estimate the thermal efficiency of the heat engine.  **[6] OR**

**2.** **(a)** State and explain Clausius inequality. Explain law of increase of entropy principle and change in entropy for reversible, irreversible and impossible process.  **[6]**

**(b)** During a Thermodynamic cycle of processes (A–B–C–D–A), the heat transferred during each process are: 120 kJ, –16 kJ, –48kJ and 12 kJ respectively. Estimate net work transferred during the Thermodynamic cycle, direction of work transfer, Change in Internal energy and Total energy during the cycle using the first law for Thermodynamic cycle.  **[6]**

**3.** **(a)** For Dual Cycle define the following by using P–V diagram:  **[6]**
   (i)   Clearance Volume  (ii)   Swept Volume
   (iii)   Compression ratio  (iv)   Cut off ratio
   (v)   Expansion ratio  (vi)   Pressure ratio

**(b)** Determine the total enthalpy and total Internal energy for the following cases:  **[6]**
   (i)   3kg of steam at 11 bar and 60% dry.
   (ii)   5kg of steam at 10 bar and 250°C.  **OR**

**4.** **(a)** Explain heating of ice from –10°C to Super heated steam at 150°C and 1 atmospheric pressure on T–h Diagram (Show sensible heating and latent heating regions clearly).  **[6]**

**(b)** A system at 400 K receives 150 kJ of heat from a heat source at 1200 K. Atmospheric temperature is 300 K. The temperature of both the system and the source are assumed to be constant during the heat transfer process, find the net change in the entropy, available energy of the heat source, available energy of system.  **[6]**

**5.** **(a)** Explain the Classification of boilers with example.  **[6]**

**(b)** In a boiler test 1250 kg of coal is consumed in 24 hours, mass of water evaporated is 13000 kg and boiler pressure of 7 bar. Feed water temperature was 40°C and heating value of coal is 30000 kJ/kg. Find equivalent evaporation per kg of coal and boiler efficiency. (Take enthalpy of 1 kg of steam at boiler exit as 2570 kJ/kg).  **[7] OR**

**6.** **(a)** What are the desirable characteristics of a good boiler (6 valid points).  **[6]**

**(b)** A boiler uses 1000 kg of coal per hour. The temperature of the hot gases inside the chimney is 650 K and outside air temperature is 300 K. The draught produced by the chimney of 25 of height is 15 mm of water column. Determine the air supplied per kg of fuel burnt, draught in terms of hot gases, mass flow rate of hot gases and the area of the chimney required if the coefficient of the velocity is 0.4.

**7. (a)** Define and explain following terms, **[6]**
- (i)   Mass fraction.
- (ii)  Mole fraction.
- (iii) Stoichiometric or Theoretical air.
- (iv)  Excess Air.

**(b)** A sample of coal has the following composition by mass : $C = 90\%$, $H_2 = 3\%$, $O_2 = 2.5\%$, $N_2 = 1\%$, $S = 0.05\%$, Ash $= 3\%$. Calculate: (i) Stoichiometric A/F ratio and Actual A : F ratio if 20% excess and air is supplied , (ii) Analysis of products of combustion by mass.

**[7] OR**

**8. (a)** Explain working of Bomb Calorimeter with neat sketch. **[6]**

**(b)** During Bomb Calorimeter test on diesel oil, the following data were recorded,

Room Temperature (R. T.) = 25°C

Weight of the crucible = 8.116gm

Weight of the crucible and oil = 8.702 gm

Weight of can = 1.051 kg

Weight of can and water = 3.492 kg

Water equivalent of can = 0.559 kg

Rise in temperature of can and water = 2.305°C

Find the HCV of the fuel. **[7]**

---

## MAY 2014

**Time : 2 Hours**                                              **Max. Marks : 50**

---

**1. (a)** State and explain Steady Flow Energy Equation and write the equation when applied to following devices (any Six), **[6]**
- (a) Throttling device.
- (b) Boiler.
- (c) Condenser.
- (d) Nozzles
- (e) Diffusers.
- (f) Turbines
- (g) Compressor

**(b)** 30 kg of copper block, $C_p = 0.386$ kJ/kg K at 95°C is dropped in 30 litres of water at 24°C. Assume perfect heat transfer, and no heat lost to the surrounding. Find the final equilibrium temperature reached for water and copper block and entropy generation.

**[6] OR**

**2. (a)** Derive the general equation for change in entropy for any thermodynamic process. Further apply the same for Constant Volume process. **[6]**

**(b)** A cylinder containing air undergoes a thermodynamic cycle through following two processes.

**Process 1:** During compression 82 kJ of work is done on the system (air) by piston and 45 kJ heat is rejected.

**Process 2:** During expansion 100 kJ of work is done by the system (air). Using the first law of thermodynamics for cycle estimate

(a)   The heat transfer during process 2 and

(b)   Direction of this heat transfer.                                              **[6]**

3.  **(a)** Explain Air standard Otto Cycle on P–V and T–s Diagram. State the formula for Compression ratio in terms of stroke and clearance volume, Expansion ratio, Net work done, Air standard Efficiency.                                              **[6]**

   **(b)** Steam at 1.5 MPa and 0.7 dry is throttled to 0.1 MPa. Find the condition of the steam after throttling. Show the process on Mollier chart.                          **[6] OR**

4.  **(a)** State different methods to determine the dryness fraction of steam. Explain working of any one Calorimeter with neat sketch for estimating the dryness fraction.       **[6]**

   **(b)** A gas turbine power plant operates between pressure ratio of 9.77. Operating temperature limits are 295 K and 1085 K. Determine Turbine work, Compressor work and Thermal efficiency.                                              **[6]**

5.  **(a)** Explain with neat sketch working and operation of Fusible plug.            **[6]**

   **(b)** The following results were obtained from boiler trial:                       **[7]**

   (a)   Feed water per hour = 700 kg at 27°C,

   (b)   Steam pressure = 8 bar of dryness 0.97.

   (c)   Coal consumption = 100 kg/hr.

   (d)   C. V. Of Coal = 25000 kJ/kg.

   (e)   Unburnt coal collected = 0.6 kg/hr.

   (f)   Flue gas formed per kg of fuel = 17.3 kg at 327 °C (Cp of flue gas 1.025 kJ/kg K).

   (g)   Room Temperature = 16°C.

   Draw the heat balance sheet on kJ/min basis and boiler efficiency.                 **OR**

6.  **(a)** Explain function and location of different boiler mountings and accessories  (three each) with the help of line sketch or block diagram.                          **[6]**

   **(b)** Determine the A: F ratio for an oil fired steam with following data,         **[7]**

   (a)   Chimney height = 40 m.

   (b)   Draught = 25 mm of water column.

   (c)   Mean Chimney gas temperature = 367 °C.

   (d)   Ambient outside temperature = 20 °C.

   Also calculate draught in terms of hot gas column and velocity of the flue gases.

7.  **(a)** Determine the method to determine air required per kg of fuel for complete combustion of fuel when fuel contains constituents C, H, S, O. Write the equations of combustion for all the constituents. Per kg $O_2$ required by each constituent, theoretical mass of air required.                                              **[6]**

   **(b)** The ultimate analysis of solid fuels is as follows:

   $C$ = 78 %, $O_2$ = 3 %, $H_2$=3 %, S = 1 %, Moisture = 5 %, ash = 10%.

   Calculate the mass of actual air supplied also individual and total mass of products of combustion per kg of fuel if 30 % of excess is supplied of combustion.           **[7]OR**

8.  **(a)** Explain flue Gas analysis by using Orsat apparatus.                         **[6]**

   **(b)** Following results are obtained when sample of gas is tested by a gas calorimeter     **[7]**

   Gas burnt in calorimeter = 0.08 m$^3$.

Pressure of gas supply = 5.2 cm of water.
Barometer = 75.5 cm of Hg. , Temperature of gas = 13°C.
Weight of water heated by the gas = 28 kg.
Temperature of water at inlet = 10°C.
Temperature of water at outlet = 23.5°C.
Steam condensed = 0.06 kg.
Find HCV per $m^3$ of gas at 15°C and barometric pressure of 76 cm of Hg.

## DECEMBER 2014

**Time : 2 Hours**										**Max. Marks : 50**

1. **(a)** State limitations of first law of thermodynamics. Explain how Clausius and Kelvin Planck statements overcome these limitations using the heat engine, heat pump and refrigerator concept. Define thermal efficiency of heat engine and COP for refrigerator and heat pump. **[6]**

   **(b)** 1 kg of ice at –5 deg. C is exposed to atmosphere at 20 deg. C. The ice melts and attains thermal equilibrium with surrounding. Determine : **[6]**
   (i) Change in entropy of the universe
   (ii) Total heat transfer during the process.
   $C_{p\ ice}$ = 2.093 kJ/kg K, Latent heat of fusion = 333.3 kJ/kg.
   $C_{p\ water}$ = 4.187 kJ/kg K. **OR**

2. **(a)** Derive expression for the following quantities for an ideal gas undergoing a constant pressure process : **[6]**
   (i) Heat transfer			(ii) Non–flow work transfer
   (iii) Steady flow work transfer	(iv) Change in entropy
   (v) Change in internal energy and change in enthalpy during the process.

   **(b)** A reversible heat engine working as a refrigerator absorbs heat from low temperature reservoir of 650 kg, when work input is 250 kJ : **[6]**
   (i) Find its COP and heat transferred to the surrounding.
   (ii) If the same device works as a heat engine, find out its thermal efficiency.
   (iii) If the same device works as a heat pump, estimate the COP.

3. **(a)** Draw P–v and T–s diagram for Otto cycle and derive the efficiency equation for Otto cycle. **[6]**

   **(b)** Steam initially at 1.5 MPa, 300 deg. C expands isentropically in a steam turbine to 40 deg. C. Determine the ideal work output of the steam per kg of steam. **[6] OR**

4. **(a)** Define dryness fraction. Explain throttling calorimeter with neat diagram for estimating the dryness fraction. **[6]**

   **(b)** 1000 kg of heat leaves the hot gases at 1400 deg. C from a fire box and goes to a steam at 250 deg. C. Atmospheric temperature is 20 deg. C. Divide the energy into available and unavailable part as it : **[6]**
   (i) Leaves the hot gases	(ii) Enters the system.

**5. (a)** Show block diagram of a boiler plant showing location of air–preheater, superheater, economizer clearly indicating the air and water circuit flow. **[6]**

**(b)** The following particulars refer to a steam power plant consisting of a boiler, superheater and economizer :

Steam pressure = 20 bar, Mass of steam generated = 10000 kg/hr, Mass of coal used = 1300 kg/hr, CV for coal 29000 kJ/kg, Temperature of feed water entering the economizer = 35 deg. C, temperature of feed water leaving the economizer = 105 deg. C. Dryness fraction of the steam leaving the boiler = 0.98. Temperature of steam leaving the superheater = 350 deg. C.

Determine :

(1)   Overall efficiency of the boiler plant.

(2)   Equivalent evaporation of the given boiler from and at 100 deg. C in kg of steam generated/kg of coal burnt and

(3)   Percentage of heat utilised in economizer, boiler and super-heater. **[7]OR**

**6. (a)** Define equivalent evaporation and boiler efficiency. Explain heat balance sheet for boiler. **[7]**

**(b)** How must air per kg of coal is burnt in a boiler having chimney height of  32.3 m to create a draught of 19 mm of water column when the temperature of the flue gases leaving chimney is 370 deg C and temperature of boiler house is 29.5 deg. C. Also calculate the draught produced in terms of hot gas column. **[6]**

**7. (a)** Define :

(i)    Mass fraction

(ii)   Mole fraction

(ii)   Stoichiometric air

(iv)   Actual and excess air

(v)    Air–fuel ratio and mixture strength. **[6]**

**(b)** The ultimate analysis of solid fuel is as follows : C = 78%, $O_2$ = 3%, $H_2$ = 3%,       S = 1%, moisture 5% and ash = 10%. Calculate the mass of air supplied also individual and total mass of products of combustion per kg of fuel if 30% of excess air is supplied for combustion. **[7]OR**

**8. (a)** Explain working of a bomb calorimeter with neat sketch for estimating the CV of solid for liquid fuels. **[6]**

**(b)** In a bomb calorimeter the following observations were recorded :

Mass of coal burnt = 3 gm

Mass of water in calorimeter = 1.4 kg

Water equivalent of the calorimeter = 0.9 kg/K

Rise in temperature of water jacket = 9 deg. C

The coal contains 3% moisture by weight and R.T. = 25 deg. C. Calculate the HCV and LCV. Consider latent heat of condensation of steam 2470 kJ/kg. **[7]**

## MAY 2015

**Time : 2 Hours**                       **Max. Marks : 50**

1. **(a)** State Kelvin–Planck and Clausius statement of the second law of thermodynamics and prove that the violation of Kelvin–Planck statement results into violation of Clausius statement. **[6]**

   **(b)** In a certain heat exchanger, 50 kg of water is heated per minute from 50°C to 110°C by hot gases which enter the heat exchanger at 250°C. If the flow rate of gases is 100 kg/min, estimate the net change of entropy. Assume no loss of heat to surroundings. $C_p$ (water) = 4.186 kJ/kg–K, $C_p$ (gas) = 1 kJ/kg–K. **[6] OR**

2. **(a)** Derive expression for the following quantities for an ideal gas  undergoing a constant temperature process : **[6]**

   (i)    Non-Flow System-Work done, Change in internal energy, Heat transfer

   (ii)   Flow System—Work done, Heat transfer, Entropy change.

   **(b)** A heat engine working on Carnot cycle absorbs heat from three thermal reservoirs at 1000 K, 800 K and 680 K. The engine does 10 kW of net work and rejects 400 kJ/min. of heat to a heat sink at 300 K. If the heat supplied by the reservoir at 1000 K is 60% of the heat supplied by the reservoir at 600 K, make calculations for the quantity of heat absorbed by each reservoir. **[6]**

3. **(a)** State the assumptions made for air standard cycle. Derive an expression for the air standard efficiency and mean effective pressure of an Otto cycle. **[6]**

   **(b)** Steam of mass 10 kg and pressure 1000 kPa, 0.85 dry, is heated at constant pressure till the volume is doubled.

   Determine :

   (i)   Final quality of steam

   (ii)  Heat added

   (iii) Change in Internal Energy. **[6] OR**

4. **(a)** Sketch and explain the construction and working of a separating and throttling calorimeter used for determining the dryness fraction of steam in a boiler. **[6]**

   **(b)** A system at 450 K receives 225 kJ/s of heat energy from a source at 1500K, and the temperature of both the system and source remains constant during the heat transfer process. Represent the process on temperature–entropy diagram and determine :

   (i)    Net change in entropy

   (ii)   Available energy of heat source and system

   (iii)  Decrease in available energy.

   Take atmospheric temperature equal to 300 K. **[6]**

5. **(a)** Describe briefly the advantages which you would expect to be gained from incorporating an economizer, air preheater, and a superheated in a steam generating plant. By line diagram, indicate the position of these accessories in a typical boiler plant. **[6]**

**(b)** The following data relates to a trial on boiler using economizer, air preheater and superheater :

Condition of steam at exit of boiler = 20 bar, 0.96 dry

Temperature of steam at exit of superheater = 300°C

Steam evaporation rate/kg of fuel = 12 kg

Room temperature, $t_0$ = 25°C

Temperature of feed water at exit of economizer, $t_1$ = 50°C, Temperature of air at exit of air preheater, $t_a$ = 70°C The temperature of flue gases at inlet to superheater, economizer, air preheater and exit of air preheater are respectively 650°C, 430°C, 300°C and 180°C respectively.

Assume that air supplied is 19 kg/kg of fuel of calorific value of 45,000 kJ/kg, find

   (i)    Equivalent evaporation with and without economizer, from and at 100°C.

   (ii)   Thermal efficiency of the boiler with and without economizer.

   (iii)  Thermal efficiency of superheater, economizer and air preheater.    **[7] OR**

**6.**  **(a)**  Define steam generator and write down the classification of boilers.    **[6]**

    **(b)**  In a certain boiler installation, a steel chimney of 30 m height produces and natural draught equivalent to 17.75 mm of water column. The mean temperature of the boiler house is 298 K and that of hot gases leaving the chimney is 633 K. If the boiler uses 1350 kg of coal per hour, make calculations for :

   (i)    Air supplied per kg of coal burnt on the grate,

   (ii)   Draught in terms of column of hot flue gases,

   (iii)  Density and mass flow rate of hot gas.    **[7]**

**7.**  **(a)**  Define mass fraction and mole fraction with example and explain the method of writing the complete combustion equation of $C_8H_{18}$ with air.    **[6]**

    **(b)**  A sample of coal supplied to a boiler has the following composition by mass :

Carbon = 87%, Hydrogen = 3%, Oxygen = 3%, Nitrogen = 1%, Sulphur = 1% and the remainder is ash. If 15% of excess air is supplied for combustion.  Find :

   (i)    The theoretical amount of air required for complete combustion of fuel

   (ii)   The mass analysis of flue gas per kg of fuel.    **[7] OR**

**8.**  **(a)**  For what purpose a Bomb calorimeter is used ? Discuss its working with the help of a neat sketch.    **[6]**

    **(b)**  The fallowing data pertains to a test run made to determine the calorific value of a sample of coal, Mass of coal burnt = 0.85 gm, Mass of fuel wire burnt and its calorific value is 0.028 gm and 6700 kJ/kg respectively, mass of water in calorimeter = 1800 gm, initial and final temperature of water = 16.5°C and 20.25°C, water equivalent of calorimeter = 350 gm, the coal contains 3% moisture by weight and R.T. = 20°C. Make calculations for the higher and lower calorific values of the coal sample. Consider latent heat of condensation of steam 2460 kJ/kg.    **[7]**

## NOVEMBER 2015

**Time : 2 Hours**                                                                 **Max. Marks : 50**

---

1. **(a)** Explain the following concepts of thermodynamics :                        **[6]**
   (i)   Thermodynamics cycle (ii) Flow work (iii) P-dV work.
   **(b)** Find the change in entropy of universe when 1 kg of ice at –5°C is exposed to atmosphere which is at 30°C, ice melts and comes in thermal equilibrium with atmosphere. Consider specific heat of ice 2.1 kJ/kgK, latent heat of fusion of ice 330 kJ/kg.          **[6] OR**

2. **(a)** What are the Kelvin–Planck and Clausius statements of second law of thermodynamic ? Also establish their equivalence.                                               **[6]**
   **(b)** Air is initially at 1 bar and 27°C is compressed reversibly and adiabatically in a reciprocating engine to final pressure of 25 bar. Find work done, change in enthalpy and change in entropy per kg of air. Assume $C_p$ and $C_v$ of air 1.005 kJ/kgK and 0.717 kJ/kgK respectively.                                                              **[6]**

3. **(a)** Draw P–V and T–S diagram of Otto cycle and derive an expression to find its thermal efficiency.                                                                    **[6]**
   **(b)** A sample of steam generated in a boiler at a pressure of 12 bar is passed through separating and throttling calorimeter to measure its dryness fraction. The following observations were recorded during the test :                                          **[6]**
   (i)   Pressure of steam after throttling – 1.2 bar,
   (ii)  Temperature of steam after throttling – 120°C
   (iii) Mass of steam collected after throttling – 1 kg
   (iv)  Mass of water collected through separating calorimeter – 15 gm.
   Find the quality of steam generated by boiler.
   Assume Cp of superheated steam 2.1 kJ/kgK.                                          **OR**

4. **(a)** Prove that when heat is transfer through finite temperature difference it causes loss of available energy.                                                            **[6]**
   **(b)** A thermal power plant works on Rankine Cycle has a boiler pressure of 120 bar and condenser pressure of 5 kPa. Steam is superheated in the superheater to 400°C. Find per kg of steam generated by boiler.                                              **[6]**
   (i)   Net work output (ii) Rankine efficiency (iii) Specific steam consumption.

5. **(a)** With the help of suitable diagram explain the construction and working of Cochron boiler.                                                                       **[6]**
   **(b)** Determine the air–fuel ratio for an oil fired steam generator with the following data :   **[7]**
   Chimney height–32 m,
   Chimney draught–12 mm of water column,
   Flue gas temperature through chimney–297°C
   Ambient air temperature, 27°C
   Also calculate the velocity of flue gas through chimney neglecting gas losses in the flow of flue gas through chimney.                                                         **OR**

---

**6. (a)** Write the function and locations of the following boiler mountings :                    **[6]**

     (i)    Blow off cock  (ii)  Fusible plug  (iii)  Steam safety valve.

**(b)** The following readings were recorded during boiler trial of 6 hour duration :

Pressure of steam generated – 12 bar,

Mass of steam generated – 40000 kg

Dryness fraction of steam generated – 0.85

Feed water temperature – 30°C,

Coal used – 4000 kg.

Calorific value of coal – 33400 kJ/kg,

Find :

(i)    Factor of equivalent evaporation

(ii)   Equivalent evaporation from and at 100°C

(iii)  Efficiency of boiler.                    **[7]**

**7. (a)** Write the complete combustion equations for $C_8H_{18}$ and $C_{12}H_{26}$. Also find theoretical air required for complete combustion of 1 kg of these fuels.                    **[6]**

**(b)** If 30% excess air is supplied for the combustion of dry anthracite of the following compositions by mass : Carbon–88%, Hydrogen–4%, Oxygen–3.5%, Sulphur–0.5%, Ash–3% and Nitrogen–1%, determine :                    **[7]**

(i)    Air–fuel ratio

(ii)   Dry analysis of product of combustion by volume.                    **OR**

**8. (a)** With the help of suitable diagram explain, how Junker gas calorimeter is used to measure Calorific value of gases fuel ?                    **[6]**

**(b)** Diesel fuel ($C_{12}H_{26}$) reacts with 80% theoretical air. Determine the product of combustion on percentage of volume basis. Considering complete combustion of hydrogen of fuel.**[7]**

### MAY 2016

**Time : 2 Hours**                                                          **Max. Marks : 50**

**1. (a)** Discuss the concept of point function and path function. Explain with examples and suitable diagram.                    **[6]**

**(b)** Steam at a 6.87 bar, 205T, enters in an insulated nozzle with a velocity of 50 m/s. It leaves at a pressure of 1.37 bar and a velocity of 500 m/s. Determine the final enthalpy of steam.                    **[6] OR**

**2. (a)** Draw the P-v diagram of various thermodynamic processes for ideal gas; clearly indicating polytrophic index or slope of each process.                    **[6]**

**(b)** In an I.C. Engine during the compression stroke heat rejected to the cooling water is 50 kJ/kg and work input is 100 kJ/kg. Calculate the change in internal energy of the working fluid stating that whether it is gain in internal energy or loss of internal energy.                    **[6]**

**3. (a)** Derive the relation for efficiency for Otto gas power cycle.                    **[6]**

**(b)** Determine the amount of heat, which should be supplied to 2 kg of water at 25°C to convert it into steam at 5 bar and 0.9 dry.                    **[6] OR**

**UQP.9**

**4. (a)** Discuss the principle and working of Throttling Calorimeter with neat labelled diagram and show the prbtess on h-s diagram. **[6]**

**(b)** An engine of 250 mm bore and 375 nun stroke works on Otto cycle. The clearance volume is 0.00263 $m^3$. The initial pressure and temperature are 1 bar and 50°C. If the maximum pressure is limit C to 25 bar, find the following : **[6]**

    (i)    The air standard efficiency of the cycle.

    (ii)   The pressure ratio or explosion ratio.

Assume the ideal conditions.

**5. (a)** Discuss the Boiler plant layout indicating location of various accessories and water, air and flue gas circuit. **[6]**

**(b)** 5400 kg of steam is produced per hour at a pressure of 750 kPa in a boiler when feed water is at 41.5 deg. C. The dryness fraction of the steam is 0.98. The amount of the coal burnt per hour is 670 kg with CV of 31000 kJ/kg. Determine the boiler efficiency and equivalent evaporation. **[7] OR**

**6. (a)** Show in tabular form boiler heat balance sheet and the formulas involved for estimating each component. **[6]**

**(b)** A boiler is equiped with a chimney of 24 m height. The ambient temperature is 25 deg. The temperature of flue gases passing through the chimney is 300 deg. C. If the air flow through the combustion chamber is 20 kg/kg of fuel burned, find

    (i)    The theoretical draught in cm of water column and

    (ii)   The velocity of the flue gases passing through the chimney if 50% of the head is lost in friction. **[7]**

**7. (a)** Derive the relation for minimum amount of air required per kg of fuel for complete combustion. **[6]**

**(b)** The percentage composition by mass of a solid fuel used in a boiler is given below : C = 90%, $H_2$ = 3.5%, $O_2$ = 3%, $N_2$ = 1%, S = 1% remaining is ash.

Find the mass of air required for complete combustion and mass analysis of dry products of combustion. **[7] OR**

**8. (a)** Discuss the construction and working of Bombs Calorimeter with neat sketch and thus derive the formula of HCV in Bomb Calorimeter. **[6]**

**(b)** The following observations were made durnig the test for finding the calorific value of gaseous fuel with the help of Boys gas calorimeter : **[7]**

Volume of gas consumed = 0.0535 $m^3$, Mass of water circulated = 20 kg,

Rise in temperature of water = 10 deg.

Condensate collected during the test = 60 gm,

Find HCV and LCV of the gas.

## NOVEMBER 2016

**Time : 2 Hours**                                      **Total Marks : 50**

**Instructions to the candidates :**

(1) Solve Q. 1 or Q. 2, Q. 3 or Q. 4, Q. 5 or Q. 6, Q. 7 or Q. 8

(2) Answer for the four questions should be written in same answer-book attach supplement if required.

(3) Net diagrams must be drawn wherever necessary.

(4) Use of steam tables, Mollier Charts, scientific calculator is allowed.

(5) Use of pocket calculator and different gas charts as applicable is allowed.

(6) Assume suitable data, if necessary.

(7) Figures to the right indicate full marks.

---

**1.** **(a)** Discuss the important points of similarities and differences between heat and work.

**[6]**

    **(b)** A reversible heat engine operates between three heat reservoirs. The engine receives 80 kW heat from reservoir A at 800 K and develops 20 kW power. The engine rejects heat to sink B and sink C. The sink B and sink C are at 300 K and 400 K respectively. Determine the heat rejected to the sink. **[6] OR**

**2.** **(a)** Derive the following equations for an ideal gas undergoing isobaric process: **[6]**

    (i) Work done         (ii) Heat transfer

    (iii) Change in entropy     (iv) Change in internal energy and enthalpy

    (v) Polytropic index of the process.

    **(b)** A heat pump is used to maintain the house at 23 deg. C. The house is losing heat to outside air through walls at 60,000 kJ/hr. Heat generated by various appliances inside the house 4000 kJ/hr. For a COP of 1.5, find required power input in kW supplied to the heat pump. **[6]**

**3.** **(a)** Derive the expression of efficiency for air standard Otto cycle. **[6]**

    **(b)** In a standard vapor compression refrigeration cycle, operating between evaporator of −10 deg. C and condenser of 40 deg. C, the enthalpy of the refrigerant. R134a at the end of the compression is 440 kJ/kg. Draw the cycle on P-h chart. Assume exit of the condenser to be saturated liquid and entry of the compressor to be dry vapor. hf (at − 10 deg. C) = 186.78 kJ/kg, hg (at − 10 deg. C) = 392.75 kJ/kg, hf (at 40 deg. C) = 256.35 kJ/kg, hg (at 40 deg. C) = 419.58 kJ/kg.

    Calculate:

    (i) Refrigerating effect

    (ii) Compressor power and (iii) COP. **[6] OR**

**4.** **(a)** Explain with neat labelled diagram separating calorimeter. **[6]**

    **(b)** An Otto Cycle engine has a bore of 80 mm and stroke of 85 mm. The clearance volume of the engine is 0.06 litre. The actual thermal efficiency of the engine is 22%. Determine : **[6]**

    (i) Compression ratio

---

    (ii)  Air standard efficiency

    (iii) Relative efficiency of the engine.

    Assume, gama = 1.4

**5. (a)** List down and discuss the function of at least 3 mountings and 3 accessories. **[6]**

   **(b)** A gas fired boiler operates at a pressure of 100 bar. The feed water temperature is 256 deg. C. Steam is produced with a dryness fraction of 0.9 and in this condition it enters a super heater. Superheated steam leaves the super heater at a temperature of 450 Deg. C. The boiler generates 1200 Tonne of steam per hour with a thermal efficiency of 92%. The gas used has a calorific value of 38 MJ/m$^3$.

    Determine :

    (i)  Heat transfer per second in producing wet steam in the boiler.

    (ii)  Heat transferred per second in producing superheated steam in super heater.

    (iii) Volume of gas used in m$^3$/hr. **[7] OR**

**6. (a)** Discuss the functions and location of various boiler mounting and accessories. **[6]**

   **(b)** Calculate the height of the chimney, velocity of flue gases and mass of flue gases flowing through the chimney when the draught is produced equal to 1.9 cm of water. Temperature of flue gases is 290 deg. C and ambient temperature is 20 deg. C. The flue gases formed per kg of fuel burnt are 23 kg. Neglect the losses and take the diameter of the chimney as 1.8 m. **[7]**

**7. (a)** Define : **[6]**

    (i)  Degree of saturation      (ii)  Saturated air

    (iii) Relative humidity        (iv)  Dry bulb temperature

    (v)  Wet bulb temperature    (vi)  Wet bulb depression.

   **(b)** Moist air of mass flow rate 200 m$^3$/min at 15 deg. C DBT and 75% RH is heated until its temperature reaches to 25 deg. C. Find the following: **[7]**

    (i)  RH of heated air,       (ii) WBT of heated air,

    (iii) Heat added to air in kW. **OR**

**8. (a)** With a neat sketch represent any three of the following processes on Pscychrometric chart: **[6]**

    (i)  Sensible heating and Sensible cooling

    (ii)  Humidification and Dehumidification

    (iii) Cooling and Dehumidification

    (iv) Heating and Humidification.

   **(b)** On a particular day, the atmospheric air conditions are recorded as 30 deg. C. DBT and 40% RH. Determine the due point temperature and wet bulb temperature of air. If this air cooled in the air washer using recirculated spray water and having a humidifying efficiency of 90%, what is dry bulb temperature and dew point temperature of air leaving the air washer ? **[7]**

ENTHALPY - KJ PER KG OF DRY AIR
SATURATION TEMPERATURE - °C
RELATIVE HUMIDITY
DRY BULB TEMPERATURE - °C
SPECIFIC VOLUME m³/kg OF DRY AIR
WET BULB TEMPERATURE - °C
DEW POINT - °C
HUMIDITY RATIO - GRAMS OF MOISTURE PER KILOGRAM OF DRY AIR
VAPOR PRESSURE - MM OF MERCURY
ENTHALPY - KJ PER KG OF DRY AIR
Linric Company Psychrometric Chart, www.linric.com

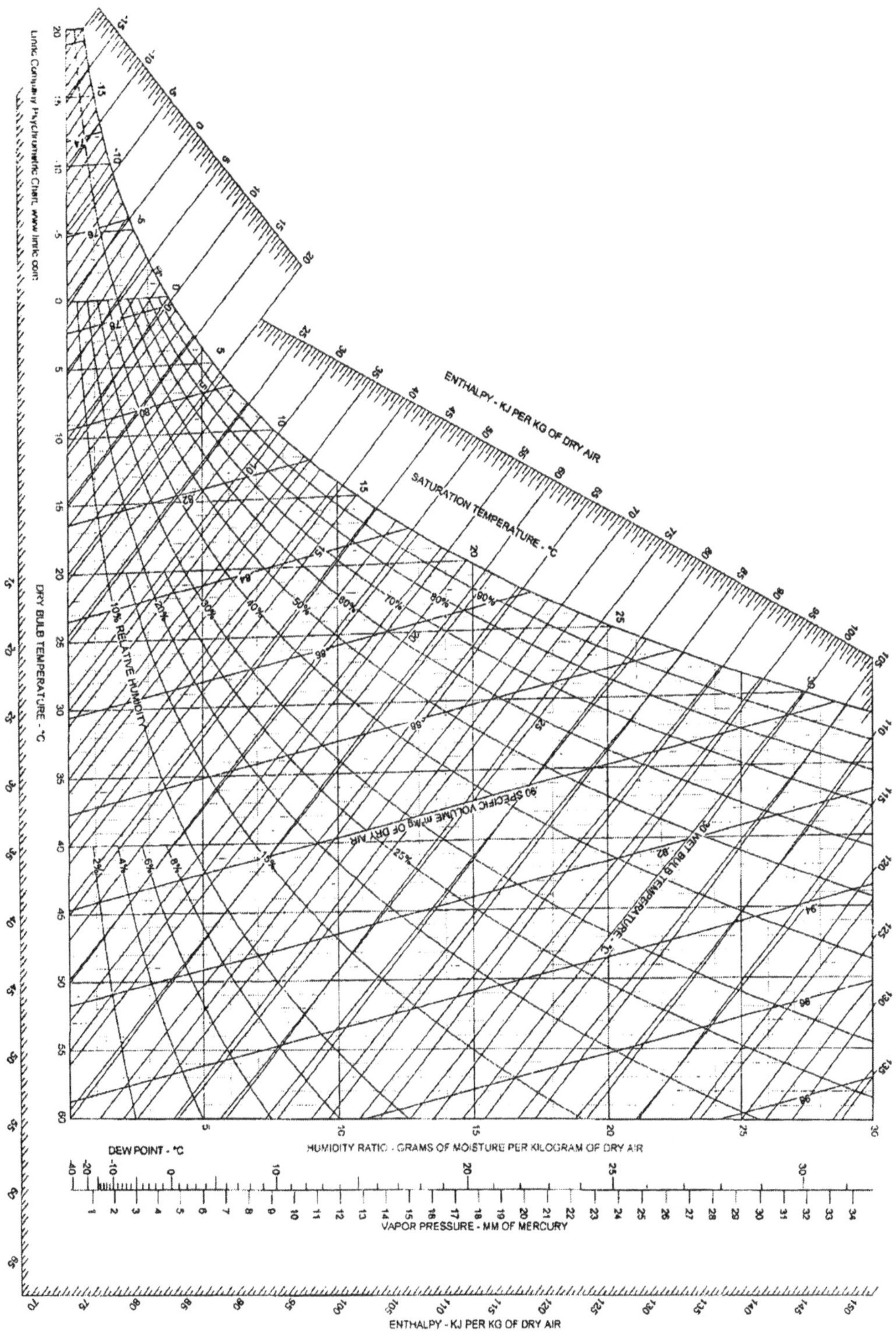

**Fig. 1**

## MAY 2017

**Time : 2 Hours**                                                                            **Max. Marks : 50**

**Instructions to the candidates :**

(1) Answer Q. No. 1 or Q. No. 2, Q. No. 3 or Q. No. 4, Q. No. 5 or Q. No. 6, Q. No. 7 or Q. No. 8.

(2) Answer for the four questions should be written in same answer-book attach supplement if required.

(3) Neat diagrams must be drawn wherever necessary.

(4) Use of steam tables, Mollier charts, scientific calculator is allowed.

(5) Use of pocket calculator and different gas charts as applicable is allowed.

(6) Assume suitable data, if necessary.

(7) Figures to the right indicate full marks.

---

**1.** **(a)** Define a thermodynamic system and surrounding. Give classification of systems with example.  **[6]**

**(b)** A fluid system, contained in a piston and cylinder machine, passes through a completer cycle of four processes. The sum of all heat transferred during a cycle is 340 kJ. The system completes 200 cycles per min. Complete the following table showing the method for each item, and compute the net rate of work output in kW.  **[6]**

| Process | Q(kJ/min) | W(kJ/min) | E(kJ /min) |
|---|---|---|---|
| 1-2 | 0 | 4340 | - |
| 2-3 | 42000 | 0 | - |
| 3-4 | −4200 | - | −73200 |
| 4-1 | - | - | - |

**OR**

**2.** **(a)** Show that $C_p - C_v = R$. Derive the relation for heat transfer and work transfer for constant pressure process.  **[6]**

**(b)** An iron cube at a temperature of 400°C is dropped into an insulated bath containing 10 kg water at 25°C. The water finally reaches a temperature of 50°C at steady state. Given that the specific heat of water is equal to 4186 J/kg K. Find the entropy changes for the iron cube and the water. Is the process reversible ? If so why ?  **[6]**

**3.** **(a)** What is a available energy? Define dead state, useful work and unavailable work.  **[6]**

**(b)** An engine working on Otto cycle, air has pressure of 1 bar and temperature of 27 deg C. Air is compressed adiabatically with a compression ratio of 7 and then heat is added at constant volume till the temperature rises to 2000 K. Find the air standard efficiency, pressure at the end of compression and heat addition in process and the mean effective pressure of the cycle. Assume, $C_V$ = 0.718 kJ/kgK, $\gamma$ = 1.4 and R = 287 Nm/kgK.　　**[6] OR**

**4. (a)** Discuss the principle of separating calorimeter with a neat labeled diagram.　　**[6]**

**(b)** A thermal power plant works on Rankine cycle has a boiler pressure of 120 bar and condenser pressure of 5 kPa. Steam is superheated in the super heater to 400 deg. C. Find per kg of steam generated by boiler :　　**[6]**

    (i)　　Net work output

    (ii)　　Rankine Efficiency

    (iii)　　Specific stam consumption.

**5. (a)** Give the function and location of any 3 of the following:　　**[6]**

    (i)　　Super heater

    (ii)　　Air preheater

    (iii)　　Fusible plug

    (iv)　　Water level indicator

    (v)　　Spring loaded safety valve.

**(b)** The following results were obtained in a boiler trial.　　**[7]**

    (i)　　Feed water per hour = 700 kg at 27 deg. C

    (ii)　　Steam produced at 8 bar and 0.97 dry.

    (iii)　　Coal used = 100 kg/hr having CV of coal = 25000 kJ/kg

    (iv)　　Ash and unburnt coal collected = 7.5 kg/hr having CV = 2000 kJ/kg

    (v)　　Mass of flue gases produced per kg of fuel burnt = 17.3 kg

    (vi)　　Flue gas temperature = 327 deg C

    (vii)　　Room temperature = 16 deg. C

    (viii)　Specific heat of flue gases = 1.025 kJ/kgK

Draw the energy balance on minute basis.　　**OR**

**6. (a)** Derive the formula for :　　**[6]**

    (i) Equivalent Evaporation and　(ii) Boiler efficiency.

**(b)** The following readings were recorded during a boiler trial of 6 hrs duration:　　**[7]**

Mean steam pressure = 12 bar; Mass of steam generated = 40000 kg

Mean dryness fraction = 0.85; mean feed water temperature = 30°c

Coal used = 4000 kg; Calorific value of coal = 33400 kJ/kg

Calculate :

(i) Factor of equivalent evaporation

(ii) Heat rate of boiler in kJ/kg

(iii) Equivalent evaporation form and at 100°C

(iv) Efficiency of boiler.

**7. (a)** What are the factors affecting Human Comfort? Discuss in detail. **[6]**

**(b)** Atmospheric air at 30 deg. C DBT and 18 deg. C WBT is cooled to 20 deg. C DBT without changing its moisture content. **[7]**

Find:

(i) Initial enthalpy and specific humidity of air

(ii) Final relative humidity of air and WBT

(iii) Sensible heat removed per kg of air. **OR**

**8. (a)** Define and discuss the significance of the following: **[6]**

(i) Wet Bulb temperature

(ii) Dew point temperature

(iii) Humidity ratio.

**(b)** Air enters a window air conditioner at 1 atm and 30 deg C and 80% RH at a rate fo $10m^3$/min and leaves as saturated at 14°C. A part of moisture which condenses during the process is also removed at 14°C. Determine the heat flow rate and moisture removed from the air. Show the process on psychrometric diagram. **[7]**

✽ ✽ ✽

www.ingramcontent.com/pod-product-compliance
Lightning Source LLC
Chambersburg PA
CBHW081323090726
47907CB00010B/2351